NEW YEAR ISLAND

PAUL DRAKER

Mayhem Press
PALO ALTO, CALIFORNIA

Mayhem Press LLC
380 Hamilton Ave #1319
Palo Alto, California 94302

Publisher's Note: This is a work of fiction. Names, characters, places, and incidents are a product of the author's imagination. Locales and public names are sometimes used for atmospheric purposes. Any resemblance to actual people, living or dead, or to businesses, companies, events, institutions, or locales is completely coincidental.

Ordering Information:
Quantity sales. Special discounts are available on quantity purchases by corporations, associations, and others. For details, contact the "Special Sales Department" at the address above.

New Year Island/ Paul Draker. -- 1st ed.
ISBN 978-1-940511-01-6

*This book is dedicated to
Carolina, Madison, Kaitlyn, and Sophia.*

*My family lived, breathed, ate, and slept this story with me for a
year.*

Sorry about all the nightmares, girls.

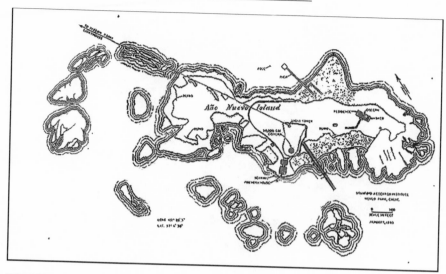

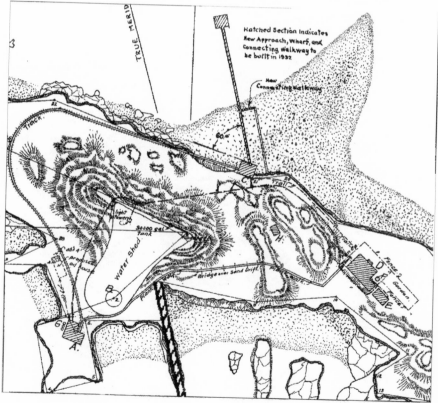

PART I

QUALIFYING ROUNDS

CHAPTER 1

Camilla

October 20, 1989
Cypress Street Viaduct, Oakland, California

"Gordon said he saw her this time—through the gap under the crossbeam, but she crawled away again."

"Gordon's wrong. It's been three days since the last live rescue." Dan Prescott looked down the black row of rubber body bags, lined up like dominos on the buckled asphalt. "Our window's closed—they're all dead."

"But the crew from Engine Company Eight heard her, too—yesterday, under the H span. She was singing."

Dan shook his head. His gaze followed the collapsed section of elevated freeway stretching a mile into the distance. The two-story spans were sandwiched together, the upper crushing the lower, resting against the crumbled concrete pylons.

"How could anyone still be alive in there?" he asked.

"I'm telling you, they *saw* her." Manuel Garcia's voice cracked. "They *heard* her."

"I've been doing this for fifteen years, and I know," Dan said. "At this point, it's strictly recovery. I'm sorry, Manny."

Black smoke billowed out of the small gaps between the roadway spans. Some of the crushed cars trapped inside were still smoldering four days after the earthquake. Two blocks away, a hook-and-ladder truck angled close to the rubble. A fireman clung to the ladder, spraying a stream of water into the narrow crack between the pancaked roadways.

Manuel stared at the constricted, smoking gap, his face drawn with anguish.

"They said she looked like a little angel, lost in the darkness," he said. "She was singing to herself."

Dan turned to the younger paramedic and laid a hand on his shoulder.

"I went home for a couple hours last night," he said. "Looked in on my daughters, asleep in their beds... and I cried. Something like this, you can't really get your head around it. You don't know what to believe in anymore. So our minds invent phantoms, showing us what we want to see. Or hear."

He looked at his junior partner and saw himself fifteen years ago. He spoke as gently as he could.

"Manny, there is no girl."

• • •

A column of names ran down one side of the clipboard Dan held, question marks after them. On the other side were detailed descriptions: gender, approximate age, hair, eyes, clothing, but no names. He stared at the list, pen in hand, but a deep voice snapped him out of his bleary-eyed focus.

"We're cutting into H section."

Dan squeezed the bridge of his nose and blinked at Ballard, the fire lieutenant.

"Waste of effort," he said.

Ballard's expression hardened. "You should go home, Dan."

Dan could see exhaustion etched into Ballard's face, but his jaw was set. The rest of the crew from Engine Company 8 came around the side of the ambulance, carrying a Hurst tool—the Jaws of Life, used to pry open mangled vehicles. Two of them lugged a large rotary concrete saw, trailing its thick orange power cable. All wore bulky knee and elbow pads.

Manny Garcia stood next to Ballard. He wouldn't meet Dan's eyes.

Ballard pointed at Gordon, his station chief.

"Gordy says she's in there, Dan. We're going in to get her."

• • •

Three hours later, Dan had check marks next to most of the fifty-eight names on his clipboard. He counted down the list of missing with his pen, pausing at the name that caught his eye again: Camilla Becker, seven years old.

Their imaginary girl?

He circled the name with his pen and continued down the list. A yell interrupted him. He looked up.

Shouts came from the hole in the concrete where Ballard's crew had gone in. The yellow of a fireman's protective greatcoat glimmered in the floodlights. They were coming out.

"Prescott, Garcia, over here." Ballard's deep voice echoed across the cracked concrete. "Now."

Dan's eyes widened. He turned to Manny, who was already hauling a stretcher from the back of the truck. He grabbed the other end, and they ran toward the gap.

• • •

"She's alive."

Dan had Dispatch on the radio. It sounded strange, hearing himself say the words, but there was no joy in them.

"Her legs—both of them," he said. "She needs to go into surgery as soon as possible."

He listened to the dispatcher while he watched the girl. She sat upright atop a stretcher near the fire truck fifty feet away. A blanket covered her from the waist down. He was sure her legs would heal, given time. The problem was the damage that didn't show.

He held the radio handset loosely. The dispatcher asked a question.

"Seven years old, I think," Dan said. "I'm not sure. She can't speak."

The girl's face was expressionless under a layer of soot. She looked like a life-size doll. Manny stood next to her, speaking to her, stroking her hair gently. Her eyes were dark glass marbles. Unresponsive. Empty.

Whoever the girl had been was gone forever, lost in the darkness behind those eyes. She was catatonic.

"No media," Dan said. "It's not a feel-good story."

The girl—Camilla?—sat like a mannequin, unaware of her surroundings. She was nearly the same age as his oldest daughter. He looked away, down at the cracks in the concrete, and tried to focus on what Dispatch was saying.

"Channel Four?" He swore under his breath. "Who called them?"

He could hear sirens in the distance now, getting louder.

"Look, Ballard's crew went back in to try and locate the vehicle," he said. "To establish her identity… to find the rest of her family."

He looked up at the hole the fire crew had cut in the concrete. They were coming out now, climbing down from between the spans. He watched them as he listened to Dispatch coordinating with the hospital. There was something odd about the way the crew was moving. Slowly. Like they all had been hurt somehow, where it didn't show.

Ballard walked toward him. Dan couldn't read his expression, but his cheeks and forehead looked pale under the dust and soot.

"Media?" Ballard asked. His voice was hesitant, not the usual commanding baritone.

Dan nodded. "Television."

"Shit."

Ballard turned away, walking faster now, and waved his crew into a huddle. Dan couldn't hear what they were saying, but they all turned to stare at the girl. Gordon and Ballard appeared to be arguing. Gordon shook his head and left the huddle to join Manny next to the girl. Dan watched Gordon lean toward Manny, speaking with quiet urgency. What was he telling him?

Ballard and the rest of the crew broke the huddle, moving with resolve. They picked up the concrete saw and the Hurst tool again.

Ballard raced over to the fire truck and opened a side compartment. He reached inside and pulled out a chainsaw.

Dan covered the radio handset with his hand. "What the hell…?"

"Not now." Sorrow and shock warred on Ballard's face. "Oh Christ, Dan, she…" He swallowed and wiped a hand across his cheeks. "Don't say a word to the media when they get here."

"But—"

"Not a goddamn word." Ballard pointed toward the girl on the stretcher. "For her sake."

He hustled away, carrying the chainsaw, and scooped up two empty body bags with his free hand. Then he hesitated, dropped them, and grabbed four smaller bags instead. Ballard followed his crew, disappearing into the hole in the concrete.

Confused, Dan looked at Gordon and Manny, standing over the girl's stretcher. Manny was still smoothing the girl's hair with one hand. As Gordon spoke to him, his hand slowed. Then it stopped moving, frozen in mid-air.

Manny slowly pulled his hand back, tucked it under his arm, and took a step away from the stretcher. Then he turned and stumbled after Gordon, who stalked away with angry strides.

Baffled by Manny's withdrawal, Dan walked toward the girl. She looked so lost, so alone now. He put his hands in his pockets and stared at her blank, doll-like face.

Are you still trapped under there, Camilla Becker?

Inside her mind, was she still crawling through wreckage and flames, surrounded by the dead and the dying? He couldn't imagine what she'd been through these last four days, or what kind of damage it had done to her. Had she given up, or was she still trying to find her way out of the darkness?

Her parents had been in the car with her, according to his clipboard. An only child. No next of kin listed. He didn't know what Ballard and the others had seen when they found her family, but in fifteen years he had never seen those guys shaken like that.

Dan tilted his head, watching her. *Maybe it's a mercy if you never come back.*

Then he frowned. Singing to herself yesterday, Manny said…

The girl was alive for a reason. She was a fighter.

Dan's throat tightened. *I gave up on you. I shouldn't have. Manny's right about me—I've been doing this so long, I'd lost hope. But you…*

His vision blurred.

You've given me a reason to believe again, Camilla. I do think you're going to find your way out of the darkness.

Something flickered in her expression.

Dan leaned closer, but it was only the red flashes from the arriving emergency vehicles reflected in her unseeing eyes. A long and difficult road lay ahead for her.

Despite himself, he reached out and touched her forearm in awe.

CHAPTER 2

J T

September 11, 2007
FOB Salerno, Northeastern Afghanistan

"The Valley of Death."

Sanchez dropped his cigarette and ground it into the tarmac. "I should have guessed. The goddamn Korengal Valley."

JT ignored him and squinted against the dust. He liked the kid, but Sanchez hadn't been with 1ˢᵗ Force Recon in Iraq. He hadn't been there for Fallujah.

Without turning around, JT raised his voice to be heard over the rotors. "DiMarco, what are we looking for out there?"

"Hell if I know. One-three brass wouldn't say. Routine patrol, they told me."

Predawn glow outlined the row of black AH-64 Apache helicopters that stretched into the distance. The 173ʳᵈ would ferry them in-country in one of the larger Chinooks, though. Its dark bulk loomed behind him, dotted with pinpoints of red—running lights.

JT would have preferred the Apache's firepower. Bringing in 1ˢᵗ Force Recon Marines for this operation meant something. This wasn't a routine patrol.

The cool, dry desert air chilled his skin, but in a few hours it would be scorching. Six years today, he thought. Six years since the planes hit the towers and the world changed forever. He had joined the Corps that same afternoon, walking away from a full engineering scholarship at U.C. Berkeley, and had never regretted his decision.

Their pilot walked across the tarmac toward them. Alone. He climbed into the cockpit.

"Saddle up, gents."

"Where's your buddy?" JT asked.

"He's in no shape to fly, Corporal. Birthday last night. I don't want him puking in my cockpit."

JT stared at him hard. "Regs say we don't fly without a copilot. You better get on that radio."

"I've got him logged as flight crew anyway, so we're good." The pilot looked flustered. JT had that effect on most people. "Cut him some slack. Brass doesn't need to know he isn't aboard, or he's looking at a disciplinary."

DiMarco's voice cut the air. "Let it go, Corporal. Let it go."

5

• • •

"They stand there looking at you…" Sanchez leaned forward, a hand on his helmet. The beat of the rotors made him hard to hear. "You're there helping 'em, right? Fixing the village's water, treating the sick, talking to the elders, and whatnot. Winning hearts and minds—all that shit. And you know. You just know."

JT watched the dark tree line of the Abas Ghar ridge slide by outside in the dim gray half-light. The kid was right, but so what? This was the new face of war. Get used to it.

Across from him, Collins nodded. "You see it in their eyes," he said. "The ones hanging in back of the crowd. But you can't do a goddamn thing about it. And then you're heading back to base, you're thinking, *sniper? IED? Or full-on ambush this time?*"

The deck of the copter bounced under their feet.

"Stop your bitching," JT said. "This is a holiday, after Iraq."

DiMarco laughed. "At least these Taliban run away when you return fire. And they fall down when you hit 'em."

JT leaned forward to slap Sanchez on the knee. "Fucking Fallujah was different. It was like *Dawn of the Dead*. Muj there were true believers, not like these sorry-asses. You'd blow their arms and legs off, they'd keep coming at you."

"An IED took out a U.S. medical convoy," DiMarco said. "The mujahideen got a huge stockpile of drugs off it. That's what we were up against."

JT nodded. "Muj were jacked on amphetamines, shooting up epinephrine—pure medical adrenaline. Word came down: head shots only. Waste of time shooting them anywhere else. I saw a guy get hosed by a SAW, musta' been hit fifteen, twenty times. Didn't even slow him down. I shot him five or six times myself. Nothing. Fucker was just laughing at us, shooting back. DiMarco had to take him out with an RPG."

DiMarco leaned forward and bumped his own fist against JT's dark knuckles. "Listen to the man. You guys are on vacation here. Relax."

"What the hell?" The surprise in the pilot's voice was alarming.

JT looked down at the valley floor. Shadows moved amid the cedar trees. Men and vehicles. A lot of them.

"That's not right," he said.

He reached over to smack DiMarco's shoulder, but DiMarco had already seen them. He stared back at JT in confusion.

"Those aren't—"

The Chinook lurched, and something wet sprayed the side of JT's face. He whipped his head around to see the pilot slump sideways. A red fan spread across the ceiling above him.

"Shit," Collins yelled. "We're hit!"

JT's eyes narrowed. He grabbed DiMarco's tac vest, pulled him close, and leaned into his face.

"Let it go, DiMarco? *Let it go?*" He spoke very slowly, holding DiMarco's eyes with his own. "No copilot now, motherfucker."

"The IFF. Get the IFF on." DiMarco's voice was hoarse. "That's an order, Corporal."

JT shoved him away and unbuckled. The Chinook tilted sideways and nosed down, bouncing and shaking like a truck riding on cross ties. Bracing himself against the ceiling, the muscles of his arms bulging, he worked his way toward the cockpit.

Sparks drizzled from the overhead switch panel. Black smoke filled the cabin. JT could hear Sanchez behind him, speaking rapid Spanish. Praying. The air stank of sweat and fear.

The pilot was dead, no question about that. JT shoved him aside, and yanked back on the cyclic. The Chinook failed to respond. Through the canopy, the ridgeline slipped by beneath them, dropping away into the next valley. Enemy territory. He grabbed the radio handset.

"Mayday. Mayday."

The radio was dead.

JT scanned the control board, locating the IFF beacon that DiMarco wanted. It would signal their location to friendlies. He flipped the switch, and a red light came on, blinking with a steady rhythm. Outside the glass canopy, the tree-dotted far wall of the valley filled his view, looming larger with every passing second.

Mounting a rescue operation would take hours, he knew—the enemy owned this valley. But first, he had to survive the crash, and they were coming down hard. He levered himself up and scrambled out of the cockpit, dragging the dead pilot behind him. Pulling himself up into his seat one-handed, he raced to buckle his harness and tighten his straps. He looked at Sanchez. The kid was mumbling, staring at the floor, face contorted with terror.

JT felt trickles of sweat rolling down his shaved head. He pulled the pilot up off the deck and draped the limp body over Sanchez's lap and his own.

Sanchez jerked his head up and stared at JT rabbit eyed. He tried to shove the dead pilot off his knees.

JT pushed down with an elbow, holding the pilot in place.

"Crash padding," he said.

He stretched his other arm past DiMarco, pulled the canvas first aid kit free, and hugged it to his chest, forcing it under his harness straps.

The Chinook tilted the other way, the whine of the rotors rising in pitch. The airframe shuddered, and JT heard the shriek of metal rending above them.

A rotor blade tore through the cabin, six feet from him, and DiMarco grunted. DiMarco's lower body and legs darkened, drenched with blood. He stared at JT in shock.

JT looked at the injury and shook his head at DiMarco. Game over.

Disintegrating blades from the aft rotor slashed through the cabin walls, coming closer and closer. The Chinook's tail slewed as the heavy craft autorotated on its remaining forward rotor. Liquid misted JT's face, stinging his eyes. The smell of aviation fuel filled the air.

Collins coughed. "We're fucked."

The Chinook plunged beneath their feet.

Sanchez's breath was coming in gasps. JT reached out and grabbed Sanchez's hand. Sanchez looked at him, and the fear in his eyes gave way to gratitude. He matched JT's solid grip with his own panicky one.

With his other hand, JT reached for Collins and held him steady.

Wind whipped through the cabin, blowing from the widening gap next to DiMarco.

JT's gaze was drawn to the light of the IFF beacon. It blinked steadily, the red rhythm slow, almost lazy, as the wall of the valley grew larger and larger in the windscreen behind it. The beacon looked like a red eye winking at him.

Then the world shredded apart in a chaos of noise, motion, rock, and flying metal.

CHAPTER 3

Lauren

August 6, 2007
Trango Tower, Karakoram Range, Pakistan

The metal piton whistled past, nearly hitting Lauren King in the head. She looked over her shoulder and watched it fall away. The four-inch angled steel spike drifted down alongside the planet's tallest vertical rock face, shrinking until it was lost from sight, invisible against the white ice of the Baltoro Glacier six thousand feet below.

Reflexively, Lauren hugged the granite tighter. She glanced up at her companions, and her eyes narrowed. *God damn it, Terry.*

After five days on the wall, all three of them were tired and clumsy, but Terry was coming apart now. He was going too fast, fumbling and dropping gear.

Trango's summit, a fang of orange rock, rose far above them. Too far. Lauren took a deep breath and turned to stare out at the ice-laden peaks around them, lit by dawn's pink rays: Uli Biaho, K2, Gasherbrum IV, Cathedral. Across the empty gulf of thin air, the neighboring spires looked close enough to touch. A cascade of fog poured through Cathedral's saddle like a silent waterfall, dissipating in midair a thousand feet down. They were on the roof of the world. No room for mistakes up here.

Her eyes dropped again to the glacier, over a mile below. Straight down. Terry shouldn't be leading this pitch—or *any* pitch on Trango. She'd seen him get in trouble trying to solo the Nose on El Cap. Dumb-ass was going to earn himself a Darwin Award, trying to climb five-fourteen. Why hadn't he said no to this trip?

Lauren knew damn well why Terry had come, though. She had caught his puppy-dog glances all summer in Yosemite's Camp 4. She'd noticed the way his voice changed whenever he talked to her.

Christ, Terry, it was never going to happen.

She wasn't sure what it was about her that attracted men, but even back in her suburban Danville high school, she had been a source of fascination for many. Maybe it was her mixed heritage—the contrast between her half-

9

Chinese features and the long, muscular limbs that let her do more pull-ups than the male jocks she routinely humiliated. Or maybe the *go-to-hell* look in her eyes was a challenge they just couldn't ignore. But whatever the reason, she knew Terry would have said yes to any trip she was going on, no matter where.

She gritted her teeth and let go with one hand, shaking her fingers to loosen them. By touch, she double-checked the figure-eight knot that tied the safety line into her harness loop, then slid her hand up the rope. Her fingers traced it past her belly, chest and shoulder, gauging the slack. A hundred thirty feet of 10.8-millimeter red and gold bi-pattern rope connected her climbing harness to Matt, who had led the pitch above her as they simulclimbed, and was now belaying both her and Terry above him.

Her gaze followed the line up the wall, counting Matt's pro—his protection: the chocks, cams, and pins that he had set into the rock every twenty feet and tied into. Hardware secured the rope at four spots between Matt and Lauren, ready to catch Matt if he fell.

Far above her, Matt met her eyes. He shook his head, pointing up at the top of their line, where Terry clung eighty feet above him.

Lauren turned away. *Don't look at me, cowboy. This wasn't my idea.*

She dipped her fingers into the bag of climbing chalk hanging from the back of her waist harness, and reached for the next hold: a narrow flake of orange granite two feet above her head.

She looked at her hands, gripping the rock. Those large, square, unfeminine hands, with their knobby knuckles and strong fingers, were her deadbeat father's. As a child, she had been ashamed of her hands. When Lauren was twelve, her mom had laid a dainty hand atop the back of Lauren's own and nicknamed her "Mi-Go," which meant "yeti"—the abominable snowman.

Those hands had gotten her in trouble, too—suspended in her sophomore year for breaking Sarah Calloway's nose in the locker room. But Lauren wasn't going to let a fucking cheerleader call her "Sasquatch" behind her back. Not after "Mi-Go."

It had been a revelation to discover that her hands were perfectly designed for gripping and pinching and jamming invisible routes on rock that defied all other challengers. Her hands were the only thing she had ever been able to count on; people always disappointed her, sooner or later.

Lauren shifted a foot, smearing the smooth rubber of her climbing shoe against a granite nub, and pushed herself higher to bring her face level with Matt's first piece of pro.

Her eyes widened.

The piton Matt had clipped their rope into was a dull, tarnished gray instead of green-painted chrome-moly steel like the ones dangling from Lauren's own harness. She knew what that meant. Matt and Terry were both rushing. They were reusing old pro, tying into hardware the last team of climbers had left behind five years ago, instead of placing their own. Her chest tightened.

You know better than this, Matt. You taught me, remember?

After five seasons of water melting and freezing in the rock, expanding and contracting in all the little fissures, the old pro couldn't be trusted.

Lauren braced herself against the rock face. She grabbed the carabiner clipping their rope to the piton's eyehole, looped two fingers through the three-inch aluminum D-ring, and yanked. To her horror, the old pin pulled free from the crack, grating in the silence.

The piton dangled from her fingers, trailing the arc of limp rope. Three more pieces of hardware dotted the rock between her and Matt, and four between Matt and Terry. Lauren grimaced, knowing the rest of the pro above her was probably no good, either.

Nice going, team.

She looked up. High above her, Terry's leg slipped, and her stomach clenched. He was losing it, which didn't surprise her, but the bad pro meant that if he fell now, he would zipper the rope off the wall and take Matt with him. They would both drop, ripping out all seven pieces above her, and then the rope tied to Lauren's harness would be the only thing connecting Matt and Terry to the face.

Her heart accelerated, thudding wildly in her chest. They would pull *her* off the wall, too.

Matt waved an arm, calling instructions down to her. His voice was bright with urgency, the words just senseless noise to her ears. Lauren shut him out and pressed her cheek against the cold orange rock. She could feel her teammates' jerky movements vibrating down the rope. It felt like the first gentle trickles of snow that signaled the coming avalanche.

The moment she'd been dreading for days was finally here. But maybe they still had a chance of surviving this.

Matt had been impatient with her all morning, saying she was taking too long to clean the route and pull the gear behind them. What Lauren hadn't told him was that she was trailing a second rope, looped through a Petzl GriGri as a self-belay. She was taking the time to sink her own anchors, sacrificing gear as they went. She was violating every principle of clean climbing because she had seen something like this coming.

But how much pro had she left in place below her right now?

Her eyes followed her self-belay rope down the granite wall. The loop dangled from her harness, hanging loosely for fifty feet to where she had threaded it through cams she'd placed in the rock. Another forty feet below that, the loop's end was tied through angle pins she had worked into a Y-shaped crack. That was it. That was all of her pro, the climber's protection supposed to catch her if she fell.

Fucking Matt. If it hadn't been for his stupid bitching that she was slowing the pace, she'd have placed more of her own gear. A lot more.

Lauren gritted her teeth and ignored the scrabbling sounds and movements above her. Her breath came in shallow pants, leaving chuffs of icy vapor hanging in the still air.

Would her backup pro be enough to hold all three of them? If not, they would drop a vertical mile. Thirty seconds of free fall, conscious the whole way. Then they would crater into a pink smudge on the glacier.

Ignoring Matt's panicked shouts, Lauren looked at her hands again. They had never failed her, the way other people always did. Maybe they could save her now.

If there was enough time, she could sink more gear, tie herself to the wall.

Letting go with her left hand, she groped amongst the nuts and cams hanging from her harness belt until her trembling fingers closed around a climber's "friend." She quickly wedged the safety device into the crack, and its opposing cams expanded to lock into place. She reached for another and jammed it right above the first. She frantically threaded her harness rope through both of them. Her fingers flew, tying a clove hitch one-handed. She needed more time.

But there was no time left. The lead rope slackened suddenly as Terry came off the wall high above her. Lauren pressed her cheek against the cold granite again, seeing the speckled rock in high relief. She listened hard but heard nothing other than the fear-monster's roar, the sound of blood rushing in her ears.

Matt had gotten them into this because he couldn't admit she was a better climber than he ever was. *That's really why we're up here, isn't it, Matt?* She forced her fingers into motion again, and grabbed a fixed nut, still attached to her harness loop. She wedged the hex nut into the crack at her waist.

Slamming more hardware in as fast as she could, she strained to hear.

When the sound came, she felt it thrum through the rope: the high, innocuous *ping* of Terry's first anchor pulling free from the rock. A couple seconds later, there came another metallic ping, followed almost immediately by a third. The lead rope was unzipping.

Her rope went taut and she was jerked up hard against the rock. Terry had torn Matt away from the face, too.

Terry plummeted past. He flashed by in Lauren's peripheral vision in eerie silence. Her hands scrabbled for a final death grip on the granite.

So none of this is your fault, Lauren? Really?

She thrust the unwelcome thought away.

Ping! That's four.

Ping! Five.

The thrums were coming through the rope faster now, the anchors tearing out more violently as gravity sucked her teammates toward the earth.

Ping! Something sparked off the rock next to her face, sprinkling her chin with rock splinters. Part of an anchor cam.

Lauren's eyes widened. They were shattering to pieces.

Matt plunged past, trailing the rope that connected them. His fingers almost touched her shoulder.

Ping! Last one.

She took a shuddering breath and locked every muscle rigid. She tried to melt herself into the rock, feeling her face contort into a tight mask of fear.

The rope through her harness ripped her away from the wall, yanking her downwards in a violent spray of broken cams and metal fragments, like she had been hit by a truck. Pain exploded through her chest and back as she tumbled head over heels into empty space.

Had she slowed them enough for the rest of her pro to catch them?

Her helmet struck the wall. She heard it fracture. A band of pain gripped her head. Sky and rock spun past over and over again. Her own self-belay rope looped thru the air behind her—when it snapped taut a hundred feet down, would her last two anchors hold?

I'm twenty-three.

She was dragged earthwards. Loose rope tangled her arms and legs.

I've barely done anything with my life.

The wall blurred past just out of reach.

I've never been in love.

Lauren gave herself fully to her terror.

I don't want to die.

CHAPTER 4

Brent

December 26, 2004
Ton Sai Bay, Koh Phi Phi Island, Thailand

The green waters rolled back, parting like a curtain to reveal a scene of utter devastation. Brent Wilson looked at his wife and son, standing on either side of him. He gripped their hands in his and held them tight as the three stood together on the fourth-floor hotel balcony, watching the waters recede.

The sea drained away from the narrow isthmus, pouring down the beaches on both sides. The churning waves drew wreckage in their wake: capsized long-tail boats, bamboo roofs, lounge chairs, beach umbrellas. And people. Hundreds of bodies swirled amid the flotsam—men, women, children—some struggling, but most limp and still.

Brent closed his eyes for a moment. So many dead.

Tourists and Thai villagers alike had been swept along when the tsunami's twin waves surged up the crescent-shaped beaches that lined either side of the island. The two waves had come together in the crowded strip of palm trees between the two beaches, where Ton Sai village's shops and restaurants clustered thickest. Most of the structures were gone now, dismantled by the crushing weight of water.

There had been no warning.

"Dad, the people that were on the beach—why didn't they run away?"

Brent heard his son's voice crack. They had booked this family trip months ago, to celebrate Brent's fiftieth birthday. He put an arm around the boy's shoulders and hugged him tight. In the face of the tragedy below, he seemed so young, so vulnerable. Fifteen—almost an adult, but in so many ways still a child. Had Brent been the same way at his age?

"I was watching them, Dad. When the bay emptied and all the boats beached, some of them actually ran closer—chasing the waterline out. Why would they do that? Didn't they know the water would come rushing back? I saw a woman pulling her kids forward. Didn't she realize they were going to die?"

Brent shared a glance with Mary. After twenty-four years of marriage, he could read the question behind her troubled look. *Will he be all right?* her eyes asked. *How badly will this scar our son?*

15

He took a deep breath. That was part of the problem, of course: she sheltered their son too much. But there were things he would soon have to face. They all would. He released the boy and tried to answer his question.

"It's human nature, son. Evolution. Most of us aren't wired for survival anymore."

"I don't understand. They weren't panicking or anything. They just stood there."

Brent laid a hand on the boy's shoulder and squeezed. "That happens. It's what nine out of ten people do in an emergency. They get confused, freeze up. I see it all the time as a doctor."

The boy nodded, unable to tear his eyes away from the carnage down below.

Brent looked over at Mary again. She was holding his black medical bag.

"Let's go," she said. "Grab as many blankets and sheets as you can carry. I'll help with triage."

He smiled. His face felt tight. He stepped over and hugged his wife, taking the bag from her. "I love you, Mary."

He knew she was strong, and she would need to be—but for a different reason than what they now faced today.

"I keep thinking of that family with the flower shop." Mary stripped the blankets from the bed and bundled them in her arms. "They were so nice to us. All these people are. I hope they're all right."

"Come on." Brent turned to his son. "We've got work to do."

Mary stiffened. "No. He should stay here. It'll be bad…"

He put a hand on her arm. "It's better if we do this as a family."

•   •   •

The first floor of the hotel was awash with sodden debris. The expansive lobby on the second floor had been converted to a field hospital. The injured lay in rows, covered by blankets and sheets. Next door, they had set up a makeshift morgue in the shell of a restaurant. Outside, seabirds split the air with raucous cries, swooping down to feast on the bounty of stranded fish that flopped amid the wet wreckage. Urgency distorted the shouts of rescuers, lending a grim cadence to the singsong Thai voices. Rescue parties brought a steady stream of casualties to both buildings.

The other doctors and volunteers deferred automatically to Brent, because of his ER experience and silver hair but also because his height and stocky shoulders cut an imposing figure among the shorter, slighter Thai. He had taken charge, directing the emergency treatment and rescue efforts.

The morgue was filling fast as well.

Brent finished stabilizing his current patient, a Thai man with two broken legs. Many of the injured had lower-extremity lacerations and breaks caused by wave-borne debris. The less fortunate had been struck higher on their bodies or crushed in the grinding wreckage. He could hear helicopters outside, ferrying the worst injured to the mainland.

He stood up and tucked his hands into his vest pockets. They had done some good here. He looked around for his son and spotted him by the window. He looked pale. He was doing fine, though, helping where he could. Brent's chest swelled in a burst of bittersweet pride. He walked over and surprised the boy with a heartfelt hug.

"Where's your mom?"

"She's trying to track down some antibiotics. We ran out." The boy suddenly pointed out the window. "Look, that guy over there in the orange baseball cap, helping search. When the water started going out, I saw him, Dad. Everyone else just stood there, but he climbed up in that big mango tree."

"A survivor-type." He looked at the man his son had indicated: a short Thai with skinny arms and bad teeth. Nothing noteworthy about the man's appearance. Brent observed him closely. "About one out of ten people is an instinctive survivor, who somehow always seems to beat the odds. This guy... well, we can learn a lot from people like that."

"What makes survivors different?"

"Nobody really knows." He continued to watch the man in the baseball cap with rapt attention. "Genetics, upbringing—these things are certainly factors. But there's no test for it, other than a real life-or-death situation like this."

"*Sa-was-dee krup,* Doctor Brent." The hotel manager stood nearby. He dipped his head in a respectful half bow. "We found a young girl. She is in very bad shape. Please, maybe you can save her."

Brent followed the hotel manager out. He glanced back at his son, a silhouette standing by the window. The boy looked insubstantial.

Son, I don't know what it takes to be a survivor. But I'm afraid I'm going to need to learn.

The icy ball of fear shifted in the pit of Brent's stomach again. It had become his constant companion lately. He hadn't told them yet. He had actually planned to break the news today, but nature had had other plans. He would have to wait a few more days now.

Brent thought about the moment, three weeks ago, when he and the fear had first become inseparable. Steve, the radiologist, had been unusually quiet, making none of his jokes. He had brought the CAT scan up on the screen, and Brent had seen the unmistakable signs: the irregular lumps and winding white tendrils where there should only be gray. The icy ball had rooted itself in his abdomen then, although his outward reaction had been angry and immediate.

"There's some sort of mistake. You fucked this up somehow." Brent had heard the irrationality of his own reasoning even as he spoke. "That can't be me, Steve. I'm a *doctor.*"

PART II

LET THE GAMES BEGIN

Day 1

Friday: December 21, 2012

CHAPTER 5

December 21, 2012
PIXAR Animation Studios, Emeryville, California

"I asked us all here so we can present a very special award, to show our appreciation for someone who, I'm sure you all will agree, is a huge part of the reason for our record-setting success."

Reuben Sasaki, the Head of Studios, lowered the wireless microphone he held and grinned at Camilla Becker. She shook her head in astonishment. Other faces were turning toward her, too. Smiling. Everyone, it seemed, knew he was talking about her. This was an ambush.

Her face flushed with embarrassed happiness. She had said no yesterday, in Reuben's office, but it seemed he had overruled her and done it anyway.

"Coming up with the right award was difficult," Reuben said. "What Camilla does here defies easy categorization. Her official title of associate producer doesn't even begin to capture all the ways she helps each of us deliver our best."

She strode past her smiling colleagues, toward the front of the auditorium, where Reuben stood at the podium, dwarfed by banner-size character art—a wide-eyed cowboy, a snarling grasshopper, a red race car—from the studio's animated movie hits. To one side of the spacious room, floor-to-ceiling windows looked out on the sunlit central quad of the studio's tree-lined brick-and-glass campus.

"Every person in this room had something nice to say about you, Camilla," Reuben said. "When we're stuck, you help us crack the toughest problems. When egos flare up, you're the one who gets us calmed down and working together again."

He acknowledged her with a welcoming nod and stepped aside to make room for her at the podium. "Whether it's story, art, technology, animation, or sound, you see the possibilities that elevate our movies from the merely great to the amazing. You make our team greater than the sum of its parts, and push us to find excellence in ourselves and each other. You care what everyone has to say. You believe in all of us—"

Laughing, she grabbed the microphone from Reuben. "Give me that, you sneak." She poked him in the chest with a finger. "I'm mad at you for this."

She turned and looked out at her team—sixty of the most talented people in the industry.

"I'm mad at the rest of you, too," she said. "Couldn't any of you have warned me?"

Reuben handed her a small statuette—a cartoonish Anglepoise desk lamp made of crystal on an onyx base. A single word was engraved on the base.

Teambuilder.

That was exactly how Camilla thought of herself and what she did, too. As usual, her mentor understood her. She threw her arms around Reuben and hugged him, thanking him. Then she turned to face her team, seeing their generous smiles. Reuben shouldn't have singled her out. He shouldn't be giving her credit for success they all had achieved together. She cleared her throat, raising the microphone.

"This award should really be for you, not me. You earned it. All of you."

She loved how these world-class talents could set aside their egos and work with her and each other, creating pure entertainment magic.

"I started here eight years ago, pretty much straight out of college—except for a year in biotech, which wasn't really my thing. Back then, our studio was a lot smaller. We've grown with each success, but the thing I love most about being here hasn't changed one bit, and that's you—*all* of you." Camilla's eyes blurred. "You're like a family to me."

She held the award up, smiling, and took a moment to regain her composure.

"Like a family, you drive me crazy sometimes. But you also inspire me. I wake up in the morning and have to pinch myself, thinking, I can't believe I get paid to do what I do, or who I get to work with. Oh god, I'd better shut up now, or Reuben's going to figure out I'd do it for free just for the privilege of working with you."

She hugged Reuben again and spoke over the applause.

"Don't think you all can distract me with this, by the way." She pointed at three smiling faces in the audience. "Jerry, Pritha, and Gianna, let's meet at two. We need to talk about the changes Gianna wants."

Movement at the entrance to the auditorium caught her eye. Remy, her administrative assistant, waved at her again and held a thumb-and-pinky phone hand up near her ear, then lowered it to flatten palm down at waist height. A knot tightened in her chest. The call was from one of her foundation kids, then. Remy's instructions were to interrupt anything she was doing when those calls came. Camilla had half expected a call today, but—thinking of the unusual invitation letter in her purse—she realized she would have to say no this time.

"Sorry, something just came up," she said into the microphone. "This celebration is really for all of you, though, so don't wait up for me. I'll be back as soon as I can."

Camilla followed Remy back to her office. Although her workspace was bright and cheery with cartoon figurines and art everywhere and windows along two walls, it lacked a door for privacy.

"I'll take the call in the conference room," she told Remy.

● ● ●

"But I don't want to go with Briana," Avery said. "I want to go with you." He sounded resigned, but Camilla could hear the tears threatening to break through.

Avery was only seven. Life had been so cruel to these kids her foundation was dedicated to: children who had lost both parents. She sat on the conference table and rested her feet on a chair, holding the phone to her ear. "Avey," she said, "sometimes, even though I want to see you, I have to do other things. But in two weeks, I promise—"

He was crying now, his muffled sobs coming through the phone. Camilla closed her eyes.

"I'll be back in two weeks, maybe even sooner," she said. "I'll come pick you up and we'll go to the zoo again. Together."

"I want my mommy and my daddy back. Why did they have to die?"

"I don't know, Avey. I don't think anybody knows that."

"Why can't you just take me to live with you?"

She had asked herself the same question, many times. But there were so many of them. Davey, Ellie, Pedro, Cassie—an endless parade of little faces. She couldn't adopt all of her kids.

"My apartment is too small, Avey. And it wouldn't be fair to the others."

For every kid her foundation tried to help, there were dozens more. The foundation was just herself, a nonprofit registration and fancy letterhead, and whatever time she could get out of Briana and Taylor—overworked volunteers on their college semester breaks. They were drowning.

Avery's sobs tore at Camilla. "I wish I was dead, too."

A fist tightened around her heart. "Don't ever say that. Never."

She wiped wetness from her cheeks with the heel of her palm, set her jaw, and raised the lid of her MacBook Air. She brought up a travel site and checked flights. Holding the phone against her ear with her shoulder, she opened her purse and fished out a credit card.

"Avey, listen to me. There's a very special place I want Briana to take you," she said. "Have you ever been to Disneyland?"

Five minutes later, she was speaking to Briana, one of her two volunteers. "Stop worrying so much. It'll be fun for you, too."

"But I can't get them to open up to me the way you do," Briana said, "I don't have your magic touch."

"You just need to be his friend," Camilla said. "That's all. Hold his hand and have fun together. Show him it's all right to be happy and to laugh again. When he wants to talk about it, he will."

She rubbed the Disney stickers that decorated the brushed aluminum cover of her laptop. "Briana, I know you'll be wonderful," she said. "I'll even share a little trade secret with you...."

For the girls, it was usually Cinderella or Snow White—beloved Disney orphans—that did the trick: letting the kids see that losing their parents wasn't the end, that life was possible again. But Avery was a boy.

Camilla smiled. "Make sure you take him on the Peter Pan ride."

After she hung up, she looked at her laptop screen. Even though she wasn't going herself this time, the Disney company would cover the park admission as usual, thanks to the standing arrangement she had worked out with them. But she had spent a thousand of her own dollars for the plane tickets and the hotel. She was doing that more and more often—more often than she could really afford—and still her little nonprofit was drowning. How could she choose who got help and who didn't?

She hated this; it was so unfair to them.

If only she could afford to hire full-time staff for the foundation, pay them, and cover the plane tickets and hotels. Then she would be able to do so much more.

She touched the invitation letter in her purse. The enclosed check would pay for five trips like Briana and Avery's this weekend. She felt guilty about sending Briana instead of going herself, but she had to see what this invitation was all about. Her heart quickened, thinking about the possibilities. Five thousand might be only the tip of the iceberg. And publicity for her foundation? All she had to do was show up tonight—no commitment—to find out more. Two weeks? It might even be fun.

She tamped down her excitement for one sober moment to consider the wording of the invitation. She really had no idea what this thing was. It might be something she wanted nothing to do with.

She would know soon enough. Right now she had to focus on other things. She pushed through the conference room door, grabbed her award off her desk, and swept past Remy's cubicle. "Call Reuben and tell him I'm coming to see him. Now."

"Hold on a second," Remy called after her. "Your eyes are red."

She stopped. "Oh god, how embarrassing."

"Don't worry about it. Just tell him you were getting high."

Camilla laughed, turning back.

Remy held a small plastic dropper bottle out to her. "Visine."

"That's sweet of you." She took it and hugged Remy. "You're a pal."

"You only like me because I don't ask questions." Remy waved her away. "Go see the boss man. I'll tell him to wait for you."

• • •

"I wasn't really kidding about being mad." Camilla held up the *"Teambuilder"* award. "I love this, but you shouldn't have. We talked about it."

Reuben smiled at her. "The test-screen audience loved the latest changes."

She blushed. "Gianna's a great writer—"

"Gianna said it was mostly you."

"She just needed a sounding board. We bounced a few ideas around."

"You convinced the texture animators to use more procedural rendering, too. We're going into postproduction three weeks ahead of schedule because of it."

Rueben pointed at the award Camilla held in her lap. "I want you to know I had mixed feelings about that. Part of me didn't want to give it to you."

"So why did you, then, Reuben? It isn't fair to the rest of the team."

"The studio is ready to ramp up another production track next year." He looked out the window for a long moment. "I want you to lead it. As full producer."

"That's not my thing. What about Kevin? Everyone loves working for him."

Reuben shook his head. "Kevin says he wants to work under you. He wants to be your AP. The only person who doesn't think you're ready is you. They all wanted to give you that award. That's why I didn't want to. We're just reinforcing this behavior."

She looked down at the award. "I don't understand."

Reuben sighed. "I think you're afraid to step out from behind the team and take a chance on yourself. You're ducking the spotlight, Camilla. Something inside you is holding you back."

Her neck tensed. Why was he pushing her like this? She was great at what she did and she loved it. He had always understood her before.

She forced herself to relax. "Look, I'm honored that you'd want to give me the opportunity," she said, "but it's really not what I do. I'm taking a couple weeks off, and I'll think about it while I'm away. That's all I can promise. We'll talk again when I'm back."

"I'm glad you're taking a real vacation," he said. "You deserve it." He made a shooing motion. "Have a little fun. It shouldn't always be about the team. Sometimes it needs to be about you."

• • •

Walking across the quad toward her office, Camilla spotted Dean headed in the opposite direction, coming her way. She suppressed the urge to avoid him and gave him a smile instead. She refused to let this become awkward. Especially at work.

Dean stopped, so she had to as well.

"Congratulations," he said, looking at the award in her hand.

"Thanks." Camilla's gaze roamed his handsome, earnest face. She had liked Dean a lot. She had let herself get attracted and started dating him, even though she knew that mixing work and her personal life was a bad idea. He was thoughtful, fun, adventurous; the sex was great; they laughed a lot together; and he had respected her boundaries—until he crossed the line.

"How's everything?" she asked.

"Painful," he said. "Confusing."

Her throat tightened. Everything had been so good, but he'd ruined it. He had no right to do what he did. Now it was over, and he needed to understand that.

She met his eyes, crossing her arms and hugging the award against her chest. "I want us to stay friends."

"We *are* friends. No creepy stalker stuff, I promise. I just care about you."

"People who care about each other don't violate each other's privacy."

"Look, I know it's over, but I wish I knew what I did that made you angry—"

"I'm not angry. But I trusted you, and you went behind my back." Her heart sped up, but she kept her voice even. "I got a call from Euclid House, saying you were asking them about my foundation, about me—"

"Because I wanted to know more about this very special person who was coming to mean so much to me—"

She shook her head. "No, Dean."

"...but who's so damn... I don't know, compartmentalized, I guess, that I couldn't really get to know you. Camilla, you're gorgeous, funny, sweet, sexy, and smart as hell, but there's only this small part of you that you're willing to share. You should be proud of what your foundation does."

"I won't talk about that with you."

How deep had he dug? Deep enough to know that she had spent much of her own childhood at Euclid House? If he had found that out, then his next questions would have taken him to the earthquake, and the dark years afterward. A chill ran along her upper arms, turning them to gooseflesh, and she rubbed them, trying to read his face.

He swallowed, looked down. "You're doing that thing again, with those beautiful, big brown eyes—"

"Don't." She let him hear the warning in her voice.

"Sorry." His Adam's apple bobbed again.

Her breathing sped up in sympathy. He had brought this on himself, prying where he had no business. Still, she hadn't meant to hurt him. She reached out and touched his forearm gently. "Friends."

He wouldn't meet her eyes. "I have to go."

"Take care of yourself, then, Dean." Camilla straightened her shoulders and strode off toward her own building without looking back.

CHAPTER 6

The clown fish grinned its cheerful, spacey grin. It seemed to be asking her, *Are you sure you want to do this crazy thing?*

Camilla was sure. She turned off the thermostat and set the alarm. Then she took one last look around her apartment. It was small, and the rent was high, but it was in San Francisco's Marina District, surrounded by trendy cafés, shops, and nightlife—a great place to live if you were a young, single professional woman. The entire Marina District was built on top of landfill and vulnerable to earthquakes, Camilla knew, but she wouldn't let fear limit her choice of where to live. She loved it here.

Except for the commute. Not the evenings, when she'd sail across the wide-open upper deck of the Bay Bridge, convertible top down, long brown curls bouncing in the wind, the water sparkling on both sides. The problem was the morning drive, which took her underneath the two-story bridge's lower deck. The low metal beams would close in overhead, and her breaths would come fast and shallow until she was back out in the sunshine again. But Camilla willingly accepted the challenge. It was a daily dragon to be slain.

The 1989 Loma Prieta earthquake lay buried twenty-three years in her past. It had taken everything from her when she was seven, swallowing her family and consuming her childhood memories in its relentless darkness.

She refused to let it have any power over her now.

For the next couple of weeks, the bridge would be a nonissue anyway. Feeling the thrill of anticipation, she scanned her tidy kitchen, the living room with its stylish urban-loft decor, and the cozy, inviting bedroom. Everything was in its place, and she would be seeing it again soon enough.

Work-wise, the timing was perfect, too. They were in postproduction right now. Besides, she had just turned thirty. She grinned back at the clown fish. A little adventure was exactly what she needed.

She looked at the figurines on her shelf: a red-haired cowgirl, a spaceman, a one-eyed green monster, a lovable boxy robot. *Wish me luck, old friends.* Camilla sometimes wondered if her attachment to these cartoon characters was entirely healthy, but it made sense to her. When she was a child, their Disney predecessors had helped her through some dark years.

On the wall above the figurines, the clown fish watched her from the glossy movie poster, surrounded by his underwater friends. Signatures from her production crew crawled around the margins. She had another poster from the same movie, but she had taken it down because the grinning shark startled too many visitors. Her brand-new award, the crystal Anglepoise lamp, now held pride of place in the center of the shelf.

Camilla loved her apartment. Still, living in the city did have its stresses. The headlines this morning had been the usual grim litany: a carjacking, another prostitute gone missing, a police shooting, a killer stalking women, financial irregularities in the mayor's campaign. It would be nice to get away for a little while.

She slid her jacket on and grabbed the handle of her rolling travel bag. Then she picked up the invitation, in its embossed envelope, from the counter.

• • •

Riding in the cab, Camilla felt a prickle of unease. The driver was heading away from the water, up Divisadero. She had expected to stay on Bay Street and curve along the waterfront. According to the news, three local women had disappeared recently... But on a Friday evening, the waterfront would be jammed with pedestrians, and it was almost the same distance either way. She watched to make sure the driver turned on Geary, then relaxed, sliding the invitation out of the envelope again.

A contestant in a reality show? Not really something she had ever imagined doing.

Camilla watched reality shows occasionally—the better ones, anyway. She was always amazed by the dumb mistakes people made, the way they alienated their peers. With her talent for teambuilding, she would make a killer contestant. Some of those shows were pure trash, though. If she smelled even a whiff of tacky, she was out of there.

The letter did not seem tacky at all. Its linen cardstock and embossing looked expensive, like a trendsetter's wedding invitation. Also, the enclosed five-thousand-dollar check had put some of her doubts about its legitimacy to rest. The money had raised other questions, though. Camilla tucked her hair behind her ear and read the letter again:

Dear Ms. Becker,

Please accept this invitation to join us as a possible contestant cast member when we reveal the details of our flagship reality entertainment project on Friday, December 21, 2012. The event will be held aboard our yacht, Leviathan, departing at 4:00 p.m. from the America's Cup Village Marina, Pier 18, in San Francisco.

The invitation is undoubtedly a surprise. Rest assured that you were not chosen arbitrarily. Vita Brevis Entertainment is a new studio—an independent venture backed by leading industry players. We've dedicated a lot of research and effort into finding the ideal mix of contestant skill sets for our show, which is a team-oriented competition. We believe that you are an excellent prospect because of your specific skills and other qualifications.

We applaud your charitable work with orphans. The competition's grand prize is a significant sum. Should you win, we will make a matching grant to your foundation as well. Even if you don't win, Vita Brevis will dedicate helpful publicity to your foundation's efforts.

Naturally, you bear no obligation to Vita Brevis Entertainment. You may attend this event and listen to the details of the show, and then choose either to accept or to decline further participation. If you do commit, you will be sequestered along with your fellow cast members for up to two weeks during the recording of the show.

The enclosed check also comes with no obligation. Even if we never hear back from you, the money is yours. Consider it a thank-you for taking the time to consider this opportunity. And also for your absolute discretion, which we humbly request: For competitive reasons, we ask that you do not reveal the fact of this invitation to anyone else.

We hope to see you aboard the Leviathan this Friday. All will be made clear then. Please bring with you clothing and toiletries sufficient for a few days.

Very truly yours,
Julian Price
Vita Brevis Entertainment

Camilla looked out the cab window. Sleazeball recruitment tactic maybe? Industrial espionage by one of the big studios? She pursed her lips, amused.

As if. She wasn't some starry-eyed intern who would get drunk and discuss her company's release road map. But she didn't think that was what this was about. Five thousand wasn't chump change, but it was too little to be an attempted bribe. The invitation was probably real. Still, she would go in with both eyes open.

The part about "team-oriented competition" told her they had zeroed in on her real talent. That seemed a little odd for a reality show. Creepy, even. She tapped the invitation against her knee, thinking. How had they found her in the first place?

A background search of Vita Brevis Entertainment had come up blank. No surprise there—major studios often launched their riskier ventures this way, creating separate labels for them at first. The studios did it to protect their established brands in case the venture failed—especially with the edgier stuff. The "leading industry players" behind Vita Brevis would stay unidentified—until the show was a success.

Camilla knocked on the glass divider. "Gough, then Golden Gate onto Sixth, and down Folsom," she said to head off any scenic-route meter padding. The driver tilted his head to listen, then nodded.

Camilla considered the invitation's vague wording again. A worm of discomfort wriggled through her thoughts. What were her "other qualifications"?

The cab cut across Market Street, headed down Sixth, then turned onto Folsom. Camilla monitored the cab's route absently, still deep in thought. She looked up as they passed the white concrete facade of Moscone Convention Center.

Survivor.

Her heart gave an ugly jolt. *What?* The word had leaped out at her from somewhere, snagging in her subconscious.

Pulse slowing again, she scanned the signs announcing convention events. The headline "2012 American Psychological Association Meeting" stood out in large bold letters. She spotted the word, lurking underneath, where it loomed from the title of an event listed for today's date: "The Survivor Personality, 3:30 p.m. Lecture open to the public."

No thanks, I'm good. Camilla felt the skin on her arms tighten. *We've got that subject pretty well covered.*

She turned her head. She wouldn't let it spoil her mood. And then they were approaching Embarcadero, the bay sparkling before them and the Bay Bridge stretching away overhead to the right.

At the stoplight on Embarcadero, her eye was suddenly drawn to a family on the wide promenade sidewalk. The mom was holding a to-go latte in one hand and her phone with the other, talking into it, distracted. Her latte hand rested on the handle of an infant stroller. But it was the other child, maybe 3 years old, who had caught Camilla's attention. The boy was pulling at his mom's sleeve and pointing across the street, bouncing with excitement. Camilla's pulse accelerated.

She was already reaching for the door handle when the boy dashed into traffic.

Horns blared. Brakes squealed. She threw open the door and levered herself out of the cab.

The boy stood frozen in the middle of the street, scared now.

A big gray truck was headed for the intersection, going too fast.

The mother screamed.

Camilla ran.

The boy stood directly in the truck's path.

She wouldn't reach him in time.

Something black buzzed past Camilla with an angry metallic snarl. It flashed across the path of the oncoming truck, right where the boy stood. A half-second later, the warm air from the truck's passing blew Camilla's hair back. She stumbled to a halt. With a scream of brakes, the truck slid to a stop a hundred feet farther up the lane of traffic. Her heart racing, she stared at the spot where the boy had been. He was gone. Then her eyes tracked farther, to where the black shape had stopped on the sidewalk.

It was a motorcycle. One of those high-tech racing-style ones, wrapped in glossy black fiberglass. Its motor burbled, now idling. The rider turned sideways, still astride the motorcycle, and handed the terrified boy to a startled passerby. He—it had to be a he—wore a one-piece black leather racing outfit. The full-face helmet swiveled toward her. She couldn't make out the rider's expression through the tinted face mask.

Camilla realized that her jaw was hanging open. She closed it with a snap.

The rider raised a hand, making a circle with his thumb and forefinger: *everything's okay.* The gesture was for her. Then he faced forward again. The passerby he had handed the boy to asked something. The rider raised his shoulders in a shrug. He leaned forward on the bike. It snarled to life and bumped down off the sidewalk, disappearing into traffic just as the hysterical mother ran up.

It all had happened so fast—the stoplight hadn't changed yet. Camilla returned to her cab, her heart rate slowing to normal. She put her hand on the top of the open door and paused, looking back in the direction the rider had disappeared. Why hadn't he stuck around?

• • •

Fifteen minutes later, Camilla was settled in at a sidewalk table in the America's Cup Village, sipping an espresso. She had a great view of the Bay Bridge overhead and Treasure Island across the water. The entrance to Pier 18 lay directly in front of her. It was the gateway to the largest and most exclusive of the new docks built for the 2013 America's Cup. These docks would provide berths for the largest superyachts and megayachts to visit San Francisco Bay during that event. Several of them were in use already.

The largest of the yachts berthed at Pier 18 dwarfed all the others. Camilla felt pretty sure it was the *Leviathan*. The name was fitting, anyway. With a sleek profile longer than a football field, and five levels of gleaming white fiberglass, smoked glass, stainless steel, and titanium, the ship dominated the waterfront. Other captains and yacht owners cast envious glances toward it. From the promenade, tourists and native San Franciscans alike pointed and speculated. Ships like that were infrequent visitors to the Bay. Two hundred million dollars? Three hundred million? She had never been aboard a ship like that before. Few people ever got the chance to.

While she waited, her thoughts drifted back to the "Survivor Personality" lecture at the Moscone Center. Seeing its title had put her subconscious to work. She remembered what she had read over the years about survivor psychology—the common personality patterns and behaviors that many of them seemed to share. Much of what she read, she had recognized in herself.

The knowledge hadn't been much help, though. She had read that a lot of survivors—even the extroverted ones—also went through periodic cycles of withdrawal, times when they just didn't feel like dealing with other people. Knowing that others experienced the same things you did was comforting. But it didn't tell you how to change those aspects of yourself.

Camilla checked the time: *3:35 p.m.* The lecture would already be under way now. She felt a tightness in the back of her neck and tried to think about something else. The incident with the little boy came back to her, the rescuer on the motorcycle. Strange, that. What kind of person saved a child's life, then shrugged it off like it was no big deal?

CHAPTER 7

Moscone Convention Center, San Francisco

"In a life-threatening emergency or a natural disaster, why do some people live, while others die?"

The lecturer paused. Outside the auditorium doors, the broad hallways of the Moscone Convention Center were quiet. His listeners sat with quiet attention. He wondered, how many of their lives had been touched personally by his topic? How many stories of tragedy and triumph lay behind the silent faces? He looked down at his notes again.

"Following in the footsteps of pioneers like John Leach and Al Siebert, psychologists have studied the phenomenon of human survival extensively. In an extreme life-or-death situation, we find that, at most, ten percent of the population is mentally and emotionally equipped for survival. Only those ten percent are able to perceive the situation correctly, to react quickly and effectively, and to make the necessary adaptations to survive. These 'survivor types' are the individuals who, time and time again, surprise us all by crawling from the wreckage or reaching the shore or walking out of the jungle alive.

"There are wide differences of opinion on whether survivors are born or made. But there is general agreement on one thing: the people who are most likely to survive in extreme circumstances share certain common characteristics."

The lecturer wrote "WILL TO LIVE" on the board. He underlined it.

"Survival is as much mental as physical. Under the most extreme circumstances, some people simply lose their will to live. They die, often without obvious medical cause. The opposite is true of survivors. Survivor types diagnosed with terminal illnesses frequently defy the odds, confounding their doctors and resuming healthy lives."

"Physical size and strength do not seem to be much of a factor. Quite frequently, smaller women or even children survive under the same circumstances where healthy, fit men perish. There are even documented cases where, to overcome some life-threatening obstacle, survivors have exhibited bursts of strength, speed, or endurance far beyond what was considered medically possible for them."

The lecturer wrote "RESILIENCE" on the whiteboard.

"People who exhibit the so-called survivor personality are flexible in the face of adversity. They regain their emotional balance quickly in response to

35

setbacks. They can let things go and start over. They actually *gain strength* from adversity."

The lecturer wrote "SELF-CONFIDENCE."

"Survivors don't need to prove anything to anyone. They don't care if what they see and think doesn't match what others around them see and think. They are competitive and tenacious and tackle problems head-on. They can be defiant."

The lecturer wrote "PLAYFUL CURIOSITY."

"Childlike curiosity and a playful, irreverent sense of humor often characterize survivors. In their daily lives, they do things to test limits, gauge reactions. They take risks, break rules. They experiment to find out what they can get away with. They laugh at threats and authority figures. They don't let situations scare them or have power over them."

The lecturer wrote "ALERTNESS."

"Survivors have a sort of personal radar going at all times. They are attuned to even slight changes in their environment. They read new developments and changing situations quickly, usually before others do. They read *people* quickly."

The door of the auditorium banged, causing the lecturer to stop. He craned his neck and stared into the dimness at the back of the room. Someone had come in. People shuffled, sending a flurry of agitated motion down the rows as the newcomer took a seat near the back.

The lecturer frowned. Trying to recapture his train of thought, he turned to the board again, and wrote "UNPREDICTABILITY."

"In almost all survivors, there is a tendency to have pairs of contradictory, opposing personality traits called *biphasic* personality traits. Survivors can be simultaneously self-confident and self-critical, optimistic and pessimistic, selfish and selfless, rebellious and cooperative. Far from being a weakness, this emotional flexibility is one of a survivor's great strengths. They are able to bring different responses to bear when situations change rapidly or become chaotic. For this reason, other people often characterize survivors as unpredictable."

The lecturer wrote "EMPATHY."

"Survivors are usually highly empathic people. They feel the pain of others strongly. In a life-or-death situation, they are often the ones doing the most to support and help others. However, sometimes not everyone can be saved. Survivors are also capable of making excruciatingly tough choices and choosing courses of action in order to survive that society at large might not deem acceptable. This 'selfish altruism' is one of the biphasic characteristics that survivors share."

The lecturer wrote "INTUITION."

"Survivors trust their feelings. They trust what their instincts tell them about situations and other people. While logical, they aren't paralyzed by analysis. They take action instinctively, quickly, often before they really know why they are doing so. This intuitive ability to read situations and people makes many survivors formidable manipulators. They are skilled at getting others to do what they want."

A bark of abrasive laughter from the back of the auditorium, followed by angry shushing and more rustling in the rows. The lecturer paused. Was somebody drunk? Or on drugs? That was the problem with opening this kind of lecture to the public. He peered out over the tops of his glasses. The commotion stopped. Then he turned to the board again.

He wrote "SYNERGY" on the whiteboard.

"Survivors are creative, intuitive problem solvers. They find easy solutions to difficult problems. That ability to make things look easy can be misinterpreted by others. When things are working well, survivors can appear lazy, disengaged, willing to let things run themselves. But when situations get dire they step in and take charge as needed. Others frequently mistake the easy competence with which a survivor approaches daily life as either laziness, indifference, or a lackadaisical attitude."

The lecturer wrote "SPIRITUALITY." He looked at his audience and cleared his throat.

"Now we come to the discussion of aspects that make psychologists and other scientists uncomfortable. But there is no denying that in the study of survivors, we see a side that is often considered mystical and unscientific. Survivors frequently describe their experiences in religious or spiritual terms. In retrospect, they often speak of faith, of an unshakable belief that they were meant to live through their experience. Some describe sensing a comforting presence when they were at their lowest ebb. Others swear that they were externally guided to do the things that ensured their survival. Unscientific? Maybe. But perhaps not.

"Our understanding of the human brain is still only rudimentary. Perhaps there is a scientific explanation for these phenomena to be found in the fact that most of us are able to tap only a small fraction of our brain's full potential. Survivors may represent those few percent who are able to access unmapped facilities of the brain that remain mostly dormant in the rest of us.

"Ladies and gentlemen, I thank you for your time and interest. Are there any questions?"

Hands went up. The lecturer pointed. The murmur of the audience died down as the first questioner spoke.

"There are limits, right? I mean, survivors don't always survive."

The lecturer smiled. "Yes, there are limits. Survivors aren't superhuman. Sometimes the objective hazards are simply too great, the conditions too extreme, for survival. Even among survivors, there is always a hierarchy. Some are more resilient than others. Every survivor has his or her own breaking point."

The lecturer scanned the audience. For the second question, he selected a raised hand near the front of the room.

"How does someone know if they're a survivor?"

"Well, there's the rub, isn't it? There's no easy answer."

The lecturer lowered his glasses, considering the question further.

"Well, actually, there is an easy answer, though it's not a particularly useful one most of the time. You can conclude that someone is a survivor after he or she survives, even thrives, under circumstances that would kill most people. Until then, your guess is as good as mine. Next question."

The third question came from the darkness at the back of the room. It sent a ripple of displeased murmurs through the audience.

"What would happen if a group of survivors ended up having to compete with each other to survive? Who would win?"

CHAPTER 8

Camilla stood at the rail on the upper deck. The megayacht glided out from under the Golden Gate Bridge and headed into open water. She watched the massive pylons recede behind her, the bridge glowing a soft red-orange in the light of the setting sun. She took a deep breath and turned her face up to the last rays.

Closing her eyes, she let the wind play through her hair. She would go inside the salon in a moment, to mingle with the hosts and meet the other contestants. It was time to start doing what she did best. To give herself an advantage in whatever "team-oriented competition" was planned, she needed to figure out who she wanted on her team. But not quite yet.

The ship sliced an arrowhead of white foam through the dark water. It cruised regally past smaller sailboats and pleasure craft, then turned south, parallel to the coast. Scattered lights were coming on along the headlands. Camilla pulled her jacket tighter against her shoulders.

"You look just like that scene from the movie *Titanic.*"

Camilla turned her head and raised a hand to hold her hair out of her face. "God, I hope not. That didn't end so well." She peered up into the easy smile of the man who had just now joined her at the rail. "This ship is amazing, though. I've never seen anything like it before. Have you?"

He looked around the deck. Another contestant? She studied him. He wore a camel-hair sport coat, pinstripe shirt, and slacks. Nice shoes, too.

"Not in San Francisco, I haven't." He grinned. "In St. Tropez, Porto Cervo, St. Barts, places like that—sure. Makes you wonder what they want from us, doesn't it?" His thin-framed glasses looked expensive. A banker?

She followed his gaze to take in the sweep of contoured white paneling, dark-tinted glass, and blond teak deck that stretched to either side of them. Blue reflections danced in the distance. "Is that a pool?" she asked.

"One of them—there's another up front." He held out a hand. "Mason Gray, by the way. I take it you're a contestant, too?"

"Camilla Becker." She shook his hand. He had short brown hair, a conservative haircut. "So what do you do when you're not auditioning for reality shows, Mason-Gray-by-the-way?"

"I'm in finance." She was right: a banker. "Fixed-income assets and derivatives. Boring stuff. You?"

"Animated film."

He smiled a wolf's smile. "Okay, Miz Camilla Becker who works in animated film, probably over in Emeryville…" *Boom!* she thought. *He's sharp.*

"Look around you. What do you see?" He was watching her closely. She took her time answering.

"Money—heaps and gobs of it."

"But what *don't* you see a lot of?"

Together they looked across the wide, vacant deck and through sliding glass doors into the brightly lit interior of the main salon. A few people were visible inside. They were scattered in small, awkward groups around the vast space. Their body language said they were all strangers to each other.

"People," she said. "There's hardly anybody onboard."

"And what does that tell you?"

"What does it tell *you?*" she replied.

He leaned back against the railing, slid his hands into his pockets, and crossed his ankles. The smile left his face. "It tells me there's a hard sell coming. And they expect to close this deal. They don't expect anyone to back out."

Feeling a twinge of apprehension, Camilla looked back over her shoulder at the Golden Gate Bridge, far behind them now.

"How can they be so sure we're all going to sign on?" she asked.

Mason pushed off the railing. He grinned again. "We should go inside, see how the land lays. Because if this was a three-hour dinner cruise, we'd be circling the bay. Instead we're headed south right now, at top speed."

CHAPTER 9

"This part was a piece of cake," Cory said. "And for a change, I'm not wet or covered in some nasty shit." The hum of the ship's engines was loud. He eyed the client. Definitely not a scientist, this one. Cory wasn't buying it. He waved a hand in the direction of the main salon, three levels above them. "Lights, camera, action—we're live now."

"Show me."

"Pay me."

He took the envelope and thumbed through the bills, counting. They were all hundreds. It took him a while, because there were a lot of them. He had earned it, though. He was proud of the work he had done. Too bad he couldn't reference it for future jobs. It was truly state of the art.

"Okay, good, that's me," he said. "But what about the other techs? We need to pay them, too."

"They've been taken care of already. Out at the site yesterday."

"They were supposed to let me know when they finished."

The client didn't say anything to that.

"Weirdest job I ever did." Cory shook his head, looking around at the gleaming chrome engines. So clean. Not like any ship he had ever been on before. He should have asked for more money. "Getting tangled up in that ropy shit, all those goddamn animals. Those big ugly things—Jesus, I was sure one of us was gonna get killed." He rubbed a thumb along his chin, looking at the client. "If I knew what we were getting into, I might've said no."

The client didn't say anything to this, either.

Cory reached into a pocket. He pulled out the controller, tapped a few times on the touch screen, and handed it to the client. "Go nuts. I watch Discovery Channel sometimes. Let me know how it turns out." He slipped the envelope into his pocket. "Well, okay then, that's it."

The client looked at the screen, slid a finger back and forth across it, and nodded. "Yes, that's it."

The pain was unbelievable. Cory fell to the floor, gasping, and watched the client's other hand slip something back into a pocket. His world faded to white.

• • •

41

"Know the rule of three?"

Cory's eyes flickered twice, then opened. It felt as though some time had gone by. The engines sounded different now. His whole body hurt. He strained to remember what had happened, but couldn't. He recognized the voice, though. It was his client. Something was very wrong here.

He tried to move and heard a crackling noise beneath him, like plastic. A tarp? His eyes flew wide. He was tied down, his arms and legs restrained somehow. He could barely twitch them. A blast of adrenaline jolted his limbs, but he wasn't going anywhere.

"Three months without human companionship."

The client's voice came from behind Cory's head. A bright light dazzled his eyes, making him squint. The light came from long LED strips running directly above him, in a ceiling fixture that seemed too close. Where was he? Sick with terror, he tried to yell, but only a wheeze came out.

"Three weeks without food."

He heard the client's steps, moving away now. He was lying on a table of some kind. He could see shiny tools and parts gleaming on the spotless walls. The ship's machine shop! But he couldn't turn his head. This was bad, really bad. A tremor ran through his body. He wheezed again, feeling the spit dribble down his cheek.

"Three days without water."

Metal clinking. Scrapes. Cory could hear his own gasping. Oh Jesus, he'd give the money back, all of it, never say anything to anyone about this ever. He needed to tell the client that. But he couldn't form the words.

"Three hours without shelter."

The client stepped into view, holding a four-foot pipe wrench. The heavy wrench thudded onto the table beside Cory. The client was wearing a plastic rain poncho now, the disposable kind.

"Three minutes without air. You should focus on that one right now."

Cory realized that even if he could speak, nothing he said would matter. He was going to die. Another heavy wrench thudded onto the table. And a third. He felt his bladder let go.

"The rule of three comes from the Air Force. It's how long the average person will survive when deprived of those things."

The client leaned into his view again, holding the shop's impact wrench now. Cory's eyes traced the wrench's pneumatic hose to its connection point above the table. Bile flooded the back of his throat, filling his mouth with its sour taste. The client grinned and blipped the wrench's trigger twice, splitting the air of the engine room with its loud auto-body-shop whizz. The sound hurt Cory's ears. Tears leaked down the sides of his face, tickling wet against his ears.

"Not everybody is average, though. That's what makes it interesting."

The client moved down to his waist. Something clinked on the table down there. The impact wrench shattered the air again—a sustained scream this time. Vibrations rattled Cory's bones as agony exploded through his hip, sending an entire universe of pain unfolding through his body. His arms and legs shook. He felt himself slide a few inches sideways. Wet pattering noises, something splashing and dribbling on the plastic tarp down at his waist. Oh Jesus, blood—*his* blood! He sucked in a huge gulp of air to scream, gagged instead, and vomited.

The client held up the impact wrench, socketed another long, sharp-tipped metal screw, and put it down again to pick up one of the heavy pipe wrenches. "Sorry, but we just can't have these things coming off of you when you go in the water."

The wrench screamed again in the closeness of the machine shop. Cory's body shook and slid on the tarp again. It went on for a while. Then the wrench was mercifully silent. He blinked. A soft burnt-hair smell hung in the air, like in a dentist's office. Vaporized bone.

His consciousness was fading. He heard the plastic tarp rustling, felt it moving against his body, and then came a ripping sound he recognized: duct tape.

"There's one last part to the rule of three. It trumps all the others. And I can see from your eyes it's going to be the deciding factor here. Do you know what it is?"

As Cory's world faded to black, the client's voice seemed to come from a great distance.

"Three seconds without hope."

•   •   •

The cold air revived Cory a little. A mist of salt spray wet his face. He turned his head and looked down into the churning black water that flowed past, just below him. His body was lying on top of the plastic tarp sheeting. The client put a foot against his side and pushed. He slid along the megayacht's rear sundeck, the slick plastic protecting the boards. Heavy metal shifted against his thighs—the pipe wrenches the client had bolted to his pelvis. His shoulders were hanging off the deck now. He teetered, balanced on the verge.

He looked up, uncomprehending. The client was a shadow silhouetted against the stars. Cory couldn't make out the face.

"It's possible to survive for hours in the water, even injured, if you put your mind to it—the weights won't help things, though. How good a swimmer are you? I'd love to stay and find out. But I can't, unfortunately." The shadow's head turned, looking toward the bright light from the main deck and salon above. "I've got to get back to the party. The other contestants might wonder where I am, and I don't want to miss our host."

CHAPTER 10

Camilla stood just inside the entrance to the main salon, with Mason Gray, the banker, at her side. The interior of the split-level space was a showcase of gleaming chrome, travertine, and cream-leather luxury. Together they surveyed the salon and its occupants. She had a good feeling about Mason. He was smart, she could tell. His eyes roamed the room, mind clearly active behind that lazy grin. She sensed confidence—cockiness, even. There was always some risk with his type, but she decided she wanted him on her team. *If* she signed on, that is.

"Your turn." She put a hand on his arm. "Tell me what you see."

"We're missing one."

"So you're psychic now?"

"Nine people, counting us. Four women, five men. They wouldn't leave the sexes unbalanced. Ten is a nice, round number."

Camilla looked at the others, bunched in twos and threes. "All contestants, then. So where are the Vita Brevis folks? Our hosts?"

Mason's eyes roamed from group to group, as if sizing them up. "What do you think of our competition?"

"Some are our teammates."

"At first, maybe. But there's only one grand prize." This, naturally, coming from a banker. "So tell me, who are they?"

Ten contestants meant two teams of five. So she needed three more besides Mason. She needed to choose carefully, though. The key to winning was having the right team dynamic—a balance, not necessarily all the best individual players.

At the other end of the salon, a curved zinc bar swooped beneath art-glass sconces, backlit by soft blue accent lighting. She focused on the trio standing by the bar. A half-Asian girl in her late twenties was talking to two guys. They looked to be around the same age.

"The girl, she's an athletic type," Camilla said. "Personal trainer, maybe. Triathlete."

Mason nodded. "Rock climber—watch her hands, what her fingers are doing around the edge of the bar-top as she talks. Acts like she's just one of the guys, but you can see she loves being the center of attention."

The Eurasian girl suddenly looked at them across the room, unsmiling, almost as if she knew they were talking about her. Her eyes were unfriendly, too. Camilla was a little surprised. "Whoa, girlfriend, lighten up," she murmured.

Mason laughed. "Amazon Girl is going to be trouble. I can tell that already."

Camilla shifted her focus to the two guys. "Guy talking to her, with the shaved head, African American. Wearing a Hawaiian shirt. He's a big dude—must spend serious time working out. A gym owner?"

"Ex-military. See how straight he's standing, like he's at attention? But she's more interested in the other guy." Mason laughed. "The guy who looks bored."

She looked at the third member of the trio: a tall Latino with short, dark hair. Her breath caught. He was movie-star good-looking. Something about him seemed familiar, too.

"Dresses like a bartender from a SoMa ultra lounge," she said. "Seriously? Who wears all black nowadays?"

But she couldn't take her eyes off the guy. Mason seemed to notice her noticing, too—she wasn't fooling him with her snide comments. She quickly turned back to Mason.

"Ouch!" he said. "You're a fashion critic, too."

She threw him a mischievous smile. But she couldn't avoid occasional glances at the dark-haired man in black. His eyes flicked in their direction. For a moment, his gaze met Camilla's. *My rider! That's my motorcycle rider!* She had no idea how she knew, but she was sure of it. He lifted an eyebrow, momentarily seeming to acknowledge her. Then he looked away.

Mason was eyeing her strangely. He'd caught that, too. Awkward. Camilla smiled, almost in apology. She couldn't think of anything to say. Then both her and Mason's eyes were drawn to a new arrival: a slim blonde, standing in the opposite doorway. Now it was Mason's turn to take a surprised breath.

"I didn't know we were doing *America's Top Model*," he said.

The arrival of the blonde woman seemed to suck all the air out of the room. Conversations stopped. *Wow!* Camilla thought. *And she's used to that.*

The woman appeared to be in her mid-twenties. She looked around, big green eyes taking in the scene, her gaze moving from person to person. Her wide, friendly, dazzling smile said, *I can't wait to meet you.* A stunned Camilla found herself smiling back. Mason was wrong. The blonde woman was wearing a designer dress and heels, but she didn't have the empty, no-personality beauty of a runway model. She was gorgeous, for sure. But there was too much excitement in her eyes, too much energy in the way she stood. She would make a runway model standing next to her look like a mannequin. At least her mouth was too wide. But even that minor imperfection simply added to her allure. *Good Lord,* Camilla thought, *the rest of us can just pack up and go home now.*

"Hi, guys," the blonde said. "I'm Jordan. Sorry I'm late."

Uh oh. Camilla looked back at the three by the bar. Her rider in black was getting up, his movements lazy but graceful, like a panther's. He excused himself from the other two. *No, no, no,* Camilla thought helplessly, amused at the same time by her own reaction. Her rider headed around to the other side of the bar. He ran an idle hand through his hair, then flipped a pair of martini glasses upright with a flourish. Jordan the not-runway-model cut across the room toward him. No hesitation.

That was bound to happen no matter what, Camilla thought. Those two belonged together. Oh well. She watched her rider—well, *the* rider, anyway—set to work mixing a pair of drinks. One of his turned-up sleeves slid higher, exposing a tattoo on his forearm.

"Hey, did I call that bartender thing, or what?" she said. Her voice sounded a little weak.

Mason was serious now. He watched the rider closely. "That tattoo looked like a Manta Ray to me... kind of unusual." He considered for a moment. "I'd say he's a swimmer or, more likely, a scuba diver. Sure is good looking, though. I bet he's in great shape."

Camilla's eyebrows went up slightly. Mason was gay? She had missed that, which was surprising. Then her amusement deepened. It was going to be *that* kind of party for her, then... she should have brought a book.

Her eyes were drawn back to the other side of the bar. She giggled. "Check out climber-chick. Oh, *man*, she's pissed now. Jealous much?" The Eurasian girl was staring at the blonde with open hostility. It actually wasn't that funny. Her eyes were slits, her mouth tight. If she were a cat, Camilla thought, her ears would be lying flat against her head right now.

Contestants were supposed to spend *two weeks* sequestered together?

Camilla hoped things weren't going to get ugly.

CHAPTER 11

Lauren glared at the blonde woman flirting with Juan. *Sarah Calloway.* Of course it wasn't really Sarah, whom she hadn't seen since high school, but Lauren knew the type. This version was named "Jordan," apparently. Fucking prom queen, all grown up. Walked into the room, and suddenly you didn't exist anymore. Lauren had really liked talking to Juan. He was a dive captain from Catalina, seemed really interesting, and so goddamn *hot*, too. But the blonde had called him to heel with a silent dog whistle that only guys could hear, and that was that. Lauren's chest felt tight, her abs tense. She flexed her fingers, concentrating on taking deep, slow breaths.

She turned her attention back to JT. Big lug was still talking. What was he saying to her?

"…team up?"

JT grinned his infectious grin and rubbed a hand across the back of his shaved head. His biceps bulged like footballs. She looked at his Hawaiian shirt. Clown probably thought he was on vacation or something. That wasn't yuppie gym muscle she saw underneath it, though. Handsome enough in a boyish sort of way, but she could see a hard edge, too, hidden beneath that grin. A crisscrossing knotwork of thick scars traced his upper arm, pale against his coffee-dark skin.

Juan the hot dive captain had a prominent scar also, right at his hairline.

And she had her own, too. Interesting.

"What if there's no teams, cowboy?" she said.

"Letter said 'team-oriented competition.'"

She rolled her shoulders, then twisted at the waist, stretching until her spine popped audibly.

"Ever do any serious climbing, JT? I like the big walls."

"You mean rocks and ropes and shit?" He looked away for a moment.

Had that been contempt in his eyes, as if she'd said "knitting" or something? When he looked back at her, the earlier boyish charm had evaporated. His eyes had gone flat and distant, and so had his voice. It sent an unpleasant chill down the back of Lauren's neck.

"Girl, I was Force Recon for four years. Marine Corps. Deployed in Afghanistan. We did some rock climbing, that's for sure. With eighty pounds of kit on—while getting shot at."

"How nice for you."

Lauren didn't want to talk about anything that had happened in that part of the world. She really didn't. It had been five years, but the thing was just

49

never going to go away, was it? She looked at her fingers, gripping the bartop, their tips white.

If this show was anything like the ones she had seen, it was going to be a straight-up competition. Physical challenges, probably—with clear rules, scores. Winners and losers, determined in a fair fight. *Her* kind of game. She looked at Jordan and Juan and felt her confidence come flooding back. Prom queen over there was in Lauren's world, now. She was in for a big fucking wake-up call.

Lauren found herself looking at Jordan's nose.

CHAPTER 12

C amilla's motorcycle rider—Mason's scuba diver—lounged on a barstool, half sitting, half standing. Jordan leaned her elbow on the bar next to him. The two of them looked so right together, Camilla couldn't really muster up much in the way of jealousy. Jordan had her head turned sideways, a curtain of blond hair hanging past her cheek as she talked into the rider's ear. Eyes moving restlessly from group to group, he nodded at something she said. Camilla's thoughts went back to how he had scooped the little boy from in front of the truck. So casually, effortlessly. She wasn't sure why, but she didn't want anybody else to know about that. It would stay their little secret.

Jordan suddenly looked right at her. *God, that smile.* Again Camilla surprised herself at how much she wanted Jordan to like her. Jordan tilted her head in apology, still smiling. She held up a finger, indicating herself and Camilla—*sorry, you and I need to talk, but I got a little tied up here*—and Camilla knew she had her team leader.

At her side, Mason chuckled. "Don't know how you do it, but it looks like you just made another friend."

Camilla felt her face split into a big, happy grin. "Come on, banker man," she said. "It'll be five on five, so let's go find the last member of our team." She glanced again at the climber-chick and her buff buddy in the Hawaiian shirt. But she got the same trouble vibe from them that Mason had, so she moved on.

"What if, for teams, they make it men versus women?" Mason said.

"Then you've pretty much lost already, banker man. Because getting a team to work their best together is what I do." She poked him in the chest. "You can get back to selling those subprime mortgages."

"Not funny."

At the far end of the salon, the floor dropped a few steps to lounge seating—all cream-leather couches and chrome. Two women were sitting near a fireplace. *A fireplace!*—Camilla had to remind herself they were on a ship at sea. The older of the two women leaned forward, talking with her hands—a lot of energy there. She was in her late thirties, her stylish dark-blond hair frosted just so with bright salon highlights, wearing jeans and a sweater—a nice cashmere. And expensive-looking running shoes. Suburban soccer mom, Camilla was willing to bet.

The younger woman was really petite, shorter than Camilla, Asian. Soccer Mom had her cornered, it seemed. She was dressed like a teenager, in a gray "SF Academy of Art" hoodie, skinny jeans, and black Converse high-top

51

sneakers. The only thing missing was a backpack slung over one shoulder. She probably cut her own hair, too, from the looks of it. Art student? She looked as though she really wanted to be somewhere else, but Soccer Mom had her trapped.

Soccer Mom was a possibility, Camilla thought. She looked capable. She might be too pushy, though—might not get along with the rest of the team.

A long travertine countertop divided the lounge seating from the upper dining area. It was loaded with platters and appetizer trays—fancy finger food. The last pair of contestants were two men, working their way along the countertop from opposite ends. At one end, a rough-looking blond guy with a sour expression on his face was poking among the platters with his finger. His longish hair was straggly, like straw, and he wore a long-sleeved black T-shirt, knee-ripped jeans, and scuffed boots. Camilla could see a small triangle of beard under his lower lip. His eyes met hers across the room, and he smiled at her.

Snake eyes, she thought, smiling back. There was something there she didn't like.

Mason snickered. "He's looking for the buffalo wings." Apparently, the guy wasn't his type, either.

The other guy, loading his plate from the appetizer trays at the far end of the counter, was older. He was a big man with broad shoulders and a thick neck, his silver hair cut short on a squarish head. He looked to be in his mid-fifties, in good shape for his age. He was dressed like he was going on a camping trip, in a sleeveless pocketed safari vest, khaki dungarees, and high-end hiking boots. His outdoorsy clothes looked brand-new: straight out of the Eddie Bauer or Timberland catalog. Camilla smiled to herself, liking the man already. She got a sense of solidity, dependability, from him—he'd be a steadying influence when things got heated. There would be no ego-driven need to assert his authority or get drawn into the usual alpha-male pissing contests. He reminded Camilla of Reuben, her mentor from work. She was drawn to his calm serenity, but there was also a hint of sadness or hidden pain about him. She wondered what his story was. But here was their fifth team member, she decided.

"Physician," Mason said. "He's a doctor."

She looked at him in surprise. "Where'd you get that?"

"In the bathroom." Mason pantomimed scrubbing his wrists. "I saw how he washed his hands." He inclined his head toward the other man at the buffet, the snake-eyed blond one. "I can't tell if that guy's a doctor, though—he didn't wash."

"Oh god, too much information."

"Always good to have a doctor on your team," Mason said, grinning. "You never know when you might need one."

CHAPTER 13

B rent stepped back from the counter to give the blond man access to the platters. He poked at this and that in apparent dissatisfaction, and Brent noted the scars on his hands and knuckles. He was tall, though not quite as tall as Brent, and lean and wiry. Active lifestyle but poor nutrition, Brent figured. Not a smoker, though—surprising for a guy like that. For the next ten years he'd probably be fine, but after that it would all be bad news. The scars on the man's hands were the result of poor suturing by indifferent doctors. Sloppy workmanship. Brent knew where he'd seen that particular kind of medicine practiced.

With his back still to Brent, the blond fellow spoke. "What's the matter, old man? You never seen somebody who works for a living?"

Brent smiled. "Brent Wilson. Pleased to meet you."

The man turned and met Brent's eyes steadily. For a long time, he didn't say anything. Then he wiped a hand back and forth on his pants leg, the way a mechanic might wipe grease off on his coveralls, and held it out. Brent shook it.

"Travis Hargrave," the man said. "Why are you here? You get a letter?"

"Looks like everyone here did," Brent said.

"What's this all about?"

"Fifteen minutes of fame. Our hosts are late, though, so you might get five to ten instead."

Travis's eyes narrowed. "Funny man." His posture had gone stiff. "I seen some of these shows. No offense intended, but you don't seem the type."

Brent laughed. "You may be right about that, Travis. I almost didn't come. But I have to say, you don't much seem the type, either."

Travis rubbed at the little triangle of beard under his chin. "Letter said prize money." He tilted his head, looked up at Brent. "From what I seen so far around here, old man, there doesn't appear to be all that much in the way to stop me getting it."

He turned his back on Brent and went back to picking his way through the appetizers.

Brent tucked his hands into his vest pockets and watched Travis move away. *Self-confidence is a good thing, my friend.* But sometimes too much of it could get you into trouble. The last eight years had been difficult for Brent. Incredibly difficult. He had lost a lot, but he had learned a lot about himself too. He now knew what it meant to be a survivor.

CHAPTER 14

Camilla had learned Soccer Mom's name: Veronica Ross. She was an attractive woman in her late thirties or early forties. But she looked a little hard, too.

"This is ridiculous," she said. "They're going to play a *video* for us? That's it? I went to a lot of trouble to be here. I could be getting work done instead."

On a Friday night? Camilla wondered, but she asked, "What kind of work do you do, Veronica?"

The large video monitor on the wall behind the head of the table looked different now. It had been there all along—part of the high-tech decor, displaying colorful abstract-expressionist art. But now the art had faded away. The blank screen seemed to be watching them like a big, dark eye.

Cups rattled on saucers nearby. Dessert forks scraped against fine china. All the contestants had gathered around the long table, except for Jordan and the motorcycle rider, whose name was Juan Álvarez. A dive captain. Camilla was eager for them to join—she wanted to meet the two key members of her dream team. But they were still on the other side of the salon, deep in conversation. In the meantime, Camilla and Mason were getting to know the other contestants. Stewards dressed in white had rolled a dessert cart in and served coffee at the long table covered in elegant white linen. A growing sense of impatience and anticipation hung in the air. The ship had left port almost two hours ago, and so far, there was no sign of their hosts.

Veronica's jaw tightened in annoyance. "I'm the director for Safe Harbor, a women's shelter, here in the city."

Camilla was surprised—seeing the designer-label clothes, salon highlights, and careful makeup, she had trouble picturing Veronica in that role. She looked down at Veronica's hands. Her French manicure was perfect.

"That's commendable," Brent said, and sipped his coffee. "Camilla, you also mentioned that your foundation does some work with orphaned children?"

She nodded. "Our invisible hosts promised some publicity, and a matching grant if I win."

Veronica was staring at her. Those eyes were her most striking feature: a pale metallic blue that was almost silver, like the glowing eyes one sometimes saw on Siberian huskies, or wolves. Camilla had never seen eyes that intense before, and now they were fixed on her, unblinking. It made her

55

uncomfortable. *Jeez, lady, relax—this isn't a competition between our charities.* But then again, she realized, that was exactly what this was.

"So what does your husband do?" Mason asked Veronica.

"I'm not married. But let me tell you something." She set her coffee cup down with a clatter for emphasis. "This is not how it's supposed to work. Not at all."

"It's a new studio," Camilla said. "Maybe they're trying something new."

"Right," Veronica said, shutting her down. "I asked around, and there are these websites where you apply for the shows you want to try out for, with descriptions of what they're about. You're supposed to send in a short video of yourself, where you talk about why you'd be perfect for this show or that show, and then they pick the contestants from those. Natalie was saying she watched..." She looked around, frowning, and snapped her fingers twice. "Where *is* Natalie?"

Natalie must be the art student. Camilla sort of remembered the girl coming to the table, but now she didn't see her. She scanned the salon, but Natalie seemed to have disappeared somehow.

Veronica looked puzzled, too. She pushed her chair back, and her pale, silvery eyes swept the room for several seconds. Then she relaxed. "There she is."

Natalie stood over by the appetizer counter. Camilla wasn't sure how she had missed her the first time she looked. The girl did have a sort of stillness to her—a tendency to disappear into the background, avoiding notice. She now made her way back, holding a Diet Coke. Camilla realized that she had never heard her speak. What an odd choice for a reality-show contestant.

"Natalie, you watch a lot of these shows," Veronica said.

Natalie dropped into her seat and hunched forward, holding the soft drink can between her hands. The sleeves of her gray hoodie covered her palms so that only her fingers showed. She looked down at the can and rolled it back and forth, not answering at first. Being the center of attention seemed to make her uncomfortable. Camilla watched her with curiosity. Her bangs were long, covering her forehead and eyebrows. She was probably twenty but looked younger, with a cute but oddly expressionless face. Finally she spoke.

"Older ones mostly, I guess. *Survivor, Amazing Race, Apprentice, Big Brother, The Bachelor... Hell's Kitchen.* The newer ones aren't as good."

"Right," Veronica said. "Did they ever do anything like this?"

Natalie shook her head. "No. People applied to them first, wanting to be contestants."

Veronica looked at the video monitor again. "Well, for this one, it looks like they just pulled whoever off the street. Incredible waste of time."

That's not quite what they did with us, Camilla wanted to disagree. But then again, how *had* they chosen the ten people now in the room? She looked around, trying to find something that connected them all: Mason, a banker; Lauren, who, it turned out, was a world-class rock climber; JT, an ex-Marine who owned a gym now; Travis, a truck mechanic; Brent, a doctor; Veronica, the director of a women's shelter; Natalie, an art student; Juan, a dive-boat captain; Jordan, a... What was it she did for a living? Fashion model, maybe? And Camilla herself, an associate producer of animated films.

Her own not-so-secret skill was getting groups of talented artists to set aside their individual egos and work together to make magic. She was good at it. Her teams achieved the kind of success that had won dozens of industry awards for their films. But how did her "specific skills and other qualifications" fit in with the others?

On the surface, the ten contestants had almost nothing in common. But Camilla was picking up something about them all. A similarity—something she found unusual for any group of ten strangers, particularly in a competitive situation. There was no loud, ego-driven grandstanding going on, no insecure posturing and jockeying for position. No idle nervous chatter, despite the strangeness of their circumstances. Instead, throughout the room she could see a general sense of confidence, a calm air of readiness. A quiet alertness, quick glances that missed very little. Familiar behaviors. She felt an odd ripple of anxiety—almost fear.

What exactly was going on here?

CHAPTER 15

Juan watched the eight contestants who were gathered around the table. He was leaning with his back against the bar, elbows on the bar top, ankles crossed. At his side, Jordan had both hands on his shoulder now. She rested her chin on the backs of her hands, talking into his ear. Her blond locks trailed onto his forearm. It felt nice. He listened to what she was saying, nodded again. He was thinking hard.

Juan was not here for the same reason as the others. He had come for a very specific purpose. He had some questions that needed answering, and he would do whatever he had to, be as ruthless as necessary, to get to those answers.

He raised an eyebrow, looked at Jordan. She lowered her eyelids a little, still smiling, and he came to a decision. He was here for answers, but there was no reason he couldn't also have a little fun along the way. He tilted his head toward Jordan and hesitated a moment. She might even be offended by what he had in mind.

Would she or wouldn't she?

There was only one way to find out.

CHAPTER 16

Camilla looked up as angry voices erupted suddenly from across the room. Problems already?

On the far side of the salon, Jordan had stepped away from Juan to face him, fists on her hips, body rigid with anger. Juan's hands were raised in apology, but he looked angry, too. His raised voice carried.

"That's not what I meant at all. It's not what I was saying. You didn't let me finish." He reached to take Jordan's arm. "Stop overreacting."

She shook his hand off violently. "Get your fucking hands off me, asshole! You're on your own." She looked ready to slap him.

Camilla's stomach sank. Her team was falling apart before it even started.

Jordan turned away from Juan and walked across the salon with angry, energetic strides. Slapping her purse down on the table, she sat down hard in the chair next to Camilla. She stared down at the tablecloth for a moment, composing herself, then turned to face the others.

"Hi. Sorry about that," she said. "That was embarrassing."

"Wow, what did he say?" Camilla asked.

"Forget it. I made a mistake, is all. I don't want to talk about it." She took both Camilla's hands and gave them a friendly squeeze. "You're Camilla. I'm so excited to meet you." The dazzling smile was back, but it looked a little forced now.

Camilla glanced over at Juan. He was still standing next to the bar but he was looking at her now, hands in his pockets. He gave a little shrug that told her nothing.

She looked back at Jordan. "How do you know my name?"

Mason asked, "And where *were* you all this time?"

"Good meeting you, too, Mason." Jordan appeared to be pretty much over her anger now. Just like that, Juan was forgotten. "Listen, guys, I'm a journalist."

"So you were interviewing who exactly?" Mason asked.

Jordan grinned at Camilla, crooking a finger at Mason. "He's smart. I like him."

She also shook hands with Brent and Veronica, whose names she also knew. Natalie was gone again. Camilla hadn't noticed her leave.

Out of the corner of her eye, she watched Juan saunter over to the far end of the table, where he joined Lauren and JT again. This was a problem. She would have to rethink her team now. It looked like she had lost her motorcycle rider. What had Juan said that upset Jordan so badly? But if

Camilla had to choose between them, she was sticking with Jordan. Veronica would have to be their fifth team member.

Jordan's smile pulled them all in. "Okay, so this whole thing's really strange, right? I got a weird feeling about it. My instincts are pretty good, and something seemed way off. So before I came in here, I did a little exploring— talked to the crew I ran into." She leaned forward. "You know what, guys? Other than the ship's crew, we're the only ones on board."

"How did you find out our names?" Brent asked.

"I can be very persuasive when I want to. The crew showed me a list with all our names. And little pictures of us, our faces. That's how they knew who to let on board."

I was right, Camilla thought. *Jordan's definitely our team leader.*

"Just the ten of us?" she asked.

Mason chuckled. "Ten Little Indians."

Camilla slapped his arm.

"There was a Cory Mitnick, too," Jordan said. "Some confusion about him. One crew guy thought he was on board, but it doesn't look like he made it."

"So what's supposed to happen here, then?" Brent asked.

Jordan pointed with her chin at the video monitor on the wall. "Their comms guy is waiting for a video transmission from somewhere. He's going to send it right to that screen."

"What else do you know?" Veronica's question sounded like an accusation. Her silver eyes were locked on Jordan now.

"There's a safe." Jordan giggled. "This whole thing is so hush-hush top secret. They're going to get a text message with the combination, open it, and hand out some paperwork inside for us to sign. Then they drop us off."

"Drop us where?" Camilla asked.

"That's the craziest part." Jordan grinned at her. "They don't know. Right now, no one on the crew has a clue where we're going. They're just supposed to take us south along the coast, until they get another text message, containing GPS coordinates…"

Mason nodded.

"Our final destination," he said.

CHAPTER 17

The monitor flickered to life. Camilla saw a montage of short video clips flash by—smash cuts through scenes from reality shows past and present. Conversations along the table died out, and heads turned.

"*Survivor*," Camilla said.

"*The Apprentice.*" Mason laughed.

"*American Idol*," Jordan said.

"And there's *Fear Factor*," Lauren called.

"*Big Brother.*" Even Natalie was calling out the names.

The scenes zipped by faster and faster, from one reality show to another. Then the sound faded out, replaced by a professional voice-over. The speaker's voice resonated through the room, friendly and earnest.

"We call this reality television," he said. "Instead of professional actors and a script created by a screenwriter, these shows bring ordinary people together in imaginative situations and exotic places. The contestants divide into teams and compete against each other for money and fame. We've all watched them, and I'm sure we've all asked ourselves the question: 'How real is any of this, *really?*'"

Camilla watched as the video montage changed. Now she was seeing behind-the-scenes footage—outtakes and production stills, all from the very same reality shows. And her excitement leaked away like the air out of a balloon.

Camera crews swarmed around the contestants now. Makeup artists touched up their faces. A row of green portable toilets stood on the beach, a few yards away from the driftwood shelters the contestants had built. Camera trucks blocked the cobbled square in front of a historic church; stacks of pizza boxes were piled next to a cooking pit.

Nobody was calling out show names anymore. Camilla looked at the faces of her fellow contestants, seeing disappointment and disgust.

JT laced his fingers behind his head and leaned back. "I knew these reality shows were all bullshit."

On-screen, a bearded man in rags sat against a palm tree. Camilla recognized him as one of the earliest reality stars, a first-season winner. The man held a cell phone between his shoulder and ear, talking into it. He was holding a white Starbucks coffee cup. Without looking, he held up his other palm, waving away the camera—waving *them* away, it seemed.

Veronica laughed. The sound of that laugh, so low and sultry, came as a surprise to Camilla.

Jordan pushed her coffee cup away. She seemed annoyed. "Well, that's just great, guys. Why are we here, then?"

The video montage faded out. The speaker appeared, life-size, on the large screen of the monitor.

"I'm Julian, your host," he said. "Welcome. Let's discuss why you're here."

From his voice, Camilla had expected him to be older. Shoulder-length black hair fell in waves to each side of an open, friendly face. His dark suit was elegant, perfectly tailored. He stood alongside another big monitor screen. On it, a three-dimensional logo spun slowly: the stylized initials "V B E"—Vita Brevis Entertainment.

"Folks, you just saw why reality television's appeal is fading." His fingers made air quotes around "reality."

"You don't have to actually *see* the fakeness onscreen," he said. "Viewers can *sense* it. They pick it up subliminally just from watching the contestants react. This is why the ratings of reality shows are dropping further with every season. You can't fool the audience."

The camera pulled back farther to reveal the end of a table in front of Julian. Camilla could now see where the video had been shot. The table was the one where the contestants now sat, and Julian stood next to the very screen they were watching. He smiled at them all.

"But you can still create truly authentic reality entertainment," he said. "We've found the answer, and it's an easy one."

Up on the monitor, he opened his arms invitingly. "Modern technology, my friends—it lets us solve the problem of making a reality show 'real.' Tiny hidden cameras and directional microphones enable the producers, engineers, and camera operators to disappear into the background. They become invisible to contestants and audience alike.

"Vita Brevis Entertainment is well funded," he said. "Our flagship venture will be a new reality show we create using this technology—a show based on a very simple premise: one hundred percent authenticity.

"What this means..." Julian clapped his hands together and leaned against the table. "Contestants experience the show exactly as the audience sees it. No downtime. No leaving the set. No meeting the crew. Cameras roll nonstop everywhere, twenty-four seven, until we have our winner.

"Which brings us to why each of you is here." He smiled. "You've been invited to participate as contestants in the pilot show. Together, we are going to reinvent reality entertainment."

On-screen, Julian paused for effect and looked away from them, as if scanning the walls, floor, and ceiling of the room. "In fact, the show has already begun," he said. "You don't see us, but our cameras have already captured some fantastic moments. If you give us your legal approval, that footage will become the first fifteen minutes of the most exciting and popular reality series ever made." He looked out at them, smiling again. "Starring *you*."

Julian disappeared from the screen, and another rapid montage of video clips began to play.

Camilla was surprised to see herself, standing at the rail and talking to Mason.

Cut to JT pointing out a window, showing Brent something.

Cut to Lauren, standing with a hand on each side of the doorway, unsmiling, sweeping the room with her eyes like a gunfighter entering a Wild West saloon.

Cut to Natalie, hands tucked under her knees, looking into the fireplace, Veronica leaning toward her, talking.

Cut to Travis tasting an appetizer, spitting it out, and putting it back on the tray.

Cut to Juan and Jordan at the bar, flirting as he mixed their drinks.

Jordan grabbed Camilla's hand and said, "Oh, no! I hope they don't use that last one." But she was laughing.

"We haven't signed anything," Brent said. He wasn't laughing. "Legally, they can't use any of this. We have to be careful here."

Julian reappeared on-screen. "Before you decide anything, let me share how you were selected." His face became serious. "Each of you has been carefully screened by our team. We knew exactly what kind of contestant mix we wanted. We went looking for you. And we found you. Each of you fits a particular profile perfectly. We looked at thousands of potential candidates. But in the end, we chose the ten of you."

He raised a hand as if to deflect any questions. "There's no obligation to participate, obviously. You have a choice to make. There is a small packet of legal paperwork to sign, including a straightforward contract. If any of you choose not to give us audio and video rights to your performance, we can edit you out of tonight's footage—the rest of us will just go on without you.

"But my friends, for those of you who do decide to sign on, I can promise the adventure of a lifetime." His eyes flashed with excitement. "The location we've chosen will surprise and amaze you. We'll be arriving shortly. Shooting the show will last between ten days and two weeks, from start to finish. You'll be competing, in teams and as individuals, toward a grand prize which one of you will win.

"And for the grand prize itself..." Julian walked forward. The camera panned back to follow him, revealing more of the table. It was piled with bundles of green bills, stacked in untidy mounds that spilled across the tablecloth, in place of the coffee cups and dessert plates scattered in front of the contestants now.

Camilla bolted upright. So much money! It stretched the length of the table. People shifted around her, voices raised in excitement, but she couldn't move. She could only stand there, staring. With that kind of money, she could take every single orphan in California to Disneyland. She could hire permanent staff. She could help *all* her kids, instead of always being forced to choose just a few. She thought of Avery's voice, how he had sounded on the call this afternoon, and her eyes stung. She sat down again.

At the other end of the table, JT was bumping fists with Juan, Lauren, and Travis. "That's what I'm talking about. Oh *hell* yeah."

Jordan let out an excited little scream, grabbed Camilla's hand, and squeezed. With her other hand, she held Veronica's. Veronica's pale eyes were locked on the screen, and her mouth hung open.

"Now, *that*..." Mason's eyes were moving, as if he was counting. "... is a lot of money."

No kidding, banker man! Camilla laughed.

Brent reached over and squeezed Mason's shoulder. He was smiling, looking at the screen. "Yes, it is," he said. "We should have expected it, after seeing this yacht. But yes... yes, it is."

Camilla's excitement was suddenly tempered with dread. She *had* to win this. She looked at her chosen teammates. She could now understand Mason's earlier comment: at some point, they, too, would stand between her kids and that money. The thought made her very uncomfortable, but she wasn't going to let her kids down.

No matter what.

"At the end of the competition, in less than two weeks, one of you will walk away with five million dollars in cash." Up on the screen, Julian rested a palm casually on the table, next to the stacked bundles of bills. "*This* cash. Oh, and one more thing." He smiled. "It's tax free. We'll cover the taxes, too, so you get every penny."

The table erupted into cheers around Camilla. Everyone was talking at once. On the monitor, Julian leaned casually back against the table, his unbuttoned suit jacket draping open, the money piled high behind him. His eyes held a glimmer of amusement. Amid the excited buzz in the room, Camilla watched him up there on the screen.

He seemed to be enjoying their reaction.

CHAPTER 18

Forty minutes later, Camilla strained to see what lay around them. The darkness was almost absolute. She could hear the soft thump and plash of waves against the rocks on both sides. The noise of the engines was fading now, the running lights of the ship's launch already out of sight. All around her, contestants stood huddled in the blackness. Too close. The skin on her arms tightened into goose bumps.

"I said I wasn't a lawyer." Mason's voice came out of the darkness beside her.

"You said that contract looked clean," Veronica said, a few feet to Camilla's left. "I swear to God, if this is some kind of a joke, I'm going to sue the hell out of these people." She shifted restlessly, the boards creaking under her feet.

"Well, there was a release of liability that we signed, too," Mason said.

"Right. You know what?" Veronica's iPhone lit Mason's face. "You're an idiot."

The light reflected off his glasses. Camilla couldn't see his eyes—only that he was grinning.

Veronica swept the phone around them like a flashlight. The glow revealed the faces of their fellow contestants, frozen in expressions of confusion and concern. They stood together in a tight cluster on the narrow stretch of dock.

Brent's voice came from behind Camilla, over her shoulder.

"What about our bags?"

"They're supposed to bring the bags tomorrow," she said. Her voice sounded little-girl-lost to her, so she cleared her throat. "They probably need to inspect them first—make sure there isn't anything the show rules don't allow."

A dim glimpse of pale foam roiling a few yards away. The breeze cut right through her dinner-party clothes. She pulled out her own iPhone. No signal. *Wonderful.*

She crossed her arms about her chest, shivering. "Everybody, stay calm," she said. "They're just trying to disorient us—"

"The money." Veronica's phone lit Mason's face again. Her voice was as harsh as ever. "What did it say about the money?"

"Guaranteed... I thought." He lost his grin. "I wouldn't have signed it, otherwise."

Veronica lowered her iPhone.

Travis spoke. "Way I read it, it said as long as we don't all manage to disqualify ourselves, one of us ten gets that five million."

Sounds erupted with frightening suddenness from the surrounding darkness. Animal noises. Loud yelps, barks, moans. The sounds drowned out the crash of the waves. Camilla could hear deeper rumbles, too. They echoed off the rocks—the sounds of something very large. The other contestants pressed in tighter, everyone facing outward. The noises seemed dangerously close. Then the sounds faded away again. A few last yips and groans trailed into silence.

Now the press of tense bodies was silent, too. She could feel her fellow contestants all around her, frozen in place, listening intently. Her own eyes strained from their sockets, staring into the darkness. Oh god, this was such a mistake. Where the hell *were* they?

The wind shifted direction.

In the middle of the huddle, someone coughed. Then there was a small choking noise that ended in a stifled sob. Natalie, maybe?

Jordan spoke for all of them. Her voice shook.

"Oh my god. What is that fucking smell?"

CHAPTER 19

Near Natural Bridges State Beach, Santa Cruz, California

Heather Stevens stood in the living room of the Swanton Drive house she shared with Jacob Horowitz and Dmitry Kuznetsov, the other two members of her research team. Heather was struggling to come to grips with what the call from Karen, their director, meant.

"What do you mean, *not going?*" Jacob, the lead scientist, asked her. "As in not going *today?* Or not going *at all?*"

Heather realized she was still holding the phone. She put it down slowly. "Karen said next season we could—"

"*Next season?* No, that makes no sense." Jacob stared at her, rubbing his beard. "It took us eight fucking months to get the grants approved for *this* season." His eyes blinked rapidly behind his glasses, showing the same confusion that Heather felt. "Besides," he said, "all our gear is already in the van, checked and loaded. How can she pull this crap at the last minute?"

"Karen didn't really give me a reason."

Jacob's face turned red. "Two goddamn weeks a year—that's all we ever get out there, and now we don't even get *that?*"

He slammed the lid of his laptop shut, shaking the small kitchen table. The waterproof tracking unit that he had been prepping rolled away. Heather caught it as it rolled off the edge, and put it back with the others. "Look, why don't we take a minute to calm down?"

"This season is different." He walked over to the window and stared into the blackness outside. "There's something *going on* out there, Heather. Out at the island. The data from the old trackers shows it clearly: a convergence pattern we've never seen before. No one has. It's a completely new behavior."

Jacob's jaw worked, and he pulled at the chest of his rumpled "UCSC Fighting Banana Slugs" sweatshirt. The last time Heather had seen him do that was two years ago, the night before his dissertation defense. Picking up her tea mug with both hands, she plopped down onto the couch. She looked down into the mug but found no answers there.

"We need to call Dmitry," she said. "He took the van this afternoon. He might already be headed to the pier."

"You do it," Jacob said. "I'm thinking."

Heather put down her tea and spread her hands. "Look, I don't want to make excuses for Karen. This is messed up. But I know she's dealing with a

69

lot of pressure from the grants committee. Maybe the funding situation is worse than we know."

"Like, how is that *my* fucking problem? Karen's the director, not me. She's supposed to be dealing with all that so we can concentrate on the science. What am I gonna do now, Heather? Put the study on hold until next year?"

"You should calm down."

"*Fuck* your calm down. Let's all go down to the Institute right now and catch her in person. She needs to tell me to my face why we're getting thrown under the bus."

• • •

A half hour later the three scientists stood in front of Karen's office door. To Heather's surprise, it was locked.

"She always used to work late." Jacob ticked a fingertip against the brass plate on the door's glass upper panel which read, "*Research Director, Santa Cruz Pelagic Institute*." "Have you seen her working late even once since she became director? Because I sure haven't," he said. "She didn't return your call, either. This is such bullshit."

Dmitry, the third member of their team, laid a hand on Jacob's shoulder. "She's not here. Come, we go now, drop off van at lab. Tomorrow morning I buy you Starbucks, and we figure out what to do."

Heather liked Dmitry. The short, stocky Russian was a thoughtful and meticulous scientist. But with his cheery grin, he was a center of calm rationality, too. That was something their team also needed, particularly at times like this.

"Inside every cloud is silver line," Dmitry said. "Instead of going to island now, maybe we finish deep-water survey, then enjoy New Year's with family, no?"

"Listen to him, Jacob. He's right. We'll be able to look at this with clearer heads tomorrow." Heather pulled out her phone. "In the meantime, I'm going to get a hold of Karen's admin, or someone from Raja's team. *Somebody* has to know what's going on."

CHAPTER 20

"I see something moving out there."

Lauren squinted and saw it again, flopping just at the edge of her vision: a faint gray shape in the blackness. She pointed it out to JT. "On the rocks."

JT's teeth and eyes gleamed white, next to her face. "I'm gonna go check it out," he said, and started down the dock, headed toward land.

She stopped him with a hand on his shoulder. "Here, take this."

"Don't want it." He handed the cell phone back. "Mess up my night vision."

Lauren watched JT's back disappear into the darkness. Several other phones lit up the small section of dock where the rest of the contestants stood. The nauseating stench came and went as the breeze shifted. It filled her sinuses, at times getting so bad it made her gag.

The animal noises rose around them again. That deep rumble came from nearby, beneath the other sounds, like liquid gargling in a giant plastic drainpipe. Her eyes met Travis's. His grimace showed teeth. *You look pretty scared there, tough guy.*

"Seals. Sea lions. That's what you're hearing." Juan's voice, coming out of the darkness behind them, was calm.

The beams from several phones swung in his direction, and Lauren could see him now. He stood at the edge of the dock a small distance away, his side to the rest of the group, arms crossed. He was looking down into the water. "If you've been to Fisherman's Wharf or Pier Thirty-nine," he said, "then you've heard them before."

She caught a flicker of amusement on Juan's lips. Asshole was just standing there laughing at them. But she could make out individual seal yips and barks now amid the noisy din.

"Great," she said, disgusted. "We're standing around terrified by a few seals." Her voice carried loudly. "What a bunch of losers."

She turned and walked down the dock with forceful strides. "Let's get going, people. Someone's gotta be waiting for us up there, wondering why we haven't shown up yet." She could see only a few feet in front of her, but that was enough to find her footing on the rocky ground where the dock ended. Now, where was JT?

A deafening roar exploded out of the darkness right in front of her. Lauren froze. Before she could react, JT came flying toward her, arms waving wild circles, running all out. His eyes were huge with fear.

"Go!" he shouted into her face as he raced past her.

Lauren pivoted and sprinted after him. Another deep bellow exploded right behind her. It sounded angry. She risked a glimpse over her shoulder as she ran.

A massive wet shape surged across the rocky ground behind her, moving with terrifying speed, rippling up and down in a violent humping motion. It reared up behind her, taller than she was, and much, much wider.

Lauren's belly clenched in terror. Oh Christ, what the hell was it?

Her feet pounded onto the boards of the dock. She whipped her head around again. It was almost on top of her now, the size of a minivan, its gray hide knotted into a cauliflower mass of scar tissue. She glimpsed an eye, red-veined with rage. Then, with a sideways jerk, the beast suddenly broke off the chase. It faded back into the darkness with another chest-rattling roar.

Lauren slowed her pace. The visible part of the dock remained empty behind her. Her heart was hammering. Her hands shook. Fucking JT! He had let that thing almost get her. She backed the rest of the way to join the others, staring fearfully at the shore.

CHAPTER 21

"Fuck, fuck, *fuck!*" JT was bent almost double, his hands on his knees. His chest heaved violently, breaths whistling in and out. Camilla put a hand on his shoulder, but he shook it off.

"Christ!" Lauren looked frantically from face to face, her mouth opening and closing. "What was that thing?"

"A seal?" Mason called to Juan. "You think?"

To Camilla's surprise, he was laughing.

Lauren took two angry steps and pushed Mason hard in the chest. He stumbled back and almost fell. She glared at him for a moment, but her hands were shaking. It looked as though she didn't trust herself to speak. Then she stalked off.

JT straightened up and looked at Mason. "You find something about this funny, asshole?"

Mason seemed like he was about to say something more, but Camilla quickly took his arm. "I need to talk to you," she said.

She led him away from JT's angry stare. Then she put her fists on her hips and rounded on him. "What were you thinking? This isn't a joke. There's something dangerous out there."

"There might be something out there, but trust me, it's not likely any real danger." Mason's voice was calm, reasonable. "Think about it. Whatever it is, they put it there deliberately, to liven things up with a little drama."

What he said made a lot of sense. It was even kind of obvious, in a way. Surprising that no one else had considered it.

"Let's tell the others, then," she said. "We need to get everybody calmed down before someone does something dumb."

She started forward, but Mason gently held her back by the arm.

Behind his glasses, his eyes twinkled. "Or we can just keep quiet instead. See how long it takes them to figure it out for themselves."

• • •

"No bars. I can't get a signal, either." Veronica sat on the dock next to Camilla, hugging her knees to her chest. The screen of her phone lit her face from below. The others were barely visible, sitting or reclining in twos and threes scattered about the dock.

"How about you?" Camilla turned to Jordan, sitting to her other side.

73

"Me, neither. Nothing," she said. "I've got Verizon. Who do you have?"

"A T and T."

A few hours had gone by. After a brief debate, everyone had agreed to wait until dawn, and see what the daylight brought. No one wanted to dare the darkness beyond the dock again. They had all settled in for a lengthy wait, doing their best to get comfortable despite the cold, the stomach-churning smell, and the sporadic chorus of animal barks and grunts.

Natalie lay on her back with her knees raised, staring at the sky. Her hands were tucked into her hoodie's front pockets. Camilla reached out and tapped her on the foot. "Natalie?"

Natalie jerked her foot away. "What?"

"Does your cell phone work out here?"

Without getting up, Natalie pulled her hand out of her hoodie pocket, holding a phone. She tilted her chin forward, peering at the screen. "Nope."

"What is it?"

"An iPhone."

"No. I mean your carrier. A T and T, Verizon, whatever."

"Sprint."

Camilla exchanged a puzzled look with Jordan and stood up. "Hey, everybody."

Faces peered up at her.

"Can anybody get a signal on their phone right now?" she asked.

Her sense of unease grew as person after person confirmed a lack of signal across the entire spectrum of mobile carriers.

"Let's all save our batteries," she said. "Turn 'em off."

• • •

Camilla lay on her side. The darkness crushed in on her from all sides, and she imagined she smelled smoke. She shivered and hugged herself. Her legs ached. She had been drowsing on and off, half asleep and half awake, for the past couple of hours. At least the cold breeze served as a constant reminder that she was out in the open, providing some relief from the claustrophobic press of the dark.

A little distance away, she could see Juan and Mason, squatting side by side. They were talking quietly about something. What? She strained to hear what they were saying, but couldn't. Juan's finger moved on the dock between their heels, tracing something out for Mason. A map? She got the distinct impression that he knew exactly where they were.

Someone dropped to the boards right next to her. It was Travis, the mechanic. Snake Eyes.

He leaned back on his elbows beside her, staring out into the darkness in front of them. "Can't really say this is what I expected." He nodded to himself. "But I guess that's all right. As long as we get our shot at that money... Camilla, right?"

She nodded. This close to her, here in the dark, he made her uncomfortable.

He pointed out over the water, at an angle from the dock. Camilla figured the shore lay in that direction. "Look right over there," he said. "Give it a minute or two. Tell me if you see something."

She peered in that direction, seeing nothing at first. But after her eyes adjusted, she thought she detected a faint flash, barely visible. It disappeared, but then she caught sight of it again. Then another one, some distance from the first. And then a third, and a fourth. They seemed to form a line, probably along the shore.

"What do you think they are?" she asked.

"Can't rightly say for sure. But I suppose I have some idea." He paused, fingering the triangle of hair under his lip. "Because what our good buddy Julian said about this thing running twenty-four-seven stuck particularly in my mind."

He looked back out at the water. "Had a job few years back pumping gas at an all-night truck stop in Bakersfield. Lonely place at night. Some bad types drifting through, time to time. Year before I started there, trucks out in the lot got broke into four times. Owner couldn't afford a security guard. So what he did, the owner, he put these cameras up around the lot. Got a break on the insurance that way. Thing was, there weren't any lights out in the lot. Place was dark as pitch at night. So the cameras, they were infrared."

Camilla shifted position, putting a couple more inches between them.

Travis pointed toward the shore. "I sometimes had occasion to go out into the lot at night," he said. "If I happened to look directly at one of them cameras when I was passing, I'd see it flash just like that. But sorry if I'm bothering you. Just trying to be friendly." He got up and moved away.

Camilla looked toward the invisible shoreline. The flashes seemed sinister now, a row of eyes hidden in the darkness. The idea of large unknown animals roaming out there had been scary enough, but this was worse, somehow. It seemed purposeful, deliberate. Like something huge watching them. Biding its time. Waiting.

• • •

Lauren's impatient pacing was getting on Camilla's nerves. She yawned and pulled herself to her feet. The air was damp, chilling her skin. According to her phone, there were still a couple of hours to go until dawn. Jordan lay fast asleep on the boards next to her, curled on her side with her blond hair pillowed on one arm.

Next to Jordan, Veronica looked up. "Do you really think this will help your little orphan cause?" she asked.

"It'll be light soon," Camilla said. *What is your problem, lady?*

Lauren was back. "As soon as it's light," she said, "I'm gonna go hunt that goddamn thing down. Find out what the hell it was." She shifted from foot to foot, shaking her arms and fingers like she was loosening them up. "Who's with me? JT?"

"Hell yeah. Sucker was big. Fast, too. But if it's still around come morning, it's gonna be one sorry motherfucker."

Brent laid a hand on JT's shoulder. "I didn't see it, but I don't think it makes sense to go challenging some wild animal. This may be its home. What do you think it was?"

"Don't know." JT shook his head. "Don't care. Walrus maybe, some shit like that."

"As far as I know," Camilla said, "walruses live up in the Arctic. Alaska, Northern Canada. Why would a walrus be down here on the California coast?"

"Because of all that global warming shit."

Lauren pushed her way between them. "It wasn't any walrus—I saw one at Marine World up in Vallejo a couple years ago. This thing was kind of similar, but different. A lot bigger and uglier." Camilla caught a flicker of fear on Lauren's face. "Like a goddamn dinosaur."

Day 2

Saturday: December 22, 2012

D awn broke slowly. A faint rosy hue spread behind the low, oppressive cover of pewter clouds, and what lay all around them gradually took shape in the dim gray light. Camilla rubbed the chill from her arms and joined Jordan and Veronica where they stood nearby. Seagulls swirled overhead and landed on the seaweed-draped rocks that stretched away to either side of the dock. The air was noisy with their cries.

Lauren and JT were pacing at the edge of a sloping rocky breakwater that blocked the view of what lay inland.

Lauren waved impatiently. "Let's move out, people."

"Be careful," Brent said. "We should all stay close together." He stood with the others at the edge of the dock, where it met land. The shore was rough here—a maze of small projections and inlets that curved out of sight in the morning mist. In the light, their surroundings no longer seemed scary. But they did look wild and desolate.

Jordan pointed a group of small seals out to Camilla. "Just look how cute they are!" she said. "Like puppies." The seals stirred lazily on the rocks and slipped into the water with barely a splash.

Veronica sniffed. "Filthy animals." She stepped off the dock to join the others. But Camilla was surprised to see her smile at Jordan, laying a hand on her arm as she went by. Unbelievable. Jordan had charmed even *her.*

Jordan grinned at Camilla. "I was wondering when you were going to wake up, sister." She clapped her hands together. "This is so crazy. Let's get rolling before the gung-ho types steal all the glory."

Camilla looked down at Jordan's feet, wobbly in stiletto-heeled pumps.

"Manolo Blahniks," Jordan said. "I've got some flats in my bag, wherever that is."

"In the meantime," Camilla said, "those are going to get destroyed."

"Whatever. I don't care about that." Jordan started toward the breakwater, then looked back over her shoulder. "Besides, after I win I'll be able to buy myself a whole closetful."

Not if I can stop you. Camilla swallowed. Teams and collaboration were more her thing than head-to-head competition, but in the end there could be only one winner here. All Jordan's "OMG, guys" and "sister" stuff aside, it was important to remember that. She followed Jordan along the shore. An avid mountain biker, Camilla was in pretty good shape herself, but Jordan moved with the athletic grace of a dancer. The thought of going toe to toe with Jordan intimidated her more than she wanted to admit. But they would be on the same team, she reminded herself. Jordan liked her, too. It was okay to want to be friends with her.

Tangled coils of rubbery brown seaweed were piled here and there, with great mounds of it along the waterline. Camilla recognized it as kelp. Knots of it floated in the water, supported by air bladders that grew along the hoselike stalks. It looked like the tentacles of some alien thing, more animal than plant. Freaky. She made an involuntary grimace but quickly changed it to a neutral expression, remembering the cameras that were probably watching right now.

At the base of the breakwater, Jordan took a tentative step onto the rocks, then another, before she stopped. In high heels, her footing was precarious. She looked stuck.

"Come on, help her," Veronica said.

Camilla shook off her misgivings and hurried forward.

Jordan already had an arm around Veronica's shoulders. She threw her other arm around Camilla's and gave her a friendly squeeze. Together the three of them joined the others making their way up the rocky slope.

Soon all ten contestants stood in an uneven line at the top of the breakwater. Nobody said anything at first. Camilla's jaw dropped in amazement as her surprised eyes roamed the strange vista in front of them, trying to make sense of what she was seeing.

Everywhere she looked, things were in motion: flopping, flapping, wriggling along the ground, or rising into the air in brief hops to land again nearby. Sleek wet heads rose up to look around, then lowered again. Mouths and beaks opened in threat, warning away other animals that came too close.

Next to Camilla, her pale silver eyes wide, Veronica stared in openmouthed disbelief. She shook her head once, as if to clear it.

"Where in the hell did these people just dump us?"

CHAPTER 23

Verve Coffee Roasters, Santa Cruz, California

"Karen's back tomorrow," Heather said. "She can meet with us then. I talked to her admin."

"That's crap," Jacob said through a mouthful of muffin. "She's avoiding us."

"Don't talk with your mouth full," she said, handing him a napkin. "But now we get to the interesting part. I also got hold of Sara, from Raja's team."

"And?" He dropped the muffin onto his plate, spilling crumbs.

Dmitry was back, with three white cups balanced on saucers, which he slid onto the butcher-block table. "They do fancy foam drawing on top, see? Is nice, but coffee tastes same like Starbucks."

"No, it doesn't," Jacob said. "I hate it when you say that. It's not even close. Anyway, Heather, go on."

"Raja's team also had their time on the island canceled with no explanation," she said. "They were freaked out at first, just like us. But Karen told them not to worry, she'd gotten their grant fully funded through next year—at a higher level. Ours, too. Karen said they could add another researcher to the team."

"Still sounds like the usual bullshit politics. Raja's team gets preferential treatment, and we get the shaft again." Jacob's voice rose, drawing stares.

"Sh-h!" Heather said. "You're missing the point. It wasn't just *our* stay that got canceled this year. It looks like none of the Institute teams are going out now."

"That's crazy," Jacob said. "Parks and Rec can't just arbitrarily revoke permits. So who bumped us?"

Heather considered. "Maybe it's the change of underwriter. Sounds like Karen found us all some new sponsor, so maybe this year's permitting grants weren't valid anymore."

"Maybe, maybe, maybe. That's all we've got?" Jacob gestured with his arm, splattering coffee on a nearby couple.

"Sorry!" Heather said, handing them her napkin. Jacob crossed his arms to fume.

Dmitry looked confused. "Okay, Karen says somebody give us money for next year? No progress review first? Is good news, then." He stirred away the fern-leaf pattern in his latte foam. "But why we don't go to island?"

81

"Somebody else is going out instead of us," Jacob said. "Bet on it." He sounded calmer. "There's no way they'd bench both Institute teams and have the station sit empty, not during December. That's when things really get cranking out there—for the pinniped and avian researchers, too."

"Look, I'm still not happy we aren't going," Heather said. "But, frankly, this new funding thing is a relief. We were looking pretty sketchy for next year; you know that. Now it sounds like it's a done deal."

"I still say we're getting screwed." Jacob wiped at his mouth. "It's the usual thing. The Institute doesn't get enough PR value out of our research, despite its importance. Our babies aren't cute and fuzzy enough for the mainstream public."

Dmitry frowned. "You should not think of them as 'our babies,' Jacob. Does not show respect. They are not pets. Very dangerous animals—you need to remember this always. If you getting careless with them, something bad will happen."

CHAPTER 24

Camilla stood at the top of the breakwater and looked down the slope at the scene in front of her, just taking it in, unable to speak. A boiling brown carpet of seals and sea lions, flecked with the white and gray of seabirds, blanketed the ground sloping away from where the ten humans stood. The downslope ended in bluffs that dropped to a small beach on the far side. White-capped waves churned the half-mile-wide channel that separated the beach from the mainland, where a sandy point faded into rising bluffs.

They were on an island, she realized. It was small—maybe a quarter-mile long and only a few hundred feet at the widest spot. There wasn't a single tree, not a single other person in sight. Only rocks and more animals than she had ever seen in one place before. In many spots, she couldn't see the actual ground itself; it lay hidden beneath the teeming seals and sea lions. Colonies of gulls, auklets, cormorants, and other seabirds hopped between the seals, adding their noise to the din. Trains of pelicans crossed the sky overhead.

"Oh my god! Someone actually *lived* here?" Jordan pointed to a pair of oversize two-story houses that commanded the high ground to their right. Both structures were ruins, their empty window frames dark. The silhouettes of dozens of large pelicans jutted like living gargoyles from the rooflines.

Brent pointed to three plainer, newer-looking structures to their left. "Those are in better shape," he said. "Some sort of warehouse or factory complex, maybe?"

Near the three industrial buildings, a rickety framework of metal beams lay on the ground alongside a pile of rubble. Some kind of tower had fallen there long ago. An eight-foot concrete seawall protected the warehouse buildings. Two other concrete structures—a windowless blockhouse and a twenty-foot concrete dome—stood a short distance inland. Seals, sea lions, and birds swarmed around it all.

"This was right here in California all this time?" Mason laughed. "Who knew?"

Lauren stood rigid, staring into the distance. Camilla's gaze followed hers to a group of larger, darker animal shapes occupying the flatter sections of the beach and downslopes. *Those* were what had chased Lauren and JT last night.

The animals looked similar to the seals and sea lions. But much, much bigger.

One of the largest reared up, lifting the front of its blubbery body high into the air. It was bigger than a pickup truck. Its blunt snout ended in a lumpy mass of flesh that hung in front of its face like a short trunk, jiggling from side to side as the animal rippled along the beach like a gigantic, obese caterpillar. It bellowed a challenge—a deep, gargling rumble that Camilla could not just hear but *feel*, vibrating through the rocks under her feet.

Its opponent, an equally monstrous creature, lumbered forward to close the distance between them. The giant combatants drove into each other, chest to chest, and struck at each other's neck and shoulders with savage bites. Short flippers waved at the air for balance as they rose even higher, trying to crush each other into the sand. The wet slaps of snouts smacking flesh echoed off the bluffs as blood streamed from the deep wounds inflicted by their sharp teeth.

"Oh god, that's horrible," Camilla said. "It's like *Jurassic Park* here." She looked away. "What *are* those monsters?"

Even Mason seemed subdued by the spectacle unfolding before them. "I guess Juan was right after all," he said.

Juan the dive captain—her motorcycle rider—stood with his hands on his waist, watching the animals fight, with an expression of mild curiosity on his face. His black dress shirt was untucked, shirttails flapping in the breeze.

"*Mirounga angustirostris,*" he said. "Northern elephant seals."

Camilla couldn't take her eyes off him.

Jordan noticed. She shook her head once, mouth tight with disapproval, and walked away.

Conflicted, Camilla followed. She found Juan fascinating, but they were on different teams now. She didn't want to risk alienating Jordan, her chosen team captain… and maybe also her new friend.

CHAPTER 25

"There's nobody here," Camilla said. "Unless they're inside one of these buildings."

Brent squinted at the two houses, then turned toward the three warehouse structures in the other direction. He scratched the side of his head.

Watching him, Camilla smiled to herself. He did that whenever he was thinking, reminding her of a big, cuddly cartoon bear wondering where the honey is.

"Where do you think they put our bags?" he asked.

"No kidding. I need to change my shoes." Jordan balanced on one foot like a stork, and reached for the other shoe. She tore off the broken heel and tossed it aside. Her designer stilettos were totally trashed, falling apart and coated with filth, but she didn't seem to mind. She was staring at the two ruined houses with a look of wide-eyed curiosity.

"I say we try those first," she said. "They look more interesting."

Camilla poked Mason in the shoulder. "I've got some news for you, my *GQ* friend, and don't forget this is coming from a mountain biker..." She grinned. "You're about to get real dirty."

"I'm a banker," he said. "I'm used to being real dirty."

"Come on," Veronica said. "While you're standing around yapping, those guys are actually doing something." She pointed to Lauren, JT, Juan, and Travis, who were already picking their way across the open space toward the houses. They moved in single file, weaving and stepping carefully between the seals and the seabirds whose nests dotted the ground every few feet.

Camilla's group followed. Jordan led the way. The remains of a wooden walkway lay scattered at their feet. A few boards were still laid out in the original railroad-track pattern, but most had been pushed aside or were missing completely. Seals waddled nervously out of their path. Birds protested their passage with angry squawks.

"There's babies everywhere, guys." Jordan was smiling. "Seal pups, chicks in the nests. This is some kind of a breeding ground, so watch your step." Her own steps wobbled on her broken stiletto heels.

"On an island like this, they're safe from predators," Camilla said.

"Except humans," Mason said.

Brent nodded. "Except humans." He frowned, a puzzled expression on his face as he stared at Lauren, JT, Juan, and Travis in the distance. But he tucked his hands into his vest pockets and followed Jordan through the living obstacle course.

Camilla and Mason exchanged a glance. Behind Brent's back, Mason raised a hand to scratch the side of his head. It was a good imitation, except for his exaggerated expression of confusion.

She shook her head at him. She liked Brent. Waving an arm to indicate the island around them, she silently mouthed, "Cameras."

Mason swept off an imaginary top hat and bowed to an invisible audience. Camilla rolled her eyes and turned to follow the others.

•   •   •

"These houses have got to be a hundred years old," Jordan said, "but no one's lived here for decades." She bent to pet a seal. "Except these guys."

"I wouldn't do that," Brent said.

Jordan smiled but ignored him.

The seal seemed to enjoy her attention. It rubbed its neck against her hand, closing its eyes. Camilla wasn't really surprised.

"He's just a wet little doggy," Jordan said. She pointed at the larger house. "I know a little about architecture. That looks like a classic Victorian, although it's in pretty bad shape. The other one was built later. It's in the Greek Revival style."

"Who cares?" Veronica said. "Neither one'll be around much longer." She pointed to a dark gap that yawned from beneath the Victorian, where part of the foundation had collapsed. "Let's find someone and figure out what the hell we're supposed to do."

The two houses had lost all their exterior paint to the elements long ago. They were weather-beaten to a uniform gray, striped white with heavy streaks of bird guano. Dozens of empty black window holes and doorways stared back at the contestants. The dormers and eaves of the larger, Victorian house were greenish with mold. Four brick chimneys jutted above, topped by the silhouettes of roosting pelicans. White seagulls and black cormorants landed and took off from the roof in a steady buzz of activity. Camilla noticed them flying in and out of the windows, too.

The other house—the one Jordan had called Greek Revival—looked plainer, but still large for a two-story. The architects had built it as an extension to the Victorian, with a shared foyer connecting the two houses. Yelping seals spilled from the doorways of both and waddled up and down the slumping porches.

"These were mansions," Camilla said. "But who built them out here? And *why*?"

No one answered.

A few smaller structures stood in the open space around the houses. A large storage shed, a chicken coop, and a laundry outbuilding stood nearby. Isolated sections of picket fencing projected from the ground. Piles of debris and wind-stripped siding lay everywhere.

The rocky bench where the houses stood extended fifty feet in each direction before steep bluffs fell fifteen feet to the roiling, splashing sea below. Both houses faced toward the mainland. On that side, bluffs dropped to the island's largest beach.

"How could anyone live here?" Camilla asked. "The animals would just overrun everything."

"There used to be a barricade." Brent pointed back the way they had come, to where a dark line zigzagged across the island, cutting it in half. "Bluffs on three sides, so the seals can't get up here from the beaches. They fenced this area off and kept it clear."

Small sections of barricade still stood—heavy logs stacked three or four high, held in place by thick fence posts. But most of it had fallen long ago. Brown logs lay scattered in piles near the broken posts.

Camilla laughed. "That wouldn't do much to keep out an elephant seal."

"Looks like the bigger ones prefer the beaches," Brent said.

Juan, Lauren, JT, and Travis stood on the porch of the Victorian now. It looked to Camilla like they were getting ready to go inside.

"Veronica's right," she said. "Let's go, team."

• • •

"Careful," JT said. "It's dark. You don't know for sure none of those big elephant things are waiting in there."

"You heard Juan." Lauren smirked. "They're only seals."

Juan shrugged. "Sixteen-foot, five-thousand-pound, aggressive, territorial seals." He started toward the doorway, but she blocked his chest with her arm.

"Ladies first," she said.

Lauren stepped into the doorway, panicking a small sea lion that was coming out at the same time. It leaped sideways into the yard to avoid her. She paused at the threshold for a few moments, squinting into the darkness, then moved inside.

"Slow down, girl." JT shouldered past Juan to follow Lauren into the house.

Camilla turned to Jordan. "Should we go search the other one?"

"Come on in, people," Lauren's voice commanded from deep inside the Victorian. "This is just gross. But it's definitely where we're supposed to be right now."

With no breeze to disperse it, the smell of feces and ammonia was far worse inside. Camilla waited until her eyes adjusted to the dimness, then followed Lauren's voice. Soon they all stood in the large central sitting room of the Victorian. Dim light filtered in through the doorways and the open windows of adjoining rooms. Abandoned nests—feather-studded piles of mud, dung, and coyote brush—lay mounded on the floor. The seals had coated the floorboards in a thick layer of droppings and mud from outside. Shuffling away from the contestants, they huddled in the corners of the central room, making restless, disturbed motions.

"Disgusting." Veronica brushed at the sleeves of her sweater. "This is absolutely *revolting*."

Sea lions moved up and down a stairwell leading to the second floor. The stairs were so thick with filth that Camilla couldn't see individual steps, just a muddy ramp. But she could see that Lauren was right.

Someone else had been in the building quite recently to prepare for their arrival.

CHAPTER 26

A large flat-screen video monitor loomed from the wall above the nest-choked fireplace. Once they were all in the room, the screen lit up and a familiar face appeared. Julian wore a different suit—black this time, and judging from its cut and sheen, another two- or three-thousand dollar outfit. It looked strange, juxtaposed with the dirty wood and pockmarked concrete of the wall they could see behind him.

"Congratulations," he said, "and welcome to the playground where our adventure will unfold. And what a playground, huh? This is a unique location, a rare biodiversity hot spot where dozens of species congregate each year to procreate and ensure their continued survival.

"You may have already met some of our larger seasonal residents." He chuckled. "I suggest you stay out of their way. It's mating season, and they can be a little touchy this time of year."

"No shit," JT muttered.

"So, again, I welcome all of you to Año Nuevo Island. We're in a restricted area not open to the general public. It's quite a privilege. We have the opportunity to witness, at close range, the natural drama that plays out here every winter."

Julian leaned back against the wall and looked at them all. "But this year, Año Nuevo will fulfill another function, too. It will provide the dramatic stage for our series of six challenges, the first of which is about to begin."

He paused, as if to ensure their attention. An expectant silence descended over the room.

Camilla looked at the eager anticipation on the faces of her fellow contestants. She knew that her own looked the same. Her legs tensed with nervous readiness.

"The Victorian-style house we are standing in was built in 1906." Julian pushed off the wall, speaking faster now. "It's the former residence of the lighthouse keeper. The lighthouse on Año Nuevo was active from 1890 to 1948—you may have spotted the wreckage of the tower. The assistant lighthouse keeper's residence is the adjoining house, right through that archway there." He pointed past the contestants.

"Both houses would frequently get overrun by the native wildlife. It was a constant battle for the island's full-time residents: the lighthouse keepers and their families.

"After the lighthouse was decommissioned, the houses were abandoned to the elements. Nature has spent the last sixty years taking them over." He grinned and pointed both index fingers at the contestants. "Now *you* are going to take them back."

Veronica shook her head. "Meaning what, exactly?"

"The rules of this first challenge are simple," he continued, ignoring her interruption. "It's a team challenge, so you'll divide into two equal-size teams. We need to make these buildings habitable again, but first we need to evict the current tenants. One team will focus on clearing this house, while the other team clears the house next door. For every seal or sea lion you usher out, you add a point to your individual score. Be firm but gentle; harming the wildlife is not allowed."

He paused. "Your scores are all-important. You start with zero points. In each challenge, you can win points. In some, you can also *lose* points. At the end of all six challenges, the player with the highest score wins the grand prize—five million dollars. So guard your points well.

"And here's how team dynamics come into play," he said. "The team that finishes clearing its building first wins today's challenge. Each person on the winning team will have twenty points added to their score."

Julian's on-screen gaze moved purposefully around the room, from person to person. "Choose your teams. Clear the buildings. Go!" The monitor went blank.

Camilla grinned at the blank screen. She already had her team—they were standing all around her. She nudged Jordan. "Come on, what are we waiting for?"

On the other side of the room, Lauren grabbed JT and Juan by the arm. "You guys are with me... and you, too, Travis, and..." She looked at Camilla's group, then at Natalie, standing against the wall alone.

Lauren's eyes slitted. "No, I don't *think so*..."

Jordan laughed—her usual giggle of can-you-believe-this amusement—but under the circumstances, it seemed a little cruel.

A digital scoreboard appeared on the screen: a grid of ten square cells, each labeled with a contestant's name, the five squares across the top and bottom outlined in different colors. Lauren's red team ran across the top, and Jordan's blue team across the bottom.

Natalie had been assigned to the red team.

"Shit." Lauren turned away.

Travis stared at Camilla across the room. "Looks like us blue-collar folks against you white-collar types. Guess y'all are most comfortable with your own kind."

"Let's go, guys." Jordan pointed through the archway. "Next door."

Camilla hustled after Jordan and crossed into the Greek Revival house next door, followed by Mason, Veronica, and Brent. Her feet slid in the muck that coated the floorboards.

Through the doorway behind them, Lauren shouted instructions. "JT, Juan, head upstairs and send 'em down. Travis and I'll shoo 'em out."

A goose-size black bird with an iridescent blue eye flapped up from the floor in a loud whir of wings and struck the side of Camilla's face, brushing her lips. She coughed and spat out a feather, tasting fishy, oily nastiness. Then she started laughing. She couldn't help herself.

Her teammates looked crazy, waving their arms and yelling, trying to shoo seals toward the open doorways. The seals seemed to be getting into the spirit of it, too. They leaped and yelped around the contestants, like eager dogs begging their owners to play. Camilla chased a seal out and went after another.

"There's another monitor in here!" Veronica yelled from deeper inside the house. "Another scoreboard." Her voice turned harsh. "The red team is beating us."

Camilla ran to find Veronica and the monitor in the second house's large living room. Jordan burst in through another doorway, a juvenile seal cradled gently in her arms.

"That's not smart," Veronica said. "It's got diseases. You don't want to get bitten."

"You wouldn't do that, would you?" Jordan stroked the seal's soft back. It looked up at her with round, curious eyes.

She stepped out of the room for a moment to set the seal gently on the ground outside. On the monitor, her score changed from 4 to 5. Then she was back. "Okay, guys, we are not going to lose. We need ideas, quickly. Camilla?"

"Think of this like soccer." Camilla looked at her teammates. "We're only covering half the field. We need to play some defense, too."

Mason laughed. "Brilliant. And sneaky. Let's do it."

Brent stood with his hands in his vest pockets, not saying anything. Did he disapprove of her idea?

Veronica shook her head. "I certainly don't think—"

"I like it!" Jordan said, clapping her hands with glee. She pointed at Mason and Veronica. "You guys, go. You know what to do. With my shoe situation, I'd be useless."

The two of them nodded and pelted out the door.

Camilla watched them go. Now that Jordan liked the idea, Veronica was a big fan, too, all of a sudden? But then, this was why Camilla had wanted Jordan as the team leader. She had seen the way Jordan could take over just by walking into a room.

Jordan wobbled on a broken shoe and grabbed the wall, smiling at Camilla. "You and Brent head upstairs," she said. "I'll clear the rest down here."

Nodding, Camilla thought of Avery and how despondent he had sounded yesterday. She had left him to come here so she could help *all* her kids. But even if she could outsmart the other contestants, how could she possibly beat Jordan?

CHAPTER 27

L auren windmilled her arms and chased another seal out the door. Passing through the central room, she glanced at the scoreboard.

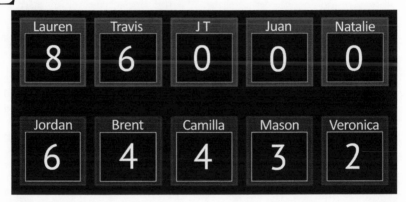

Lauren	Travis	J T	Juan	Natalie
8	6	0	0	0

Jordan	Brent	Camilla	Mason	Veronica
6	4	4	3	2

She smirked—she was killing them. Thumping noises came from upstairs, along with cursing and the barks of distressed seals. Juan and JT had chased five or six of the slippery, stinky animals down the stairs for her to shoo out, but they didn't seem to be having much luck with the last few.

"What are you clowns doing up there?" she shouted. She was eager to finish and wipe that smile off Jordan's face. Would the losing team have to pick someone to send home? Julian hadn't said anything about that.

Juan skidded down the stairs behind his last seal. "You need to let JT and me up front now," he said, pointing at the scoreboard. "So far, we've been taking one for the team while you rack up points."

"You'll get your twenty when our team wins."

"What?" JT slid down the stairs to stare at her. "Fuck that, Lauren. We need to start scoring *now*."

"Fine. Be my guest." She looked around. Hadn't she cleared this room already? For some reason, it seemed to be full of seals again.

She chased one toward a doorway and bumped into JT, who was driving his seal the same direction. Both their seals escaped back into the house.

"God damn it, girl," JT said, "you need to back the fuck off."

She stepped up and pushed JT. "Listen, cowboy, nobody—"

93

"Hey!" Travis's shout echoed from the other side of the building. "Get over here. These sons-a-bitches are cheating."

Lauren plunged through the house to find Travis, silhouetted in an open doorway to the outside. He had his arms braced against the jambs and his knees wide to block access, but the room was already full of seals.

"Where the hell were you?" he shouted. "Not much use now."

From over his shoulder, Lauren spotted Mason and Veronica outside, herding a big crowd of seals in front of them. Waddling across the open ground and waving their arms, they drove the seals toward the doorways Travis wasn't covering. A riot of slippery black and gray shapes spilled into the room.

"You gotta be shitting me," Lauren said, and rushed to intercept. Through the empty frame of a window, Mason laughed at her.

Juan jammed a jagged hunk of plywood across a doorway, and JT tried to cover the other side, but there were too many openings.

Lauren couldn't see the scoreboard. Was the blue team catching up?

"You two!" she yelled. "Go do the same thing to their house."

"Hell with that." JT nudged a seal back out with his knee. "I need points."

"God *damn* it." She slapped the doorframe. "Where the hell's Natalie?"

Cheering erupted outside, and her chest tightened.

She looked at Juan. He slowly shook his head at her. How could he act so calm about it? They had just lost. She slammed a fist into the wall and stepped outside. Her team joined her to stand in silence, watching the other team celebrate.

"Awesome! Go, blue team!" Jordan jumped around outside the other building like an excited schoolgirl. She hugged Mason and Veronica, welcoming them back. "My heroes! You guys won it for us."

Lauren's hands balled into fists. Beaten by a fucking *cheerleader*. She had to look away. To her surprise, she saw Natalie shoo a seal out of their building. And another.

"Real nice," Lauren said. "Scoring yourself some points?" She crossed her arms. "You're pretty useless, you know that, Natalie? You let us down big-time."

Juan shook his head again. "She's not why we lost."

Natalie give him a grateful glance, and Lauren turned away in disgust.

Mason waved at the red team from fifty feet away, surrounded by his own happy blue teammates.

"Look at that," JT's jaw clenched. "Motherfucker's laughing at us."

"Let him enjoy it." Travis stared at Mason with cold eyes, rubbing the triangle of beard under his lip. "Payback's a bitch."

CHAPTER 28

"You look ridiculous." Veronica laughed—that unexpected sexy purr again.

Camilla looked down at herself. Her white shirt was now mostly brown, with smears of gray she didn't want to think too hard about. Her jeans were so caked with mud and seal crap, she couldn't tell they were once blue. She smelled like a zoo.

Jordan put an arm around her. "We all look ridiculous," she said. "But we won."

Their blue team had gathered in the central room of the Victorian house again. Matted hair stuck to Camilla's cheeks, crusted with mud and stuff she didn't want to think about. She rubbed her face, and her hand came away coated with brown grime. She needed to get cleaned up—she must look like a cartoon street urchin. She eyed Jordan, who looked like she had just stepped off the pages of a magazine. How had she stayed so clean? Except for her shoes, which were a disaster—pretty much falling apart.

"Julian and the crew are in those other warehouse buildings," Camilla said. "Hopefully they've got some showers over there."

"And some lunch," Jordan said. "I don't know about you guys, but I'm hungry."

"Aren't you both forgetting something?" Mason said. "One-hundred-percent authenticity, remember?"

"What are you saying?" Veronica stared at him. "You don't think they plan to feed us? They'll just leave us rolling around in the mud here like..."—she indicated Camilla with a manicured fingernail—"...dirty animals?"

"I assume the ship will pick us again." Brent put his hands in his vest pockets and leaned back, scratching his spine against the wall like a big old bear against a tree trunk. "Otherwise, where are we going to sleep?"

Camilla looked up as Lauren's red team filed in to take their places against the opposite wall. They were quiet. Too quiet, she thought. Their resentful stares cut across the room.

Her eyes sought out Juan. Unlike the others, he didn't look resentful. Just thoughtful. He slouched against a wall with his hands in his pockets, like a teenage slacker. She smiled, picturing irritated teachers telling a younger Juan to stand up straight and pay attention.

The scoreboard flashed once. Their scores stared out at them:

95

A pulsing blue frame, labeled "Winning Team," appeared around the bottom row of the scoreboard. The blue team's scores spun upward by twenty points.

Jordan let out a whoop and hugged Camilla again.

"Who wants to make a wager?" Mason called across to the other team. "I say we'll find our grand-prize winner in the bottom row."

Camilla slapped his shoulder. "Stop it."

The scores faded, and Julian reappeared.

"My congratulations to the winning team," he said. "With this win, each of you is starting strong. But remember, this is only the first contest of many, and fortunes can change quickly.

"To members of the other team, I say, don't take this first defeat too hard. You will have plenty of opportunities to earn points in the coming days—more than enough to outscore the current leaders if you rise to the challenge.

"There may be some questions about contest rules, tactics, and such. Let me reassure you about that. If I didn't specifically disallow something, it's fair and legal play." Julian's face took on a serious look. "I am sorry to say, however, that we did see one transgression against my instructions. For that, there will be a penalty applied to the whole team."

Veronica's mouth snapped into a thin line. She grabbed Camilla's elbow. "Your stupid idea just cost us, young lady," she hissed.

Camilla pulled free. "Why don't we see what he says, first?" She stared at the monitor and rubbed her arm, ignoring the chill of Veronica's icy glare against her cheek.

The room brightened as the monitor changed scenes, showing the front of the Victorian house instead of Julian. On-screen, Lauren chased a seal out of the doorway and disappeared back inside again to a soundtrack of muted barks and shouts. Then Travis appeared in the doorway, pushing a sea lion out with his knee. It turned to duck back in, and he gave it a vicious kick in the side, sending it flying off the porch steps. "And *stay* out, you dirty son of a bitch!" He dusted off his hands, and ducked back inside as the screen went dark.

See? Camilla wanted to say to Veronica, but she bit her cheek instead.

"Oh, that's just great," Lauren said. "*We* get a penalty?"

Without taking his eyes off the screen, JT grabbed one-handed for the front of Travis's shirt, but he wasn't fast enough. Travis scooted out of his reach and backed toward the open archway. His flat gaze shifted rapidly from person to person, and he held his hands at waist level. He didn't look scared; he looked ready to fight—even if it was many-on-one.

"Ease up, guys," Lauren said. "Let's not make things worse."

The scoreboard reappeared, a pulsing red frame labeled "Penalty" around the top row. The red team's scores spun through a five-point decrease.

JT crossed his thick arms, refusing to look at Travis.

Julian returned to the screen. "Folks, Año Nuevo is a nature preserve. My earlier instructions not to harm the wildlife were quite clear.

"But now we can move on to the next step together. It's a cooperative activity, not a competitive one. No points are at stake here. Think of it as a team-building exercise."

From the screen, he waved a hand to indicate the rooms around them. "Your new accommodations are now vacant, but they lack curb appeal—they're the ultimate fixer-uppers."

Camilla's jaw dropped. *Accommodations?* She mouthed the word silently at Jordan.

"In the storage shed behind these buildings," Julian said, "you will find tools, lumber, and rolls of plastic sheeting. Most importantly, you'll find two high-pressure washers with plenty of fuel. These buildings will be your homes for the next couple of weeks. Let's get them cleaned up, weatherproof, and animal proof so we can move in."

CHAPTER 29

Camilla swiped an arm across her sweaty, filthy forehead, and put down the wrench. She grinned at Jordan. "That's the last one!" she shouted over the deafening roar of the pressure washer next door.

Together, they looked at the metal cot frame they had assembled: angle-steel beams held together by four-inch bolts, an open grid of spring-mounted wire on the top to support a mattress. It was cheap stuff—something you'd see in a dormitory or institution... or a residential youth group home, Camilla thought, suppressing a shiver.

The two women stood in an upstairs bedroom of the Greek Revival house, which their blue team had cleared of seals. The red team had taken over the many-dormered Victorian structure next door.

Camilla looked up at a ceiling corner, where eight inches of sky showed through a ragged hole in the naked wood lathing.

"Looks like my room comes with air-conditioning." She had to shout to be heard over the pressure washer.

Jordan unrolled the khaki-colored mattress pad she held, and tossed it on top of the cot. "Feels like I'm back at Camp Karolyi."

"What?"

"Gymnastics summer camp." A shadow crossed her face. "Never mind."

After several hours of the motor's rattling roar, Camilla was dying to give her ears a break. "So you're a journalist," she shouted. "How about we go do some investigative reporting?"

On their way out, Camilla looked in at Brent next door, braced against the back pressure as he aimed the nozzle of the heavy power washer around the corners of the room. For an older guy, the big, blocky doctor looked strong and vigorous. She felt a tug of affection, watching him tirelessly blast away the mud and animal filth with a firehose-thick stream of water. The whole house smelled like the sea now—salty, fishy, and wet—but it was a huge improvement over the earlier rotting-zoo miasma.

She headed down the stairs with Jordan, avoiding as best she could the filthy river pouring down the steps alongside them. The torrent of brown slurry had a hazy white surface sheen that made Camilla pause. Kneeling, she dipped a couple of fingers into it and held them to her nose, smelling only seawater.

"Slippery," she said, rubbing her fingers together. "I don't know... With all the wildlife, are we sure it's okay to use this detergent stuff in the washers?"

99

Jordan giggled. "It's biodegradable and biosafe, according to the label. You actually think they'd allow us to spray something harmful here?"

Ten minutes later, the two of them stood in front of the first warehouse building. Seals and disgruntled seabirds moved around at their feet, ignoring the muted roar of the power washers in the distance. Waves crashed behind the concrete seawall on their left.

Camilla rattled the door of the first building. "Locked. Figures. But Julian and the others are in there. See?" She slid a hand along the slick, wet siding, then wiped her slippery palm off on her thigh. "Same stuff. They washed these three buildings yesterday for the camera crew to use."

Jordan nodded. "Let's find another door or some windows. It must be afternoon by now. I'm getting really hungry and thirsty."

There were no nests underfoot to watch out for here; the warehouses sat on a hard section of yellowed limestone. Camilla took a step back and looked over the three A-frame structures. They all were connected. Two single-story buildings in front backed onto a larger two-story building that loomed like a factory. Unlike the two mansions, they had been built simply, with shiplap siding that still retained most of its gray paint. Someone had boarded up the square window frames from the inside, so she couldn't see in.

"What's that?" Jordan pointed at a thick pipe, almost three feet in diameter, which poked straight out at ground level from the wall of the largest building. It extended fifteen feet inland before disappearing under the rising slope of dirt and rock.

"No clue," Camilla said. "It's too thick to be a water or sewer line."

What kind of factory had this been? Her eyes traced the path of the underground culvert, following it uphill. It rose to the surface again in places, forming a broken ridge like a backbone before ending in a pile of concrete rubble at the top of the hill, alongside the fallen lighthouse tower.

She pursed her lips, thinking. "Maybe some kind of gas vent?"

Whatever it was, it hadn't been used in a very long time. In places, the ten-foot sections were misaligned after years of neglect, leaving crescent-shaped openings that gaped black in the rocky dirt of the hill. Camilla watched a seal crawl into one of the gaps. A big, ungainly-looking bird—some kind of petrel, maybe?—popped out of another. The underground segments would be clogged with debris and nests.

Jordan shook her head. "Whatever. Let's go."

They cut between the buildings and the seawall, which deflected the rougher waves from the open ocean, visible in bursts of white spray above the concrete edge.

"It's a little creepy the way the show's crew is hiding from us," Camilla said. "Do you think we're on camera right now?"

"Bet on it," Jordan said.

They circled all three buildings. Every window was boarded up from the inside. The other two doors were also locked.

Camilla slipped around the corner where they had started—and froze. Right in front of the door she had rattled earlier lay a plastic shrink-wrapped bundle. The ground where the bundle now sat had been bare only five minutes ago.

She grabbed Jordan's arm. "Is that what I think it is?"

Jordan laughed and clapped in delight. She rushed forward, teetering on her wrecked high-heels, and knelt to rip the plastic off a twelve-pack of plastic water bottles. Tossing one to Camilla, she twisted the cap off another for herself and glugged down half.

Camilla took a gulp from her own, gasping with relief as the water hit her parched throat. "I was starting to worry," she said. She leaned against the door, trying it again. Locked. "So *that's* how this is going to work…"

Jordan swigged again, wiped a forearm across her mouth, and grinned. "Julian Claus and his invisible little elves."

Camilla tucked the twelve-pack under her arm. "We're about to be the most popular girls at the party."

"Let's get the lay of the land first." Jordan high-stepped around a cluster of sea lions and started uphill. "The others can wait."

• • •

The slope was gentle, but the seals and ground-nesting seabirds made it difficult going. Camilla actually had to step over the backs of juvenile seals at times. She pointed at the crumbling concrete dome as they passed it on their way up. "What do you think that was?"

The rim rose above their heads, ten feet high at least and open at the top. A sunken area of cracked concrete bigger than a basketball court sloped downhill above it.

"An old water cistern." Jordan didn't seem very interested. "Whenever it rained, the water would run down this catchment basin and collect inside."

Camilla wrinkled her nose at the mess the seals and birds had made amid the broken concrete slabs. A rotten, mildewy odor wafted from the cistern dome—sickly sweet, even fouler than the sharp zoo smell that permeated the rest of the island. She gagged, squeezing the bundle of water bottles tighter under her arm. "At least Julian's giving us water," she said. "I'd hate to have to drink out of that—it smells like something died in there."

"It'd probably kill us, too," Jordan said. "Don't get too comfy about the water situation, though. I shouldn't have chugged mine."

Camilla groaned. "He's going to make us work for every sip, isn't he?"

They passed the last manmade structure on the island: a small concrete blockhouse the size of a two-car garage. It stood on its own, a couple of hundred feet from the warehouse buildings and set at an oblique angle to them—an outcast exiled to live in disgrace. With no windows, it looked like a miniature prison.

"If anyone misbehaves, that's where we stick 'em," Camilla said.

"A 2012 Zimbardo experiment?"

"What?"

"Nothing. It's locked, anyway." Jordan pointed at a bright new steel padlock hanging from the door of the concrete blockhouse.

A few minutes later, they reached the highest point on the small island. Standing next to the legs of the fallen tower, Camilla raised a hand to her forehead to shield her eyes. She turned in a complete circle, seeing the entirety of Año Nuevo Island for the first time. Her original impression had been correct: it was tiny.

Shaped sort of like a seahorse which had turned its back on the mainland, the island was maybe a quarter-mile long and two hundred yards across at its widest point. Projecting from the seahorse's lower belly, the dock where they had spent last night pointed toward open ocean. The three factory or warehouse buildings sat on the edge of the upper belly, protected by two hundred feet of curving concrete seawall.

Closer to the seahorse's narrow neck, the concrete blockhouse also sat on the open-ocean side of the island. Farther inland lay the dome of the ruined cistern.

On the opposite side of the island, along the seahorse's back, a wide swath of beach faced the California coast. Vertical bluffs twenty feet high dropped from the main body of the island to the sand, which was dense with sleeping sea lions and seals. A concentration of larger, darker shapes covered the beach's northern end.

Camilla pointed them out to Jordan. "That must be the main elephant seal rookery. Those really huge monsters—the alpha bulls—see how each has his own territory?"

Each of the immense bulls lay at the center of its own separate group, surrounded by dozens of smaller elephant seals. Yards of empty beach isolated the sprawling groups from each other.

At the shoreline, a solitary giant emerged from the waves. An even larger bull raised its head from the center of one of the groups. It bellowed a challenge at the newcomer.

"Harems," Jordan said. "That's what they're fighting over. It's about females, not territory."

"I'm glad they don't come up here much," Camilla said. "It looks like they mostly stay on the beaches."

The steep bluffs continued along the back of the seahorse's half-coiled tail, around the south end of the island. Halfway down the tail, huge fans of filthy water ran from the many doors of both houses and spread across the rocky ground. Both teams were making great progress toward getting their houses habitable. Hanging out of an upper window at the back of each house, thick intake hoses trailed a short distance across the open ground before dropping over the edge of the bluff to suck up seawater from the ocean fifteen feet below.

Lauren hung out of an upper window of the Victorian, gripping the upper sill with one hand. She had the nozzle braced under her other arm, blasting decades of filth and old nests away from the windowsills, chimneys, and roofline. It looked dangerous, but she seemed very much in control, navigating the window ledges with confident ease.

In the foreground, Juan and JT were rebuilding the seal barricade.

"JT's even stronger than he looks," Camilla said. But she was actually watching Juan. He held the end of a heavy log while JT hefted it into place and then leaned against it, swinging a hammer to nail it against the uprights.

"JT's smart," Jordan said. "But he hides it."

"I guess this is the part where we talk about the other contestants," Camilla said.

Jordan laughed. "What's there to say, really?"

"Juan... I'm so curious. On the ship, what happened between the two of you?"

"Don't ask." Jordan's eyes narrowed. "Sometimes people aren't who you think they are." She looked back toward the houses. "As far as I'm concerned, Juan is right where he belongs: on a team full of losers. And the hell away from us."

Camilla followed her gaze. Juan's black clothes made him stand out against the island's chalky gray-brown soil. Maybe Jordan was overreacting. Maybe she had misunderstood whatever Juan had said. Camilla found it hard to believe anything bad about someone she had seen save a child's life. Most men she knew would be telling that story over and over again—maybe playing it up with fake modesty, but still milking it for all it was worth. But Juan had simply shrugged, given her the okay sign, and ridden away. She needed to talk to him, but she felt torn by her loyalty to Jordan, who would be disappointed in her if she did.

She was here to win, though. Her kids were counting on her. And the last thing she could afford was to drive a wedge between herself and the team captain she had selected. Reluctantly she shifted her gaze.

In the distance, Veronica and Mason came around the corner of the plainer of the two houses—the Greek Revival, now the blue team's quarters. Mason held a roll of clear plastic tarp under one arm. He gestured with his other hand, as if he was explaining something. Even at this distance, Veronica's impatient stride made it clear she had no interest in what he was saying. She held something shiny—a staple gun—which she used to staple the clear plastic that Mason held across the empty window frames.

"Why does Veronica dislike me so much?" Camilla asked Jordan. "To be honest, I'm not really used to getting that from people."

"I don't think she knows, herself." Jordan grinned. "But I do. She's intimidated by you."

"I don't understand. Why?"

"You really can't see it, can you?" Jordan put an arm around her shoulders and hugged her. "That's why I like you so much, sister. But if Julian asked me to pick the one person here that I thought could give me a real run for the money, I'd have to say it's you."

She hugged Jordan back, and the two women stood there for a moment, looking toward the mainland.

Camilla's vision blurred a little. Jordan always called her "sister." She had never had a real sister, but if she had, this was exactly who she would have wanted her to be.

Jordan let go of her and started back toward the houses with brisk, wobbling steps. "Let's go finish helping our team before we get accused of social loafing."

"I'll be right there." Camilla needed a minute to herself first. Then, nestling the bundle of water bottles under her arm, she turned to follow—and noticed the bird.

It lurched across the open ground, a large gray auklet, its entire breast soaked in crimson. The bird stumbled forward in hopping steps, moving slowly but with clear purpose. A terrible injury gouged its upper chest; bright blood soaked its downy gray-white feathers and coated its feet.

Camilla exhaled sharply. What could she do? She stared after Jordan, who was already a hundred yards away, too far to help.

She stepped closer and squatted next to the hurt bird. The wound looked like a dog bite—it must have gotten too close to a seal. She reached for it. Then she stopped.

There was nothing she could do for it.

The auklet ignored her and staggered steadily along, leaving a trail of blood. It was on its way somewhere—back to a nest, to its chicks, maybe. Camilla's throat locked up and she had to look away.

The bird didn't understand what was happening to it, even now.

It didn't realize it was going to die.

CHAPTER 30

Natalie stood at the edge of the bluff, her back to the two houses, and watched the surging crowds of elephant seals and sea lions on the beach twenty feet below her. Wooden steps angled down the bluff, ending in a rickety span of elevated walkway six feet above the sand. From the bottom of the steps, the narrow walkway projected straight out from the bluff, supported by old creosoted log piers, to split in a Y after fifty feet. One leg of the Y continued past the surf line, extending another thirty feet over the water.

The rickety walkway had no handrails. It didn't look safe at all. Boards were missing, leaving gaps you could drop a foot through, breaking your ankle.

The bigger elephant seals had to duck to pass beneath it.

Natalie's skin crawled—a nasty, unpleasant sensation that told her someone was watching her from nearby. *Too* close.

Careful not to move her body, she slowly turned her head to scan the open ground to her right.

Travis leaned against the back of the chicken coop, ten feet away, hidden from the houses by its weathered plywood wall.

Surprise made her clamp her thighs together, but she kept still. How had he gotten so close without her noticing?

"Natalie," he said. "Come over here for a minute."

She stayed put and watched his eyes, seeing what he was. *Knowing* it.

"I just want to ask you something," he said.

Natalie turned and walked back toward the houses, keeping the chicken coop—and Travis—in her peripheral vision the entire way.

CHAPTER 31

A blurry orange sunset shone through the plastic tarp covering the windows. The room felt damp and smelled like seawater. Camilla sat on the floor with her back against the wall, eyes shut, listening to the muted conversations around her, and the crinkle of plastic water bottles. She knew she should go back to her own building and change out of her filthy clothes, but she was tired. Jordan had left a couple of minutes ago to change shoes—the straps on her designer high heels had finally broken, and she couldn't walk in them anymore.

Camilla and Jordan's gift of water had helped ease the tension between the teams, but the water was pretty much gone now. Camilla knew that Julian couldn't afford to let them get too dehydrated, but she would still suggest rationing the next batch more carefully.

Travis had found everyone's luggage, stashed inside the chicken coop. Camilla's bag was now in her own room—next door in the Greek Revival house. She had dragged it upstairs before coming back across the foyer to rejoin the others in the Victorian's vast central room—red territory, but a gathering place for both teams as they waited for Julian to reappear on the monitor. The red and blue teams weren't mingling much—not surprising, really, after the way the first challenge had gone. But Camilla's blue team had done well. She was proud of them.

Her heart still ached for the wounded bird she had seen. It was probably dead by now. Just a part of nature. She wouldn't think about it anymore; she'd think about something else. The cameras, for instance—where were they hidden? She scanned the walls and ceiling. Something tiny darkened a corner high above, where two walls met the ceiling. Squinting up at it, she couldn't make out any details, but she was sure there was a tiny lens behind it.

Across the room, Juan sat slumped against the wall next to his teammates, forearms on his raised knees. His gaze, too, slowly roamed the corners of the ceiling. Then his eyes dropped to meet hers, and he nodded in confirmation. Moving only a finger, he indicated another spot—a knothole on the wall next to the monitor screen. Another camera.

Camilla glanced toward the archway of the foyer between the houses, but Jordan wasn't back yet, so she tilted her head to indicate the monitor itself and mouthed a silent question to Juan. "Power?"

His finger moved a couple of inches to indicate the floor alongside the fireplace, beneath the monitor, then pointed downward. *Look beneath,* his gesture said.

107

Camilla bounced up and walked toward the monitor. Squatting, she stared beneath the inch-wide gap between the floorboards, into darkness. Although she didn't want to waste her phone's limited battery life, she turned it on briefly to aim the brightness through the crack where floor met the wall. A quarter-inch cable descended below the floorboards, dropping four feet to disappear inside a row of shoe-box shapes wrapped in clear plastic.

Of course. She switched off her phone and grinned at Juan. "Car batteries—"

"Guys, this is so weird…" Jordan burst through the archway, and stopped, her gaze flicking from Camilla to Juan, then back. Her puzzled expression vanished.

Camilla stood up, not liking the way Jordan's eyes had changed. "*What's* weird?"

"My other shoes are missing," Jordan announced to the room, her face showing cheerful surprise again. She was barefoot. "I brought six pairs of shoes with me, but now they aren't in my bag."

Lauren sneered. "You brought *six* pairs of shoes?"

Camilla tried to remember whether she had packed an extra pair Jordan that could borrow. She didn't think so. "Veronica," she said, "do you have something she can wear?"

"No, sorry." Veronica pushed herself upright and glared at her. "You were so sure you knew why Julian wanted to search our bags."

Feeling a growing disquiet, Camilla raised her voice. "Everyone, go check your bags. Maybe they accidentally stuck her shoes in someone else's luggage."

The room emptied rapidly, and Camilla turned to meet Veronica's glare. "So I was wrong about that," she said. "Now I'm wondering what else I was wrong about."

CHAPTER 32

JT pulled his tote bag from beneath his cot and dropped it on the mattress pad. With a glance at the doorway to make sure it was still clear, he unzipped the tote and reached inside. He relaxed when his fingers closed on the hard metal edges they were looking for.

He was actually surprised to find it. Julian's crew must have been rushing when they searched the bags, and missed it somehow.

JT had been a model Boy Scout growing up, and the Scouts had taught him to be prepared, just as the motto said. His years as a Force Recon Marine had only broadened his thinking about the types of situations he needed to be prepared for.

There was probably a camera here in his room, too, watching him right now. He pulled his hand out and rezipped the bag, then wadded it under his cot.

He lay down and crossed his arms behind his head, staring up at the ceiling, thinking. For now the competition was pretty tame—a joke, really. But he could already see that Julian and his crew, with their limited civilian mind-set, didn't understand what they had set in motion here. Things were going to get dicey soon, the way they always did in situations like this.

When they did, he'd be ready.

CHAPTER 33

In the room next door to JT's, Lauren had spread the contents of her backpack across her mattress pad. Clothing, toothbrush and toothpaste, deodorant, and underwear were separated into organized piles, each pile aligned with the others, just the way she liked it. Everything she had packed was here.

But there was something else, too.

Something she didn't remember packing.

A lone climbing carabiner—a large aluminum D-ring— sat on the mattress. She had set it apart, a good distance from her clothing and toiletries, as if it might contaminate them somehow.

She stood staring down at it, troubled. It was a brand she hadn't used for many years. She must have missed it when she cleared out her backpack to get ready for this trip.

She picked it up and rubbed the side of it, feeling the sandpapery roughness where it had scraped against rock. How long had it been there, hidden in her backpack, tucked away in a fold somewhere? She felt her chest tighten. She didn't think the pack was that old.

The carabiner nagged at her subconscious, glinting silver in the room's dimness…

Like ice crystals on a granite wall just out of reach. Blood streaking the vertical rock.

Muted sobs from below. Weak voices calling her name.

Pain. A vise crushing her head.

Blood dripping in her eyes.

Upside down.

So cold.

The carabiner's shiny metal gleamed in the fading light.

•   •   •

How long had she just been standing here, staring at it?

Lauren looked up, surprised to find herself in near darkness.

CHAPTER 34

Veronica sat on her cot with her back against the wall, knees raised in front of her, holding a thin stack of typewritten pages. Her Louis Vuitton travel bag lay open on the mattress, by her feet. She had pushed the bed against the same wall as the empty doorframe, so it couldn't be seen from the hall outside.

Her eyes strained against the dimness as she scanned the lines of text. She folded over the next page and read the last few paragraphs. Her mouth hardened, and she deliberately relaxed it. She didn't want to give herself wrinkles—Botox was expensive.

She wasn't really surprised by what she had just read, though. Not at all.

A dog-eared manila folder lay by her hand, its flap open. She checked the front of the folder again, where a thick diagonal ribbon of red-and-white label tape cut across the corner. She reread the label:

CONTENTS INCLUDE CLASSIFIED INFORMATION

Sliding the report back into the folder again, Veronica shoved it into the pocket of her travel bag.

CHAPTER 35

C amilla's upright rolling bag lay open on her bed. A large object, wrapped in newsprint, lay nestled among her familiar clothes. She gave it a tentative poke.

"Is anything wrong with *your* luggage?" she called out.

"No," came Veronica's sharp reply from next door. "Nothing missing."

"Mine, either." She prodded the newspaper-wrapped shape again. It was about eighteen inches long and hard, like metal. Definitely not Jordan's missing shoes.

What on earth had Julian put in her bag?

The newspaper crinkled in her hands as she lifted the heavy item out. The paper wrapping disguised its outline. Peeling back the wrinkled columns about budget overruns and missing women, she peered at the mysterious object. It looked like a large machine part—a metal armature or lever of some sort with a gear on one side. Camilla crumpled the wrapping one-handed and tossed it away. With her other hand, she turned the metal shape this way and that, trying to identify it. She had absolutely no clue what it might be.

She hefted the heavy chunk of metal, holding the lever part like a handle, not liking how the jagged teeth of the gear jutted from its end. Then she dropped it to the floor, struck by a disquieting thought.

It felt like a primitive weapon.

CHAPTER 36

Everything Brent had packed in his overnight bag was present and accounted for, including his meds. He stood at his room window, watching the last of the fading light and listening to the distant barks, groans, and rumbles on the beach below. The island was noisy at night, but at least the wide area of flat ground outside the houses was now free of seals.

Juan and JT had rebuilt the zigzag log barricade that cut across the center of the island from bluff edge to breakwater. All ten contestants had worked together to herd the seals out, and the southern half of the island had once again been reclaimed by humanity.

Brent shook his head. The others were failing to see some obvious things about their situation. Warning flags. Things that, at this point, they all should be starting to get very concerned about.

For example, no one was questioning the glaring lack of safety precautions. Their complete dependence on their hidden hosts for such basic survival needs as drinking water. The apparent lack of any protocol for dealing with injury or illness. The dangers presented by the native wildlife— and even by some of the contestants themselves.

He needed to bring these things to the group's attention soon. He would have to raise the subject if no one else did, but he was reluctant to be the first. As the oldest contestant present, trying to fit in with others half his age, he knew how quickly someone like him could turn themselves into an outsider. But he would say something if he had to.

They all needed to understand that there was something very wrong going on here.

CHAPTER 37

C amilla sat up with a gasp and stared into darkness. The creak and screech of torn metal echoed in her ears, and her heart thudded in her chest and neck. Head fuzzy with confusion, she gulped a few breaths of air, smelling smoke. Where was she? Her legs hurt. She was so cold.

She could still hear the screams, the groans, the hopeless sobbing. Lots of different voices overlapping. But the sounds were different now. Farther away. They didn't really sound like people anymore. They were only animals. Barks and yips in the distance. *Seals.* Camilla remembered where she was.

Stars glittered, uninviting and cold, through the ragged hole in the ceiling.

She put her feet on the ground and sat on her cot with her head in her hands, covering her ears, as the last wisps of the dream faded. She got her breathing and her heartbeat under control, and pushed away the lingering sadness.

The empty plastic bottle skittered away underfoot when she stood up.

She was so thirsty. But there was no water.

Camilla stepped out into the hallway, navigating by touch as her eyes adjusted. She could now hear deep breathing from the open doorways of neighboring rooms. A few steps down the hall, a board creaked underfoot and she stopped, listening. Sleep sounds came from Jordan's room, and she peeked in.

A small patch of starlight gleamed through the plastic-covered window, lighting Jordan's face. She was sleeping peacefully, curled on her side. Camilla remembered the cold look she had seen flicker across that face when Jordan caught her talking to Juan. She was sure she hadn't imagined it. She needed to be more careful.

The next doorway was Veronica's. As she passed it, moving down the hall, she sensed the breathing change. She hurried by, feeling like a teenager sneaking out at night.

Mason's room was next. She could hear him breathing in there. He sounded asleep, but she didn't look in.

A deep, slow rumbling came from the last room. Brent was snoring. She grinned. Sleepy bear hibernating. No, what he *actually* sounded like was—she pinched her nose shut and leaned against the wall to keep from laughing out loud—an elephant seal.

Her urge to laugh suddenly disappeared, because she could see something at the end of the hall. A shape crouched in the corner, hidden by darkness.

119

What was it? It looked too big to be a seal, but small for a person. Camilla stared at it, straining her eyes, not daring to move.

Could it see her, whatever it was? The skin on her arms crept. She forced herself to breathe slowly and silently as her eyes probed the darkness, trying to make out the shape.

Long minutes went by. Now she could tell that it was a person—a small person, sitting in the corner, hugging her knees to her chest. Natalie. Why wasn't she saying anything? Did she need help?

Natalie's eyes glittered in the darkness. She sat motionless as a statue, as if waiting for something. In the gloom, Camilla couldn't make out any expression at all on her face.

A red team member, sneaking into the blue building at night... why? Camilla started forward. A small motion shifted the darkness ahead of her. She stopped, blinking. The corner was empty now. Natalie was gone.

She reached the end of the hall, placed a hand on the damp banister, and looked down the dark stairwell. It was the only place Natalie could have gone. Feeling a little nervous, she edged down the stairs to the first floor.

Downstairs, with fewer windows, the gloom pressed in closer. Not much chance of finding Natalie now. Navigating by touch, Camilla made her way to the front of the house, where the starlight filtered in through the windows, the clear plastic rustling lightly in the night breeze. What if she was on camera now? Those infrared ones? She composed her face in the darkness; she didn't want to look scared.

Through the window, she could see a black shape moving outside. A man's silhouette, edging along the shadows, headed past the house she stood in. Moving to the window, she pressed her nose against the plastic, but the shape remained too blurry to make out. She reached up, pulled the edge of the sheeting free from its staples. Easing it open a narrow crack, she put her eye to it. The cold air chilled her cheek and made her want to blink, but she could see the man's back in the starlight as he headed toward the barricade. It was Juan.

Where was he going in the middle of the night? Camilla felt a rush of curiosity. Her motorcycle rider was up to something. He turned to look back toward the houses, and she instinctively stepped back so he wouldn't notice her. Then she pressed forward again, eager to see.

Juan put a hand on top of the four-foot seal barricade and vaulted over, into the seal territory beyond. Was he heading to the factory buildings? To the dock? She had to go find out.

Camilla reached for the door to open it... and stopped.

Maybe this wasn't such a great idea, sneaking after a man she didn't know, across a deserted island in the middle of the night. She had seen this movie before: the plucky heroine follows the mystery man, alone and unarmed, and something terrible happens. It was so clichéd that Hollywood screenwriters called the story trope "too dumb to live."

Still, she might get a chance to talk to him without worrying about Jordan's reaction. She knew she'd be safe with a man who would casually risk his own life saving a stranger's child. Well, *probably* safe. No. She was smarter than this.

Camilla reluctantly turned away from the window, and the darkness shifted right in front of her face. She threw her body backward, slamming her back against the door with a thud. Travis grinned at her. He had been standing right behind her in the darkness, almost on top of her. For how long?

"Easy, easy," he said. "I didn't mean to scare you."

"You didn't."

He raised his hands, palms out in surrender, and took a step back. "I wanted to ask you something. Your team killed us today, but I can't say I feel right about how y'all won. What your buddy with the glasses did was pretty low. But then, it's about what I'd expect from a banker."

Sending seals into the other building? But that had been her idea, not Mason's.

"I think you should go now," she said.

His eyes narrowed. "You got no call to be rude to me. I'll say one more thing: I heard your buddy didn't come up with that idea all on his own."

Travis took a step toward her, and she bumped against the door behind her again. Her mouth went dry. If he got any closer, she'd yell for Veronica.

"I'm telling you now," he said, "that five mil's not going to end up with somebody who wins by cheating. It don't matter if that's okay by your rich buddy Julian, because it ain't all right by me. We clear on that?"

"I said you need to leave," she said.

He pressed in closer, crowding her against the door, his face inches from hers. "Maybe I ought to make sure you understand."

He had no right, bullying her, terrorizing her in the dark this way. Furious, she balled her hands into fists to hide their shaking. Even if she got hurt right now, she wasn't going to let herself get intimidated like this.

"Listen carefully, you snake-eyed creep, because I'm only going to say this once." She took a deep breath. "I'm not afraid of you. Get away from me right now, or I'll kick you in the crotch so hard you won't be able to *move* tomorrow—then we'll see how much your score improves."

"You little whore…" His bared teeth gleamed in the dark.

Travis suddenly jerked backward as he was pulled away from her and shoved aside.

A voice rumbled out of the darkness behind him. "You heard what the lady asked, Travis. Better get going now." She could see the gleam of silver hair, a blocky shape towering over Travis. Brent was a big man.

Camilla sagged against the door in relief. She had never been in a physical fight in her life. She was sure Travis wouldn't hesitate to hurt her.

"I see you white-collar types do all stick together," he said. "You think you can still kick some ass, old man?"

Brent sounded calm. "Keep after her and we might just find out. The home audience'll love it."

"I don't want you to have a heart attack—they might shut the whole show down before I get that money." Travis's voice trailed back from the foyer connecting the two houses. He was leaving. "Sleep tight, y'all. I expect we'll be having a big day tomorrow."

Camilla closed her eyes and slid a little way down the door. Her legs were trembling. Then she felt a big hand on her shoulder.

Brent peered at her with a concerned expression. "Are you all right?"

"I guess so." She let out a shuddering breath. "But I think I made an enemy tonight."

"People like that are their own worst enemies." He took his hand away and tucked both hands into his vest pockets.

"You're a brave one," he said. "I don't mean to tell you what to do. Heck, my own son is almost your age, and God knows *he* never wanted to listen to me, either, so why should you?" His eyes were friendly but worried. The sadness was there, too, deep down—it seemed to be a part of him always.

"Sorry to drag you into that," she said.

"Camilla, please be careful here," he said. "This isn't just fun and games anymore—not with so much money at stake." He looked toward the yawning darkness of the Victorian's archway. "I don't know how a person like Travis slipped through their screening, but he's not someone you should take lightly."

Camilla felt touched that he was worried about her. She stood up on her tiptoes and hugged him. Her arms barely fit around the big man.

"Thank you," she whispered in his ear. Then she let go and went up the stairs.

Camilla lay on her bed, listening, but she didn't hear Brent come back up to his room. Older people often couldn't sleep because of insomnia, but she didn't think that was why. Picturing him sitting at the bottom of the steps, she smiled to herself and curled up tighter, getting comfortable. His son was so lucky, she thought as she drifted off.

Camilla felt safe.

She knew that Brent was watching over his team right now. Like a big silver sheepdog. Guarding them from harm while they slept.

Day 3

Sunday: December 23, 2012

CHAPTER 38

"Sorry, no Starbucks for you this morning."

Camilla stopped rubbing her eyes and stared at Lauren in surprise. She had never seen the ultracompetitive rock climber smile, not even when making a joke. But judging by the hostile look on her face now, maybe she didn't understand what she'd said was funny.

"What I really need is water," Camilla said. "We all do." Her tongue stuck to the roof of her mouth. She felt light-headed.

"And I'd like a spinach-and-gruyere omelet *and* a basket of croissants," Jordan said. "I've never been so hungry in my life."

Jordan looked as if she were coming downstairs for brunch in a five-star bed-and-breakfast, instead of standing barefoot in a ruined house on an island covered with noisy, smelly wild animals. Her hair was pinned up, and her short-sleeved knit shirt and capri pants looked crisp and ironed. How could she be so fresh and clean with no running water? Camilla looked down at Jordan's bare toes, pink against the waterlogged floorboards, and wished she had a pair of shoes to lend her.

Most of the contestants from both teams were gathered around them now, standing in the central room of the red team's house and glancing at the blank monitor screen above the fireplace, waiting. Mason looked clean and presentable, too. Wow, he had even shaved somehow! Camilla swept her limp and tangled curls behind her ear, thinking of how she had dry-brushed her teeth just minutes ago. She felt like a dirty street urchin again. With no visible crew or cameras, it was easy to forget they were being recorded. She really ought to try harder to look more presentable.

Brent and Veronica came in from outside, and the morning sounds of the island's yelping, squawking, barking animal population filtered in behind them. Elephant seals rumbled in the distance, accompanied by the soft thump of waves.

The monitor screen crackled to life.

"Good morning, folks," Julian said. "I trust you enjoyed your breakfast?" He grinned at them. "Just kidding."

"Son of a bitch…" JT's voice trailed off in surprise.

"You're no doubt feeling hungry and thirsty," Julian said. "These are good feelings to be having right now. Invigorating. *Motivating*. They'll give you the drive you need to excel in this morning's challenge, where we finish filling out the bottom level of Maslow's hierarchy."

Camilla remembered Maslow from freshman psych—a psychologist who had defined and categorized human survival needs. She leaned forward, listening.

Julian swept a hand about him. "We draw our inspiration from the island's wild residents as they go about fulfilling the requirements for survival. The first requirement is shelter, which we addressed yesterday. Today we must focus on the next few basic requirements: food, water, warmth."

He paused with a chuckle. "Sex is usually considered another basic survival requirement in Maslow's hierarchy. I must tell you, though, we have no challenge planned for that one—you're on your own. The only advice I can offer on the topic is this: make sure you don't forget about the hidden cameras—they're everywhere."

As if, Camilla thought. But she couldn't help sneaking a glance at Juan.

"Back to today's event," Julian said. "This is an individual challenge—a scavenger hunt, if you will. Scattered across the island, vital supplies and other necessities of life have been cached."

He smiled. "Yes, there is water. Yes, there is food."

Camilla exchanged an excited glance with Jordan. She could see the same urgency on the other faces around the room.

"There are thirty caches in total," Julian said. "Some are plainly visible; some are hidden. Each is worth from one to twenty points.

"In the storage shed outside, you will find ten handheld supermarket-style scanners. They are labeled with your names. There are no teams today.

"Each of the thirty supply caches is tagged with an electronic identity tag. Find a cache, scan its tag, and the points are added to your individual score. The supplies you find inside the cache are yours and yours alone, to use any way you see fit."

Julian's face sobered. "For this challenge, there is only one new rule, or prohibition. It pertains to the buildings on the other side of the island. These buildings are off limits. None of you may enter them under any circumstances, either during the challenge or afterwards."

Camilla thought of how she and Jordan had rattled the doors of the crew's factory buildings. Was Julian's prohibition because of their actions? Or had Juan done something over there last night to earn his displeasure?

The digital scoreboard once again replaced Julian on the screen. Both rows of scores were now outlined in gray rather than the red and blue team colors. An additional square box appeared in the center, labeled "Caches" and displaying the number 30.

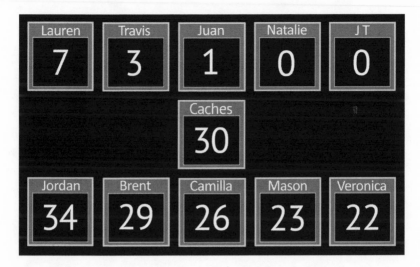

"And now, you know the drill," Julian's voice said. "I wish you all happy hunting. Grab your scanners. Go!"

CHAPTER 39

The impact came from behind, knocking Mason off the porch steps of the Victorian house and sending him sprawling face-first on the rocky ground. His glasses flew from his face. He got up on his knees and scrabbled frantically through the dirt, trying to find his glasses. His fingers closed around a yellow construction boot, its heel planted, its toe held an inch or two off the ground.

"Sorry, bro." JT's weightlifter muscles bulged under another colorful Hawaiian shirt. He didn't look very sorry.

Mason glanced around and saw the backs of the other contestants crowding through the door of the storage shed. No one was looking in his direction. Beneath JT's raised toe, he could see a wire curve—the earpiece of his glasses. All JT had to do was roll his weight forward, and they would be crushed.

Mason looked up at him. Waited.

JT stared impassively at him for a beat. Then disgusted amusement spread across his dark face, and he said, "Piggy."

Mason was amused, too. He nodded. "Jack."

"Aw, hell." JT blew out a breath and shook the toe of his boot, jarring Mason's fingers loose. He swept the glasses aside with his boot and ran toward the shed.

Mason crawled in the direction JT had kicked his glasses. He wiped them on his sleeve, slipped them on, and stood up. Then, dusting off his torn slacks, he jogged to the shed.

Contestants streamed out, each holding a yellow pistol-shaped scanner in one hand. As he pushed through them, Mason thought he heard, coming from inside the shed, the crunch of something breaking.

Stepping inside, Mason looked down. The shed was now almost empty of people. As his eyes adjusted to the dimness, he could make out a scattering of yellow plastic shards on the floor of the shed, with a crushed scanner in the middle. Unsurprisingly, the scanner was labeled with his name.

He turned toward the doorway to see Travis stop halfway out.

Travis turned his head to the side, revealing a mirthless half smile. "Well that's a damn shame," he said. "I guess yours was defective." He continued out, disappearing from sight as Mason watched.

• • •

Fifteen minutes later, Mason threw a leg over the seal barricade and climbed over. Under his arm, he held the aluminum cylinder he had found under a scrap of plywood. It looked something like a large can of spray paint. The seals seemed more agitated today, perhaps because of all the human activity yesterday. He knew he probably looked ridiculous, tiptoeing and high-stepping around all those yelping animals in his slacks and pinstriped shirt, but he needed to find some water now, and some food.

Moving along the remains of the boardwalk, he spotted Juan, squatting in front of a semicircular opening where the rim of an underground culvert stuck out of the thin, rocky soil.

Juan reached inside, pulled out a small bundle wrapped in black plastic, and scanned the attached tag. Then he put the scanner on the ground and tore the plastic open. His eyebrows rose, and he looked up at Mason with dry amusement. He pulled a stack of green U.S. currency out of the bundle and riffled through it with his thumb. It was half an inch thick.

Mason laughed. Ten thousand dollars, if the bills were hundreds. But here, it was just paper.

Juan raised the back of his shirt, shoved the money under his belt, and walked away.

Mason went the other direction.

He came across Camilla, crouched near a jumble of broken concrete slabs a few yards from the barricade. She reached one arm into a crevice to ease a large backpack from between two slabs of stone, and he heard a clink of metal. Curious, he stepped over a nest, ignoring the bird that darted out to peck at his ankles, and walked closer.

Camilla looked up, eyes wide with alarm.

"Just me," he said.

She smiled. "What do you have there?"

He pulled the cylinder out from under his arm and turned it so she could read the label.

"Bear spray?" Her expression of concern was funny. "What are we supposed to do with *that*?"

"I can guess, but I'm hoping I'm wrong. What do you have?"

He crouched alongside her, and she unzipped the backpack. Coils of blue nylon rope, maybe a third of an inch thick, took up most of the space inside. She pulled it out to reveal a jumble of bright, shiny metal underneath. Mason leaned forward as she spread the pack open. The bottom was a nest of climbing gear: carabiners, cams, and belay devices piled haphazardly along with a harness.

"Lauren might have a use for it," she said.

"Not much to climb around here," he said. "I'm beginning to like Julian's sense of humor." But he had spotted something else, about fifty feet away.

"Happy hunting," he said, and left her repacking the climbing gear.

The triangular pennant stood a foot high. Its plastic flag was colored a muted gray that blended into the background, instead of the usual bright orange. He pulled it up and inspected the attached package.

A dozen shiny space blankets were wrapped in individual bundles inside, each one a sheet of gold-colored aluminum material folded in a package no bigger than a candy bar. He tucked the package under his arm with the bear spray and stood up.

From the other side of the barricade, Jordan waved to him.

"I know there are no teams today," she said. "But can I talk to you for a minute?"

He sauntered over and threw a leg over the barricade to join her on the seal-free side.

"What's that?" she asked.

"Bear spray."

"Oh. Anyway, we're both at a disadvantage here. You don't have a scanner, and me, well…" Jordan linked an arm through his. She lifted a bare foot to point at the sole, where blood was spreading from a cut on her arch. "…this is slowing me down some."

Mason guessed where she was going with this. He nodded for her to continue.

"How about we work together? Whatever we find, I'll scan the points but you keep the stuff."

"Sorry, Jordan," he said. "I don't really see what's in it for me. I'll be able to move faster on my own."

Her face fell. "I guess you're right. Well, if I see a chance to help us both anyway, I will. Good luck."

He patted her on the arm, slid his own arm free, and grinned.

"If I can help us both, I will, too," he said. "But you don't need to worry. After yesterday, you're leading the pack in points, and closest to the five million right now." With another friendly pat, he walked away. But he watched her out of the corner of his eye.

Jordan paced to the edge of the bluff, near the wooden staircase. She didn't seem to be limping. She looked down at the beach, and Mason followed her gaze to where the larger elephant seals shuffled back and forth. He studied her face surreptitiously. Jordan's jaw was set, her green eyes steeled in fierce concentration.

She looked as if she was struggling with a decision.

CHAPTER 40

JT hopped from rock to rock along the breakwater, paralleling the high-tide waterline and surveying the cracks in between the rocks, yellow scanner in hand. So far, he had found a heavy pair of leather gloves—useful, but not very.

He squatted to probe at a large tangle of rotting kelp, whose outline looked too regular to be natural. A dense cloud of small black flies rose buzzing into the air, and he waved a hand to disperse them. Parting the rubbery stalks of kelp, he exposed the corner of a black plastic case with a familiar-looking waterproof shell. He pulled it out of the squishy brown knots and scanned the attached tag.

A "3" lit the scanner's small gray screen. Hell, another forty points and he might actually start to catch up with the leaders.

Popping the latch on the case, JT lifted the lid. A pair of shiny green lenses stared up at him from the contoured foam padding inside, their short stalks projecting from a black visor with rubber straps. JT grinned at the night-vision goggles—he had used them frequently in the field. A third-generation NVD like this cost several thousand dollars—hopefully the goggles would give him an edge in an upcoming challenge.

Carrying the case, he angled up toward higher ground.

Reaching the flat section of dirt, he spotted something yellow about forty feet away. Juan had seen it, too. His eyes flicked up to meet JT's, and he exploded into a sprint, scattering seals as he ran for the yellow thing.

JT was closer to it, though. With a curse, he burst into a run, also.

Juan reached it first.

JT slid to a halt a few yards away, and he and Juan stood eyeing each other. Juan held the cache—a yellow plastic case about the size of a briefcase.

"Give it here," JT said. "Don't make me come get it."

Juan shook his head and dropped into a wary crouch.

JT was surprised. "You sure you want to do this, motherfucker?" He let the NVD case and gloves fall to the ground and circled toward Juan, arms ready.

Juan circled away, keeping his distance.

Shit, JT thought. But he needed those points. The yellow case had been closer to him than Juan, anyway.

133

Movement in his peripheral vision—other contestants coming their way from different directions. JT was reminded of high school and the crowd of rubbernecks that always gathered whenever there was a fight. He himself had never been among them; he'd usually been the one fighting.

"That's enough," Brent said, taking his hands out of his vest pockets. He moved in on JT's right.

"Stay out of this," JT said.

Brent stopped.

Behind him, Veronica stood watching JT with an expression of disgust. Her intense silvery-blue gaze bored into him.

He ignored her and locked eyes with his opponent. Juan's face was neutral, his eyes alert with calm readiness. Why did he look so relaxed? JT reached down one-handed to pick up a brick-size rock. Juan's face didn't change. No fear.

"Last warning," JT said, but now he was wishing he could defuse the situation somehow. Cameras or no cameras, things were about to get ugly.

There was no chain of command here. Nobody official to step in and resolve conflicts. No one was going to decide this for them. All the contestants were hungry, thirsty, and fixated on winning. With five million dollars at stake, they would take stupid chances, just as Juan was doing.

Feeling trapped, JT started toward him, unable to back down now.

Juan held the yellow case with one hand and ripped the tag away with the other. "Points or prize, JT—which'll it be?"

JT stopped. "Points."

Juan tossed the tag toward him. He caught it and scanned it, sensing the others relaxing around him as he did. Someone released a breath they had been holding.

"What's in the box?" JT shouted, glad things hadn't gone further.

Juan shrugged and knelt to pop the latches. He lifted the lid of the yellow case and let it fall back.

JT and the others moved in closer to see. A foot-long orange cylinder nestled inside, topped with a thick, black, rubbery wand.

Veronica tossed her hair, shaking blond highlights out of her face, and squatted next to Juan. "What the hell is it—an ice-cream maker?"

"An eepurb." Juan pulled out a folded paper instructions manual and read the cover. "GME AccuSat 406 Cat 2 EPIRB." He looked up. "An emergency position-indicating radio beacon."

Veronica snorted, stood up, and walked away.

JT gave a barking laugh. "I was hoping for a George Foreman grill and some burgers," he said. "But we can fire this up instead and tell the Coast Guard to bring pizza when they get here."

Ten more days like this, together, stuck here?

His eyes met Juan's. The dive captain regarded him with the same lazy, unshakable calm as always.

You and me, JT thought, *we're going to have a big fucking problem.*

CHAPTER 41

Jordan wiggled her toes in the cool sand and looked back up the wooden stairs. The bluff's edge cut off her view of whatever was going on up above. From down here, she couldn't see any of the other contestants. The beach around her was as crowded as St. Tropez or Majorca on a hot July day, but instead of European tourists on towels, she had seals and sea lions lolling all around her.

Across the channel lay the mainland, its sandy bluffs and sea grass-covered dunes sloping up into the redwood-covered hills of Big Basin and Chalk Mountain beyond. Her parents' home in Woodside, where she had grown up, was less than thirty miles away—just on the other side of the mountain range. So was most of the Bay Area's population of seven million. But from where Jordan stood, she could see no signs of civilization other than a lonely, abandoned-looking farmhouse a mile inland. This particular stretch of coast was mostly protected wilderness, so it was like traveling back in time.

After the rocks and gravelly dirt of the island's elevated surface, the beach sand felt soothing under her feet. She would be able to move fast here.

She eyed the dark shapes of the elephant seals in the distance. In the surf, three or four large males basked in the sun while keeping their distance from each other. One raised its head to shuffle a few yards up the beach, and Jordan's breath sped up slightly. Now that she was down at their level, the alpha bulls looked impossibly huge—monsters that weighed forty times what she did. She would have to be careful.

Stepping around a cluster of sea lions, she moved north, scanning the surrounding beach. Just ahead, one branch of the elevated wooden walkway crossed her path. Extending from the bluff staircase, it ran six feet above the sand, stretching all the way across the beach to where it ended over the water. Creosote-log piers supported the walkway every fifteen feet or so. Beneath the walkway, next to the concrete base of a pier, something gleamed white.

She wove through the seals and sea lions, getting closer, until she could make out a large white Tupperware container tucked next to the pier. *Food!* Gray elephant seals surrounded the pier, but they were smaller ones—females, not the huge, aggressive males.

Jordan crept forward. The elephant seals shifted nervously as she approached, watching her with suspicious eyes. She slowed, changing the rhythm of her steps, and the seals seemed to relax.

Pushing through the last group of seals, she knelt in front of the container. The seals around her suddenly erupted into motion, scrambling away in a panic.

She scooped up the slick plastic carton, shot to her feet, and tossed it onto the walkway above her head. A deep basso roar sounded from behind, vibrating through her chest and shaking the beach beneath her feet. Grabbing the walkway's edge with both hands, she pulled herself up in a single smooth motion, her waist at the level of the wooden beam. Her legs dangled below, vulnerable.

No judges here, no trophies, and no second place—she would only get one shot at this.

Certain that she would feel sharp teeth closing on her ankle or calf at any moment, Jordan kicked her legs out to the sides and thrust herself up with her arms—executing a perfect straddle beam mount. Her bare feet thumped onto the walkway.

She crouched there, arms outstretched for balance, and gasped in relief.

A massive dark shape slammed into the pier below.

The impact shook the boards beneath her feet and tumbled her to one knee. The Tupperware container lay on its side in front of her. She grabbed it and tucked it under one arm as a wet bulk rose three feet above the rim of the walkway next to her.

Kneeling, Jordan found herself staring a bull elephant seal right in the eye. It roared, blowing a blast of foul breath into her face.

Go!

Gagging on the smell of rotting fish, she sprang to her feet and sprinted down the walkway toward the bluff.

The bull's teeth splintered the boards behind her, sending chunks of wood flying.

Jordan hurtled along the catwalk, leaping over the gaps where the planks were missing, her bare feet slipping and skidding on the slick gray-and-white bird droppings. Roosting birds launched themselves out of her way and went flapping into the air.

Churning through the sand alongside the walkway, the elephant seal tried to head her off. She felt its teeth tear into the wood just behind her bare ankles as she bounded from board to board, desperately trying not to fall.

Reaching the edge of the bluff, she hurled herself up the stairs that led toward the flat ground above. The elephant seal roared again in warning and turned to shuffle back to his harem.

Breathing rapidly, Jordan collapsed on the steps. Adrenaline coursed through her body.

She watched the seal retreat, and her breaths slowed to a calm evenness. Eyes narrowing in concentration, she replayed the encounter in her head. The elephant seal had been surprisingly fast, given its bulk—she had no doubt it could outrun her in a straight line on open ground. But its reaction times were slow. It wasn't very smart.

Looking down at the Tupperware container in her arms, she peeled back its lid. A couple of dozen candy bars lay stacked inside, "Snickers" written on their brown labels. Her shoulders stiffened. Reclosing the lid of the container, she pulled the scanner from her belt and scanned the container's tag, earning eight points.

Jordan stared after the departing bull seal again, and her jaw hardened with resentment.

When an elephant seal lifted its chest to charge like this one had, it wouldn't be able to see what was right in front of it. *Her* seal had a distinctive zigzagging scar under its right eye, and a pale patch on its trunk.

She'd be able to recognize it again.

Mouth tight, she sat on the steps watching the seal that had chased her for a long time.

CHAPTER 42

Lauren stood beneath the rusted framework of the fallen lighthouse tower, flexing her fingers and looking up. A cylindrical bundle hung from one of the tower's higher spars, thirty feet off the ground.

She could climb it, no problem. But the spars were rusty steel, badly corroded and flaking from the salt air—would they hold her weight? She bounced on her toes and looked around to see what the other contestants were doing.

Some sort of huddle was breaking up by the breakwater. Juan closed a yellow plastic case and stood up. Then he, Veronica, Brent, and JT all headed their separate ways.

Lauren looked up again. The bundle was about the size of a liter water bottle, and that decided it for her. Grabbing the nearest spar, she levered herself up onto the scaffolding. She scanned for hand- and footholds, ignoring the ominous creak of metal, and soon was twenty feet above the ground.

Glancing down, she tensed. Right below her, a tangle of rebar spikes stuck out of the broken concrete. She would be impaled if she fell. She reset her feet and pulled herself higher on the fallen tower, angry with herself. Why was she sketching out? This was nothing.

A burst of liquid, sexy laughter from below startled her, and she tensed again. Veronica better not be laughing at *her*.

She wasn't. Lauren watched her pull something from a section of broken red-clay sewer pipe and hold it up, still chuckling. Rolls of toilet paper, still in their plastic wrap. Veronica scanned the tag and stood up, brushing the dirt from her jeans. With a moue of disgust on her face, she inspected something smeared on the arm of her sweater.

A high-maintenance type for sure, forty but trying hard to look twenty. She wouldn't last much longer here. Lauren felt a brief twinge of sympathy for the older woman, then turned her attention back to the bundle above.

A couple of minutes later, she released her grip and dropped the last short distance to the ground, landing lightly on her feet. The cylinder in her hand—a plastic mailing tube—was disappointingly light. She shook it but didn't hear anything. She scanned the tag for five points, then tore the end cap off and peered in.

Disappointed, she scissored with two fingers and pulled out the sealed envelope rolled inside. She squinted at it in confusion. The plastic address

139

window was taped over with black friction tape, but she could read the letter's return address:

California Department of Corrections and Rehabilitation
2100 Peabody Road
Vacaville, CA 95696

Lauren frowned. *What the fuck?*

CHAPTER 43

Even though Travis wasn't visible right now, Mason knew he was still lurking close by, shadowing him. In the distance, JT, Juan, Camilla, and Lauren made their separate ways across the rocky northern end of the island. Mason watched them for a few seconds, then hopped down into the cracked concrete catchment basin. Shifting a piece of broken concrete that lay in the shadow of the dome overhead, he pulled out a briefcase-size white plastic case with a red cross painted on top.

Mason laughed. He stood up inside the concrete basin, like a man waist-deep in an empty swimming pool, and a shadow fell across him from the rim above.

"A first-aid kit." Travis rubbed his chin, grinning down at Mason. "Why, I reckon that'll come in handy sooner or later. Hand it on up or you'll be needing it yourself real quick."

Mason looked around. No one else was in sight.

"And while we're at it," Travis said, "I'll take anything else you're carrying, too. I don't suppose you've scanned them, so according to the rules, they ain't really yours."

"I wonder if there's any baking soda in this first-aid kit?" Mason kept his voice easy, conversational. "That's supposed to provide relief from pepper spray."

He brought his other hand into view, holding the black cylinder, and smiled. "But this is *bear* spray, actually, so it's a little more powerful. Not really intended for use on people. I suspect it'll cause some lasting damage—leave you blind, maybe?"

CHAPTER 44

V eronica reached up and tore the padded envelope loose from under the eaves of the small concrete blockhouse, where it had been taped. She turned it over in her hands and scanned the attached tag. The scanner registered zero points. Sweeping the blond tips of her hair out of her face, she scanned it again. Zero points.

A wordless growl escaped through her gritted teeth.

Frustrated, she looked around her. From where she stood, hidden by the corner of the blockhouse, she couldn't see anyone else. She tore the end off the padded envelope and fanned it open, letting the compact object inside slide out into her hand. An old-fashioned black text pager—the kind Blackberries and smartphones had made obsolete—sat on her palm. Her eyebrows rose.

She checked that the pager was set to vibrate rather than beep, and turned it on. The display lit up, and a short text message ticked across it:

STAND BY FOR INSTRUCTIONS...

Veronica looked around again to make sure no one had seen her, then slid the pager into a front pocket of her jeans.

CHAPTER 45

Lauren shaded her eyes with her hand and looked to where Juan was pointing. Her heart gave a thump of excitement.

"Hell *yes* I see 'em," she said. "You think we can swim it?"

Juan shook his head. "No. It'd be like climbing inside a washing machine filled with sharp rocks."

"Chicken?" she sneered. "I thought you were some kind of bad-ass scuba diver."

A wave exploded against the jagged rocks below them, throwing spray into the air and sprinkling her arms with droplets.

"Look at the rip current pouring through this channel down here," he said. "It'll beat us to pieces, then sweep us out into the strait before we're a quarter of the way there."

At the island's northernmost edge, the ocean foamed white over a tumble of broken rocks extending from land's end. The rocks disappeared and reappeared as green waves crashed over them with unrestrained violence and spiraled outward in eddies of white foam.

Lauren shifted restlessly from leg to leg, probing the roof of her parched mouth with her tongue, feeling peeling sandpaper.

"Well, shit, cowboy," she said. "What bright ideas do *you* have?"

A loose trail of rocks and boulders curved away from the island like a giant question mark. Breaking waves slammed against them, sending eruptions of spray shooting skyward. The last boulder, three hundred feet out from the island, was the size of a house. It rose several feet above the spray, and on its dry, flat top stood a dozen or more white plastic gallon jugs.

Water—it had to be drinking water.

"There has to be a way," she said. "I mean, Julian wouldn't make it *totally* impossible..."—her abdominals tightened—"...would he?"

Juan didn't answer at first. He stood very still, arms crossed, dark eyes staring at the faraway jugs. Lauren could see salt crusted on his jaw—from dried sweat or seawater. He had shaved, she noticed, and changed his shirt, too, although this one was also black. She liked the way he smelled: sweaty but not rank. Her gaze traced the corner of his jaw, his cheekbone, his small ear, his face in profile.

"Neither of us can get that water on our own," he finally said.

• • •

145

"We don't know for sure what that is." Mason grinned. "Those jugs might turn out to be full of sea water. Or paint thinner."

Camilla grimaced. "Oh, *shut up*, Mason. It's drinking water."

Fabulous, Lauren thought. *Nice going, Juan.* These fucking yuppies were going to be a huge help, she could see. Time to call in her own reinforcements. She turned and yelled across the island.

"Yo, JT! Get your ass over here!"

"Anyone thirsty?" Camilla spread the top of the backpack she held. "Here's how we go get those."

Seeing the rope and climbing gear, Lauren took an excited breath. "That was supposed to be for me," she said.

"I'll let you borrow it," Camilla said. "But we all share the water."

"You'll get yours." Lauren turned away from her to meet Juan's eyes. He seemed more energized now. She joined him at the water's edge.

He pointed to the nearest rock. And then another one, twenty feet up-current.

She nodded. "Belay point." She pointed to a jagged four-foot fang of black rock just as it disappeared in a detonation of surf. "Tough transition there."

"Not only that." He pointed. "We can't grab hold anywhere. Sea urchins."

Lauren could the holes now, dotting the rocks every few inches, purple-black balls of spikes nestled inside. Involuntarily, she pulled her fingers to her chest. "Oh Christ."

JT slid down the short slope to join them. "I'll let you use these." He held out a pair of thick leather gloves. "But it'll cost you."

"We need you to belay us from shore," she said. "*Earn* your share."

She turned to Juan. "You ready?"

He grinned. "Let's do it."

"Everybody shares that water," Camilla said.

Lauren frowned, and stepped up to her, toe to toe. "Listen up, Dora the Explorer. This isn't some staff meeting you're running, where we vote on things." Reaching back with both hands, she swept her hair into a ponytail and tied it with a piece of shoelace, matching Camilla's angry glare with her own. "Your team killed us yesterday, so unless you feel like getting wet yourself right now, Juan and I go get those jugs. We can discuss who keeps what when we get back."

Mason smiled, holding up the first aid kit. "Someone may need this before we're done. Am I in or out?"

"Oh god, not you, too, now." Camilla turned and grabbed the first-aid kit from him.

Lauren laughed.

Juan stepped forward. "Here's the plan: Lauren and I rope up and go. JT and Mason belay us from shore. When we get back, they each get a jug, and so do you, Camilla. Lauren and I flip a coin for the points, and the two of us split the rest of the water."

Silence followed.

"Anyone else want to go instead, then?" Juan asked.

Nobody said anything.

"That's what I thought."

• • •

Lauren crouched on the rock nearest shore, trying to keep her balance. A wave slapped her in the face, pushing her body sideways with irresistible force. It would have peeled her off, but the ropes held her in place. Blinking salt water out of her eyes, she raised her ungloved hand and gave a thumbs-up. JT paid out more rope as Juan pulled back on his, stabilizing her.

She looked at the next rock, about fifteen feet away, disappearing and reappearing in the surf, and felt her footing slip beneath her. Taking a deep breath, she relaxed her body and leaped forward, plunging into the churning water, trailing the two ropes behind her in a V. The surge grabbed her and dragged her under, yanking her hard and bringing both lines taut.

Kelp roiled in the surrounding foam—she didn't want to get tangled up in that. She kicked and stroked hard for the next rock. A wave broke above her, pushing her under again. Tumbling over and over beneath the green-lit water, she clawed her way to the surface.

"Left," JT shouted. "On your left!"

Her gloved fingers fought for a hold on the wet, slippery rock. The icy surge was stronger than she had expected, terrifying. It seized her like a giant hand and dragged her body sideways again, scraping her calf across something sharp. The injury stung—sea urchin, probably. Lauren gripped the rock one-handed and pulled her shoulders and head out of the water. Groping underwater with the ungloved hand, she located a gear loop on the waistband of her harness and unclipped a cam. She jammed it into a crevice in the rock, slotted a hex alongside it, and clipped into both.

Secured now, she leaned back to hangdog a quick rest, letting her arms and hair dangle loosely in the waves. Whitewater detonated against her, and the world disappeared in a chaos of foamy white, then reappeared. The two pieces of gear held her in place.

Joy washed through her body. She could feel her muscles pumping, her calm, deep heartbeats, her breaths coming free and easy and strong. Lifting herself higher on the rock, she looked back at the shore. The others were cheering for her. Lauren grinned. She hung from one arm and waved, giving another thumbs-up.

Juan was tying the rope around his waist and shoulders, watching her.

Tilting her head to the side, she pursed her lips and crooked a finger, beckoning him.

"Come on in, cowboy," she shouted. "The water's fine."

CHAPTER 46

A half hour later, Juan's ungloved fingers slipped off a sea urchin-free section of rock. He glanced up at Lauren, braced in position five feet above him, as the current pulled at his legs, prying him away from the boulder. Kelp swirled about his chest. Dragged by the surge, his toes slid across rock, and he tried to reset his feet, scrambling for a foothold. No luck.

He reached for the rock again with his free hand, but it was too far—the surge held his body away from it. Clinging with his remaining hand, he tilted farther and farther from safety. Waves exploded against the boulder, hauling at his chest, trying to tear him loose. His gloved hand was slipping, too. He had miscalculated—maybe even killed himself. Any moment now, he would be swept away and under. Juan took a deep breath, preparing to fight for his life.

A hand clamped around his wrist.

He looked up, surprised to see Lauren leaning down toward him. She was grinning. Blood streaked the side of her calf and stained her shoe, but her grip felt as strong as a vise. He relaxed.

She shifted her body, and the muscles in her shoulder and arm bunched as she lifted him out of the water and up onto the boulder's slope. One-handed.

He leaned back against the rock next to her, his feet trailing into the water, and caught his breath. "Thanks."

"De nada, amigo." She slapped his shoulder. "Come on, I'll buy you a drink."

Rolling over, he followed her up onto the boulder's flat surface.

The jugs clustered around their feet. Lauren picked one up, and Juan did the same.

Unscrewing the cap, he sniffed. Then he tilted it up to his mouth. The water sluiced down his dry throat—clean, cool, delicious. He sighed involuntarily, stopping for a breath, and chugged again as Lauren did the same. She wiped a forearm across her mouth and smiled at him, her eyes dancing with delight. She seemed a completely different person out here: in her element now and happy. Juan could understand that. He stared down into the clear water, at the bright orange sea stars and green anemones beneath. Underwater, with a tank on his back and a regulator in his mouth, he was someone else, too—someone he liked better.

Shouted questions drifted across the water, the words impossible to make out. He made an "okay" sign with his thumb and forefinger and raised it high. Beside him, Lauren waved her arm in broad sweeps and gave a thumbs-up. Cheers erupted in the distance, and the small figures on shore started jumping around, giving each other high-fives. It seemed that everyone else had gathered to watch—Juan did a quick count and came up with seven—*almost* everyone, then.

A purple bruise was forming on the side of Lauren's forehead, and she was covered in abrasions and cuts. He was too. Blood from the cut on her calf spattered droplets onto the rock, but she didn't seem to mind.

He lowered himself to sit at the edge of the boulder, water jug in hand, and dangled one leg. Lauren dropped to sit beside him. The sun sparkled on the waves. She put her hand on his knee.

"You realize that was insane, of course," he said.

She laughed. "Not compared to some climbs I've done."

Juan looked at the C-shaped trail of ropes that curved back to the island from boulder to boulder, anchored in seven or eight places to rocks poking above the roiling surface. Two more ropes stretched directly over the water, straight back to the island, hanging in taut arcs.

"What was the hairiest?" he asked.

Lauren's face changed. "Trango Towers. Pakistan." It was almost a whisper.

Juan waited.

"It didn't end well." Her smile was gone now, as if it had never existed. Drawing in a sharp little breath, she took her hand off his leg.

"I spent a couple days hanging upside down next to the wall—with cracked ribs, internal bleeding, a skull fracture, and a concussion. Three weeks in the hospital once I got back Stateside. And I was the lucky one…"

She stared at her hands, and her body seemed to curl in on itself. "I lived."

An awkward silence hung in the air. Her eyes met his and widened, and the corners of her mouth turned down. She seemed to be probing his expression, looking for something there. Juan had no idea what.

Then her eyes hardened, as if shutters had suddenly slammed down behind them.

"Get up." Lauren sprang to her feet. "We have a delivery to make."

CHAPTER 47

"**Y**ou left the water out there."

Camilla's voice was a dry croak. She cleared her throat and stepped toward Juan, who was the first to come ashore. Her mouth was so dry it hurt. She could hear angry voices behind her, and she knew she should be angry, too, but the tightness in her throat wasn't anger—it was disappointment. Betrayal. Her motorcycle hero wasn't planning to share the water.

"We're all so thirsty." She didn't like the way her own voice sounded: weak and whiny. She spoke with more force. "I saw you two tying a rope through the handles on the water jugs. We all did. But then you left them there. Why, Juan?"

Juan's expression was neutral. He raised his hands in a placating gesture, and Camilla felt a little better. Maybe this wasn't what she thought. Then he shrugged and pointed back at Lauren, climbing up out of the surf behind him.

Lauren shook the water out of her hair. She looked at the semicircle of angry, bewildered faces, smirked, and turned to Juan.

"Looks like no one else found any water," she said. "Isn't that a bummer?" Her smirk didn't change as everyone tried to shout at her at once. Juan just looked bored.

Camilla turned away to avoid saying something she would regret. She couldn't believe that Juan was going along with this. She tried to catch Mason's eye, but he was grinning at the water jugs in the distance. Of course *he* would think it was funny, but she didn't—not at all. She looked for Jordan but couldn't see her. Weird. Everyone else was here…

"Hold on," Brent's voice commanded. He held up a hand, and the angry shouts quieted. "Lauren, dehydration is a serious health risk. These people need water. Don't play childish games with this."

"Relax," Lauren said. Shouldering past him, she grabbed one of the two ropes that stretched over the water. And pulled.

Camilla's eyes followed the rope to its other end, where a white train of water jugs was tumbling one by one off the edge of the distant rock, to hang suspended over the water. The jugs dangled from the second rope, which had been threaded through their handles. Lauren began hauling the rope in, hand over hand. The train of water jugs moved toward them, sliding along the second rope like laundry on a clothesline. JT stepped up next to Lauren to help pull.

151

Camilla looked around, noticing they were still one contestant short. "Where's Jordan?" she asked Veronica.

Veronica shook her head. "Haven't seen her all day."

Lauren jerked her head in an impatient come-here gesture. "Mason. Camilla."

Camilla hesitated, not liking where she saw this going.

"Come on," Mason said. "Lauren's got the right idea here. She knows what she's doing."

He walked over to join Lauren's group, and Camilla reluctantly followed.

JT pulled the first water jugs off the line. He handed one to Camilla and one to Mason, then opened his own and took a long drink. Camilla did the same. The water felt wonderful splashing down her parched mouth and throat. Knowing she should slow down, she drank gulp after gulp, unable to stop until she needed a breath. Then she lowered the jug and started toward Brent, Veronica, Natalie, and Travis who stood a small distance away.

"Hang on." Lauren laid a hand on her shoulder, stopping her. "Not so fast."

Camilla pushed the hand off her shoulder. She walked over to hand her jug to Veronica who smiled at her, those silver eyes momentarily kind. But Veronica immediately handed the water to Natalie. Tipping the jug up, Natalie took several huge gulps, then handed it back to Veronica with a muffled thank-you. Veronica drank and passed the jug to Brent.

The jug was more than a third gone now. Knowing she had done the right thing by sharing, Camilla tried not to monitor how much was left.

Before Brent could drink, Travis reached for the jug. "Old man, you better—"

Brent handed it to him without protest and tucked his hands into the pockets of his vest. He met Camilla's eyes, and she could see his approval. Good. Brent, too, understood what Julian was trying to do here. And he didn't like it, either.

"Well, Doc," Travis said, tossing aside the empty jug. "Seems like we just ran out of water. But on the odd chance you're thirsty, too, you might want to take it up with the lady over there." Grinning, he pointed at Lauren.

Camilla shook her head in disgust. Travis had finished her water. Watching Mason squat behind Lauren to stack the jugs in a pyramid, she realized that team loyalties didn't matter to anyone right now. These dynamics were much simpler: the haves and the have-nots. Lauren's "haves" controlled all the water. Deliberately spurning her own place among the haves, Camilla had joined the have-nots in protest, and she was proud she had done so.

Juan leaned against a rock nearby. He looked like a bored lifeguard to Camilla, but his position near Lauren, JT, and Mason made it clear which group he was with. Trying to catch his eye, she willed him to put a stop to this. *Say something, Juan. Take charge. I know Lauren will listen to you.* But Juan seemed to be only half paying attention.

If Jordan were here to see him, Camilla thought, she would have an I-told-you-so look on her face. But where was she? A worm of worry spiraled through Camilla's gut. Could Jordan have gotten hurt somewhere while everyone else was focused on the water? But there were cameras everywhere, supposedly. If something bad had happened, Julian and his crew would have seen it on-screen and would have come out. She looked over her shoulder toward the warehouse buildings, but they remained silent and still. No activity. Maybe Jordan had given up and gone back inside one of the two houses, then. It wouldn't be easy for her to move around the island barefoot.

And there was that, too, wasn't there? Would Julian and his crew *really* have taken Jordan's other shoes? Camilla looked at Juan, remembering the fight he had with Jordan aboard the yacht, and her gut tightened. But taking Jordan's shoes was such a petty, spiteful thing to do. She couldn't imagine many guys even *thinking* of it. No, she was getting paranoid. She focused on Lauren.

Lauren seemed to be counting the water jugs. She frowned. Did it again. Her eyes narrowed. Then she stared at Juan. He shrugged. For a moment, it looked as if Lauren was about to say something to him. Her face twisted in indecision, and then she turned to face the "have-nots" instead, holding up a jug of water.

"Okay, people, listen up," she said. "Half this water's mine, and half belongs to Juan." She raised her voice to drown out the protests. "We went out there and earned it the hard way. Risked our lives. Besides, you heard the rules this morning, same as we did—"

"I don't care about the rules," Camilla said, stepping forward. "You're better than this, Lauren."

"Don't worry, we plan to share the water with you all. But it isn't going to be free. Fair is fair. We've got twelve jugs left. Who's thirsty?"

"I'll pay cash." Veronica's voice was loud, like a bidder at an auction. She held up a fan of hundred-dollar bills. "A thousand dollars for two jugs."

Lauren laughed. "Don't be cheap. The island's Seven-Eleven isn't open, and this may be our only water for the next ten days."

Camilla's discomfort deepened. Only twelve gallons of water? But it was possible Lauren was right.

At Lauren's side, JT laughed. "A thousand? This shit is worth a lot more than Cristal right now."

Mason stood up behind them. "It's a closed economy, so basic laws of supply and demand apply here." He pushed his glasses up on his nose, addressing Veronica. "All of us found plenty of cash. And even though, as a banker, it pains me to say this, none of us have much use for it right now." He winked. "But hang on to it. It might come in handy in a couple of weeks."

"This is just idiotic," Veronica said. She crumpled the bills in her fist and jammed them into her pocket.

"What else do you have?" Lauren asked her.

Veronica looked down at the small pile of caches she had found: toilet paper and binoculars.

"I'll take the binoculars." Lauren held out her hand.

Veronica's mouth was a tight line.

Mason laughed. "And in case you're thinking of holding us all hostage for toilet paper later, don't bother. We can just use our cash instead."

• • •

Camilla and Mason sat with their backs against a rock, twenty feet away from the others. She had two jugs of water between her feet; Mason had one. She watched the trading with interest, noting the caches that people had found, as they exchanged them for water.

"That was weird," she said. "Natalie actually traded one of her water jugs *back* to get that stun gun."

She watched Natalie press the trigger of the small handheld unit, sending crackling arcs of electricity dancing between the two metal prongs at the front. Looking a little surprised, Natalie jammed it into the belly pocket of her hoodie.

"What does she want with that?" Camilla asked.

"Well," Mason said, "Natalie's quiet, but she's not dumb. And on the red team, she's like a lamb among lions. They're a rough bunch."

"Back on the ship, when we chose our teammates…" She watched Natalie drift to the side of the group. "Should we have—"

"No." He laughed. "Definitely not. Save your charity for when it isn't likely to cost you five million dollars."

"A lot of this stuff Julian hid for us is kind of odd, and not just the stun gun." Camilla pointed to Mason's bear spray and first-aid kit. "Scary, even." She thought about the other items she had seen: disposable rain ponchos, rolls of duct tape, space blankets, a flashlight, a roll of thin-gauge wire, camping cookware and forks and spoons—ironic, considering that no one had found any food. What were they supposed to do, eat the wildlife?

She looked down at the large packet of candles in her lap. "At least some of it's useful."

Mason laughed. "Pretty useless, actually, without matches. Unlike *that*." He pointed to the LED camp lantern that Travis was handing to Lauren.

"Juan got the matches," Camilla said. "But you're right: that lantern will come in handy."

"For the red team, not us," Mason said. "Nice of you to give Lauren that big folding knife, too."

"I needed to get the extra jug of water, for Jordan," Camilla said. "I'm worried about her. We should go look for her."

"She's fine," he said. "If there's one person here you don't need to worry about, it's our team captain."

The trading had died down now.

"Anybody got a coin?" Lauren asked. Brent tossed her one, and Camilla remembered that Lauren and Juan planned to flip for who got the points.

Juan seemed to have perked up. He reached for the coin, but Lauren shook her head, handing it to JT instead. "Call it in the air," she said to Juan.

Juan won the toss. He didn't react much. As he scanned the ten-point RF tag that had been zip-tied to one of the water jugs, Lauren gritted her teeth. She looked like she wanted to hit somebody. Instead, she bent to gather her caches and her water. Others were doing the same now.

Camilla leaned back against the rock. "Excitement's over, I guess."

"Okay, that's my cue, then." Mason stood up and walked into the center of the group with his hand high, like a scalper hawking Giant's tickets in front of AT&T Park. Camilla's face split into a grin of surprise when she saw what dangled from his upraised hand. Without a working scanner, he had pocketed the RF tags off the caches he found. He now held five or six, waving them for all to see. Juan and Lauren both froze in place, staring at the tags.

"I'd like to buy a vowel," Mason announced.

Five minutes later, Camilla was grinning and shaking her head, looking at Mason. He had five jugs of water at his feet, along with three rolls of duct tape and the bear spray. He had traded his RF tags, along with the space blankets and the first-aid kit, to Juan and Lauren for the water. Camilla looked around, realizing that Mason had now cornered the island's water market. Other than her, with the jug she was saving for Jordan, he was the only person with more than one jug.

She poked him in the chest with her finger. "All I can say is, you better share when people need it, buddy. Or you'll have *me* to answer to."

"Want some free financial advice?" Mason pointed at the jugs at his feet. "Always invest where there's limited supply and high demand."

Jordan appeared suddenly from around the corner of the bluff facing the mainland, jogging barefoot along the beach with a large Tupperware container in her arms. A big bag of trail mix was balanced on the top. She smiled her dazzling smile.

"Guys, I know where all the food is."

CHAPTER 48

Zelda's Beachside Restaurant, Capitola, California

"A *film crew?*" Jacob asked. "Is it those Discovery Channel guys again?"

Karen Anderson looked at Heather for help.

There beneath the big white-and-maroon-striped umbrella on the restaurant's open sundeck, the soft, ocean-scented breeze was just cool enough to feel good on Heather's face. She wanted an explanation as badly as Jacob did, so she didn't say anything. Dmitry didn't, either.

"What the hell?" Jacob said. "Why aren't we out there as technical advisers at least, making sure they don't disrupt things?"

The beach in front of them was crowded with tourists and locals. Children played in the sand and ran in and out of the surf in half-zipped wetsuits, screaming with delight. On the other side of the esplanade, a pastel-colored row of faux-adobe haciendas—beach rentals—nestled against a backdrop of eucalyptus trees.

Karen pulled out a pack of cigarettes and a lighter. She looked around at the surrounding tables, then put the pack and the lighter back in her purse with a sigh.

"Try and see how this looks from our perspective," Heather said to her.

The waitress, a twenty-something blonde with a streak of purple in her hair and turquoise nail polish, arrived with their burgers and salads. Dmitry smiled at her, and she smiled back at him from behind oversize dark sunglasses.

The Santa Cruz coastline curved away out to sea in both directions, revealing miles of beach-and-bluff coastline under a wide blue sky spotted with cotton-puff clouds. The tall coastal bluffs to the south were ridged with white-painted houses interspersed with eucalyptus and cypress woods.

The focus of their conversation lay just a few short miles up the coast in the other direction, to the less-populated north: Año Nuevo Island.

Karen picked up a fork and put it back down. "Look, I'm disappointed, too," she said. "I really look forward to our stay out on the island every year. But there are financial considerations as well. A little flexibility from you guys would be helpful."

"Last time Discovery did that segment, I didn't like the way they made us look," Jacob said. "They're not interested in the science; they only want ratings. They play on people's fears."

"Your food's getting cold," Karen said, and started on her salad.

157

Heather looked down at the weathered decking at her feet, worn to a rounded smoothness except for the knuckle-size bulges of harder knots in the wood. A small brown sparrow bobbed near her ankle, looking up at her hopefully. She dropped an inch-thick home-style french fry, and the sparrow hopped toward it.

"I didn't invite you here to argue," Karen said. "I wanted to give you some good news. Team, we're fully funded for the next eighteen months. So extend the study. *Expand* it. We have last season's tracker data to work with now…"

A rhythmic tinging rose from the table, stopping her in mid sentence: Jacob tapping his fork against his plate. He was looking out at the waves, jaw working like he was chewing something he couldn't swallow.

"Why didn't you tell us until the last minute?" Heather asked Karen.

"This thing just came together," she said. "The stars aligned."

"That's no answer."

"You guys need to grow up a little." Karen's voice took on a little heat. "We were almost three hundred thousand dollars short heading into next year. Projects were on the chopping block. Including yours…"

"What?" Jacob snapped out of his sullen reverie.

"Yes, it was going to get cut." Karen said. "I found a way to save it, and all you three can do is bitch."

In the silence that followed, something fluttered at Heather's feet. She looked down to see the brown sparrow whirr into panicked flight and shoot between the yellow-painted railing that separated Zelda's Restaurant from the beach. The big gray pigeon that had chased it away waddled back to the abandoned french fry at her feet. It regarded Heather with its beady black eye for a moment, then began to peck at the fry.

Jacob sounded agitated. "Think of the damage those Discovery assholes will do, running around out there unsupervised."

"I never said it was Discovery Channel. In fact, I can't tell you too much more right now."

"I don't get it." Heather stared at her. "Why the secrecy? That's *weird*, Karen—really weird."

"No, it's bullshit." Jacob tossed his half-eaten burger onto the plate. "I don't accept that. You *have* to tell us who's out there."

The purple-haired waitress was back. She dropped off the check, then slipped Dmitry a folded piece of paper with her turquoise-nailed fingers. He grinned at her, tucking it into his shirt pocket, and she walked off with an exaggerated wiggle.

"Nice," Heather said to him. "Can we focus here?"

"I don't need pressure from you, too," Karen said. "I get enough of that from the board. And the grants committee is just…" She put her empty glass down with a thump and pulled her wallet out of her purse. "Trust me, I'm taking good care of us here."

Dmitry leaned back in his chair, not smiling now. His eyes were on Karen. "Who is going to island, Karen? They are already there? You should tell us."

"That's not the point," Karen said. She put three twenties on top of the bill, looked at her watch, and got up. "Guys, it's the holiday season, and my plane leaves soon. It'll be Christmas in a couple of days. Wrap up the surveys, turn 'em in, and then take a couple weeks. *Enjoy* yourselves. Visit family; have some eggnog; sing some carols; get drunk. That's what I'm going to do. I'll see you back at the Institute in January." She walked away fast, heels clicking against the boards.

Heather looked down at her plate, stunned. Then her attention was drawn back to scrabbling motion near her feet. A big gray-and-white herring gull darted at the pigeon, which fled, bumping into a chair leg before flapping away across the beach.

The seagull picked up the french fry in its cruel beak and turned its yellow gaze on Heather for a moment. Then it hopped up on top of a nearby piling, flipped the fry around lengthwise in its beak, and gulped it down.

Scavengers and predators, she thought. Nature's hierarchy in action— even here, with the soft murmur of children's laughter in the background. The sun went behind a cloud, and a gust of wind blew across the patio, chilling her. Not hungry anymore, she looked at Dmitry and Jacob.

"Karen's family's local," she said. "They live in Berkeley. So why exactly is she headed to the airport?"

CHAPTER 49

Jordan lifted the jug two-handed and drank, the cords in her slim, elegant neck standing out as she swallowed. She lowered the jug and looked down the beach.

Camilla took another bite of Snickers bar and followed her gaze. A few hundred feet away, the beach widened to a blunt tip pointed toward the mainland. Huge gray shapes moved restlessly in the early-afternoon haze, galumphing across the sand at the heart of the elephant seal rookery. Alpha males patrolling their harems roamed the waterline, chasing off interlopers. Challenges rolled across the beach and echoed off the bluffs behind them—deep bass rumbles that she could feel as well as hear.

Everything at this end of the beach was on a giant scale. Even the newborn pups lying next to their mothers were the size of German shepherds. The older juveniles were larger than Camilla herself.

"I couldn't get close," Jordan said. "It was a big crate with one of those 'perishable' stickers on it, buried partway in the sand." She pointed. "Right there."

Camilla looked, and her legs suddenly felt weak. "Oh god."

From behind her, where the other eight contestants stood in a semicircle, she heard groans of dismay. She turned to stare at them, eyes wide. What was Julian *thinking*? He couldn't possibly intend...

Lauren collapsed to a sitting position on the sand and hugged her knees. "No way," she said, shaking her head vigorously. "They can't make us do this. Fuck that shit—it's flat-out suicide."

Camilla turned back to where Jordan was pointing. The crate sat right in the center of the island's biggest harem of elephant seals, its upper half just visible behind the bulk of a basking female. A monster alpha bull shuffled back and forth, guarding his turf, a massive flipper brushing against the crate with every pass.

Jordan turned to face them all, looking frantic. "Guys, we've just got to. There's no other choice." Her bare feet stamped the sand, like a toddler throwing a tantrum. "We *need* that food." She sucked in a breath and smoothed her hands against her stomach, looking at the crate.

"Jordan..." Veronica took her by the arm, her voice filled with concern. "Have you eaten anything *at all*?"

Tears suddenly spilled over Jordan's eyelids, and her mouth turned down at the corners. She shook her head and looked down at her feet.

Camilla looked at the empty Tupperware container by their feet, at the residue of trail mix in the crumpled bag, the Snickers bars in the other contestant's hands. Hadn't Jordan already taken her share?

"But why not, dear?" Veronica asked.

Jordan was crying hard now. She looked from person to person, her face desperate.

"I'm severely allergic to peanuts," she sobbed. "I could die."

• • •

"Well, your plan has the virtue of simplicity, at least," Mason said.

"Shut up, Mason." Camilla looked at Jordan, a dozen yards away. The tears were gone now, and Jordan's jaw was set. Okay, then. They would do this, for Jordan and for themselves. The candy bars Camilla had eaten had restored her strength. Still, what they were about to do was far more dangerous than anything she had ever seen on a reality show. They were all being incredibly stupid here. Including Julian.

But Jordan had shared the Snickers bars and trail mix she found with everyone. She hadn't asked for anything in return. Even Juan had taken a couple of Snickers bars, although he hadn't thanked her—hadn't even acknowledged her. Camilla was starting to have her doubts about Juan. After all, she hadn't actually *seen* the rider's face when he rescued the child.

Glancing at Juan briefly, she squatted next to where he, Mason, JT, and Lauren were huddled.

"Here's how we do this," she said. "Grab *that* thing…" She pointed at the ten-foot metal spar she had asked them to retrieve from the tower wreckage. Then she handed Mason a large metal carabiner from her backpack. "Duct-tape this onto the end, and run the rope through it."

"We'll be like the mice trying to hang a bell on the cat," he said, fingering the carabiner's one-way spring-loaded gate.

"No, you won't, because the rest of us will lure that monster away from you four," she said. "Once you get close enough to the crate, JT uses the pole to clip through the handle. Then everyone retreats, and we haul the crate back to us with the rope. Easy."

"Easy, huh?" Mason laughed and held up the canister of bear spray. "Safety precaution, in case the rest of you can't keep that beast away from us."

Hefting the spar one-handed, like a javelin, JT stood and pointed to his left side. "Lauren, you there. Mason on my right. Juan, you behind me, steadying the pole."

Camilla stood and walked toward the others, who were spreading out in a wide semicircle around the crate. Jordan, studying the bull elephant seal and the crate beside it, didn't look up.

"Everyone, move in slow," Camilla called. "Be careful—we don't want anybody hurt."

They converged on the crate cautiously, from all sides. The crate's guardian reared up and tossed its head, lurching from side to side, trying to keep them all in view. Camilla watched the seal grow more and more agitated.

She braced her feet, ready to bolt, but it wasn't moving away from the crate. She started circling sideways, getting closer.

A roar came from behind her, and she whirled about, heart racing, to look over her shoulder. She had accidentally edged too close to another male's territory. Weaving between the female seals and juveniles at her feet, she quickly scrambled away, breathing a sigh of relief when the second seal didn't pursue her. This was going to be tricky.

"Travis," JT called. "Buddy, now's your time to shine."

Travis didn't make any move. Camilla wasn't really surprised. She would have to do something to break all their paralysis. She looked at Brent. He scratched the side of his head, watching the seal, then met her eyes and shook his head. She knew what he was telling her: *too dangerous*. But Jordan needed food, and soon enough, the rest of them would, too.

She wove between the pups and smaller female elephant seals. *Smaller?* They were still ten or twelve feet long. But they weren't giants, like the old bull stationed in front of the crate. Camilla eyed it carefully as she got close. It had to be over sixteen feet long. Holding its head eight feet above the beach, it watched her. Looking at it made her legs feel weak and shaky again.

"Camilla," Brent called from behind her, "Stop. There's a difference between brave and stupid."

She raised a hand in acknowledgment, not taking her eyes off the bull… and crept forward. She hoped Brent understood; she couldn't let fear control her actions. Not once. Not ever. She had decided that a long time ago.

When she was fifty feet away, the bull suddenly lurched forward, bellowing as it charged. Camilla pivoted and ran, her feet kicking up the sand. But her spin was clumsy, and she stumbled. The beach shook under her knees, and she bounced to her feet, knowing the monster seal was close behind her. The chocolate bars were back in her throat, threatening to come up—oh god, she was dead now. Camilla ran.

"Hey, hey! Over here!" Brent shouted.

Out of the corner of her eye, Camilla saw Brent running forward, waving his arms above his head. The elephant seal turned to chase the bigger target, and Brent shambled away.

To Camilla's horror, she realized that Brent wasn't very fast. She yelled wordlessly and ran back toward the seal.

It turned toward her again, then spun and humped back toward JT's group, who had gotten within twenty feet of the crate. Lauren ran, and the rest scattered, too. The bull took up its post in front of the crate again, bobbing its head and roaring at them all.

"Lauren!" JT shouted. "You're supposed to have my back."

"Like you had *my* back the other night on the dock, first time we saw one of these babies?" Lauren shook her hands loosely, limbering up her fingers. "I seem to recall you running past me like I wasn't there, JT."

Mason laughed.

"He's right, Lauren." Juan raised his voice, addressing them all. "We need to work together. If we don't, somebody'll get killed."

Camilla racked her brain, trying to think of a solution. If only they had something to drive the seal off without hurting it... Fire! That was the answer. Grinning, she turned to Jordan to share her idea.

The expression on Jordan's face stopped her cold.

It was a look Camilla had seen before, but never in person. She had seen it on TV, on world-class runners waiting for the starter's gun. On champion figure skaters about to enter the arena. On professional boxers eyeing an opponent. The laser-focused concentration of someone for whom winning was everything—the *only* thing in the world that mattered. It transformed Jordan's beautiful features into a mask of fierce determination, her eyes into green ice. Jordan's nostrils flared. She bounced in place once, setting her feet, and then sprinted directly at the crate and its terrifying guardian.

"No!" Camilla shouted. "Wait." She started after her, but it was futile. Jordan ran with the light-footed grace and speed of a trained athlete; she couldn't keep up. The distance between them grew.

The alpha seal swung its head in Jordan's direction and exploded into motion. It came on like a bulldozer, with shocking speed. Sand flew. Jordan didn't even slow down.

Skidding to a halt, Camilla clapped a hand over her mouth. Her team captain had gone absolutely crazy.

Jordan ran straight into the oncoming seal's charge. The slim young woman and the five-thousand-pound behemoth came together like a bicycle running head-on into a bus. Camilla screamed.

The massive alpha bull slammed its chest forward, toppling onto Jordan, and she pivoted away to the side. A slender white hand snaked up to deliver a vicious slap across the elephant seal's eye.

Camilla's scream cut off in mid breath. Who was this woman?

And then Jordan was sprinting along the waterline with the angry elephant seal in pursuit, hurdling over smaller seals in her way as she led the giant bull away from the crate.

Several of the smaller juveniles failed to get out of the bull's path in time. They disappeared under its bulk to lie injured or dying in its wake, crushed into a bed of crimson-stained sand.

Camilla looked away, closing her eyes. Then she opened them again. On the open sand, the monster was faster than Jordan.

"Jordan!" she screamed. "Back this way!"

Jordan didn't turn back. The alpha bull was closing the gap, only a few yards behind. Camilla had a horrifying premonition of seeing Jordan's body crushed and bloody in the sand.

Jordan looked over her shoulder at her pursuer, her face a mask of angry resolve. Then she dived to her hands and knees, rolling over and over sideways as another massive shape reared up from the sand directly in front of her.

The second alpha bull roared, sending lesser seals scattering as it drove into the intruding bull. Chest to chest, the two behemoths slammed together and tore into each other. Forgotten by her pursuer, but still in danger, Jordan dug her heels in and scrambled backward. Gouts of blood spattered the sand around her as the two monsters towering above her sank their teeth into each other's scarred flesh. Jordan scrambled to her feet and ran back toward Camilla.

Camilla stared at her, torn by conflicting emotions. Jordan had somehow managed to avoid getting killed or injured. But she had hurt the elephant seal's eye and led it into a bloody fight with a rival *on purpose*.

Jordan staggered and put her hands on her knees, letting her head hang forward. She swayed, her blond hair curtaining her face, so that Camilla couldn't see her expression. But she looked like she was about to throw up or pass out.

Concerned, Camilla rushed forward, but before she could get there, Jordan stood up straight again. Flipping her hair back from her face, she glanced back toward the battling alpha bulls a hundred feet behind her, then walked toward Camilla with her usual cocktail-party poise and grace.

A deep male voice interrupted before Camilla could say anything to her.

"Of all the stupid things I've seen people do to land themselves in the ER," Brent shouted, jogging toward them, "that had to be the dumbest—"

"Brent, she's *hungry*." Veronica stopped Brent with a light touch on his elbow. "Don't forget how young she is."

Veronica's pale blue eyes swept over Camilla, and her mouth pulled into a grim line. *But you should know better,* her eyes said. Putting an arm around Jordan, she walked her away.

Camilla's throat tightened, and she stared after Veronica in surprise.

CHAPTER 50

Holding the ten-foot spar like a spear, JT fished with it for the crate's handle. Tension thrummed through his legs and arm muscles. His gaze flicked back and forth between the carabiner at the end of the spar and the sand dune the bull elephant seal had disappeared behind. The snorts, roars, and slaps of a titanic battle rose from beyond the dune. It wasn't hard to guess what Jordan had done. JT didn't know many Marines with the guts to try something that crazy.

The carabiner's gate kept sliding past the handle of the crate without opening deeply enough to catch, and Juan's steadying hand at the back of the spar wasn't much help. Sweat dripped down JT's cheeks. Swearing, he wiped his face with the crook of his elbow and tried again.

"Come on, come on, come on," Lauren's urgent monotone grated in his ears. Bouncing up and down on his left, her ponytail swinging, she looked ready to run at the first sign of the monster seal. On his right, Mason stood calm and steady. Even without looking at his face, JT was certain he was grinning. *Something seriously wrong with that guy.*

And this fishing bullshit wasn't working.

"Hell with it." Sliding his hand loosely along the spar, JT ran forward until his fist closed around the D-ring at the end. Dropping to a crouch directly in front of the crate, he reached for the handle. The noises from behind the dune suddenly changed, growing louder.

"It's coming back!" Lauren screamed.

The elephant seal bull burst over the dune, fifteen feet away, humping toward him with blood streaming from its chest and flanks. Gritting his teeth, he reached forward to clip the carabiner to the crate's handle, but he was jerked up and away by a hand on his biceps. Juan pulled him to his feet, and together they stumbled backward.

The elephant seal didn't even slow. Chest held high, it charged them, shaking its great, ugly head from side to side. Its trunk rippled back, pink gums with three-inch yellow teeth yawning wide above JT's head.

Shoving Juan one-handed, JT thrust him out of the seal's path. With his other hand, he raised the steel spar like a lance.

The elephant seal lowered its head, then snapped its neck upward, sending the spar flying end over end through the air. Knocked backward, JT landed on his butt in the sand. He looked up to see a monster the size of a deuce-and-a-half truck dropping forward onto him. Game over, now—he was fucking dead.

A sharp hissing noise came from behind him, and the air filled with a cloud of orange-red fog. Stepping forward over JT's legs, Mason aimed the black canister of bear spray up into the monster's face.

Recoiling, the elephant seal curled backward over itself and ground its face into the sand. A tail flipper the size of a car door caught Mason broadside, sending him flying. The seal's roars turned to high deafening squeals and it retreated over the dune again, heading toward the water.

A wisp of orange-red mist from the cloud of bear spray settled over JT, and needles jabbed his eyes and the inside of his nose. Gagging and wheezing, he slapped his palms over his face. Agony blanketed his head—like getting stung by hundreds of wasps at once. Fire burned his cheeks and powdered glass shredded his mouth and throat.

Something cool splashed in his face. Water. Through a blurry red haze, he saw Juan swinging the jug of water toward him again.

"Thanks," he croaked, and a fit of coughing racked his chest. Juan pulled him to his feet and walked over to Mason, who lay facedown on the sand nearby.

Shaking his head to clear it, JT retrieved the spar. He clipped the carabiner D-ring through the handle of the crate and looked about him with watering eyes.

Mason was standing now, brushing the sand off his clothes and rubbing his shoulder. Juan scooped Mason's glasses out of the sand and handed them to him. Putting them on, Mason grinned at JT.

Something really *wrong with that guy*. JT rubbed at his eyes. Now, where was Lauren? Spotting her about fifty feet away, he clenched his jaw in anger. She had run. Again.

From the other side of the dune, the monster's receding squeals were drowned out by the angry roars of another elephant seal. The sounds of a fight erupted once again.

The crate temporarily forgotten, JT ran up to the crest of the dune, with the others right behind him.

It was ugly. Blinded by the bear spray, the retreating bull was no match for its rival.

Sinking teeth into the blinded seal's neck, the challenger ripped back and forth with animal fury, sending blood pouring from gashes in the other's throat.

The vanquished bull sank to the sand as the victor threw its head back, rumbling its roars of triumph across the beach.

JT glanced at the other contestants, standing in a small group at the crest of a nearby dune. Camilla looked pale. She met his gaze and turned away. Brent's face was red. Biting a thumbnail, Jordan stared at the dead seal, unable to tear her eyes away.

Other large elephant seals shuffled in the haze. The natural order had been disrupted, and soon they would be challenging each other for the dead bull's territory and harem, JT knew. He rubbed his eyes again, and walked back toward the crate. Everybody followed. Nobody said anything.

The animals on the beach gave the dead elephant seal a wide berth.

It lay there silent and unmoving, a huge black mound rising from an empty circle of brown sand.

CHAPTER 51

The crate was a large cube, four feet on a side, made of high-impact olive-hued plastic. Camilla could see a big white sticker on the lid: an hourglass, surrounded by the outlines of fish, grapes, flowers, and beef carcasses. The word *"PERISHABLE,"* in boldface at the bottom of the sticker, made interpreting the symbols unnecessary—it pretty much had to be food. Camilla looked at Jordan, relieved on her behalf.

Kneeling in front of the crate next to JT, Jordan wore an expression of hungry anticipation. She rubbed her palms down her stomach, like she was smoothing the front of a wrinkled dress.

Staring a warning at the others, JT used his handheld scanner to read the tag on the crate. No one challenged him. Over his shoulder, Camilla read twenty points off the scanner's display. Snapping open the latches, he lifted the lid of the crate.

Jordan's eyes grew huge.

Hundreds of brick-size packages, individually wrapped in brown plastic, were stacked in neat rows inside the crate. JT laughed and pulled one out, tossing it to her.

"MREs," he said. "Meals Ready to Eat. 'Meals Rejected by the Enemy,' we used to call 'em. Taste like shit, but they'll keep us alive."

Camilla reached in and grabbed a package: Thai-style chicken. Flipping it over, she read the small print on the back, afraid of what she would find.

Beside her, Jordan tore open her own MRE.

Camilla grabbed her wrist, stopping her. Turning the open foil package in Jordan's hand, she pointed at the fine black print. The fifth ingredient, after water, chicken, mushrooms, and food starch, was peanut oil.

"Oh my god." Jordan dropped the package onto the sand. She pawed through the crate, flipping over packets, reading the backs, and tossing them aside.

"No. No. Shit. Shit. No. Oh my god." Her voice cracked.

Camilla put a hand on her shoulder, but she shook it off. Digging to the bottom of the crate, she pulled out a package and read the back. She flung it away and stood up. Her mouth opened, but there was no sound. Raising an arm, she wrapped the crook of her elbow around her mouth, and her eyes widened even further.

"We'll figure something out," Camilla said to her. "I'm so sorry."

Jordan let out a strangled cry and shook her head. Then she turned and ran south along the beach, her receding sobs echoing off the bluffs.

"Someone should go after her," Veronica said. "After what we saw from her earlier, there's no telling what she might do now."

Camilla started forward.

"Not you," Veronica snapped, freezing her in place. "You *encouraged* her. You almost got her killed."

I did? Camilla just stared, too stunned to answer.

"We're going to have a talk about this later, young lady." Veronica's eyes bored into her, shrinking her like a naughty child. "Did you even bother to see what condition her feet are in?"

"Veronica, that's enough," Brent said. Then he turned to Juan, leaning against the bluff nearby with his caches piled next to his boots. "Give me that first-aid kit. Right now. No more stupid games."

Juan shrugged and handed it over without a word.

Brent jogged up the beach toward where Jordan had disappeared.

CHAPTER 52

Brent found Jordan sitting at the foot of the wooden steps that connected the elevated beach walkway to the bluff. Sitting with her chin on knees, her arms wrapped tight around her shins, she stared across the channel at the mainland. It was quiet; the only sounds were the soft whoosh of the surf and the lonely call of the occasional seagull.

She didn't look up as he approached. He knelt down next to her, laying the first-aid kit flat on the ground.

"We need to do something about those feet," he said. "They're going to get infected."

He lifted one of Jordan's feet by the heel. It was covered with sand, seal filth, and guano, and blood welled from cuts and abrasions on her toes. A skin avulsion marred the arch of her foot, where a half-inch flap of skin had torn loose and folded back.

Opening the first-aid kit, he set to work cleaning and dressing her injuries.

Jordan's vacant expression was a look that Brent had seen often enough in ERs, on the faces of patients in traumatic shock. She didn't even flinch as he swabbed the blood and dirt away from a deep cut in her sole and applied a dab of neomycin/polymyxin-B ointment.

"You'll get through this," he said. "Think of something happy."

Raising a hand to bite at her thumbnail, Jordan continued to stare across the water.

Working on her foot, Brent studied her face with his peripheral vision. "Surely a lovely young woman like you has someone waiting for them at home," he asked. "Married?"

"No." A faint smile appeared on her lips, but her eyes were still fixed on the mainland.

"Fiancé? Boyfriend?"

"I was engaged for a while." She looked at her nails, then dropped her hand.

"Lucky young man." Brent wrapped a length of elastic bandage around her heel and arch. "He must have thought the world of you."

"I suppose. But we grew apart."

"It happens," he said. "I know a little bit about that, myself."

"So what's there to say, really?"

He started working on her other foot. "There must've been some good times, though. Tell me about one of those."

173

"We were at Stanford together. He was premed, and I was majoring in communications, so we both studied all the time, but every Friday we'd go to this Mexican place on University Avenue, a whole group of us. They made great margaritas there. Then afterwards we'd all end up at Nola's—a crazy New Orleans bar kind of place—or we'd head up to the city and hit a few clubs."

"Sounds like you two really had something special," Brent said.

She gave him a sharp glance, then looked away again.

"Are you still in touch?" he asked.

"No, he passed away. It was very sad."

"I'm sorry, I guess I'm not doing a very good job of cheering you up. I'll shut up."

"That's okay. At least it's taking my mind off being hungry." She raised her thumb to bite at the nail again. "Besides, we'd already broken up by then. This guy... well, we weren't really right for each other. You know how it is, one of those mistakes you make when you're young. I had moved on. He needed to."

"You probably broke his heart," Brent said.

"Hey, I thought you were trying to cheer me up." Jordan pulled her foot away and stood up.

"Sorry. Let's change the subject, then. I'm not too happy about what you did back there, risking your life like that."

"Whatever."

Turning away, she padded up the steps without a backward glance.

CHAPTER 53

"Our rooms don't have doors," Camilla said. "How will you keep the rest of the water safe?"

"Here's a pen," Mason said. "Put your initials on your jug, and mark the water level."

He hadn't really answered her question. Camilla looked at the armful of MREs she held—Mason's share of the food from the crate—and tumbled the packages down onto his cot. Warm amber light bathed the drying wood walls of his room and glowed from the remaining wet spots on the bare floorboards of the upstairs hallway. Outside the window, the sun was setting. Shadows stretched across the narrow yard in front of the two houses. The air was turning chilly.

Camilla had stashed her own MREs and caches in her room already. If she rationed herself, the food supply wouldn't be a problem. Vita Brevis giving them enough food made sense to her; as a mountain biker, she knew what a difference a mid-ride energy bar made. Too little to eat now would leave the contestants lethargic—and in the end, this was about entertainment, wasn't it? She looked around at the walls, wondering which knotholes and cracks hid cameras. Watching people with no energy lie around would make for a boring show, and she figured Julian knew it.

But what could they do for Jordan? Could a person eat raw kelp? *Ew-w.* Probably not. The crew would now be aware of the situation, and they would have to do something about it.

Or would they? Her thoughts drifted back to the dead elephant seal they had left lying on the beach. Julian's crew hadn't intervened then, despite the danger.

She couldn't get the picture of the dead seal out of her mind. The way it had looked, just lying there, so still... They had caused its death—all ten of them together. It was her fault, too. Camilla tasted acid in her mouth, and swallowed.

"What about this other stuff we found?" She pointed at Mason's duct tape and bear spray. "What's to stop someone from taking it?"

"Everyone knows who has what. If something disappears, it'll be pretty easy to find the culprit."

"Unless they stash it in someone else's room."

Mason grinned. "You're giving me ideas."

175

"Veronica left the toilet paper in the outhouse for everybody. Even Juan left us six of the space blankets that you traded him. He put them on our doorstep."

"Your point is?"

She pointed at the water jugs stacked next to his cot. "When are you going to share that water? If people start running out, it'll be a magnet for trouble. You can't guard it all the time."

"We can trust our teammates for now," he said. "Later, maybe not so much."

CHAPTER 54

Jordan crouched on the rocks by the water's edge, next to the dock where they had spent the first night, and faced the open ocean. A seagull overhead pierced the air with its lonely cry. There was no one else in sight, which was perfect because she wanted to be alone.

She splashed a double handful of seawater on her face and tipped her head back to let the chilly trickles run down her neck and ears. It felt good—distracted her from the gnawing emptiness in her stomach. This kind of hunger was a new experience, and not one she liked. Cupping her hands, she poured water on her face again and let it soak down her chest and belly, wetting her blouse. The cold was refreshing, tightening her skin almost painfully. She did it again, not caring how soaked she got, and smoothed her wet hands down her stomach.

Hiking up the knees of her capri pants, she extended her legs and let her calves dangle into the water. The cold water hurt at first, then it numbed her injured feet. She sighed, and looked at the green-brown kelp floating in the water and strewn on the rocks. Glistening in the sun, the slimy leaf blades tapered to translucent air bladders. The kelp stipes knotted and coiled on the rocks like garden hoses and varied in size, from pinky-width to the circumference of a soda can. Gross. Just gross.

She needed to wash her hair, too. How would that work?

"Hey, Blondie." Travis's voice came from nearby.

She slowly pulled her feet out of the water but she didn't turn around. His boots clumped to a stop on the rock right behind her.

Too close.

"Thought you might be interested in this," he said.

Still seated, she turned her head. Her eyes widened. Travis stood less than a foot away, his belt buckle at the level of her face. The thumb of one hand was hooked into the pocket of his jeans, his fingers trapping a red and white plastic bag against his thigh. Beef jerky.

"Oh my god," Jordan said. She reached for it.

Instead of releasing the packet when her hand closed around it, Travis tightened his fingers to hold it in place.

"Yep, I thought we might be able to work something out...," he said, bringing his belt buckle an inch closer to her forehead. "...first."

They were alone. Even the seagull was gone now.

She looked up at his face. He was grinning, but his eyes were cold. Distant.

177

Her gaze dropped to his boots. He shifted his feet wider. The silence stretched to fill the air between them.

Then she laughed—a high, bubbling tinkle of genuine amusement.

"Oh my god, that's just so pathetic," she said. "The saddest part is, you're probably serious." She pulled her feet under her and stood up in one quick motion, almost smacking him in the jaw with her head.

He stumbled back a step but didn't release the beef jerky. His mouth twisted into a snarl.

"This ain't some safe little sorority house, Blondie, where you can just mouth off to me like that." He looked left and right. "This island's a dangerous place, and I don't see anybody in charge. Accidents can happen. People can get hurt."

Jordan's eyes narrowed. "Yeah, they can. How about I yell rape, Travis?"

She took a fast step toward him, and he backpedaled. Shoving her face into his, she spoke in a fast singsong hiss: "Oh my god, guys, help, he tried to rape me, oh my god, he hurt me, oh, I'm so scared, help me…" She raised her voice. "How about we try *that*?"

With a savage jerk, she tore the bag of beef jerky from under his grip.

Stepping back, he raised both hands, palms out like a traffic cop. "Now, wait just a minute—"

Jordan threw the bag in his face. Hard. The smack of plastic on skin echoed from the rocks. "Pick that up and get lost, you disgusting slimebag. Before I actually get mad."

Travis scooped up the beef jerky and backed away fast, boots slipping and skating on the rocks.

She glanced down at the kelp. No matter how gross, it was only seaweed—like the wakame salad at sushi places. Let them all think she was starving; she could eat *that*.

Travis's voice echoed off the rocks. "You're a fucking bitch."

"Oh, you have no idea," she called after him. "Truly no idea at all."

CHAPTER 55

"Young lady, come here." Veronica gestured toward the open doorway. "Let's go for a walk."

Even though Camilla knew she had done nothing wrong, she had trouble meeting Veronica's eyes. She followed her out of the blue team's house, and together they walked to the edge of the bluff overlooking the main beach.

She calls Jordan by name, Camilla thought. *Why am I always "young lady"?*

Barks and yelps drifted up to her ears—the seals on the beach below jostled and pushed, huddled together, settling into their places for the night. A chill breeze blew off the channel, and the skin on her arms shrank into goose bumps. The sunset lit Veronica's face beside her, painting her pale eyes yellow-orange.

Camilla started. "We've somehow gotten off on the wrong foot—"

"Right." Veronica cut her off. "I had a talk with Brent. About you." She looked away, shifting her piercing gaze toward the mainland, and her lips compressed.

"Why?" *And what business of yours is it to talk about me, anyway?*

"Brent's concerned about you." Veronica continued to stare into the distance. "He told me Travis tried to push you around, but you stood up to him. He thinks you antagonized Travis unnecessarily."

Camilla stared at her in surprise. Brent was unhappy with her? But she had thought…

"Brent and I don't agree about that," Veronica said. She placed a hand on Camilla's forearm for a moment—a kind gesture, almost affectionate. Veronica continued to scan the distant shore across the channel, but her eyes were softer now, defocused. There were faint lines at the corners.

"I think I might have misjudged you, Camilla."

Veronica pointed across the water at something—Camilla wasn't sure what. Then she crossed her arms. "Most of the women I take in at Safe Harbor are silent victims," she said. "They're afraid, which is understandable, but their abusers take advantage of that fear—often for years and years, until something finally snaps."

She turned and met Camilla's eyes. "If Travis ever bothers you again, you talk to Brent and me about it. But don't ever be afraid to stand up for yourself, either. A woman's got to be self-reliant."

Camilla felt something relax inside her. She smiled at Veronica, glad to have finally earned her respect. What Veronica did for a living every day—it made her own job in animated film seem so frivolous and self-indulgent.

"Come on, let's head back before we miss something," Veronica said. "But I'd like to talk more later—get to know each other a bit. Jordan likes you a lot, you know."

Camilla's face split in a big grin. She and Jordan got along great, but she had never been sure how Jordan really felt about her. Following Veronica back toward the houses, she could see movement through the plastic-covered windows of the red team's Victorian quarters—everyone was probably gathered there now, hoping to hear from Julian. A faint orange glow flickered in the windows, throwing shadows on the plastic sheeting. Someone had started a fire.

She turned to Veronica. "I want you to know I really respect the work you do."

"Thank you." Veronica pursed her lips, holding the Victorian house's door open for her. "But don't you also do something similar, for children?"

Camilla nodded. She didn't like to talk about her foundation, her kids, but she would have to overcome that now, wouldn't she? One of the implications of Vita Brevis's publicity was that she would have to take an active front-person role, speak in front of crowds and cameras. And if she managed to win the five million dollars—ten million counting the matching grant—she would be able to make a real difference in the lives of so many more. She swallowed.

"Tell me about it," Veronica said, stepping into the hallway.

Camilla realized that this was perfect product placement opportunity. The hidden cameras were rolling. Oh god, she should have thought about this, had something prepared to say…

"I take kids who have lost both their parents to Disneyland," she said. "It's easy to lose hope when you've had everything snatched away from you. What these children need more than anything is—"

"Disneyland?" Veronica's voice turned harsh, rising in pitch and volume. "*That's* your big contribution? *Disneyland?*"

The murmurs of conversation next door stopped. Camilla froze as faces appeared in the archway. Her mouth opened and closed, but no sound came out, and she knew that the cameras were getting all of it.

"You don't understand…" Again she heard Avery wishing he were dead, and her eyes began to sting. She could see all their little faces in her mind's eye right now—a whole parade of her kids, pale and quiet. Some were defiant at first, most only sullen and withdrawn, but she reached them all in the end. She held them through their tears, taught them it was okay to laugh again, to be happy again. The bond she shared with her kids was special, forged in her own childhood pain, and right this second, she was failing every single one of them. She forced the words out. "What they *need* is a reason to believe again."

Veronica snorted. "And you give this to them how, exactly?"

"I take them on rides…" She stopped, realizing how lame that sounded. "I mean, the ones where—"

"Rides? Really." Veronica swept an arm behind her, glaring. "I'm saving women's lives out there, and you're going on *rides?* What are you, seven years old?"

Behind Veronica, pale ovals filled the gloom beyond the archway—Brent, Juan, Jordan, Lauren, Mason—all staring at the two of them. Mason seemed to be grinning. Camilla's eyes blurred, and she couldn't make out expressions anymore.

"How dare you patronize me!" she shouted at Veronica. "You don't understand what it's like. They... I..."

She drew a deep breath and tried to compose herself. "No, wait. Listen, why don't we just—"

"I think I've heard quite enough." Veronica's voice was a calm, velvety purr now. Turning her back on Camilla, she pushed past the others and disappeared through the doorway.

Following her into that room was hard, but Camilla made herself do it.

CHAPTER 56

Camilla studied the scoreboard, avoiding the eyes of the other contestants. Her face still felt hot. She refused to look at Veronica, who stood nearby, talking easily with Natalie and Lauren. Part of her wanted to shrink into the floor and disappear, but the back of her neck was tight with anger. The way she had embarrassed herself and made her charity foundation look like a joke... well it hadn't been an accident.

Veronica had set her up.

Camilla wanted to march over to her now, say the things she should have said the first time, instead of babbling about rides like she was brain-damaged. She would talk about the kids. How their little faces would light up, their dull eyes would become bright again. How Walt Disney's imaginary magic could turn into real, *healing* magic.

But she knew what would happen if she tried. Veronica's silvery, contemptuous gaze would freeze her, and her words would dry up in her throat. Again. Then Veronica would say something patronizing in that velvet voice edged with broken glass—maybe ask her if she was feeling all right, or if she perhaps needed to go lie down for a bit—and Camilla would look even sillier. So instead, she focused on the scoreboard while her face burned, and tried not to hear the conversations around her.

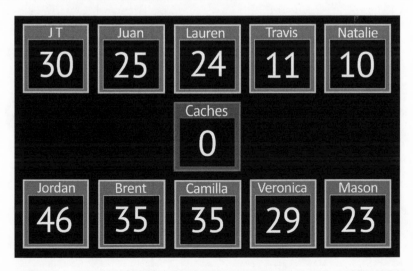

Camilla's thirty-five wasn't a surprise; she had kept track of her score in her head as she scanned the caches. But she was surprised to see that only Jordan had a score higher than hers. Sure, she had looked like an idiot in the hallway with Veronica, and Julian would certainly play it up for laughs in the final edited footage. But if she did manage to win the grand prize, then none of that mattered, did it? Her foundation would get the money regardless.

And if she won, Veronica's Safe Harbor women's shelter would get nothing. That didn't seem fair. Right then Camilla decided: if she won, she would share the money with Veronica, donating a substantial portion of it to Safe Harbor.

For now, though, she would keep that decision to herself. Before opening her mouth again, she would wait for the perfect time and plan the right words.

Veronica had really hurt her, but Camilla had set herself up for it, too.

Mason dropped to sit on the floor next to her, and leaned back against the wall. "Relax," he said. "It's just a game."

"Oh god, I must've sounded so…" Realizing she was probably still on camera, she composed her face. "Veronica shouldn't have done that to me. We're *teammates*!"

"For you, it's always about the team, isn't it?" Mason smiled and patted her knee. "I'm guessing Julian probably isn't your biggest fan right now."

"Well, right now I'm not his, either… Wait a minute—why would Julian be mad at me?"

"Today was supposed to be an individual competition, but you turned it into a cooperative event instead. You had all ten of us work together to get the water and the food."

"Oh, that was all *my* doing?" She playfully shoved his shoulder. "Shut up. Now I know you're just messing with me. Besides, how else could we have done it?" But then again, maybe she *had* acted as a catalyst for the others…

"And don't mind Veronica too much," Mason said. "All of this is harder on her than she's letting on."

Camilla's gaze roamed the room to settle on Brent, who was working on Lauren's leg. She watched him apply several butterfly bandages to the gash on Lauren's calf with abrupt, angry motions. His face looked red.

"Brent's been moody ever since we got back, too," she said. Was he mad at *her*? She needed to talk to him and find out.

Mason must have seen something in her face. "Lighten up," he said. "You're taking things way too seriously. And don't worry about your team so much." He winked. "Remember, the grand prize isn't a team award."

CHAPTER 57

A half hour had gone by, and it was almost dark outside now. In the central room of the Victorian house, people came and went, waiting for Julian to make another on-screen appearance. A small fire crackled in the fireplace, putting out a meager warmth that Camilla barely felt. Next to her, Jordan sat against the still-damp wall, looking listlessly at one bandaged foot. Camilla wanted to talk to her, but she didn't look up.

After several minutes, Jordan spoke, her tired voice barely loud enough to hear. "There's a place up in Calistoga called Solage. They have a great spa."

Camilla nodded. "I've been there, after biking Boggs Mountain. Got a deep-tissue massage, swam in the mineral pools... Oh god, can you imagine being there right now instead of here?"

"We should go," Jordan said. She turned her head sideways, resting it on her knee, and smiled. "Just the two of us. After all this is over, let's plan a girls' weekend up there in wine country. I did some articles about the Napa wineries two years ago. They'll remember *me*—they'll roll out the red carpet for us."

Camilla smiled back. "I'd love to go." Jordan's eyes sparkled with friendliness, but Camilla could see dark crescents beneath them. How long had it been since she had eaten?

Jordan tipped her head back against the wall. "We'll let them valet-park the Lamborghini we'll be driving, since one of us is going to win this thing."

From where he sat on Camilla's other side, Mason spoke. "Since you'll be able to afford it, will you take me, too?"

"Sorry, *sir*," Camilla said. "Girls only."

"I'm hurt." Mason stood up, then winced and bent over, hands on his knees. "Ouch! I really *am* hurt." He rubbed his lower back.

Camilla remembered how the blinded seal had knocked him to the sand... the seal they had killed. She looked down at the damp floorboards. Here she was, just a couple of hours later, talking about going to the spa with her new friend, while the poor seal lay dead on the beach.

Brent crossed the room toward them, frowning at Mason. "Is your back injured?"

"Not really, but this must be what getting hit by a bus feels like," Mason said. "I hope Julian doesn't intend for us to mix it up with one of those monsters again."

"Does this hurt?" Brent probed his back brusquely with strong, practiced fingers. "No? Well, you got off luckier than that seal did."

Shame tightened Camilla's cheeks. "I feel so terrible about what happened," she said. "Nobody wanted for it to *die*. It was sort of an accident, wasn't it?"

"It was no accident." Brent's raised voice brought conversations around the room to a halt.

Mason laughed. "So you're saying I deserve a penalty for using the spray Julian himself gave us? He'll take five of my points for harming the wildlife? Hey JT, maybe I *shouldn't* have sprayed that seal. What do you think?"

"Points? Penalties?" Brent shook his head, looking disgusted. "No, I'm saying that it's a miracle somebody wasn't killed or severely injured out there today." He turned to address the whole room. "And what about when one of us does get hurt?"

"If it's a real emergency, I'm sure they'll send someone," Camilla said. She didn't like the uncertainty she heard in her own voice.

"I'm a doctor," Brent said. "Believe me when I tell you that in a life-or-death medical emergency, the outcome is determined by how quickly a patient receives appropriate care. So how long do you think it'll take the first responders to reach us out here? An hour? Two?"

Camilla dropped her eyes, knowing that Brent was right. But she had abandoned Avery to be here—her kids were counting on her to win. What was a little danger compared to what those kids had suffered? Especially when she weighed the risk against how much she'd be able to help them if she won...

"And it's not just the lack of basic safety." Brent tapped the on-screen scoreboard. "It's these stupid little competitions themselves. They're presented so innocuously, all fun and games. But they're ugly. Julian's designed them to bring out the worst in us. To set us at each other's throats, make us take crazy risks. By putting the food where it was, he deliberately set things up so a violent confrontation with that animal was inevitable.

"This whole thing is criminally irresponsible—I think you're all just too blinded by the money to see it."

Mason straightened up from his pained crouch. "Very melodramatic, Brent." His voice was light and friendly. "I think you're probably right that OSHA might not approve of some of the dangerous working conditions here. Hmm..." He rested his chin in his hand in a parody of thinking. "But you know what?" he said suddenly, grinning. "I think five million dollars is pretty decent hazard pay."

"High stakes," Lauren said. "Makes sense it'd be a tough game." She looked at Brent with hostility in her eyes. "Doesn't sound like you have the stomach for it, though. Shoulda' stayed home."

"Not all of us are high-paid doctors," Veronica said. "My shelter can use the money to help a lot of women—do some real good."

Camilla looked at Brent, wishing he would leave it alone. Instead, he stood in the center of the room, turning in a circle, looking from face to face. He scratched the side of his head. Then he pointed at Jordan.

"What about her food situation? You think that's an accident, too? They did profiles of us, remember."

"That's just silly." Camilla shook her head. "So they knew about Jordan's allergy and they're trying to poison her or something?"

"Nah." JT held up his half-eaten MRE. "Military puts peanut oil in everything. Know why? It's the cheapest shit they can buy."

Brent ignored them both.

"Jordan, look at me." He dropped to a crouch in front of her and took one of her hands. "You're smarter than this. You need to listen to me. When Julian shows up on that screen, tell him you're out. They need to come pick you up before you get sick or collapse from malnutrition."

"No." Jordan's voice was quiet but firm. "Thank you for your concern, but I'm not quitting." With eyes of green ice, she pulled her hand away.

The sound of slow, deliberate clapping rose from the archway, and Camilla turned to stare.

Travis leaned against the door frame, applauding, but his eyes were on Brent not Jordan. "Old man, I gotta hand it to you," he said, grinning. "You had me going for a while there. Folks, this here's a slick one, make no mistake."

He pushed himself off the doorjamb with his elbow and stepped into the room as Brent stood up to face him.

"I may not have a medical degree," Travis said. "Didn't go to a fancy college like I'm sure most of y'all did. But I've been around some… Enough to learn how things really work."

He slowly circled the room as he spoke, never taking his eyes off Brent's.

"Seen lots of high-and-mighty folks—doctors, judges, lawyers—telling people how they ought to live. Makes you feel all warm and fuzzy, don't it? Knowing they care so much. Like Dr. Brent here, watching out for the rest of us."

Meeting Travis's gaze steadily, Brent tucked his hands into his vest pockets.

"But look a little closer, and you know what you find? Every single time?" Travis stopped near the monitor. "They got their own reasons."

The muscle in Brent's jawline twitched. The air crackled with hostility, like dry static.

Travis grinned. "And those reasons usually have something to do with money." He reached behind him and tapped the scoreboard on the screen.

Camilla's eyes widened.

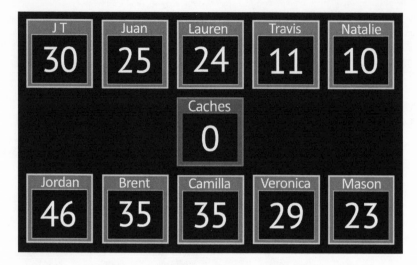

Travis sounded amused. "Let's say Jordan was to listen to doctor's orders—pack it in and go home. Who'd be closest to winning the five mil then?"

CHAPTER 58

Full dark outside. The fireplace beneath the blank monitor screen was down to embers, softly pulsing their red-orange glow. Camilla had her space blanket wrapped around her shoulders. Leaning against her, Jordan had drifted off to sleep at her side. Camilla did the math: her friend hadn't eaten for two days now. Opening the crinkling reflective blanket, Camilla wrapped it around Jordan's shoulders, too. The room was growing cold.

The other contestants were scattered about the edges of the room, also sitting or lying down, except for Brent. He had walked out after Travis's accusation, shaking his head in disgust, but Camilla couldn't help wondering. Five million was a lot of money for anyone, even a doctor.

Nobody was talking. Everyone looked as exhausted as Camilla felt. Pulling out her iPhone, she slid the power switch and waited. The glow from the screen splashed her face, but there was still no signal. She had about a quarter of her battery left, so she switched the phone off again to conserve power.

The glow from a larger screen lit the room. Camilla looked up at the monitor screen.

"Good evening, my friends. What a day we had today!" Julian wore an immaculately tailored suit as usual, this one sharkskin gray. He stood against a backdrop of machinery: valves, vents and pipes, glass-fronted gauges. Everything looked old—rusty, decrepit, and out of date. Behind him, a six-foot metal wheel valve jutted into the camera's field of view.

Camilla felt Jordan shift beside her, suddenly alert. She sat up straight, eyes locked on the screen.

"Physical survival," Julian said.

Camilla looked at Jordan. They needed to get some food for her. Clearing her throat, Camilla scooted forward. She opened her mouth to interrupt Julian's speech, and felt a hard shove—almost a blow—to her ribs. Shocked, she turned to stare at the person she wanted to help.

Green eyes burning, Jordan shook her head at Camilla. "No," she whispered.

"But…"

"I said *no*." Jordan pulled away from her and looked at the monitor.

Camilla's face flushed in anger, and she turned back toward the screen. If Jordan wanted to be stupid, it was her choice.

"The famous psychologist Abraham Maslow characterized human survival needs as a pyramid," Julian said. "Physical survival is the bottom level. We took care of those basic necessities yesterday and today: shelter, food, water, warmth. For tomorrow's competition, we move on to the higher and more interesting levels of the pyramid. But we're getting ahead of ourselves so let's worry about that in the morning. You've all earned your rest tonight.

"So instead, we'll do something fun right now: a little getting-to-know-you activity. A social icebreaker that will help us bond with our fellow contestants as we participate in this game together."

Julian's smile took on an unpleasant edge.

"Tonight we'll start with one of our key players, someone who had a lot to say today. He's full of advice for all of us, so let's find out a bit more about who he is, shall we?"

Their host faded from the screen, replaced by a still picture. A smiling boy of about 6 years old held a toy stethoscope against the chest of a friend who lay on his back, arms at his side, also smiling. The picture looked old: the boys were outside, in a fenced backyard, wearing T-shirts and corduroy pants. The cuffs of their pants were wide, almost bell-bottoms.

Julian continued to speak in voice-over, like a newsreel announcer. "Even as a young boy, Brent Wilson knew he wanted to be a doctor."

Just like a TV documentary biography—an A&E special, Camilla thought as the picture changed. Now a twenty-something Brent, his hair dark, stood in black cap and gown with a row of others dressed the same way. A commencement exercise.

"Graduating fourth in his class from the prestigious Johns Hopkins medical school, Brent specialized in emergency medicine. His early career was spent in ERs throughout northern and southern California."

Images drifted across the screen: Brent in scrubs and white coat leaning over a curtained hospital bed. Brent in a group of other doctors and nurses, pushing a gurney.

"Brent Wilson epitomized the American dream. He married his high-school sweetheart, and they had a son together, who was soon studying to follow in his father's footsteps."

"Hey," a deep voice rumbled from behind them. "What's this?"

Standing in the doorway, his face white, Brent stared at the pictures of himself up on the screen. "Wait a minute. I never said they could—"

"But then tragedy struck," Julian's voice continued, talking right over the interruption. "Following a bout with a life-threatening illness, Brent spiraled into a pattern of narcotics dependency—a problem all too common in the medical field."

A picture of an angry Brent appeared on-screen, raising an arm to cover his face as he ducked back through the glass doors of a hospital.

"Stop!" Brent shouted. "You can't do this. It's wrong…"

But Camilla thought he looked scared beneath the anger. And guilty, too.

"Scandal followed when a patient's family sued. Brent soon found himself defending against charges of medical malpractice. His problems with drugs and gambling worsened after a bitter divorce in 2005, when his wife of twenty-four years left him, and he became estranged from his son. But he would not give up his family. A court-mandated restraining order was necessary to ensure that they could resume their lives in peace."

"You son of a bitch!" Brent shouted, rubbing at his left shoulder. "I'll sue you!"

Julian's upbeat newsreel-style narration continued over a still picture of a hospital entrance sign. "In October 2006, under a shadow of scandal, Brent was summarily dismissed from the staff at Highland Hospital. There were accusations of moral turpitude. In April 2007, the medical board permanently revoked his license to practice medicine, for conduct unbecoming a physician."

The MRE that Camilla had eaten felt like a brick in her throat, tasting of chemicals and grease. Julian had no right to do this to Brent. No right.

Her breath caught. Did their host have a similar profile of her, too, cued up and ready to play? Oh god, what did *hers* say?

"You son of a bitch…" Brent's voice trailed off, weakening. He swayed, leaned against the doorjamb, and dragged a hand across his cheeks.

Julian's face reappeared. "I hope you've enjoyed this first contestant profile. Perhaps we'll make these into a regular feature over the coming days. And now, I wish you all a pleasant night."

The monitor went blank.

CHAPTER 59

"That was illegal." Brent spoke with a shaky voice. "Wrong, malicious, and illegal."

The others stared at him and he stared back, the silence stretching, filling the darkened room.

Camilla stood up. Julian could take his stupid game and go to hell, for all she cared. Enough was enough. "Brent, we all want you to know that—"

He held up a hand, stopping her. Running a trembling palm across his cheeks again, he reached back to grab the door frame behind him with his other hand and slid down into a seated position on the floor.

"What he said is more or less true." Brent cleared his throat. "A one-sided picture, granted. But it's true I had some problems. In 2004, I was diagnosed with peritoneal mesothelioma, a rare and highly malignant form of cancer. The five-year survival rate is less than ten percent."

He looked out a window, into the darkness beyond. "When you're a doctor, you can get to believing you're above the laws of nature. You determine who is sick and who is well, who will live and who will die. It's magical thinking, but you don't realize that until afterward.

"Now I was the patient. The chemotherapy was brutal. It took its toll on us all. I wasn't very easy to live with. Mary, my wife, left me. She took my son…"

"I'm so sorry," Camilla said.

"*Are* you?" Brent glanced at her and then looked away. "A five-year-old girl died on the operating table because I was high on Versed at the time and couldn't see what I was doing."

Her gut tensed as if he had punched her. All she could think of was little Avery's face, and her other kids. She had *trusted* Brent? Thought he was keeping them *safe*? She wanted to throw up.

"The drugs I self-prescribed let me carry on with a semblance of normality," he said. "After a while, they were the only thing that kept me going at all. My addiction spiraled out of control, but I kept it hidden—until I killed a little girl."

He stared up at the screen, defiant now.

"Somehow, even with all of that, I found the will to survive. I beat the odds. I beat the mesothelioma. Then I beat the drugs. If your 'profile' of me was any good, you'd know that, Julian, you slandering son of a bitch."

The screen remained blank.

193

Lowering herself to huddle against the wall again, Camilla turned away from the others and pressed her nose against her upraised knee. Everything was so ugly now. She didn't want to listen to any more. She wanted to go home.

"What about the gambling?" Mason asked.

Just shut up. She rocked her forehead against her kneecap, not wanting to hear the answer. But needing to.

"Doctors gamble with human lives every day," Brent said. "Doing it with money instead was a poor substitute. Even so, I found the gambling harder to stop than the drugs, but I got control of that, too."

Heavy shuffling. She felt the floor creak as he stood up.

"The mesothelioma almost took my life, but I'm a survivor," he said. "I learned that about myself, the hard way. I made some terrible mistakes, and they cost me a lot. But they cost others more. I don't blame my wife and son for never wanting to speak to me again."

Nobody else said anything.

Heavy footsteps moved away, and Camilla looked up as Brent stopped in the doorway. He spoke with his back to them.

"I'm sorry for misleading you about still being a doctor. Pride, I suppose, and God knows I don't have very much to be proud about anymore. I'm going upstairs now. Tomorrow, I'm going home..." Turning toward the blank screen, he raised his voice. "...and getting a good lawyer."

"I'm truly sorry I lied to the rest of you." His eyes swept the room. "But you should be thinking about this: whose turn is it next time? And what's Julian going to say about *you?*"

CHAPTER 60

Leaving her upstairs room in the Victorian house, Natalie found Travis leaning up against the wall outside her door. Dropping her eyes, she tried to scoot around him but he pushed off the wall, blocking her way.

"Natalie. Hold up a minute. We need to talk."

She stopped and stood staring at her toes.

"You saw the scores down there," he said. "You and I, we're not doing too hot right now."

She pushed at the floorboards with the toe of one black Converse high top. "Maybe things'll get better tomorrow," she said.

"See, that's exactly what I mean. You and I need to work together. Otherwise, neither one of us stands a chance of winning this thing."

She edged away. "I'm okay on my own."

Putting one palm against the wall, Travis leaned over her. He was much taller than she was. Feeling his breath on the top of her head, she put her hands in the pockets of her hoodie and went very still. He was going to touch her.

"I got some ideas how we can turn this thing around together," he said. "You need me, Natalie. I can help you."

Yeah, she needed him, like she needed that cancer Brent had. She had heard this one before—far too often.

"Leave me alone." Hunching her shoulders, she ducked past him and slipped down the stairwell.

CHAPTER 61

Lying on her back on her cot, Lauren stared at the ceiling in the semidarkness. She was thinking about earlier in the day, when the elephant seal had come charging back. She hadn't meant to run, but instinct just sort of took over.

Nobody said anything about it afterward, but later in the day she had caught a look between JT and Juan that she didn't like. She was sure they had been talking about her.

Thinking about it, she felt her abdominals tense. Tomorrow's competition was probably going to be teams again, and she needed to make sure those two clowns didn't get any ideas. Her red team needed a win.

She pictured Jordan's face and made a fist. So right now, that walking, talking Barbie doll was the front-runner of the overall competition? Tomorrow, Lauren would change that—teach the snotty cheerleader bitch what it felt like to lose. And if Jordan wanted to do something about it? Well, that would be fine with Lauren, too.

She stuck her hands in the pockets of her cargo pants, surprised to feel something damp and crumpled. With a jolt, she remembered the letter she had found up on the wrecked tower. In all the excitement with the water and the food, she had jammed it in her pocket and forgotten all about it.

Christ. The letter had gotten soaked when she and Juan went after the water jugs. It was all wadded up in there, falling apart.

Unzipping her pants, Lauren slid them carefully down her legs. She straightened the half-dry cargo pants on her lap and held the pocket open loosely, probing with her fingers. Easing the envelope out of her pocket, she gritted her teeth in frustration as chunks of paper came loose.

She hoped all the ink wasn't washed away, but it was too dark to see now anyway, and she would have to dry the letter before trying to open it.

"Like a washing machine filled with rocks..." She remembered Juan's description of the whitewater they had crossed. She had done this before—accidentally left papers in her pockets before when she put clothes in the wash. There was only one thing you could do when it happened.

Spreading the closed envelope on the driest area of the floor, next to her cot, she smoothed it against the boards in the half-darkness. In the morning the letter would be dry. Or drier, anyway.

But would it be legible?

With a sense of growing unease, Lauren considered the return address she had seen on the envelope:

Department of Corrections

Day 4

Monday: December 24, 2012

"Security." On the monitor, Julian held up two fingers. "Security defines the second level of Maslow's hierarchy of survival needs, which come right after the first-level requirements for physical survival. Security is the focus of our next challenge. It's a team competition."

A ray of pale sunlight filtered through a window, striping across the screen, making their host hard to see. The morning sounds of seals and birds filtered in from outside. Camilla glanced at Brent. She had tossed and turned all night, torn about what to do. She wanted to talk to him—to try to understand—but she was afraid she might say something they both would regret. Even now thinking about it made her stiffen with anger. She turned away.

Brent was still here, though—he hadn't asked Julian about going home. Mason had explained it to her this morning, telling her why. As ugly as it was, Julian's little player profile had been perfectly legal. Brent couldn't sue anyone for slander because he had basically admitted that all of it was true.

It was disgusting what they all would tolerate for a chance to win that money. Last night, she had come to a realization about herself, too. She was sticking this out. Even if it got nastier. Even if she found that nastiness directed at her. Tied for second place with Brent, she couldn't quit now. She would never forgive herself if she walked away from the chance to turn her little joke of a foundation into something real.

"Today's event is a zero-sum game," their host said. "For every point someone gains today, someone else loses one. At the end of the day, some of you will have more points than you have now, and some of you will have fewer. During today's challenge, everybody's points are at risk."

Camilla stood up straighter and tightened her jaw. *Be honest,* she thought. *There's another reason you can't quit now.* Whatever Julian had in his profile of her, she refused to let him threaten her with it, or let it dictate her actions. She would not be cowed.

To quit now would be to admit she was afraid.

At her side, Jordan shifted restlessly from foot to foot. She hadn't eaten for almost three days now. Her eyes looked a little sunken, but Camilla saw a weird hyperactive energy on her face. Manic.

Julian smiled from the screen. "There are different kinds of security, but I think we'll all agree on what kind of security matters most right now: protecting those all-important points. The player with the highest point score wins five million dollars. That makes your points valuable indeed.

"The team that is victorious out there today guarantees its end-of-day point totals. They gains the security of knowing those points can never be lost again.

"For members of the losing team, there will be no such assurance."

He clapped once and leaned forward.

"The challenge itself is a fun one. It's a live-action game of capture the flag, with our lovely island home as the arena. Here's how it works.

"Each team's territory includes half the island. The border between red territory and blue territory is the seal barricade. Deep in the heart of each team's territory, you'll find a base with the team flag. The red team's flag is red; the blue team's is blue.

"Go get the other team's flag. Bring it back to your own base, and plant it next to your own flag. If both flags are present at the same time, the player who plants the enemy flag earns ten points, and his or her teammates all earn five points. Each member of the other team loses six points. As I said, it's a zero-sum game.

"Anytime you are in enemy territory, the other team can tag you out, and you lose a point. The person who tagged you gains a point. But if you are carrying the flag at the time, you lose five points and they gain five. So don't get caught with the flag.

"If you do get tagged, you are out of play until you run back and touch your own base. Then you are back in."

Their host looked at his watch and back at them.

"The first team to plant the enemy flag three times wins the challenge."

Julian's image faded, replaced by the scoreboard. The red team's scores filled the top row; the blue team's scores ran across the bottom. Between the rows, in the center of the screen, a long irregular shape faded in, rendered in bold white lines. A red X appeared on one end, a blue X appeared on the other end, and a white line zigzagged down the middle—the seal barricade. The whole thing was a map of the island.

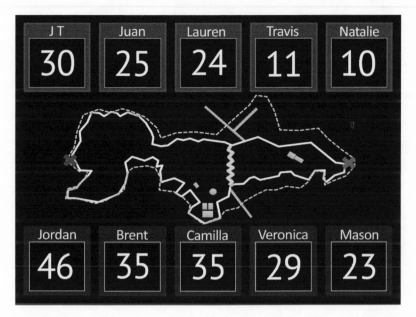

Their host's voice came from the monitor. "Blue team's base is behind these houses, at the bottom of the bluff. Red team's base is on the small beach at the far side of the island, where you staged from to get the water. The game starts when both teams reach their bases. Good luck to you all, and may the best team win. Go!"

CHAPTER 63

Lauren had her eye on Travis as the five members of the red team hurdled the barricade and jogged toward their base on the far side of the island. He ran with a loose, easy arm-swinging stride: surefooted despite the rocks underfoot and the cowboy boots he wore. How did he end up being her problem? Still, for five million, she'd deal with it.

Natalie was hanging back, keeping her distance from the others. Not that Lauren could really blame her, but it meant she wasn't going to be a lot of use today. Why did Julian have to stick her useless ass on Lauren's team?

She turned her attention back to Travis, thirty feet ahead of her, and her eyes narrowed. She had to talk to Juan and JT as soon as possible; she needed a moment alone with the two of them.

Ahead lay the narrowest section of the island: a fifty-foot causeway like a neck, with bluffs on each side that dropped to sections of beach. A choke point, easy to defend.

"Travis," she called. "You're defending. Stay there."

Muscles thrumming with impatience, she waved Natalie forward across the causeway. "And you cover this end. The blue team has to come through here to reach our flag. Tag 'em."

They stopped at opposite sides of the causeway, a hundred feet apart, watching her. Perfect. Lauren hustled after Juan and JT, who were already sliding down the rocky slope to the small beach at the island's northern end.

Her feet hit the sand, and she stared at the wide red rectangular banner waving atop a ten-foot steel pole: their flag. Julian's hidden crew had been busy last night, sneaking out to set this up for them. The flagpole rose from a hole in a black plastic cone, like the base of a patio umbrella. Another hole waited to receive the blue flag, which they needed to go and capture right now. But first things first.

"Listen, you two." She waved them over. But why did JT need to look at Juan first? Why did Juan give him that little nod? She frowned. "Something you need to know about—"

"I'll captain us today," JT said.

Son of a bitch. All of a sudden, Lauren's chest was so tight, she couldn't breathe.

"Bullshit." She stepped up into his face, her hands curling into fists, what she wanted to tell them irrelevant now. "I'm captain, and that isn't changing, so get with the program."

"Capture the flag?" JT waved a hand at the red banner behind him. "Fucking C-T-F? Girl, I *own* this. In Afghanistan, when we weren't on patrol, my squad played CTF twenty-four seven. Beat every other unit on base. Call of Duty, Modern Warfare, Halo, Counter-Strike, whatever, didn't matter—we always won."

"So y'all sat around playing video games? Real nice. No wonder it took us ten years to get Bin Laden." Her fists clenched and unclenched. "Video games mean nothing, asshole."

"You had your shot at captain," he said. "We fucking lost, remember?"

Lauren looked at Juan. "You tell this clown—"

Juan stepped forward, silencing them both with an abrupt "cut" gesture across his throat. "I'll do it." His voice was hard with command, the finality of his tone absolute. "Now, both of you stop arguing, and let's go win this thing."

Fists uncurling, she stared into his dark eyes, speechless. Couldn't he see how badly she needed this? "Juan, I…"

His eyes held hers, and she could see no compromise in them. None. A bitter, sharp-edged plug clogged her throat. He had kicked her to the curb and taken team lead, just like that.

Juan's hands flexed restlessly at his sides. He was energized again, the way he had been yesterday when they went after the water together—so unlike his usual look of bored disinterest. He pointed at her and JT, then stabbed a finger upslope, the direction of the blue team's base.

"Get their flag. I'll make sure no one takes ours. If we let ourselves lose again, we might as well go home."

CHAPTER 64

At the narrow southern end of the island, the blue team gathered around their flag. Their base occupied a small bench of smooth sandstone at the foot of the bluff. Waves crashed on the rocks a few yards away. A slippery sandstone ramp led up to the seal-free zone surrounding the two houses, fifteen feet above their heads.

Camilla looked around their base. It would be easy to defend. On the ocean side, the rocky bench dropped away into the water beneath vertical bluffs that curved out of sight around the edge of the island. On the side facing the mainland, the sandstone yielded to a narrow strip of sand that wrapped around below the bluffs to join the main beach. A few seals basked on the strip, like dogs guarding the blue base's back door.

Jordan waved them into a huddle. Camilla monitored her other teammates in her peripheral vision: Brent's deep slow breathing, Veronica's ready stance, her intense pale stare locked on Jordan. Would they all be able to work together today the way they needed to, to win this? She glanced at Mason and almost rolled her eyes—he had added a tie to his pin-striped suit. Still, his inability to take anything seriously also made him drama proof. She knew she could count on him.

The morning sun backlit Jordan's hair, turning it into a halo of molten gold. "Okay, guys, an easy blue team win again," she said. "Camilla, what're you thinking?"

"Mason and I go out on offense," she said. "We get the red flag and bring it back. Veronica and Brent defend, inside our territory. And you..."

She looked at Jordan's bare, scab-encrusted feet and winced. Their captain's speed would have made her unstoppable playing offense, but the island's rocky surface meant that was out of the question. Those missing shoes were going to hurt the blue team badly today.

"You better stay with the flag. Be our goalie."

"Don't worry." Jordan laughed. "As long as you guys don't let the whole red team through at once, I can handle any of them."

• • •

Reaching the top of the ramp first, Camilla sprinted past the two houses and headed for the seal barricade. Lauren and JT were already coming her way, hurdling the barrier into blue territory.

"Do we tag them?" Mason called.

"No!" she yelled. "Leave 'em for our teammates." Angling away to avoid them, she threw a leg over the logs. An angry shout rose from JT. Straddling the top of the barricade, Camilla turned to stare in surprise.

Near the edge of the oceanside bluff, Lauren suddenly dropped to her belly and slid her legs over, disappearing from sight. Those bluffs dropped straight onto rocks and whitewater—what on earth was she doing?

Cursing, JT ran to lean over the edge, staring after her. Mason took advantage of his distraction, doubling back to grab one of his biceps.

"Tag."

"You sneaky four-eyed motherfucker." JT shook him loose.

Camilla laughed and threw her other leg over the barrier, dropping into red territory. Travis tried to intercept her, but she darted around a group of sea lions, avoiding him.

"Get that little bitch, Natalie!" he yelled.

Passing the fallen lighthouse tower, she crossed the narrow causeway where the island pinched into a neck. Natalie chased her halfheartedly for a few steps but couldn't even get close.

A minute later, Camilla stood staring at the red flag, waving fifty feet away at the bottom of a short rocky slope, and felt a burst of excitement that sent her pulse throbbing in her neck. Even though she couldn't see Juan, she knew he was down there somewhere, guarding the red team's flag.

Go for it. Skating down the rocks, she caught her ankle at the bottom and sprawled onto the sand, hands splayed to catch her fall. She scrambled to her feet, facing the flag.

And there he was, pushing off the bluff face where he had been leaning beneath an overhang, hidden from above. He dusted off his hands and walked casually forward to a spot on the sand opposite her. The red flag rose between them, flapping in the wind. Neither said anything for a moment.

Juan's faint smile of acknowledgement looked open and friendly. Camilla was struck by how relaxed he appeared. Realizing she was panting slightly after her run across the island, she willed her breathing to slow.

She eyed the flag, watching for an opportunity to rush it. Juan matched her distance exactly. She knew that his relaxed demeanor was deceptive: he was ready to tag her as soon as she tried.

"I know it was you," she said. "Your motorcycle is black, too." Wow, *that* came out sounding really intelligent. She tried again. "I mean the kid in the street—you saved his life."

Juan shrugged, still smiling. God, he was good looking.

Shouts rose in the distance—several voices yelling, furious threats. She heard Veronica's voice, strident and angry, but couldn't make out the words.

Juan turned his head to look in that direction. "Sounds like things are getting rough out there," he said.

"Not surprising." She started to circle around the flag. "People want that five million."

He looked at her feet, as if measuring the distance, and backed a few steps away from the flagpole. And then a few more. What was he doing?

The distant shouting continued.

"Makes you wonder exactly who the intended audience is," he said. "Doesn't quite seem like something that would air right after *Glee,* does it?"

"Where did you go the other night?" she asked.

She shifted from foot to foot, watching him retreat, leaving the flag exposed. Was he giving her a fair shot at taking it? Why? And where was Mason?

"Cory Mitnick," Juan said. "What do you think happened to him?"

She drew a momentary blank on the name, then remembered: the eleventh shipboard invitee, whose name Jordan had wangled out of the ship's crew.

"Guess he had someplace else to be," Camilla said. "He wasn't a contestant, anyhow."

"Why not?"

"Five men and five women," she said. "He'd have made eleven, and anyway, he wasn't on board, according to the crew."

Giving her a speculative look, Juan took two more steps back. "What if he actually *was* on board when we left the dock…"

She remembered Jordan's exact words: *"A Cory Mitnick, too—some confusion about him."*

"…but then later on, he wasn't?"

"What, you think this Cory guy jumped overboard?" she asked.

Juan watched her closely. "Maybe he had some help."

Camilla imagined floating in the cold ocean at night, watching the yacht's running lights getting farther and farther away. It reminded her of something—an old story she had once read. Despite the warmth of the morning, a chill raced down her arms.

"You're just trying to freak me out," she said. "But if somebody did end up in the water that night, they'd have been dead in half an hour."

A strange look passed over Juan's face. "Not necessarily."

He looked down at his feet, which meant he wasn't looking at her. Or the flag. She sprinted for it, her sneakers throwing up sprays of sand.

Juan blurred into motion, too. He was fast, she realized—a lot faster than she had expected. Suddenly, he was right there, reaching forward to tag her.

Diving under his arm, she wrapped a hand around the flagpole and yanked it out of its base. She spun to run, but her foot skidded and she lost her balance. Juan's arms wrapped around her as he tackled her to the sand.

He immediately rolled to the side to avoid crushing her under his body, and she rolled with him and somehow ended up lying on top of his chest. Camilla lay there panting for a moment, her face inches from his. Seen from this close, his eyes were light brown. He smelled good: his own clean scent and a hint of aftershave. Her chin tingled where it had brushed the line of his jaw. She really should get up. Right now. As soon as she caught her breath.

"Tag," he said, but he didn't move, either. A flicker of amusement danced in his eyes.

The moment stretched, and Camilla's heart sped up. This was getting awkward. Why was she just lying on him, like she was brain damaged or something? Someone was bound to come around the corner and wonder what was going on between them. Mason would never stop teasing her, and he would get a real kick out of telling their team captain, too. What would Jordan think of her *then*?

Camilla's heart pounded so violently, she felt it pulsing in her neck. And surely Juan felt it, too. How could he not? Her chest was pressed against his.

Remembering the cameras all of a sudden, she gasped. She needed to get off him. Right now.

"Sorry," he said.

She jammed the fist that still held the flagpole into the sand, and felt the sharp grains bite into the backs of her fingers as she pushed herself up.

"No, *I'm* sorry," she said.

Now she was sitting astride him. Oh god, this probably looked even worse.

Juan shook his head. He pointed at the flag in her hand. "Five points."

Realization dawned on her slowly. That was why he had backed away to let her grab the flag first, before tagging her. She had lost five of her points to him, not just one.

"Oh, great." Mad now, she slapped his chest and rolled off him. She stood up, and he rolled to his feet as well. The calm friendliness in his eyes seemed genuine.

He reached for the flag she held. Took it.

"Whatever happens here, you can't take too seriously," he said. "It's just a game. But you're a nice person, and it's not a very nice game, Camilla. Be careful."

Unable to think of anything to say, she stood there facing him, her feelings in turmoil. What had he meant by that?

JT came sliding down the slope behind her, his construction boots sending rocks skittering across the sand. "Fucking Lauren went AWOL," he said to Juan. "Again."

He paused to catch his breath and turned to point back across the island. "And Travis... dumb son of a bitch tagged himself out. But he did it using his elbow, right into the doc's face."

CHAPTER 65

Clinging to the small ridges and knobs of the bluff's vertical face with her fingers and the toes of her shoes, Lauren edged around the southern end of the island. A few feet below her heels, whitewater churned against mussel- and starfish-encrusted rocks. She peered around the corner to see the blue flag, in the center of a flat sandstone shelf. Swinging her body around, she dropped onto the shelf and shook her hands to loosen them.

Jordan stood barefoot next to the flag, staring at her with cold eyes. Then she raised a sculpted eyebrow.

All right, bitch. Lauren tilted her head, cracking her neck. *It is on.*

A small, superior smile appeared on Jordan's face. She pulled the blue flag out of its base. "Want this?"

She tossed the flag toward Lauren, and it clattered down onto the rock surface between them.

Mocking me. Bands of rope tightened around Lauren's chest. *Like I'm some kind of a joke to her.* This was Susan Calloway in the high school locker room all over again. Well, she would break *this* bitch's perfect little nose, too.

Springing forward, she scooped up the blue flag and ran for the rock ramp that led up onto the island's plateau, with Jordan sprinting after her. Gritting her teeth, Lauren spun, swinging the end of the steel flagpole like a baseball bat, aiming for Jordan's face.

But the flagpole swished through empty air—Jordan wasn't there anymore. Running three sideways steps up the bluff wall, in seeming defiance of gravity, she launched herself at Lauren from above.

They crashed to the ground with the flagpole trapped between them and rolled apart. Realizing that Jordan had just taken five points from her, Lauren stood up fast, fingers clenched into fists.

On her hands and knees, Jordan looked at her and laughed. Then she pushed off and bounced to her feet.

Lauren threw a punch, and Jordan bobbed back, avoiding it, still laughing. Weaving and feinting, they circled each other, stepping over the flag that lay on the ground between them.

Somebody was going to get hurt bad here, Lauren realized. That was for goddamn sure. She swung at Jordan again, but her heart was no longer in it.

Jordan danced back again, and her eyes narrowed with dislike. She raised her own hands in some kind of a martial-arts stance—karate or some shit. Jordan wasn't laughing now.

Lauren's stomach sank. For the first time, she wondered if she would actually be able to beat Jordan.

"Cut that out!" a deep voice shouted behind her. "Right now."

Jordan's eyes shifted to look over Lauren's shoulder. And widened.

Lauren turned around to see Brent stumbling down the sandstone ramp toward them, his large frame supported by Mason on one side and Veronica on the other. Blood streamed from his nose and mouth, covering his chin and staining his collar and fisherman's vest. "Get away from each other!" he shouted.

Lauren looked at Veronica in shock. "Who hit him?"

Pale eyes like the blue flames of a propane camp stove burned into hers. Angry. Accusing. "Travis." Veronica practically spat the name.

"Oh Christ." Lauren ran up the ramp.

Crossing the island toward her own team's base to tag herself back in, she wondered how something this obviously out of control could end well for anyone.

CHAPTER 66

"I'm all right." Brent rubbed his sleeve across his lower face, streaking blood on the clean shirt he had changed into. "God damn it, I'm fine."

Camilla noticed with some alarm that he was massaging his left arm when he thought no one was looking. *Oh god, his heart?*

"You should take a break," she said.

Veronica gave her a slight nod, her features taut with concern. She had seen it, too.Leaving Jordan with the flag, they had helped Brent inside and he had gone upstairs to change. Now he sat heavily on the stairs, his jaw already starting to swell.

Although she felt guilty for checking scores, Camilla's eyes flicked to the monitor on the wall.

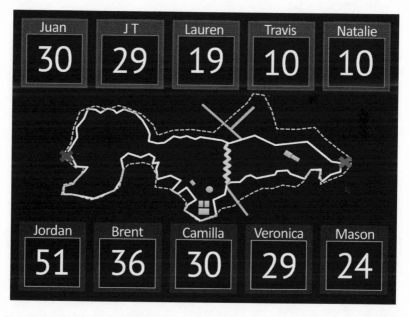

Juan's tag had cost her. If she wanted her foundation to get the money, she would have to start doing better. But the game was turning rough, now. Camilla didn't want anyone else getting hurt.

"We need an ice pack." Veronica snapped her fingers at Mason and Camilla. "And you two, don't just stand there like idiots. Do something."

"Okay, where's the first-aid kit?" Camilla asked.

"No." Veronica waved her away, looking furious. "I'll take care of him; I've got some nursing experience. You two need to go after their flag again."

"But Julian has to give us a time-out, because Brent got hurt—"

"A *time-out?*" Veronica said. "Don't be ridiculous. What are we, playing beach volleyball here?"

"Oh god. Come on, Mason. She's right." Camilla headed for the door—the red team would be going after the flag right now, with only Jordan in their way. "Let's go."

Brent's voice, slurred but strong, followed her out the doorway.

"Remember who you are. Don't stoop to their level. That's exactly what Julian wants."

• • •

Once they were both outside, Camilla grabbed Mason's arm.

"We have to do something about Travis," she said. "Take him out of play before he hurts someone even worse. Any ideas?"

"Maybe one or two." Mason reached behind his waist to pull the black cylinder of bear spray from under his suit jacket.

"Oh god. But I think we need to do this."

He grinned. "It'll be fun…" A furious scream from the direction of the blue base interrupted him.

"I'm going to kill him!" a woman's voice shrieked. "I'm going to fucking *kill* him."

Camilla stared at Mason in alarm. "That's Jordan."

She sprinted toward the top of the ramp, arriving just as Jordan crested the slope, hair soaked, her wet dress plastered to her body.

"That son of a bitch." She took a deep, shuddering breath, and Camilla was surprised to see she was near tears. "What happened to you guys? You left me alone out here."

Camilla put a hand on her back to calm her. "Brent was hurt—"

"Bastard netted me with a bunch of kelp to avoid a tag—threw me in the water like a fish he didn't want." Sniffling, Jordan rubbed at her forearm. "I landed on rocks."

"Travis?" Camilla asked.

Jordan shook her head. "Juan."

"Oh, no." Camilla pictured his face so close to her own a few minutes ago, seeing his calm, sardonic smile. Her cheeks felt hot. "I'm so sorry."

Jordan dropped suddenly to sit on the ground near their feet. She swiped an arm across her eyes, then hugged her knees and looked away. "Where *were* you guys?"

"Did Juan get the flag?" Mason asked.

She didn't answer, but the sound of cheering from the far side of the island answered for her.

"Why didn't you call for help?" Camilla asked. "Maybe we could have caught him."

A stricken look bloomed across Jordan's face. "Oh my god." She dropped her face into her arms.

She hadn't even thought of it, Camilla realized. They were all falling apart here.

• • •

"You hang back a little," Camilla said to Mason.

Lurking just inside red territory, Travis leered at them from behind the seal barricade fifty yards away. He rubbed at the triangle of beard under his lip.

"I'll make him chase me," she said. "You come up behind him and spray him. Then we both run like hell."

"Don't be shy!" Travis shouted. He grinned, beckoning her forward. "Bring your fag buddy, too."

Mason laughed. "That's our cue. Just don't let him catch you."

Camilla sprinted forward, and Travis shifted along the barricade to intercept her. He looked like he would enjoy hurting her. Mason wasn't kidding.

She feinted to one side, pivoted, and scrabbled up the rough round logs, getting splinters in her palms. The heel of her sneaker caught on the top, tumbling her headfirst into red territory, and her face smacked against something wet and rubbery.

Yelping, the seal Camilla had landed on wriggled out from under her as she rolled aside. She scrambled to her feet and took off running, with Travis's boots clattering on the rocks close behind her.

Slaloming around seals, bird nests, and rocks, she was forced to watch the ground ahead of her skidding feet. This didn't seem like such a great idea anymore. What if Mason couldn't catch up with them?

Passing between the cistern dome and the fallen lighthouse tower, she glanced toward the locked warehouse buildings. No one had come out when Travis injured Brent—this was definitely a rough game. But by pepper-spraying Travis in return, were she and Mason about to make things even worse?

And where was Mason? All she could hear was Travis, almost on top of her now.

In the middle of the causeway, Natalie raised her hands, looking uncertain. Dodging around her with pathetic ease, Camilla ran for the red team's base. Juan was there. He could protect her until Mason caught up. She would be safe with Juan.

Or would she? She pictured Jordan—soaked, hurt, and humiliated—and realized she had made a big mistake.

"You stupid little bitch!" Travis's yell came from far behind. "Why did you just *stand* there?"

What? Slowing, Camilla looked back.

Travis had Natalie by the arm. He shook her violently, sending her head whipping back and forth. "You let her run right past you again."

Camilla skidded to a halt in shock. She didn't see Mason anywhere.

Travis grabbed the front of Natalie's sweatshirt with his other hand, bunching it in his fist and lifting her onto her toes. "What use are you? Huh?"

The sweatshirt rode up, exposing the stark whiteness of Natalie's bare stomach and ribs.

"Let go of her!" Camilla shouted, running toward them.

A loud, ugly crackling sound reached her ears. Travis convulsed suddenly and fell to the ground, releasing Natalie. She squatted next to him, pressing the stun gun against his neck, and the crackling sound came again. Travis's back arched and his legs jerked, kicking at the rocks. Then he lay still.

Camilla stopped twenty feet away.

Natalie pulled her sweatshirt down, covering herself. Lips trembling, she met Camilla's eyes. She looked about to cry. Then Mason appeared at Natalie's side.

Still squatting, Natalie looked up at him. He gently held out a hand, and she touched his palm. Then she scooted backward and stood up.

Why had Mason let Natalie tag him? Rooted in place, Camilla stared in confusion. Events were moving too quickly, leaving her stranded like a traveler lost in a strange country whose customs she no longer understood.

Placing a foot against Travis's side, Mason shoved, sliding him toward the edge of the oceanside bluff. Travis's eyelids fluttered, but his arms and legs didn't move.

Camilla's eyes widened.

Mason pushed again, sending him tumbling over the edge. Camilla winced, remembering that the drop to the beach was eight or ten feet at least. But after what Travis had done to Brent, to Natalie, she was okay with this.

Lifting the back of his jacket, Mason fished a roll of duct tape from behind his belt. He looked at Camilla and gave her a wide wolf's grin.

She hesitated for a moment, then nodded. *Take him out of play.*

She gave Mason a thumbs-up.

He jumped down after Travis.

CHAPTER 67

"You can think of it as getting benched for unnecessary roughness."

Someone was jostling Travis's body, rolling him over and over—sharp grains of sand pressing against his forehead and cheeks, then daylight shining bright orange through closed eyelids, then a faceful of cold, dark sand again... the continuous rip of tape coming off a roll, like an icepick in his ears. Hands lifting his legs. He groaned, every muscle of his body throbbing and tingling with remembered agony.

"I mean, we can't start behaving like savages, can we?" Hands rolled him onto his back and Mason leaned into view, squatting next to his head. Smiling.

Travis lurched to grab him but managed to rise only a few inches off the sand. His arms didn't move. Neither did his legs.

Tilting his chin, he looked down his own body and saw a man-size cocoon of silver. Panic jolted through him like another blast from the stun gun. Cocksucker had him wrapped up like a mummy in duct tape: legs together, arms against his sides, wrists behind his back—had to be a couple of rolls' worth at least.

He sucked in a breath to shout, and gagged as Mason trickled a fistful of sand into his mouth. *"Mmmphh."*

"What?" Lifting Travis's head, Mason pressed duct tape against his lips. "Sorry, I didn't quite catch that."

Choking, he tried to shake his head loose, but Mason pulled the tape tight, looping it several times around his jaws and the back of his hair. Pasty sand scraped Travis's gums and trickled into his throat, tasting like mildewed salt packed against his tongue. Something small—a worm or a tiny sand crab—wriggled against the roof of his mouth.

Thrashing helplessly, he sucked air through his flared nostrils. He narrowed his eyes and stared into Mason's shit-eating grin. *"GGGILL OOO, GGAAGGGTHUGGERR!" Kill you, cocksucker.*

"We don't want to end up like the Roman gladiators here," Mason said. "Still, you're lucky Camilla gave me a thumbs-up. Thumbs-down, and I might have misunderstood. I might have done *this*..." He slapped a strip of tape across Travis's nostrils.

Arching his back, eyes wide with terror, Travis scanned the unbroken line of the bluff top above. Nobody was there. Nobody could see him.

His lungs spasmed. Bright spots danced in his dimming vision.

He was going to die.

217

Laughing, Mason ripped the tape loose. Travis nearly passed out anyway, unable to suck air through his nose fast enough.

"Hope you don't catch a cold before your teammates come find you." Mason pinched Travis's nostrils shut and looked into his eyes. "But then again, maybe they won't bother. I don't think they like you too much."

Letting go, he stood up and dusted off his hands. "You know, you look kind of sexy there, all wrapped in gray, like a female elephant seal. It'd be funny if one of the big bulls came along and thought so, too, wouldn't it? I'd give up half the five million just to see that."

Icy terror gripped Travis, sending a jolt down his arms and legs. He managed to roll onto his side, accidentally snorting sand into his nostrils. Eyes bulging, he blew his nose clear and rolled onto his back again.

"Well, what have we here?" Mason's voice came from the direction of the bluff, sounding genuinely surprised. Then he was back, smiling down at Travis. "Looks like you'll be sitting out the rest of the game."

Lifting Travis's feet, Mason dragged him into the shadow of the bluff and crammed him through a foot-wide vertical crack in the rocky wall. He tumbled into darkness, thumping his head against rough stone.

A humming sound vibrated through the rocks beneath him. Light from the narrow opening reached a few feet into the cave, illuminating uneven walls of sandstone that stretched into foul-smelling darkness.

Then the light dimmed as Mason's silhouette filled the entrance, heaving the first rock into place to block the bottom of the opening.

CHAPTER 68

Camilla and Veronica stood at the top of the ramp, staring down at their own base. The blue flag waved, lonely and unattended. Jordan was missing.

"*Now,* where is she?" Camilla asked, alarmed.

Frowning, Veronica paced along the bluff with impatient strides, staring down at the narrow strip of sand below. Camilla followed her. The strip widened to join the large mainland-side beach, and they scanned the seal-covered expanse of sand. Veronica suddenly laughed her throaty laugh and pointed.

"There."

Jordan sprinted barefoot along the beach, hugging the face of the bluff, weaving between the harems of elephant seals as she headed their way. She held the red flag in her arms, its cloth banner rippling and flapping behind her as she ran. A great bull rose from the sand with a roar to lurch after her, but she was already out of reach.

Racing across the high ground above, JT and Lauren paralleled Jordan below. They pointed and shouted to each other, looking over the edge as they ran. Camilla knew that the steep bluffs hid Jordan from them most of the time. She would be visible only when crossing below ravines or diverting around clumps of seals at the cliff base.

Realizing they would never catch her, Lauren slid to a halt, her features contorted in fury. She grabbed JT's thick bicep to stop him, too, before they got close enough for Camilla and Veronica to tag them.

Camilla looked down again, seeing Jordan round the corner below. Then she ran toward the ramp, arriving just in time to watch Jordan plant the red flag next to their blue one. *Score!*

Blue team and red team were now tied, one to one.

Camilla laughed out loud as Jordan waved to her, beaming that dazzling smile. Their team captain had evened up the score single-handedly. But *how?*

CHAPTER 69

"What the fuck, Juan?"

Lauren jammed her fists onto her hips and stared down at Juan, lying prone at her feet. JT stood beside her, arms crossed, not saying anything. *Him* she could count on, at least.

Juan groaned. He shoved himself up onto his hands and knees, letting his head hang for a moment. Then he tried to stand but sank back to his knees, one hand pressed against his temple. Blood smeared the side of his face, spreading in a sand-caked trickle from beneath his hairline. He swabbed angrily at it with the tail of his black dress shirt.

With his other hand, he indicated a jagged piece of broken concrete that lay nearby.

"She cold-cocked me with that. How'd she get past all of you? She's *barefoot,* for Christ's sake!"

"Same thing she did yesterday," Lauren said. "Dropped down to the beach, stayed close to the cliff so we wouldn't see her. That's gotta be against the rules—out of bounds or something."

Juan laughed, then doubled over in pain, holding his head. "Against the rules? It doesn't look like there are any."

He pushed to his feet. "Still no sign of Travis?"

"Fuck him," Lauren said. "We don't need his type."

Juan looked at her, surprised. Then he pointed to the rock again.

"Jordan's completely out of control. Now I'm really wondering about Travis. Maybe that crazy bitch killed him."

CHAPTER 70

Camilla skidded to a halt next to the fallen lighthouse tower, her sneakers sliding on dirt. The island's highest point gave her a 360-degree view across the rocky surface and most of the large beach below. Jordan ran along the beach now, holding the red flag again. She had said she would stay to defend their own flag, but clearly she hadn't.

Mason had taken way too long to tie up Travis. Camilla was glad to see him climbing the breakwater toward her. But now Veronica was in red territory, too. Why wasn't anybody protecting their base? Teamwork was breaking down; everyone was doing their own thing. She needed to get them working together again before it was too late.

Sure enough, Lauren came tearing up the ramp from the blue base, holding their blue flag. She sprinted toward the barricade, crossing blue territory unchallenged.

"Mason, we're defending!" Camilla shouted. "Tag Lauren!"

Action down on the beach drew her eye. JT now stood between Jordan and the blue base, blocking her. Juan rounded the other corner, and they had Jordan trapped.

Dodging and weaving among the seals, Jordan cut toward the water as the red team closed in from both sides. Then, to Camilla's surprise, she threw the red flag into the surf and sprinted away, leaving JT and Juan staring at their soaked banner—and the angry bull elephant seal she had thrown it in front of.

How did *that* help the blue team? Camilla felt disoriented again, as if everyone else were playing a different game from the one she was playing, with rules no one had explained to her. She closed her eyes and concentrated. What was going on?

The first team to plant the flag twice more would win, but nobody was defending their bases. Nobody was trying to tag members of the other team coming after their flag. Her fellow players were smart, too. What was she missing here?

In her head, Camilla heard Reuben's words after she won her *Teambuilder* award: *"It shouldn't always be about the team."* And Mason's last night: *"The grand prize isn't a team award."* Oh god, it was all so clear now. Julian had been clever, calling this capture the flag game a *team* challenge. Because it wasn't really a team game at all. Her own team-oriented mind-set had blinded her. Julian's scoring rules meant that only three things really mattered to your own individual score: planting the flag yourself, tagging someone carrying your flag, and not getting tagged while carrying theirs.

Camilla opened her eyes and grinned. She needed to tag Lauren before her teammate Mason did. She sprinted toward Lauren as Mason closed in from the other side.

Lauren's face crumpled, realizing they had her trapped against the edge of the bluff.

JT's voice drifted up from the beach. "Lauren, throw me the flag."

"No," Lauren shouted back. "I'm taking it all the way."

"God damn it, girl, they *have* you."

Throwing the flag off the bluff, Lauren spun on Mason and swatted him hard in the ear with her open hand, knocking him to the ground.

"Tag." She stalked off.

Camilla helped a stunned-looking Mason to his feet. "You didn't have to do that," she called after Lauren. "You really hurt him."

"Whoops." Lauren didn't look back.

Mason shook his head to clear it, and a trickle of blood ran from his ear. Picking up his glasses, he stumbled to the bluff. Camilla followed, and they stared down at the beach.

Juan had recovered the red flag, avoiding the elephant seal somehow. JT now held the blue flag Lauren had thrown him. Together, they ran around the corner.

Camilla's neck tensed as cheers erupted in the distance; JT had planted their flag.

They were now losing, two to one.

If the red team scored again, the game would be over.

CHAPTER 71

Running along the beach, staying close to the bluff, Camilla followed Mason as they dodged around clusters of seals. He was laughing, with the red flag gripped in his hands—they had found it unguarded, and he had reached it seconds before she had. Jordan stood on the raised walkway ahead, waving them forward. They rounded a corner and skidded to a stop, almost colliding with the red team coming the other way.

Lauren, JT, and Juan slid to a halt ten feet in front of them. The blue flagpole was clenched in JT's fists.

The two teams faced each other, holding each other's flags. Whose territory were they in? Camilla glanced up at the bluff, trying to figure out which side of the seal barricade they were on. She couldn't see.

Jordan jumped off the walkway and ran toward them.

"Give me our flag," JT said. "Don't make me come get it." The threat in his voice was clear.

"Here you go," Mason said, still laughing, and suddenly the air between the two teams was filled with a cloud of orange.

Camilla spun toward Mason, who held the black canister one-handed, waving it back and forth, spraying Lauren, JT, and Juan. Screaming in agony, all three dropped to the sand holding their faces, the blue flag still entangled in JT's arms.

Too shocked to say anything, Camilla slapped Mason's arm aside.

He didn't stop laughing. Tucking the black cylinder of bear spray into his belt again, he ran forward, gave Lauren a friendly clap on her shoulder where she knelt choking, and scooped the flag out of JT's arms in the same motion. With a flag in each hand, he took off down the beach, running toward the blue base.

Coughing and gagging, the red team scrambled to their feet with tears streaming from their eyes. Lauren seemed to have gotten the worst of it. It looked like she was having trouble breathing. Juan threw her arm over his shoulder, and they stumbled toward the surf line. Cursing, JT stood and ran after them.

"Oh god, sorry," Camilla called after them. "I didn't see that coming."

Jordan had stopped twenty feet away. Hand over her mouth, she stared after Mason, her eyes widening in shock.

White-hot anger coursed through Camilla's body. Mason shouldn't have done this; it was totally wrong. She sprinted after him.

225

• • •

Camilla caught up with Mason as he rounded the corner onto the limestone bench at the southern end of the island, where their base lay. Without letting herself think too hard about what she was doing, she dived at his legs and wrapped her arms around his shins. He crashed to the ground, glasses flying, dropping both flagpoles as he tried to break his fall with his hands.

She scrambled forward, grabbed both flags, and slid to her knees in front of the blue base. Dropping the blue flag, she used two hands to jam the red flagpole into the base. Then she picked up the blue flagpole and stood it vertical, but her hands were trembling now. She couldn't believe what she had just done: she had tackled her own teammate.

She tried to jam the blue flag into the base, but the end wobbled, missing the hole. She glanced toward Mason, who was sitting up now.

Swallowing, she tried again. The end of the flagpole skated around the edges of the hole, not going in. She concentrated, staring at the pole and steadying her hands. In her peripheral vision, Mason was walking toward her now.

Camilla took a deep breath and slid the end of the flagpole along the surface of the base. It dropped into the hole, and she felt a wash of relief. Standing up quickly, she faced Mason.

She had just seen him pepper-spray three people. He was like one of the problem kids that Euclid House sometimes sent her way: he just did whatever he wanted, with no fear of consequences. What if he was mad at her?

Unsmiling, he stopped six feet away. She could see no expression on his face at all. His glasses were dusty, so she couldn't even really see his eyes. Was he angry? Mason had lousy posture and a habitual stoop, probably because he spent all his time in front of a computer, but that made him look smaller than he really was. For the first time, she realized that he was a lot bigger than she was. He could probably hurt her pretty easily.

For a long, awkward moment, neither of them said anything. Then he lowered his head and turned away, walking over to the water's edge.

"Mason?"

He didn't answer, didn't look at her.

Camilla's throat was suddenly tight. Mason wasn't angry; he was upset. She hadn't realized how much she had come to enjoy her irreverent buddy's company. What had she been thinking? Now she had destroyed their developing friendship.

Then she pictured Lauren, gagging and choking in the sand, Juan and JT scrubbing at their faces. Eyes narrowing, Camilla marched forward and yanked the bear spray out of his belt. Stepping back, she whipped her arm sideways and threw the black cylinder out into the crashing whitewater.

"I don't care about Julian's stupid rules," she said. "Here's mine, Mason: you don't get points for hurting people."

Behind his glasses, he blinked.

She stared up into his face, defiant.

Then he grinned. Wincing, he bent down to rub his knees. "No points for hurting people, huh?" The elbows and knees of his suit were torn. Blood showed through the rips and welled from the abrasions on his palms.

Camilla flushed; her tackle had done all that. She was such a hypocrite.

Slowly, painfully, he dropped to sit on the ground. "I'm not giving you any more advice. It seems I've created a monster."

"Oh god, Mason, your hands! I'm sorry, but you—"

Laughing, he waved her away, rubbing at his injuries. "Congratulations. I guess you and our team captain are two of a kind."

Sensing someone at the top of the ramp, she looked up to see Veronica staring at her. She had been standing there all along. Her pale, silvery eyes bored into Camilla, icy with judgment. Camilla couldn't believe she had actually mistaken this woman for a soccer mom. But shame washed over her, making her face hot.

She couldn't meet Veronica's gaze.

CHAPTER 72

Splashing sounds. Coughing and gagging next to her. Her own choking noises, too. She couldn't breathe. A strong arm around her shoulder, holding her steady. All she could see was red. Then a blurry glimpse of JT on his knees, cupped hands scooping seawater onto his face. Oh Christ, she couldn't take a breath. Steel bands cinched around her chest, crushing. And the pain, like frostbite thawing all over her face.

Lauren threw up.

She sucked in a gasping breath, hearing it wheeze into her lungs. She heaved again, tasting acid and the peanut sauce from the last MRE. Her legs buckled. Juan supported her, splashing more water into her eyes with his free hand, scrubbing her face like a little kid's.

Shoving him angrily aside, she fell to her knees in the surf.

She threw herself facedown into the water and held her eyes open with shaking fingers. The salt water was cold, soothing. She could hear Juan nearby, his voice a hoarse croak, talking to JT:

"Stay with me, man. We need to focus."

"I swear I'm going to kill that little shit," JT rasped. "I can't see."

Lauren rolled onto her back, hyperventilating, chest spasming. The sky was a blur above her. Her eyes stung, throbbed. Her face was on fire. She wiped her nose, and her wrist came away coated with snot. Then her wrist started burning, too.

She lay there, panting, until she got her breathing under control.

"Score's two-two," she said, staring up at the sky. "We're going to win this thing, and I don't give a fuck what we have to do to them to do it."

• • •

Cracking her knuckles, Lauren watched Camilla jog away after handing the red team's flag back to Juan. Little Miss Politician thought her apology was worth something? Lauren had just glared at her. That must be how it worked in the corporate world: lie, cheat, and steal; then send the doe-eyed ones to say "sorry." Real cute. Psycho Barbie was probably running toward them along the beach already, coming to steal their flag again.

JT ground the heels of his hands into his eyes. They were bloodshot almost solid red. Lauren was pretty sure hers looked the same.

229

"All right, *Captain*," she said to Juan. "*The plan.* You've got one, right? Astonish us with your brilliance." Her eyes narrowed. "But you and JT both scored already. This time, *I* plant the blue flag."

Juan nodded. Then he pulled the red flag out of its base and walked to the water's edge. The ropes they had used yesterday to go after the water jugs still trailed across the waves toward the distant boulders. Grabbing a rope with one hand, he braced himself. Then he plunged into the whitewater, taking the flag with him.

A minute later, he stood in front of JT and Lauren again, dripping onto the rocks. He was no longer holding their flag. Tilting his head, he cleared water out of his ear with a twist of his finger. Then he pointed toward the blue base.

"Now we *all* go."

• • •

Mason was alone, standing next to the blue flag. Grinning.

"I'm sorry, could you repeat that?" Lauren said. "We should try not to hurt you too badly *why*, again?"

He reached behind him. "I wonder if anyone's ever been bear-sprayed twice in one day before? Once is probably enough for most people."

She flinched, then stepped forward, angry with herself. "Do it and I kill you."

"Take the flag. Just please don't hurt me."

"Chickenshit." She grabbed the flagpole, but before she could yank it out of the base, Mason's other hand darted forward, tapping her wrist.

"Tag."

He scooted back fast, looking ready to yank the bear spray out from behind him.

Oh Christ, he had just taken five points from her. "You little asshole." Lauren's fists clenched. "You're dead."

Juan laid a hand on her shoulder. "Back up, Mason," he said. "Now." His voice was mild, but Mason retreated a few steps.

Juan waved Natalie forward. "Natalie, grab the flag."

Lauren stared at him. Why was he giving the flag to the most useless member of their team? But he only pointed up the ramp.

She met Mason's eyes. "Later for you." Then she followed JT's broad shoulders up the slope.

Sprinting ahead of the others, Lauren looked back, smirking at how slow Natalie was. Running flat out, she hurdled the barricade, and her foot came down on a bird nest. She winced at the crunch of eggs and fragile bones beneath her shoe, but she didn't stop. Mason had tagged her out... but once she touched her own base, she would be back in play.

CHAPTER 73

"Where's their flag? Camilla asked.
"They hid it." Jordan's eyes widened in surprise. "Oh my god, Julian never said we couldn't."

Veronica snorted. "What kind of imbecile dreamed up these rules?"

They stood staring down at the empty plastic cone that was the red base. A scrambling noise came from behind, and Lauren shot down the slope beside them.

"Back up, everybody," Camilla said. "Don't let her tag you."

But Lauren ran to the red base. When she knelt and slapped it with her hand, Camilla understood that Mason had tagged Lauren again. She looked so angry—didn't Mason understand he was going to get himself killed here?

Juan skated down the slope and stopped next to Lauren, his eyes narrowing when he spotted Jordan. JT slid to a halt beside the two of them.

Juan pointed at Camilla and her teammates. "Tag them," he said. Then, to her surprise, he plunged into the water.

Jordan pointed up the slope the red team had descended. "That means Natalie's got our flag up there," she said. "Get her."

Camilla charged up the slope, spotting Natalie a short distance away, out of breath, the blue flag drooping in her arms. She looked up, an expression of resignation on her face, and then her gaze flicked past Camilla's shoulder.

Camilla tried to dodge, but too late. A hand caught the back of her shirt, jerking her backward, and a thick arm wrapped around her upper arms and chest.

JT laughed. "Tag." But he didn't let go. Instead he hoisted her off her feet, and she found herself being carried under his arm like a misbehaving child.

"Put me down." She tried to wriggle free.

"Nah," he said. "Can't trust any of you to play fair." The muscles of his arm tightened like a python coiling around a deer.

"Get your hands off her *right now*," Veronica said from nearby.

Camilla's face flushed. This was embarrassing enough, being carried like a doll. Having Veronica rescue her would be even more humiliating. She struggled but couldn't move.

"I mean it." Veronica's tone turned jagged. "Let her go."

JT jerked forward, jouncing Camilla against his arm. "Gotcha. Double play." Veronica's face was suddenly inches from Camilla's, and JT's other arm was wrapped around Veronica's shoulders, pulling her against his chest.

231

"Take it in, Natalie!" he yelled. "Lauren, cover her. I got these two."

Veronica had been trying to help her, and now JT had them both. "Sorry," Camilla said to her.

Blazing with icy blue fury, Veronica's pale eyes met Camilla's for a second; then she looked down. She raised a knee high between them and stomped hard, raking the side of her shoe along JT's shin, like a skateboarder grinding a rail. Her foot smashed into the top of his arch with crushing force, and he let go of both women. Camilla fell to her hands and knees and drew in a gasping breath.

Veronica spun on JT and raised a finger, leveling it at his face. "Don't you ever lay a hand on one of us again. Not ever."

Veins stood out on the side of JT's shaved head. He turned and walked away, limping slightly. Veronica stalked after him, continuing to berate him in a low, angry voice.

Natalie stood fifteen feet away, eyes wide, mouth open. She hadn't moved. Lauren materialized at her side and grabbed the other end of the blue flagpole. "If you're just going to stand there like an idiot," she said, "give that to me."

Natalie shook her head, refusing to let go.

Watching the two red-team women struggle over the flag, Camilla shook her head in disbelief. Then she thought of what she herself had done to Mason earlier.

It was all of them, really. Julian had turned them into animals.

Tinkling laughter trailed past her ear as Jordan ran forward, clapping a hand on Natalie's shoulder as she went by: a tag. Natalie's face crumpled, and she released the flag, sending Lauren stumbling back with it. Falling to her knees, Lauren immediately threw the blue flag away before Jordan could tag her, too.

But Jordan didn't stop. She scooped up the flag and continued down onto the beach, where the red base was.

"Where are you going?" Camilla shouted after her.

Jordan should have taken the blue flag to safety, not closer to danger. Mason was stuck back at their base, unable to run, after Camilla's own tackle had injured his knees. And JT had tagged both her and Veronica out—by the time they made it to their base and back, it would all be over. This was all down to their team captain now.

"Jordan, get it out of here!" Camilla yelled.

Shaking her head, Jordan tossed the blue flag onto the sand next to the red base. Cheeks flushed, eyes bright, she took a few barefoot steps back toward the water and settled into a ready stance, facing Lauren. The flag lay between them.

"You dropped something," she called to Lauren.

She was baiting Lauren, wanting her to pick it up so she could tag her. But from the expression on Lauren's face, Camilla could see what a bad idea this was. She ran forward.

Lauren's mouth pulled into a snarl. She took a few steps to the side and crouched, reaching down by her feet. Then she straightened, holding a four-foot length of steel pipe with a jagged chunk of concrete at the end. It looked like a medieval mace.

Jordan's eyes widened.

"No worries—I found it," Lauren called back. "But thanks."

"Stop it right now!" Camilla shouted at them.

Jordan glanced at her. "Stay out of this, sister."

"Listen to your captain," Lauren said, moving toward the flag, steel pipe held ready. "She's got the right idea."

Camilla got in between them and stepped toward Lauren, hands raised. "Can't you see what's going to happen here?"

Out of the corner of her eye, she saw something black and red rising out of the water behind Jordan.

Camilla screamed.

Jordan whipped around, too late. An arc of red knocked her legs out from under her with a wet slap, and she crashed to the ground, flat on her back. A black figure whipped the soaked red flag upright and swung a leg up onto the rock behind her. Then a dripping Juan pushed himself upright and swept past Jordan, thrusting the base of the flagpole into her stomach as he went by—a quick, vicious jab, like a downhill racer planting a ski pole. She doubled over onto her side, arms wrapped around her midsection, and pulled her knees to her chest.

Camilla ran to her, passing Juan as he bent to grab the blue flag. She dropped to her knees by Jordan's side. "Oh god, are you okay?"

Jordan rocked back and forth, hugging her stomach, eyes screwed shut. Her face was red, and the cords in her neck stood out. Camilla laid a hand on her forehead, and Jordan grunted one word: "Bastard."

Juan planted both flags in the red base and stepped back.

Lauren's voice rose behind them. "God *damn* it, Juan." She sounded upset.

Camilla didn't know why—after all, the red team had just won. But she didn't care about that. She stared at Juan, dripping water from his short black hair, and a fist tightened around her heart. Fighting to keep her composure, she gently brushed her injured friend's hair back from her forehead.

"Why?" she asked. "Why, Juan?"

Juan's expression was neutral. He rubbed at his temple. Then he shrugged.

CHAPTER 74

Pelagic Institute, Santa Cruz, California

In the lab, Heather hunched in front of her widescreen Samsung monitor, sipping tea from the oversize mug she held. Jacob leaned over her shoulder. The fronds of a small spider plant dangled from the shelf above, touching the corner of the screen, and he slapped them away abruptly. She hated it when he got like this.

He pointed. "Just try and tell me you don't see that."

On the monitor, glowing trails stretched behind moving dots—each dot labeled with an alphanumeric designation. The trails arced and looped, tracing out their patterns against a background of fainter lines, like the contour lines on a topographic map. A digital clock at the bottom of the screen spun through a five-day period on fast-forward as she watched first one, then two, then *four* labeled dots appear at the edges of the screen to swirl into a circling pattern at the center.

"I see it," she said. "Your convergence pattern. They're not supposed to do that."

"This is only last year's tags," Jacob said. "There may be even more of them. Nobody's ever seen this shit before, Heather—it's a totally new behavior. And we're sitting here with our thumbs in our asses." He pounded his fist on the worktable, sloshing tea out of her cup. "What the fuck is *going on* out there?"

She pushed back from her workstation, getting a little space between her and Jacob, when the door to the lab swung open with a creak.

Dmitry leaned inside the doorway. Looking pleased with himself, he cracked a Diet Coke. "I find out who is on island."

"Who?" she asked.

Dmitry's grin spread. "My cousin Sasha, he sometimes drives truck for Institute. I get him job—take care of family. Sasha tells me, last week he took Karen down to Monterey Aquarium to help with new exhibit. Is not eating, this one. She give it checkup so they can keep on display longer than last one. Bring more visitors, more money—"

"Yes, yes, the fucking tourists love it when they have one." Jacob waved an impatient hand. "Go on."

"Sasha said Karen is talking on cell phone whole way, sounding very nervous. She keep saying, 'What assurances you give me?' and 'Can I get in writing?' Sasha pretending not to listen, but hearing everything."

235

"So who is on the island instead of us?" Heather asked.

"Is reality show."

Jacob laughed and dropped into the beanbag chair beside the desk. "You mean *documentary*. They're making a documentary. 'Reality show' means something else, Dmitry."

"No." Dmitry looked offended. "I know what is documentary. They making *reality show* on island right now, like *Fear Factory. Survivors. American Idols.*"

"That's the stupidest thing I ever heard. Your cousin misunderstood."

Heather nodded. "I'm afraid he's right, Dmitry. Parks and Rec would never allow it."

"Is true," Dmitry said. "Sasha say Karen talk about money, too, asking when they sending the wire transfer for Institute. But then she ask about different wire transfer, too."

Heather tensed. "You know, the weird way Karen was acting, the way she cut out yesterday, I could almost believe something like this."

"You've got to be shitting me." Jacob blinked rapidly. "This month—"

"Of course they'd do it this month," she said. "Any other time, there's no way they could get away with it."

"I don't understand," Dmitry said. "Island is closed to public *always*."

Heather remembered that he was new to the team. "In December, they close down the whole shoreside state park, too," she said.

He nodded in understanding. "Because of elephant seals arriving. Mating season." His hands moved in a graphic gesture that she didn't want to try interpreting.

Jacob bounced out of the beanbag and paced to the window, grabbing the front of his sweatshirt. "For the next two weeks, Año Nuevo is the most isolated stretch of coast in California. That island might as well be in fucking Antarctica somewhere. They could be doing *anything* out there right now, and nobody would see. We have to check it out."

The monitor suddenly switched to screen saver, startling Heather. She twitched, spilling her tea, and its sweet, herbal scent filled the air. "I think they paid Karen off," she said. "Bribed her. This is so wrong... Raja's team spent four seasons hiding in blinds to avoid disrupting the animals' natural behavior. A bunch of TV people running around—that'll set the mammal studies back years. *Years.*"

Jacob pointed at the monitor again. "This is why we have to go out there. The convergence pattern. Whoever they are, they're causing it somehow."

Dmitry shook his head. "Is not good idea. We get fired."

"Why'd they choose Año Nuevo, anyway?" Heather twisted a lock of hair between her fingers, then caught herself doing it and stopped. "I thought they liked tropical settings with everyone shirtless, in bikini tops. Did Sasha catch the name of which studio is behind this? Maybe we can call them."

"Sasha is good listener. He hear name of company sending wire transfer: Vita Brevis Entertainment."

"Oh, shit," Jacob said. "It's really true."

Heather spun back to her monitor. "Let's see what Google has to say about Vita Brevis Entertainment."

• • •

A few minutes later, she turned back to the others, puzzled. "This just keeps getting better and better. I found some old quote they probably got the name from, and a couple similar-sounding companies, but no Vita Brevis Entertainment."

"That's a waste of time." Jacob crossed the lab with angry strides and turned her monitor off. "I'm telling you, we need to just take the fucking boat and go out there."

CHAPTER 75

With only four people sitting and leaning against the walls, the great room of the Victorian house now seemed a vast empty space. Lauren stared down at her hands. Her eyes still itched from the bear spray. The blue team had stayed in their own building instead of joining the others—smart of them, considering the way Lauren and her teammates felt right now. The midafternoon sun filtered weakly through the dull gray overcast outside.

Her chest tightened every time she glanced at Juan. He should have let *her* plant the flag. The scoreboard glowed from the monitor above them all, taunting her.

Somehow, she had ended up in the bottom three. How the Christ had that happened?

Nobody felt much like talking, it seemed. Lauren certainly didn't. JT kept rubbing his shin. In the corner of the room, Natalie was almost invisible with her knees tucked up in front of her chest. She never took her eyes off the doorway.

The fifth member of their team—Travis—was still missing, but Lauren didn't give a shit about that. If he never came back, that would be just fine with her.

"We got that security thing," JT said. "We won today, so we can't lose these points now. The other team can still lose theirs."

"Big deal," she said. "I don't have many to lose, but I see playing captain worked out well for *somebody* today." She glared at Juan. "Don't get too comfortable, though. Your pretty little barefoot princess next door is still ahead of you, *amigo*. You should have spiked her harder."

Juan had changed into dry clothes—all black, of course. What was with that, anyway?

He shrugged. "Julian had a second monitor screen in the other house all along," he said. "That tells me he expected things to get tense between the teams. For this amount of money, perhaps it was inevitable."

Lauren looked down at her hands again. It was easy to stay angry, to psych herself up. But maybe it was time to listen to the small voice that she had been hearing for the past two days, growing more and more insistent with every passing hour. The others had to be thinking the same thing, even if no one else was willing to admit it.

"This situation," she said. "I've been here before. You take a bunch of ultracompetitive people together and put a crazy challenge in front of them, nobody's gonna back out. You ignore what your instincts are telling you. Next thing you know, people are dead. Something real bad is gonna happen here. I know it. And you know what else? It almost seems like Julian *wants* that."

Juan looked thoughtful. "Maybe something has already happened. Nobody's seen Travis since the beginning of the game. We should go out, look for him."

"Yeah, Travis." Lauren made a sour face. "Here's a little something about our good buddy Travis you might find interesting."

Reaching into the pocket of her cargo pants, she pulled out the envelope she had dried out last night. Most of the ink had washed away, but this morning she had read the parts of the letter that were still legible. It was enough. She handed the envelope to Juan.

"JT, Natalie," she called. "Come over here. You ought to see this, too."

Juan looked at the return address, and his brows arched. Then he pulled the letter out of the envelope. JT and Natalie looked over his shoulder as he scanned the faded paragraphs, reading aloud.

"Lewd or lascivious conduct with a minor fourteen or fifteen years of age... rape using threat of force... aggravated assault... counts of sodomy... the defendant, Travis Hargrave, represented that... sentenced to a state correctional facility for no less than... parole eligibility in four years... registration as a sex offender..."

JT let out an explosive breath. "Where'd you get this, Lauren?" His voice was unusually quiet.

"One of the caches from the second day's competition. It got soaked, so I didn't read it 'til this morning."

A look of surprise crossed Juan's face. "A rapist, a child molester. And clearly, Julian knew." He tapped the letter with the back of his other hand. "He's telling us."

Lauren glanced at Natalie, seeing no surprise at all in her expression.

JT got up and walked to the big front window, rubbing the back of his shaved head. His voice was pitched high, incredulous.

"What kind of fucked-up reality show is this?"

CHAPTER 76

In the Greek Revival house, the blue team was gathered around the monitor. Camilla sat next to Jordan, peering at her in concern. "You could be—I don't know—bleeding internally, or something," she said. "Please let Brent have a look at you."

Jordan shook her head. She was acting like a stubborn little girl, and Camilla knew how to deal with those. She changed the subject.

"You're way ahead of everybody," she said. "What are you going to do with the money if you win?"

"*When* I win." Jordan looked away.

"When you win. How will you spend it?"

"I don't know. I don't care about that." Jordan rubbed her stomach. "For me, it's never been about the money." Her megawatt smile reappeared, eyes sparkling with enthusiasm, and Camilla felt her own excitement return. Maybe she was being too much of a worrywart. She sneaked a glance at the scoreboard:

WINNING TEAM

Juan	J T	Lauren	Travis	Natalie
43	34	18	13	9

Jordan	Brent	Camilla	Mason	Veronica
53	28	26	24	20

At least she was still in the top five, and she wasn't going to be naive anymore. Teams didn't matter; it was every person for herself. She had dropped the ball today fooling herself about that, but tomorrow she was going to play harder, smarter. Her kids were counting on her. They really had no one else to fight for them. She pictured Avery's tear-streaked face, Cassie's sullen stares, Ellie, Davey—all of them. By taking their parents, life hadn't played fair with them, had it? She was here to try to make up for that. So why should *she* play fair?

Jordan was going to be very, very hard to beat, but even if she won, that might be all right, too. If she didn't care about the money, then maybe Camilla could convince her to care about something else. What if Jordan joined the foundation's board? What a spokesperson she would make for the kids! And as a journalist, she could get their stories out, find people who wanted to help.

Camilla laid a hand on Jordan's arm. "I've got an idea I'd like you to think about. You don't have to answer now…"

The room brightened, and Julian appeared on the monitor.

Sitting on Jordan's other side, Veronica held up a warning hand. "Quiet, everybody."

Their host smiled at them from the screen, looking relaxed. "I must give my congratulations to today's winning team," he said. "You all played very hard out there. A gripping contest—our most exciting day yet. Team spirit was strong.

"But there are also the individual gains and losses." His eyes roamed the room. "It's at this point that the winners start to sort themselves from the losers. Look around you, at your fellow players. One of you will walk away with five million dollars. Ask yourselves the question: 'Will it be me? Or them?'

"The winning team's points are now secure, and this gives them some advantage in future competitions. But for members of today's losing team, if you push yourselves, you can easily overcome the edge the other team's victory has bought them.

"And now, since last night's contestant profile was such a hit," Julian said, "we bring you another one. She's a steadying influence, a quiet source of calm strength for us all. Let's find out who she is, what she's had to overcome to become the person we see today."

Camilla blew out a breath as the screen went blank. She wasn't ready for this. She could *never* be ready for this. Her thoughts whirled and collided.

Not me, please not me. Let it be anyone but me.

The face that appeared on the screen wasn't hers. Her pounding heart slowed as she stared in surprise.

On-screen, a teenage girl of 16 or 17 raised a middle finger at the camera. The photograph was slightly faded but still clear enough. A black Goth-rock T-shirt stretched tight across her chest: an image of rock star Marilyn Manson in an obscene pose. Rips and holes tattered the shirt and the cutoff jean shorts she wore, deliberately exposing broad areas of skin. The girl's hair was tar black and cut short in a spiky wild shag. Pale makeup caked her sneering face, and a half-inch silver hoop pierced one nostril. Thick black eye shadow and mascara surrounded piercing silver-blue eyes that burned with fierce anger. An hour earlier, Camilla had stared into those same eyes and seen that same fury in them.

"Veronica Ross grew up in San Francisco's Sunset district," Julian said in a cheery voice. "As a teen, she had frequent run-ins with the law and spent time in several juvenile detention facilities."

"...about which the court records were sealed. Making this illegal." Veronica's voice sounded calm, but her hands were trembling. She stared at the floor and raised her knees to her chest.

Jordan reached over and gripped one of Veronica's hands. She squeezed back but didn't look up as Julian continued.

"Unlike many troubled teens, Veronica was able to turn her life around. She found stable employment and built a life for herself, studying toward her nursing degree at night."

The picture changed to show a waitress in her early twenties taking an order outside a sidewalk café: Camilla recognized the North Beach location. Veronica's hair was dark blond—her natural color, probably—and her waitress dress was short, showing off her toned legs. Her smile looked genuine.

"Veronica's first marriage, to Dominic Taylor, was not a happy one." The monitor showed Veronica in a white wedding dress, standing next to a handsome, dark-haired man in a tuxedo. "Local police found themselves frequent visitors to the Taylor household. Hospitalized twice in what was clearly a pattern of domestic violence, Veronica always refused to press charges.

"One January night in 1998, following a Super Bowl party at the Taylors', things took a tragic turn. Police officers, summoned by a neighbor's complaint, found Dominic dead of multiple wounds sustained from a kitchen knife. Veronica required hospitalization for her own extensive injuries and was taken into custody after treatment." An arrest photo showed Veronica's bruised face, one eye swollen shut, stitches extending below her hairline. She held the traditional mortarboard with booking number and department information.

"Given the history of abuse that officers could attest to, the judge was very sympathetic to her case. Veronica was charged with involuntary manslaughter. She performed extensive community service at a local women's shelter and her sentence was suspended.

"There was one happy outcome from her terrible experience. Over the course of the trial, she and one of the police officers from her case became very close. A year later, the young widow married SFPD rising star Leo Cannetti." A second wedding photo showed a laughing Veronica in a stunning wedding dress, hair longer now, smearing cake into the face of her grinning groom.

Veronica sat watching herself on the screen. She wore a distant, icy expression, but it looked as though she was struggling hard to hold her composure. Tendons stood out on her arms and in her neck, and the hand that Jordan wasn't holding trembled in her lap.

Despite the way Veronica had treated her yesterday, Camilla hated to see her suffer this way. Julian's mocking tone was so cruel, making fun of her personal tragedy. This was as bad as Brent's profile had been, and they were all just sitting here letting it happen.

"I'm turning this off," Camilla said, standing up.

"Leo and Veronica were married for ten years," Julian continued. "The life of a police officer is a stressful one, and sometimes that can spill over into family life, but the couple seemed very happy together. It was not to last, however."

Camilla crossed the room with rapid strides. She inspected the frame of the monitor, but there wasn't an obvious off switch. Reaching up, she ran her hands along the top and sides but found nothing there, either.

"In December 2010, Leo was killed in the line of duty," Julian said. "Following up a lead in a current case, he visited a confidential informant after hours. What transpired is unclear, but Leo and his informant were each struck by several shots fired at close range by an unknown assailant. Leo died at San Francisco General without regaining consciousness, and Veronica found herself a widow again. To this day, the case remains unsolved."

Grabbing the corner of the monitor to yank it down from the wall, Camilla realized she was too late. Julian's voice trailed off into silence and the screen went dark, so she dropped her arms and faced her teammates once again.

Veronica let out the breath she had been holding. She stared at the blank screen, avoiding everyone's eyes. Jordan put her other hand on Veronica's shoulder.

Brent sat staring with a stony expression, his hands in his vest pockets. Camilla was sorry now that she hadn't supported him yesterday. This was obscene.

"We can't let Julian treat us like this," she said. "It has to stop. We need to stand up for each other and tell him—"

There was a loud static pop behind her, and the monitor lit up again.

The scene it now showed was the luxurious salon of the megayacht. Camilla could see herself and the other contestants sitting around the long table, smiling, laughing, joking with one another. The sight jarred her, seeing the excitement and anticipation on all their faces, on her own face grinning wide-eyed from the screen. Everyone looked so happy. Only three days ago, but it already seemed like a distant memory, impossible to reconcile with the depression and misery that weighed her heart now.

The scene shifted to a different view of the same room. Juan and Jordan filled the foreground now, standing next to the bar, dressed in their dinner-party clothes. In the background fifty feet away, Camilla could see herself and everyone else at the table. Juan's voice was low, but the hidden microphone had amplified the sound well.

"Okay, ready?" he said on-screen. "Let's make this look good."

Camilla's jaw dropped.

The on-screen Jordan giggled quietly, a hand over her mouth. Then she composed her face into an angry expression and put her hands on her hips.

Juan held up a finger and looked toward the table where they all were gathered. A grin was visible on his face, too. Then he turned back and raised his hands.

"That's not what I meant at all," he said in a loud voice. "It's not what I was saying. You didn't let me finish." He reached to take Jordan's arm. "Stop overreacting."

On the monitor, she shook his hand off violently. "Get your fucking hands off me, asshole! You're on your own." She stormed away, toward the table.

The monitor went blank.

Veronica abruptly jerked her hand out of Jordan's. She didn't take her eyes off the screen, but her mouth pulled into a thin line. Her nostrils flared. Camilla was afraid of what she might do next if that icy control gave way.

Jordan got up slowly, and Camilla turned to stare at her. Her friend—no, a friend would never do this—the *blonde woman* met her eyes. Jordan looked just as shocked as Camilla felt. A rushing noise rose in her ears, drowning out the sound of Mason's laughter. She had been stupid, stupid, stupid. So trusting, so gullible.

The scoreboard reappeared.

Jordan's eyes flitted from face to face.

"Guys," she said softly, "I think I'm going to go upstairs now."

"You're not welcome here anymore," Camilla said. "Get your bag and leave."

Brent's voice was milder. "I do think it would be best if you found somewhere else to stay from now on, Jordan."

"Guys," Jordan said. "Listen…"

Veronica's eyes were still fixed on the blank monitor, but her voice was jagged with broken glass and razor blades.

"*Get out.*"

CHAPTER 77

Juan was on his feet. So were JT and Lauren. He faced the two of them, watching their expressions but aware of their hands, too. He had to be careful here.

Lauren's hands bunched into fists, opened, and clenched again.

"I am trying really hard, Juan," she said. "*Real* hard. But I can't come up with an innocent explanation for what we just saw. Maybe you can help us out here? Because you gotta admit, it looks pretty bad."

JT stared with eerie calmness, his features frozen in a mask of mild curiosity, as if he was waiting for Juan to explain something that puzzled him. It was quite scary, actually, because of the way veins bulged on JT's neck and forehead.

"All day long," Lauren said. "Back and forth, you and that Barbie-doll bitch racking up the points with your bullshit grudge match. I guess we should have caught on sooner, but hey, we were all a little preoccupied."

JT shifted positions. Juan watched his shoulders, readying himself to move fast. They were angry, and angry people were unpredictable.

"Tell me," Lauren asked, "is Travis a part of your little charade, too?"

Without relaxing his guard, he shook his head.

"Don't say a word." She pointed at the door. "You want to leave right now, Juan. Before JT kills you." Her voice cracked. "Or before I do."

• • •

Juan walked out the front door of the red team's house, carrying his duffel bag in one hand and his jug of water in the other, with the case containing the EPIRB beacon tucked under his arm. Squinting into the late afternoon brightness, he spotted Jordan waiting in the middle of the yard, her travel bag and a jug at her feet. She raised a hand to shade her eyes, then struck a hipshot pose and stuck out her thumb like a hitchhiker.

Juan grinned.

"Come on," he said. "I know where we can stay."

She laughed out loud. "You would, wouldn't you?"

He led her over the seal barricade and past the three warehouse buildings and ruined catchment basin with its dome, to the small concrete blockhouse that stood isolated from the other buildings. The steel door had a solid latch and a heavy padlock. He fished a key from his pocket. Then he stopped and looked at her, thinking.

She raised her eyebrows. "What?"

"Give me a minute," he said.

Unlocking the blockhouse, he stepped inside, pulling the padlock out of the latch as he went by. Why take an unnecessary chance?

Leaving Jordan outside, he swung the door shut. The windowless blockhouse was dark, but it had been even darker the last time, at night. He had memorized the layout.

He slid his hand along the rough wood cabinet top until his fingers closed around the hilt of a dive knife. Feeling along the rough wood, he located a handle and crouched to open the cabinets below.

The dive knife had a flat chisel tip instead of a point. Working by touch alone, Juan used it to pry up one of the cabinet's floorboards. He probed the six-inch gap between the cabinet's base and the concrete floor, finding enough space for what he needed.

Still working blind, he opened other cabinets, feeling around inside. He stashed everything he found within the hiding space he had made.

Another thought occurred to him. He crossed the blockhouse and crouched near the wall, sweeping his hands along the ground until he located the pile he remembered. Sorting through the things his fingers brushed against, he collected an armful of soft, rubbery objects and slipped these inside the hiding place as well. Then he lowered the cabinet floorboard into place again, using the pommel of the dive knife to hammer it until it was wedged tight, and closed the cabinet doors.

Jordan would be getting impatient by now.

He walked to the door and swung it open, letting light into the blockhouse.

Jordan strolled in, pulling her travel bag. She stopped in the center of the room and turned in a complete circle, almost twirling.

"The presidential suite, I see. You take me to all the nicest places."

Juan reached outside for his duffel and dropped it inside the door. He slid the EPIRB beacon case onto the cabinet top. The countertop work surface ran the length of one wall, its rough cabinets painted an ugly green. A flimsy yellow tube-steel-and-formica table stood against the wall, surrounded by three lightweight plastic chairs. A pair of wooden cots anchored the blockhouse's far corners—makeshift wooden frames covered by threadbare blankets. Closer to the door, a pair of sawhorses supported a ten-foot board: a drying rack. Several black wet suits hung from the rack above a pile of equipment on the floor: dive fins, gloves, dive knives in scabbards, collection bags, a speargun.

Jordan dragged her bag over to one of the cots and sat down. She rolled onto her stomach and propped her chin on her hands, facing him, kicking her ankles up behind her. Her feet were bleeding again, he noticed.

"They forgot to put the champagne on ice," she said.

"The Four Seasons it's not."

"How did you know this was here?"

"The night after we cleaned out the houses, I did some exploring."

A hopeful look crossed her face. "Did you find some food?"

Juan shook his head.

Suddenly, she was crying. "Oh my god, Juan. I'm so hungry. I'm dizzy and my head hurts. What am I going to do?" Tears streamed down her cheeks. She pointed in the direction of the warehouse buildings. "I'm sure Julian wants me to go pound on his door and beg, but I won't do it. I can't quit, especially now."

Her eyes were so green. Juan liked looking at them. He didn't say anything.

Just as abruptly as she had started crying, Jordan stopped. She regarded him curiously.

"O-kay, then," she said.

Neither of them spoke for several minutes.

Jordan looked at the wet suits. "Can you catch me a fish?"

He thought about it, watching her face.

Her mouth curled into a smile. "Any time now, my chivalrous knight."

"No air tanks," he said. "And no fish close to shore, because of all the seals."

"Crabs? Lobster?"

Juan shook his head again. He walked over to the wet suits and picked up something from the floor. Time to find out how badly she wanted this.

"I'll get you something to eat," he said. "But don't expect it to be pleasant."

Her eyes widened as he slid a narrow stainless-steel shaft into the long barrel of the speargun. Sunlight glinted on the sharp point with its vicious barbs. He stepped into the doorway.

"No," she said in a small voice. She shook her head. "Oh, no, I don't think so."

"You've got to eat. It's been three days. Wait here for me."

Jordan stood up, and the color drained from her face. She walked across the room and put her hands on the counter. Her back was to him, but he could read the tension in her arms and shoulders. Throwing her head back, she stood there for a long moment, arms trembling. Her breath hitched.

Moment of truth, he thought. *Let's find out who you really are.*

Then she was coming toward him fast, stopping in the doorway next to him. One slim hand wrapped the barrel of the speargun, and she raised her chin, thrusting her face toward his.

From inches away, Jordan's eyes held his. Cool and arrogant. Unsmiling green steel.

"Give me that and get out of my way," she said. "I'll do it myself."

CHAPTER 78

Travis stood in the darkened hallway, rubbing his wrists. He stayed in the shadows, watching Lauren through the archway. Half-Chinese bull dyke was just sitting there, with her head in her hands. JT moved across his field of view, pacing. Big black dude looked pumped, pissed off—but not half as pissed as Travis was.

His hands still tingled—the duct tape around his arms had cut off the blood flow for hours. It had taken most of the day to work free, scraping himself against the rock.

Staying hidden, he watched his former teammates. He knew that Natalie was in there with the others, hiding in the corner. He had heard the shouting earlier and seen Juan exit, so it was just the three of them in there. Travis wasn't entirely clear on why they had kicked Juan out. But it would make things easier, because he knew one other little Judas who had also turned against her own team—and who was now keeping quiet about what she had done.

He remembered how the little bitch's eyes had followed him as Mason rolled him off the bluff. No expression, as if she were watching Mason drop a bag of garbage into a dumpster. She had said nothing to the rest of the team while Travis lay trussed and helpless in the cave's darkness for hours.

He shivered, rubbing his arms. Being tied up like that had brought back unpleasant memories. His mind had drifted away for a while, and he was back in the narrow darkness behind Cell Block 4's laundry machines. The noise of the washers had been very loud, thudding and rattling next to his head. They had masked the sounds of violence, the laughter and grunts, and Travis's screams. The guards had known exactly what was happening, but they waited several hours before pretending to discover him, bleeding and half dead. The prison infirmary was not equipped to deal with the extent of his internal injuries, so they had rushed him to an outside hospital for surgery—almost too late to save his life.

But after he had healed, inside and out, he had gotten payback. If there was one thing Travis believed in, it was payback. One at a time, he had gotten to all of them, paid them back with interest. Always when they were alone, not expecting it.

He had put Deacon in a wheelchair for life. Angel had lost both hands in the machine shop while Travis whispered into his ear. The bleach had torn DelRay's insides apart. And Plug now spent his days in a low-security ward, staring sightlessly out the window and drooling. Nothing could be proved, but word got around, and nobody had messed with Travis after that.

After making parole, he had tracked down Lyle, the shift guard, too. He wouldn't be rattling any more cell bars with his baton. Lyle's baton was buried in the mud at the bottom of the Sacramento Delta now, wedged inside Lyle himself.

Travis thought of Natalie. That little bitch, he knew exactly what to do with. He'd take his time with her. She might even enjoy it.

Then he pictured Mason's grinning face. *I got something* you *might like, too.*

His fist tightened around a handle wrapped in layers of the same duct tape Mason had tied him with, and he looked down at the shiv he had sharpened out of a split piece of steel rebar.

Four inches of jagged, rusty metal projected from his fist.

CHAPTER 79

Juan knelt at the base of the concrete seawall, making the fire.

Jordan held the little seal's lifeless body in her arms. She sat cross-legged on the ground with her back to Juan, rocking soundlessly back and forth, looking away. The steel spear still protruded from the seal's neck, and her clothes were soaked with its blood. For some reason, she didn't want Juan to see her face right now. He felt an unfamiliar tightness in his stomach every time he looked at her.

The fire crackled, its orange tongues dancing as he fed it a dry piece of driftwood. The seawall sheltered it from the wind. Juan was very aware of the boarded-up factory building directly behind them, its featureless two-story facade looming over his shoulder.

I know you're watching us right now, Julian. You and I will talk soon. You know things you shouldn't, and you're going to tell me how. And why.

He stepped over to Jordan, and she turned her face away from him. Was that wetness glistening on her cheek? Kneeling beside her, he gently tried to take the seal from her. She hugged it tighter to her chest, shaking her head stubbornly. But she still refused to look at him.

Juan shrugged and handed her the dive knife. Then he stood up and walked away.

CHAPTER 80

Lauren sat on a rocky slab at the island's highest point, beside the wreckage of the lighthouse tower. Año Nuevo Point was visible a half-mile away, across the wave-churned strait that separated the island from the California coast. JT sat behind her, facing the other way, not saying anything. She leaned back against his broad, muscular back. He felt solid, dependable, and rock steady behind her, and she needed that right now.

The setting sun painted the dunes of the beach and the rocky bluffs around them with its orange light. The water was a little calmer today, gleaming silver in the oblique rays of sunset. Patches of sea grass and coyote bush waved in the gentle wind that ruffled her hair. She reached down, running her fingers through the dirt.

On the beach, looking small in the distance, the seals were oddly quiet. They did that around sunset, it seemed, and the island became relatively peaceful for an hour or two. Lauren found Año Nuevo's rugged and barren beauty taking her by surprise. She tried to relax and forget about everything that had happened, enjoying JT's silence and his company. His mood was different now. It had scared her earlier, the way he had gone all calm and ready, eyeing Juan with dark, speculating looks. She had kicked Juan out because she was angry, but she had also done it to protect him from JT. She had been afraid of what might happen if he stayed any longer.

"Natalie's moving to the other building," she said.

"Makes sense." JT's muscles shifted against her back, his lats flexing. "If I was her, I wouldn't want to stay near Travis."

"I've been thinking about what Brent was saying last night. If he's right, putting someone like Travis in the show might make sense, although it's really sick."

"Just 'cause the doc lied to us don't mean he's wrong."

"And Veronica. Christ! She killed her first husband ten years ago. *Knifed* him. But you'd never know it—she looks like a Menlo Park soccer mom now. Scary."

JT didn't say anything, but she felt him nod.

"There's some reason they picked these people," she said. "Julian said they screened thousands. Some reason they picked us, too. What were they looking for?"

"Hardcore competitors," he said.

"Really? *Natalie?*"

"Okay, people willing to take chances, maybe. People who aren't going to quit or cry foul when the game gets rough."

"Somebody's going to get hurt or killed here." She closed her eyes. "I've seen it happen before. This feels exactly like it did then."

JT turned his head. She could see the side of his face, his eyes roaming the shore. "You said you had a climbing accident," he said. "What happened?"

Lauren looked out at the water, knowing she had to talk about this. History was repeating itself here. And she felt comfortable with JT. If anyone could understand what she'd been through, it was probably the big ex-Marine. She leaned her head back against his hard, shaved skull.

"I got my American Mountain Guides Association certification six years ago," she said. "Started teaching rock climbing in Yosemite, but the Valley was too tame for me. I was good, JT. Really, *really* good. A couple of the other instructors—buddies of mine I was tight with—we always used to talk a big game, how we were going to do some adventure travel, tackle some really exotic walls together. The whole Yosemite scene had become like Disneyland, crowded with tourists, day-trippers—a real circus. Climb a half mile of granite, you don't want to look down and see a traffic jam of Winnebagos and minivans. The three of us, we were ready to step up to the big leagues, make a name for ourselves.

"One of the crew, Matt… he cooked up this crazy trip to the Baltoro Glacier in Pakistan. At first it was just campfire talk, but we kept egging each other on. Then he actually got the permits, and suddenly it wasn't a joke anymore. We were going to do this thing—blaze a new route up Trango Tower, come back celebrities. How hard could it be, right?

"Next thing I knew, we were in Pakistan, on the road from Islamabad to Skardu. A twenty-eight-hour bus ride, but nobody could sleep. Matt kept talking names—climbers who'd pioneered famous routes. It was going to be talk shows for us. We'd write books, get gear endorsements. But by the time we were actually trekking into Paiju, after seven more hours of bumping along in a jeep, reality was starting to sink in."

Lauren's eyes went out of focus as she remembered how it had been. Her chest was starting to tighten.

"This was a whole different ball game than we were used to. JT, these mountains were *bigger. Much* more intimidating. Jagged, pointy peaks like shark's teeth. Covered with giant ice fields, cracks the sun never reached.

"All the climbers we passed were world class. They made us feel like amateurs. After the first couple of conversations, we stopped telling anyone what we were planning. But for each other, we were still putting on a brave face. I wasn't going to be the one to back out, and neither was Matt, and neither was Terry."

"Trango Tower itself was like nothing I'd ever seen before. This giant granite finger pointing into the sky, as tall as a couple of El Capitans stacked on top of each other. Sheer drops on every side. We were in way over our heads, and I knew it. So did Matt and Terry, but we kept talking ourselves into it. We'd be okay as long as we were extra careful.

"I almost backed out on the last day's approach to the Tower. Even getting to the base was hairy, trekking across a glacier and then the couloir, avoiding crevasses, constantly watching for rockfall. We couldn't breathe properly—hadn't acclimated to the altitude—and we hadn't even started to climb yet."

"As things were, we actually got fairly far up before the accident. We started up the southeast face—a route called Eternal Flame. Terry was the weakest climber of the three of us, so Matt and I traded off leads for the first few days. I was terrified the whole time, but I told myself that was good—it would make me careful. I think the others were telling themselves the same thing. We almost made the summit, JT.

"It all came apart for us on the fifth day."

Lauren stopped and took several deep breaths. Oh Christ, her chest was so tight her back hurt. Pressing her spine against JT, she forced herself to go on.

"It was bound to happen. The three of us really had no business being up on Trango. Terry popped off a foothold and his arms were pumped, shaky from the altitude and four days on the rock. He came off the face. But he'd also been sloppy—hadn't placed enough protection to hold his weight in a fall. He peeled Matt, and then me, off the wall with him. My pro held all three of us. We bounced off the face a few times, dangling from the ropes. Matt and Terry were both killed in the fall.

"I was luckier, but I'd cracked three ribs and ruptured my spleen. I'd also hit my head hard. The helmet saved my life, but I had a skull fracture and a concussion, and hanging upside down didn't help things any.

"When a climber falls in Yosemite, a couple hundred people see it happen. Rescuers are on their way before you stop swinging. A helicopter scoops you up and whooshes you to a hospital. But we weren't in the Valley. We were in the middle of Bum-fuck Nowhere, in a remote corner of Pakistan, and the southeast face of Trango can't even be *seen* from any of the camps below.

"JT, I hung there upside down for two days. The nights were awful. I don't remember most of it. But there's worse."

She was going to throw up. Her back was shaking now, her arms. She could manage only a whisper.

"Even after I got right side up again, I couldn't pull myself up the rope to get back onto the rock. Matt's and Terry's bodies were three hundred fifty pounds of dead weight hanging on the line attached to my harness, dragging me down. It was windy, and *cold*—we swung and twirled against the face like a wind chime. I knew I was going to die. I had no choice."

Her chest heaved. Once, twice. She was going to puke for sure. Why didn't he say something, anything at all?

"I cut them loose. Oh Christ, I cut 'em loose. I *had* to. Their bodies fell thousands of feet to land somewhere on the rocks and ice below—they were never recovered. I watched them go, getting smaller and smaller until I couldn't see them anymore. Then I jumared up the rope—a hundred, hundred twenty feet. I was in a lot of pain, but after dozens of rappels off shit anchors, I managed to make it down off the face. Alone. I think I was hallucinating the whole way down."

Lauren gritted her teeth, clamping down on a whining sound that wanted to escape from her throat. Her hands were shaking. She put them in her lap and knotted her fingers together, forcing the words out.

"I kept seeing Matt or Terry. They'd be right below me or above me on the wall, not moving, watching me go by. Sometimes they would talk to me, but mostly they just looked at me, and there was something wrong with their eyes.

"I don't remember too much after that. There was a Polish team at the base. They got me out of the mountains, and the embassy flew me back home, where I spent three weeks in the hospital.

"And I lied to you when we first met, JT. I haven't done any real climbing since the accident."

She took a deep breath, and her face pinched together. But she felt relief, too, as if she had puked out something rotten—something that had been choking her, poisoning her inside. JT stayed silent, but that was all right now. He hadn't stiffened up, hadn't pulled away from her. Feeling his deep, slow breaths through her back, she felt a swelling of gratitude toward the big lug, knowing that he was thinking about what she'd said. Maybe together they could figure something out, because things were going to shit here, fast, and if they didn't do something about that, people were going to end up dead.

JT spoke. He sounded tired, older, to Lauren.

"My second tour in Afghanistan ended when our chopper got shot down over the Korengal." He didn't say anything for a while after that, and she thought of the pink network of scars she had seen, traced across his shoulder and left arm.

"Some tribesman hit the pilot with a lucky shot from the ridgetop. Copilot was hungover, in no condition to fly, so even though we'd logged him as flight crew, he stayed back on base. Long story short, the chopper went down the next valley over, about ten klicks outside the pacified zone."

"We came down hard. My arm was busted in two places—open fractures, bones sticking through the skin. Scapula was shattered; they had to screw it back together—final screws just came out last year. My face was all bashed up, lots of other little shit, but I was in good shape compared to the others. Three other guys survived the crash. It was pretty clear DiMarco wasn't going to make it. He was messed up real bad—just about cut in half. Collins's back was all fucked up, and one of his legs. Sanchez—he was this nice kid—both his legs were busted bad. All three were conscious, but they couldn't walk. I didn't know whether to go try to get help or stay there with my squad mates, but I had to decide fast. In that valley, the smoke from the crash was going to draw the wrong kind of attention *real* quick."

She felt him shifting behind her, and turned her head again to see him staring across the water. A muscle twitched in his jaw.

"Toughest decision I ever made, leaving my guys. But they knew it and I knew it—we were all going to die if I stayed. This way, there was a chance."

The muscle in his jaw twitched, smoothed out, twitched again.

"Three days in that heat, my arm got infected—swelled up like a sausage. Talib were looking for me... knew I was out there. Once they even found me, but I got the dude with a rock—pancaked his head before he could yell for his buddies. Eventually, I stumbled across the One-sixtieth, running a patrol. Spooked 'em—after making it through all that, I almost got shot by our own guys.

"Maybe being in a situation like that changes you somehow, I don't know. Maybe it doesn't. Maybe it just lets you find out who you were all along, what you're capable of doing to survive."

Lauren nodded to herself, staring into her lap. There was nothing more to say. Without looking up, she reached out to the side and found JT's hand on the ground beside them. He laced his fingers thru hers. Neither of them said anything. They just sat there, back to back, watching the sun's rays fade and the shadows lengthen around them.

Day 5

Tuesday: December 25, 2012

"Belongingness," Julian said. "Being part of a community, tribe, or family. These group-focused survival needs form the third level of Maslow's hierarchy."

Camilla watched their host on the monitor. She kept her gaze away from the doorway, where Jordan and Juan now stood like uninvited guests.

"Look what the cat dragged in," Veronica had said when they showed up a few minutes earlier. Then she had turned her back on them, and the rest of the blue team had pretty much ignored them, also. Camilla was still angry with both of them, even though she now realized that Juan had tried to warn her yesterday.

Still, they needed to hear Julian out, she reminded herself. Listen to what he had to say first. Then, as they had discussed last night, they all would decide together what to do.

"For today's challenge," he said, "it's time to slow things down. Today's competition will be a quiet one. There will be no physical contest. Today is all about emotional intelligence instead."

Camilla exchanged a glance with Brent and relaxed. They had discussed this last night with Veronica and Mason, and the four of them had agreed: if any of them felt that what Julian proposed was too dangerous or risky, they all would refuse to play. She had watched her teammates' reactions carefully and felt that Brent was with her all the way. She wasn't too sure about Veronica, who hadn't had much to say—Julian's insensitive profile of her hung over them all like a cloud, making any conversation awkward. Mason had just grinned as usual. But he had nodded—while rubbing his injured knees, which only made her feel guilty all over again.

What Julian was talking about here sounded pretty tame, though. Even better, it sounded like a competition geared toward Camilla's own strengths. She listened closely.

"As I said, the theme of today's activity is belongingness. Gift-giving traditions have evolved in every culture, to celebrate belonging, and our little island community will be no different."

Julian's voice took on a conciliatory tone. "Yesterday things got quite intense—maybe a little out of hand, even. So relax, everyone. Merry Christmas. No teams today, no running around the island, no high-energy stuff. We'll keep it low key—just a small group of friends exchanging presents. But I warn you, you will have to think today.

"Fifty small gifts are distributed along the edge of the seal barricade. There's no time element here. For this game, it really doesn't matter which gifts you take. Just grab the first five you see, and head back—no more than five per person. Then we'll all gather for the gift exchange."

Fifteen minutes later, Camilla stood in the main room of the Victorian house, looking down at the small collection of objects she held: a plush toy— a stuffed blue cartoon Porsche with big eyes—a small pocketknife made of silver, a refrigerator magnet shaped like a Coke bottle, an elaborate platinum friendship bracelet, and a snow globe with a miniature Golden Gate Bridge inside—which was especially dumb since it never snowed in San Francisco. The gifts definitely hadn't been out there yesterday. Julian's hidden crew had been busy in the night again.

All ten contestants were gathered in the great room now. Tension buzzed in the air, but Camilla was glad to see that everyone seemed subdued and quiet today—yesterday's descent into violence must have sobered everyone. Looking around the room at the items the others held, she tried to anticipate what the game would be. Each gift was monogrammed—silk-screened or printed or engraved—with a player's name.

Each gift also had a miniature two-sided LED flashlight attached to it. Camilla flicked the switch on one, and green light splashed over her hands. She flicked it the other way, and the light glowed red. Shutting it off, she met Brent's gaze. He raised his eyebrows, looking more curious than concerned— apparently he didn't see much to worry about here, either. But she would reserve judgment until she heard the rules of the game.

She glanced at the others, reading the dynamics. Juan and Jordan were isolated from everyone else. They were unquestionably a couple now. It still hurt to see them, so she moved on.

Travis kept his distance from everyone also, focusing his gaze on the floor—like he had withdrawn into a shell. Getting electrocuted and tied up yesterday probably had something to do with it. Hopefully, he had learned his lesson. Camilla and Mason were on the opposite side of the room from Travis, but she was sticking close to Mason anyway. She never knew when he was going to say the wrong thing and get someone angry, and she felt oddly protective of him—maybe because she had injured him herself yesterday.

There was something new about Lauren and JT, too. They stood close together, shoulders brushing. Were the two of them an item now? But no, Lauren's body language looked wrong: shrunken somehow, very unlike her usual gunfighter stance. It seemed almost like she was hiding behind JT. Her face was pale, making the light freckles across her nose and cheeks stand out. Lauren's eyes moved restlessly from person to person, widening when they met Camilla's.

She was afraid, Camilla realized. No, actually, she was *terrified*.

From across the room, Lauren stared at her in a mute appeal. For help? What could have scared this tough, confident woman so badly? Camilla needed to talk to her right after the game, to get to the bottom of this. She tapped her wrist, then subtly indicated first Lauren and then herself—*let's talk later*. Lauren nodded and seemed to sag with relief.

The monitor above the fireplace lit up, and Julian smiled out at them once again.

"During our time here, we've all gotten to know each other a little, and formed impressions and opinions of one other. Today, we see how effective each of you has been at earning the acceptance and regard of your peers."

Camilla looked down at the friendship bracelet she held, and her jaw tightened: it was engraved with Jordan's name.

"But first, check the names on the gifts you hold. If any of them have your own name, you will lose an opportunity to affect another contestant's score, so now is your chance to get rid of those gifts. You have exactly three minutes to trade gifts, and then the contest begins." Julian faded from the screen.

The plush toy car that Camilla had was labeled with her own name. She turned to Mason. "I have to trade this. Do you have—" She stopped in mid sentence. "Wait a minute…"

"Shhhh." Mason grinned and handed her a pewter souvenir of London Bridge, engraved with her name on it, then pointed at the pocketknife she held, labeled with his.

She handed it to him, hiding a smile. The others might catch on, and they had only a couple of minutes to act, so she walked quickly over to Brent and Veronica. "I'll trade you Juan's gifts for Mason's gifts."

Veronica frowned at her but handed over a gold money clip inscribed "Mason," in exchange for the snow globe labeled "Juan."

All around Camilla, people were trading away the gifts with their names. She traded Natalie the Coke-bottle refrigerator magnet with Juan's name for another Mason gift: an executive bar set with delicate silver tongs, corkscrew, and ice pick. The three minutes were almost up now, so she quickly rejoined Mason, handing him the money clip and bar set in exchange for two gifts that bore her name. It was a gamble, but she was fairly sure she had seen through Julian's deviousness, and Mason figured it the same way she did. She took a deep breath.

"What are you two doing?" Veronica was staring at the gifts in Camilla's hands now, reading the names on them. Her eyes widened, and she sucked in her breath. "Oh, shit."

Heads swung toward them.

Veronica's voice rose. "I want the gifts with my name. All of them. Right now."

"Aw, fuck me!" JT got it, too.

Before anyone could move, Julian reappeared on the monitor. "Time's up. No more trading. Now we begin."

Panicky faces stared at Camilla from all around the room. Expressions darkened. At her side, Mason laughed.

"Here's how this works," Julian said. "I'll call you up to the screen, one by one. You have an opportunity to say whatever you want to the audience and to your fellow contestants. Tell them how much they've come to mean to you, make promises for the future—whatever you like. Anyone else is welcome to share, too, if they have something to say about you. Then you will receive your gifts."

On the screen, Julian held up a small teddy bear.

Anyone that holds a gift with your name will present it to you. But first they must make a choice." He turned over the bear, flipping the switch on the attached LED light to demonstrate. "A green gift will increase your score by five points. Red will reduce it by five points."

His smile turned mocking, contemptuous.

"Your fates are in each other's hands. If you find the outcome of this contest not to your liking, you have only yourself to blame for the impression you've made on your fellow contestants." Julian's image faded away, replaced by the scoreboard.

Alarm bells clanged through Camilla as she realized how ugly this was likely to get.

Julian's voice called the first name. "Jordan."

Camilla's eyes narrowed. Fist tightening around the friendship bracelet she held, she watched Jordan walk to the front of the room. Jordan's "53" dominated the scoreboard behind her. She had cheated to get it. She didn't deserve it. Camilla stared at the woman she had naively considered a friend. Right now Jordan was about to learn that what goes around comes around.

A deep voice rumbled in her ear. "Don't play into Julian's hands. This is meant to turn us against each other."

Camilla looked up at Brent in surprise. She had been so focused on Jordan, she hadn't noticed him joining her. "*She's* the one who turned on us," Camilla said. "Julian had nothing to do with it."

"Then don't give him the satisfaction of making us behave like animals for the cameras." Brent's swollen mouth made him slur a little. There was something new in his eyes: a glitteriness she didn't like. She turned her back to him and concentrated on Jordan's performance.

Jordan attempted a smile, but it died quickly when her eyes met Camilla's. She looked at her feet instead, holding her hands together before her, fingers laced—a cartoon picture of demureness. Her voice was soft and tentative.

"I'm not going to apologize for what we… what I did," she said. "All of us knew going in that this was a reality show, and we've seen enough of those shows to know it's the surprises that keep them interesting." Her eyes moved from person to person around the room.

She was *still* trying to manipulate them, Camilla realized. Bitterness rose like bile in her throat.

"When Juan and I met on the ship," Jordan said, "we both thought a secret alliance would give us an advantage. We knew it would make us entertaining to the audience, too. Even if other contestants were eliminated, we figured Julian would keep us in the running until the end, because of our secret. Instead, he outed us.

"But he's not sending anyone home, so it looks like we're all in this together until the end. I can understand if you're a little mad at me, but I hope you can see it from my perspective, too. It's just a game. We all want to win. Any of you probably would have done the same thing if you had thought of it."

Jordan bowed her head.

Camilla stepped forward with the friendship bracelet. "You were our team leader, Jordan. I looked up to you." Her throat was tight, making it an effort to speak. "We counted on you, and you betrayed us."

Jordan wouldn't look up from the floor. Her reply was a whisper. "I'm sorry, sister."

Sister? Camilla forced her fingers into motion, and red light splashed across her hands. The scoreboard behind them flickered as Jordan's score dropped to 48.

Camilla held out the bracelet. "This is for you... *sister.*"

Jordan took it from her without looking up.

A minute later, three other red-lit gifts lay at Jordan's feet, surrounding one lonely green one from Juan. Her score was now 38; she was no longer the lead player.

Julian called the next name: "Juan."

Juan stood before them all and shrugged. "Jordan said everything that needed to be said. You might not be happy about what I did. But if you were on the red team yesterday, you benefited from it."

He accepted a green gift from Jordan but drew reds from everyone else. His score stayed at 43, though. Camilla was momentarily puzzled, and then she remembered the security the red team had won yesterday.

JT was next. He rubbed a hand across the top of his head, meeting their eyes. "I guess y'all know I compete hard. It's what I was raised to do, and what the Corps trained me to do. But I play fair."

He stared hard at Juan. "Honor means something to me, compadre. *Semper fidelis*—always faithful—"

Veronica snorted. "I don't know about the rest of you, but that's enough bullshit for me." Marching up to JT, she snapped her gift to red and dropped it at his feet. Lauren and Natalie gave him green gifts, and Jordan gave him a red gift. Travis tossed a red at JT's feet. His points remained unchanged at 34—third place now—protected by the red team's security.

Brent didn't say anything when Julian called him up to the scoreboard. His injured face looked painful, like he had a mouthful of walnuts under those bulging purple lips. He accepted his gifts with a quiet dignity that gave Camilla hope. Maybe they could get through this game without further ugliness.

It was her turn next. How would the others react to what she had done?

Mason winked at her from the sidelines as she stood in front of the monitor and cleared her throat.

"I don't know if this is going to work," she said. "But Julian didn't actually *say* we had to get rid of our own gifts. I think he was being tricky. So..." Looking over her shoulder at the scoreboard, she flicked the switch on the London Bridge souvenir to light it green. Her score climbed to 31. Grinning, she moved on to her next gift, and the one after that. A moment later, her score was 46—the highest on the board.

It dropped to 41 almost immediately as something soft bounced off her knees and fell to the floor. She looked down at a plush otter—another stuffed children's toy. Red light spilled across the floorboards from a soft starfish held in its paws.

Someone had thrown it at her.

"Cheatin' little whore." Travis's dull monotone carried across the room from the wall where he leaned, sneering at her. "Making no end of trouble for yourself."

Camilla was more shocked that no one had come to her defense. No one would meet her eyes. But she hadn't cheated—she had just played smart.

Julian's voice called the next contestant's name.

Clapping her on the shoulder as he took her place with an armful of gifts, Mason addressed them all.

"Dot-com bust, subprime meltdown, government bailout—in the finance industry, we never let any of it interfere with the bonuses that we paid ourselves. So doing this feels quite natural..." He flipped four of his own gifts to green.

Veronica had the bad luck to draw gifts mostly from the red team. Her score plunged to 5. The scoreboard now read:

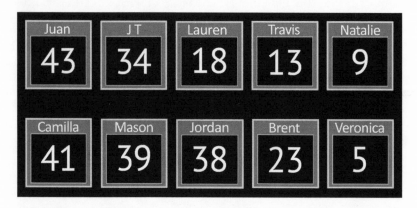

Juan	J T	Lauren	Travis	Natalie
43	34	18	13	9

Camilla	Mason	Jordan	Brent	Veronica
41	39	38	23	5

Veronica's icy gaze swept the monitor and then, bright with dislike, fixed on Camilla.

Lauren didn't say anything when it was her turn, accepting her gifts—mostly red—without comment. Because she was a member of the red team, her score was also secure and didn't change. She seemed relieved to retreat to her spot next to JT again. Camilla was eager to talk to her, to find out what was wrong.

"Travis," Julian called out.

Sauntering up to the monitor, Travis rubbed the triangle of beard on his chin. He looked over his shoulder at his score and nodded. "I guess what I say about myself right now don't really matter overmuch. My score can't go down—there's really not all that much room for it to go down, besides. And I'm betting you good people ain't exactly looking to help me push it up. So there it is."

His flat gaze slid over Camilla and Mason to stop on Natalie.

"So instead I'll talk about someone else," he said. "Blondie and *el capitan*, they weren't the only two that betrayed their teammates yesterday. What those two did, sure, it's sneaky as hell, but I can get myself past it. I don't blame 'em for it, really. Maybe any of us woulda' done the same. But what do y'all say about somebody who sucker-punches a teammate from behind with a stun gun and hands 'em over to the other team? Leaves 'em tied up, hurt, and in pain all day without saying anything?"

He pointed an accusing finger at Natalie.

"This one here's a little scorpion, a poisonous spider. Don't let her quiet act fool you—she's a vicious, coldhearted, nasty little cunt. I even offered to help her out earlier, and that's how she repaid me—"

"You piece of shit!" Natalie shouted. She took three steps forward, arms straight at her sides, hands clenched into fists. "I know what you are, Travis. I saw it right away." She drew a gulping breath. "I'll kill you if you even come near me again." Natalie's whole body was trembling now. "I'll *kill* you!"

"Whoa!" Brent stepped between her and Travis, holding up his hand. "What's going on here?" he demanded.

"I'll tell you." Lauren pushed off the wall and strode forward. "Travis here is a child molester. He's a convicted rapist who just got out of prison."

Without taking her eyes off Travis, Camilla reached back and grabbed Mason's wrist. They were in *way* over their heads here. She squeezed hard, willing him to be silent and not make things worse.

Travis spun on Lauren. "Someone's been lying to you, you f—"

"Fuck you." She stepped up into his face. "I want you off my team, and I want you off this island—right now, you fucking dirtbag."

Mason's laughter rang out, loud and gleeful in the sudden silence.

Travis froze.

Oh god, here we go. Camilla tried to block Mason with her body, but he slipped his wrist free and stepped closer.

"This is so Jerry Springer of us," he said. "Sharing our feelings—I'm getting all warm and fuzzy inside. I do have a quick question, though—"

"Mason, stop." Camilla grabbed his arm again.

"I've always wondered…" He was grinning at Travis now. "I've heard child abusers have a rough time in prison, that they usually get a dose of their own medicine from the other inmates. On the *receiving* end. Can you comment on that, Travis? Is it true?"

Travis's face went white.

Camilla pulled a laughing Mason away, shoving him behind her, as Travis launched himself toward them.

Her vision blurred for a moment; then she realized she was sitting on the floorboards. Feet moved around her, scuffling. Shouts rose above her. She raised a hand to her face, where the sensory memory of a dull thud was just registering, and her eyes widened in shock as red wetness doused her fingers. A sharp ache spread through her cheekbones, concentrated in the center of her face. Her nose.

Arms and legs thrashed against the floor in front of her: Travis and Mason on the ground, Travis on top, elbows flailing as he drove punch after punch into Mason's face. Mason cowered, trying to ward off the blows with his forearms. His glasses flew off and smashed against the wall.

All around them, people crowded forward to intervene.

Camilla rolled onto her hands and knees. Blood pattered onto the weathered floorboards beneath her face. Pushing forward, she squeezed through the forest of legs in front of her and grabbed one of Travis's arms. She threw her weight against his shoulder, shoving him off Mason, who scrambled clear.

"Off me, you little whore," Travis grunted, whipping his other hand behind him to yank something out of his belt. He pulled Camilla off balance, and she fell to her knees in front of him. The panicked shouts took a moment to register.

"Knife!"

"He's got a—!"

"Watch out...!"

Travis's arm whipped forward, and something shiny flashed toward Camilla's belly.

Suddenly, no one was moving anymore. Silence fell over the room.

She looked up, meeting Lauren's eyes. Lauren stared back at her, face ashen with shock—the same shock Camilla saw in the other blurry faces all around her.

Oh god, did he just stab me?

Camilla looked down.

CHAPTER 82

A jagged spur of sharpened metal trembled in midair, less than an inch from Camilla's stomach, clutched in Travis's fist. But it wasn't coming any closer. A large, dark hand gripped Travis's wrist, holding it in place, preventing the improvised blade from plunging into her belly.

JT's other fist clutched a handful of hair at the back of Travis's head, yanking his neck backward. He pulled the hand holding the blade away from her and twisted it up behind Travis's back. Lifting Travis and stepping back, he held him off the ground.

Travis's boots kicked helplessly above the floorboards. One struck Camilla in the knee. The knife dropped from his fingers and rattled onto the floor. She scooted forward and kicked it away, sending another rain of red droplets from her face onto the floorboards. Staring up at JT, she cupped a hand below her nose, feeling her palm fill with blood.

JT's expression was serene. Shoulders flexing, he yanked Travis's wrist higher and higher between his shoulder blades until a wet, ugly tearing sound echoed through the silence of the room, followed by a liquid pop.

Travis gasped, and his face went slack. JT released him to fall facedown onto the floorboards. He curled onto his side, his arm twisted behind him in an impossible position. "Oh Jesus, my shoulder," he moaned. "You broke my shoulder."

Camilla took a deep, shuddering breath, followed by another. The image of that vicious rusty spike hovering inches from her belly chased away all other thoughts.

So close. She had almost died here. It had been so close.

The shakes hit her hard.

Wrapping her arms around her shoulders, she threw her head back, trembling so violently her teeth chattered. Her lower lip curled into a grimace, making her injured face hurt. Feeling the rivulets of blood from her nose running down her chin and neck, she had to fight to keep from crying. People were talking to her, kneeling next to her. She shook like she was on a bike bumping down a rocky trail. There were hands on her shoulders, concerned faces leaning into her own. She stared at the ceiling, unable to talk without breaking down, hugging herself and shaking like she'd never be able to stop.

CHAPTER 83

Brent held the cold pack against Camilla's nose, making a light-blue blur in the center of her field of vision. Around its edges, she could see people leaving the room. The first-aid kit lay open at her feet, filled with bandages, syringes, and phials neatly laid out in their compartments. Sitting with her back against the wall, she was surrounded by discarded gifts from the abandoned game. The shakes had tapered off to an occasional shudder now. Her nose hurt, but the pressure in her swelling face bothered her more than the pain did.

Veronica knelt by her other side and squeezed her shoulder—another caring gesture—and again Camilla felt like crying. Jordan had walked out without a word, without even checking to see how she was doing, but Veronica had been there for her. The woman who had embarrassed her in front of everyone, who had patronized her and treated her so coldly, had also been the first to help her. She had hugged Camilla and held her until she stopped shaking, then helped her stand.

Veronica spoke to Brent now, over Camilla's head. "She needs an X-ray."

"I can see that." He sounded irritated.

"Doc, when you're done helping her, I think I might need a stitch or two over here." Mason's tone was cheerful despite his own facial injuries. "Don't worry, I promise not to sue."

Camilla turned her face away from Mason's voice. This was mostly his fault. Why did he derive so much enjoyment from antagonizing people—even dangerous people? As a kid, he must have gotten beaten up constantly.

Brent glowered at Mason from under his brows. "You're a real comedian. How's that working out for you, friend? I don't see anybody laughing here."

From the corner, Travis groaned and muttered something Camilla couldn't hear. Brent had immobilized his arm against his chest with a sling and given him a shot of something. JT and Lauren stood over him, arms crossed, watching him like prison guards.

But Travis didn't seem to be in any shape to do further mischief. His face was drawn, and cold sweat sheened his forehead. "Doc," he called in a weak voice. "Got something stronger? This ain't doing all that much for me."

"What'd you give him?" Veronica asked.

"Clindamycin."

She snorted. "Nothing for the pain, then. What about fentanyl? That might shut him up, and we seem to have a lot of it in there."

275

Brent frowned, and closed the first-aid kit with a snap. "Do you want to risk his going into respiratory arrest?"

Veronica's mouth pursed. "I could care less if he did, really."

The conversation back and forth over Camilla's head was starting to bother her, making her feel like a child. She was a responsible adult; it was about time she started acting like one. This wasn't really Mason's fault, as obnoxious as he had been, or even fully Travis's fault. The true blame for what had happened rested elsewhere.

"I want to talk to Julian," she said. "In person. Right now."

Brent nodded. "Something we should have done much sooner." With a crackle of knee joints, he stood up and faced the monitor screen.

"Okay, Julian, fun and games are over," he called out. "We've got a dislocated shoulder here and a nose that's almost certainly broken. Let's get some transportation double-quick and get these folks to a hospital. I also suggest you call this entire ill-conceived show a wrap right now, before you have something even worse on your hands to deal with."

The monitor remained silent. Their scores stared back at them.

Brent raised a hand to scratch the side of his head. "Did you hear me? I said we have a medical emergency here. You can be legally liable for withholding medical care from the injured—one of whom, I might add, has also demonstrated repeatedly that he poses an ongoing threat to the lives and safety of others here."

The monitor remained mute.

Holding the cold pack against her face, Camilla pushed to her feet, catching first Lauren's eye and then JT's. Making sure she had both their attention, she pointed toward the north end of the island, where the locked factory buildings stood. They looked at each other and then walked over to join her. Together, the three of them headed for the door.

"Hey!" Brent called after them. "Somebody needs to watch Travis."

"Just sedate him," Veronica said, and she walked over to join Camilla and the others. "Or JT can do his other arm, too."

Brent turned back to face the monitor. "Julian, you can't just ignore this situation and hope it goes away. Last warning."

"Forget it," Veronica said. "The idiots are back there panicking about this. Calling lawyers. That's why Julian isn't answering: they don't know what to do."

• • •

"Open up!" JT shouted. "Open the motherfucking door." He slapped the wood, but the panels were solid, tight, and flush against the frame.

Lauren held the four-foot length of pipe she had found yesterday. The heavy plug of concrete on one end made it a crude sledgehammer. Hefting it, she stared at Camilla expectantly. Whatever had scared her earlier, she seemed to be over it. She just looked angry, eager to confront Julian.

Camilla scanned the boarded-up windows of the first factory structure. No little bottles of water on the doorstep today. Instead, the blank facade seemed to be mocking them all. She nodded to Lauren. Sounding like she had a bad cold, Camilla raised her voice, loud enough to carry into the building.

"Break it down."

Shouldering JT out of the way, Lauren raised the pipe and swung it sideways two-handed, slamming it against the wood with a splintering thud. The door shuddered on its hinges, but it held. She swung again.

A crowd had gathered behind them now. Everyone was here, except for Travis. Even Juan and Jordan stood on the edge of the group, watching. Camilla faced them all and lowered the hand with the cold pack, not really liking what she was seeing on their faces.

"We're all together on this, right?" she asked. "Even if they take Travis away, it'd be crazy to go on."

Nobody said anything. Some of them wouldn't meet her eyes.

"Natalie," she said, shocked. "*You* can't seriously be thinking of staying."

"Nobody is staying." Brent powered on his phone, frowning as Lauren swung another sledgehammer blow. "It's time we involved the authorities, instead of escalating the situation ourselves like this."

He tapped at the screen, waited, then shoved it back in his pocket. "God *damn* it!" he shouted. "Right now, can *any* of you get a signal on your phone?"

Lauren wound up again, raising the pipe over her shoulder, and slammed the concrete plug against the wood. The door sagged, giving way.

"Be careful," Brent said. "We don't know who else is in there. Julian might have security people, too. They could perceive this as a threat."

"That might be smart of them," Lauren said, and swung again.

JT eased Brent aside. "We've got it from here, Doc."

With a splintering crash, the door swung wide.

Lauren stepped into the doorway.

And stopped. And stared.

The steel pipe fell from her fingers, ringing loudly against the concrete at her feet.

CHAPTER 84

Lauren wasn't exactly sure what she had been expecting to find on the other side of the door. A nervous Julian, probably, pacing back and forth with a satellite phone to his ear. Frightened camera operators sitting in front of screens showing different views of the island. Maybe even the security crew Brent was so worried about, rushing toward her. *Some* kind of activity, at least. But most definitely not the still, silent space that lay in semidarkness before her. Motes of dust floated in the air, dancing in the rays of light from the open door. The sound of her dropped pipe echoed through the emptiness within, fading into silence. She could smell a musty, closed-up odor like an old attic—the smell of long abandonment.

People were gathering in the doorway behind her. She stepped forward, moving deeper into the building's single room. Her eyes were adjusting now. She could make out some sparse furnishings: a pair of tube-frame cots and an old drainboard counter with a hole for the missing sink. Along the counter, she could see ring binders and composition notebooks, shelves of bound reports, stacks of loose papers. Rolled posters or maps lay on the tables, next to a scattering of pens and pencils. An animal skull, vaguely like a dog's, stared from atop a shelf: probably a seal. A much larger skull sat beside it, three times the size of a grizzly bear's: clearly an elephant seal. The bigger skull was strangely misshapen, fractured as if crushed in a giant vise.

Lauren's mind swirled in confusion. This was bad, finding the buildings empty. *Really* bad. After what she had found this morning, how was it even possible?

She picked up a quarter-inch-thick report from the counter, flipped open the light blue cover, and tilted the pages to catch the light from the door. A scientific report—a survey of some kind of marine wildlife. Useless. Dropping it to the floor, she headed for the back of the room, to a doorway that led into the neighboring building. She could hear a murmur of conversation rise behind her as the others examined the room she was leaving.

There *had* to be somebody in here. Maybe they were hiding.

The second building was even emptier than the first. Pencil-wide stripes of bright sunlight angled from between the boards on the windows, slicing across more cots and a rickety table with beat-up chairs.

If, the whole time, nobody had been in here…

279

Lauren's forehead tightened in confusion. She tried to think past the noisy static that was filling her head now: the voice of the fear monster, the rush of blood in her ears.

It had been lying there on her mattress, right in front of her face, blurring into focus as soon as she opened her eyes this morning. The memory of it hit her again like a punch in the gut, scattering her thoughts. Prickles ran up and down her arms and legs.

A doorway at the back of the second room led through an empty alcove and into the largest building: the two-story factory structure. She stepped through as crashing and splintering noises echoed from the rooms behind her—JT probably, breaking the boards away from the windows. Staring into the large space before her, lit only by pencil beams of light from the holes in the roof and walls, she saw dark rows of machinery. *Old* machinery—probably from a hundred years ago or more.

A cavernous two-story space lay in front of three narrow aisles running between ceiling-high clusters of gears, pipes, vents, glass-fronted needle gauges, and metal tanks like the vats in a brewery. It all looked ancient, covered with layers of dust. Nothing here had been used in decades. A ladder of wooden steps led up to a loft above the machinery, shrouded in darkness. A six-foot metal valve wheel, meant for cranking the machinery by hand, was mounted on the central block of gears, pipes, and gauges. She had no idea what it was for. But none of it mattered.

Julian wasn't here. Neither was the crew. There was no one here at all.

As the implications hit home the prickles racing over her arms and legs intensified, racing down her back, freezing her where she stood.

Her breathing locked up.

Lauren turned and pushed blindly past the others coming through the doorway. Someone asked her something, but the words were just noise without meaning now. She shoved her way back through the other two buildings, all the faces and rooms she passed registering as only a blur.

She needed to get away from the others.

She couldn't trust any of them now.

CHAPTER 85

"What do you think this was?"

Brent was looking at JT, as if he should know.

JT rubbed his palm across his chin. It was dark in here. He walked up to the nearest block of machinery, where the giant valve wheel was mounted. Leaning close, he looked at the round, glass-fronted gauges and wiped the dust off one of them with his hand.

"Somebody should go get a light."

Brent handed him a phone, and he used the screen to light up the gauge.

"Pressure gauge," he said, ticking a fingernail on the glass cover. "Needle shows PSI." He stepped back and pointed. "That big tank in there's a boiler. This part's a pump."

Handing the phone back, JT grabbed a handle on the rim of the huge valve wheel and pulled hard, his arms and shoulders flexing with the strain. The wheel didn't budge. It was frozen, rusted in place.

He grabbed it with his other hand, too, braced his legs, and grunted, straining against the resistance. It gave with a rusty creak, turning a few inches. Letting go, he stepped back and looked the machinery up and down.

"Beats me. I think I've seen something similar on old aircraft carriers, but I thought this was a lighthouse station." He raised an eyebrow and looked at Brent. "Travis could probably tell us more. But I ain't about to ask that piece of shit for anything."

Brent thrust his hands in his vest pockets and shook his head. "He's in no position to answer, anyway. I put him under before leaving—easier on all of us."

JT nodded. This was probably a good time to bring up what been worrying him all morning. He led Brent over to the wall, out of earshot of the doorway.

"Something else, too, Doc: Lauren. I think you should talk to her. She's not handling this well. Seemed fine last night, but this morning she was acting real freaky all of a sudden. Wouldn't tell me why." He rubbed the back of his head. "Girl puts on a tough front, but she's scared real bad."

"I can have a word with her," Brent said, "but it's the police we really need to be talking to at this point." He tapped his phone again and the screen lit up. "Still no signal at all. Do you think maybe they—?"

"Shine that over here." JT was staring at the section of wooden siding next to them, which held a faint sheen in the light of Brent's phone. He ran his fingers over it. "If Julian's crew isn't staying in these buildings…"

281

He rubbed his fingers together, feeling a trace of tacky detergent residue. "...then why'd they wash the walls?"

CHAPTER 86

Lauren hustled along the beach, headed north along the waterline, moving fast but without real purpose. Her heart was beating hard, her emotions in turmoil. Her arms seemed to have a life of their own, now grabbing at her hair, now slapping her thighs restlessly as she took long strides along the sand. She needed space from everyone right now, to get her thoughts under control and figure out what she needed to do.

Large, dark shapes lay on the beach just ahead: the main cluster of elephant seals. She didn't want to run into those so she swung around and headed south.

Someone had left it for her—laid it next to her face while she slept, knowing it would be the first thing she saw. Ten-point-eight millimeter red-and-gold bi-pattern, the color faded as if by long exposure to the weather, one end unraveling where a sharp knife had sliced through it.

She had recognized that rope—oh yes, she had *definitely* recognized it.

With both shaking hands entangled in her hair, Lauren reached the beach's southern end and spun about to go north again.

Who could she talk to?

Who could she trust?

She had even caught JT looking at her strangely this morning.

The factory buildings had been empty. There was no one else on the island.

Turning south again to avoid blundering into the elephant seal rookery, she stared across the strait toward the mainland.

The waves were calmer today under the gray sky, without their usual white-capped turbulence. Beckoning to her across the short stretch of open water, the beaches and bluffs of the mainland seemed close enough to touch. She shook her head, trying to clear the panic, realizing she was talking to herself.

"It's impossible—I saw them fall. I fucking *saw* them."

Something dark on the bluff above drew her attention. She looked up, and suddenly she couldn't breathe.

Near the fallen frame of the lighthouse tower, a figure stood silhouetted against the bright sky, silently watching her.

She couldn't tell who it was.

CHAPTER 87

"The way I see it, there are two possibilities," Mason said.

Camilla was still angry at him, so she didn't answer. She sat on one of the cots and picked up the first of the reports she had stacked beside her. Light streamed in through the window now, brightening the dusty room. The boards that JT had pulled away from the frame lay jumbled in a corner.

"Possibility number one: Julian is on the ship, anchored out of sight just up the coast. There's a soundstage on board, fitted with old stuff to look just like one of these rooms."

Possible, Camilla thought, but pretty unlikely. She continued ignoring Mason and thumbed open the beige cover to read the first page. The report in her hands was dated 2010, three years ago, and titled *Pinniped Population Study*. Elephant seals and sea lions. The white-bound ones were surveys of bird species. She shuffled through the pile of reports: 2012, 2011, 2009... So the station—because this had to be a remote biology station—was still in use from time to time.

"Possibility number two," Mason said. Then he stopped, letting the silence expand. He was grinning.

She found she just couldn't stay mad at him. "Okay, fine," she said. "I'll bite. Possibility number two?"

"A submarine."

"Oh god, shut up." She stood and walked to the window, pointing toward where the mainland lay hidden by the island's upslope. "I saw an old farmhouse about a mile inland, across the channel from us. Probably built around the same time as these buildings. Julian and his crew are in there."

Mason nodded. "That's what I'm guessing, too." His glasses were broken, one of the lenses shattered, the eye underneath it swollen and purple. He had an ugly cut on his chin, and bruises on his jaw and cheekbone. *What a pair we must make,* she thought. She probably had two black eyes herself: the swollen bridge of her nose was a blurry pinkness intruding on the bottom of her view.

He picked up a rolled poster and unrolled it on the counter near the window. "A submarine would have been cool, though—"

"Wait a minute," Camilla said, pointing at a scientific report that lay on the floor. Dust lay thick on the concrete elsewhere, but it was disturbed where the report had been dropped facedown, cover open. The binding on this report was blue, unlike the beige or white ones she had seen so far. Staring at it, she felt a ripple of anxiety tighten the back of her neck.

"Hand me that one," she said. "It looks different."

CHAPTER 88

L auren came to a stop and dropped her arms to her sides. She had come to a decision. She would not stand by powerless again while the situation around her spiraled further and further beyond recovery.

It felt good to take control, to take action.

Bouncing in place with nervous energy, she stared across the water at the mainland. Only three-quarters of a mile—a little longer than the swim in a sprint-length triathlon. The crosscurrent would make it more tiring, but she could do this. Easy.

Although the beach seemed extra crowded with seals today, the channel itself was surprisingly clear of them. That would make things easier for her.

She took two running steps into the surf and broke the water in a clean forward dive, surfacing just beyond the shore break to take a deep breath.

Strong kicks and even, powerful strokes of her arms carried her out into the strait.

Lauren struck out for the mainland, leaving Año Nuevo Island and its terrible uncertainties behind her.

CHAPTER 89

Mason handed Camilla the blue-bound report from the floor and then went back to the poster he had unrolled on the counter.

The blue-black corner of a photograph stuck out from between the center pages of the report. Camilla folded back the light blue cover, and her disquiet grew as she read the title page.

Año Nuevo 2011-2012 Seasonal Tracking and Predation Survey
Santa Cruz Pelagic Research Institute

Karen Anderson, PhD
Jacob Horowitz, PhD
Heather Stevens, PhD
Dmitry Kuznetsov, DSc

"You need to see this," Mason said. He was no longer grinning.

She flipped the report closed, holding her place with her finger, and carried it over to the counter to look down at the map he held spread beneath his palms. The familiar seahorse shape of the island was a blank white space in the middle, surrounded by expanding contour lines showing ocean depth. Scattered amid the contour lines, dozens of X's were jotted in pencil, with dates and coded notations beside them, clustering most densely in the channel between island and mainland.

He raised his eyes to meet hers. "There's something else out there."

"I know," she said. "Something bad."

A distant shout sounded through the open window: Jordan's voice—an urgent command, with none of her usual coquetry.

"Juan, get over here. Right now!"

Through the window, Camilla watched Juan join Jordan at the top of the bluff. She pointed at something Camilla couldn't see down below, on the beach or in the water. Raising his hand to shield his eyes, Juan stared where she was pointing. Then he grabbed her arm, and the two of them ran for the wooden stairs that led down to the beach.

Mason stared after them. "We'd have *heard* a boat..."

"Not a boat." Camilla's stomach clenched. "Lauren."

She flipped the report open to the center, where several pages of taped photographs thickened the paper. One glance confirmed what she was afraid of. Camilla turned it so Mason could see the photographs. His eyes widened.

"That's a lot of blood."

289

CHAPTER 90

Stroke, stroke, stroke, breath. Stroke, stroke, stroke, breath...

Splashing through the waves, Lauren could hear indistinct shouts. On her next breath, she looked back over her shoulder. A cluster of figures stood at the end of the elevated walkway where it projected out over the water. At the front of the group, a tall man swept his arms over his head like a railroad signalman. Juan. The cheerleader stood beside him. In front of them, Camilla—the stripe of white tape across her broken nose visible even from here—was waving her back, shouting something. Lauren couldn't make out the words. Mason was there, too, doing something weird: sticking his arms out in front of him and clapping his hands together straight up and down, with fingers hooked. Playing charades. *Have fun, buddy.*

Camilla grabbed at Mason. Jumping up and down, she pointed toward Lauren, her voice rising in pitch. She sounded hysterical now; the woman was practically *screaming*. Camilla thought swimming the channel was too dangerous? She didn't get it at all. The real danger was there on the island with her. Christ, it might even *be* her.

Others were clambering down the stairs from the bluff: JT, Brent, Veronica... It looked as though everybody wanted her to turn back. Fuck that. She switched from a three-one rhythm to two-one, speeding up.

Stroke, stroke, breath. Stroke, stroke, breath.

She couldn't trust any of them. Someone had put the carabiner in her pack. Someone had left the cut climbing rope on her pillow.

Oh Christ, she couldn't think about that—not *now*. Lauren gasped, flooding her mouth with seawater.

In her mind's eye, she could see Matt's eyes clearly, bulging in terror as he stared up the line at her, seeing the knife in her hand, realizing what she intended.

"Please don't do it, Lauren," Matt sobbed. "I don't want to die."

Farther down the rope, Terry's head hung back. His helmet was cracked, but his eyes were open too, staring at her out of his mask of blood. The glacier glistened white, a mile below his dangling feet. He shook his head from side to side, trying to speak, his eyes widening in horror as he watched Lauren slash at the line connecting the two of them to her waist harness, dragging her down.

Close to the middle of the channel now, Lauren sobbed. She pushed herself to swim even harder.

Stroke, stroke, breath, stroke, stroke, breath...

CHAPTER 91

"Fuck!" JT yelled, pushing past Camilla to grab Juan's shoulder. "She can't hear us. She's not turning back."

"She's past the halfway point." Juan changed his arm motions, waving Lauren forward.

Camilla's legs shook. She reached behind her, groping for Mason's wrist.

"She's got this," JT said. "She's got it. Go on, girl—"

The water beneath Lauren erupted.

She was lifted high into the air, carried at the front of a gray-and-white torpedo shape the size of a small aircraft. It hung suspended above the water for a frozen second, crescent pectoral fins slicing through the air as it defied gravity. Then the massive shark fell back into the water with a deafening slap that echoed off the bluffs behind them. Plumes of white spray flew skyward.

Lauren was gone.

Camilla realized she was screaming: a high, piercing shriek that rolled out of her mouth, going on and on. She was powerless to stop it. Her fingers dug into Mason's wrist.

JT dropped in front of her, knees thudding down onto the boards of the walkway. He grabbed the top of his shaved head with both hands. "Aww, hell no! Please, aww, no…"

A billowing red stain spread across the water where Lauren had disappeared.

"Oh my god." Jordan had both hands clamped over her mouth. Then she pointed. "She's still alive."

Camilla watched in horror as Lauren surfaced in the middle of the red stain, one arm flailing at the water.

Something floated on the surface at Lauren's side. At first, Camilla's mind refused to interpret what she was seeing; then she realized she was looking at Lauren's legs. Lauren's lower body was not aligned properly; it had come partially detached from her upper body, which still tried weakly to swim.

The cloud of red continued to spread, dyeing the water in a growing circle around her.

As if in the slow motion of a nightmare, Jordan's pointing finger shifted. A short distance from the struggling swimmer, a disturbance swirled the water, then a gray triangle broke the surface. Glistening in the afternoon sun, it arced slowly around Lauren. A wide gray back, like the top of a car, crested beneath the dorsal fin, followed by the towering tail.

293

Down the shore, the elephant seals were in panicked motion, humping up the beach to get farther from the water. Even the alpha bulls seemed small, clumsy, and harmless to Camilla, now that the true apex predator had announced itself.

Sickle tail sweeping from side to side in a leisurely motion, the great white shark circled its prey.

CHAPTER 92

Lauren felt her mind growing sluggish. She wasn't exactly sure what had happened, but she understood that she wasn't going to make it across now. Sounds faded, getting farther and farther away, until all that was left was a muted whoosh in her ears, like the lingering aftereffect of a loud rock concert.

She had gotten hurt somehow. Very badly hurt—the water around her was red, and she could smell the sharp metallic tang of her own blood.

Somehow, she had also gotten turned around to face the island again. As her eyesight faded, she looked at the group of darkening figures on the walkway. They seemed to be watching her, their outlines blurring.

One of them was a liar, pretending to be someone they weren't. But which of them was it?

Her last coherent thought broke apart.

CHAPTER 93

The shark circled Lauren. Her elbow splashed weakly once, twice, then stopped moving.

Mason gently pulled his wrist from Camilla's grasp. Her fingers ached, and she realized she had probably hurt him. She looked away, meeting Veronica's eyes.

Veronica's expression was hard, her mouth pursed like she had bitten something bitter. She slowly shook her head.

Brent's face was gray beneath his silver hair. He tucked his hands into his vest pockets and lowered his head, breathing heavily.

Juan released the breath he had been holding, and seemed to deflate. He put his hands on his hips and looked down at his feet.

A large seabird descended to splash at the edge of the expanding red circle around Lauren. A second bird followed, then a third. Hungry beaks snatched at scraps and tugged at loops of something floating in the water.

Camilla covered her mouth and began to weep quietly, staring at the nightmare scene unfolding in front of her.

Then the seabirds scattered, flapping away into the air again with raucous cries.

The great white shark tightened up its slow circle, moving in to feed.

"...wrongful death, caused by your studio's willful, unbelievably gross negligence." Brent stepped forward, rapping the screen of the monitor with a knuckle. "I know you can hear me, Julian. The authorities need to be notified, right now. There are eight witnesses here." He swept an arm to indicate all the contestants gathered in the central room of the Victorian house: everyone but Travis.

Everyone but Travis *and Lauren*. Camilla snuffled, wiped her running nose, and winced in pain, then looked absently at the blood on her hand. Did Julian even *know* what had just happened here?

"Every minute you delay just makes it worse," Brent said. "All of us can corroborate the fact that you were repeatedly asked to send help for an earlier medical emergency. *Repeatedly*. This is—God damn you, *somebody* answer me!"

The monitor continued to display the scoreboard, mocking them with its silence.

Veronica shook her head, fear lending added intensity to her electric gaze. "It's no good. They won't let us talk to anybody until they figure out how to spin this."

"They may not even know about Lauren," Camilla said. "Whoever's in charge over there probably turned off all the feeds the second Travis attacked me, and sent the camera crew home. They're probably sitting in a conference room somewhere with Julian, planning damage control for a few injuries—not for getting someone killed."

JT shoved Brent aside and faced the monitor.

"Listen up, you motherfuckers..." His tone was cold, cold. "Send. Somebody. Right. *Now*." Veins stood out on his forehead. "Or I'm going to come track you down. I'll find out who you are. I'll find you all. You'll pay for what happened to her—every sorry-assed one of you."

Leaning against the wall with his arm around Jordan's shoulders, Juan shook his head at JT in warning. Jordan herself looked upset, though surprisingly dry-eyed, and Camilla was struck by the memory of her tears on the day of the scavenger hunt. Shock over Lauren's death had deadened Camilla's emotions. Looking at Jordan no longer hurt. She could finally see her for who she really was: an icy beauty who could cry over her own hunger, but not over another person's death.

The monitor blinked, going black for a second; then the scoreboard reappeared.

The room went silent.

The score in one cell began to change.

It scrolled rapidly down from eighteen, spinning through the teens, then through single digits, to stop at zero. The zero blinked slowly inside its square cell.

Lauren's score.

Then Lauren's entire cell disappeared from the scoreboard, leaving only nine scores showing.

PART III

ELIMINATION ROUND

CHAPTER 95

JT dropped his tote bag on the cot and unzipped it. He looked up at the corners of the ceiling, at the walls, but it would take too long to find where the cameras were hidden, or even how many of them there were. Fuck it.

He reached into his tote and pulled out the Glock. The thick-framed polymer handgun was chambered in .45 ACP—subsonic and heavy-hitting. Keeping his finger safely outside the trigger guard, he popped the full thirteen-round mag out and eyeballed the visible round. Then he butted the magazine back into the grip's mag-well and hefted the firearm's familiar, comforting weight.

Something had scared Lauren, but that wasn't what made her run. She had run when she realized they were all alone on the island. He, too, understood what that meant.

Holding the Glock in a firing grip, he tapped the bottom of the magazine with the heel of his support hand and then racked the slide, releasing it to slam forward again. A quick press check showed the shiny brass of a chambered round. Then he raised the tail of his Hawaiian-print shirt and tucked the gun into his belt, snugged into the small of his back.

Somebody here was playing a different game than everybody else.

That person was responsible for Lauren's death.

He or she would pay for it.

JT walked out of the room and down the stairs to join the others outside.

CHAPTER 96

"Microphones. Keep your voices low." Camilla dropped the hidden camera onto the hard dirt at their feet.

The contestants stood outside in a circle, behind the two houses. The dark, moldering eaves and empty windows loomed over them, bearing silent witness. Everyone stared at the black object she had thrown down. A square plastic wafer with a shiny dome of glass in the center, it was connected by short wires to a plastic cube and a tiny metal cylinder. Lens, antenna and battery—the entire assembly would fit inside a matchbox.

Brent stepped forward and crushed the camera under his heel.

Juan dropped three more. "There are hundreds of them. Hidden everywhere."

"These are too small to transmit far." Camilla kept her voice to a whisper. "Julian and the crew are in that farmhouse, across the channel."

Brent scratched the side of his head. "We've got to get someone's attention. Get them to come." He looked past the houses, toward the mainland. "I mean, Highway 1 is *right there,* on the other side of the headlands. It's less than a mile away."

"That's why I wanted us to come out here," Juan said. "I have a couple ideas, but I don't want to give anyone a chance to interfere. I'll be right back."

A chance to interfere? Camilla watched Juan hurdle the seal barricade, heading toward the blockhouse he now shared with Jordan. What did he mean by "interfere"?

In a minute, Juan was back, carrying what looked like a black hard-shell attaché case.

"The EPIRB I found during the scavenger hunt." He patted the case. "They wanted us isolated, even jammed our cell phones. But Julian made a mistake, giving us this beacon. It'll broadcast a marine distress satellite signal to the Coast Guard, with our GPS location. We turn it on, and they'll be on their way in minutes."

"How do you know it actually works?" Camilla asked.

Juan gave her a grim smile. "I've been turning it on four times a day to make sure, checking the signal, running the self-check diagnostics. It was factory sealed. They didn't tamper with it."

"What are we waiting for, then?" JT said. He had rejoined the group. "Fire it up."

305

Juan nodded. He knelt and set the case down, unsnapped the catches, and raised the lid. Then he froze. He looked up at them, a strange expression on his face.

Camilla's gut tensed. What now?

Wordlessly, Juan turned the case around for all to see.

Nestled in the form-fitting foam lining was a shattered mass of fractured yellow plastic, pieces of antenna, and clipped, half-stripped wires. Broken shards of green circuit board hung out of the cracks in the beacon's shell, dangling from loose wires.

"No, that's not right." Looking at the wreckage, Camilla felt a lead ball drop in her stomach. "We can't fix that, can we?"

Juan shook his head.

Mason leaned forward to look into the case. "Travis smashed my RF scanner right before the scavenger hunt. Just saying…"

"When's the last time you checked it?" Camilla asked Juan.

"This morning." He stood and shoved the case with his boot, sliding it into the center of the circle, where it sat like a mute accusation.

Camilla stared down at the wreckage of the beacon, understanding what it meant. Lauren had figured it out before the rest of them had. And now she was dead.

Juan looked from face to face, his expression hard. "One of you knows something about this. I'd like to hear it right now."

Camilla pushed the case away with her toe. She looked at the circle of faces. "It's obvious when you think about it," she said. "The scanners, the flags, the gifts, and then the empty buildings…"

"Just say it." Veronica's eyes bored into hers. Her face was drawn with fear.

"One of us never got a letter," Camilla said softly. "One of us isn't really a player. One of us has been working with Julian all along."

CHAPTER 97

"Well, we know it wasn't Lauren."

"Oh god, shut up, Mason. You're not helping." Camilla looked from person to person—strangers really, all of them, despite their five days together. She could see her own fear and confusion reflected in each of their faces, but how could she tell what was really going on in their heads? The ball in the pit of her stomach shifted.

Mason waved a hand toward the house behind them. "But the fact that someone like Travis—"

"I doubt it's Travis," Brent said. His mouth was still swollen from Travis's elbow. "He called too much attention to himself."

"But he's an *ex-con*," Camilla said, liking the idea of the spy being Travis. She could handle that. She wouldn't have to be afraid, the way she was now. Afraid to look too closely at the faces in front of her, scared of what she might see there. Her voice sped up.

"Julian could have used Travis's past to blackmail him—"

"And then let us all know about it?" JT shook his head. "No." His eyes drifted from face to face. "Makes no sense."

"Someone doesn't want the rest of us to leave," Juan said. He shoved the case back into the center of the circle with his boot, and the broken beacon seemed to accuse them all over again. "Someone did this."

"How do we know you didn't do it yourself?" JT asked. Muscles bunched in his thick shoulders.

Jordan slid a hand around Juan's upper arm: a warning.

JT raised his eyebrows at that. "Hell, maybe you *both* did it. Maybe that secret-alliance shit was just a smokescreen—"

"Wait a minute, guys." Jordan turned to look at Veronica. "You were up near the blockhouse this morning, after the fight. What were you doing there?"

The back of Camilla's neck tightened. "Stop it, all of you." she said. "Accusing each other isn't solving anything—"

"No, little lady, you're wrong." Veronica's sharp voice silenced her. "It's exactly how we get to the bottom of this." Her ice-hard silver eyes swept the circle. "Because we're looking for a person who has done something like it before—someone with a history of doing things like this."

"What the hell are you talking about?" JT's voice was different now, his tone cautious.

"Wait here," Veronica said. "I've got something to show you all." She turned and strode into the Greek Revival house.

A minute later she was back, holding a tabbed manila folder. Camilla's eyes widened when she saw the red-and-white "Classified Information" label.

Veronica flipped it open and read aloud.

"Summarized Record of Trial of Corporal James Tyrone Washington, by Special Court Martial. Convened by Commanding Officer, First Reconnaissance Battallion. Tried at Marine Corps Base Camp Pendleton, California, on November sixth, 2007—"

"Where the hell did you get that?" JT grabbed for the folder, but Veronica backed away. Brent laid a hand on his shoulder, stopping him.

"Those transcripts were sealed," JT said. "That operation was *classified*. You're breaking national security laws even by having those in your possession. Give me that…"

Veronica waved the folder out of his reach.

"Your chopper was shot down in Afghanistan," she said. "Three others from your squad survived the crash also, but they were hurt worse than you. They couldn't move. You were supposed to stay with them until an evac team arrived, weren't you? *Semper fidelis*, JT—"

"Shut the hell up, woman—"

"—it means 'Always Faithful'—"

"—you don't know. You don't have *any* idea—"

Veronica's voice rose, harsh and strident, overriding his. "—*doesn't it?*"

"That valley was hot with Taliban." Thick veins stood out on JT's neck. "We were *all* going to die."

Juan stepped up beside Brent, getting between JT and Veronica. "Back off, JT."

"You panicked." Veronica flipped to the end of the file folder, rustling the white pages as she rifled through them. "That's what the military judge concluded. The chopper's radio beacon meant that rescue was on its way. You were supposed to stay with the casualties, JT—stay until help arrived. But you couldn't wait."

"You weren't there! *Hell*, you didn't *see* what—"

"You needed an excuse to leave them." Veronica's eyes blazed with contempt. She slapped the folder with the back of her hand. "So you created one."

Flipping the folder open again, she read aloud: *"It is the conclusion of this court that Corporal James Tyrone Washington did willfully and deliberately disable the IFF radio beacon before abandoning Staff Sergeant DiMarco, Corporal Sanchez, and Sergeant Collins with the disabled aircraft. Corporal Washington's inexplicable sabotage of the radio beacon prevented a rescue operation from being successfully mounted, and was a likely contributory factor in the deaths of DiMarco, Sanchez, and Collins. The military judge recommends that Corporal Washington be stripped of rank and discharged from the Marine Corps without honor forthwith, and that the Marine Corps officially refrain from involvement in any civil actions that follow."*

Pushing forward between Juan and Brent, Veronica let the folder flap shut. Jaw outthrust, she stared up into JT's face. "But why *our* rescue beacon? There's nowhere you can run to here. No, I think we all know why…"

She turned away, disgust on her face.

"…because there really is only one possible explanation, isn't there?"

JT moved with explosive speed, knocking Juan and Brent aside, sending both of them sprawling to the ground. Seizing a startled-looking Veronica by the neck, he wrapped his big hands around her throat. The file folder fell to the dirt as he lifted her to her toes, then off her feet completely, throttling her.

"I… didn't… *do* it," he grunted.

Camilla ran forward, grabbing his wrist, but it was like grabbing the limb of a tree. Wrapping her arms around his elbow, she let her body hang, trying to pull his arm down using her weight. But it was futile. She had been carried under one of those arms yesterday; she knew how strong they were.

"Somebody help me!" she cried. "Oh god, he's going to kill her."

Veronica's eyes bulged from her reddening face, so near Camilla's. She shook her head, sending blond highlights feathering across JT's corded wrists and Camilla's cheeks. She cried out—a strangled noise, cut off in mid gargle as he tightened his grip.

It was over before anyone else could react.

CHAPTER 98

Slapping her palms together as if in prayer, Veronica drove the wedge of her joined fingers straight up in front of her, between JT's forearms. Then she slammed her elbows down onto his arms, spreading them apart and bringing his face within range.

Camilla fell away, pain exploding where Veronica's elbow had brushed her broken nose. She looked up from the dirt to see Veronica's hands dart forward.

Veronica dug her hooked thumbs into JT's eyes and her fingers curled to seize his head and ears in a clawing two-handed grip. She pulled his head forward, driving her forehead into his face with a brutal snapping motion—once, twice, three times—each blow sounding like a brick hitting a melon. Ropes of blood flew from JT's nose and mouth to spatter in the dirt and across Camilla's jeans.

Camilla's vision blurred. Her nose was white-hot agony. She gasped, hyperventilating. A hand on her shoulder... someone—Brent—dragging her up, shouting past her ear.

"Stop, God damn it! Stop right now!"

"My eyes!" JT screamed. "You blinded me, you fucking witch!"

Coughing, Veronica danced back, bouncing on the balls of her feet in a low ready stance. Her forehead was smeared with blood, JT's and her own, soaking into her blond hair.

Amazingly, JT was still on his feet, too. Camilla looked at his eyes and flinched. He slapped his hands over them, and blood welled from beneath his fingers. Then he whipped a hand behind him, under the tail of his Hawaiian shirt.

"Gun." Mason's voice sounded calm, but his arm came up in front of Camilla's chest, shoving her back protectively as he took a step back himself.

JT held the blocky black pistol one-handed, covering an eye with his other hand. The exposed eye blinked furiously in a socket filled with blood.

He leveled the gun in Veronica's direction, but she was in motion again, bounding forward and grabbing the top of the gun's slide with one hand. She twisted her body, rotating the gun and JT's arm between them.

Her other hand snaked forward to stab extended fingers into his neck, then dropped to curl under the gun in a two-handed grip. She pulled hard, rotating against his already-twisted wrist, and the gun came free.

Stepping back, Veronica raised it two-handed and pointed it into JT's face. She held it steady, overlapping thumbs parallel below the slide, as he gagged

311

and grabbed at his throat. Her eyes were frighteningly wide, luminous with fury. Her lips pulled away from her teeth.

Camilla was sure she was about to pull the trigger.

"Veronica, *no!*" she shouted. "Don't do this. Please don't do this."

Veronica blinked, seeming to come back to herself. Holding the gun on JT, eyes still locked onto his stunned and bleeding face, she turned her head to the side, coughed twice, and spat a mouthful of bloody saliva to the ground.

"I told you..." Her ragged voice died with a croak. She coughed and tried again.

"I told you never, ever to lay a hand on one of us again."

Taking two steps back, she whipped her arm in a sideways arc, sending the gun sailing out over the water.

"Oh my god, what a mess," Jordan said.

Camilla turned to stare at her. Jordan's face was white. Standing beside her, Juan was looking away. Camilla followed his gaze to the spreading ripples where the gun had splashed into the ocean, sixty feet from shore. His dark eyes were active, narrowing in concentration as his gaze jumped from the rippling circle to the nearest seaweed-covered rocks and then to more distant boulders. Triangulating...

She caught his eye and shook her head at him. *Don't.*

Expression neutral, he held her gaze.

Veronica turned her back to the group and walked away, shoulders hitching. Natalie broke away from the group and followed Veronica though the doorway of the blue team's house.

"I can't see." JT swayed on his feet. "I *can't see*, god damn it!" He sat down hard in the dirt, his ruined, swelling face unrecognizable. "Oh hell, Doc, she blinded me, I think. I need a medic."

"Don't move," Brent said. "I'll get the first-aid kit." Looking haggard, he glanced at Camilla and shook his head.

It was too much for her. She needed to get away from this, get away from everyone, to gather her equilibrium and think. She had to find somewhere to be alone. Camilla turned and stumbled toward the seal barricade. But then she stopped. There was really no place to go. There was no escape. They were trapped.

Lauren had felt the same way, too. She had tried to run. And look what happened to her.

●　●　●

Camilla squatted near the top of the oceanside bluff with Mason, Juan, and Jordan, the four of them making a small a circle fifty feet from where Brent was tending to JT—the first-aid kit open yet again. Her own nose ached and throbbed, but even from a distance she could see that JT was in far worse shape. One of his eyes looked like a blood-soaked tennis ball, swollen completely shut.

Brent held a gauze pad in one hand, a bottle in the other. "I have to clean it up," he said, "or you'll lose the eye for sure. Right now I'm giving you fifty-fifty odds, and that's only if we can get you to a hospital quickly."

Swallowing, Camilla turned back to face her small group. "You said you had a *couple* of ideas, Juan. *Plural.*"

"If time wasn't a factor," he said, "we could arrange rocks or boards to spell out 'SOS' in large letters. On the ground here, or up there"—he pointed to the pitched roof of the Victorian house—"where a passing aircraft would see it, or a hiker on the mainland would."

She shook her head. "We can't afford to wait that long."

"I agree," he said. "Things are headed downhill fast. Lauren killed herself, but soon we'll be killing each other. By the time somebody notices an SOS and the Coast Guard gets here, they'll have to hose what's left of us off the rocks."

"I have something a little more primitive in mind," Camilla said. "The oldest distress signal known to mankind."

Looking at her through his broken glasses, Mason grinned. "Now, or wait for night?"

"It'll be more visible at night," she said. "But let's get ready for it now. We'll gather all the wood we can, stack it in a giant pile at the top of the hill, where the lighthouse tower used to be."

Jordan stared at her without a trace of friendliness. "Why bother?" Her tone made Camilla feel like the slow kid in class. Jordan waved a dismissive hand toward the houses behind them and the empty factory structure across the barricade.

"We can just set one of these buildings on fire."

• • •

Camilla ran a hand along the side of the chicken coop. Her palm encountered the same glossy slickness that had coated the walls of the factory buildings. The same slickness that she had felt sliding her hand along the logs of the barricade. The same whitish residue that she could now see drying on the still-damp walls of the houses they had washed three days ago.

Biodegradable, bio-safe detergent? She didn't think so.

She wasn't sure what it was, but she had a pretty good idea.

Five minutes later, she had gathered everyone in the open space in front of the houses. She had collected a few boards and scraps of plywood, which now lay at her feet.

"Juan, let me see those matches."

He tossed her the small pack. She squatted, striking a match only to have the breeze blow it out.

"Everybody, gather around." She waved them closer to form a tight circle of legs around her, blocking the wind. "You need to see what we're dealing with here."

The next one stayed lit. She held the shrinking match against the splintered end of the board until it was about to burn her fingers. Then she shook it out and dropped it. The shiny surface of the wood had discolored slightly but was otherwise unaffected.

Tossing the board to the ground, she stood and dusted off her palms. She handed the matches back to Juan and looked around the grim circle of faces.

"It's a good thing we have gasoline," she said. "Other than a few scraps of driftwood, not a single structure or decent-sized piece of wood on the island will burn. Julian's crew fireproofed everything before we got here. Except for our two houses…"

Camilla looked behind her at the two looming, two-story wooden structures. She closed her eyes.

"We fireproofed those *ourselves.*"

CHAPTER 99

The ORCA bounced across the waves. Heather gripped the topside wheel, standing at the helm as she steered the thirty-foot research vessel along the coast. Santa Cruz harbor, where the ORCA had been tied and berthed, lay behind them, to the south. The late afternoon sun glinted gold on the water as they headed toward Shark Station Zebra, Año Nuevo Island.

A thump below the hull sent up fans of white spray, wetting Jacob and Dmitry, who hunched at the stern rail. Heather met their eyes, and Jacob blinked, his face a mask of indecision and dread. It was a little late for that, she thought. They had made their decision to come, and he had been the most insistent. Dmitry, on the other hand, looked serene, and seeing his calm helped her, too. Resisting the nervous urge to twirl a lock of hair between her fingers, she kept both hands firmly on the wheel.

They had disobeyed Karen's directive. By taking the boat, they had commandeered Institute property without authorization. But neither of those things worried Heather as much as what she was afraid they would find when they reached the island. The shark researchers of the Pelagic Institute—her team—shared the old station buildings with the bird and mammal research teams, who had studies running concurrently. The scientists all took care to respect each other and avoid disrupting each other's work. She cringed at the thought of the damage that a reality film crew may well have already done.

And then they were there. Año Nuevo Island lay before them, the two lighthouse keeper residences visible as Heather swung the ORCA seaward, coming around to the dock. She stared in disbelief, the fingers of one hand rising to twist a curl of hair as Jacob's shout rang out behind her.

"Un-*fucking*-believable."

Drastic changes had been wrought on the south side of the island. The two residences, given over to crowded seal habitat for decades now, once again stood on empty ground. Clear plastic sheeting—deadly to seals or seabirds, which could become entangled in it or choke on swallowed shreds—flapped in the windows. The zigzag log barricade had been torn down many years ago to give the animals free access to the entire island. Now, for some crazy reason, it had been rebuilt, rendering fully half of Año Nuevo's high-ground habitat inaccessible, denied to the wildlife that so desperately depended on areas like this for breeding and survival.

Her eyes widened in helpless anger.

Someone had even washed the pelican and cormorant nests away from the roof peaks and chimneys, leaving them bare of life. This went far beyond interference. It was wanton, reckless habitat destruction. This coastal island area, part of the unbelievably few acres to be found along this stretch of California's shore, was a critical factor in the life cycles of many interlinked species.

"We need to document this." Jacob fumbled something in the back of the boat, dropping it. Heather felt the thud through the hull, but she couldn't tear her eyes away from the scene of devastation before them.

"We have to show the other directors." Jacob's voice broke. "Karen should go to jail for this. To fucking *jail*."

"They give some fines. That's all." Even Dmitry sounded unhappy. "Like last time, when they tease sharks to make Discovery show—"

"This is so a thousand times worse." Heather's hand shook on the wheel. She felt like crying. "The fines are a joke. They only paid a few thousand—oh, shit, Raja's going to have a heart attack when he sees this. Get the Nikon."

As she bumped the ORCA up against the dock, a terrible thought struck her.

"What if Karen tries to play dumb and pretend she had no idea what they were going to do?"

Dmitry laid a hand on her shoulder, and the other on Jacob's. "We go to station now," he said. "Collect papers, bring them back to boat. Then we find somebody in charge, talk to them, make them understand. They help us put back the right way. To restore."

"It's too late," Jacob said. "The pinniped populations will take decades to recover from this, and that'll impact our babies, too." He clumped down the dock with fast, angry strides, toward the three old warehouse buildings that made up the station. Then he burst into a run. "Oh, *fuck*, the station's wide open!"

Heather and Dmitry had trouble keeping up with him. In the distance behind them, she could see people spilling out of the two houses to the south and running toward them. But Jacob was focused on the yawning door of the science station. His voice shook with anger and disbelief.

"They bashed our fucking door in!"

A slim blonde woman whipped around the corner of the station building, aiming something she held in her hands: a speargun. Heather froze. The woman's face and hair were dirty, but underneath the layers of grime, she was stop-traffic gorgeous. Still, Heather found it hard to focus on anything but the pronged stainless steel spear that swiveled in a tight arc between her own chest, Jacob's, and Dmitry's. The woman holding the speargun wore a ragged, stained dress that ended just above her knees. Shockingly, her feet were bare and covered with dirt, scabs, and bloody abrasions.

"Who the hell are you guys?" she demanded.

"Who are you?" Heather asked in surprise.

Ignoring her question, the blonde woman stepped closer. "How did you guys get here?" Anger hardened the line of her jaw and crackled like electricity in her wide green eyes.

"Jacob...," Heather said in a warning voice.

But Jacob was too agitated to realize the danger. "Do you have any idea what you've *done*?" he shouted. "How many laws you've broken?"

The woman took two steps forward and touched the speargun's point to the hollow of Jacob's throat. "Shut the fuck up. I don't care." She looked toward the breakwater, which hid the dock from view. "How big is your boat? We all need to get out of here."

"So, you think you can just run away?" Jacob's eyes twitched with uncontrollable blinks. "It's not going to be that easy. You people are going to pay for this."

"You've got them," a man's calm voice said from behind Heather. "Keep them here. I'll make sure the boat doesn't leave without us."

Startled, Heather whirled about to stare at the dark-haired man standing behind her. Where had *he* come from? She realized he had flanked them, coming around the seawall and up behind the three of them while the woman held their attention.

Was everybody here so good-looking? The man was dressed head to toe in black, and he and the woman looked like a matched set. Undoubtedly TV people—actors—but they weren't acting the way she imagined TV people would. Heather's eyes widened, noticing the dive knife the man held in his hand, inches from Dmitry's spine.

These people were dangerous. She could see Dmitry understood that, but did Jacob?

To her relief, the man in black turned away and stalked toward the breakwater. He moved like a jungle cat: fast and without a single wasted motion. Standing at the top and shielding his eyes with his hand, he looked toward the dock for a moment, then headed back. More people were coming down the path from the old lighthouse keepers' houses.

A man and a woman arrived first, together. The man wore a suit. Lawyer, maybe? The woman was dressed in jeans, petite and pretty with dark, curly hair. Both were injured—they looked as though they had taken quite a beating. Cuts and bruises discolored the man's mouth and chin. One lens of his glasses was shattered. The curly-haired woman's nose was swollen and taped—probably broken—and her eyes were ringed with purple. She sounded angry—scared, too.

"Don't point that at them, Jordan," the woman with the taped nose said.

"Whatever. Just go get everyone." The blonde woman prodded at Jacob with the speargun, forcing him back, jabbing the point right beneath his bobbing Adam's apple. His eyes widened, and at last Heather saw fear in them. Good. It looked like Jacob had finally realized what would happen if the blonde woman—the one called Jordan—were to pull the trigger.

Eyes steeled with anger, she nestled the spear point in the hollow of Jacob's throat again. "How could you possibly think you could keep us here after what happened?"

The woman with the broken nose stepped forward and wrapped a hand around the barrel of the speargun. "Put it down before you kill him."

Jordan's eyes narrowed. "Let go, *sister*."

Two more women jogged up the path: a well-dressed blond woman in her late thirties or early forties, and a Japanese or Korean teenager in a gray hoodie.

"Are these Julian's people?" the older woman demanded in a hoarse, ragged voice. Purplish bruises ringed her throat. The cold ferocity burning in her pale eyes scared Heather even worse than Jordan's speargun.

"No, Veronica," the woman with the broken nose said. "They aren't."

"Who's in charge here?" Jacob asked, belligerent again.

"Looks like nobody." The man in black was back. He reached out and, to Heather's relief, pushed the tip of the speargun away from Jacob's neck. Jordan looked at him, a question in her eyes.

"Boat's at the dock," he said. "No one on board."

He looked at the three scientists, his dark eyes intense. "You need to get on the radio, get the Coast Guard out here right away."

Jacob rubbed his neck. "Goddamn right we do. Dmitry, go call them. Everyone needs to see what you people have done to this place." He pointed at Jordan, who still held the speargun ready. "And she assaulted me with a deadly weapon just now—"

"Jacob...," Heather warned.

Dmitry looked at the man in black, who nodded a curt approval, and then set off at a jog toward the breakwater, almost bumping into a big, husky gray-haired man coming up the path. The big man turned to stare after him, scratching the side of his head. Then he looked at Heather and Jacob, and his eyes widened. The man grimaced when he saw the speargun in Jordan's hands. Then he sighed.

"I should be grateful. It seems we've managed to avoid more injuries. But thank God you're here. We need your help."

Jacob put his hands on his hips. "You people are in a lot of trouble."

The curly-haired woman with the broken nose stepped forward, holding out a hand to shake. "Jacob, right? I'm Camilla."

Jacob glared at her but didn't take her hand.

"And I'm Mason," the man in cracked glasses said. "You must be Karen? Or Heather?"

"Heather," she said with surprise. "How do you know our names?"

"You're the shark experts," Camilla said. "We saw some of your papers."

The man with glasses—Mason—nodded. "So perhaps one of you can shed some light on something for us. This morning, a woman—"

"Whoa!" Jacob held up a hand. "What the fuck?" He took a couple of quick steps away from them, then a couple more, squinting at something near the base of the seawall. "No fucking way. I am *not* seeing this."

He turned back and beckoned, his voice dropping to a horrified whisper. "Heather?"

Nervously she pushed forward to see what he was staring at. A blackened fire pit, recently used, surrounded by large dark flayed shapes... She swung back to face the TV people, her throat convulsing with the sudden urge to vomit.

"You sick freaks!" she said. "What is *wrong* with you all? I mean, seriously, you're killing and eating the *seals*?"

The Jordan woman's face hardened, and her eyes went steel cold. She raised the speargun and pointed it at Heather's face. Everyone froze.

In the tense silence, Dmitry's voice floated up from beyond the breakwater. "Jacob, radio is not work. I try, but no signal."

Jacob frowned at Heather, ignoring the spear aimed at her head. He ran to the seawall, grabbed the top, and pulled himself up. Getting his head and chin over, he yelled, "Go! Just go get them. These people are fucking crazy!"

"Go?" Dmitry's faint voice asked.

"Right now! The Coast Guard. Santa Cruz Auxiliary or Monterey. *Hurry!*"

The man in black suddenly broke away from the group and sprinted toward the breakwater, then up and over it to disappear from sight, descending toward the dock.

From beyond the breakwater drifted the sound of the ORCA's engines revving. Everybody was headed in that direction now, jogging or running. Heather followed.

When she reached the top of the breakwater she could see that the man in black was too late. The ORCA pulled away from the dock, leaving a trail of white froth as the powerful engines churned the water, widening the gap. Halfway down the dock, the man in black slid to a stop and stared after the departing boat.

At the wheel, Dmitry gave a small wave as the ORCA picked up speed.

CHAPTER 100

Camilla stopped at the top of the breakwater and watched the boat pull away. Seeing it leave without them, she felt her heart beating uncomfortably fast in her throat, even though she knew that was silly.

Juan was a black figure on the dock below, staring after it.

Brent exhaled heavily next to her.

"The Coast Guard will be here in an hour," she said to him.

"It's about time. *They* can sort this mess out." He squatted and eased himself down to sit on the rocks. "We'll need to get law enforcement involved, too." This was hardest on him, she realized. Anytime anybody got hurt, he probably felt that it was his fault.

The ORCA churned through the water, now fifty feet away, now a hundred, heading for the open ocean. The stocky blond scientist was braced in the cockpit, his hand jamming the throttle forward.

Mason spoke beside her ear.

"What's that line in the water behind the boat?"

Before she could say anything, the line suddenly snapped taut, springing up out of the water to throw a fifty-meter line of white spray connecting the back of the boat to the end of the dock. For a frozen second, a thick chain of shiny silver links stretched arrow-straight above the water, shedding a shower of droplets as the boat was pulled up short. The pilot was hurled forward against the console, and a loud, splintering crash echoed back to the breakwater. Revving now to a higher, screaming pitch, the outboard engine ripped completely free of the boat, snapping up into the air in a wide arc.

The dock, jerked by the chain, heaved under Juan's feet, throwing him to the boards as Camilla watched, stunned.

In his hurry, had the scientist forgotten to untie the line? But that made no sense. It was a chain, not a rope. And it was too long.

The engine splashed into the water fifty yards away, tied to the end of the chain. The boat coasted a few yards more, now powerless, its rear deck a split wreck of torn and splintered fiberglass.

The pilot struggled to his feet in the cockpit as the boat glided to a full stop. He shook his head as if dazed, staring back at the island as water rushed over his feet and ankles.

Camilla's eyes widened. It was sinking. He had to get off before the boat pulled him down with it.

"Swim!" she screamed at him. "Get away from it."

Then she thought of Lauren.

321

．　．　．

The boat went down fast, listing to its side as it sank. From the breakwater, everyone was shouting instructions.

"Raft!" From the dock, Juan hollered through cupped hands. "Grab the raft!"

Standing next to Camilla, Heather shook her head. "He can't reach it," she said. "It's underwater already."

Camilla didn't answer. She was scanning the water around the boat in wider and wider circles.

The scientist leaped from the listing boat with an awkward splash. Surfacing, he swam toward a five-foot section of the boat's wooden swim platform, torn loose when the chain wrenched the stern of the boat apart and floating some twenty feet away. He scrambled onto it as the top of the boat's cabin disappeared beneath the waves behind him.

Paddling the platform like an awkward surfboard, he labored toward them, his progress slow—*so* slow.

And then Camilla spotted what she was looking for—what she had dreaded seeing: the dark triangle of a fin slicing through the water, coming around the northern side of the island.

She grabbed Heather's arm, pointing. "We have company."

As she watched, the distant shape slipped under the rippling surface, disappearing from sight.

Heather didn't seem too bothered. "They have good hearing," she said. "It's just coming to investigate the crash."

"It killed and ate a woman this morning," Camilla said.

"No," Heather gasped. She shook her head. "That doesn't happen. A test bite, perhaps… a mistake…"

Camilla understood the scientist's confusion. She knew a little bit about great white sharks herself, because of the clown fish. One of the other characters in that film was a shark. Even though it was an animated children's film, she had insisted that her studio do their homework. She even flew an expert in from the Woods Hole Oceanographic Institution to hold a private seminar for her whole team. She had been fascinated and had learned a lot. Her team made their animated shark scary, but that was mainly because the other characters were fish—its normal prey.

In real life, great white sharks also preyed on seals and sea lions, but attacks on humans were extremely rare—usually cases of mistaken identity when a diver or surfer in a wet suit looked like a seal to them. Fatal attacks were even rarer; most of the time, the shark broke off the attack after one exploratory bite.

Squinting, heart pounding, she swept the surface with her eyes, in a line between where the fin had dipped and where the man was paddling the piece of wreckage. Nothing. Knowing it was coming but not being able to see it only made it worse.

What they had witnessed this morning—Lauren's death—did not jive with what the Woods Hole expert had presented. However, the *way* the shark attacked did match the seal predation behavior the expert had described. The shark would dive deep, then attack vertically from below—invisible to a seal swimming at the surface until it was too late. Even so, half the time the seals escaped. They didn't actually see the shark coming, but they sensed it, leaping away as soon as they felt the...

Camilla's eyes widened. She cupped her hands and screamed out to the man on the water. "Pressure wave. *PRESSURE WAVE!*"

The man stopped paddling and scrambled up onto the piece of wreckage, balancing in an awkward crouch.

Camilla closed her eyes in relief; he understood her. Then she opened them again, unable to look away. The man wobbled on the broken section of platform, watching the water at his feet. His paddling had closed about half the distance with the dock, but he still looked very small and vulnerable to her, with a wide expanse of open water all around him.

Time stood frozen again; the seconds stretched as nobody moved, nobody spoke.

Then the man hurled himself forward in a wild leap as the platform exploded out of the water beneath his feet, lifted by a pointed snout and gaping jaws that knocked him cartwheeling through the air. Rising out of the water to almost its full length, like a missile launched from an underwater submarine, the shark dwarfed him, holding the crushed platform in bathtub-size jaws ringed with serrated triangular white razors. Spitting out the splintered wood in a spray of water, it slid backward to disappear beneath the waves again.

The man splashed back into the water and spluttered to the surface immediately.

"Swim, Dmitry!" Heather screamed, next to Camilla's ear.

Eighty feet from shore, he flailed at the water, not making much progress.

Camilla's eyes were drawn to Juan, braced near the end of the dock, leaning forward over the water as if ready to jump. But he just stood there. Dmitry thrashed and struggled, getting closer but obviously needing help. What was Juan waiting for?

"Go!" she shouted. "Go help him!"

Without turning his head, Juan held up his hand—*I heard you*—but still he didn't jump. Her throat tightened. She had seen him risk his life to save a child; was he just going to watch this man Dmitry die now?

She wasn't a great swimmer, but *somebody* had to help him. Camilla bounded down the breakwater, leaping from rock to rock, risking a bad tumble.

As she drew closer, Juan backed up several steps on the dock, then ran forward, picking up speed to split the water in a clean dive. The tightness in her heart loosened—she wasn't wrong about him. But long seconds went by, and he didn't resurface. Oh god, had the shark...?

Popping up alongside Dmitry, Juan rolled him onto his back and looped an arm over his chest. As he stroked toward the dock, hauling the scientist, Camilla searched the water around them, looking for a fin, a disturbance, seeing nothing. A few minutes later, they reached the shallows and pulled themselves up onto the rocks.

Camilla scrambled toward where the two men lay on their backs, but before she could reach them Juan slapped Dmitry on the shoulder, rolled over, and stood up.

He headed for the dock, and she followed.

Pushing roughly past her, the bearded scientist named Jacob grabbed Juan by the arm. "That was sixty thousand dollars of Institute property—"

Juan shook off his hand, ignoring him, and lay down at the end of the dock. He reached an arm into the water, shoulder deep, fishing around by touch, and pulled a six-foot loop of steel chain out of the water. He stood up, dropping it on the deck. It lay in a puddle of water, glinting in the sun, its shiny two-inch links solid and heavy-looking. Camilla stared at them as the others crowded the dock behind her.

"Brand-new," she said. "This was put there recently."

Juan nodded. "No tarnish at all. I felt an eyebolt under the dock, too."

"The end of the chain probably had a hook on it, hanging from that," she said. "Whoever did this would have needed only a few seconds to reach underneath, grab the hook, and connect it to the engine's frame. It hung out of sight in the water until the boat ran out the full length of the chain—"

"Whoever did this'?" Jacob thrust himself forward again, leveling a finger at her. "Don't try to deny it. It was you people!"

Stomach tight, Camilla looked at them all. "He's right. One of us did it. There's no one else here. But Mason was—" *...with me the whole time,* she was going to say, but Brent held up his hand, cutting her off.

"Before we all start accusing each other again," he said, "I'd like you all to remember what happened last time someone thought that was a good idea."

Veronica's face darkened. "What's *that* supposed to mean?"

"It means I'm getting pretty tired of treating serious injuries under these conditions. We should focus on getting rescued and let the police sort out who did what." Brent dusted his hands together, looking at the scientists. "How long until you're missed? How soon will your colleagues come looking for you?"

Jacob turned to look at the other two scientists. Dmitry sat on the edge of the dock, breathing heavily. He shook his head. Camilla watched Heather's face blanch. *No way.* It couldn't be...

"Uh, yeah," Jacob said. "We... well, we..."

"Nobody knows we're here," Heather said. "Normally, we're here for a couple of weeks in December, but this year, at the last minute, we got told to stay home. Then we heard about a reality show being shot out here, and we wanted to make sure our research was safe and the animals weren't being bothered."

The look on her face made Camilla's cheeks feel hot. She looked down at the ground.

"Nobody knows we're here," Jacob said. "Oh fuck, nobody knows we're out here."

Brent sagged. "Then we have a real problem."

CHAPTER 101

"So let me get this right," Jacob said, rubbing his beard. "You've all been here for five days, on your own, doing whatever stupid shit some guy on this TV screen tells you to?"

Camilla closed her eyes and nodded. "It sounds so dumb now."

"Yeah. Darwin-award-level dumb."

Blank now, the monitor screen stared from the wall above the fireplace, mocking them all. The entire group, including the three new arrivals, had gathered in the central room of the Victorian house. Jacob paced back and forth, asking questions, and Camilla didn't like the answers she had for him.

"What happened to your face, by the way?" he asked.

"Everyone's under a lot of strain," she said. "Some of us aren't handling it too well."

"I don't get it." Heather looked from Camilla to Mason, to Veronica, to Brent, taking in all their injuries. "You did this to *each other?*"

The worst part was, Camilla could see it all from the scientists' perspective. She felt again the rattling impact of Mason's body striking the ground with her arms wrapped around his shins, and her face tightened in shame. They all had crossed the line and let things get out of control, allowing themselves to be manipulated by Julian.

They *had* done this to themselves, really.

She heard little Avery again, wishing he were dead, and her eyes prickled. She had come here for the best of reasons, but she had done things she *knew* were wrong, and she had rationalized them to herself. And now people were hurt. Now Lauren was dead.

Heather stared at her. "I mean, what kind of people *do* this?"

Camilla crossed her arms and stared at the floorboards. "I can see how it looks—"

"Look," Brent said. "I'm a doctor. Stop with the petty judgments for a minute and listen to me. You three don't have the full picture. We've got two people upstairs who are seriously injured. I've sedated them, but we've got to get them to a hospital right away. And earlier today, a woman was killed trying to reach the mainland."

"She drowned?" Jacob asked.

Brent shook his head. "One of your research subjects ate her."

Heather's face changed. She turned to Camilla and cupped a hand over her mouth. "You said that. I remember now, but in all the confusion, I—"

325

"Who saw it?" Jacob asked. "Did you see any distinguishing marks? Scars? On the shark that attacked her?"

"Jacob!" Heather gasped.

Brent shook his head, a disgusted expression on his face. "Try your phones," he said. "Let's hope they work—none of ours can get a signal."

"Nonsense. Mine works fine here." Jacob pulled out a phone and looked at the screen. He frowned. "Well, it always did before."

"They're jamming the signals," Camilla said. "We're cut off."

"But why?" Jacob asked.

"Julian, the host, told us we'd be isolated for two weeks." Something else was bothering her now—something they needed to do right away, but she couldn't quite remember what it was.

"Why would you agree to this craziness?" Jacob asked.

She looked away, not wanting to answer.

Brent spoke for her. "The grand prize is a substantial sum."

"How much money?" Jacob sounded angry. "How much money did they promise you, to ruin decades of conservation and scientific progress here?"

"Five million dollars."

"Five million? five…" Jacob's eyes flickered in rapid-fire blinks. "*Fuck* you people. Seriously. We have to scrounge every year for pennies to keep our research going, because nobody seems to understand how important it is, but they have no problem paying a bunch of idiots five million dollars to kill themselves on TV—"

"Please, Jacob," Heather said. "Their friend died—"

"The gasoline," Camilla said, uncrossing her arms and straightening as she realized what was gnawing at her. Whoever Julian's spy among them was, he or she would know about the plan to send a signal. It would be easy to sneak away. "We need to go get it out of the shed right now. We need to keep an eye on it and make sure nothing happens to it before it's dark enough."

"Dark enough?" Jacob asked. "Dark enough for what?"

• • •

"I can't let you do this," Jacob said, jogging alongside Juan and Mason. "There's been too much damage already."

Mason patted Jacob on the arm and grinned at him. Juan ignored him completely.

Camilla led everyone across the open ground toward the storage shed. Juan pulled open the shed door, and he and Mason went inside. As the shadows deepened and lengthened around them all, the others gathered in a wide semicircle outside the doorway.

A moment later, Juan was back empty-handed. Camilla felt the familiar sinking in the pit of her stomach again as he leaned against the shed wall with his hands in his pockets, eyeing them all, not saying anything. She could smell gasoline.

Mason stepped out of the shed, holding a large red gasoline can out in front of him by one fingertip. He tossed it the ground, where it landed with a hollow *thunk*. "Okay, this isn't funny anymore. Who has something to share with the class? Speak up."

"Cute," Veronica said, stalking forward. "You probably did it yourself—"

"Veronica," Brent rumbled.

"He hasn't been out of my sight all afternoon," Camilla said, stepping between her and Mason. "He couldn't have chained their boat, either."

Veronica speared her with that pale-silver stare. "Maybe both of you did it, then."

"It could have happened hours ago," Juan said. "Before we even talked about a signal fire."

"And you were the first to think of that, weren't you?" Veronica's voice was dark velvet, rich with insinuation. She turned back to Camilla. "Or was that *you*?"

The back of Camilla's neck tensed. Her belly tightened. She had seen what Veronica was capable of.

"Or maybe I did it," Brent said. "Or even Natalie here. The point is, it could be anyone. Let's go inside, put our heads together, and see if we can come up with some answers that make sense."

CHAPTER 102

"Let's start at the beginning," Brent said. "None of us went looking for this. Vita Brevis came to us. What made them choose *us* specifically?"

The seven contestants sat in a wide circle on the floor in the great room of the Victorian house—the red team's former quarters. It was nearly dark, and the temperature was dropping. Lauren's LED camping lamp sat in the center of the floor.

Camilla could see their breath: small puffs of vapor that glowed in the lamplight before vanishing. She rubbed her arms, trying to shake off the chill, which seemed to come from deep inside her rather than the cold air. Her heart thudded in dread as she considered what she would have to tell the others: her most private secret. She didn't want to talk about this—she had even dumped Dean for digging into her past behind her back. But she had to set aside her personal discomfort now. The others needed to know.

At least the three scientists weren't with them—that would have made it worse. But they had taken the other lantern to the science station, to gather and protect their work.

Camilla took a deep breath. "Brent's right. Why we were selected—I think that's the key to understanding this."

The camping light threw shadows across the faces of her fellow contestants, distorting them and making expressions unreadable. Like kids on a campout holding flashlights under their chins and telling scary stories. She shivered, looking from face to face. One of them knew what she was going to say already. But which one?

Mason spoke, sounding oddly serious. "The night before we were dropped off, on the ship, I noticed something unusual. Nobody made any calls telling loved ones, friends, or roommates what they were doing. That seems unlikely for an entire group of ten people. I don't have any family that would want to hear from me, but the rest of you?"

Camilla shook her head and looked at the floor. "Where are you going with this, Mason?"

"Listen, it's got to be said, so I'm saying it." The lantern's white light reflected from his broken glasses, making his eyes invisible. "We need to at least acknowledge a possibility here. This whole 'reality show' thing"—he air-quoted it with two fingers of each hand—"may not be exactly what we've been led to believe."

"Meaning what?"

329

He waved a hand. "Call me morbid, but ask yourselves this question: what kind of reality show wouldn't immediately pull the plug after contestants maimed each other, and one died in a horrible accident—maybe even live on camera, given the high-tech setup here?"

Veronica snorted. "That's ridiculous."

"I hate to burst your bubble," he said, "but I think we all need to keep an open mind. What if the reality show was a pretext, and this is what Julian intended all along? Am I the only one thinking this?"

"Oh god, Mason..." Camilla shook her head. "There really is something wrong with the way your mind works."

"I agree," Juan said, and she glanced up. "You sound paranoid."

"But it can't be a coincidence," Mason said. "Think about it for a moment. They chose people who wouldn't tell any—"

"No," Camilla said. "There's another reason they wanted us. I think we all have something else in common—something much more unusual."

"You think you know why we're here?" Veronica said, her voice harsh. "Then just say so. Why did they choose *us*?"

Camilla opened her mouth, but the words stuck in her throat. She couldn't talk about it. She just couldn't.

Thankfully, Brent spoke for her.

"What's the most terrible experience of your life, Veronica?" he asked. "What defines who you are today? I think we've all got some idea, thanks to Julian's nasty little profile. And we saw how you were able to handle JT."

"Don't you even—"

Brent raised a hand, silencing her. The light from the lantern lent him a terrible gravitas, making his face look ancient and forbidding.

"We've all heard a distorted version of my story," he said. "And about JT's last tour in Afghanistan. Lauren walked away from a climbing accident that cost two people their lives. In prison, child molesters usually don't survive a month, but Travis did. He's out on parole after a five-year sentence. Do you see the pattern here?"

Camilla found her voice.

"We're survivors," she said. "It's what we have in common. Each of us is still alive because, at some point in the past, we've beaten incredible odds. That's why they selected us."

Brent nodded. "The seven-year survival rate for mesothelioma is less than five percent. I was diagnosed in 2004, and eight years later, here I am, alive and healthy, my cancer in full remission. But you said 'we,' Camilla, and I sensed something about you, too, when we first met. Tell us why you're here."

There was no turning back now. She looked into the lantern's cold blue-white LED, its harsh light providing no warmth, no relief from the bleak sadness that washed over her. She stared at it so she wouldn't have to see the faces of the other contestants as she spoke.

"I lost both my parents in the Loma Prieta earthquake when I was seven," she said. "A two-story freeway collapsed in Oakland and our car was underneath. Somehow, I lived..."

Her voice was flat, affectless. Hearing it scared her. She had never told anyone this before, never let anyone get close enough to her to ask. Never.

"But I don't remember any of it." Why had she felt compelled to say that so quickly, the words tumbling out of her mouth? Why was her heart beating so fast? Was it *really* the truth, or was it only what she had convinced herself of?

"When I got older, someone told me I was trapped in the car for four days. It took rescuers that long to clear enough wreckage to find us and get me out. They had to cut me out of the car... Both my legs were broken."

Her shins were aching now. Shuddering, Camilla hugged her knees and closed her eyes, hearing an echo of the tortured creak of metal that haunted her dreams. Metal tearing, then awful wet, sloppy sounds and her own horrified shrieks. She wanted to find a corner, curl up, and just go away for a while.

"You've known you were a survivor ever since you were a child," Brent said. "Somebody else now... Juan. If we're right, then why are you here?"

Camilla perked up at the sound of his name. Opening her eyes, she took a deep breath and forced herself to let go of her knees. She watched Juan with curiosity. Jordan sat at his side. He didn't answer at first, and when he did his voice was low.

"I'd rather not talk about it. But it fits the pattern."

"This isn't group therapy," Mason said. "We aren't sharing because we're caring. Nobody believes me, but I think Julian made sure—"

Veronica shushed him with an impatient gesture. "Why would you try to hide something?" she asked Juan.

He seemed to consider this. "That's fair, I suppose. It's meaningless to worry about concealing an unsavory past right now. I was born in another country, in South America. I grew up on the streets. Things were different there—or perhaps not so very different from our worst inner cities here. My neighborhood was poor, and gangs ruled everywhere. You had to join one because, if you tried to go it alone, you wouldn't last a day.

"Gang life is the same wherever you are. It's not glamorous. We had to do ugly things every day to survive, and I'm not proud of that. At nineteen, I saw a chance to get out, and I took it... but the past has a way of catching up with you."

Camilla had never heard Juan speak that much before. She wished she could see his expression more clearly, but shadows painted the planes of his cheeks and turned his eye sockets into pools of inky blackness. The dark clothing made him almost invisible—a ghost in the corner of the room.

"One of my old gang found me a couple years later. I had made a new life for myself in Long Beach, working as a deckhand on a dive boat. He booked a charter under a false name. You can imagine my surprise when he came aboard, but he had a gun."

Juan's voice was emotionless. "The captain was dead as soon as we left port. My old friend held the gun on me, making me drive the boat. He told me I had betrayed them all. He shot me in the chest twice, and once in the head. Then he threw me overboard, five miles out to sea."

Jordan shifted beside him and put a hand on his forearm, rubbing it. Her face, too, was an unreadable mask of shadows.

"How did you survive?" Camilla asked, surprising herself.

"I was lucky. The Coast Guard was monitoring radio traffic and heard something suspicious. They boarded the empty boat, then started a search. They found me—pulled me out of the water before I bled out."

"Doesn't sound like it was just luck," Brent said. "How long were you in the water?"

"A little more than five hours."

"I rest my case." Brent's eyes roamed the room. "Natalie, how about you?"

Tucked next to Veronica, she shook her head. She didn't look up at them. "Natalie…?"

"Leave her alone." Veronica's voice split the cold air. "She grew up getting passed around from abusive foster home to abusive foster home, okay? Some really sick people out there. You don't need to hear any details— it was ugly. Just use your goddamn imagination."

Natalie sagged, shrinking into herself. Her head dipped, and she buried her face in Veronica's shoulder.

Veronica put an arm around her. "This poor girl is more of a survivor than any of us."

"Okay, I accept that." Brent tucked his hands back in his vest pockets. "How about you, Mason? Or are you going to turn this into a joke, too?"

Camilla sat up straight, suddenly very curious. What had Mason walked away from that would have killed most people?

But he only shook his head. "I might be the exception that invalidates your little theory here. I didn't escape the Twin Towers when the planes hit, didn't eat my companions after an avalanche, or anything like that. I'm not sure how I fit the picture."

Brent frowned. "It's no coincidence that you're one of the top scorers in this sick little competition. You're usually one step ahead of the rest of us. Some people might find that very suspicious under these circumstances, Mason, but I think it's only because you're a survivor, too. I can see it in you—takes one to know one."

Camilla caught herself nodding in agreement. Even Mason's irreverent sense of humor was a characteristic frequently found in survivors.

"I'm a survivor in the dog-eat-dog corporate jungle," he said. "But surviving layoffs is not the same thing as what you're talking about."

"Maybe it's not that different," Brent said. "Tell us."

"Well, three years ago I worked for a New York boutique investment bank, on the fixed-income side. My department specialized in mortgage bonds. Subprime… Yes, you're welcome." Mason laughed. "Maybe you saw some of the bad press. The company was Dorer, Bradshaw, and Jameson. We were a smaller house but more leveraged than most—which was saying a lot back then.

I saw the warning signs early. Lots of people did, but most were too greedy to pull back—there was too much money to be made. But by the time the whole thing came crashing down, I had already divested my own interest.

Our senior partners lost everything, though. And then the SEC raided us. Six of our board members were indicted for insider trading. Dorer, the senior partner, took a high dive out a corner office window. Bradshaw and Jameson went to jail. I got a slap on the wrist, then accepted a position with a retail bank out here and moved to California."

The light glinting off Mason's glasses hid his expression. "I feel a little silly even telling you this, but that's my deepest, darkest survival story."

"I suspect there's something you're leaving out," Brent said. "How many of your peers managed to avoid being tainted by the scandal? How many were able to make a clean transition?"

Mason grinned. "Touché. I came out of it better than most."

Camilla thought about it for a moment. It made sense. They were all survivors, but of different things: cancer, domestic violence, accidents, war, natural disaster, prison, child abuse, gang violence, corporate scandal, and...

"Jordan, how about you?" she asked.

Jordan leaned forward, draping herself over Juan's back and letting her arms dangle over his chest. She rested her chin on his shoulder.

"I've been thinking about this while you guys were talking, but I can't come up with anything. In fact, the last few days here have been the roughest in my entire life. Could I have been some kind of mistake?"

"I don't believe that for a second." Brent waved a hand at the gifts scattered across the floor, the monitor on the wall. "This whole thing has been orchestrated too carefully for a case of mistaken identity. There must be something that explains your presence here. Maybe, as in Mason's case, yours wasn't literal life-or-death survival."

"I've led a fairly sheltered life, especially after hearing your stories. I've always gotten what I wanted, and people have been really nice to me. Could your theory that Julian chose survivors be wrong?"

"The math says it can't be wrong," Mason said. "Let's say the odds of a person being a survivor are—"

"One in ten." Camilla sat up straight. "No, wait, I'm wrong. One in ten people is a survivor *type*. That's different. We're actual *survivors*."

Brent nodded. "Say ten percent are survivor types—the people likeliest to make it through a life-or-death situation. But most of them never end up facing those situations. Actual proven survivors? We're much rarer. I don't have the numbers."

"Even at one in ten," Mason said, "just do the math, Jordan. Statistically, only one of the contestants here should have been a survivor type. But eight of us were not only survivor types, but proven survivors. The odds are—"

"I get what you're saying. Less than one in two million," Jordan said. "Less than one in a *hundred* million if we count your story, too. But it still doesn't change what I'm saying." She held her hand up, displaying it. "It's not that nothing bad has ever happened to me. I broke a finger once..."

Her pinky *was* a little crooked. Camilla had never noticed it before.

Jordan dropped her hand. "But that's about the worst I can come up with."

A sudden thought struck Camilla.

"Control group," she said, recoiling from the awfulness of the idea even as she spoke. "What if this is some kind of sick psychological experiment and you're supposed to be our control group?"

Jordan shook her head. "Psychology experiments have to pass ethics review boards. I took a grad psych class at Stanford, and we had a guest lecture from Phil Zimbardo—you know, the 'Zimbardo experiment' guy? Back in the seventies, he had half his subjects play prison guards and half play prisoners, but he had to shut the whole thing down because the mock prison guards turned abusive for real. Nowadays, an experiment like that would never be allowed. Psychologists can't even come close to doing the stuff reality shows do—that's why they love to analyze them."

"Besides, you're no control group," Brent said. "You're definitely a survivor type; your performance in Julian's stupid games proves it. Your shoes, your food situation—these additional handicaps should have put you at a *huge* disadvantage, but up until today you were ahead of us all. The real question is, how did Julian know you were a survivor—or a survivor *type*?"

Jordan rubbed her crooked pinky with her other hand, thinking.

"I was a competitive gymnast. That's how I broke this. But I quit after high school." She shook her head. "I don't know. There's nothing, really."

"There's *got* to be something." Brent scratched the side of his head. "You told me about your fiancé passing away. Maybe Julian chose you because you're a survivor of emotional trauma."

"But I wouldn't say I was traumatized by it. He wasn't my fiancé anymore, and we were long over by then. I was seeing someone else. Sure, I was a little sad for him when I heard—anybody would be. But I can't really see what that has to do with being a survivor type."

"How did your fiancé die?" Brent asked.

"*Ex*-fiancé. He killed himself, actually. Like I said, it was pretty sad. He was smart and had a bright future ahead of him, but he obviously had some problems and couldn't deal with them."

"Frankly, that sounds kind of cold, Jordan. But I suppose it's not surprising given what else we've seen from you here. Think about what that says about you."

"About *me*?" Anger hardened her voice. She detached herself from Juan and sat up straight. "I don't remember asking for your opinion, but let's pursue this a little, shall we? My ex kills himself and I don't let it ruin my life, so I'm callous; I'm a bad person. On the other hand, you get high, chase off your family, and kill somebody's kid. Then you lie to us all. But because you feel all sorry and regretful, that makes you a good person? That gives *you* the right to judge *me*, you fucking junkie?"

"That's enough, Jordan." Camilla raised her voice, hearing Brent's breathing coming heavy and fast.

"I'm not finished yet." Jordan shook off Juan's hand, too, and stood up.

"For your information, Brent, my ex, Jonathan, was a fucking drug addict, too, so I'm getting pretty tired of listening to *your* sanctimonious bullshit. The only difference I see between you and him right now is one overdose, but who knows? The night is still young."

Camilla stood up, too. "Both of you. Let's stay focused on why we're here, instead of attacking each other."

Juan reached up and took Jordan's hand and pulled her down to sit beside him again.

"That's better." Camilla spread her hands, looking at them all.

"So why would Julian specifically seek out survivor types as contestants? Who is Vita Brevis Entertainment, and what are they *really* trying to do here?"

CHAPTER 103

The hiss of pouring rain rose out of the gray fog, drumming on the awning that covered the distant huddle of black-clad mourners. The chaplain's eulogy, delivered in Spanish, drifted across the wet grass and shining headstones. It floated up the hill to where JT stood alone under a leafless tree.

The dying tree provided him no shelter. Rain pelted the hood of his poncho. Water streamed down his arms as he watched the honor guard fold the flag into a neat bicorn triangle and present it to Mrs. Sanchez. Her expression was invisible behind the heavy black veil, but JT could see, even from fifty yards away, how the two younger women at her side struggled to hold her upright and quell her shaking.

The Marines of the honor guard—JT's former platoon mates—saluted Mrs. Sanchez. Sobbing, she shuddered before them, head bowed, her body hunched in spite of the relatives supporting her arms at each side. The Marines held the salute, and JT felt the urge to salute, too, to honor the kid's memory. But he couldn't; the gesture would have been unwelcome. He knew that the honor guard was aware of his solitary presence on the hill, even though they refused to acknowledge him.

He watched, silent and impassive, as the bugler raised his instrument. The mournful, lonely notes of "Taps" reached his ears. They gave him no solace, no sense of release as they faded away. Their finality only made the weight that sat in his chest grow heavier. He closed his eyes against the comfortless gray as the hiss of the rain also faded to silence.

Someone moved close by, stealthy in the darkness.

JT came awake with a jolt of adrenaline. Tingling sensations rippled down his arms and legs. Where was he? Unimportant. Focus on the threat.

Semiconscious, he strained to clear his head but couldn't shake the muzziness that fogged his thinking. The comforting black cloud of slumber would be easy to slide back into, and that scared him. He was drugged, anesthetized, lying on his back. The dull pain in his face throbbed in time with his heartbeat. Sharp spikes stabbed behind his left eye, into his head. He could feel scratchy gauze on his cheek and brow, tape pulling taut on his forehead and cheekbone.

JT stared with his right eye, desperately trying to see. The room floated in the deep gloom, its blurry outlines visible, but he could make out no details. Something or someone had awakened him. He could sense a presence nearby.

337

He tried to reposition himself on the cot without making a sound, but his arms and legs were sluggish and failed to respond.

"It's all fun and games until someone loses an eye, huh?"

Travis's voice came from the side, near his head. He tried to scramble to a sitting position, but his drugged limbs betrayed him again. He couldn't move.

His heart hammered violently in his chest.

"I wonder who did it," Travis said. "Funny thing is, wouldn't really surprise me to find out it was any one of 'em. A real prize group, ain't they all?"

Something rustled near his head, and JT twitched. His leaden limbs wouldn't respond.

"But I could always finish what they started, I suppose." A sharp point touched his cheek. "How 'bout I shiv out your other eye?"

Terrified, he strained his muscles and managed a weak flop, shifting an inch or two.

"Or I could gut you, leave you to die hard."

A sharp point touched and trailed down his stomach, but the paralysis held him to the cot. He couldn't move, couldn't speak.

"You and me, we have unfinished business together. That's a fact." Travis's voice moved away. "But our business, it'll have to wait."

JT could see him now, silhouetted against a dim rectangle in the darkness—the doorway of the room.

"I've got some other business to attend to first," Travis said. "But keep an eye out for me. Yep, keep an eye out." He chuckled.

Then he was gone.

JT felt cold sweat trickling down his scalp, turning chilly in the night air. He tried again to move, muscles fighting against the lingering paralysis from the anesthetic, but he could manage only a few more inches. Then the fog closed over him again, washing everything away.

CHAPTER 104

"It's Latin, obviously," Veronica said. "Like *'semper fidelis.'* *'Vita Brevis'* means... 'brave life,' maybe?"

"No." Jordan sounded calmer but still angry. "Think 'brevity,' 'abbreviated.' It comes from a famous quote by Hippocrates. *'Ars longa, vita brevis.'* 'Art is long, life is short.'"

Camilla sat up straight.

Jordan noticed her surprise. "The benefits of a liberal arts education, I guess. I got my master's at Stanford, in communications."

"But 'art is long, life is short,' though?" The lead lump turned over in Camilla's stomach again. "That sounds like a sick joke, considering what happened to Lauren. Almost makes you think there's something to Mason's creepy theory, like they're throwing it in our faces."

"Get a grip." Veronica waved her hand, as if dispersing a bad smell. "Someone dies accidentally, and now we're in some kind of a... I don't know... *snuff film*? Is that what you two think?"

"I'm keeping an open mind," Mason said.

She snorted. "Look, I'm sure those things exist, and that there's a market for them—sickos probably buy them over the Internet. But you're talking about shaky Handycam footage of hookers getting murdered in dirty basements—not something like this. Are you people forgetting that yacht? That's millions and millions of dollars of boat. And the money we saw... Who would go to this level of expense to make a snuff film? The whole idea's asinine."

Camilla flushed. "Mason's got quite an imagination, and I'm not saying he's right, but I can't explain—"

"Two possibilities." Veronica held up her finger, looked at her hand, frowned, and scraped something from under her thumbnail. "Number one— which I think is most likely—a runaway train wreck of stupidity. Some Hollywood son of a bitch who I'd love to get my hands on, well, he thought it would be more entertaining to watch people who fit your survivor profile compete with each other, instead of average folks. We'd be tougher, less likely to quit, more resourceful, et cetera. Studio execs loved the concept, so they green-lit it, handed him a big budget. They went out and found us; then they dangled the cash in front of us like a carrot. But it didn't work out as planned. There was violence. Someone died."

Camilla shook her head. "But why would they keep—"

"The people in charge panicked at first, but then they decided the damage was done. A few more days wouldn't change their liability exposure, or they could buy their way out of trouble later—pay us off or something. Idiotic, but this *is* Hollywood we're talking about. I can see it happening."

"No," Camilla said. "I work in the film industry. No studio would ever—"

Veronica raised a second finger, cutting her off. "Possibility number two, if we're thinking out of the box. It's personal. Revenge. One of us pissed off somebody very rich and powerful, and this whole thing is some kind of elaborate setup. Maybe getting revenge any other way would be traceable back to that person, I don't know. Maybe the rest of us were meant to be witnesses to an "accidental" death in one of these games that wasn't really going to be accidental. But no one could have anticipated Lauren's *real* accident, and it's thrown everything off."

Mason looked at Brent. "Doc, the kid you killed—was her dad by any chance a rich Hollywood entertainment mogul?"

"I'm not going to dignify that with an answer." Brent's eyes glittered oddly in the lamplight as he stood. "I'm going to go check on my patients. But, Mason, maybe your dead senior partner Dorer had a relative who didn't like how you managed to duck any responsibility for what your firm and your whole bloodsucking industry did to us all." He trudged out of the room with heavy steps.

"Jordan's right, you know." Veronica's voice held a harsh edge. "Brent's using again. Look closely at his eyes when he gets back. His pupils should be dilated in this low light, and instead they're pinpricks."

Camilla's hands tightened into helpless fists. "The first-aid kit."

"Another cute little present from our hidden hosts." Even in the dim light, Veronica's expression looked bitter. "Knowing Brent's history, they loaded it with class-A restricted pharmaceuticals. I saw fentanyl, propofol in there, OxyContin—the kind of scheduled drugs you normally keep under lock and key, even in a hospital."

"I did notice something different in the way he's been acting," Camilla said. "How do we stop him from taking them?"

"This isn't an episode of *Intervention,*" Mason said. "So long as he isn't a danger to us, I don't see that it's a priority."

"No, that's not fair." She thought about the injured people upstairs, the toll it must be taking on Brent. "We all need to try to help him."

"He'll be fine." Jordan stood up, pulling Juan to his feet also, and headed toward the door. The sarcasm in her voice cut through the room. "Like he said, he's a *survivor,* remember?"

CHAPTER 105

Inside Shark Station Zebra's old buildings, Jacob sat on a cot with his head in his hands. Heather watched him out of the corner of her eye as she gathered stacks of their notes and documents. She could hear him mumbling, and occasionally he shook his head. But he never looked up.

On a nearby cot, Dmitry lay with his arms crossed behind his head. He seemed to be thinking. The light of the battery lantern was dim, but they had been able to collect most of what they needed.

The TV people had scattered their notes and reports. Pages were folded, dog-eared, torn. Even though there were bigger problems to worry about, this still bothered Heather a lot—a little respect for others went a long way in this world. The nice woman, Camilla, had at least had the decency to give them some prepackaged meals and a quarter jug of water. She looked sad about it, and Heather wondered why until she realized that the food and water probably belonged to the woman who died.

"I'm putting in for a transfer to San Diego," Jacob said into the silence. "You guys should, too."

Dmitry sat up. "Okay, is very nice idea. But what should we do *right now*? Some of these people, they are not safe to be around."

Heather agreed. "There's something off about all of them. Like we're dealing with a group of sociopaths. And none of them trust each other—did you notice that?"

"We're leaving tomorrow first thing," Jacob said. "Beyond that, I can't think. Karen shouldn't get away with this. The press will be all over the shark attack. It'll be 1994, the kayak guy all over again, but ten times worse because this was a fatality."

She stopped sorting papers and turned to look at him. "Worrying about that is not really important right now." Was he confused?

Dmitry was squinting at Jacob with a puzzled expression on his face.

"How exactly are we leaving?" Heather asked. "There's no boat. No Coast Guard drive-bys, because you told them last year it interrupts the animals' natural behavior and disrupts our studies. No working radios or cell phones. So what's the plan?"

"Fuck." Jacob shook his head without lifting it from his hands. "I just don't know."

Dmitry settled back and crossed his arms behind his head again.

"Looks like we stucking here."

CHAPTER 106

"Travis is gone."

Camilla glanced up sharply to see Brent in the doorway again, his hands in his vest pockets. She could see the unnatural glitter in his eyes, the tiny pupils. Veronica and Jordan were right.

Veronica made a wordless sound of disgust. "I thought you sedated him."

Next to her, Natalie slipped her hands inside her hoodie pockets and slid a little closer.

"I did," Brent said. "But I couldn't risk a code blue—this isn't a hospital, in case you hadn't noticed."

"What about JT?"

"You're concern is touching. I'll be sure to tell him." Brent half-turned toward the doorway. "He's dozing again, but he had dragged himself halfway off the cot."

"Maybe you should have paid more attention to your dosing, Brent."

"Maybe you should have shown a little more restraint when you enucleated him, Veronica."

Camilla stood up. "But Travis... we can't leave him stumbling around outside, half-drugged, with a dislocated shoulder—"

Mason raised a hand. "I'm okay with that."

"Oh god, shut up already." Camilla grimaced at him. "Who's coming with me?"

Veronica stood up also. She looked down at Natalie for a moment, then nodded to Camilla.

"I'll go with you—mostly because I don't like the idea of him creeping around at night while we're asleep. But just inside the barricade; if we don't find him, he's on his own." She dusted off her hands. "Are you coming, Brent?"

"No, Travis has caused me enough headaches for one day." His eyes rose, moving back and forth between the two women, and Camilla's heart sank, seeing how wide his irises were, the pupils drowning in a glittering sea of blue.

Brent's gaze locked on Veronica's face, and his brows tightened. "Just make sure you don't kill him."

CHAPTER 107

Juan sat at the edge of his cot, staring out the open doorway of the blockhouse he shared with Jordan. He would close the door again tonight and padlock it from within, but for now the cool air wafting from outside felt good. With no windows, the blockhouse got stuffy quickly once the door was closed, and the cloying odor of mildew bothered him in a way that the strong natural smells of the seals didn't.

Ordinarily, he enjoyed the animal noises, too—the barking, yelping din of the seals lulled him. But he had developed a feel for Año Nuevo's rhythms, learned the normal nightly cycle of its seal populations, and he could tell they had changed.

Something was not right.

He closed his eyes, listening, letting his mind free-float. He had sensed the strangeness on the second night—an ill-defined unease rippling through the barks and yips that swelled and subsided through the dark hours, until dawn. The third night, it was worse. The seals' cries were more muted, cutting off faster, the silences in between deeper. Juan had initially ascribed the change to the contestants' own presence; with ten humans moving about the island during the day, the seals would no doubt find their activity disruptive.

But now he was sure, it was more than that. Because by the fourth night, he could put a name to the change in Año Nuevo's night rhythms, to the new tentativeness in the barks and yips of the seals.

Fear.

Nightfall on Año Nuevo had become a time of terror.

• • •

The flickering yellow light of a candle lit the blockhouse. The door was closed, shutting out the night. Shadows danced on the walls. Soft light glowed from Jordan's high cheekbones, her straight nose, her elegant neck, her wide sensuous mouth. She sat cross-legged on the other cot, watching him, very still. Juan liked how she didn't feel the need to fill the silence. He liked the way she watched him. Last night, he had woken more than once to see her lying on her side with her cheek on her forearm, watching him from across the dim room. He had wanted to go to her, but something inside had stopped him. He thought of what he had hidden from her, under the cabinet

345

floorboards, and rolled onto his back to stare at the ceiling. His throat was suddenly tight.

With a gentle rustle, Jordan uncurled her legs and stood up. She glided over to the counter and stopped there, her back to him. Juan admired the graceful way she moved—like a dancer, a ballerina, but with an aggressive purposefulness that made most dancers look like pale, flighty imitations. She intrigued him, puzzled him.

Jordan raised her hands in front of her. Her shoulders moved gently, rhythmically. He couldn't see what she was doing, but he knew she was rubbing her finger—the pinky she had once broken. It was an unconscious gesture he had learned to recognize, an indication of stress or indecision. The Jordan he was coming to know was a very different creature from the vivacious, bubbly, outgoing woman she had first seemed. He had to admit, he did not understand her at all. And that scared him.

She turned and glided over to his cot, sitting on the edge where he lay. Her slim fingers brushed his hair, slowly sweeping it away from his forehead. Juan's heart sped up. He looked up into those large emerald eyes, their irises flawless. Her pupils were very large in the candlelight, her unsmiling face beautiful in repose.

Jordan's index finger traced the scar at his hairline, rubbing it gently, softly, barely making contact. Juan turned his head away and swallowed, feeling the old sorrow rise up inside him. Gently grasping his chin, she turned his face toward hers again, and her mouth drifted toward his. She stopped an inch from his lips and slid upward until her full lips brushed his scar in a light, feathery kiss. Then she pulled back and tilted her head, staring down at him.

Her expression didn't change. He reached for her face to trace its lines, its contours, but her hand rose between them to intercept his, palm to palm. Lacing her fingers through his own, Jordan squeezed hard. She curled her wrist, drawing his wrist toward her chest, and laid the back of his hand against her heart. He could feel her heart beating, fast and forceful, through their joined hands.

Jordan's head dipped again, bringing her lips to his.

• • •

The air was filled with her scent. Their scent. Juan opened the door, enjoying the coolness of the night breeze for a moment, before returning to her. The wind swirled through the blockhouse, drying the sweat on their bodies. He inhaled, enjoying her musky, clean smell. The dive knife in his hand was a distraction but, with the door open, an unpleasant necessity.

"You realize we probably gave them quite a show," Jordan said.

He nodded. He wasn't too concerned about cameras right now. Listening to the sounds outside the doorway, he relaxed. The seals he had startled by opening the door were settling again—they would provide him some warning if anyone approached. Lying beside Jordan, he placed the knife on the ground next to them. She raised herself on one elbow, running a finger down the center of his chest. Then her curious fingers traced the circular scars on his chest and abdomen.

"I saw you change your shirt yesterday. I wondered about these."

She tapped the center of his chest twice with her finger. "I'm *still* wondering about them. Your story was bullshit."

He slid the side of his thumb down her spine, feeling the bumps and recesses, the smooth, firm muscle to each side. "Why?"

"Oh, I'm sure there's some truth to parts of it. Not bad for something you made up on the spur of the moment. But Juan..." Her fingers stroked his chest, the sides of his neck. "No ink."

"Tattoos can be removed."

"There's also the way you speak. Diction. Your vocabulary. Your manners. I give it exactly zero likelihood that you grew up on the streets. You went to very good schools, learned flawless English young enough to have no accent at all."

"So you think I'm Julian's plant? The fake contestant?"

"No." Jordan put a finger on his lips. "You're not."

She kissed him, lingering, and his hands buried themselves in her hair, holding the sides of her face.

"I trust my instincts about people," she said when they stopped to breathe. "I think your reasons for keeping quiet are your own, and not Julian's."

Juan kissed her again. It would be so easy to lose himself in this bubble of suspended time with Jordan, to forget why he had come. He stared into her eyes, wondering what she was thinking.

What about after this was all over? What would happen then?

He remembered the hurt, betrayed faces of the other contestants when Julian outed the two of them, revealing their shipboard deception. Best not to set himself up for a similar betrayal, game or no game. He pushed the thought away, not liking the sharp pang it sent through his chest.

Jordan's fingers spread behind his head, gripped his hair tight. Her mouth opened, hungry against his. Juan rolled, and she moved beneath him.

\

CHAPTER 108

Travis stumbled through the darkness, across the open ground. Ahead lay the barricade, a low-lying line of darker black. Every step sent an explosion of pain through his shoulder, neck, and chest, making him want to puke. But he had survived worse. Much worse. The shoulder wasn't actually broken, he reckoned; it was dislocated.

The pain wasn't the worst of it. The sickening pressure yanking at his shoulder and arm was worse. He knew it came from ligaments and tendons and what-all, stretched out of place by a bone that wasn't where it was supposed to be. That old crackhead hadn't fixed it; he'd just given Travis some weak shit to knock him out. Son of a bitch was probably saving all the good stuff for himself.

Travis shook off the light-headed feeling the drug hangover had left him with. He knew what needed to be done. Fuck the doc. He had learned to rely on himself for a lot of things, and he could take care of this by himself, too.

Getting over the barricade one-armed hurt like hell. Grunting with pain, he rose from a squat on the other side, sending seals skittering away from him. Gritting his teeth, he took a couple of steps after one of them, overtaking it. Travis kicked it as hard as he could, feeling bone give beneath the toe of his boot. The pain that detonated in his shoulder dropped him to his knees but he grinned through the agony, listening to the injured seal's cries.

How do you like them *apples, Julian?*

He struggled back to his feet.

• • •

A few minutes later, Travis stood at the island's highest point. Tilting his head back, he looked up at the rusty scaffolding of the downed lighthouse tower. The night sky was featureless and overcast, a lighter gray than the ground and sea below. Cold wind rippled his jeans and work shirt, making crisp crackling sounds in the near-silence.

Trying to brace himself for what he had to do, he found himself dallying. But then he thought about Natalie.

Unknotting the sling from his injured arm, he held it in his teeth and grabbed his bad wrist with his good hand. Resting his forehead against the cool metal of a rusty spar, grunting and gasping with the pain, he lifted his bad arm in front of him to head height. Bracing it against the metal, he took the fabric sling from his mouth and looped it around his wrist a few times, tying it securely to the spar.

He took a deep breath, then another. This was going to hurt like a bitch—he couldn't let himself think about it for too long.

Skidding both feet forward, he let his body drop. He collapsed to a half-sitting position at the base of the tower wreckage, hanging from his bad arm.

The explosion of pain unfolded through his body, worse than he had expected, but his shoulder popped back into place. Throwing his head back, he slammed it against the metal of the tower over and over, gasping. He sucked in a huge breath, scrambling to get his legs back under him. The pain expanded like a red wave, crashing over him, washing him away, but it felt almost good, now that the terrible pressure in his shoulder was gone.

Travis passed out, slumped at the base of the tower with one arm tied above his head.

CHAPTER 109

Camilla pulled herself through the orange-lit darkness, surrounded by screams and sobs, dragging her useless legs behind her. Patches of fire glowed here and there, seen through the rubble. The broken roof pressed in overhead, crushing down onto the warren of broken, soot-stained tunnels she crawled through. She hit dead end after dead end, where fire reflected off the shiny hubcaps, crumpled car panels, and fractured, sloping walls of concrete. It was always the same, this terrible place of her dreams, almost comforting in its familiarity. Voices, echoing and muted, cried out in the orange dimness, calling the names of loved ones, pleading for help.

There had to be a way out. But she had never found it.

Somewhere under here, she had also lost her little mermaid doll. She missed it, even though it had gotten all dirty and yucky: sticky with something dark.

But there was a difference this time. She wasn't alone. Something else was in here with her, moving amid the fire and screams, crawling through the darkness close behind. A person, an adult. She looked over her shoulder to see who it was, but for some reason, she could never turn her head quite far enough to glimpse a face.

Camilla pushed ahead, driven deeper into the maze by her pursuer. She was in unfamiliar territory now. Or was she?

Up ahead, a slight clearing, hazy with smoke. A familiar blue car, crushed beneath the lowered ceiling that brushed her head. The upper half of the driver's-side door, the window frame bent outward, folded almost double. Dark wetness trailing down the lower half of the door in thick, syrupy streams. Small, dark handprints everywhere.

She turned her head away.

The fire cast just enough light for Camilla to finally see her pursuer: a man with long black hair, in an elegant suit smudged with blood and soot, his adult frame looming over her child's body. He raised his head, meeting her eyes.

Julian grinned at her from above. His mouth gaped impossibly wide, cheeks tearing with a meaty rip, skin peeling back as his jaws cracked apart, splitting his face, ripping his head open until she was staring into a yawning, bloody cavity lined with jagged, triangular white razors.

Shark's teeth.

CHAPTER 110

Juan lay on his back. Jordan moved above him in a slow rhythm. She was leaning forward over him, her elbows straight, her palms atop one another, pressing down on his heart as if she were trying to restart it. She watched him, her face serious, her eyes sometimes glazed, sometimes widening, sometimes fierce with concentration.

Hours had passed. The candles had burned down to stubs. They had found a place together that was no place, where there were no words, where the passage of time had no meaning. Juan's eyes wanted to close, to let him be carried away by sensation, but he didn't want them to. He wouldn't be able to see her, then—wouldn't be able to look into those bottomless green eyes.

Her breathing quickened. She slowed their rhythm, and a tiny furrow of concern appeared between her eyebrows. He reached up and smoothed it away with his finger, but it reappeared. Her gaze flicked back and forth, from his left eye to his right; she was almost frowning. Then her eyes flickered and glazed over, the way a shark's nictating eyelid closed white to protect the only place it was vulnerable, the second before it struck.

Jordan went rigid, shuddering above him, her muscles locked. He laced the fingers of both hands through hers, and her eyes widened, deepened, pulling him in. Juan gasped, drawn into the expanding ripples where their bodies joined. Arms shaking, he held her suspended over him as the waves washed through them as one. He fought to keep his eyes open, staring up into her perfect face.

Timeless, the moment. Endless.

Jordan's body relaxed, slumping down on him a little at a time. She lowered her head, the waves of her hair falling forward in a curtain that hid her expression.

There was silence. When she spoke at last, her voice was inflectionless.

"I've never felt this way before," she said. "Not ever."

He tensed. What did she mean?

She looked at him, trembling, eyes wide with fear.

"I'm scared, Juan."

He relaxed, but a needle of disappointment wormed its way through his chest.

Her unblinking eyes were fixed on his face now. She didn't breathe.

He raised a hand to her cheek. "I am, too, Jordan."

Her expression softened.

353

He looked out the open doorway, toward the darkness they had escaped together for a few hours, and thought about it.

"I think we all are," he said.

Jordan rolled off him suddenly, a blur of motion, moving toward the door. Scooping up her dress with one hand and the speargun with the other, she exited, leaving him staring at the empty, dark doorway.

A hollow sense of loss spread through his chest and tightened his stomach. Had he said something wrong?

She was gone.

CHAPTER 111

Travis blinked, his consciousness returning. The moonless sky above him was now diamond clear, lit by millions of bright pinpoint stars. From the change in the sky, and the way the sweat had cooled on his body, chilling him, several hours must have gone by. The broken scaffolding of the tower loomed above, blocking some of the stars. His shoulder still hurt like a motherfucker, but the pressure was gone.

Staggering to his feet, he untied his wrist from the spar. Then he sat down again, with his back against the tower's wreckage. His forehead ran with fresh sweat from the pain, but he found he could move his bad arm a little and flex his fingers. Lifting his knees, he cradled his injured arm in his lap, looking at the stars. They stared down from above, silent eyes watching him, cold and indifferent. They didn't care what he did here—what *anybody* did here. A million years from now, they still wouldn't care.

All around, the island lay dark and silent. The shapes of seals shifted restlessly around him, but most lay huddled, sleeping. He sat a while longer, thinking of camping trips in his childhood, so long ago. Then he stood up.

He retied the sling around his shoulder. Down the slope, he could see a change in the factory warehouse buildings where Julian's crew had been hiding. Faint light gleamed from a window that the boards no longer covered.

Who was in there? Not that it mattered anymore—they had *all* fucked him over. Julian and his crew had, too. Travis owed them all now, but he wasn't going to make the same mistake as last time. He would find a safe place to hole up... catch them one by one.

It was time for some payback.

CHAPTER 112

Juan found her an hour later, sitting by herself on the shale beach of a narrow cove near the north end of the island. The sun was coming up, painting the edge of the horizon in pink and peach. Jordan sat very still, holding the speargun across her knees, watching the sunrise. She seemed smaller somehow, shrunken, huddled against the cold. A train of pelicans crossed overhead, looking like pterodactyls, visitors from a bygone age.

He settled himself on the sand next to her, and she leaned against him. He pointed.

"*Zalophus californicus*. Sea lions. See the ears? And over there, harbor seals—*phocidae*. Offshore in the kelp, you'll find otters, too. They're quite playful when you come across them underwater."

Jordan took his hand and held it to her cheek.

"Julian was clever," she said. "The contract had no nondisclosure clause, no grant of exclusivity on distribution. When I saw that, I figured they'd slipped up. Do you see?"

He nodded. "The ultimate scoop. You'd be able to report the story any way you saw fit, even before the show aired. They'd be at your mercy. You'd be able to dictate your own terms to them."

"Especially if I won. They gave us half an hour on the ship to look at the papers, and I was jumping up and down, eager to sign before they caught on to their mistake. I fell for it, Juan."

"This isn't what it was made out to be."

"I know that now," she said. "But I don't know what's really going on here."

He slid his hand free, tossed a pebble into the water. "I'm going to find out."

Curling against him, she tucked her forehead into his cheek. Her hand sought his again, lacing their fingers into one. "We'll find out together."

Then she stiffened. "Your hair is wet, Juan."

"I know."

She leaned away, looking up into his face, surprising him with the vulnerability of her soft gaze. Then she lowered her eyes.

"Juan, I... I think I'm in..." She squeezed his hand.

"I..." Her voice had lost all inflection again. "...trust you."

He looked at her feet, bleeding into the sand again. At the speargun across her lap. Face stiffening, he closed his eyes and held her to him.

"I know."

Day 6

Wednesday: December 26, 2012

CHAPTER 113

Morning. Camilla stood on the boardwalk at the top of the bluff, a breeze rippling her hair as she looked down at the beach below. Elephant seals moved back and forth, shuffling along the sand, but they seemed to be staying well back from the water—something she didn't remember them doing before. Did they sense the shark, lurking somewhere nearby just offshore? Fragments of last night's dream came back to her, and she shivered.

But she recalled the long-ago Woods Hole shark expert saying that great whites didn't stick to one location for long, preferring to cruise up and down the coast. In all probability, the shark that had killed Lauren and tried for Dmitry was long gone.

No, they had other predators to worry about now. *Human* predators. Travis was still lurking somewhere, and none of them would be safe until they found him.

"Didn't we catch him this way once already?" Mason's hushed voice drifted out of the chicken coop behind her. "I doubt he's dumb enough to fall for it twice."

"Be quiet," Camilla said in a loud whisper, without looking in his direction. "I'm thinking maybe *you* should've been the bait this time."

Mason laughed. "No doubt. But then again, I *am* the one with the bear spray."

"I thought I threw that away, by the way."

"A secret admirer left another can of it by my bed. It was there when I woke up."

"Oh god, you must be lying. Does this mean you're Julian's spy?"

"No."

"Would you tell me if you were?"

"No. Probably not."

"Wonderful."

Could Mason be Julian's spy? She had to admit, his actions made him a good candidate for it. If he was lying about the bear spray now, though, it was a pretty weak effort. He definitely hadn't chained the scientist's boat, either. Still, there was a pattern to Mason's outrageous behavior. He had antagonized people, angered them, pushed them until they reacted with violence. Her stomach coiled as she remembered the blade that had come so close. Mason's taunts had almost gotten her killed yesterday. And these morbid theories he kept spouting...

361

But what *was* Julian trying to accomplish here? That he had recruited proven survivors was beyond a doubt, but that wasn't all he had done. There were other patterns visible in the specific mix of contestants he had chosen. Disturbing ones.

A violent child molester, a girl who had suffered sexual abuse as a child, and a woman who reacted to abuse with lethal violence?

A recovered drug addict provided with a tempting supply of drugs, and an outspoken young woman who had lost her drug-addicted fiancé to suicide?

There was no reason to include a rescue beacon in the scavenger hunt, unless its destruction had been intended all along, to throw suspicion onto JT—who, she was now sure, hadn't broken it.

Camilla thought of little Avery and her other kids, the bond she felt with them, and how she had reacted when she heard about the child Brent had killed. It had been hard for her to keep silent. A bitter taste soured her mouth, and she looked at her feet.

If Julian's goal had been interpersonal conflict and strife among the contestants, he had chosen them all well.

"...*and other qualifications*," the Vita Brevis letter had said.

She felt violated.

They all had given Julian exactly what he wanted, too, playing into his hands right up to the point where Lauren died. But things were completely out of control now. Why were the producers allowing this to continue?

If Mason was Julian's spy, was he also here as a catalyst, to instigate more problems? If so, this plan to catch Travis, which she had talked him into this morning, could very well blow up in her face.

"Forget about it," she called. "This is a waste of time."

"That's what I said an hour ago." Mason ducked out of the chicken coop. "Travis probably crawled into a hole somewhere to lick his wounds... unless he decided to swim for it and save us all the trouble."

"Mason, that's awful. Can you try acting like a normal person for a few hours? For *my* sake?"

"Name one normal person on this island." He paused. "Well, okay, maybe our three new guests. But then again, how normal is it to make great white sharks the focus of your life? Normal is overrated, Camilla. If you believe Brent, normal people aren't survivors."

"You called the SEC, didn't you? You're the one who brought them in. To investigate your own firm."

Mason grinned. "I hated to see the taxpayers bear the burden of such irresponsible corporate greed."

"You're so bad." Camilla shook her head. "I don't know what I'm going to do with you."

Movement drew her gaze to the narrow southern end of the beach below. Two human figures, small in the distance. Veronica, demonstrating something to Natalie. Teaching her. Camilla's stomach tensed, watching their movements.

"Krav Maga," Mason said, drawing up beside her. "A martial art developed by the Israeli Defense Forces." He chuckled. "Makes sense that the most picked-on, most abused people in history would come up with the deadliest form of self-protection. And that Veronica would be drawn to it."

"I've never heard of it." Camilla found it disturbing to watch.

"That's because there's no way to turn it into a sport like karate, jiu-jitsu, et cetera. Krav Maga's all business—strictly killing and maiming." He pointed at the women down on the beach. "Watch. There aren't any purely defensive motions. Every single move includes a counterattack."

"When JT grabbed her yesterday, I was terrified," Camilla said. "I thought for sure she was dead."

He nodded. "Hindsight's twenty-twenty, but this does make a lot of sense after what happened in her first marriage. She made sure she'd never end up in the same position again."

"Julian's profile was a bit vague about her second marriage."

"I wondered about that, too." He smiled. "But I think it's safe to say that Veronica can take care of herself."

Camilla watched Veronica correct Natalie's stance, holding her shoulder and guiding her elbow through a short arc. Even from a distance, she could see that Natalie appeared eager to learn but lacked any kind of physical aptitude. Veronica seemed patient with the younger woman, encouraging her.

"It makes me sad to watch this," Camilla said.

"Yeah, she is a pretty hopeless student, isn't she?"

"That's *not* what I meant…"

Footsteps pounded the boardwalk behind them. She looked up as Dmitry came to a stop beside them, red-faced, catching his breath.

"You see Heather this morning?" he asked. "Jacob thinks maybe she went for walk. But I look everywhere."

The concern in his face deepened into fear.

"I can't find her."

CHAPTER 114

"When and where did you see her last?" Brent asked.

"Last night," Jacob said. "She was right next door to us, trying to get some sleep in the other room of the station."

Brent tucked his hands into his vest pockets and glanced at Camilla. He was high again, she could tell. If anything, his eyes were worse now than last night.

Everyone was gathered on the flat ground outside the houses, except for JT, who was still sedated upstairs, and Travis. And, of course, Heather.

From their brief meeting, she had seemed a nice, thoughtful person. Camilla's heart sped up. If something had happened to her, then Camilla herself was to blame. She'd been right there at the seal barricade last night when Veronica turned back.

"Travis is where he belongs," Veronica had said, wrinkling her nose. "With all the other animals. You can do what you like. I'm going to bed."

Peering into the darkness, Camilla had pointed toward the dim outlines of the factory buildings. "We really should go tell those three."

"Right." Veronica waved a hand in dismissal. "Be my guest."

She walked back toward the houses, and Camilla had followed her.

Camilla had been afraid. And now she felt guilty.

This was her fault.

"There's something we should have told you," she said, addressing Jacob and Dmitry. "Travis, our missing contestant, is dangerous. He's a convicted rapist, a felon—"

"And now this happens." The way Jacob stared at her made her drop her eyes. "Couldn't any of you have had the basic decency to warn us when you lost track of him?"

"There was a lot going on yesterday," Brent said, but his eyes flicked toward Camilla again.

She looked away. It would have been so easy to hop the barricade and run to the station, pound on their door and yell a warning, and then sprint back. Just a couple of minutes. But it had been dark, hard to see. Travis could have been lurking anywhere, ready to grab her. He was strong—even one-armed, he could have covered her mouth and dragged her away, to where the noise of the seals would cover her screams while he did anything he wanted to her. She remembered the malice in that flat gaze.

And now Heather had paid the price for Camilla's cowardice.

365

"Let's start where she disappeared," she said. "At the station. See if we can find something that gives us an idea what happened, and then we'll sweep the whole island again."

Two minutes later, Jacob led them inside the station's second room.

"She normally sleeps in here," he said. "When there aren't too many rapey criminal types roaming the island unattended, that is."

He pointed back through the doorway to the first room. "And we were in there."

Camilla looked around Heather's small sleeping space. Sunlight streamed into the un-boarded window, illuminating a cot with tangled blankets trailing onto the floor. The only other furniture was the small worktable with its two cheap plastic chairs, all stacked with binders and notebooks. One stack had spilled onto the floor, creasing the pages and covers of several reports, but otherwise there was nothing to see.

"Did you check in there?" Juan pointed through the room's other doorway, into the largest building—the factory filled with old machinery.

"We yelled for her," Dmitry said. "Shining light around, but she didn't answer."

Jordan looked at Juan, and hefted the speargun in her hands. They were inseparable now, Camilla saw, moving in unspoken synchronization, like two halves of a whole. Even under these circumstances, Camilla felt a faint pang of something like jealousy. Juan raised a hand, peering inside. Then he motioned forward, and the two of them disappeared into the factory building together.

"Hey. Hey, now." Brent frowned and pushed through after them. "Make sure you don't aim that thing at anyone…"

Dmitry picked up the lantern from the table and grabbed Jacob by the arm. "Come. We don't want her to shoot Heather by mistake." The two scientists hurried after Brent, sending lantern light bouncing across the walls and ceiling.

Veronica's quicksilver gaze lingered on Camilla and Mason for a moment, as if assessing how useful they were likely to be. Then she shook her head and plunged into the factory building with forceful strides, followed by Natalie.

Camilla and Mason were left alone. She walked over to Heather's cot and straightened the wadded blankets.

"Heather *did* seem a little too OCD to leave the bed unmade," Mason said.

Near the edge of the blanket, a patch of dark maroon the size of a half-dollar crusted the tattered fibers. Camilla's heart gave a jolt. "Mason," she whispered, although she wasn't sure why she was whispering. "Look at this." She held it to the light.

"Heather's a woman," he said. "There might be another explanation for that."

"No." Camilla shook her head. "If it were in the middle maybe, but not here on the edge."

He stepped closer to see. Something tiny skittered away from his shoe across the concrete floor. He glanced down at it, and his face changed.

"Tell me if this is what I think it is," he said.

Shouts erupted from the darkness beyond the doorway: Travis's drawling profanity, a sharp command from Juan, followed by Brent's angry rumble. They had found him.

She looked down at the small white fragment lying in a patch of sunlight near Mason's shoe. The surface of its unbroken side was smooth, and there was a dot of red in the center where it had fractured.

It was a tooth.

The skin on Camilla's arms tightened. She was looking at a piece of Heather. Sickened, she turned away. "What did he *do* to her?"

Mason glanced toward the doorway. "Here comes Veronica."

"Oh, no." Alarm raced through Camilla's body. "Mason, she's going to *kill* him if she sees this."

Veronica burst through the doorway, bouncing on the balls of her feet, energized. "We got him."

Camilla took a deep breath and stepped forward, covering the tooth with her foot. Out of the corner of her eye, she saw Mason straighten up. Thank god, he got it. He understood what she was doing, and for a change, it didn't look as if he was going to try to make things worse.

Veronica glared at them. "We got that animal, no thanks to you two. But we still don't..." She trailed off, her pale eyes igniting with suspicion as she looked back and forth between them. Her voice slowed, turning liquid, insinuating.

"What are you two up to in here?" Her gaze speared Camilla.

"We were thinking—" Mason started.

Without turning her head, Veronica held up a palm, silencing him.

"Young lady, I believe I asked you a question."

Camilla could feel Heather's tooth poking into the bottom of her shoe. Her legs started to tremble.

"Why did you leave last night?" Camilla blurted. "If anything happened to her, it's our fault, too. Yours and mine. We could have warned them."

Veronica blinked like an owl. "I thought you—"

"No you didn't. You didn't care. And I was *scared*. I was so scared he'd hurt me again."

Veronica's shoulders slumped. "Dear God."

She turned on her heel and ran back into the darkness. Male voices rose in shouts and threats from the direction she had gone.

The breath Camilla was holding whistled out of her. She collapsed into one of the chairs, grinding the heels of her palms into her eyes. She hadn't wanted another death on her conscience—not even Travis's. She felt bad enough about Heather as it was.

"You have a real talent for deception," Mason said.

"Oh god, shut up." She pointed at the tooth, gleaming from the floor. "We need to save that for the police. Do you think there are cameras in here?"

"Probably," he said. "Even if there aren't any, they can do some of that CSI magic to nail him. Lauren was an accident, Camilla. But this is murder."

"You're so sure she's dead."

"We didn't find her, did we? And it wouldn't be hard to dispose of a body here."

She winced, thinking of Lauren. "No, it wouldn't. Come on."

She got up, picked up a notebook, and tore several blank pages from it. Squatting, she slid them under the tooth, not liking the way it rolled across the paper toward her fingers, as if it had a life of its own. She folded the corners over and picked it up, folding it again, making a little package.

Ugh. She didn't want it in her hands any longer. "Here, hang on to this—"

Mason stepped away, holding his hands up. "No thanks, I'm good."

The shouting was getting louder now. Veronica's voice, harsh and strident, rose above the others.

"Oh god." Camilla tucked the folded papers with the tooth into the pocket of her jeans, grimacing. "Let's go."

CHAPTER 115

"You got no right." Travis twisted, but Juan and Brent held him tight. "I already told you ten times, I ain't seen no fucking Heather."

Heather's cot was a few feet away, a mute reminder of what had happened here. Camilla had mussed the covers to hide the blood spot before the others herded Travis in. She stared at his face now, probing his expression. Travis's features twisted into a snarl.

"The fuck you looking at me all googly-eyed for, bitch?"

Veronica stepped in front of her. "Because she's never seen a piece of shit talk before. For the last time, what did you do with Heather?"

"Y'all must be real stupid. Or deaf." He jerked again, trying to shake loose.

Juan's fingers tightened on Travis's shoulder, and he dropped to his knees in front of them, gasping.

"Watch him," Juan said to Brent. Then he and Jordan left together.

A moment later, Jordan passed the window outside, heading toward the blockhouse. She was alone.

Travis tried to stand, but Brent wrapped a big hand around his shoulder and pushed him down again.

"I advise you not to move," he said. "Your rotator cuff is torn. It'd be very easy to exacerbate your injury—or dislocate the shoulder again."

"...kill you," Travis gasped.

Veronica turned away, her expression bleak. "He did it, all right. She didn't just wander off and drown."

Camilla glanced at Mason out of the corner of her eye. He was inspecting Travis the way an entomologist might study a strange bug. But at least he wasn't grinning or saying anything inappropriate.

Veronica took a step toward Travis. "I know this animal is responsible. We may not be able to *prove* anything..."

Brent leaned forward, looming over the kneeling man. "That's not our job, Veronica."

"I know," she snapped. "But until he's in custody, he's a danger to every woman on the island. And frankly, I don't trust you to sedate him again."

"Now, wait a minute—"

"Please," Camilla said. "Let's not argue. Isn't it more important to get Julian to send help?"

"I'm all ears," Veronica said.

Camilla had been thinking about this.

369

"I think you're wrong about them panicking, Veronica," she said. "Yesterday, Julian wiped Lauren off the scoreboard. That was very deliberate. I think he was saying something to us. He was telling us that the competition would go on without her."

She looked around the room. She had everyone's attention now.

"But Julian needs our cooperation for that," she said. "And we're not going to give it to him."

She pointed in the direction of the houses. "We have food left. I've still got a tiny bit of water. Even if you've finished yours, Mason's got five more jugs hidden. That's a half gallon each.

"We can wait him out if we have to. He's not going to get what he wants, so he has no reason not to send help."

Camilla took a deep breath. They were all listening to her. Good.

"I know one of us is a spy. One of us is working with Julian. But it actually doesn't matter who it is. Not anymore. Because…" She paused to look up into the corners of the ceiling. Were those dark spots the cameras? She chose one, stared into it, and raised her voice. "… as of *right now,* the rest of us—"

"—refuse to play," Juan finished from the doorway.

He shoved something shiny off his shoulder, and it cascaded onto the concrete floor in a trill of loud clinking. Wet chain, coils and coils of it—no doubt the chain that had destroyed the scientists' boat.

Jordan appeared behind him. She held out a slender hand, fingers hooked through a half-dozen heavy padlocks, and dropped them onto the pile of chain.

Travis tried to scramble to his feet. "Not locking me up like a fucking animal again." Brent's fingertips whitened on his shoulder, and he sank to his knees, groaning.

Juan glanced at Dmitry. "How long until someone comes?"

Jacob pulled at his beard. "From San Diego, it takes—"

Juan silenced him with a chopping gesture of his hand through the air. "Dmitry, how long?"

Dmitry was staring at Jacob, his face perplexed, but he pointed out the window, in the direction of the mainland. "Day after New Year's, park on shore opens to public again. Visitors, rangers walking there, they see us from shore. January two."

Juan looked at them all. "Seven days."

"I've got bad news," Mason said. "We only have three."

CHAPTER 116

"You're a liar." Veronica pointed a chipped fingernail at Mason. "You dumped the water yourself, just like you dumped the gasoline."

Neck tense, Camilla watched Veronica pace in front of the dark monitor screen, like an angry, caged tiger. The look on her face was scary. The air crackled like dry static, waiting for a wrong movement or word to set off a spark that would explode into violence again.

Mason slid his hands into the pockets of his slacks. "Blaming the messenger doesn't help, I'm afraid."

"Why didn't you say something earlier?" Camilla asked.

The contestants had gathered once again in the great room of the Victorian house. Travis was chained up back at the station, where he would stay, with the two scientists watching him, until help arrived. It was better than leaving a contestant to guard him, Camilla had reasoned. Veronica was a poor choice for obvious reasons, and so was Natalie, and so was Mason. But none of them could be trusted with him, really. If they accidentally left Julian's spy in charge of Travis, that person might set him free.

"I was going to find who took the water, and cut a deal with them," Mason said. "But after Lauren and everything else happened, it didn't matter anymore."Veronica stopped pacing, and her eyes widened. She turned to stare at him. "So you've known it was gone since *yesterday?*"

"I had it hidden," he said. "I buried it. No one could have known where it was, except Julian's spy."

"Right," Veronica said. *"You."*

"Mason isn't the spy," Camilla said. "He couldn't have chained the boat."

Veronica's eyes snapped toward her. "And *you're* always defending him. The way you two pal around, it wouldn't surprise me if you were *both* in on it."

Camilla glanced at Juan and Jordan, leaning against the back wall, only half participating. There was no help there. It was as if Jordan had inherited Juan's laconic personality, his silent watchfulness. She turned back to Veronica.

"Without water, we can only last three days," Camilla said. "I think that works both ways. Unless Julian's willing to let us die of thirst, then *he's* only got three days, too."

"What if Julian *is* willing to let us die?" Mason asked. "Sorry, but I think you're being naive here. One of us got killed yesterday. Another woman got murdered last night..."—he paused—"...*probably* murdered, I mean..."

371

Camilla's eyes flicked toward Veronica, who was watching Mason with her mouth pursed.

He swept a hand at the monitor screen. "...and *they* haven't done anything about it. Try and explain *that* to me."

"I can't," Camilla said. "But I think it means we need more leverage."

What Mason said before had given her another idea. Someone in the room wasn't going to like what she had to say next, but she didn't know who—not just yet, anyway. She took a deep breath.

"I was wrong earlier," she said. "We *do* have to unmask Julian's spy. Right now. Then Julian has no way of influencing events here, and it's over."

She pointed at Mason. "Everyone, think about what he said. Only Julian's spy could have known where the water was..."

Veronica shook her head impatiently. "Enough with the stupid word games."

"The spy didn't see where the water was hidden," Camilla said. "The cameras did. Julian did. That means they can communicate with each other."

She let that sink in, watching their faces.

"A working phone," Mason said. "It makes sense."

"It wouldn't even have to be two-way," she said. "The cameras let them see and hear everything that's going on here. They would only need to be able to send instructions."

He nodded. "Text messages."

"I'll go first." Camilla walked to the front of the room.

Standing in front of the monitor reminded her too much of yesterday, when she had done the same thing during the gifting game, and what that had led to. The fight. The knife. Was this a mistake?

No, they had to do this. She took off her jacket and laid it on the ground.

"Somebody search me," she said.

Mason's eyes widened behind his glasses. Why was he surprised?

Oh god—Heather's tooth!

Her stomach contracted. She could feel the awful lump in her pocket, pressing into her thigh. How could she have forgotten?

Mason started forward. "I'll do it—"

"Not you." Veronica's luminous eyes cut from him to Camilla, paralyzing her, like a mouse frozen in the gaze of a snake.

She had to explain herself—*before* they found it—but she knew that Veronica wouldn't believe her. No one would. Camilla's breath caught. With everyone so angry and keyed up now, the true danger she had so blindly placed herself in dawned on her.

They might even think *she* had killed Heather.

Veronica's eyes probed hers. She struggled to keep her face calm.

"Natalie," Veronica said. "Check her."

Camilla almost sagged with relief. She wouldn't have Veronica's deadly hands prodding at her. She wouldn't have those terrible, unblinking pale eyes inches from hers, dissecting her every facial twitch.

Natalie stopped next to her, looking unsure how to begin.

"Here," Camilla said, reaching into the other pocket for her iPhone.

"No," Veronica commanded. "Let *her.*"

Natalie's shy fingers plucked her phone from her jeans. With a look of concentration, she pressed the On switch, and prickles raced across the back of Camilla's neck.

What if, after five days of dead air, it suddenly got a signal *now*?

Natalie dialed a number. Held the phone to her ear.

Camilla tensed.

"No signal," Natalie said. She picked up Camilla's jacket and checked its pockets. Laying it back down, she looked at Veronica.

Camilla's pounding heart was slowing to normal. Her face tried to stretch in strange directions, to laugh, even though she knew how bad that would look.

Somehow, Natalie had missed it. Trying to hide her relief, Camilla exhaled slowly, blowing through her mouth because her broken nose was blocked.

"Check her other pocket," Veronica said.

Oh god.

Tentative fingers probed her thigh, and Natalie pulled the folded lump of paper from her jeans.

Camilla raised her hands. "I—"

"I *knew* it. A note." With forceful strides Veronica crossed the floor and snatched it from Natalie's hands. "Let me see that."

Veronica was two feet away now. Picturing those hooked thumbs punching into JT's spurting sockets, Camilla closed her own eyes. She squeezed her legs together, fighting an overpowering urge to cringe. If she weren't so dehydrated, she'd probably end up peeing herself right now.

It was absolutely the wrong thing to think of. An inappropriate urge to giggle seized her, and she bit the inside of her cheek to stifle it. *Don't laugh. Don't laugh. Oh god, don't laugh at her—she'll kill you.*

The urge worsened.

Paper rustled. Veronica drew a sharp breath, a foot from her face.

"It's blank," she said. "What is the meaning of this, young lady?"

Camilla opened her eyes.

"Why are you carrying this wad of paper in your pocket?"

Everyone was staring at her. She looked at Veronica and swallowed. Opened her mouth. Couldn't think of a single thing to say.

Mason laughed.

Veronica's head swung toward him. "Maybe *you* can enlighten us, then."

"Do you really need a *man* to explain it to you, Veronica?"

She stared at him, and her brows knitted. Then she snorted. "Some man *you* are."

The tension in the room seemed to be dissipating, though. Camilla stared at her in confusion. Veronica's expression was a mix of pity and disgust.

"For God's sake," she said, shaking her head at Camilla. "A woman your age should have learned by now to be prepared. It's disgraceful."

Her face softened, and she laid a hand on Camilla's forearm. "Come see me afterward. I've got some in my bag."

Her period—*that* was what Veronica thought the paper was for. Camilla's face flushed.

Now everyone—Juan, Jordan, Brent—would be wondering about her hygiene. She was mortified. But she didn't dare correct the misunderstanding. In fact, she ought to be grateful for it. She looked down at her feet.

Heather's tooth lay on the floorboards in plain view, halfway between Veronica's toes and hers. Her eyes widened, and the awful urge to giggle came back stronger than ever. Veronica would notice her staring at it for sure. Camilla jerked her head up, staring wall-eyed into Veronica's face.

"You don't want to get an infection," Veronica said. "Not here."

CHAPTER 117

"What have we here? Naughty, naughty, naught-ty."

Camilla uncrossed her arms and looked up at the sound of Mason's voice, giving her full attention to the front of the room. She had retreated to a corner, and the past five minutes were a blur. Her legs were still shaky, her face hot. She couldn't tell whether she was going to laugh, cry, or throw up.

Heather's tooth lay on the floor, right in front of everyone. It seemed impossible that no one had noticed it. She had to get it back, save it for the police.

She had only half listened while Mason was searched, and now Mason and Veronica were searching Brent.

"Got a prescription for these?" Grinning, Mason held a bundle of pills and several syringes in the air, displaying them to the other contestants like a courtroom lawyer grandstanding with exhibits. Brent looked disgusted.

Mason read the labels. "Fentanyl, Demerol, and propofol...And what about this? Modafinil? Hey, I've heard of this stuff. Silicon Valley startup execs use it to work nonstop twenty-hour days." He laughed. "Wow, that's quite a cocktail, Doc. You might want to ease up—none of us can be much help if you OD."

"Don't worry about me," Brent said. "I know my own tolerances. Let's not get distracted here." He pointed at the pills and syringes. "Check my phone, and give those back."

"We have power," Mason said, manipulating the phone. "Wait for it... wait for it... but no. I was going to call the AMA on you, Doc, but there's no signal."

Mason pulled his own iPhone from his pocket. "Do yourself a favor and buy one of these. That big Microsoft clunker of yours is an old-man phone."

Brent's face was dark. Breathing heavily, he snatched the pills and syringes from Mason. Stuffing them back into the pockets of his vest, he walked away.

"Don't forget your old-man phone," Mason said, holding it out to him and laughing.

Veronica turned abruptly and walked across the room, away from the arched doorway. Camilla looked through the arch, where JT now stood.

He laid a hand on the frame and surveyed the room. A thick gauze bandage and tape covered one of his eyes. His nose looked the way Camilla's felt.

375

"Big waste of time," he said through split, swollen lips. "Easy to modify a phone so you need a code to activate the signal."

"Do you have a better idea?" Camilla asked.

JT's eye swept past Veronica, and his knuckles tightened on the doorway, but his fierce glare settled on Juan.

"Maybe I don't need one," he said. "Maybe I already know who we're looking for."

Jordan's grip tightened on Juan's arm.

"Then you won't mind if they check *you*," Juan said.

"Hell, why not? I've got nothing to hide." JT stepped fully into the room and raised both arms above his head. His eye flicked toward Veronica. "Anyone but her."

JT's phone was dead. Mason and Brent found nothing else on him.

"Now you," he said, fixing Juan with a stare.

"I'll go." Jordan detached herself from him and walked to the front of the room.

Veronica waved Natalie forward and curled a finger at Camilla, but kept her distance from JT. The air thrummed with tension.

At the front of the room once more, Camilla tried not to look down at Heather's tooth while she searched Jordan. Jordan's phone had a little bit of battery life left, but no signal. Camilla handed it back with an apologetic shrug, but Jordan's cold expression gave her nothing.

"We might as well search you now, too, Natalie." Camilla looked at the younger woman with sympathy, remembering what Veronica had said about her history.

Natalie nodded, looking down at the floor. She pulled her hands from her hoodie pockets, holding an iPhone and the stun gun.

Camilla was as gentle as possible, but Natalie shrank from her touch and Jordan's. Her phone was dead. Head down, Natalie retreated to a corner, and Jordan returned to Juan's side.

"Your turn, *compadre*." JT's voice was deadly calm. "I've seen you at night. Down by the dock."

"You're wrong," Juan said, backing toward the doorway. "But I won't be searched. I'm leaving now."

Camilla's breath caught. Not him. Please not him. And Jordan, too? But here was her chance, while all eyes were on Juan. She knelt rapidly as if tying her shoelace, pinched Heather's tooth between her fingers, and slipped it inside her shoe.

"What are *you* doing now?" Veronica's voice froze Camilla before she could stand.

"Back up." Juan's command sliced across the room, and they both turned to stare.

He had a gun in his hand. Black and blocky, it was held low in front of him.

"Mo-ther-fucker!" JT's voice rose in surprise. "That's *my* gun."

Camilla stood. She had seen Juan gauging the distance yesterday, memorizing the spot where it had hit the water. She had hoped he would understand that it should stay there at the bottom, where it belonged. Bringing it back onto the island was sure to get somebody killed.

But was he Julian's spy? She again saw him scooping the little boy out from in front of the truck. Her heart wouldn't let her believe he was.

"Juan, put it down," she said. "This is only making it worse."

"You're holding it wrong," JT said, edging toward him. "And the safety's on."

"No!" Camilla shouted.

Juan raised the gun, hard-eyed. Finger on the trigger, he aimed it at JT's face. "There's no safety on a Glock. Now, back up, JT. Last warning."

Mason laid a hand on JT's shoulder. "You should be getting used to this by now," he said. "Statistics do say that when gun owners get shot, it's usually by their own guns. But let's hear him out."

JT plucked Mason's hand off his shoulder without taking his eyes off Juan. "Because of you, Lauren's dead."

Juan shook his head. "It had nothing to do with me. She made her own decision."

Bitterness washed over Camilla. She pushed in front of him, ignoring the gun. "You could have said something." She stared into Juan's dark eyes, searching for the friendliness she remembered, not finding it. "You could have warned us all about the sharks."

"I'm not your tour guide." Juan's eyes never left JT, but he waved out the window with his other hand. "Besides, I can't really explain that."

So a divemaster thought the shark attack was strange, too. But even if he wasn't Julian's spy, his indifference was equally hurtful.

"How can you be like this?" she asked.

"You're a nice person, Camilla."

Coming from Juan, it stung. It sounded like a dismissal.

"Stop saying that," she said. "I don't want to hear it. Especially from you."

His face didn't change. "What I mean is, none of us are responsible for each other here."

Camilla saw the flicker of hurt in Jordan's eyes.

"You need to understand that," Juan said. "Before you get yourself injured again. Or worse."

"Not my brother's keeper, Juan?" Her disappointment in him was choking her. She nodded toward Jordan. "Why don't you ask *her* how she feels about that?"

But Juan was staring at her now, and the look of pain blooming in his eyes stopped her dead. He had let her down, and she had hurt him terribly in return—but she had no idea how.

He made no attempt to disguise his sorrow. She wanted to look away, but his dark eyes held her, drowning her in his private pain. She knew the patterns of grief well. She could tell this was an old wound—one he had carried for so long that it had become a part of him, defined him.

"Search me." His voice was hoarse. He lifted his arms away from his sides, the gun still held on JT, but his eyes on her.

Camilla stepped close. She glanced at Jordan, who was biting a thumbnail and looking away, lost in some separate worry. Camilla searched Juan's pockets, looking down at her hands the whole time, very aware of his wounded eyes on her. When she reached her arms around his waist to check his belt he tilted his head toward her, probing her expression, and she swallowed. This close to him, she could hear his pained breathing, sharp and shallow through his nose. But she sensed no menace directed at her—only that bottomless well of unhappiness. Her own breath sped up in sympathy.

Juan's phone had a quarter battery charge left, but no signal. She found nothing else.

She looked up at him, wishing she could take back whatever she had said that hurt him. "So it was just the gun you didn't want us to find?"

He nodded.

"You're wasting your time, girl." JT glared. "He's the one."

Taking a deep breath, Camilla stepped back. Juan's eyes followed her.

"Okay," she said to the room. "That got us nowhere…"

"I want my gun back," JT said. "Give it to me, and maybe I don't kill you."

Jordan spoke. "Juan isn't with Julian. I know that."

Camilla raised her voice. "Please, JT, can you sit down before someone gets hurt? And, Juan, can you put that away?"

"You're making a mistake," JT said. But to her relief, he backed up and sat down against the wall.

Juan gestured with the gun. "Legs out in front of you."

JT stretched his legs across the floor, and Juan relaxed, letting the gun drop to his side. He kept his finger on the trigger, though.

"So what next?" he asked her.

She had no idea. Her plan was a bust. But wait—they hadn't searched *everyone* yet.

"Veronica," she said. "It seems we missed you somehow—"

Veronica cut her off. "There's a problem."

CHAPTER 118

"I swear to God I had no idea," Veronica said.

The silence in the room was overwhelming. Camilla stared at her in shock, seeing fear in those pale eyes. *Veronica* was Julian's spy?

Brent raised a hand to scratch the side of his head, but she found nothing cute about the gesture anymore. "What are you talking about?" he rumbled.

"If I had known what was going to happen to Lauren... to Heather... I'd never have done it." Veronica's hands were shaking. "I swear to God."

"What did you do?" Camilla asked her.

"Sit down, JT." Behind her, Juan's voice held a note of warning, but Camilla couldn't look away.

"I have a communications device," Veronica said. "It's been used to send me instructions."

Camilla was surprised at how betrayed she felt. Veronica had hugged her when her nose was broken. She had intervened when JT was manhandling her. Veronica frightened her, but Camilla had looked up to her, too— admired her for her fearlessness and directness.

That she had been lying this whole time made Camilla very, very angry. "What instructions?" she asked.

"I can see what this looks like, but I'm not the spy. I'm not working with Julian."

"*What* instructions?"

Veronica reached into a pocket and pulled out a clunky, old-fashioned text pager. She held it out with a shaking hand. "I found this during the scavenger hunt."

Camilla took it from her, and read the first message: "STAND BY FOR INSTRUCTIONS." She hit the button that scrolled to the next message, read it, and something coiled in her gut. She stared at Veronica.

"What does it say?" JT's voice held an edge like fingernails on a chalkboard.

"Sit down, JT." Juan spoke louder this time.

"Why?" Camilla asked Veronica. "Why would you do this to us? People are dying now."

"I was losing. I was in last place. I need that money." Veronica's eyes hardened. "Safe Harbor is bankrupt. If I don't win, I have to shut down the shelter." She looked at Mason. "The bank is taking the property out from under me, you grinning vulture. Leaving those women no place to go—"

"That's not good enough." Camilla locked eyes with her. "Ask Lauren. Ask Heather."

"There is no money *now,* Veronica." Brent's large hand closed over Camilla's, and he gently took the pager from her. "You can be sure of that." He leaned forward, squinting to read the message on its screen, and stiffened.

"Doc." JT's voice cut through the room. "Tell us *all* what it says. Right now."

"'DESTROY EMERGENCY BEACON ASAP.'" Brent dropped the pager to the floor. "That's what it says." He put his hands in his vest pockets and stared at Veronica with contempt. "I hope you realize what you've done. Two women are dead because of it."

"It's not like that." Veronica's mouth tightened. "You wouldn't understand."

"JT. Sit. Down." Juan's voice—calm, but with cold finality. "Last warning." Camilla sensed the room about to explode behind her, but she didn't look away from Veronica's eyes. "What you did to JT, setting him up like that—it's disgusting enough if you *are* the spy," she said. "If you aren't, it's even worse."

"I... oh, shit. Forget it." Veronica spun and stormed off, disappearing through the doorway to the other house.

Natalie half-stood, staring after her.

Mason grinned. "Not the best role model, Natalie. But hey, she sure can teach you to look out for number one."

"You're just going to let her go?" JT said. "She fucking *blinded* me. Doc says I'm never going to see out of this eye again. Did it occur to any of you to ask how she happened to have my court-martial transcript?" He sat against the wall, staring at Camilla with his one remaining eye, restrained by the gun in Juan's hand. He had saved her life when Travis tried to stab her. He didn't deserve this.

"I'm sorry," she said. "But no more violence. Nobody else dies here."

"They threw Travis into the mix to distract us from her," JT said. "She's a killer, remember? Murdered her first husband. None of us is safe as long as she's running around."

With a pop and crackle, the monitor on the wall behind Camilla came to life, lighting the faces in front of her with stark, artificial contrast. The room went silent. She looked over her shoulder.

The screen showed the same room they now stood in, but empty of people. The floor was littered with small objects, instead: the gifts from the previous contest. In real life, the gifts had been shoved to the corners, their LEDs all dark, batteries dead now. But on the monitor, lights still glowed from them: a few green, but mostly red. It was a scene from yesterday, Camilla realized. She braced herself, knowing that whatever Julian wanted them to see was sure to be bad.

On-screen, a small figure entered the room, moving with caution. She seemed to be sorting through the items on the floor, occasionally adding one to the small pile in her arms. She glanced up toward the camera for a moment. Natalie.

She had missed her turn, Camilla remembered now. With the lowest score, she would have gone last. But then Travis had attacked them, and events had taken their awful course, and the game had been abandoned.

But not by everyone, it seemed.

On the monitor, Natalie moved to the center of the room, crouching to dump her armful of gifts in a clear spot on the floor. She reached down, manipulating them as a green glow spread from the pile, growing in intensity. Natalie looked up and out at them from the center of the screen, her face lit green from below. She seemed to stare directly at them, checking something.

Mason laughed—an unrestrained bray of amusement. "You're watching your score, aren't you?" he said. "To see if it goes up."

Camilla looked at the real-life Natalie, standing beside her. She seemed paralyzed by the sight of herself up on the screen.

On the monitor, she finished what she was doing. Staring up toward the camera again, she nodded once, as if satisfied with what she saw. Then she stood and swept her pile of gifts aside with her foot, scattering them among the other items. With a final glance at the camera, she left the room. The screen went black, and the scoreboard appeared on the monitor.

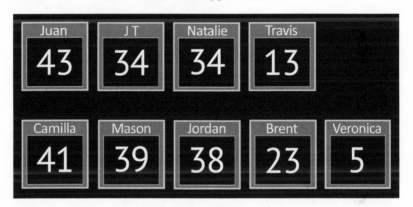

Hunched in her hoodie, Natalie looked guilty. And scared. Her score had been in the single digits before, Camilla recalled.

She stared at the floor. They had no leverage over Julian. They were doing this to themselves and each other while he sat back, laughing at them and recording it all. She thought about what she had just seen Natalie do, and a surge of acid vomit gushed into her throat. Forcing it back down, Camilla spoke without looking up.

"Tell me, Natalie, did you do that *before*—or *after*—Lauren died?"

Natalie dropped her head and walked away fast, exiting through the same doorway as Veronica.

"Well." Taking a deep breath, Camilla raised her eyes to see Mason, Brent, JT, Jordan, and Juan watching her now, as if they were waiting for her to do something. She focused on Juan, who still held the gun at his side.

"If we have any more secrets from each other," she said, "I suggest we get them out on the table *now*. Before something worse happens…"

The scoreboard faded, and the monitor lit up behind her. Camilla turned and found herself staring into Julian's easy grin.

CHAPTER 119

"Good afternoon." Julian's voice, like his expression, was calm and friendly.

"You son of a bitch!" Brent shouted. "How *dare* you smile at us!"

Everyone surged forward, crowding in front of the monitor, their angry yells rising all around Camilla.

"Let me talk to him," she shouted, waving them back. *"Let me talk!"* The room quieted down.

Julian gazed from the screen, his serene smile unchanged. He steepled his fingers in front of him and tapped his joined index fingers against his lips, as if trying to decide how to begin.

Camilla wasn't going to give him that chance. "If you say another word, I'm going to pull this monitor off the wall and destroy it. And the one in the other house, too. And then I'm going to start ripping out cameras." Her throat tightened. "I don't know how many of us will help, but I won't be doing it alone."

Julian's grin turned rueful. His gaze floated somewhere over her shoulder, not meeting her eyes. Ignoring her.

"Whatever you think you can make us do to each other here," she said, "I promise you, it isn't going to happen. You need to listen right now."

He looked down at the ground, shaking his head and holding up his palms, still smiling. Why wasn't he taking her seriously?

"I'm pulling the plug, then." She grabbed the edges of the screen and thrust her face toward his, feeling her features stretch in an unfamiliar snarl. "We'll build a raft if we have to—"

"I can't hear you now," Julian said, interrupting her. "I can't see you either. After getting to know you all, this is a bit awkward to be speaking to a blank screen."

What?

The room fell into a shocked silence.

Camilla's legs went loose and rubbery beneath her, and she grabbed the wall for support. Julian was *right there* in front of her, but she couldn't even talk to him. They couldn't even *beg* him for help.

"Over the last few days," he said, "we've come to realize that it's insufficient to merely isolate our cast of actors and hide the behind-the-scenes workings of my production crew. We've learned we also need to isolate the production staff, including myself, from you."

Camilla turned away and pressed her forehead against the wall. They were trapped, buried alive on this tiny island. Chest heaving, she sucked in breath after breath, unable to get the air she needed. She was buried alive all over again, trying to escape, unable to find a way out.

Get a grip. What Veronica had said to her last night—she needed to get a grip now, before she lost it totally. She rolled her body against the wall to face the monitor again, forcing her breaths to calm, making herself listen to what Julian was saying.

His face changed, becoming serious.

"You see, we chose you well indeed. You are an amazing group of individuals—true survivors all. You've proved you can thrive even under these adverse circumstances. I am honored to be hosting this show with you. Deeply honored."

He looked thoughtful. "And therein lies the problem. I myself, as well as the other crew members, now risk being influenced by you. We all have our favorites—I definitely have mine.

"Each of you has…"—Julian waved a hand to indicate something off-screen to either side of him—"…*fans* here on the production crew, rooting for you to win. This makes it hard to keep the contests fair. We needed a way to make sure that none of us, deliberately or inadvertently, provide cues or hints or make biased contest rulings, giving someone an unfair advantage. And this was the only way to be sure. So from here forward, until we've declared our winner, this show will be run double blind."

Spreading his hands, Julian gave them another rueful smile.

"As you can imagine, this decision was disappointing to me, but I understand the reasons. To make up for it, the producers have authorized me to share some good news with you. First however, we must talk about yesterday's unfortunate disqualification…"

"Disqualification?" JT said. "She *died*, motherfucker. And so will you. Very soon." He looked at Juan. "I'm getting up. *Now.*"

Juan gave him the "okay" sign, and he stood up.

Watching them, Camilla had missed some of what Julian was saying.

"…legal department reviewed yesterday's events in detail, engaged outside counsel, and heard multiple legal opinions consistent with our own. We've received assurances that the show can continue. Legally. The release that each of you signed was clear and explicit about individual responsibility and assumption of risk."

Mason's eyebrows went up. "He's saying it was Lauren's own fault."

"I'll kill him." JT's voice was flat calm. Like a robot's voice. It sent fingers of ice down Camilla's back. "All of them are dead. *All of them.*"

Oblivious, Julian grinned at them, his eyes filled with excitement. A bitter plug jammed Camilla's throat. Julian really couldn't hear them.

"For today's game," he said, "we move up to the fourth level of Maslow's hierarchy. After the basic physiological survival needs, after security, after love and belonging, comes the need for esteem. To survive, we must earn respect from others—and, most importantly, from ourselves. Today you will demonstrate self-reliance, competence, and control in what is, naturally, an individual competition rather than a team one."

He reached off-screen to pick something up.

"The actual game is one that was popular in high schools and colleges during the more innocent pre-Columbine era. You may even have played it before: assassin."

Julian held up a black gun shape. It was larger and bulkier than the gun in Juan's hand.

Camilla knew that even if she destroyed the monitor, Veronica and Natalie were watching this on the screen in the other house. She bit her lip, fighting the tremors in her legs that ran up her body and made her nose ache. They were on their own here. There was no help coming. None.

"The game of assassin is a game of stealth and strategy. You will earn esteem by proving your mastery over your fellow contestants, until only one winner remains: the last assassin standing. Given the outdoor venue, our version of this classic game will be played with paintball markers."

Turning, Julian fired a shot against the wall behind him, leaving a starburst of gray paint.

"The rear wall of the storage shed is false," he said. "Behind it, you will find your own personal paintball guns. The eye protection provided is not optional—it's mandatory for everyone."

He held up a small blue envelope in his other hand.

"Each of you will also find an envelope addressed to you. It contains a single name: the name of your first target. But while you are stalking him or her, don't forget that someone else has your name and is stalking you."

Controlling her breathing, Camilla studied her fellow contestants. Mason was staring at the screen, unsmiling. Could she count on him? Or not? She didn't like the speculative look on his face.

"Any paint on your target counts as a successful kill," Julian said. "Kill your target, and your score increases by five points. Your target loses five points and is eliminated from today's game. You take their envelope, and their target becomes your new target, and so on. The circle closes until only two assassins remain, stalking each other. The last assassin standing is the winner of today's contest, earning a bonus score of fifteen points with his or her final kill."

JT's eyes were still on Juan, taking his measure in that scary, calm way, ready to explode into violence the moment Juan lowered his guard. Not good.

"Assassin is meant to be a game of stealth. There can be no more than one other witness to each kill. If there are multiple witnesses, the target is still eliminated—dead, after all, is dead. However, the assassin's cover is also blown, and you become a free target. Anyone can kill *you* to earn five points."

Juan's fingers flexed and tightened on the grip of the *real* gun he held, his gaze locked on Julian. Camilla felt a dull ache spread through her chest. Juan wasn't going to look out for her, or anyone else. None of them were responsible for each other, he had said.

"Kill the wrong person, and you become a free target for everyone."

Jordan stood with one hand curled around Juan's bicep, watching Julian with icy composure. Whatever doubts had troubled Jordan earlier, they weren't on display anymore. Calculations ticked behind her cold green eyes. Camilla's "sister" didn't spare her so much as a glance.

"Kill your own assassin—the person stalking you—and you earn ten points. Your assassin loses ten. But listen carefully, because this is important." Putting down the paintball gun, Julian held up a finger. "He or she must shoot at *you* first. No preemptive strikes. No guessing. Or else, you become a free target."

Brent sat slumped against the back wall, his head down. Camilla frowned. Was he all right? He tucked a hand into his vest pocket, and his fingers moved beneath the fabric, patting the contents against his chest as if for comfort. His drugs. Saddened and angered, Camilla looked back at the screen.

"The rules are simple," Julian said. "But the game is as complex as the creativity and ingenuity you bring to it."

Their host's face turned serious again.

"We understand that keeping you so completely in the dark has its downside. Uncertainty can be paralyzing. Right now you are wondering who Vita Brevis Entertainment really is. What kind of show this is. What we all stand to gain—or lose—through our continued participation. You want answers. You deserve them."

Julian steepled his fingers before his lips again.

"And if you dedicate yourselves to playing today's game well, I will give them to you. Tonight. The answers to all your questions. Together, right after the game, we will strip away the mystery—but only if all of you participate. I promise you that what I have to reveal will surprise you."

Why *had* they been selected? Why were they being subjected to this ordeal? Camilla stared at him, needing it to make sense somehow, desperately wanting the answers he promised, but knowing they could never trust his word.

But had Julian ever actually *lied* to them? She thought back and couldn't come up with a single instance where something he said turned out to be untrue.

"For those of you growing tired of our lovely island home, keep this in mind, also," he said. "Today's game is the penultimate challenge. There is only one more after this one. If you all participate, play hard, and focus on beating these last two challenges, we will be going home tomorrow, with one of you crowned as our grand prize winner."

Camilla tried to force away the hope blooming unbidden in her heart. Her little apartment in the Marina, her job, her coworkers and friends, her normal life—it all seemed like a memory from long ago. And her kids—she *had* to get back. She heard Avery's sobbing again, saw his face instead of Julian's, and understood at last that Veronica was right. Avery and the rest of her kids—they didn't need Disneyland.

What they needed was Camilla herself, to teach them that life was possible again, that they could be happy again. She straightened up, jolted by the sudden, awful realization of what would happen if she died here. She would be doing the worst thing she could to her parentless kids: abandoning them.

"And now for the good news that I promised." Julian walked a few steps to the side, and the camera followed him to reveal a waist-high stack of green bundles, the size of a large hay bale. He laid one hand on the bale, and she realized she was looking at money: a massive stack of currency—much more than he had shown them aboard the ship.

"In recognition of unforeseen events that have made this competition more difficult than we originally anticipated, we are increasing the grand prize," Julian said. "Doubling it, in fact. The overall winner, the person with the highest point total at the end of the final competition, will receive ten million dollars. Tax free."

Pulling a bundle off the bale, he thumbed through it. "But even if you don't win the grand prize, you won't be leaving empty-handed. Second place earns three million dollars. Third place earns one million. The rest of you will receive three hundred thousand dollars. Each."

He tossed the bundle of money back onto the bale.

"As I said, this new policy of double-blind isolation was a keen disappointment to me personally. I had looked forward to sharing this experience with you, just as I have so far. So I made a request, and our producers granted it.

"The final game has been kept a secret even from me. I can't give anything away. So I asked our producers if I could join you on the island tomorrow, and they agreed."

Julian looked humble now, as well as excited. Camilla searched his face for the lie. She couldn't see it.

"Play well today, my friends, and tomorrow we finally get to meet in person. I look forward to hosting our final game live, together with you, there on New Year Island."

CHAPTER 120

Juan was the first to break the silence. "He's coming here."

Camilla stared at him. Juan's eyes were distant, remorseless. The eyes of a shark. The sorrow had been set aside, buried again.

"Maybe," Brent said, raising his head. "*If* Julian isn't lying. And *if* we're stupid enough to stick our necks in the noose again today. But we aren't."

"I want to ask him something personal." Juan didn't brandish the gun he held. He didn't have to. His meaning was clear enough: if he didn't like Julian's answers, their host would die.

"I have some questions for him myself," Mason said. "Ones that I really doubt he plans to address tonight, up on that screen."

"Man's got to answer for Lauren. For the scientist girl." JT pointed to his eye patch. "And for *this*."

"I'd like to interview him." Jordan's eyes were green ice. She held a sheathed dive knife in her hand. "Do some 'cutting-edge' journalism."

They all knew the cameras were rolling, Camilla realized. But none of them cared who heard them anymore. And she didn't, either—not now.

She had to get back to Avery, no matter what.

What were her alternatives? She could try to swim, like Lauren had done. They could try to build a raft, even though she had seen the shark smash a wooden platform to pieces to get at Dmitry. They could simply refuse to play—her original plan—but that was no good, either. It meant languishing for days with a chained-up murderer on their hands, losing strength until they were helpless from dehydration, getting more and more desperate, terrified the whole time that Veronica would do something bad to them. Or that they would do something bad to each other.

Camilla was *not* going to die here, like that.

Not of thirst.

Not afraid.

She pictured Julian's smug smile, heard his sarcasm, his taunts, those awful profiles of Brent and Veronica. No doubt there was one of her, too, ready to be shown, mocking her childhood tragedy and those of the children who needed her help.

She thought of the things they had done to one another here, while he sat there, so smug, laughing at them. And that was the worst part, wasn't it? He had made them do this to *themselves*. He had made Camilla betray what she believed in, do things she was ashamed of. He had made her think less of herself.

389

How arrogant and cruel did somebody have to *be*, to do this to people?

She remembered Lauren. Dead. Heather. Dead. They would never know what that poor woman had suffered at Travis's hands, all because Julian had refused to send help. Camilla would never be able to forgive herself for not warning the scientists about Travis, and *Julian* was the one who had put her in that position.

She had been so scared here. He had made her afraid all over again. Camilla hated being afraid more than anything in the world. As a child, she had spent *years* drifting in and out of the darkness inside her head, too terrified to live. Last night's dream came back to her: Julian's gaping shark jaws. It made perfect sense now. He had done the worst thing possible to Camilla, a woman who had to confront her childhood terror every day of her life, refusing to back down: he had made her feel helpless and afraid again.

And now he was smiling at them like he was their *friend*, claiming he would join them, as if this were some fun adventure? A hard knot formed in her chest. Whatever the others wanted to do to Julian was fine with her. He deserved it.

But they had to get their hands on him first.

If he did come, she knew he wouldn't come alone. Still, no matter how many bodyguards he brought with him, if there was any chance they could lure Julian to them, they had to take it.

Camilla was sick of being afraid.

"Let's play the game," she said.

CHAPTER 121

The scoreboard reappeared.

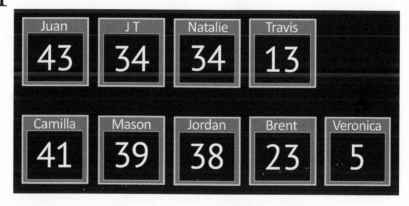

"Camilla, I expected more from you," Brent said. "The money's a lie, and so is everything else. Julian is toying with us." He took a deep breath. "Look at the psychology of this. We're all sick of feeling like victims. It's not our nature, given who we are, what we are. He's using our own survivor mind-set against us."

She didn't respond. What was Brent's answer, then? To sit around taking drugs while their situation got worse and worse? Sometimes you had to decide to risk everything, she knew. It was something that all survivors knew. You had to choose to push *forward* while blackness closed in all around you and the ceiling pressed down overhead. You had to accept the risks and the danger and make them your own. You faced the darkness on your own terms, instead of waiting to be dragged into it, because to do otherwise was to die.

The scoreboard blinked.

The score in one cell spun through a change.

CHAPTER 122

Standing alone with Natalie in the blue team's Greek Revival house, Veronica watched her own score climb. Her eyes widened as the digits spun past, faster and faster, to stop at 45—a forty-point increase. Her score cell slid left, switching places with the others. She was no longer in last place.

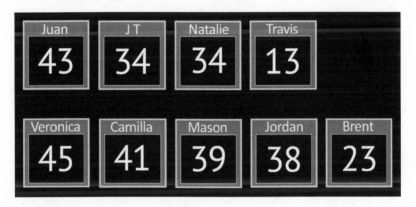

Julian had rewarded her for destroying the beacon.

She was in first place now.

If she could hold on to it, she would win ten million dollars.

Veronica drew a deep breath through her nostrils. She would pay off those vultures from the bank. Pay off the lawyers. She would buy outright the property that Safe Harbor occupied. She would open a South Bay shelter, and one in the East Bay, too. With so much travel to do between the offices, she also would need to get a new car: one of those nice little Mercedes SLK's would be just right. She'd pay off the Platinum MasterCard. She would...

"There's no way the others will go along with this," Natalie said. "Not after how the last game ended. Not after Lauren."

"Don't be ridiculous," Veronica said. "Of course they're going to play. They can't help it. It's who they are. It's who *we* are. Survivors. And now you're going to help me win."

CHAPTER 123

Camilla looked at the scoreboard, where Veronica's score now dominated them all.

"Oh *hell* no." JT said. He chuckled—a hollow sound—and shook his head slowly, eye patch gleaming white against his dark-mahogany skin. "That's *not* going to happen."

"Can't you see what the purpose of this game is?" Brent said. "He wants us all—"

"—to split up." Camilla nodded. "Yes, I get that. Julian wants us all moving around the island on our own... running into each other alone."

Brent took his hands out of his vest pockets and stared at her. "And you don't think that's a bad idea?"

Jordan's voice was cold. "Go do your drugs, Brent. No one cares what you have to say anymore."

"If you do this," Brent said, "it's probable that someone else will die here. *Today.* Are you ready to face that, Camilla?"

She took a deep breath.

"Julian chose us because we were survivors," she said. "Let's find out if he was right."

CHAPTER 124

"So where's this mandatory eye protection?" Mason asked.

Camilla scanned the back wall of the storage shed. The *real* back wall, revealed now that the plywood panels covering it had been pulled loose and laid aside. Veronica and Natalie had done that a few minutes ago, she knew.

When Camilla had led the others outside, she saw the two women leaving the shed. Each held a paintball gun and a blue envelope. Natalie slunk past them, head down, like a teenager caught smoking. But Veronica held her head high. As the two groups passed each other, her contemptuous silver glare cut across the space between, spearing Camilla. If Veronica felt sorry for what she had done, Camilla couldn't see it. Veronica carried the paintball gun with the same practiced ease she had demonstrated holding JT's gun yesterday. She had been a police wife for ten years, Camilla remembered—once she had a target in her sights, she wouldn't miss. Veronica's eyes were bright with hate. Was Camilla's name in the envelope she held? Surrounded by the others, she had held Veronica's gaze, refusing to be afraid, until Veronica and Natalie disappeared into the houses.

On the wall of the storage shed, seven paintball guns hung on hooks. Taped to the wall above each was a blue envelope and a spare ammunition cartridge. Camilla could see two empty hooks. She spotted her name on one of the envelopes. But Mason was right: no eye protection at all.

"I guess they forgot the safety glasses," she said.

He laughed. "It's all fun and games until..."

JT's head whipped toward him, and Camilla was surprised to see Mason shut up. Maybe he did have a survival instinct after all.

The muscular ex-Marine reached for his paintball gun and the envelope beneath it, never taking his eye off Mason. He tapped the envelope. "Could be it's your name in here."

Camilla noticed that JT never looked at Juan. And that Juan was careful never to end up within JT's reach. Juan still held the real gun down at his side. The thought of those two coming face to face with no one else around filled her with dread. She was the one who had pushed for this. But was Brent right?

Before her group left the Victorian house, he had looked at her with stony eyes, and then settled himself on the stairs.

"Do what you like. I refuse to be his puppet."

"The game doesn't work unless everyone plays."

"Bring me the envelope, then," Brent said, "but leave that stupid toy behind. I don't have any use for it."

He patted the steps beside him. "I'll be waiting right here for whoever shows up. I'll give the envelope to them."

Camilla's heart went out to the big man. He looked defeated. Broken. Were his hands shaking?

"Brent, I want you to know—"

"Just go." He looked away. "Please leave."

Jordan thrust her face toward him. "Enjoy your fix."

Brent wouldn't meet Camilla's eye as she led the others outside. She knew there was a possibility that she might not see him alive again. But she tried not to think about it.

In the storage shed, she lifted her paintball gun off the hook and looked it over. A Tippman TPX according to the markings on the side, it was heavy and awkward. She fumbled with the gun until she found the button that released the magazine, and pressed it. A boxlike ammunition cartridge slid out of the grip, and she barely caught it with her other hand before it fell. A green ball the size of a large marble was visible at the top of the cartridge. Camilla pushed it back into place and looked at the others.

"Let's make sure these things really shoot paint and not something else."

She pointed the gun at the back wall and pulled the trigger. There was a snick of compressed gas, louder than she had expected, and the gun bucked in her hand. A bright starburst of neon-green paint splattered against the wall. She raised her eyebrows.

"I don't know much about paintball, but that seemed a little overpowered."

"Nah," JT said. "It's about right. That's why the eye protection."

Which they didn't have. She looked at his eye patch and cringed inside.

JT stepped up to the wall and sniffed the green paint. Then he touched it with a finger. Watching them one-eyed, he held his finger up as if feeling for something. Then he dabbed it to his tongue. After a few seconds, he spat on the ground.

"Just paint."

The others took their paintball markers, spare ammunition, and envelopes. One gun was left on the wall. The envelope beneath it read "Travis."

"What do we do about that?" Mason asked.

Camilla considered. "I think it's a forfeit. Whoever has Travis as a target, come and take his envelope."

"Better get some paint on him first," Mason said. "Or else it may not count as a kill."

Camilla nodded, and thought of the two scientists guarding Travis. What would they make of this? They would probably think the contestants were crazy, doing this. She wasn't so sure they were wrong, either.

But the alternatives were worse. She had no idea who Julian and his people—Vita Brevis's producers—were, but they were definitely not any kind of legitimate studio. Veronica's idea, the Hollywood hubris scenario, was flat wrong—had to be. What was happening here had progressed far beyond any possibility of legality. People were dead.

The room was suddenly noisy with the barks of paintball markers. A rainbow of different-colored splats appeared on the wall. Yellow, pink, orange, and black starbursts joined Camilla's green mark. Each contestant had been assigned a distinct color of paint.

"Looks like they all work," JT said.

Camilla took Brent's gun off the hook with her other hand. She fired a purple starburst onto the wall next to the others, then tossed the gun aside—he didn't want it. She tucked his envelope into her pocket to give to him.

"Aim low," she said. "Let's shoot for the legs whenever possible. And all of us need to stay in tight control of our emotions. No fights, no violence, no matter what happens. No matter who wins or how they do it. Even if the money's real—ten million is a lot, but it isn't worth dying for."

Camilla took a deep breath, looking from eye to eye. The terrified voice in her mind screamed at her to stop this madness before it was too late. It told her she needed to convince them all to put the guns down before someone else got hurt—or killed. It told her to gather everyone together and not let anyone out of sight until help arrived, because, surely, someone *had* to come and save them before they succumbed to thirst. Julian couldn't possibly leave them here to die.

It was the voice that said that this couldn't really be happening. The voice that, in situations like these, led 90 percent of people to their deaths.

She knew better than to listen to that voice.

Camilla was a survivor.

"I suggest we all split up and open the envelopes when we're alone," she said. "And, Juan?" She dropped a hand to his wrist, which held the real gun—the Glock—aimed at the floorboards. Next to him, Jordan stiffened. Camilla ignored her and looked Juan in the eye. "Don't get confused about which gun is which."

Juan held her gaze for a moment.

Then he nodded.

"Let's roll."

PART IV

SEMIFINAL ROUND

CHAPTER 125

"Poetic justice. Do you think I'm wrong?"

Jordan wouldn't meet Juan's eyes. They stood in the blockhouse, facing each other, looking down at the envelopes they held, putting off the moment.

Juan knew she was right. He nodded. "Julian wouldn't pass this opportunity up. Either your name is in this envelope, or my name is in yours."

"I never cared about the money," she said. "It doesn't matter to me. And I don't even care about winning. Not anymore."

He looked up, surprised. Because if there was one thing about this fascinating, extraordinary, incomprehensible woman that he had been certain of, it was that to Jordan, winning was everything.

"I just don't want anything to happen between us, Juan. To change what we have. To ruin it."

She said it plainly, softly. Her usually expressive face was still. Juan was pretty sure he was seeing a Jordan that few ever saw—perhaps a Jordan no one else had ever seen.

He reached out and brushed the hair away from her face, and she took a quick, sharp breath. Her eyes—so wide, so green—stared into his own. She looked afraid.

His throat felt tight. He wanted to wrap his arms around her to chase away the fear. Hold her close, bury his face in her hair, and not let go. But he couldn't yet, because there was something he needed to do first. What Camilla had said after they found Veronica's pager: time to get all their secrets out in the open before it was too late. She had been looking right at *him* when she said it.

What he had hidden from Jordan, beneath the cabinet just an arm's reach away, was like a wall between the two of them. The longer he waited, the worse it would be when she found out. She would understand his reasons, he thought—she was the same as he in so many ways. Besides, he had done what he'd done days ago. The situation had changed since then—on the island, and between them. A lot had changed.

Jordan looked down at her bare feet. They were bleeding again, from the walk across the island. Seeing them made Juan feel even guiltier.

She was rubbing her badly healed broken pinky again. She looked so vulnerable, so fragile to him now. Her voice was a whisper he could barely hear.

"This isn't easy for me to say."

Juan's heart sped up. He was afraid, too. Very afraid of what was coming. "Jordan…"

"I don't use these words lightly… anymore." She took a deep breath, looked up into his face.

"Juan, I—"

He stopped her, placing a finger on her lips. Heart pounding, he knelt and opened the cabinet, pried up the floorboards, and reached underneath.

Scooping up an armful of the things he had hidden, he deposited them on the counter. Then he walked over to the doorway of the blockhouse, knowing that his words wouldn't make a difference right now. He was afraid to look at her, to see the hurt that he knew would be spreading across her beautiful face. He put a hand on the door frame, closed his eyes, and hung his head, hoping—praying—that she would understand.

"You utter bastard."

It was a hiss—unexpected, grating, filled with hate. He had never heard Jordan sound like this before. He whipped around, and the pair of black neoprene scuba booties smacked into his chest, sending him staggering back. Jordan had thrown them hard, and the thick rubber soles hurt.

"You had these the whole time." She hefted a metal can in one hand, reading the label. She picked up another and looked up at Juan, her green eyes slits, incandescent with fury.

"Tuna? Beans? Peaches?"

He ducked as heavy cans thudded against the door frame around him. Jordan threw with force and accuracy. A can hit him in the midsection, knocking the wind out of him. Juan sat down hard. Another can spanged off the concrete wall next to his head. He crabbed along the wall to get away, but Jordan was out of cans.

"You worthless son of a bitch." She grabbed the speargun.

Juan's eyes widened. She thought he was with Julian? Reflexively, his hand crept behind him, where the Glock was a hard lump under his belt. "No, you don't understand…"

"I actually thought…" Her whole body shook, at the edge of control. "I actually thought you and I, we—"

"It's not what you think." Juan raised a hand, fingers spread in supplication. "I *found* the food and the booties on the first night. I'm not Julian's spy."

She spotted his other hand moving toward his belt, and her lips spread in a horrible rictus, baring teeth. The speargun came up, and he froze.

Jordan's beautiful features were unrecognizable now, distorted with hate. She spoke very slowly, each word a sibilant hiss.

"*Spy?* You really think I care about that? You just don't get it, do you, Juan?" She leveled the speargun at him. "Good-bye."

Staring at the spear point aimed at his face, he realized she was about to kill him.

But Jordan spun away, scooping up her paintball marker and blue envelope with her free hand. In the doorway, she paused one last time, looked at the envelope she held, and then back at Juan with a depth of hatred that chilled his spine.

Then she was gone.

CHAPTER 126

"I know where Heather is. She's fine. There's nothing to worry about."

Jacob's comment caught Dmitry by surprise. He looked up from the reports he was tying into a bundle, wrapping them in both directions with a length of twine, the way he had carried his books to school as a boy. But instead of relief, he felt a deepening concern at Jacob's words.

The voice of the bad man—the criminal—came from the room next door.

"I told all of 'em I didn't touch your friend." Chains rattled. "Now, let me loose before I get mad!"

Dmitry's eyes flicked to the keys on the counter. But he ignored the criminal's voice and focused on Jacob.

"*Slava bogu,*" he said. "We are very worried, with all these crazy people here. Why you didn't say before where she is?"

"I just figured it out myself," Jacob said. "It's where I'm headed, too, just as soon as we finish packing up."

"But where is Heather? Where she is gone?"

"San Diego." Jacob smiled, and Dmitry felt a spike of fear shoot through him.

"No, Jacob, listen to me." Dmitry tried to read his eyes but couldn't. "Heather is not in San Diego. She was here on island yesterday. With us."

Jacob patted him on the shoulder and gave him one of the patronizing looks he disliked so much. "That's just what she wanted us to think, Dima. But she left for San Diego already. She doesn't like the way Karen sold us out any more than I do."

Dmitry grabbed both of Jacob's upper arms.

"You are confuse," he said. "Nobody is in San Diego. We don't know where Heather is, but I am thinking maybe she is dead. We are in bad trouble here, Jacob. Bad trouble."

Jacob blinked, and an expression of mild frustration crossed his face. "Have you not been listening to what I've been saying, Dima? Heather made the right decision. I don't blame her for leaving. Karen compromised our work here with sloppy protocols. She brought in all these other scientists from God knows where—no integrity at all."

He pulled loose from Dmitry's grip and barked a laugh, waving a hand toward the room where the criminal was chained.

"Did you see these people? I mean, really? No proper scientific discipline—worse than first-year grad students. I've never heard of any of

407

them before. This is who the Institute is hiring now? Jesus, Dima, the blonde one didn't even have *shoes* on."

Dmitry shook his head.

"No. You have to think, Jacob. Remember. These people making reality show. Not scientists. Yesterday, boat is broken." His voice was rising, and he fought to control it. "People are hurt, people are *dead!*"

"See, that's exactly the kind of talk we don't need." Jacob walked over to the window of the science station and looked out. "You have to face reality sometime, Dima. The tracking study is ruined now. There's no further reason to stay."

He pointed in the direction of the breakwater and the dock beyond.

"The San Diego director's sending a boat. They're damn glad to have serious researchers like us. We need to hurry to the dock, before we miss them."

Dark wings of fear unfolded in Dmitry's belly. He looked closely at Jacob's face, trying to make sense of what he was saying. He could see a sheen of sweat glistening on Jacob's forehead. It didn't match the unconcern in his expression and voice.

"Jacob, please try to understand," Dmitry said. "I am your friend telling you this. You are upset, thinking wrong. Nobody is coming. We need Coast Guard, *politziu.*"

Jacob shook his head. "Well, then, that's your choice. You can come or you can stay, but I'm going to the dock." He picked up an armful of binders and bound reports and tucked them under his arm. In the doorway, he turned to face Dmitry.

"I don't think I can convince them to wait long. So if you want to come, you better hurry."

CHAPTER 127

"Who's your target, Natalie?" Veronica looked out the window, cradling the paintball gun in her hands. Her back was to the large foyer of the Greek Revival house, where she and Natalie had returned to prepare. She scanned the open ground outside, watchful for movement. But most of her attention was focused on the sounds behind her. The slow, careful tear of paper. She tilted her head, aligning her ear to catch the slight intake of breath. It came from farther to the right. Natalie had moved a few steps in that direction.

"Maybe we should split up now," Natalie said.

Veronica spun, snapped her arms up, and pulled the trigger. The snick of compressed air was loud in the room.

Natalie staggered back, a splatter of red paint dead-center on the chest of her hoodie. She drew a couple of gasping breaths and stared in shock at Veronica.

"Sorry, Natalie." Veronica lowered the gun and walked toward her. "But it's just a game."

"But you can't do that! I didn't try to shoot at you first. You didn't *know* you were my target."

"I knew. I heard it in your voice. It's a righteous kill. Now, give me your gun."

Head down and shoulders hunched, Natalie held it out to her.

Turning, Veronica fired a shot from Natalie's gun. A starburst of blue paint appeared on the wall beside the monitor, and she handed the gun back.

"Besides, you *did* shoot at me first," she said.

Natalie looked at the gun in her hand, at the blue paint on the wall, and then her face crumpled like a sheriff's subpoena in an angry woman's fist.

Veronica snorted in disgust. "Grow up, Natalie. I don't have time for this. If you want to make a big deal out of it, you can go complain to Julian."

The monitor on the wall flashed, and the scoreboard appeared. The cell around each of their scores was outlined in white again, rather than the red or blue team colors. Veronica stared, mesmerized, watching her own score spin up ten points.

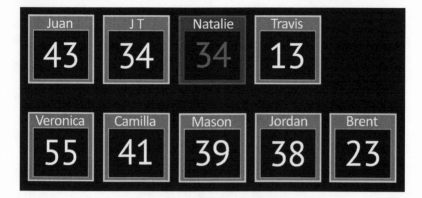

Natalie's cell blinked. Then the outline around it faded from white to gray. She slid down against the wall, hugged her knees to her chest, and buried her face.

Veronica turned her back on the room and marched upstairs, ignoring Natalie's sobs.

She didn't have time to babysit.

Women in need were counting on her.

• • •

A few minutes later, Veronica stood in her room. The paintball gun and envelope lay on the cot in front of her, but she was looking at her hands, turning them this way and that. She realized she had been doing that for several minutes, spacing out while her mind wandered. She had been thinking again about Leo, her second husband... Time to get with the program here. Her French manicure was a mess—nails split and cracked. She had forgotten to put her makeup on this morning. Her hair was filthy, knots of it hanging in front of her eyes. She was falling apart. At this rate, she'd look like a street person soon, dreadlocked and disgusting.

Ah, Leo, dear, I'm sure you would have loved to see me in this state.

She raised both arms and tried to comb through her hair with her fingers. They caught, hung up in the knots and tangles.

Her eyes snapped into focus and zeroed in on her Louis Vuitton travel bag. She crossed the room with aggressive strides, flipped it open, and unzipped the upper compartment where, four days ago, she had been surprised to find JT's court-martial transcript tucked away. Reaching inside, she dug deep until her fingers closed around the black Spyderco tactical folding knife she had brought.

Veronica flipped it open with a practiced one-handed motion, and three inches of matte-black case-hardened steel locked into place. With her other hand, she reached up to grab a tangled lock of hair.

CHAPTER 128

Brent loosened the surgical tubing he had wrapped around his upper arm, and rolled down the sleeve of his plaid shirt. Letting out a pent-up breath, he picked up the three syringes, now empty, that lay on the step beside him. Out of habit, he turned his head, looking for the sharps disposal, but of course there wasn't one. He chuckled and let the syringes fall from his fingers to roll down the steps, their bare needles pointing every which way.

He dumped a packet of pills into the cup of his hand and slapped his palm to his mouth, dry swallowing them. Reaching into his vest pocket, he grabbed another packet and tossed them down, too.

"Stop it. Please stop." The voice came from the top of the stairs.

Brent looked up to see Camilla standing there, eyes huge, like a little girl who wanted to go downstairs at night but was afraid of monsters. She held something white in front of her chest, two-handed, the way a Japanese pharmaceutical rep held a business card. He squinted. It was a folded-up wad of paper—perhaps the one that had been in her pocket earlier.

"What's that?" he asked.

Her face was sad. "Something I wanted to talk to you about, but it's not important now." She tucked it back into her pocket and came down the stairs to sit beside him.

She looked into his eyes and winced. "Why are you doing this to yourself, Brent?"

He didn't have an answer for her.

She laid a hand on his arm. "Talk to me."

Brent looked toward the distant windows. The light streaming through the plastic sheeting shimmered and danced, making patterns on the floor. Across the room, the scoreboard glowed from the wall monitor.

He pointed at the paintball gun tucked under Camilla's arm. "Can you imagine what those scientists think, seeing us running around with those things?"

"I don't want you to die."

Brent laughed. He could imagine how it probably looked to her, what she thought. He squeezed her knee.

"You needn't worry about this old man. I'm not killing myself."

"I don't believe you. I saw." She pointed at the syringes, the empty pill packets scattered on the steps. "So many…"

Brent sighed. "I suppose that would be enough to kill somebody—probably even enough to kill the rest of you put together."

411

He leaned toward her, trying to see her face clearly.

"Tolerance builds up over time, you see. Your physiology adapts."

"What if you make a mistake? Out here, that could kill you."

She sounded like Mary now. Loneliness washed over him, and he looked away.

"I'm a survivor, Camilla. I've faced my own mortality. Death doesn't scare me anymore."

He stared at the shimmering, dancing light again.

"Living the rest of my life alone does."

CHAPTER 129

Mason leaned against the wall inside the chicken coop, shrouded in shadow, watching the two houses through the open doorway. Glancing at the blue card in his hand, he read the name of his target: Juan. A half-smile played across his face. The paintball gun hung loosely in his hand, loaded with balls of neon pink—Julian's sense of humor on display once again.

Mason wondered what Camilla was doing right now.

Motion at the entrance of the Greek Revival house caught his eye. A woman stood in the doorway, bracing her fists on the edges of the doorframe, her own paintball gun gripped in one hand. Her body vibrated with restrained energy as her fierce silvery gaze swept the open area outside, probing the shadows.

Mason's eyebrows rose in surprise. It had taken him a moment to recognize Veronica. She looked different now.

Her hair had been chopped short. The bright salon highlights were gone. Standing up in spikes and radiating from her head in a rough shag, her hair looked almost black in the distance. She looked very familiar to Mason, now, though. Apart from her clothes and the missing nose ring, Veronica looked exactly the way she had as the angry teenager in the picture from Julian's profile.

Only deadlier.

Her nostrils flared. Her mouth was slightly open, in an expression of hungry anticipation. Mason watched her chest rise and fall. She looked like a predatory animal readying for the hunt.

Your mask is slipping. I can see what you really are. Even if you yourself don't know.

Her pale eyes bored into his across the empty space, and Mason drew back against the wall despite himself. He grinned. Even though he was sure she couldn't see him, the urge to hide had been involuntary, instinctive.

He wondered whose name was in Veronica's envelope. He hoped it wasn't Camilla's.

Veronica stalked away from the house, disappearing into the lengthening shadows as she made her way toward the barricade.

After a moment, Mason slipped out to follow her.

CHAPTER 130

JT ripped another strip from the black T-shirt. It required almost no effort, as if the tough cotton were tissue paper. The bloody white gauze of his eye patch gleamed up at him from his cot. It would make him a target, visible in light or darkness. Reaching up, he wrapped the black strips of clean cloth around his head and over his dead eye, winding them into a bandana that also covered one side of his face. He double-knotted it behind his head.

The Hawaiian shirt lay on the cot. In its place, he wore another long-sleeved black T-shirt. The desert camouflage of the multipocket tactical vest that covered his chest was a decent match for the island's dirt and rock, as were the tan fatigue pants he wore.

He double-laced his boots—combat boots now, also in desert tan—and listened to the quiet sounds that echoed through the Victorian house.

JT himself made no noise at all. Silence was his specialty.

One dark night in the Korengal, DiMarco had dubbed him the "shadow of death." The nickname had stuck. But the Taliban themselves had no nicknames for him. The ones he had encountered on patrol didn't have nicknames for anything anymore.

JT flipped open a small green plastic compact one-handed, shielding the mirror inside its lid with his hand to prevent reflections from bouncing off the walls and ceiling, visible from the hallway or outside. Without looking down, he dabbed two fingers into the compact and striped the dark greasepaint under his eye. He dipped again, coming up with a lighter color.

He finished the interlocking pattern of light and dark that now covered his face, head, neck, and wrists, then slipped the compact back into a vest pocket.

Then he picked up the blue card that had been inside his envelope. His eye flicked down briefly to read the name of his target.

The card and envelope went into another pocket of his tactical vest. He picked up the night-vision goggles from his cot.

JT clipped a Benchmade tactical folding knife, also striped in camouflage, to his pants pocket. Then he slipped through the door, disappearing into the darkening hallway.

He would be a shadow once again.

CHAPTER 131

Crouching by the breakwater, Jordan ripped upward with the dive knife. She sliced through the half-dry seal hide, which she had carefully scraped clean of putrefying flesh, and cut another long strip. Sheathing the knife at her waist, she ripped the last few inches by hand. The end of the strip refused to separate, and she tore it free with her teeth.

Her anger burned inside, white hot, incandescent, making her stomach hurt, her jaw clench, her heart ache, her eyes sting.

She scanned the area all around her. No one moved—only seals and birds. She thought of how he had pointed them out to her on the beach this morning, teaching her their Latin names, and a choked sob suddenly erupted from her mouth. Tears splashed the backs of her hands, burning them.

Bastard.

Swiping her forearm across her eyes, she strangled the sobs that wanted to come, that threatened to leave her curled helpless on the ground, a pathetic loser for others to pity and feel superior to. That wasn't her. It would never be her.

She would make that bastard sorry.

Gritting her teeth, fully in control of herself again, Jordan stared at the paintball gun, the speargun, and the envelope that lay on the ground beside her.

She would make him regret what he did.

Grabbing a long strip of sealskin, she shifted onto one knee and wrapped the strip around her opposite ankle, heel, and foot in a figure-eight pattern, layer after layer, pulling it tight they way a gymnast did after a sprain. She tied it off and shifted position, switching knees so she could wrap the other foot.

She didn't need his fucking scuba shoes.

Ignoring the stench of rotting blubber, Jordan looked at the three sealskins in front of her and thought of tuna and peaches.

Or his fucking food, either.

She stood and grabbed the hooded sealskin cape she had fashioned, sliding it onto her shoulders and tying the reeking folds of it about her like a full-length Burberry trench coat.

Or his cozy fucking blockhouse. He could keep it all. He could rot in there. She didn't care.

Her new outfit felt sticky and awful against her skin, but it would keep her warm enough, even in December. After all, this was California.

417

Jordan slung the speargun across her back and picked up the paintball gun. She ripped open the envelope, and her shoulders sagged in disappointment. Her target was Mason. Then she straightened.

That meant Juan had her name. He would have to come after her.

And if Juan didn't have the guts to come after her, she would still make him sorry. Her eyes narrowed. After she took out Mason, she would only have to eliminate six others to close the circle.

Then Juan would be her target, just as she was his.

She was going to look that son of a bitch in the eyes and make him regret that he ever met her.

CHAPTER 132

Juan stood inside the blockhouse, next to the drying rack, facing the open doorway. The light outside dimmed, and a chill wind tickled his bare chest and shoulders. Clouds were gathering above the island. They were sparse now, only thin wisps and streamers, but he knew they would thicken and darken over the next few hours.

The storm was coming.

Thrusting both arms into the form-fitting black wetsuit that covered him from the waist down, he shrugged his shoulders and felt the neoprene drape his chest. He reached behind him to grab the lanyard and drew the zipper up his back. Kneeling, he zipped up the left neoprene bootie, then the right. Their heavy-duty rubber soles were ridged on the bottom and sides, for stable footing on wet rock.

She hadn't given him a chance to explain, to tell her how he felt about her. But now what was done was done. Best not to think about it anymore.

He stood and pulled the black neoprene gloves over one hand, then the other. Flexing his fingers, he watched the space beyond the door. Nothing but seals.

He had hurt her pride.

Lifting a heavy nylon belt threaded with square lead weights off the drying rack, he swung it around his waist and buckled it into place. Then he shrugged into a slim buoyancy-compensator vest and tightened the straps about his chest. Without a tank to inflate it, the BC vest wouldn't be much use for its primary function of providing buoyancy. But its many pockets, D-rings, and buckles had other uses. He attached a clear face mask to a D-ring near his shoulder, letting the mask dangle at his collarbone.

She had let her guard down. She had left herself totally open to him. After what she had been through already—her fiancé's suicide—that must have taken incredible courage.

The oversize swim fins on the drying rack—Beuchat Mundial Carbon Pros—were each almost a yard long. They were designed for free diving and for powering through strong currents with minimal effort. Rubber struts ridged their black carbon-fiber blades like the long, bony fingers of a bat's wing. Juan lifted one over his shoulder and snapped it through a ring of the BC, letting the fin hang down his back, out of the way. Its mate went over his other shoulder.

He had been afraid to trust his own feelings. Now it was too late. She would never forgive him.

He slid the serrated dive knife into the black plastic locking sheath strapped to his calf. The spare paintball ammunition—yellow, in his case—went into a side pocket of the BC vest. Wedging the paintball gun barrel-first into a diagonal chest pocket, he left the grip exposed so he could draw it one-handed. Left-handed.

Perhaps, deep down, he had known that he didn't really deserve her.

But he couldn't undo what was done, and it didn't matter how sorry he was. He would focus on the job at hand—the true reason he was here. He ignored the way the corners of his mouth tried to pull downward. No more distractions.

With his right hand, Juan picked up JT's Glock. A day of immersion in salt water had done the polymer handgun no harm at all. He had wiped the brass cartridges dry and reinserted them into the magazine, but he was fairly sure even that precaution had been unnecessary. The Glock would probably even shoot underwater. He slid the blocky handgun into the improvised drop-leg holster strapped to his thigh, which he had made by cannibalizing parts from another BC vest. A rubber strap snapped into place, holding the gun securely until it was needed.

Juan smiled grimly. Now he could operate in the frame of shallow water that surrounded the island, too, while everyone else was limited to moving on the rock-and-sand picture within that frame.

With the serrated dive knife, he sliced through an empty water jug, cutting away the top to leave a large opening. Then he grabbed another empty jug and did the same. That one had belonged to Jordan.

His eyes swept the blockhouse, inspecting the walls and ceiling corners, until settling on a sunken divot in the concrete. He was reasonably certain he could make out a small black dot in its shadowed center. Staring at it, he drew the paintball gun.

Unsmiling, Juan raised his other hand to present a raised middle finger to the camera. Then he aimed the paintball gun. It bucked once in his hand, and the divot disappeared under a splatter of yellow.

Grabbing a jug with each hand, he carried them to the doorway, ready to drop both and grab for either gun. After scanning the area outside the blockhouse, he slipped cautiously outside and knelt to brace the two jugs upright between rocks.

Juan stood up. It was time for some answers.

The storm was coming.

CHAPTER 133

An unnatural stillness reigned over the island. Camilla lay flat on her back, watching the sky. It was what she liked to do at the midpoint of a mountain bike ride. She would reach the summit, legs shaky, breathing hard from the climb, and find a nice place to stretch out. She would take her helmet off, tousle her sweaty hair to let it breathe, and watch the clouds while she gathered herself for the downhill run. Getting ready.

Because on the downhill run, anything could happen to her.

Camilla liked to go fast. *Crazy* fast.

She would dare the mountain to do its worst to her and she'd laugh, bombing down the trail without ever touching her brakes, leaving her riding companions far behind, because flying free with the sky wide above her and the wind whipping her face while trees flashed past on both sides was the exact opposite of being buried in darkness and smoke and death and screams while crumbled walls of rock and metal pressed in on you from all sides and crushed down on you from above and you were crawling, lost, crawling, crawling, dragging yourself, unable to find a way out...

She would wait for her companions to catch up in the parking lot, drinking water and smiling a quiet smile, with her bike already racked atop the Prius. She would smile when they tried to talk to her about safety and told her they were worried about her. She would smile while they called her a reckless maniac, and ask her if she had a death wish.

Nobody would go riding with her more than once. Mostly she went alone.

Camilla watched the light play through the clouds, dimming and brightening as they passed. The sun sparkled off the ocean in a band of blinding whiteness that made her squint. She let her hand drift to the paintball gun that lay at her side. Sometimes, it was like the song said: to survive, you had to get a little crazy. She knew that the stillness was an illusion. All around below her, her fellow contestants would be moving about the island, hidden and stealthy. Or they would be hunkered down, concealed from view, like trapdoor spiders waiting to ambush their prey. In the minutes and hours ahead, short bursts of human activity would erupt with shocking suddenness and play out with desperate energy, only to have the stillness return once again. But she wasn't quite ready to join that dance yet.

Camilla thought about what Brent had said about living life alone. She was thirty years old already. She was an extrovert, she knew. She liked people, liked spending time with them, liked helping them. And people liked her. But she also liked to keep them at a comfortable distance. She did a lot of things alone. She pushed her friends and even boyfriends away when they got too close, when they wanted more of her then she was willing to share. The terror of her childhood tragedy was always going to be there inside her, a part of her forever. She had buried it as deeply as anyone could. But it still threatened to cripple all that she had become, if she allowed it to get a grip on her mind again and drag her back into its unrelenting darkness.

She thought about Veronica, a woman with her own darkness to fight. Perhaps that was why, despite all Veronica had done, despite how badly she had treated Camilla, Camilla still couldn't find it in her heart to hate her. She was even admirable in an awful sort of way... No. Camilla stopped herself. She was doing what she always did: being too nice.

Watching a cloud go by, she wrinkled her nose and shook her head. "That woman is an incredible bitch."

But even Veronica had been happily married for ten years. How would Camilla ever meet the right person if she kept pushing people away, afraid of getting too close, afraid of letting them find out what had happened to her when she was a child? Was she afraid that talking about it would give it power over her again? Or that others would see her differently once they knew? That they would start treating her like a freak?

Juan, Brent, Mason, JT, Jordan, even Veronica and Natalie—they had all heard her story, but none of them seemed to act any differently toward her because of it. She felt strangely close to all of them, like they were a weird dysfunctional family. Maybe that was because they were survivors, too. They understood her. Tomorrow, they would all face Julian together; they were her team.

A noise caught her ear—a faint rustle from beneath. She pushed her rambling thoughts aside and strained her ears, concentrating on the quiet movement she could hear below.

Camilla was ready.

The downhill run had begun.

CHAPTER 134

Moving silently through the shadows that draped the rooms of the Victorian house, Juan passed through darkness into light and back into darkness again. Motes of dust floated before his eyes, dancing in the fading rays that slanted through the clear plastic tarp over the windows. He paused near the archway that led into the great room, ignoring the bluish glow from the monitor on the wall. The stairwell wound around the corner in front of him. Easing around, he raised his paintball gun.

"Hello, Juan."

Brent's deep voice had a strange, hollow timbre.

White cylinders and irregular crumples of shiny foil lay scattered on the lower stairs: syringes and empty pill packets—a half dozen of each. Brent sat on the landing above, his legs stretching down the steps. A beam of light spilled over half his body, leaving the other half in darkness. His wrists hung loosely between his knees, the blue envelope held in one hand. His head was tilted back so that Juan could only see his throat and chin. Brent stared up at the ceiling as if something up there was very interesting.

A starburst of yellow paint exploded across the center of his chest, and Juan lowered the paintball gun.

"Listening to the angels, Brent?"

Brent didn't move, didn't lower his head.

"Oh, I think I can hear at least one of them," he said. "My guardian angel, maybe. Or perhaps the angel of death. I'm not sure which."

Brent's chin and Adam's apple moved as he spoke, but he continued to stare upward. Juan couldn't see his face.

Quick strides took Juan up the steps. He shoved the muzzle of the gun into the base of Brent's neck. But it was the Glock, rather than the paintball gun, which he now held.

"Let's find out which angel it is," he said. "Two questions, Brent. Answer without hesitating, or I kill you right here. No second chance."

Brent's chin tipped forward slowly. His eyes were eerie blue marbles, unmarred by visible pupils, which stared through Juan without really seeing him. Juan's stomach coiled in disgust.

"What would you like to know?" Brent said.

"How did you know about Lauren's climbing accident?"

"Yosemite Climbers Die in Tragic Pakistan Fall." It sounded like a headline, the way Brent said it. "Trango Tower Claims American Lives, 2007." He tilted his head to peer at Juan with that opaque blue gaze. "Lauren

King—that's an easy name to remember. But I guess you young people don't read newspapers anymore."

Juan pointed at the pills and syringes scattered about his feet.

"Why are you taking drugs again?"

"That's not the right question," Brent said. "The right question is, did I ever really stop? And the answer is no, I never did. But there's something you should know."

He reached into a vest pocket and pulled out a foil pack of pills.

"These I brought in my luggage. It's modafinil—Provigil—for treatment of narcolepsy and, more recently, Alzheimer's. Almost no side effects or aftereffects. It keeps you going on minimal sleep, alert and at full mental capacity, without an amphetamine crash later. It also sharpens brain function. A key ingredient of my 'cocktail,' as Mason puts it."

He reached into another pocket and pulled out a similar foil pack.

"This is from the first-aid kit. It's labeled 'modafinil,' too. But that's not what it is. In fact, I have *no idea* what it is. Something new, probably experimental, certainly not FDA approved yet. A catecholamine booster like modafinil. But much, much stronger."

Brent's jittery eyes turned inward, and Juan had to resist the urge to strike him across the face with the pistol. He had seen that expression of euphoric wonder before. The doctor was cataclysmically high.

"I feel like Superman," Brent said. "If I wanted to play Julian's stupid game, I could have taken you all instead of letting myself get eliminated. I could even take that gun away from you right now with ease."

"I'd like to see that," Juan said. "Go ahead and try."

"No, I don't want to. I'm feeling too good right now. I haven't slept for three days, but I'm still ready to, take on the world. My amygdala is on fire. My brain…"

His strange eyes searched Juan's face, as if struggling to put his sensations into words.

"…my brain is in overdrive, Juan. I can practically see what you're thinking, how slowly your thoughts move, by reading the cues on your face. All my senses are amplified. I can hear and feel every little thing going on around us. I can tell you who is moving around outside right now and what they're doing."

Juan reholstered the Glock against his thigh. "You're delusional."

"No. You need to try this. You need to feel it to understand. You think you're a survivor? This compound is the chemical essence of what *makes* you a survivor—distilled and amplified. My norepinephrine and epinephrine levels must be off the chart. I wish I could run labs on myself right now, do a full blood workup. I feel decades younger."

Brent reached out and grabbed his wrist.

"Just imagine what a soldier this stuff could create, Juan. A human machine that could fight for weeks without sleep. Smarter, faster, stronger, more ruthless, more relentless than anything else on the battlefield. Unstoppable."

Juan's expression hardened. "I've heard cocaine abusers say the same sorts of things right before going into toxic shock. How much of this shit did you put into yourself?"

Brent chuckled. "A lot."

Juan jerked his arm out of Brent's grip. "Is this really what you want? To die here?"

"Look." Brent turned over his wrist to display his forearm. Veins bulged under his skin, throbbing in a rapid cadence. "My resting pulse is over two hundred," he said. "At my age, it's amazing my heart doesn't burst."

He leaned forward into a beam of light, illuminating an eye that looked solid blue, like a robin's egg. Inhuman. "They are going to make billions with this drug, Juan. Billions."

Juan shook his head slowly. *"Quem deus vult perdere, dementat prius."*

He faded back down the stairs and into the darkness, leaving Brent sitting alone at the top of the steps.

CHAPTER 135

Squatting in the crawlway beneath the house, JT tracked the whisper of Juan's departing footsteps. Juan was not his target... yet.

He silently unwrapped an MRE and scarfed it down, thinking about what he had heard. Brent's words had taken him back to Fallujah, where he had seen firsthand the muj's drug-fueled zombie suicide runs, their superhuman ability to shrug off devastating injury.

Juan had been quick to dismiss everything Brent said.

JT wondered about that.

But despite all Brent's talk of enhanced senses, he had seemed completely unaware that JT crouched silently in the darkness fifteen feet below him. Perhaps Juan's Euripides quote had been right on the mark: *Whom the gods would destroy, they first make mad.*

JT gently touched the skin around his ruined eye. Could a corneal implant repair the damage Veronica had done? Civilian surgery would be expensive, and his dishonorable discharge prevented him from using the VA hospitals. *"Billions of dollars,"* Brent had said. JT didn't need billions.

He would settle for ten million. Tax free.

He considered the name on his target card again. Threat assessment had been an integral part of the training in his military specialty, and he had watched his opponents here carefully over the past five days. He knew who the most significant threats were, standing between him and the grand prize. Veronica was dangerous in every sense of the word, and she had a substantial point lead over everyone else right now, but he didn't expect it to last much longer. No, there were two people JT considered far greater threats than the woman who had blinded him.

One of them was Juan.

The other one's name was written on his target card:

Jordan.

CHAPTER 136

Mason shuffled through a large cluster of sea lions, moving toward the narrow saddle section near the highest point of the island. The fallen lighthouse tower lay dead ahead, its base a high pile of broken concrete rubble. It would be a good place for someone to hide.

He turned and, pushing his cracked glasses higher on his nose, looked back along the path he had traversed. Nothing moved except for the wriggling, writhing mass of seals, sea lions, and birds.

A large black cormorant flapped into startled flight from the ground near his feet.

Looking after the departing bird, Mason held an index finger to his lips and whispered, "Ssshhh!" Then he giggled.

He continued toward the base of the tower, twenty feet ahead. Something blue on the ground near his feet caught his eye. An envelope.

Bait.

Movement rippled in his peripheral vision. Mason spun, and his mouth opened in surprise.

One of the seals he had passed on the trail contracted unnaturally and rose from the ground in a single graceful movement to stand upright. Black paint splattered across Mason's chest.

He laughed. "I thought I was seeing fifty million years of evolution happen in fast-forward."

Jordan threw back the crude hood of her sealskin cape and lowered the paintball gun. Her eyes were cold.

"I can smell your new couture from here." Mason reached into the inside pocket of his suit jacket and withdrew his own blue envelope. "Your new target." Squatting, he placed it carefully atop the other envelope, covering it. Then he continued along the path.

As he came parallel with the broken base of the tower he grinned.

"But wait," he called, turning back to look at her. "Why are there two envelopes instead of one?"

Jordan was leaning forward at the waist, one arm outstretched to pick up Mason's envelope, when he turned. Her green eyes flicked up toward him, going wide with sudden alarm.

Mason moved aside, still grinning.

Next to him, Veronica stepped out from behind the base of the tower.

CHAPTER 137

Veronica pivoted on her feet, swinging her paintball pistol up two-handed to aim it at Jordan's face. She pulled the trigger.

But instead of the hard snick of gas expanding behind a high-velocity paintball, the gun made a muted *phhht*. A few drops of red paint sprayed from the gun barrel to sprinkle the ground, falling well short of Jordan. The look of triumph on Veronica's face twisted into surprised anger.

Jordan didn't hesitate. She scooped up Mason's envelope and the second envelope beneath it. With the other hand, she swept her gun around to fire at Veronica.

Jordan's gun *also* malfunctioned with the same *phhht* sound.

Veronica's left hand slapped upward beneath the pistol grip and then whipped over the top to grab the frame of the gun. She yanked back hard, holding the gun steady with her right. The movement was lightning fast, a reflex, but her left hand slipped off the plastic.

Tap-rack. Muscle memory. Jordan knew Veronica's years of firearms training had just betrayed her. The Tippman TPX wasn't a real gun. It didn't have a working slide. Jordan's own finger was already on her magazine release, dropping the faulty ammunition cartridge toward the ground at her feet. But when it hit the dirt her feet weren't there anymore.

Pulling her arms in close to her body, Jordan spun away, letting go of the envelopes. She pirouetted like a dancer, grabbing her spare ammunition cartridge and shoving it into her gun as she whirled.

Six feet from where she had stood a second ago, she raised the gun.

Veronica was in the middle of a combat reload, striding sideways, slamming a new cartridge into the grip of her gun. The jammed ammunition cartridge floated near her knees, dropping in slow motion through the air, as Jordan pulled the trigger twice.

Two black flowers of paint bloomed on Veronica's chest. Her jammed ammunition cartridge bounced off the dirt, spattering her shins with red droplets.

Jordan raised the gun a few inches.

Fuck you and your useless training.

Veronica's head snapped back as black paint exploded across her forehead.

Jordan dipped to scoop up both the envelopes she had dropped.

Veronica threw her paintball marker aside, sending it skittering across the rocks. Black paint streaked her face and frosted the spikes of her short hair.

431

Raising both hands in front of her, she stared at them in stunned incomprehension. Then her fingers hooked into claws.

She shook her head violently, like a wet dog, sending streamers of paint flying in all directions. Then she screamed—a wordless, full-throated, guttural cry of fury that made the tendons stand out on her neck. Her chest heaved, rising and falling. Bulging from their sockets, her luminous eyes locked on Jordan's own.

Then her lips curled up at the corners in a terrifying, openmouthed smile.

Jordan's own anger melted away.

She's insane. How did I not see that before? Veronica is fucking psychotic.

Veronica screamed again—a hoarse, liquid sound, more mountain lion than human, echoing off the rocks and distant buildings.

Jordan turned and ran, with Veronica close on her heels.

CHAPTER 138

Juan levered himself up to balance in a squat at the top of the seawall. He watched Mason stroll through the corridor between the seawall and the factory building, ten feet ahead and eight feet below, seemingly oblivious of Juan's presence. His nonchalant act wasn't very convincing, though. Juan half expected him to start whistling. Mason knew perfectly well that someone was behind him.

Juan dropped into the corridor, and Mason turned to face him with an expression of mock surprise.

"Whoops, wrong gun," he said. "Besides, your paramour already got me."

"I have a few questions," Juan said, training the Glock on Mason's navel. "When did you move here from New York?"

"November 2008."

"Why?"

"Change of scenery—"

Juan jabbed the gun barrel into his solar plexus, and he doubled over with a grunt.

"Why did you move to San Francisco?"

"Lifestyle choice." Mason rubbed his midsection. "San Francisco's nightlife is a great playground for people of my, um, ..."—he grinned—"...persuasion."

"I'm sure." Juan looked at him closely. "What did your Vita Brevis letter say, Mason?"

"What did *yours* say?"

"Things about me that aren't common knowledge," Juan said. "Things that *would* have become common knowledge if I declined Julian's offer."

Mason nodded. "The SEC wasn't the only three-letter government agency interested in my career in New York. My letter was similar to yours."

CHAPTER 139

Jordan was frightened. She was a fast runner and had expected to outpace the older woman quickly. Instead, she found herself pushing hard to maintain a slim lead. Veronica came on relentlessly.

Seals scrambled out of Jordan's way. Birds exploded up from nests at her feet, jetting away in bursts of feathers. Veronica was panting behind her. But not in an exhausted way, Jordan thought.

She sounded excited, actually.

Jordan realized she had made a bad mistake. And by letting herself get chased in the wrong direction, she had just made it worse.

She skidded to a halt, and Veronica did the same, fifteen feet away. A few steps beyond Jordan's heels, the sandstone bluff dropped straight to the beach twenty feet below. Veronica had her trapped against the cliff.

The two women faced each other, breathing heavily. Veronica wore a carnival funhouse grin, open-mouthed and panting.

Jordan looked over Veronica's shoulder, scanning the terrain. Mason was gone. There was no one else in sight. She was alone with Veronica.

It would be impossible to get past her.

"You *know* something." Veronica's voice was saccharine—cloying and sweet. "You lied to us last night."

Jordan didn't answer. She tucked the paintball gun into the waist of her sealskin wrap and grabbed the speargun that hung across her back, leveling it one-handed at Veronica.

Veronica's funhouse grin only widened.

"You shouldn't keep secrets from *me*, Jordan. I want to help you, but I can't if you won't talk to me."

Keeping one eye on her, Jordan glanced down at the envelopes. Veronica's name was printed on one. Jordan slid the target card out far enough to read her own name. No surprise there.

"Look at me when I'm speaking to you!" Veronica's voice rose, harsh and strident. "What didn't you tell us?"

Jordan looked at the target card inside the second envelope, the one with "Mason" printed on it. His target was now her new target. She read the name and sucked in a sharp breath. *Juan.*

The anger was back, like a stone in her heart, burning her eyes, filling her arms and legs with ice. She would make him sorry. She would humiliate him. She would make him suffer.

She would make him wish he had never been born.

435

Veronica screamed at her. "I asked you a question, Jordan!"

She looked at Veronica, who was wasting Jordan's time right now.

"I told the truth, you washed-up old hag, but I guess you're just too fucking senile to understand that. Now, get out of my way." Jordan raised the speargun.

Veronica charged her.

The speargun discharged, sending its two-foot steel shaft flying toward Veronica.

It arrowed over her shoulder, whizzing through open air inches from her throat. She didn't even break stride.

Jordan turned, took three running steps, and launched herself off the bluff. She plunged, thick seal cape billowing, legs still taking running steps through the air as the beach rushed up at her from twenty feet below.

Tuck and roll. Jordan landed hard, and the impact sent sand spraying. She bounced forward into a somersault, rolled, and came out of the tuck to spring upright. Pain exploded through her ankle, and her leg buckled.

Broke it. *Broke my fucking ankle.* She hopped a few steps to regain her balance. Panicked seals, apparently unused to having people fall out of the sky, scrambled away from her.

The sand had been soft. It had absorbed much of the impact. Her injuries could have been a lot worse than a broken ankle. Gritting her teeth, she nocked another shaft into the speargun. She pushed the tip of the barrel into the sand and leaned on it, using it as a crutch while she stretched the elastic charger back to full cock. Reloaded and ready now, she looked up at the top of the bluff.

Veronica stood silhouetted against the sky, watching her. Then she drew back, disappearing from sight.

Jordan bent to pick up her paintball marker, which had been knocked loose in the fall. She shoved it back into the waist of her sealskin wrap and hobbled south, limping between huddled sea lions and elephant seals, poking the speargun into the sand with every step. The elevated walkway and wooden stairs lay ahead. They would take her back up onto the island's rocky surface. Somewhere up there, her new target lay hidden.

She thought about how he had tricked her, used her, and lied to her, and how she had stupidly let him do it, and the beach blurred in front of her eyes.

Bastard.

Her fist tightened on the speargun.

CHAPTER 140

Dmitry looked out the window of the science station. The situation was degenerating. People were acting strangely, doing things that were hard to understand. He had seen some of the TV people running around outside earlier. He had heard shouts. Angry screams.

The animals, too, were acting unpredictably. The shark that had knocked him out of the water yesterday should not have done that. Seen from below, the shape of his body could have looked nothing like a seal. And the island's seal population was thinner than it should be at this time of year. Nature's delicate balance was tipping here, in a direction he couldn't predict.

Dmitry looked up at the clouds gathering in the darkening sky above. They matched his mood.

He was a realist. He knew that Heather was dead. The criminal tied up next door was a murderer, and Dmitry would see that he paid for what he had done to her. He would guard the criminal until he was in custody, and talk to the police when the time came—tell them everything he could remember, give evidence. But why had the rest of the TV people left the criminal with the scientists? Shouldn't *they* be responsible for him, rather than Dmitry?

The keys to the chains lay on the table near his hand.

And now Jacob had left him, too. Jacob's odd behavior was worrisome, but at least Dmitry had some idea what that was about. Not everyone handled danger and stress the same way. Unable to face Heather's death, the environmental disaster here, and the destruction of their research, Jacob was retreating into his own fantasy world. His complete inability to face the reality of their situation meant that he would be worse than useless. Dmitry was on his own.

The criminal yelled at him from the next room again. He was getting tired of the man's taunts.

"Hey, Russkie. *Tovarish!* I'm talkin' to you. *Preev-yet,* man. I know you're there. You have to untie me. I'm innocent, I swear. I never touched her."

Dmitry knew how this would be handled in Russia. Criminals were not coddled. He thought about threatening the chained man himself, forcing him to admit what he had done to Heather, what he had done with her body afterward. His arm was injured. He was tall but skinny. Dmitry could probably beat him in a fight.

But then he remembered the man's cold, snakelike eyes. No, this was for the police to do.

437

"Okay, tell you what," the criminal yelled. "Let me go, and I'll take you to see her—her name's Heather, right? I know where she is."

Yob tvayu mat. Dmitry stood up, face flushed with anger, and grabbed the keys to the chains. He would see what the man had to say, and then he would ask some questions of his own. But there was something he needed first. It would make the criminal more talkative. He remembered seeing it earlier, lying in the dirt just outside the station. Dmitry opened the exterior door and stepped out to fetch it.

The heavy three-foot steel pipe with the thick lump of concrete at one end was sure to be very persuasive.

• • •

Travis stared down at the Russian lying sprawled on the floor of the science station, his bleeding head inches from Travis's boot. A prod from his toe, and the concrete-plugged steel pipe that lay next to the Russian rolled aside, oscillating in diminishing arcs to come to a stop again.

Travis looked at the keys in his hand, laughed, and dropped them on the floor. It had surprised the hell out of him when they were tossed through the doorway, landing next to his feet.

He now turned his attention to the two objects lying on the cot in front of him: a big plastic toy pistol he recognized as a paintball gun, and a blue envelope with his name printed on it. Picking up the envelope one-handed, he slid out the card, and read the name on it. *That little whore.* He grinned.

Travis scanned the corners of the ceiling until he spotted a likely dark spot, which he figured was a camera. Tucking the envelope under his bad arm, he raised his hand to his forehead and threw an ironic salute toward the camera.

Then he picked up the paintball gun.

With another curious glance at the Russian's prone form, he left the science station to track down his prey.

CHAPTER 141

The clouds above Camilla were thicker now. Their edges had gone gunmetal gray, and the afternoon light had a brittle, flat quality. The air tickled her arms with a staticky stillness that she associated with impending thunderstorms. Lying spread-eagled on her back, she felt the muscles of her left calf tingling—after hours of immobility, the leg had gone to sleep. She stretched her foot and pushed against the brick of the chimney with the toe of her sneaker, working away the cramp. She had spent the afternoon in her rooftop perch, tucked away between the dormers and chimneys of the Victorian house, staying flat, invisible from below. She wondered whether Julian had cameras up here, too. She couldn't see any, but she figured they were there.

Her strategy was simple. She knew that everyone would have to come back to the houses sooner or later to check scores on the monitor and find out who was still in play. She wasn't a skilled shooter, she wasn't the fastest runner here, and she certainly didn't have the best reflexes—she was actually kind of clumsy when it came to this sort of thing. But what she did have was patience. She would let the other contestants eliminate each other while she stayed hidden and safe. The circle would close. Eventually, there would be only one other player left, looking for her—and also her target, worth fifteen points to Camilla because then she would be the last player standing.

Her rooftop aerie was hidden and had a 360-degree field of view that let her track everyone's comings and goings. She knew that both houses were empty except for Brent, who hadn't left the Victorian. Juan had come and gone some time ago—he had given her quite a jolt when she peered over the edge of the roof. At first she hadn't been sure what she was looking at, her heart pounding with fear as she watched a slick, dark shape with black wings folded across its back, stalking through the shadows. It looked like a giant insect, or a fallen angel from a Renaissance painting. Then she had realized that what she'd mistaken for wings were actually swim fins. Juan didn't have an air tank on his back, but he probably wouldn't want to go deep anyway, with the shark out there. He was no doubt using the safer shallows surrounding the island to move about unseen. And right now Juan's point total put him in second place.

Fifteen minutes ago, Camilla had checked the scoreboard herself. Making sure the coast was clear, she had crawled across the connected rooftops to reach the hole she had widened in the shingles—her own private escape hatch. Dropping through it, she landed back in her own upstairs room in the

Greek Revival house. No one was around. She slipped quietly down the stairwell to peer at the monitor in the empty living room, memorizing the current scores. Then she returned to her room and stood her cot on end, leaning it against the wall.

Earlier, she had tied a leftover piece of climbing rope from her backpack around the upper end of the cot's frame. Now she tucked the loose end of the rope into her belt and climbed up the cot's wire mesh like a ladder. Thrusting her head and shoulders through the hole in the roof, Camilla pulled herself up. Then, lying on her stomach, she used the rope to lower the cot silently to its original position.

Now, hidden and safe again, she thought about the scores she had seen.

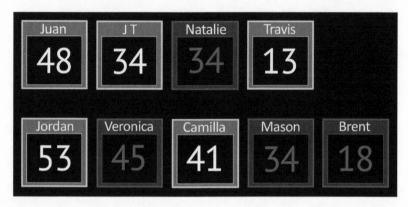

Four of them were still in play, plus Travis, who, she was surprised to see, hadn't been eliminated yet. That made no sense to her.

Jordan was, unsurprisingly, in first place again.

Camilla looked at the target card in her hand: Natalie, her original target. But Natalie had been eliminated early in the game. According to the rules, Camilla needed to track her down and ask for her envelope. Then she would learn the name of Natalie's target, who had become Camilla's new target. It wasn't going to happen. She wasn't planning to leave her rooftop nest and put herself at risk.

Besides, she could probably figure out who her current target was without chasing down envelopes. She considered the scoreboard again.

Camilla hadn't eliminated Natalie. Which meant that Natalie's own target had eliminated her, earning ten points by doing so. Juan was only up five, so it wasn't him—he had taken out either Mason or Brent, who were each down five. Jordan was up fifteen. That meant she had either taken out three targets in a row or eliminated one target plus her own assassin. It couldn't be three targets in a row, because then she and Juan would account for all eliminations, and that wouldn't explain Veronica's unchanged score. Veronica had been eliminated, but her score was unchanged, so it had gone up first, then come down by the same amount when she was eliminated.

There was only one possibility.

Veronica had been Natalie's target originally. She had taken Natalie out instead, becoming Camilla's new target. Camilla breathed a sigh of relief, realizing that Veronica's elimination meant she wouldn't have to face her.

The scores told the whole story.

Jordan was now Camilla's target.

Camilla stared up at the clouds. Her conflicted feelings about Jordan confused her. Had Jordan's friendliness to her *all* been an act? She couldn't believe that. She was usually great at reading people, and Jordan's betrayal had blindsided her, shaking her faith in herself. They never had a chance to talk after that. Jordan and Juan had been ostracized, and now people were dying, and, oh god, how important were her own silly hurt feelings in the face of that? She and Jordan needed to reconnect and try to figure out what was going on here.

But Jordan didn't take her seriously. It hurt to acknowledge it. Maybe after she beat Jordan and took first place from her, she would have to respect *that*.

Camilla realized her original strategy was flawed now. If she waited and Jordan eliminated all three of the others, then Jordan would be ahead in overall points even if Camilla eliminated her to win the assassin game.

The same was true of Juan, also, because of the security the red team had won in capture the flag. Juan's points wouldn't go down when she eliminated him—making him just as much of a threat as Jordan.

No matter who won, though, they would finish this game. They would get Julian to come, and... what? Hold him hostage? Threaten him? *Kill* him?

Maybe. Camilla would do whatever was necessary to get back to Avery and the rest of her kids. They needed her. Vita Brevis had committed crimes against everyone here, endangering their lives. If they killed Julian, it would be self-defense. And when they left the island, they would find out who else was behind Vita Brevis and make them all pay for this.

Brent believed the prize money was a lie, and she figured he was probably right. But she didn't think that mattered. She had seen that yacht, worth hundreds of millions of dollars. Whoever they were, Vita Brevis had money, even if they didn't plan to make good on their promises. Camilla had been lured here by the promise of help for her kids; Vita Brevis *owed* them now. She would rally the other contestants and file a civil suit in addition to the criminal charges. Even if Vita Brevis had to sell its stupid luxury yacht to settle, she would make sure her kids got every penny they were promised.

But if she wanted to be at the top of the scoreboard when this game ended, it was time to change her plan before either Juan or Jordan swept the scoreboard and made it impossible for her to win. It was time to go on the offensive.

Now.

She rolled slowly to the side... and froze in place. A faint, uneven scraping drifted up from below. Raising her head slowly, she peeked one-eyed over the edge of the roof.

Her breath caught. A seal was walking upright toward the houses, lurching across the open ground. Camilla rolled onto her back, eyes wide, heart pounding again. That *couldn't* be what she had seen. It was impossible. So what had she *really* seen?

Its loose hide had flapped as it walked. Through the gap in its hide, she had glimpsed dirty pink skin, human legs. Despite the terrible limp, it moved with a limber grace that she recognized as Jordan's.

Camilla closed her eyes and listened, tracking Jordan's approach. Then she rolled to the side, extending her head and arm over the rooftop to take aim at the shape fifteen feet below her. She pulled the trigger over and over again, as fast as she could. Light green paint spattered the ground around Jordan. It spattered her sealskin hood and cape and streaked her legs. Excitement coursed through Camilla, and she laughed. She had beaten Jordan.

Jordan's paintball gun dropped from her fingers and bounced once, landing in the green-spattered dirt at her feet. Her other hand held a long black tube, which she leaned on, its point buried in the dirt. She stood with her hooded head lowered, hiding her face, but her body vibrated with tension. Her free hand rose to disappear under the hood. Camilla thought she heard a faint noise from her—a muted cry that shook with fury and despair, which was quickly stifled. Balancing on one leg like a stork, Jordan swept the end of the black tube up to point it at the roofline.

Camilla ducked away and rolled onto her back, eyes wide. Had Jordan been about to shoot her with a *speargun*? She slid her body a few feet and cautiously peeked over a different part of the roof edge.

The point of the speargun was jammed into the ground again. Jordan reached up and swept her hood back, looking around her with an icy, remote expression on her face. But she didn't look up, didn't acknowledge Camilla. She turned her back on the buildings and limped to the edge of the bluff, where she sat at the top of the wooden stairs that led down to the beach. She lay the speargun across her knees.

They just needed to talk.

Camilla slid down the sloped roof of the Victorian and swung her legs over the edge, lowering herself to hang from her arms. She let go and dropped. Her landing was a little clumsy, but she stood up and dusted off her hands and knees. Then she walked over to sit on the steps beside Jordan.

Jordan stared out over the water, toward the mainland. She never looked at Camilla. Through the thickening clouds, a band of sunlight made a stripe of ocean glow silver, bright enough to make Camilla squint. Seabirds hopped near their feet. Jordan's ankle looked swollen. Painful. Camilla wanted to ask about it. But instead, she just watched the waves, the changing patterns of brightness, and held her tongue. She would leave it up to Jordan to break the ice first.

Neither of them said anything for a while.

Jordan flicked her wrist and two blue envelopes fluttered to the step at Camilla's feet. She spoke without much life.

"You were under a collapsed freeway for four days? Is that true?"

Camilla nodded.

Jordan looked away toward the north. The silence stretched between them again.

Camilla swallowed. As difficult as it would be, she was ready to talk about what had happened to her, if that was what Jordan wanted. She would answer her questions. She didn't want it to be another source of awkwardness between them.

Jordan spoke again.

"I want to go home."

CHAPTER 142

Jacob sat cross-legged at the end of the dock, with his back toward the island. He waited patiently, facing the churning, frothing vastness of the Pacific Ocean. The most essential pieces of his research were piled beside him on the dock, next to his thigh. He stared out at the roughening water, not thinking much, reminiscing about surfing—he had done a lot of surfing in high school.

San Diego had some good surf spots. Maybe on the weekends he'd take it up again, once he got settled in down there.

There was a great surf break off the south side of the island here, too. No one really surfed it, though. For the life of him, Jacob couldn't imagine why.

A footstep sounded behind him on the dock. A shadow fell across him.

He turned his head to look over his shoulder and smiled, reaching to take the offered hand.

"*You're* the San Diego director?" he asked.

In answer, a bulky gray pistol shape like a power drill was pressed lightly against his forehead.

Jacob frowned.

His confusion disappeared in a wet, splintering thump that echoed off the rocks of the breakwater.

CHAPTER 143

Camilla stood facing the corner of the Greek Revival house, steeling herself. A black gap yawned in front of her, close to her feet. The structure had settled, separating from its foundation, leaving a seal-size opening into the darkness beneath. She didn't want to go in there.

Jordan had limped away without another word, leaving her alone at the top of the steps, so she had slipped back inside the Greek Revival house for another peek at the scoreboard.

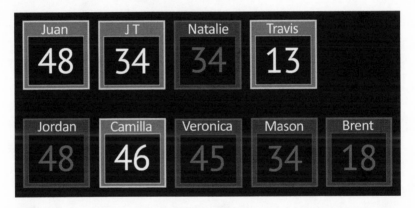

Now she could afford to play the waiting game again, but her rooftop hiding place was no good anymore. Jordan had seen it, and Jordan would tell Juan. So Camilla would go underground instead. She could watch both entrances and the entire flat area surrounding the houses, through the small gaps in the foundation.

The others all knew about what had happened to her when she was seven. Hiding *underneath* the house was absolutely the last place anyone would expect her to be. To win this game, she would face her terror, her childhood nightmare, head-on.

Juan and JT were the only two left. Travis had to be JT's target, but JT had ignored him for some reason, probably saving him for the very end. But whichever of the two—Juan or JT—prevailed, when they returned she would surprise them by firing from the darkness below.

She looked at the hole again, steeling herself to enter it. The longer she stood here in indecision, the greater her risk of being seen. But it was difficult, oh so difficult, to make herself enter that narrow, black space. She squatted in front of the gap and closed her eyes.

Sliding her legs through, she rolled over onto her belly and eased backward through the gap. Her breath caught in her chest as darkness closed over her head. She turned and crawled deeper under the house to check the view from the other gaps, but the pinholes of light where they opened to the outside seemed dim and distant now. The blackness she moved through felt suffocating, like a blanket. Her heart sped up, thudding in her chest and throat. She looked back over her shoulder. The entrance was still visible behind her, but it seemed faraway and fragile.

Oh god, what if it disappeared? What if something blocked it? She stopped crawling and froze. Dread flooded her limbs with weakness, and she bit her lip. She had to get moving again. But she couldn't force herself forward.

Keep going. You can't freeze up now. Arms and legs. Move!

A bulky shape emerged insect-eyed from the darkness beside her.

One strong hand clamped over her mouth, holding her head immobile. The other hand reached out and took her paintball gun from her. Camilla's eyes bulged with fear as an inhuman face with green, telescoping eyestalks leaned into hers. Its mottled skin made it impossible to make out other features.

"Brave girl, coming down here," JT said. "Where did Jordan go?"

The night-vision goggles and camouflage facepaint made him look alien and terrifying. The hand over her mouth relaxed slightly.

Sagging against his fingers, Camilla sucked in a ragged breath. Her heart felt like it was going to explode. "I don't know," she gasped, muffled by his palm.

"I never figured you for a cheater. But I guess money can do that to anyone."

"What are you talking about?"

"You took out Jordan," he said. "I think you're a free target now, Camilla. Five points for anyone."

"But why? She was my assigned target."

"Show me."

With shaking fingers, Camilla rummaged in her pockets. She pulled out two envelopes, thankful that Jordan had left her Veronica's envelope as well as her own. Camilla had transferred Veronica's target card into her own envelope—one of the two she held out now in the near darkness.

JT plucked them away, and she heard paper crinkle. The stalks of the night vision goggles aimed downward, and JT chuckled.

"Jordan was after Juan. I wish I could've seen that."

Then he opened the other envelope. Hers. He stared at it silently for a while. Then his fingers released her face.

Camilla fell to her hands and knees in the dark crawlspace, gasping. She strained to see. She could hear paper crinkling again, then JT spoke in a cold, emotionless voice that sent a chill down her spine.

"Look at this."

"I can't see."

"Shit." He laughed. "I forgot. Come over here, then, where you can see."

A large shape blocked the light from the gap momentarily, and her heart constricted. Then the shape shrank as JT crawled away. She followed.

In the slanting light from the gap, he held three envelopes. One was labeled "JT," and another was hers. He slid the target cards out of them.

Both cards said "Jordan."

"Something is wrong here," JT said.

"Just about *everything* is wrong here," she replied.

He nodded. Then he turned over the third envelope—Jordan's—and pulled out the target card with Juan's name. JT slid it into his own envelope and tucked that into his vest pocket.

"I'm going to go talk to Juan..." He pushed his night vision goggles up onto his head, and his eye held hers for a moment.

"...but for you, Camilla, I'm afraid it's game over."

CHAPTER 144

JT picked his way across the breakwater, staying low, the waves foaming at his feet. Passing the empty dock, he looked up at the angry clouds gathering above the island. Thunder rumbled in the distance. He stood still for a moment, watching the changing sky. Without being obvious, he used his peripheral vision to scan the terrain behind him.

There was no sign of the small shape he had noticed earlier, flitting from rock to rock behind him, keeping low and in the shadows, trying to stay out of sight.

There's no reason to follow me, girl.

He pulled Camilla's paintball gun out of his combat vest. Wrapping a hand around the frame of the gun, he squeezed hard, feeling the plastic splinter under his fingers. He folded the wreckage of the gun in half and tossed it out into the water.

I hope you saw that. You weren't going to get it back, anyway. Now, leave.

He pulled out his own paintball marker and scanned the rocks ahead.

This was between Juan and him.

He stepped onto a rocky finger that jutted out into the water. Kelp and foam rose and fell in the narrow channels on each side, swirling just below his feet. JT looked south toward the dock again, his paintball marker held in a two-handed grip. Then he looked down at the water below him. Something glinted near the bottom, catching his eye. Taking a few steps forward, he aimed the paintball gun at it.

Something struck his leg on the other side—his blind side—followed by rapid impacts to his hip, chest, and arm. He whipped his head around in time to see the last paintball fly up out of the water from the opposite channel, striking his shoulder and spattering him with more yellow paint. *Shit.* Ambushed.

But now I've got you, amigo.

Overlapping ripples spread across the dark water where the paintballs had erupted from the surface. JT could see nothing beneath. He stayed still, waiting, watching.

Water dripped on rock behind him. He turned very slowly.

A dark, wet shape hauled itself up out of the first channel and onto the ledge, crouching there for a moment. Then Juan stood up to face him, silent and ready.

JT inclined his head. "No bubbles."

"I can hold my breath for a long time."

451

"Where's your air tank?"

"If I had a tank, I would have been out of here a long time ago."

"You're a liar." JT rolled his neck from side to side, cracking it. He dropped his paintball marker, letting it slide down into the water. "I've seen you out here with a tank on. Sneaking around, night after night."

"Now who's lying, JT?"

JT shifted, holding his arms out to his sides, ready. "I want my gun back."

"Not going to happen."

"We'll see about that." JT inched toward Juan, who stood at the edge with the water behind him.

"What did you think of Brent's superdrug talk?" JT kept his voice casual.

"Brent's lost the plot," Juan said. "But I do have a couple questions for you."

JT took another step, and Juan aimed the paintball marker at his good eye. "Last warning."

JT stopped fifteen feet from him. "Ask away."

"Why was your final mission classified?"

"'Classified' means I can't tell you, hombre."

Juan fired, and JT whipped his face sideways to protect his eye. He felt the sting and the spatter of paint against his ear, but he didn't flinch. Then he slowly turned his head back to face Juan again.

You just killed yourself, amigo.

"Why was it classified?" Juan repeated.

"Because the shot that brought the chopper down came from one of our own. Friendly fire. It happens, but the unit that shot us down wasn't supposed to *be* in that valley. They were operating off the books—without official sanction from our so-called regional allies. It would have been a political shit storm if it got out, so they covered it up. For my silence, I got to walk away." JT's hand drifted to his pants pocket. "You're not going to walk away from this, though."

Juan tucked the paintball marker into his BC vest. "How did Veronica get hold of your court-martial transcript?"

"You put it in her luggage." The Benchmade tactical knife was in JT's hand. "She's a killer, but she's not Julian's spy, Juan. *You* are." He flicked his wrist, and the blade locked open.

Juan's hand whipped toward his thigh and the grip of the Glock, but stopped in midair. He crouched, his other hand dropping toward the dive knife sheathed on his ankle. But again he froze, and pulled his hand away. He straightened up slowly.

"Afraid of me?" JT asked. "Force Recon trains killers—you *should* be."

Juan shook his head. "It's not that." His hand drifted to the buckle of his weight belt. "I'm trying to figure out how to avoid killing you."

He whipped off the belt, and let the heavy lead dive weights dangle from his right hand. Eyeing JT, he shifted the belt to his left hand.

Shit.

Juan now held the belt on JT's blind side.

CHAPTER 145

A minute later, JT lay crumpled at Juan's feet. Juan pulled a blue envelope from JT's pocket and stepped back. Blood dribbled from the slash across his shoulder and upper chest where the tactical knife had sliced through his wetsuit. Backing up to the edge of the water, he buckled the weight belt around his waist again. Then he slid JT's target card from the envelope and read his own name.

He and JT had been each other's targets. Full circle. Juan was now the last person standing—the winner of the assassin game.

He wouldn't have to face Jordan.

His shoulders sagged in relief, but his throat felt tight again.

JT was moving, pushing up to his hands and knees. Juan found it surprising, considering the blows he had taken from the lead weights.

JT shook his head as if to clear it. Then he raised his neck, and his one-eyed gaze met Juan's. He got his legs under him, getting in a position to spring.

Time to go.

Juan stepped backward and let himself fall, half-turning as the dark water closed over his head. Pushing off the rocks with his feet, he coasted parallel to the bottom. Corkscrew rolling twice, he pulled the fins from his shoulders and slipped them onto his feet as he spun. Then he slipped the mask over his face and cleared the water from inside it with a sharp exhale through the nose. He knew JT would see the bubbles, but he was already a dozen yards from shore. With powerful kicks, he headed away from the ledge.

• • •

Thunder rumbled overhead. Juan sat alone on the large boulder, three meters above the churning waves. Año Nuevo Island lay in the near distance behind him, silent under the darkening sky. He had hauled up onto the last of the scattered rocks that trailed away through the rough water at the island's northern end, very aware of what patrolled the deeper blue beyond.

Sitting where he and Lauren had found the water jugs three days ago, Juan now raised a full jug to his lips and drank. Then he set it aside.

A chill wind blew through his hair, drying it. He let one leg dangle over the edge. Raising his other knee, he rested his chin on it, leaning forward to watch the roiling sea. The swim fins hung behind his shoulders once again, out of the way for now. He glanced back over one shoulder at the island, separated from him by a hundred meters of whitewater. Nothing moved there. Even the seals had abandoned the rocks.

Paradise lost.

Juan faced forward again, looking out to sea and sitting very still, taking in the seething tumult of the ocean before him. The light of day was fading, even as the angry clouds closed over it, blotting out the sky.

A large cormorant flitted down to settle on the water twenty meters beyond the boulder. He watched it dispassionately.

A splash from below his feet made him look down. A lone seal wriggled onto the rocks below, hauling its rear flippers as far out of the water as it could. It looked around, nervous, and Juan smiled a grim smile, understanding why.

I know you're out there right now.

Ripples spread across the black water in concentric circles where the cormorant had been moments before. A single feather floated at their center. The large seabird was gone, taken silently when Juan had looked away. He leaned forward, focusing intently on the open water in front of him.

Show yourself.

A dozen meters out, the ocean rippled. A large gray fin broke the surface. His eyes tracked it as it slid below the waves again.

We have much in common, you and I.

Thunder rumbled. Distant lightning fired the clouds. Another fin, larger than the first, sliced the water off to his right. Then a third.

You are also a survivor. Sixteen million years of evolution have left you unchanged.

The water roiled, and a juvenile elephant seal struggled to the surface in a spreading circle of red. A flash of white belly slid past as meter-wide crescent jaws clamped onto the seal to drag it under.

Untroubled by conscience, unburdened by remorse, impervious to pain... What would you teach me if you could speak?

Great whites passed before the boulder. Fins crisscrossed the waves in front of Juan. Tails slapped the water, warning other sharks away when they came too close.

Lightning flashed.

Sharks fed.

The sun sank lower and lower in the sky.

And then it was dark.

Juan stood on the boulder, facing the island again. Año Nuevo hunkered against the dusky sky, a silent black outline now, willing to kill to protect its secrets.

But soon enough, he would have the answer to one of them.

CHAPTER 146

Mason looked out a window into darkness. "It's going to rain soon," he said.

Lightning flashed, lighting up the rocky ground outside. He turned away and walked through the living room of the Greek Revival house, passing Brent, who sat in a corner. He went upstairs.

Coming down the stairs a few minutes later with five empty jugs, he passed Jordan, sitting on the bottom step with one leg stretched out in front of her, a dead expression on her face. She held the speargun draped over her knee, its point resting on a stair.

"That ankle looks bad," he said. "Why don't you have Brent look at it?"

Jordan didn't respond, didn't even glance at him, so Mason continued down the stairs and walked over to Brent.

"I need something sharp."

Brent regarded him for a moment with eyes that were almost normal again, and then lifted the first-aid kit onto his lap. He opened it and held out a scalpel.

"One of those jugs is mine, I presume."

Mason used the scalpel to cut away the top of each jug. "Yours, mine, Camilla's, Natalie's, Veronica's. Hope you don't mind. They were all more or less empty."

Brent shrugged. "Veronica is next door, I think. You can ask her for permission if you like."

Mason grinned. "Thanks, but I'll pass."

Carrying the jugs outside, he looked up at the faint outlines of the roof, silhouetted against the roiling clouds. He placed the jugs below corners where the planes of the roof met to form valleys. They would collect a lot more water this way.

The shingles up there weren't clean, though. He ducked back inside.

Ten minutes later, he was on top of the dark roof with a roll of clear plastic sheeting in one hand and a staple gun in the other. Working by the light of the LED headlamp he had found in Lauren's bag, Mason lined the valley between dormers with clean plastic. Something caught his eye: a footprint discoloring the brick chimney. He raised his head to shine the light on it and grinned, because he recognized the sneaker tread.

Camilla.

She was easy to underestimate. A lot of people here had already made that mistake. But he wouldn't.

Once he was back in the main room, he looked at the scoreboard.

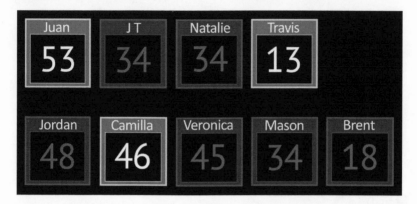

"Hey, Brent," he said. "Travis is still in play. What do you make of that?"

"I have no idea, and I can't say I much care."

Brent shifted positions to look up at the scoreboard. His eyebrows rose. "It does look as though your boyfriend is showing you up, however, Jordan."

"He's not my boyfriend." Her voice sounded dead. "He's nothing."

Mason laughed. "I guess this show just went into reruns."

Jordan pushed herself upright in a single graceful motion and hobbled up the stairs.

"Trouble in paradise, I guess." Mason watched her go. "But for real this time."

Brent shook some pills into his hand. "Maybe Jordan's starting to learn that there are people who won't dance like a puppet whenever she flashes that smile at them."

"You don't like her very much, do you?"

"No. I don't."

CHAPTER 147

Lightning flashed, illuminating the empty dock that jutted over black water. In the afterglow, Juan waited for a longer break between flashes, then thrust himself up onto the end of the dock. Crouching in place for long seconds, he scanned the dim outline of the breakwater and the jumbled rocks below. Nothing moved. He stood and walked forward until he reached the foot of the breakwater.

Large, tangled masses of kelp draped the shore, piled high in knotted skeins where the waves had left them. Stopping at the base of the breakwater, he panned his vision across the top, noting the flashes from infrared camera lenses. But the rocks were otherwise still.

Something grabbed his ankle.

Juan jerked his foot to the side and leaped away, grabbing for the Glock. He stood balancing on his other foot, one hand on the gun's grip, seeing nothing where he had been standing.

The touch had been gentle, without any real force. He looked down at his elevated ankle, surprised to see a long smear of bright green paint visible against the black neoprene of his wetsuit. Relaxing, he put his foot down and moved his hand away from the gun.

Where he had stood a moment earlier, a tangle of kelp moved. A face pushed out between the yellow-brown leaves and coils of seaweed, and Camilla smiled up at him. She crawled out of the pile, pushing the strands of kelp away from her shoulders and arms.

Juan held out a hand, and she took it. He helped her up to stand beside him on the rocks.

"Ewww." She brushed at her hair and clothes, sticky from the kelp slime, and made a comic face of disgust. Then she looked him up and down.

"I was wrong," she said. "You look good in black. It suits you."

She pocketed the spare paintball ammunition canister she held, and wiped her green-smeared hand on her pants.

He looked at the green paint on his ankle again. "I didn't expect that. But I think I'm beginning to understand."

She looked at him without guile. "I was waiting a long time. I was so worried when you and JT... Where did you go afterwards? What were you doing?"

"Thinking." He looked at her with curiosity. "So *I* was your target?"

"Not originally. I think this is how it went. Mason was after you at first, but then Jordan got Mason, and I got her."

457

"*You* got Jordan? She was your original target?"

"No, Natalie was. But Natalie was after Veronica, which was a pretty uneven matchup, don't you think? So naturally, Veronica took out Natalie. Jordan was originally Veronica's target, but she took her out instead. Thank god I didn't have to go up against Veronica myself."

"And JT comes into all of this exactly where?"

"He took my gun away. And the target card with your name. But, Juan"—she poked his chest with her index finger—"he did that because I had already eliminated his original target."

He nodded grimly. "Jordan."

Camilla's face was serious, too. "I know this sounds stupid, but something really strange is going on."

He thought about it for a moment. "You go on up to the houses. The rest of them should be there already, waiting for us."

"What about you?"

"I'm going to check on something first."

"What?"

"How Julian pays his utility bills."

CHAPTER 148

Three suspicious faces looked up at Camilla when she walked into the living room of the Greek Revival house.

"You got him," Jordan said. It wasn't a question. She looked down at her feet.

"But where's JT?" Camilla asked, starting to worry.

"He never came back," Mason said.

Juan and JT were both still out there. After the fight she had seen, the thought of another confrontation between them chilled her blood. But they weren't the only ones missing.

"What about Veronica and Natalie?" she asked.

"Next door. But the game isn't over yet..." Mason pointed at the scoreboard.

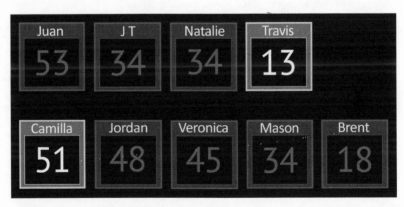

"Travis must have been Juan's target," he said, "so now he's yours."

"No." She shook her head. "This is all screwed up."

She pulled out a green paintball and tapped it against a projecting nail on the wall, puncturing it.

"Let's see what we have," she said.

Drawing a four-foot circle of letters on the wall in green paint, she wrote the first letter of each of their names, except for the three "J" names, which she wrote as "Jo" for Jordan, "Ju" for Juan, and "JT" for JT. Stepping back, she considered the diagram.

Then she drew green arrows connecting each assassin in the game to his or her original target.

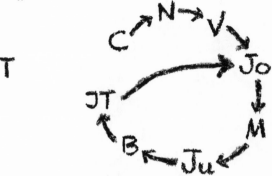

Although it was more or less a circle, there were some interesting discrepancies.

Veronica's and JT's arrows both pointed at Jordan.

Camilla's arrow pointed at Natalie, but there was no arrow pointing at herself.

The "T" representing Travis was completely isolated, with no arrows pointing either to or from him. She tapped the wall under the "T," thinking.

"Mason, can you please go get Travis's envelope?"

A minute later he was back.

"Someone already took it," he said. "And his paintball gun, too."

Camilla's eyes widened. "That's not good."

Brent stood. "I don't much like the sound of that, either."

"Where's Natalie?" Veronica's harsh voice cut through the room like a razor. She stood in the archway of the foyer that connected the two houses, eyes darting frantically around the room.

Little hairs prickled at the back of Camilla's neck. "You mean she wasn't over there with you?"

Veronica's gaze speared her. "*I thought she was in here with you people!* Why didn't you check with me instead of just assuming?"

"Come on," Brent said. "Let's go find her—and check on Travis, while we're at it. We shouldn't have left the scientists in charge of him. He's too dangerous."

Mason waved a languid hand at the windows. "It's raining out there now…"

"So stay." Veronica cut across the room and out the front door into the downpour, moving fast.

Camilla started to follow.

"Hold on," Brent said. He reached into a pocket of his fishing vest and tossed her a small vinyl packet. Then he did the same for the others. She looked at hers. It was a disposable rain poncho, from the scavenger hunt four days ago. Nodding thanks, she unfolded it to slip it on.

Jordan batted hers away. She didn't stand, and her expression of disinterest didn't change.

Mason and Brent slipped their ponchos on and followed Camilla out into the wet night.

•   •   •

"He's breathing."

Hearing Brent's words, Camilla sagged with relief. Seeing Dmitry stretched out on the concrete floor of the science station with blood coating the side of his face, she had been sure he was dead.

Kneeling beside him, Brent looked up. "We shouldn't move him, though."

Moaning, Dmitry rolled onto his back, eyes still closed. His face contorted into a grimace of pain.

"Blyad," he said. "The criminal—he is gone?"

"Get up, you imbecile." Veronica crowded forward. "Why did you let him go?"

Dmitry sat up and pushed away Brent's hand, ignoring her.

Camilla looked around. "Where is Jacob?"

"I don't know." Dmitry blinked, looking at their faces. "Jacob, he is not thinking right. *Nu pai yehkhal chelavek.*" He focused on Veronica, and his face darkened. "I tell *you* about this already, many hours ago, but you say to me fuck off and not bother you right now. Now it is dark outside—all of you must help me find him."

Veronica exhaled a wordless noise of frustration and turned away. "Useless."

"Let's get him back over to the houses," Camilla said. "You need to look at his head, Brent, and then we'll organize a search party. For Natalie, Jacob, and Travis. And JT."

"You're wasting time," Veronica snapped. "She could be hurt out there."

Veronica's clothes were soaked. Water dripped down her face from the short, wet spikes of her hair. Her eyes were wild.

Brent pulled out a poncho to hand her, but she was already out the door again. His eyes met Camilla's, and she turned away from the stony reproach in his face. *This is your fault,* Brent's expression said. *You encouraged them to play this game.*

A bitter metallic taste filled her mouth.

She had forgotten all about Natalie. While the rest of them chased each other around the island, Natalie was all alone.

She could hear Veronica's raised voice outside, strident with fear, calling Natalie's name.

•   •   •

Back in the living room of the Greek Revival house, Camilla watched Brent stitch Dmitry's scalp with skillful hands. She could hear Mason going from room to room, upstairs and downstairs in both houses, calling Natalie's name.

"We need Juan and JT now," she said. "They can handle Travis without anyone else getting hurt—"

A voice from the doorway interrupted her.

"A real shame they ain't here, then."

Travis walked into the room. Water soaked his clothes and hair and dripped from the sling around his right arm. He waved the paintball gun in his left hand at Brent.

"Y'ought ta open up a regular clinic here, Doc. License or no license, it looks like you're getting plenty of business. I guess beggars can't be choosers, and people sure do have a way of getting hurt on this island."

Brent stood up. "What do you want, Travis?"

Camilla stepped closer to Brent, her heart pounding in her chest as she stared at Travis. She couldn't breathe. He had killed Heather. Oh god—and maybe Natalie, too, now? Was Brent right? Had *she* caused this?

"I just want to talk," Travis said. "Seems there's some misunderstandings between us. We need to clear the air."

"You hit me from behind like bitch." Dmitry pointed to his head. "I never see you. How you can open chains without key?"

"I don't know what you're talking about, *Toe-varish,* but you looked like you were taking a nice nap there. Person who read you your good-night story musta' wanted me back in the game pretty bad." He looked at the scoreboard. "Seems I'm pretty late to the party, though."

"Where's Natalie?" Camilla asked, feeling her throat constrict.

Travis's snake eyes fixed on her, and he grinned an unpleasant grin. "Camilla. Scoreboard says it's just you and me left, so…"

He raised the paintball marker and fired.

Brent raised a hand in front of Camilla's face, and brown paint splattered across his palm; he had intercepted the shot intended for her. He stepped forward, blocking her completely with his body, and swung his open hand to slap the paintball gun away. It clattered into the corner with a sound of breaking plastic.

Travis shoved him one-handed, sending him staggering back against the wall.

"You're about to be real sorry you did that, old man."

"I'm not sure about that, Travis. Look around you."

Camilla was relieved to see Mason walk into the room. And Jordan now leaned against the doorway, one ankle raised, the speargun in her hand.

Mason held something gray wadded in his hands. Clothing.

"Julian won't come unless we finish the game." He smiled at Camilla. "Your assassin tried and failed, so now he's all yours…"

"Fuck you, faggot." Travis's hands clenched into fists.

Mason ignored him. "Where's your gun, Camilla?"

"JT broke it—"

"God damn it!" Brent shouted at her. "Five people are missing right now. Hasn't your foolishness cost us enough?"

"*TRAVIS!*" The ragged shout froze everyone in place.

Veronica burst through the outside door, letting in a spray of rain as she crossed the room with rapid strides. Camilla stepped aside as Mason did the same, the two of them parting to let Veronica pass between.

She came to a halt a foot in front of Travis, her fingers curling and twitching like the legs of a spider. Dangerous lights flickered in her pale, bulging eyes.

"Where *is* she?" Veronica screamed into Travis's face. "Tell me now!"

Eyes narrowing, lip curling, he stared at her.

Mason spoke into the silence. "Veronica…"

She ignored him.

"Veronica," he repeated.

Camilla turned and stared at the gray object Mason held spread in front of him. Natalie's hoodie. Spatters of wet brown paint smeared the front, overlaid on a dried starburst of red.

"I found this in her room," Mason said.

Camilla's throat locked up.

Brent looked at the brown paint dripping from his hand. Then he looked at Travis.

The silence that filled the room was thick, pregnant, like the pause between lighting's flash and the boom of a thunderclap.

Veronica looked up into Travis's face again. Her voice changed to a liquid, velvety, sexy purr.

"Where is she, Travis?"

"Why do you care, bitch?" Travis sneered. "What're you, her mom?"

Veronica spun away from him, and something seemed to blur in front of his neck with an ugly, meaty crunch.

Travis dropped straight down, collapsing behind her like a puppet with its strings cut.

At first Camilla was confused. Then she realized that Veronica had used the momentum of her turn to snap a back elbow into Travis's throat. It had been faster than a striking snake—almost too fast to see.

On the floor, Travis sucked in a ragged gasp of air as his face darkened. Veins on his neck bulged, and his next breath tapered off into a whistling wheeze. His eyes widened, filled with awful realization. He groped weakly for Veronica's calf.

She shook off his hand without looking down—impatiently, as if she was dislodging the claws of a too-playful kitten.

"Natalie's out there somewhere," she said to them all. Her chest heaved. "This *animal* hurt her, or worse."

Travis's face was purple now. He clawed at his throat, ripping at the collar of his shirt.

"Oh god, he's choking!" Camilla said, grabbing Brent's arm. "Please *do* something."

Brent pulled loose from her and pushed past Veronica. Kneeling beside Travis, he unsnapped the first-aid kit and reached inside.

Veronica ignored the activity behind her.

"Now, who's coming with me?" she asked.

Light glinted off the blade of the scalpel in Brent's hand. Camilla's eyes widened as he hunched over Travis. She couldn't see what he was doing, but a bubbling whistle rose from Travis, followed by another.

"Tracheotomy." Mason laid a hand on her shoulder. "Opening his airway."

Veronica turned her neck and looked down at what Brent was doing behind her. Then she raised a knee and stomped backward with her running shoe. Hard.

Travis's back arched.

Brent tumbled on to his backside, falling away from his patient, his hands covered with blood.

More blood jetted from the hollow of Travis's throat, where the scalpel was now buried with only the last inch of handle protruding. A geyser of blood sprayed the wall, soaking Camilla's painted diagram of the game, obscuring her green letters and arrows with looping red ribbons and spatters.

Travis's boots kicked at the ground. His hands clawed at his throat. Brent stared up at Veronica, incomprehension darkening into fury as he scrambled to his feet.

Veronica spoke slowly, like she was explaining something to a dull child.

"*Natalie* should be your priority, Brent. *Not* this piece of human garbage. Now, let's go find her."

Brent's hands shook. He turned away from Veronica and stumbled up the stairs, leaving them all.

With a last bubbling whistle, Travis's body shuddered and lay limp.

Camilla's arms and legs were blocks of ice. She met Veronica's eyes. "You killed him."

"He deserved it." Something dark capered in Veronica's luminous gaze. *Glee.* Her chest rose and fell in slow, deep breaths. Her mouth hung half open. She wiped the back of her wrist across one side of her mouth, and her eyes moved slowly from person to person. Camilla could see an awful relish in her gaze.

"All people like him do." A threat.

The scoreboard on the wall flashed once. The box around Travis's score dimmed to gray. His score changed, spinning down from thirteen, passing through single digits to stop at zero. Then the entire box and Travis's name disappeared, wiped from the scoreboard. Just like Lauren.

Camilla raised a hand to cover her mouth.

Her own score blinked.

Needles of irrational fear skewered her stomach. She was about to fade and disappear, too. But instead her score spun upward to pass Juan's. "WINNER" appeared in the frame around her name. She was now in first place, leading all the other contestants in points.

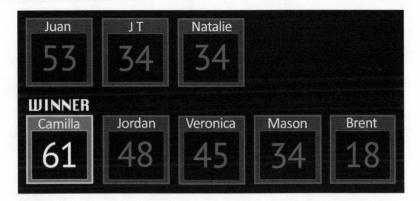

"No," she said. Her voice sounded small in her ears, like a child's. She shook her head. "No, I didn't want *this*."

Jordan stood up. Surprisingly, her face held a look of impatience, as if she was disappointed in Camilla.

"Don't you get it?" she said. "Natalie is still alive." She limped out of the room, turning her back on them all.

Camilla looked at the scoreboard again. Natalie's name stared back at her from the monitor.

Alive.

Did Veronica realize what she had just done? On camera? Camilla glanced in her direction. She was surprised to find Veronica's pale eyes lingering on *her*. But they flicked away immediately, turning up to stare at the monitor.

● ● ●

Mason tossed Camilla an MRE. As if she could eat right now.

"And then there were eight," he said.

"Not funny, Mason." She grimaced. "Besides, right now it looks like it's just the two of us. Brent's shooting up again."

Jordan was next door, sitting on the stairwell of the Victorian, where she could see the other monitor. Camilla had tried to talk to her, but Jordan just looked away, acting annoyed. So she had given up and returned to the Greek Revival house.

Veronica was gone. Again she hadn't waited for anyone to join her before resuming the search.

Mason nodded at Travis. "We can't just leave him here."

Camilla closed her eyes for a moment. "Help me, then."

She walked over and grabbed a boot. Mason did the same on the other side. She pulled, and Travis's lower body slid along the floor, but his head and neck didn't move at first, resisting her. She pulled harder, and he came unstuck, sending her staggering backward. Sickened, she realized why.

"Mason, he was pinned to the flo—" Her throat convulsed. Dropping Travis's leg, she clapped a hand over her mouth and ran outside, gagging. The remains of the morning's MRE spurted through her throat and nose, spilling onto the muddy ground. She closed her eyes and drew a gasping, burning breath. Dropping to her knees, she heaved again, bringing up only a weak dribble of stomach acid this time.

Rain pelted the back of her poncho. Camilla refused to let herself cry.

Avery, Cassie, Davey, Pedro—all her kids—they needed her. The only thing that mattered right now was getting back to them. She had to be strong.

They had finished today's game. Julian had promised them answers tonight if they did. And tomorrow he was coming to the island.

They would teach *him* what it meant to be afraid.

A gentle hand grasped her elbow, helping her up. Mason handed her a heavy plastic jug, its top cut away, sloshing with liquid. She took it in both hands, staring at the dark surface.

"Drink," he said.

Camilla gulped. The water was clean and delicious, renewing her parched mouth and throat.

"More," Mason said. "As much as you want. They're overflowing."

"Thanks," she gasped.

"It's your own jug. I refilled it. Oh, and I moved Travis into the next room, so you don't have to see him anymore."

Camilla put her jug down, threw her arms around Mason, and hugged him. Her body started shaking, but she wasn't crying. She refused to cry.

Lightning flashed, and she felt Mason's body tense. He patted her back—a warning—and she released him to step back. He was staring out into the darkness, with no expression on his face.

The lightning flashed again, lighting up the flat, muddy plain surrounding the houses. A pair of figures was approaching from the direction of the seal barricade. One of them was clearly Veronica. She jogged sideways next to the other one—a man, tall, covered head to toe in shiny black. Veronica kept touching something he held cradled in front of his chest, dangling on both sides. Then darkness returned.

The next lightning flash illuminated Juan's face clearly as he stepped up onto the porch. Camilla grabbed Mason's wrist, seeing the limp form Juan carried in his arms. Natalie's lower legs hung loosely over Juan's left forearm, bouncing with every step. Her head lolled back bonelessly over his right elbow. One of her bare arms dangled toward the ground; the other lay across her chest. She wore a white T-shirt, soaked through, and her eyes were closed. She looked so young, so very small.

Natalie's breathing was shallow, her face milk white.

Camilla turned and ran inside. "Brent!" she called. "Brent!"

She found him in his room, sitting on his cot, his face in his hands.

"I can't do this anymore," he mumbled.

"Not good enough." Camilla grabbed his hand, pulling him forward. "You must."

Downstairs again, she watched Juan kneel and lay Natalie gently on the floor against the wall. He stepped back, crossed his arms, and looked down at her prone body lying below Camilla's defaced diagram, like a sacrifice at the altar of Julian's terrible game. Juan's face was grim.

She pushed Brent forward, and he stumbled.

"You must," she repeated.

Veronica looked up from where she knelt beside Natalie, one hand on her forehead, the other holding her wrist. Camilla was shocked to see tears streaming down Veronica's face.

"Brent, help her. She's fibrillating, I think." Veronica's voice was choked with emotion. "I don't know what to do."

Brent's shoulders slumped, and then he straightened, moving forward. With practiced efficiency, he did a quick assessment, his face going grave as he held two fingers to Natalie's neck. From the first-aid kit, he brought out a large syringe and a glass ampoule, which he shook once before drawing its contents into the syringe. Holding the syringe in one hand, he probed the ribs to the left of Natalie's breastbone with the fingers of the other hand.

"What's that?" Suspicion joined the anguish on Veronica's face.

"Intracardiac injection of epinepherine." Brent drove the needle deep into Natalie's chest. "Not ideal, but she's arresting and we don't have a defibrillator." He depressed the plunger.

Natalie's eyes flew wide, and her body jolted. Her splayed fingers scrabbled at the floorboards as she took rapid, heaving breaths. Fear distorted her face, and she clamped both wrists between her thighs, curling onto her side. Her eyes closed, and her breathing slowed as her body slumped bonelessly again.

Brent thumbed an eyelid open, but Natalie didn't respond. She was out.

"She's got a fighting chance now." A bitter expression twisted his features as he pulled the needle out of Natalie's chest and tossed the syringe aside. "And don't forget, she's a survivor."

Veronica pushed him away and pulled Natalie's limp form onto her lap, wrapping her arms protectively around her. She lowered her forehead onto Natalie's.

"I'm sorry." Veronica's shoulders began to heave, wracked by stifled sobs. "I'm so sorry."

Camilla had to look away.

Juan stood with his arms crossed, staring down at the two women.

"I found her in a cave on the west side," he said, "Near the end of the breakwater. The entrance was hidden behind a rock pile. But that's not all I found in there."

He pointed at the wide-screen monitor on the wall.

"It was so obvious, and we all missed it. Those car batteries should have died days ago. They were just window dressing—empty battery cases. The power cable ran underneath them, buried shallow. I followed it to the cave, where I found the generators that actually power these monitors." His jaw clenched. "Gas-powered generators, along with plenty of gas. But it isn't all that much use for sending a distress signal *now*."

Camilla looked at the driving rain that lashed against the plastic-sheet windows and pelted the ground outside, visible through the open doorway. She closed her eyes.

"Four hours too late," she said. "We missed our chance by *four hours*."

Mason laughed.

CHAPTER 149

"Look." Camilla pointed at the monitor. Large white digits now blinked at the corner of the screen, ticking steadily down from "15:00." Fifteen minutes until their host appeared, she figured, looking at the others. Veronica had mastered her emotions after a few minutes. Sitting against the wall and holding the limp Natalie in her arms, she avoided Camilla's eyes.

Juan leaned against the wall, arms crossed, seeming lost in thought.

"We must find Jacob, too," Dmitry said.

"I covered the whole island," Juan said. "He's gone."

Mason sat next to Camilla. Jugs of water lined the wall next to him. He had gone next door to retrieve JT's and Travis's, refilling them, too.

Brent sat apart from the others with his head back against the wall, eyes closed. Camilla could hear a quiet, ragged murmur under his breath—he was humming to himself.

"What about JT?" she asked.

Juan shook his head. "He's on his own."

"I'll go get Jordan," she said.

Juan seemed to wilt, but he didn't say anything.

She found Jordan next door, sitting on the steps of the Greek Revival house, staring at the monitor with a bleak expression on her face.

Camilla squatted on the steps next to her. "You shouldn't be in here all alone. Come join the rest of us."

Jordan stared past her. "Go away."

What had happened to the friendly, sparkly personality that Camilla liked so much? It was gone without a trace, set aside like a once-fashionable coat that its owner no longer felt like wearing.

"Fine," Camilla said, standing up. "We don't have to be friends. But we really should talk, Jordan."

Once she was back in the Victorian, Mason stood up and dusted off his hands. He stood in front of her defaced diagram and, using a pink paintball, drew an arrow from the "T" to the "C." But there were still no arrows pointing at Travis, and two arrows pointed at Jordan.

Intrigued again despite herself, Camilla joined him, like a co-presenter at a studio green-light meeting. Mason turned to face her. He tapped the diagram as if it were a whiteboard.

"What can we infer from this?" he asked.

"Number one," she said. "By leaving Travis unassigned to be anybody's target, Julian kept him in reserve until the very end."

She looked around the room at Brent, Veronica, Natalie, Juan, Dmitry, and Mason. She had everybody's attention now—except for the unconscious Natalie's, of course.

"Number two. Instead, his assassin was reassigned to someone else. That's interesting in itself, since it effectively doubled the odds against that person.

"Number three. Travis got loose. Or someone *let* Travis loose and put him into play, injuring Dmitry in the process."

"So was Travis Julian's spy?" Mason asked. "Or not?"

"I don't know," she said. "I have trouble picturing Travis setting up the flags and other games for Julian, but there's no reason he couldn't have. He was the one that supposedly found our luggage, remember? As for freeing himself—he was in the prison system for years, after all. He might have been able to. But I'm only speculating."

Mason pushed his glasses higher. "So one of us might still be a spy…"

She nodded. "We can't rule it out, I'm afraid.

"Number four," she said. "I was Travis's assigned target—"

"So for most of the game, no one was after you." Veronica's voice cut the air. "And *you* won. That seems fair, doesn't it? But at least we know who Julian's favorite is."

Camilla felt her face flush. "Bear with me, please," she said. "Number four. Travis was supposed to come after me. And he did, eventually. But first he got up to some extracurricular activity…"

"Natalie," Mason said. "He grabbed her and stashed her for later." He looked at Juan. "She owes you, my friend. Travis must've used her own stun gun on her—again and again, getting his revenge. It's a good thing her heart was young and strong."

"This man… this criminal," Dmitry said. "I am glad he is dead." His voice turned gloomy. "What about Heather?"

Face sober for a change, Mason shook his head. "I'm afraid he had more time with her. I'm sorry, Dmitry."

"But why Jacob? I mean, Jacob is not woman."

"I don't know," Mason said. "Travis definitely didn't like men. I'm sure of that…"

Veronica interrupted. "Maybe he thought Jacob had seen him take Heather."

"No," Camilla said as a horrifying possibility occurred to her. "Travis set off my alarms from the first moment I saw him. What if he was something even *worse* than we know?"

Mason looked at her. "Like what?"

"Fava beans and a nice Chianti," Brent rumbled from the corner without opening his eyes. "Travis? Now he was a serial killer, too, Camilla? And I thought *I* was the one on drugs."

"Don't be so quick to discount her," Mason said. "These things are outside my experience—I just don't know—but I've seen the same movies you have. Hollywood dresses it up some, sure, but there really *are* people like that out there." He laughed. "Veronica, I think you might have done the world a service."

"Because he liked to hurt men, too?" she said. "Great. Makes no difference to me. Typical that you men would see it that way, though. Now all of a sudden, he's a *real* bad guy."

"I didn't mean it that way—"

"You think I have any regrets about what I did? Any at all?" Veronica's eyes flashed. "If Travis stood up and walked in here, I'd kill him again."

"You might want to watch what you're saying," Brent said. "You're upset." He opened his opaque, drugged eyes and pointed a thick finger at the ceiling and walls. "We should assume this is all being captured on video and will be admissible in court."

"And I should give a shit?" Veronica snorted. "No jury would ever convict me. They'd give me a fucking medal, instead. He had just kidnapped this poor girl, nearly killed her. Travis was a sadistic rapist, a child molester, a murderer, and now, according to you boneheads, maybe even a serial killer. *Not* a fine, upstanding, highly decorated police captain on a first-name basis with the mayor..."

Camilla froze in mid breath.

In the sudden silence, Veronica's eyes widened in horror. Her jaw snapped shut, and she tucked her chin down to stare at the floor.

"Oops," Mason giggled.

Veronica had killed her second husband, the police captain, too. Camilla found she wasn't really surprised. Veronica had killed *both* her husbands.

Camilla felt a pang of sympathy for Veronica, trapped in an inescapable cycle of abuse and violence, driven to seek it out over and over again because it was the only love she knew.

"Serial killers are astronomically rare," Camilla said, speaking to defuse the situation and take the focus off Veronica. "Maybe I *am* being silly. After all, what are the odds that Vita Brevis would accidentally recruit a serial killer as one of ten show contestants?"

"Perhaps it wasn't an accident," Mason said.

"Oh god, you're not helping, Mason."

"I can just imagine the Craigslist ad." Dark amusement flickered in Juan's eyes. "Serial killer with a preference for underage girls wanted. Must be proven survivor and look good on camera. Ten million for two weeks' work, room and board included..."

"Look." Mason sounded exasperated. "We know Julian recruited Travis specifically because he was a convict. They even made his résumé a prize for Lauren to find."

He laid a hand on Camilla's shoulder. "Besides," he said, "the percentage of serial killers in a prison population, no matter what they were arrested for, would be much higher than in an average cross-section of humanity. So even if it was an accident, maybe the odds aren't quite as astronomical as you seem to think."

Mason tapped the "T" on the diagram. A streak of Travis's blood looped beneath it, underlining it. "But like I said, I don't really think it was an accident. We already know Julian deliberately recruited a convicted child molester for morbid entertainment value. So how much of a stretch is it to believe Julian actually wanted Travis because he was a serial killer?"

"That's utterly ludicrous." Veronica stroked Natalie's unconscious head, which rested on her thigh. "And you didn't really address Juan's point, either. How would they go about finding a serial killer when the police and FBI chase them for years and can't catch them?"

"The black widow speaks." Mason said.

Veronica's eyes ignited.

"Sorry, sorry." He held up his hands in a gesture of mock contrition. "Okay, that's actually a fair question, but I don't think it would be all that hard, theoretically."

Veronica's voice was dry. "I can't wait to hear this."

"You'd have to be willing to do something police and FBI can't: use live bait."

"Policewomen frequently pose undercover as prostitutes to entrap predators," she said. "It almost never works."

"That's not the same as live bait. You let the bait actually get taken by the fish."

"I hesitate to even ask what you mean."

Mason turned to Dmitry. "Your sharks—I read some of the surveys in the station and looked at your data. You obviously can track them quite well. How?"

"We using the GPS." Dmitry sat up, cupping his hand around an imaginary cylinder. "Satellite tracker unit show us where is shark—"

"These tracker units—how did you get them into the sharks in the first place?"

"First we try to poke them into shark's back with harpoon. Very hard to do. Trackers coming off too soon. No good. But Jacob, he is persistent." Dmitry smiled. "Two years ago, he figure out very good solution. We put tracker unit *inside* bait—seal carcasses we find. Shark, he eats bait. Then we track him easy."

Mason looked at the others. "There you have it, then."

Camilla was appalled. "So you're saying Vita Brevis put GPS trackers inside *prostitutes* to catch a serial killer? Travis abducted one of them, and *that's* how Julian found him?" She grimaced in disgust. "How do you even come up with this stuff?"

Mason grinned.

"He's just trying to get a reaction out of you, Camilla," Brent said. "He finds it gratifying for some reason."

She glanced away, seeing the countdown tick from 04:46 to 04:45. Less than five minutes from now, they would have the answers they sought—*if* Julian delivered on his earlier promises.

Juan shook his head. "Even a drugged-up prostitute might notice someone putting a GPS tracker unit inside them, no matter how high they were. Am I right, Brent? You seem to be the authority around here on being high."

"Perhaps I am, Juan. Perhaps I am." Brent leaned forward. "But I'll play."

His eyes were jittery blue, pupilless. "I would imagine that prostitutes are often desperate for money to buy drugs, are they not? And Vita Brevis seems to have no shortage of money. What if, in Mason's scenario, the prostitutes were told that Vita Brevis was buying a kidney from them? Some might be willing to go along with that. Then, instead of taking a kidney out, Vita Brevis could implant a GPS tracker and stitch them up. Does that work for you, Mason?"

"Enough!" Veronica said. "I'm about to throw up. It's disgusting that you people can sit there making jokes about this. And don't try to make things complicated when they aren't. It's actually real simple."

She pointed at the next room, where Travis's body lay. "Travis kidnaps Heather and rapes her—a crime of opportunity. But he's angry and frustrated by his injuries, and under these circumstances he takes things too far and kills her. Later, Jacob confronts him about Heather and accuses him. He thinks Jacob knows something. So as soon as he's free he kills Jacob, too, disposing of the body the same way as Heather's: feeding them to the sharks.

"As for Natalie…" Veronica's arm curled over her protectively. "That animal has been after her since the first day on the island—probably since he first saw her on the ship. That's how their minds work."

She snorted. "Hannibal Lecter, my ass. Travis was a garden-variety trailer-trash piece of shit. Common as dirt. Kick over a rock, you'll find three guys just like him."

The monitor suddenly brightened the room.

Camilla found herself staring at their host.

CHAPTER 150

Julian straddled an old office chair, resting his chin on his forearms, which were crossed atop the chair back. His suit was a rich maroon. With his loosened tie dangling over one arm, his body language was relaxed—a teacher having an informal chat with a few favored students. But his customary playful smile was gone. In its place, his features conveyed a solemn sense of gravitas.

"My congratulations to the winner of today's contest, the last assassin standing…"

Camilla winced. He meant her.

"…and to all the rest of you, who have unquestionably earned your current rankings today. Only one more competition remains tomorrow, and rest assured, I will indeed join you for it. But now, as I promised, let us peel back the veil of mystery together. Here are the answers you seek."

Julian leaned back and spread his arms wide. "We live in an exciting era of technological transformation. The Internet age is rewriting the rules of entertainment forever. The old gatekeepers of our industry—the studios, distributors, cable companies, and traditional media outlets—are being swept aside by the new and truly innovative.

"Today's entertainment audience is global, affluent, and hungry for novelty. Amateur self-publishing channels, YouTube, and the like are only the first wave of the coming change. Vita Brevis represents the other end of the spectrum. We are multinational, professional, well financed, and independent. Today we have access to direct distribution—and direct monetization—on a scale unprecedented in human history. Vita Brevis operates outside the control of the mainstream media, ungoverned by the arbitrary laws and regulations of any country or jurisdiction.

"We know what the people want. And we will give it to them.

"Tomorrow's stars aren't actors and musicians, athletes and models, the superficial creations of a tired oligarchy that grows more irrelevant by the day. Nor are they the so-called reality stars, elevated above their mediocre lives and humdrum backgrounds for fifteen minutes of fame. No, we can do better."

Laying his forearms back down on the chair back, their host canted forward and rested his chin again, smiling—a pleased coach congratulating his team after a winning season.

"Tomorrow's stars will be drawn from the exceptional amongst us. They are the individuals who can adapt, thrive, and win under any circumstances, no matter what the odds are. They are survivors."

He paused to let that sink in.

"No traditional cable or television channel will ever air this show. No traditional studio will ever make the decision whether to censor any part of it. But I promise you this: each of your amazing performances, your struggles, your victories will be seen by more people than you ever dreamed possible. As I said, our distribution channel is direct, and our business model is equally nontraditional. We plan to make a lower-fidelity, partial version of our product available for free. How? By uploading it to file-sharing sites, video hubs, peer-to-peer networks, and dozens of other free high-traffic channels.

"Our audience will spread it like wildfire because the content is so utterly compelling. Have we not created the ultimate viral video?

"And we will also make the full-length, high-fidelity version—the director's cut, if you will—available for a fee. A *substantial* fee, I assure you. High enough to cover the extra security precautions that we must take for payment collection, to ensure anonymity both for the customer and for ourselves. But the demand is there, my friends. And where there is paying demand, innovators like Vita Brevis will arise to satisfy it."

Camilla felt the bile rise in her throat. This was a sick and cynical nightmare, but in its own horrifying way, it was inevitable, too, wasn't it? Sooner or later, in the brave new world of the Internet, someone was bound to try an experiment like this.

And she herself had been selected for it because she was a freak, a sideshow act—all because of a terrible childhood tragedy that she could do nothing to change. The person she had fought for twenty three years to become—the person she thought she *was*—didn't matter.

Julian had chosen Camilla because she was a monster.

Her hands rose to cover her ears, but she forced them down to her sides, fighting against crushing despair. She wanted to find a quiet corner away from everyone, curl into a ball, and escape into nothingness.

This wasn't what she was. What had happened to her could have happened to anyone. The horrible things she remembered from so long ago were impossible. They were the disturbed nightmares of a traumatized child. She simply remembered them *wrong*.

Julian rose, and the camera followed him as he walked a few steps to stop in front of the massive bale of currency. He picked up a packet of bills and fanned through it with his thumb.

"I assure you that your generous prizes represent only a tiny investment for us. Especially compared to what Vita Brevis stands to *earn* in this venture. But there will be other compensations for you as well. We acknowledge that this is an entirely new entertainment model. You are its very first stars, a bright constellation that will light the way for all those who follow. Consequently, we place no restrictions upon you. You will have full rights to exploit and benefit from your experience here in any way you please."

He bowed, courtly and sincere.

"We are deeply indebted and grateful to you all. But there is one among you to whom I owe especial thanks—one without whom this would have been impossible."

Camilla's eyes widened. Julian was talking to his spy now.

On the monitor, he placed a hand on the center of his chest.

"I will name no names, but you know who you are. As we discussed beforehand, you will be joining me in a different capacity after the show. Your future with Vita Brevis is assured."

The despair redoubled. Someone—probably someone in the room right now—had betrayed them for the promise of an illegal career with Julian. That person was equally to blame for the deaths of Lauren, Heather, Travis, and perhaps also Jacob and JT.

Was it Brent? Maybe. Julian could be using the drugs to manipulate him.

Veronica? A truly terrifying possibility.

Mason? Very plausible, even though she was sure he hadn't chained the scientists' boat.

Or was it Travis? The two-way-isolation rule meant that Julian was talking into a blank screen again. Double blind. He might not even know that Travis was dead.

Juan? She glanced at him. Oh god, maybe.

Jordan, who had now isolated herself from the rest of them? It fit so well.

What about JT?

Camilla was driving herself crazy thinking about it. It could be any of them.

Julian clapped his hands together sharply, startling her.

"Now, all of you, rest well and prepare. The final challenge lies ahead—a most dangerous game indeed. It will push each of you to the limits of your abilities. The previous challenges, much like the lower levels of Maslow's hierarchy upon which they were modeled, have laid the foundation and prepared you well for this final one. Tomorrow we reach the top of Maslow's pyramid. But tonight we will relax and entertain ourselves with two more contestant profiles. Enjoy them, and I look forward to meeting all of you in person tomorrow."

Their host faded from the screen.

The faces all around Camilla were a blur. She braced herself, terrified of seeing her own childhood face staring back at her from the monitor.

Instead, an image of a sprawling city nestled at the base of lush, rain forest-covered mountains bathed the room in a greenish glow.

The voiceover continued in Julian's narrator voice, so familiar from the earlier profiles of Brent and Veronica, so hateful to Camilla's ears.

"Roberto Martín Antonio y Gabriel topped Colombia's power structure in the 1990s. A major exporter of luxury agricultural goods, he collaborated with his closest competitors to establish fair pricing for their product worldwide, building an impressive business empire and amassing vast wealth. But family was Roberto's true legacy. His eldest son, César Juan Antonio y Gabriel, grew up among Bogotá's aristocratic elite."

A picture of a young man, maybe 18 or 19 years old, appeared on the screen, and Camilla gasped.

Wearing a tailored white silk shirt and designer sunglasses, he stood with arms crossed in front of a silver cigarette boat docked in front of a multistory waterfront villa. The contoured twin-headlight fairing of a racing-style motorcycle was visible in the villa's open garage, alongside an exotic yellow sports car—a Ferrari or Lamborghini. The young man's face was different—his features a little less sharp, less handsome—but the bored-lifeguard posture was unmistakable.

She was looking at a younger Juan.

"Groomed to take over the multibillion-dollar business empire, it soon became clear that César would have to navigate far rougher business waters than his father had. Times were changing. The economic interference of a Northern Hemisphere superpower was making the business climate far more competitive than in his father's heyday."

Juan had said he grew up on the streets. Hardly.

Camilla's eyes flicked back and forth between the aristocratic young man on the screen and the wetsuit-clad Juan—her child-rescuing motorcyclist—now leaning against the wall in the same slacker pose. His face was far more striking now, the nose and cheekbones more angular, the jawline sharper. Plastic surgery?

Unlike in the photograph, there was no arrogance in Juan's expression now. She read resignation in his dark eyes, in the slump of his shoulders. She was shocked to find that Julian's revelations didn't change her opinion of Juan—she still believed in him.

"Perhaps young César Juan was unprepared to step into his father's shoes, but Roberto Martín's tragic death during a business negotiation left the family little choice. César was expected to assume the reins of the empire. Instead, he disappeared. His family—and his father's business competitors as well—all searched in vain for the young man. No trace of him was ever found. He was assumed to be a victim of a kidnapping gone wrong—a common enough fear among Bogotá's wealthy. Shortly thereafter, competition in the agricultural sector intensified. Things went rapidly downhill for the Antonio y Gabriel family."

Sadness filled Juan's eyes as images flashed past on the screen. A burning Mercedes riddled with bullet holes. The luxury villa, strung with police tape, with half its facade blackened by fire. A sprawled shape lying in the street, covered by a bloodstained sheet, surrounded by uniformed officials.

"César's younger brother, Álvaro, attempted to hold things together in the face of a deteriorating business climate but could not. Soon the Antonio y Gabriel business empire was no more. Tragic accidents claimed the lives of César's mother and younger sister. Álvaro fled Colombia. But he never gave up the search for his older brother."

Juan put his hands on his hips and stared at the ground. His lack of defiance—his quiet, dignified sorrow—pierced Camilla's heart.

A small island, postcard familiar, appeared on the screen. Pleasure boats floated in the harbor, lined up in pleasing arcs on the cobalt blue water. White hotels and restaurants dotted the green hills that climbed from the harbor to the wooded hillsides above.

"Álvaro eventually found his brother on Santa Catalina Island in California. César was living under a different name, working as an independent dive-charter captain. Álvaro chartered his brother's boat for a surprise reunion, but any reconciliation between the two was brief. César was rescued from the sea by the Coast Guard, a victim of multiple gunshot wounds. Álvaro was never found."

Camilla's eyes stung. *Not my brother's keeper, Juan?* She had actually said that to him. If only she had known... His all-black outfits made sense to her now: he was a man in perpetual mourning. Juan would not let himself forget.

Like her, he, too, had lost his entire family. Fleeing a toxic legacy, he'd had to reinvent himself. They were so much alike, the two of them: both survivors, both refusing to let their past define who they were.

"Juan, look at me," she said. "It doesn't matter. I'm so sorry."

Head down, Juan walked across the room and out into the downpour.

CHAPTER 151

Jordan sat alone on the steps. The monitor on the wall glowed. The cavernous central room of the Victorian house felt empty around her, though not as empty as she felt inside. Learning the truth about Juan, what he really was, had hurt her more than she had thought possible. Not his family background—she didn't care about that. What hurt was what the profile said about *him*. What she had already found out for herself.

What Juan was really like.

She wished she had never come, never met him. She wanted to go home.

A deep voice rumbled from the dark hallway that led deeper into the building.

"Fuck me." It sounded darkly amused. "An honest-to-God no-shit Colombian drug lord."

A pair of glowing green circles emerged at head height from the darkness of the hallway, followed by a muscular body. JT's face and arms were striped with camouflage paint. His teeth glowed white as he pushed the night-vision goggles onto his forehead.

"You sure know how to pick 'em, girl. But at least now we know where they got the money. The kind of money we saw on the ship. The kind of money it would take to put this thing together. The kind of money we all found just lying around during the scavenger hunt."

A bundle of hundred-dollar bills slapped the floor by Jordan's feet.

"*This* kind of money," JT said. "Drug money."

Jordan ignored him.

Catalina Island faded from the monitor screen, and Julian's voice returned, rising in pitch and volume.

"And now, folks, we come to perhaps the most interesting contestant of all, and by far the favorite of the home crowd to win the grand prize. She's smart, she's sassy, and she's popular with her peers. But under that drop-dead gorgeous exterior beats the heart of a true competitor—a true survivor."

She would not let anyone—JT, cameras, Julian, *anyone*—see a reaction on her face. She kept it expressionless as she pushed herself upright, balancing on her good foot and using the speargun as a crutch.

On-screen, a picture appeared. She could see herself, hair in a bun, muscles taut, standing on the balance beam with the concentrated expression her gymnastics coach always called her gold-medal face. She remembered that picture: the state semifinals. She had won it all to qualify for the finals.

Putting a bored expression on her face now, Jordan turned her back on the monitor and headed up the steps.

Behind her, she could hear Julian's voice, campy with canned excitement.

"Yes, folks, you guessed right! We're talking about... Jordan... Vaughan!"

CHAPTER 152

Camilla listened with a heavy heart to Julian's breathless delivery. She listened for a clue, a hint, an explanation for why Jordan had shut all of them out—now even Juan, too.

"Jordan grew up in Woodside, California, on her parents' country estate. She attended exclusive private schools and had the very best tutors. Her parents prepared her well for life. From an early age, she excelled, competing in swimming, ice skating, debate, horseback riding, skiing, math, tae kwon do, and lacrosse. Elected class president in her senior year of high school, Jordan was also an all-state gymnast and soccer team captain. Academically and socially, she dominated. A straight-A student, she graduated as class valedictorian and was also voted homecoming queen by her peers—easily the most popular girl in her school."

A montage of still photos accompanied Julian's words. Jordan in riding boots, sitting on a horse, concentration in her eyes. Jordan churning through the water in swim cap and goggles, shoulders lifted in a butterfly stroke. Jordan onstage in a stunning dress, accepting an award of some kind, her broad, friendly can-you-believe-it smile—the one that Camilla missed seeing—sharing her joy with the audience.

"Jordan was accepted to prestigious Stanford University, where she continued to excel, earning her undergraduate degree in English, summa cum laude, and a master's in communications, also summa cum laude."

Julian's voice paused, leaving Camilla staring at a picture of Jordan in cap and gown at a graduation ceremony. The camera had caught her at an unexpected moment, and the smile was not in evidence. Jordan's eyes stared at something out of frame with fierce, hard-jawed concentration. Camilla recognized the expression. She had seen it when Jordan charged the giant bull elephant seal.

"But always, just outside the bright spotlight that followed Jordan through her mounting successes and accomplishments, trouble and tragedy lingered. The salutatorian from her graduating class, outshined in every way by her exemplary peer and ostracized by Jordan's social circle, committed suicide on the Caltrain tracks by lying down in front of an oncoming train. Less than a year after graduating, Jordan's ex-boyfriend from high school died in an alcohol-related car crash. After her first romantic breakup in college, the young man dropped out of school and left the state. Jordan's thesis adviser's marriage fell apart amid accusations of inappropriate relations with a student. But mean-spirited rumors and jealous talk were not enough to keep a promising young Stanford premed student from proposing to the vivacious, well-spoken debutante. Jordan and Jonathan were soon engaged to be married."

On the screen, a young couple sat at a table in an outdoor garden café. Dark sculptures and manicured hedges blurred the background. Camilla recognized the tall rectangle of Rodin's *Gates of Hell*—Cantor Art Center at Stanford. Jordan's smile beamed from the monitor, but it was only for the handsome man she held hands with. Her eyes were bright with happiness, and Jonathan's eyes shone with adoration that was apparent even in the photograph.

Camilla's heart ached with sadness for them both. She knew how the story ended—she had heard the rest of it last night.

Julian's tabloid tone was disgusting. She could hear the glee in his voice. Camilla pictured their host's grinning face. He *dared* to come face them after treating them like this? He could not be allowed to walk away, no matter how much money he threw at them—or at his lawyers.

"Jonathan idolized his young fiancée. He had overcome his own troubles, including a devastating struggle with addiction, before turning his life around. He looked forward to their building a life together, but for Jordan, after a short period of reciprocity, boredom soon set in. She broke off her engagement to take up with the editor of the technology blog she now worked for. Jonathan spiraled into depression and drugs, which landed him on academic probation. He died of an overdose a few weeks later."

Camilla's hands clenched into shaking fists, and she closed her eyes. Julian had brought Brent here and supplied him with drugs as a spectacle for Jordan, to throw her tragedy in her face over and over again. No wonder she had withdrawn from everyone, hiding her pain behind that cold, hard mask. She wouldn't give Julian the satisfaction of seeing her suffer.

"But Jordan is a true survivor in every sense of the word. Time and time again, she has remained untouched by the troubles and tragedies around her. Her uncanny ability to avoid the misfortunes of other, lesser people continues to serve her well in this competition. Folks, she's in it to win it. So it should be no surprise that the official betting line puts the odds heavily in Jordan's favor to take home the grand prize."

As the screen went dark Camilla opened her eyes. Her bitter anger hardened into steel inside her. Julian's cruelty was unforgivable. After what he had done to them all, he could not be allowed to walk away from this alive.

If she had to, she would kill him herself.

CHAPTER 153

"'**P**aranoid.' That's what Juan called me," Mason said. "'Ridiculous. Ludicrous'—Veronica, those were your exact words. But it turns out I was right all along."

"Now, just hold on." Brent cleared his throat. "Julian didn't exactly *say* this is a snuff film, did he?"

"No…" Camilla spoke without looking up. "Not exactly…"

"Huh?" Mason sounded like he was at a loss for words. "We're splitting hairs over *semantics* now? Somebody please explain this to me, then."

Camilla stared at her hands. She was thinking of the vengeful direction her own thoughts had taken. Of the way anger and violence became a black hole, a cycle impossible to escape once you let yourself get dragged in. She thought of Veronica…

And Veronica spoke, summing it up for them all, sounding angry but also darkly amused.

"Well, you have to give Julian credit for originality, at least. A drug-addicted doctor. A disgraced banker the audience can hate. A survivor of systematic child abuse." She stroked Natalie's hair. "An earthquake survivor. A violent sex offender. A woman with… my history. An AWOL special forces soldier. A Colombian ex-drug lord. And a silver-spoon valedictorian cheerleader. Pitted against each other in an illegal Internet pay-per-view event. The World Series of survival…"

She chuckled, and the bitter self-loathing in her voice made Camilla shudder.

"Oh, we've given them what they want, haven't we? Better than MMA, UFC, cage fighting—did I leave anything out?"

Camilla said, "Lauren."

"Right." Veronica waved her away. "I agree with Brent. I don't think the main purpose of this is watching us die. But if some of us do, it's definitely part of the entertainment."

Camilla was thinking about something else Julian had said. The skin on her arms tightened into goose bumps.

"Julian lied again," she said. "This isn't pay per view at all." Her voice sounded loud in the sudden silence. "He said '*the official betting line*…'"

"Gambling." Brent cleared his throat. "It stands to reason, doesn't it? That's also why they cut off Julian's ability to see and hear us. For the kind of money that's being illegally wagered, they don't want anybody rigging the game."

485

"And it means something else, too: a live broadcast." Camilla looked at the walls around her, the skin on her arms crawling. "People are watching us *right now*. Betting on who lives and who dies."

She stared at Dmitry. "That's why Heather and Jacob were murdered."

Dmitry nodded, his face dark with anger. "*Ya panimayu.* Some of it I do not understand, but this I do. That man, he ordered the criminal to kill my friends."

"Julian didn't want you scientists interfering," Mason said. "And besides, you're witnesses—he can't let you leave."

Camilla nodded. "That makes a lot more sense than your serial killer silliness, Mason. Travis killed the scientists on Julian's orders. But why did he take Natalie?"

"She was a present." Veronica's eyes burned with hatred. "Julian gave Travis a bonus."

Natalie stirred on Veronica's lap and murmured something.

"Shhh. You're safe now." Veronica stroked her hair. "What is it, dear?"

"...ot ...ravis," Natalie slurred. She sat up, blinking like someone waking from a deep sleep.

"Thank God you're all right." Veronica took Natalie's hands in hers. "That animal won't ever touch you again. He's dead."

Natalie spoke again, clearly this time in the silence of the room.

"It wasn't Travis."

Veronica's voice changed. "What are you talking about?"

"The person who took me away... it wasn't Travis." Fear transformed Natalie's features as she stared from face to face, blinking. "I couldn't really see who it was, because they were behind me, and then I don't remember. But whoever it was used both of their arms."

Veronica's body went rigid. Her eyes widened. She was on her feet, stepping in front of Natalie, before the significance of what Natalie had said dawned on Camilla.

The person who had taken Natalie might be in the room *right now*.

"All of you. Get out." Veronica's luminous eyes shifted from person to person. Her body vibrated with coiled tension. At her sides, her fingers curled like angry scorpion tails.

"I'm giving you two minutes to get your stuff."

Camilla stood slowly, not wanting to trigger an explosion. Veronica was afraid. It was in her eyes. But Camilla could see something else in them, too.

Veronica's nostrils flared. She looked from Brent to Mason to Dmitry, probing each of them with a cobra's speculative gaze. Her tongue curled up to slide along her teeth. She spoke, her voice rich and velvety, dripping with menace...

"Two minutes. That's it. After that, I kill anyone I find still here."

...and, oh god, anticipation, too.

"Veronica..." Camilla held up a pacifying hand. "Please—"

"You, too, little lady." Veronica's tone dripped poison. "I never liked you very much, anyway."

Camilla led the others out into the rainy night, carrying their bags and water jugs, as Veronica's full-throated yell chased them from the doorway behind.

"Keep going! Out past the barricade and don't come back. I swear to God, if I ever see any of you over here again, you'll die."

Slinging a leg over the stacked logs to straddle the top, Camilla paused, looking back toward the houses.

Lightning flashed, illuminating Veronica on the porch of the Victorian, her face raised to the darkness.

"The others... you tell them. Tell them *all*."

Veronica's scream rang from the bluffs and echoed across the rocky ground, reaching every corner of the island.

"From now on, anybody I find on this side of the barricade, *I kill!*"

CHAPTER 154

Rain lashed Jordan's face and streamed off the shoulders of her sealskin cape. The wind whipped her wet hair back and forth, slapping her cheeks. She gripped the wobbling flagpole with both hands, balancing the heavy weight on top that threatened to topple it, taking her with it. Gritting her teeth, she drove the pole downward, plunging it into a crack between the hunks of broken concrete at her feet. Her bad foot struck the ground, and white-hot pain erupted through her broken ankle. Clenching her jaw, she ignored it.

Lightning flashed, illuminating the fallen lighthouse tower above her. She hugged the pole to her chest, gripping it firmly with her hands, and let herself hang on it, using her body weight to drive it deeper into the crack, wedging it tight.

Rivulets of rain streamed down the pole, mixed with something darker, staining her hands with the stickiness that washed down the shaft. She let go and hopped back, wiping her palms on the sides of her cape.

In the next flashbulb burst of lightning, Jordan looked up at her handiwork—a picture definitely worth a thousand words.

She glanced toward the houses, their dark bulk rising from the gloom on the other side of the barricade. Either the others would understand what she was telling them, or they wouldn't. She didn't really care either way. She was done with all of them.

She knew she was displacing her anger, but it was better than the alternative.

Baring her teeth again, she stared at the other building, the one closest to her—the blockhouse.

His blockhouse.

Jordan patted the shaft of the flagpole. *This should have been you, you bastard.*

When the lightning flashed again she was gone.

CHAPTER 155

Camilla knocked on the frame of the open doorway. "Can we come in?"

Juan looked up from the cot, where he sat contemplating the flinty gray triangle in his hand. It was a pendant, perhaps a large arrowhead, that he wore around his neck. Tucking it back into his shirt, he waved them in without enthusiasm.

Camilla entered the blockhouse, glad to get out of the rain. Brent, Mason, and Dmitry crowded in behind her.

Taking off her rain poncho, she sat on the opposite cot. Juan didn't appear to be in the mood for conversation, and she felt like she was intruding. She was curious, though.

"Was that a tooth?"

He nodded listlessly. "*Megalodon.* A gift from someone. A long time ago."

"But it's *huge.*"

"*Da, Carcharodon megalodon,*" Dmitry said. "Prehistoric ancestor to great white shark. Looks almost same, but two and half times long. Fifteen times heavy."

"That's a pleasant thought." Camilla shuddered. "After what happened to Lauren, I don't even want to try to picture that."

"How long ago are we talking?" Mason sounded intrigued.

"*Megalodon* first appeared twenty-eight million years ago. Still alive one million years ago."

"So the modern white shark is a million years old?"

"No, *sixteen* million. They living same time."

"Great whites are nature's ultimate survivors," Juan said.

Dmitry shook his head. "No, my friend. They are endangered. We ruining our oceans, destroying their habitat."

Juan looked at him. "You come here every year? To study them?"

"I come last year. Before that I was in Phystech. Moscow."

"This time of year—December—it's high season here, isn't it?"

Dmitry nodded. "Elephant seal mating time, having pups. Is like buffet for shark."

"How many?" Juan asked. "At any given time, how many great whites do you expect to see here at Año Nuevo?"

"They are pelagic, so they come and go—solitary predators. Usually one. Other times, none. But sometimes we see two. Last year, for three days, we had two different sharks—lots of predation events."

Juan looked at his wetsuit drying on the rack. "I counted fourteen out there today."

Dmitry chortled and shook his head again. "No, no. Is too many. You see same shark over and over again. *Whole season,* we get maybe five, maybe ten, but not same day. At most two."

"I counted fourteen different individuals," Juan said. "Different sizes, fin profiles, distinguishing marks, scars."

"Is impossible." Dmitry looked skeptical. "Whole California coast has total great white population of only two hundred, maybe two hundred fifty sharks."

Juan shrugged and looked away. He stood and walked over to crouch in front of a small yellow piece of machinery that sat beside the table—a generator, Camilla realized, probably from the cave where he found Natalie. Juan poked at it, ignoring his guests.

"You should come with us," she said. "To the station buildings."

He shook his head. "I'll stay here."

"Will you be safe?"

"Safe enough." He shifted the map that lay on the table next to him, and Camilla saw the black polymer grip of JT's gun peeking out from underneath. It had been within inches of his hand the whole time.

"What about when you sleep?" she asked. "Heather disappeared while everyone was asleep."

Juan seemed to think about it. "Not an issue," he said. "From now on, *no one* sleeps."

He straightened, turning to Brent. "Time to open up the pharmacy. What was that stuff that lets you skip sleep with no side effects?"

"Modafinil," Mason cut in. "The Silicon Valley round-the-clock brain booster."

Brent nodded. "Popular with the medical profession, too."

Juan watched his face closely. "How much of it should we take?"

"Four hundred milligrams every twenty-four hours should keep you alert for a few days."

"How much do you take, Brent?"

"A little more than that." He chuckled. "About nine thousand milligrams. But I don't recommend you try that yourselves—the results wouldn't be pretty. I've had years to build up a tolerance."

He tapped the inside of his elbow. "I'm also relying on the modafinil to counteract the high levels of opioid analgesics I'm injecting. That isn't a factor for the rest of you." Reaching into a pocket of his fishing vest, he withdrew a handful of foil pill packs and dropped them on the bed.

Juan picked up a few and pocketed them. Camilla dubiously did the same, followed by Mason and Dmitry.

Juan dusted off his hands. "Well, if that's it, then—"

Camilla grabbed his wrist. "Juan, people are betting on us right now. Illegal gambling."

"It fits."

"And Natalie—Veronica may only be trying to protect her, but what if we're wrong? What if Veronica herself took Natalie?"

Mason laughed. "You really haven't figured Veronica out. She's a mystery to you, isn't she?"

Camilla stared at him surprise.

"She's very high functioning considering what she is," he said. "I'll grant you that."

"Mason, it's been a long day…"

"Veronica's a sexual predator, Camilla. She likes to kill men." Mason grinned. "I'm lucky, I suppose. For some reason, she doesn't really consider me a man."

Was this another one of his morbid theories? Camilla looked at Brent.

Brent shrugged. "I'm not a psychiatrist. I suppose it could make sense."

"But that means Natalie…"

"…is safer with her than with us," Mason said. "Because if JT or Jordan didn't take Natalie, then somebody in this room did."

Troubled, Camilla thought about it. Travis's paint color—brown—had been smeared on Natalie's sweatshirt. Whoever had taken her had probably also freed Travis. And then deliberately framed him, using paint from his spare ammunition cartridge the same way Camilla had used hers on Juan after JT destroyed her paintball gun.

Juan spoke. "Veronica's a danger to Camilla and Jordan as well."

Remembering the sneaky way Veronica's eyes had skittered away from her earlier, Camilla felt the skin at the back of her neck tighten. Veronica hadn't wanted Camilla to catch her looking. And there had been something dark and calculating in that silvery gaze, hadn't there?

"I think Juan's right," she said. "Veronica wants the ten million, and we're both ahead of her in points."

Mason nodded. "I hadn't considered that. But it's scary, given what she learned tonight by killing Travis…"

Camilla finished his thought.

"There's more than one way to move up the scoreboard."

CHAPTER 156

Veronica stood at the window. Staring through a narrow gap where the clear plastic had pulled away from the frame, she scanned the rain-washed darkness outside. A flash of lightning illuminated the open ground before her. All clear. She walked briskly through darkened rooms to another window at the back and checked the flat area behind the houses. Clear.

Natalie was upstairs. Resting. She was safe.

He—whoever he was—wouldn't get past Veronica again.

She felt guilty. The lure of money had caused her to lose track of her priorities, and poor Natalie had suffered for it. The person who had done it... Veronica would punish him as soon as she found out which of them he was. She would make him crawl. Make him beg. Make him bleed. Her breathing sped up, and tingling warmth spread through her body.

She found herself hoping it was Juan.

After all, a man who could do a thing like that to his own sister, to his own mother—abandoning them to die... A man like that might be capable of doing *anything* to a woman. Her chest heaved. Anything at all.

Painful things. Disgusting things. *Sick* things.

Things that would make her bleed.

Letting her eyes unfocus, Veronica raised a hand and traced her mouth with her fingertips, brushing them against her lips.

Things that would leave permanent scars inside her.

Things she couldn't even *imagine*.

The tingling intensified, localized, sharpened. She could hear herself panting now, and she hated herself for it.

A small noise came from the other side of the room. From the stairs.

Her gaze hardened, snapping into focus. The ground around the houses remained clear. Face warm, mouth dry, Veronica continued to stare out the window.

"Where do you think you're going, dear?" she asked the room behind her.

No answer.

She turned around.

Natalie held the banister, swaying slightly, unsteady on her feet.

"You should be resting right now," Veronica said. "You have to give your heart time to recover."

"I'll be right back." Natalie wouldn't meet her eyes. "I won't be long."

"Natalie, you can't go outside. It's too dangerous for you. Whichever one of them it was, he's going to try again."

495

Natalie looked at the floor. "I know."

"So why are you doing this?"

"I need to."

"No. Absolutely not. I forbid it."

Natalie shuffled her feet, pulling the sleeves of her paint-stained hoodie over her hands. She looked everywhere but at Veronica.

A ribbon of fear, bright and electric, laced Veronica's spine.

"Please, Natalie." Her voice broke. "I can't protect you if you won't listen to me."

CHAPTER 157

Jordan pulled her sealskin cape tighter around her. Lightning illuminated the backs of seals sleeping on the dark beach that stretched below the crack in the bluff where she had made her shelter.

The blue canopy overhead kept off the rain, and the sandstone walls on each side kept the wind away. The greasy smell of cooking seal rose from the small fire in front of her. She avoided looking at the fire, which would blind her to anything sneaking up on her from the darkness beyond, making the speargun across her knees useless until her eyes adjusted again.

She reached up and twitched a corner of the sloping blue cloth she had spiked between the walls above her—the game flag, which she had cut from its pole. The curtain of water cascading from its surface parted to give her a clearer view of the beach, where small groups of seals huddled together for warmth. There were fewer of them than before, and she wondered about that a little. Why were they leaving? The seals didn't seem to notice the little bit of hunting that she was forced to do for survival, or even the crazy thing she had done, angry, earlier tonight. She didn't think it was the sharks, either. The seals would be used to them—a natural and familiar hazard here. Something different was thinning their crowds on the island.

Juan could probably explain it to her. He could sit by her side here, his arm around her, and they could talk about it. He could point things out to her in that calm way...

Worthless lying bastard.

She didn't care about the fucking seals. She wanted to go home.

Jordan's broken ankle hurt. Her toes, purple and swollen under their covering of dirt, looked like cocktail sausages. When she got back she might need surgery to avoid permanent damage. But for now, there wasn't much she could do beyond binding it as well as she could. And she would just have to deal with the pain, but pain was something she had taught herself to ignore.

Her finger had hurt when she broke it, too.

She rubbed the crooked pinky, remembering. She had caught it on the bars in a bad transition during the state semifinals, in her senior year of high school. She had landed and looked at her hand, eyes going wide with shock at seeing her pinky poke sideways with an L bend where there shouldn't be one. Covering it with her other hand, she had walked to the locker room before the tears could start. Sitting on the bench, she kept it covered when the coach brought her parents in.

497

Her coach looked apologetic. "I can drive her to the emergency room for you—"

"Hold on." Her father held up a hand. With the other, he raised his phone to his ear again and turned away, listening. Malcolm Vaughan ran a tech hedge fund, and the phone was stuck to his head most of the time.

"I can't right now; I'm watching my daughter win a trophy…" He paused, nodding. "Of course we are. We're shooting for 2008, but 2012 is more likely. No point rushing unless she's ready to win the gold… Look, can I call you back—wait a minute, they want to *what?*" He waved the coach away, and stuck a finger in his other ear. "No, they can't do that! Tell them Kleiner and Sequoia committed already…" He walked out into the hallway, his voice growing heated. Shaking his head, he waved her mother forward to deal with her situation.

Jordan realized that her father hadn't looked at her once. She turned toward her mother.

Colleen Vaughan spoke to Jordan's coach in a voice ripe with concern.

"Does this mean she won't qualify for the finals?"

Jordan's eyes narrowed, and she stood. Grabbing the athletic tape off the bench, she marched into the restroom, into a toilet stall. Steeling herself, she looked at her hand, ignoring the knock at the stall door.

"Are you all right?" Her coach.

"A tantrum doesn't solve anything." Her mother.

Jordan lowered the lid and sat. Gritting her teeth, she grabbed her injured finger with her good hand and yanked the bent pinky straight. The bolt of pain made her arm shake, and her elbow slammed against the side of the stall.

"Kicking the wall?" Her mother again. "Very mature, Jordan."

Silent tears ran down her face as she wrapped her throbbing pinky and her ring finger in layers of tape, binding them together.

"Answer me when I'm talking to you. Remember our conversation the last time? Do you want me to sell all the horses?"

Jordan scrubbed her forearm across her face and composed her expression. Then she opened the stall door, ignoring her mother.

"It was only sprained a little. I'm ready now."

Her coach shook her head. "I saw your finger."

Jordan looked at her with contempt. "Get the fuck out of my way."

On the way home in the back of the Bentley, Jordan ignored her parents' questions. She had qualified for the all-state finals, using the pain that throbbed up her wrist to her elbow to drive herself relentlessly, winning every event. She held her trophy on her lap as she looked out the window, her fingers manipulating the little golden figure on top. Jordan kept her face expressionless as she snapped off its plastic arms, legs, and head.

She never spoke to her father again.

CHAPTER 158

Inside the station building, Camilla sat on a cot with her back against the wall. She huddled under her space blanket, trying to stay warm. The scientist Heather had been taken from the adjoining building—a fact that never left her mind. But at least she wasn't alone now. Brent, Mason, and Dmitry crowded the room around her, lounging on the other cot or sitting on the floorboards. Nobody spoke much.

She held in her hands a bound report, *Archaeology and History In Año Nuevo State Park,* which she was reading by the light of Lauren's LED lantern. She had found it among the zoology surveys, and Dmitry hadn't recognized the Parks & Rec Cultural Heritage publication. She turned the pages, partly to keep her mind occupied but also to look for anything that might help. Exactly what she was searching for, she had no idea, but anything was better than letting her thoughts run wild in frightened and exhausted circles, as they had for the past few hours.

Julian had made an offhand comment about tomorrow's game, calling it *"a most dangerous game indeed."* At the time, she hadn't thought anything of it, but now his words haunted her. Camilla had an awful suspicion that she knew what tomorrow's game was going to be. But she didn't dare to discuss it with Brent or Mason, for fear that either of them might be Julian's spy.

The Most Dangerous Game…

Long ago, she remembered reading a short story of that name. Written in the 1920s, it was a classic about a famous big-game hunter who falls off a ship and washes up on an uncharted island owned by an exiled general. Claiming he hunts only "the most dangerous game," the general invites the hunter to join him. Upon learning the intended prey is human, the hunter refuses, only to find that he himself has become the hunted.

Was Julian planning to show up tomorrow with a pack of dogs and a hunting rifle? Would there be multiple hunters? Would the spy unmask himself or herself and join the hunt at Julian's side?

The pages rattled in her hands and the Mylar space blanket crinkled around her arms and shoulders. Closing the report, she grabbed her knees to hide her shaking. A few hours ago she had been ready to kill Julian herself, and couldn't wait until he arrived so they could grab him. She had been so hopelessly naive.

Vita Brevis didn't blink an eye at murder. Quibbles about terminology aside, Mason was right: Julian had brought them all here to die.

All but one of them.

Who was his spy?

Veronica was the only one who could see the monitors. Julian could be speaking to her right now, giving her instructions. She was a multiple murderer. She had killed Travis right before their eyes, with no more remorse than if she were swatting a fly. She had nearly killed JT—a Force Recon Marine—with her bare hands. She was lethal enough without a weapon, but if Julian gave her one…

The only gun they had was in Juan's hands. What proof did she *really* have that he wasn't the spy? It was even possible that he had grabbed Natalie himself, then brought her back to confuse them. And he had said something very odd to Camilla during the flag game.

He had mentioned Cory, the missing shipboard guest. When she asked if he thought Cory had jumped overboard he said, "*Maybe he had some help.*" At the time, it had vaguely reminded her of a story. With growing terror, she now realized that the story was "*The Most Dangerous Game.*"

She had seen Juan fight. JT had a knife and had clearly been trying to kill him. Even though Juan had the gun, he hadn't even felt the need to draw it, subduing JT with a diver's weight belt instead. Maybe she was blinded by her inability to think anything bad about someone who had risked his life to save a child.

JT had never come back. What if he and Juan had crossed paths again after she left Juan and returned to the houses? Where *was* JT? Had Juan killed him? Or was JT lurking outside right now, staring at their window, walkie-talkie in hand, speaking to Julian?

And Jordan—what if Camilla was wrong about her? Had her cheerful personality been an act all along? It hurt to believe that, but she could easily picture this new, cold-eyed version of Jordan side by side with Julian, hosting another of these terrible games together.

Brent and Mason were in the room with Camilla, seemingly lost in their own thoughts. They seemed oblivious of her inner struggle. Could one of them be faking it—watching her secretly from beneath half-closed eyes?

Or even both of them? What if Julian had more than one spy?

Dmitry would seem to be the only one she could trust for sure, but earlier, she had heard him admit that he was new to the shark research team. Could he be a Vita Brevis plant?

Even without the modafinil she had taken, there was no risk of her falling asleep.

They would see Julian tomorrow.

Pushing aside the space blanket, she rose and walked through the doorway into Heather's empty room.

There was something she had to do.

CHAPTER 159

Kneeling on Heather's cot, all alone in an empty room lit by a single flickering candle, Camilla took out her iPhone. Watching the dark doorways, she thought about little Avery, waiting for her to come see him. Like she had *promised*.

Right after he said he wished he was dead.

She pressed the power switch on her phone. The battery indicator showed only a narrow sliver of red—she had a few minutes left at most. No signal, but she hadn't expected any. Brushing her hair away from her forehead, she took a moment to compose her face and held the phone out in front of her. She activated the camera app, centered her candlelit live image on the small screen, and pressed the record button.

"Anyone finding this phone, please make sure this message gets to Briana Kent. Her contact info is in the phone's address book.

"Briana, if you are listening to this, it means that I'm... I didn't... It means you need to take charge of the foundation. I'm counting on you, and so are the kids. With this message, I'm leaving you whatever money I have. I know it's not much, but it's enough to pay yourself a salary and cover expenses. Please tell Avery I didn't..."

She had to look away. Gaze roaming the ceiling, she fought to control her face. She took a deep breath and looked into the phone again.

"Tell him I didn't abandon him," she said. "Tell him I would have done anything to get back. I tried, Avery. I tried *so hard*—"

Unable to continue, she tucked her chin into her shoulder and stared at the floor, pressing her other wrist against her nose and mouth. She lowered the phone and pushed Stop.

Angrily, Camilla erased what she had recorded. Holding up the phone at arms-length, she pushed the button again.

"Anyone finding this, make sure it gets to Euclid House and someone plays it for Avery Sanger, seven years old."

She forced a smile onto her face. Made her voice sound cheerful.

"Avery, I really wanted to be there with you. If there had been any way I could, I would have. But something bad happened, and I couldn't come. You already know life isn't always fair to us. People get taken away from us sometimes, and it's not our fault. When it happens, it's okay to be sad for a little while. But you can't stop trusting everyone. You can't give up hope—"

The battery indicator blinked three times.

The phone went dead in her hand.

CHAPTER 160

Sensing someone standing in the doorway of the blockhouse, Juan looked up from the map spread on the table in front of him. Seeing who it was, he relaxed and slid his fingers forward, pushing the Glock out of sight beneath the map again. He put down the pen he held in his other hand.

Natalie stood at the side of the door frame, watching him.

Juan returned his attention to the map, and she came into the room with shy, hesitant steps to stand alongside him. He pointed at the pen marks he had made at different spots along the shoreline.

"The cave where I found you," he said. "It might not be the only one."

But Natalie was not interested in conversation, it seemed. She raised her arms and draped them around his neck, molding her body against him and raising her face to his.

Juan broke the kiss and shook his head. "I don't think—"

Natalie clung to him, her mouth soft on his neck, his ear. He took a step back, bumping the edge of the cot with his calves. Placing her hands on his shoulders, Natalie pushed him back onto the cot. She stood in front of him, and her eyes held his, dark and serious, as she slowly pulled down the zipper of her jeans.

Juan remembered what Veronica had said about Natalie's history. She was probably trying to express her gratitude, thanking him in the only way she knew how.

He shook his head again. "This isn't a good idea." He reached for her wrists but she stepped backward, reaching behind her to lean against the table.

Natalie wriggled her hips, and the jeans slid a couple of inches lower.

Juan kept his eyes on her face, refusing to look down but unable to avoid noticing the stark whiteness of skin in the open V of her zipper.

"No, Natalie." He kept his voice gentle.

Unsmiling, unblinking, she held his gaze for several seconds.

It suddenly occurred to him what the past half minute would look like to Jordan, played on the monitors for everyone to watch, perhaps even interspersed with footage of him and Jordan making love.

What could she possibly think of him *then*?

Juan closed his eyes and lowered his head. Unable to speak, he waved Natalie away.

He listened as she rezipped her jeans, slid away from the table, and backed toward the door. Then he looked up.

503

Standing in the doorway again, she watched him with no discernible expression on her face. And then she was gone.

He stared after her, realizing with a sinking feeling that he had allowed himself to get distracted. He had let his guard down.

He reached under the map for the Glock, and his fingers brushed across empty tabletop.

The gun was gone.

Day 7

Thursday: December 27, 2012

CHAPTER 161

The storm had broken a few hours before dawn. Camilla was surprised that she felt alert, without the brittle, spacey feeling she remembered from college all-nighters. Standing outside the dripping walls of the station building, she looked around in the dim gray early-morning light.

Mason stepped out to join her, looking oddly cheerful. She glanced at the shattered lens of his glasses, at the cuts and bruises on his chin, and touched her own broken nose. They had to get ready; Julian could arrive anytime.

Would he come by boat? By helicopter? How many others was he bringing? Had people *paid* for the privilege of hunting Camilla and her fellow contestants? The thought sickened her, and it made her angry, too.

"Let's go up by the tower," she said. "I want to see if we can spot Jordan anywhere."

"Did Julian look South American to you?" Mason asked, walking beside her. "Like, maybe, Colombian?"

She shook her head. She was no expert, but Julian's features told her he maybe had some French or Italian ancestry.

"No," she said. "But last night I realized there is something else we all have in common, besides being survivors. I think it's significant."

"All of us were dumb enough to let ourselves be marooned in a place we didn't know in the middle of the night?"

Exasperated, she rolled her eyes at him. She just couldn't see him being Julian's spy.

"Normally," she said, "reality shows pull their contestants from all over the country, don't they? The diversity tends to make it more interesting—you root for your hometown heroes and all that. But everybody here is from California."

"I'm from New York."

"You're from California *now*."

"That's actually quite interesting," he said. "It means the candidate selection process couldn't have been this big, anonymous nationwide search Julian indicated it was."

She nodded. "Could there be some other connection between all of us? None of us seem to know each other, but Julian got hold of our names *somehow*. And he knew enough about each of us and our stories to get him interested in digging further."

"News," Mason said. "If I was looking for proven survivors, that's where I'd start. California news stories. Lauren's accident would have been in the

507

news. Your Loma Prieta earthquake, obviously. Veronica's first husband would have made the news, although it wouldn't have been a big story. Same with Juan, because there's no way the Coast Guard uncovered his identity."

She nodded. "'Billionaire Drug Lord's Sons Kill Each Other at California Resort Island'? Juan would have been an absolutely *huge* news story if they knew who he was. They never found out. JT would have also been in the news—local Marine in helicopter crash. But what about you?"

He frowned. "My name did appear in some articles, but who would look for survivors in the financial news? And then there's Natalie. Sad to say, but child abuse isn't really newsworthy."

"What about police reports, though?" Camilla brightened with excitement, but then her enthusiasm faded. "No, that doesn't really work, either. Brent's cancer was hardly a police matter. Or your SEC and IRS shenanigans."

"IRS...?"

"I know you, Mason."

"Okay, fine, but Jordan wouldn't have shown up in news or police reports, either. How did Julian find her? Based on his profile, she's easy to dismiss as a rich-kid overachiever with a short romantic attention span—"

Camilla grabbed Mason's wrist in shock.

At the top of the hill above them, a meaty dark lump had been spiked atop a red-stained pole.

"Oh god..." She covered her mouth.

From the top of the seven-foot pole, the head of an elephant seal stared back at her with eyes like dull marbles. The severed head was as big as a rhino's—clearly an alpha bull, one of the five-thousand-pound monsters that ruled the beach below. A zigzag scar marred the hide beneath the right eye, and a pale patch stood out on its rubbery trunk of a nose.

Camilla stared at it in horror. Jordan had done this. The woman she had once wanted to call her friend was having some kind of breakdown. Why else would she take such a risk, challenging a dangerous animal alone and in the dark for no reason at all? What kind of mental state was she in, to do a thing like that?

It wasn't right for Jordan to be abandoned and alone now.

Camilla felt a wave of sorrow wash over her.

"Jordan's totally lost it," she said. "We have to find her and help her. Something's happened to her mind. When we get back, she'll need counseling. Professional care."

"This head is for the beast." Mason chuckled. "It's a gift."

"Not funny, Mason. Not now."

"You've got this all wrong," he said, pointing at the grisly banner. "Jordan's telling us something here. Trust a Stanford communications major to do it with a literary reference."

"Mason, please. Julian's coming and we don't have a lot of time."

"I'm disappointed in you. It won the Nobel Prize for literature, and you haven't read it?"

"What's she telling us?"

"*Lord of the Flies*," he said. "Maybe there is a beast... Maybe it's only us."

CHAPTER 162

"More caves is logical." Dmitry stood next to Juan in front of the table in the blockhouse, looking down at the map. "Because of faults— lots of faulting in this part of coast."

"Show me." Juan handed him the pen.

Dmitry tapped the table at a spot beyond the eastern edge of the map. "San Andreas Fault." With the back of the pen he traced a long course. "Big 1989 Loma Prieta earthquake, caused by San Andreas Fault."

He drew a line on the map, along the mainland near the coast, which cut past Año Nuevo Point. "San Gregorio Fault, part of Alquist-Priolo Earthquake Fault Zone. Branches off San Andreas Fault up in north, runs down to here."

Moving his pen closer to Año Nuevo Point, he added another, shorter line, connecting to the first. "Año Nuevo Creek Fault."

Closer to the point and the channel that separated it from the island, he added yet another. "Frijoles Fault."

Two more, each shorter and closer to the channel than the last. "Green Oaks Fault. Año Nuevo Thrust Fault."

Dmitry added another fault line, which ran through the channel separating the island from the mainland. "At least one fault in middle of channel. Probably more, here under island, also."

He tapped the island with his pen.

"That's why finding cave is not surprising. Probably lots of cave under island. When Coast Guard built lighthouse hundred forty years ago, they block some cave with cement to keep water out, control erosion."

Juan thought about it, but he couldn't concentrate. Jordan's rolling travel bag was still next to her cot. Why had he let her go? He should have gone after her. He pictured Jordan's beautiful expressive face, her myriad expressions: Jordan happy. Jordan thoughtful. Jordan serious. Jordan moving above him, looking at him with a half frown of concern on her face. Jordan in the throes of ecstasy, eyes open and vulnerable, sharing herself completely with him.

Jordan's face at the end, so angry, so utterly furious with him. He had deserved it. He had treated her so badly. He had ruined everything.

He was missing what Dmitry was saying.

Face tight, Juan forced himself to concentrate. He studied the map. Año Nuevo Island sat at the juncture of a converging network of geological faults. The fault lines increased in density the closer they came to the island.

509

"So this would be a really bad place to be when California's big one hits?" he asked.

Dmitry nodded. "Bad place for earthquake. Very bad."

CHAPTER 163

Camilla stood on the elevated walkway, watching the elephant seals on the beach below. She needed to find Jordan and speak with her, get her to rejoin the others before it was too late.

The sun was climbing over the horizon now. They would be face-to-face with Julian soon. They didn't have much time, and they needed Jordan's help.

Camilla scanned the crowds of seals. There seemed to be fewer than before, which made it easier to spot what she was looking for.

Despite the dread that weighed her limbs and sat like a brick in her gut, she couldn't help feeling a certain awe as she watched Jordan move among the seals. Her motions mimicked those of the animals around her: long pauses, languid stretches, followed by short bursts of shuffling, limping forward motion. The elephant seals that Jordan passed did not react even when she brushed against them or pushed them as she went by. They seemed to accept her as one of them.

She did not look like a person who had lost her mind.

Relieved, Camilla let out the breath she had been holding and lowered herself to drop from the walkway to the sand.

The seals around Jordan scattered at Camilla's approach. Jordan stood up from her crouch, balancing storklike on one leg. She leaned on the speargun, using it as a crutch. Neither friendly nor unfriendly, her face was set in an expression of stony indifference. She didn't say anything.

Camilla found herself at a loss for words. She swallowed.

"Julian's coming."

Jordan looked away, and her lips twitched in annoyance, as if she was disappointed in Camilla.

"Don't shut the rest of us out this way," Camilla said. "We need your help. Maybe together we can figure out who Julian's spy is, before he gets here."

"Oh, that." Jordan turned away and limped along the beach, giving a dismissive wave behind her. "We've had the answer to *that* ever since the first presentation on the ship."

"I don't understand."

"The company name. Vita Brevis." Jordan's pace was brisk, despite her limp.

Camilla hurried to keep up. "What was that quote again?"

"Ars longa, vita brevis, occasio praeceps, experimentum periculosum, iudicium difficile."
It was strange to hear Jordan pronounce the rolling Latin syllables, tossing
them over her shoulder with indifference.

"But what does it *mean?*"

"It's not important."

Camilla grabbed her arm. "Please, Jordan!"

She answered in a bored monotone. "Art is long, life is short, opportunity
fleeting, experiment dangerous, judgment difficult."

"So this is a sick experiment of some sort? Or we're being judged
somehow? What does it *mean?*"

"*What* isn't important. *Who* is."

"*Who* is what we're trying to figure out here," Camilla said. "I'm mystified.
How does the quote tell us that?"

Jordan just shook her head. But then she stopped for a moment and
looked at Camilla—really looked at her. And smiled.

Her wide, dazzling smile lit Camilla's face like the sun, and she felt a burst
of hope as the knots in her heart started to loosen.

Jordan reached out and touched her forearm.

"You don't give up on people, do you?" she said. "I'm really sorry he
brought *you* here, Camilla, because you don't deserve this."

"Julian's coming to kill us all," Camilla said. "It'll be much easier for him if
we're all separated like this, angry at each other. We need you with us right
now, Jordan. *I* need you. *Juan* needs you."

At Juan's name, Jordan's face changed, turning ugly. Her fingers gripped
Camilla's forearm like a claw.

"Juan needs me?" Her attempt at a sarcastic laugh sounded more like a
choked sob. "Juan doesn't need *anybody,* sister. Don't you forget that. And
don't you *dare* trust that bastard."

Pushing Camilla's arm aside, she turned and limped away down the beach
with fast, angry strides.

Watching her receding back, Camilla closed her eyes.

"Oh god," she said to the empty beach. "We're all going to die here."

CHAPTER 164

"**D**id you find JT?" Camilla asked.

Brent shook his head. But he didn't stop—just continued wagging his head back and forth much longer than would be normal. Camilla looked at his eyes, and her heart sank. His blue irises were wide and almost without pupils—he had injected himself again.

She threw Mason a questioning glance that asked, *Why didn't you stop him?*

Mason shrugged and gave her a rueful grin. Then he pointed toward the narrow, bridgelike causeway of rock separating the northern part of the island—the seahorse's head—from where they now stood.

"We found an orange line in the sand," he said.

Camilla had gathered everyone she could—Mason, Brent, Juan, and Dmitry—near the fallen lighthouse tower to come up with a plan. Tamping down the rising panic inside that screamed at her to run, run, run because Julian was coming to kill them all, she thought about what Mason had just said.

"Orange was JT's paintball color," she said. "He's alive."

"But a line in the sand means only one thing," Mason said.

She nodded. "Cross at your own peril. He's over there, in hiding, telling the rest of us to keep away or else. But that's no good. We need his help."

"Unless he's with Julian," Mason said.

Camilla walked over to the middle of the causeway, and the others followed. An irregular orange line, marked every few feet by a crushed orange paintball, cut across the narrowest section of dirt and rock, running its full forty-foot width.

Heart pounding, Camilla hesitated for a moment. Then she stepped over the line and strode to the northern end of the causeway. She scanned the rocky ground beyond, seeing only emptiness.

"I know you can hear me, JT," she shouted. "We need your help. Julian's coming to kill us all."

Silence greeted her in response.

"Please, JT. Protect us. We need you."

Nothing but echoes.

JT had abandoned them to die. Camilla tasted bitterness in her throat. This must have been how his wounded teammates felt in Afghanistan.

Juan laid a hand on her shoulder. "The orange line may be a decoy. He could be behind us. Anywhere."

She stared at him, tense with doubt. Had *Juan* draw this line?

513

"I know what you're thinking, but I didn't kill him." Juan took his hand off her shoulder. "I'm not a killer, Camilla."

What about your brother Álvaro?

And now Juan had given himself the last name *Álvarez.* Oh god. If JT was still alive, maybe he was hiding from Juan.

She was going about this all wrong—trying to pull her team together, when they were probably the people she should be most scared of. Maybe Veronica, JT, and Jordan had the right idea, and Camilla, too, should be getting as far away from the others as possible.

Brent cleared his throat. "What you were reading last night, about the history and archaeology of this place? Well, I read a little of it, too."

"Maybe your book club can meet a little later, then?" Mason said. "Right now isn't a good time."

Brent ignored him and pointed out to sea. "When Spanish explorer Sebastián Vizcaíno sailed past here four hundred years ago he was already losing his crew to scurvy. Not a whole lot of medical knowledge back then."

"Yeah," Mason said. "No modafinil to get them so high that they'd babble to each other about history instead of coming up with a plan."

Brent frowned at him. "I guess you didn't take any of the pills, or you'd know there aren't any euphoric effects associated with modafinil. My pupillary constriction and general feeling of well-being comes from other things—fentanyl and hydrocodone, mainly."

"You're a credit to the profession, Brent."

Brent waved him away and pointed across the channel.

"Vizcaíno's chaplain, Father Antonio de la Ascensión, had given last rites to half the crew by the time he looked out at Punto Año Nuevo and named it. Vizcaíno's sailors made no attempt to communicate with the natives—Costanoan Ohlone people—they saw hiding on the shore, watching the ship go by."

"I'm guessing this is eventually going somewhere," Mason said.

Brent kept his eerie gaze focused on Camilla. "The cure to what was killing Vizcaíno's men was growing wild all along these shores. *Fragaria chiloensis*—beach strawberry—was a staple of the native diet, and so were gooseberries. Scurvy is caused by acute vitamin C deficiency, and both types of berries are very high in C.

"The Ohlone hid amongst the berry bushes until Vizcaíno's ships were out of sight. But they were less fortunate in their next encounter with the Spanish: a military expedition led by Gaspar de Portola. I do wonder how differently history might have turned out, if…"

"…if Vizcaíno's men and the Ohlone had trusted each other," Camilla said. "But they didn't, and so they died."

She turned to Juan. "Let's all go to your blockhouse," she said. "*Together.* I want to see that map."

• • •

In the blockhouse, Camilla looked at her companions. Dmitry held the four-foot concrete-capped steel pipe she had seen days ago in Lauren's hands. He carried it over his shoulder like a medieval mace. Juan wore his wet suit again, and a dive knife on his ankle. She couldn't see the gun.

She looked at the can of bear spray in Mason's hand and shook her head. "That's not going to be enough."

He reached into his pocket and pulled out a silver pocketknife that she recognized as one of the presents from the gifting game, two days ago. The blade was less than two inches long—it looked pathetic.

"Oh god." Rolling her eyes, Camilla took it from him and tossed it aside. Picking up one of the heavy dive knives on the counter, she handed it to him.

"Thanks," he said. "I think."

Seeing the awkward, tentative way he held it, Camilla's face tightened into a grimace. This was her army.

"Brent?" she asked.

He shook his head and tightened his grip on the first-aid kit. "I know what it feels like to kill accidentally," he said. "I won't do it on purpose."

Camilla took a dive knife for herself, too. She strapped its sheath to her upper arm like a workout iPod—upside down, so she could grab it in a hurry with the other hand. The thought of using the knife to defend herself—stabbing another human being with it—sickened her. But unlike Brent, she was ready to do it if necessary. She would do anything she had to, to get back to Avery—and to make sure Julian didn't get away with this.

"Juan, what about the gasoline you found in that cave?" she asked. "I know none of the houses or other wood will burn. Julian made sure of that. But we have gas now, and it isn't raining. Maybe we can light a pile of dried seaweed or something to make a signal fire."

He was shaking his head. "It's diesel."

"So?"

"Julian thought of everything." Juan tapped the generator on the counter with a knuckle. "Diesel fuel doesn't ignite easily outside a high-compression engine. It would actually put *out* a small fire—we'd need to get something big burning hot already before it would be useful as an accelerant."

"Everyone over here, then," she said. "Let's take a look at the map."

The five of them looked down at it. Like movie generals strategizing for war, she thought. And wasn't that pretty much what they were doing, after all?

Borrowing Juan's pen, she crosshatched the area south of the barricade, where the houses were.

"Veronica and Natalie," she said. "Red territory."

"The black widow's lair," Mason said, laughing.

Camilla ignored him and hatched diagonal lines across the seahorse-head shape of the island's northern end. "Orange territory—JT."

She drew wavy lines over the island's main beach. "Black territory—Jordan."

She tapped the center of what was left. "That leaves the five of us with this territory," she said. "Our paintball colors were green, pink, yellow, and purple, so we'll call it rainbow territory."

"'Rainbow' works for me," Mason said. He traced their territory's outline with his finger. "Julian's main advantages are the cameras and—if you're right—the guns he brings. To level the playing field, we need to take those advantages away from him."

"We don't have time to find and destroy all the cameras," Brent said. "That would take days, and even then we'd never get them all."

Camilla nodded. "But we don't *have* to get them all. Clearing one small space is enough, if we can force Julian to come after us there."

"This blockhouse?" Mason asked.

Juan shook his head. "The walls are concrete, which is good, but it's small—no maneuvering room. And it's exposed. They could breach a wall and pick us off from a distance."

Camilla tapped the wooden station buildings on the map. "These are even worse. Too many ways in—doors and windows—and the walls won't stop bullets. Julian could hunt us room to room, killing us one by one."

She stepped back and took in the whole of rainbow territory, from the seal barricade in the south to the causeway in the north, bounded on the west by the dock and breakwater, and on the east by the bluffs dropping to the beach.

The blockhouse and the station buildings wouldn't work. The big factory warehouse would turn into a carnival shooting gallery, with them as the targets. The lighthouse tower was a twisted wreck of rubble…

Her eyes drifted to the center of rainbow territory, where a circular structure was marked, and her heart gave a sudden leap. She stabbed down at the map with her finger.

"There's our answer."

• • •

The five of them stood around the broken concrete rim of the cistern dome, looking down into the darkness. At the cistern's top, the opening let in a shaft of light to illuminate a circle of rocks and broken rubble twenty feet below. The patch of light faded into the black emptiness on each side.

"Not the most pleasant smell," Mason said.

Camilla took a deep breath, ignoring the foul odor that wafted from below.

"It's bigger on the inside," she said. "That's good."

Juan nodded. "It extends underneath the edges of the spillway, six or seven meters in each direction. They won't be able to shoot us from above. They'll have to come in after us."

Mason looked at him. "Or smoke us out with tear gas."

"I don't think Julian will do that," Camilla said. Her voice turned bitter. "It wouldn't look good on camera."

Near her feet, the edge of the dome had crumbled, creating a rocky slope instead of a sheer drop. Camilla crouched down and slid forward, jumping the last two feet to stand at the wet bottom. The smell was much worse inside—even after getting used to the ever-present miasma of the seals, it almost made her gag.

She looked up at the others, silhouetted around the circle of light above her.

"Come on down, team," she said. "Let's get to work."

• • •

"JT's muscles would be useful right about now." Mason's voice echoed in the hollow void of the cistern. He shifted another rock.

"Hold on," Camilla said, lifting up the lantern. "Another one." Pulling the tiny camera free of the crack in the cistern's curved wall, she dropped it to the concrete floor and smashed it with a softball-size rock.

The moving lantern threw wild shadows against the moldy walls. Working nearby, Brent, Juan, and Dmitry cleared wet rocks and chunks of concrete from the slimy corridor circling the inside edge of the cistern. By piling the rubble into sofa-size barriers, Camilla hoped to make a rock maze at the bottom of the pit, like the foxholes in a war movie. Julian's guns wouldn't be much use to him in the tight underground space. It would be close-quarters trench warfare.

If only they had JT with them…

"Why is JT hiding from us?" she called.

Juan wedged a large rock into place. "Because he thinks I'm Julian's spy."

"Why?"

Juan stood stock-still with another rock in his hands. He slowly turned to look at her with realization dawning across his face. "He had a good reason to. He even told me what it was, but I missed its significance."

"Blyad!" Dmitry stumbled away from the rubble where he was digging, and backed into Juan. *"Miertvoh tyelah.* Is dead body under here!"

Down here? Camilla's heart sped up. "Is it Heather or Jacob?"

"No, no, not them. Is another man. I don't know him."

Juan's face darkened. "JT, then." He stepped forward. "Come give me a hand with him, Brent."

The lantern shook in Camilla's hand, sending shadows bouncing against the walls of the cistern. Juan and Brent shifted rocks away. The gag-inducing smell of decomposition sharpened. A dense cloud of flies rose from the curled, still shape nestled in the muck and swirled into the air around them.

Half-carrying, half-dragging the slumped, wet form between them, the two men pushed forward. The sickly-sweet stench of putrefaction made Camilla gag.

Juan and Brent let the body slide to the floor in the center of the cistern, where it lay framed in a halo of light from above. Neither said anything. Juan rolled the body onto its back, faceup. Then he stiffened.

Brent took a few steps backward, away from the corpse. He raised a hand to scratch at the side of his head.

Baffled, Camilla stared at the body lying in the circle of light. What she was seeing made no sense at all. The dead man wasn't JT.

She recognized him, though.

The dead face stared up at the sky, grinning a skull's mirthless grin, bright white teeth visible through the rotted lips and cheeks. Maggots boiled in the empty eye sockets. More of them squirmed in the matted, damp black hair. His coat twitched and squirmed with loathsome movements. Beneath the mildew, the suit looked as elegant and expensive as the one she had seen him wearing on the monitor yesterday.

Camilla forced a breath through a throat like a pinhole.

"We were wrong… *so* wrong."

She raised her eyes to look at the others.

"Julian's not coming. He's been down here all along."

CHAPTER 165

Juan climbed out of the cistern and stood at the rim, staring down at Julian's corpse—a grinning scarecrow in a four-thousand-dollar suit. Camilla, Mason, Brent, and Dmitry climbed up after him and spread out around the edge, making a circle. They stared down at Julian, too, their faces frozen in expressions of shock and disbelief that no doubt mirrored Juan's own.

"We had this backward," he said.

"Prerecorded." Mason's face showed no expression. "Every word and pixel of it."

One of Brent's lower eyelids started to spasm. "There's only one possible reason I can come up with for that," he said.

Juan nodded. Brent may be high, but he was lucid enough to understand just how bad this was.

Looking at the others around the circle, Juan read their faces and saw that Camilla, Mason, and Dmitry also understood what this meant.

"This is what Jordan was trying to tell us," Camilla said.

He glanced sharply at her, but her eyes were still riveted to the corpse. Her face was as white as Julian's.

"There's nobody else," she said. "*Nobody* is watching us right now. This whole time, we thought it was Julian's *spy* we were trying to uncover..."

Juan nodded. "...when who we were really looking for is Julian's *boss*."

With one last look at the grinning corpse below, he turned away. It was time at last, he knew. He had waited as long as he could, but he no longer had any choice. The objective hazards here had now become too overwhelming.

It had been the same ten years ago, with *el jefe*—Juan's father, Roberto—lying dead in the street and none of them knowing who had ordered the killing: Montoya's men, the Ramírez brothers, Guillermo el Loco, or even one of *el jefe*'s own trusted lieutenants. Juan had looked into all their faces during the emergency meeting in Cartagena and understood the same thing he understood now.

To stay was to die.

With his back to the others, he walked down the slope and away from the cistern.

"No!" Camilla shouted after him. "Can't you see? This is just what he wants!"

Without turning, Juan raised a hand in farewell—and kept walking.

"He?" Mason's voice sounded high and squeaky. "We have no idea if the person we're looking for is a *he*."

That was what Mason sounded like when he was afraid, Juan thought. Really, truly, finally afraid at last. He continued up the hill, past the blockhouse.

"It could be a *she*, Camilla," Mason said as Juan left them farther behind. "It could even be *you*."

Juan headed down the small slope toward the shale beach, and the crest of the hill hid the others from sight. Mason was right: it could be any of them… including Mason himself.

The answers that Juan had come for no longer mattered. He no longer cared how Vita Brevis had found him, how they had uncovered his true identity, or who else they had told. It didn't matter anymore; the profile they had done of him had rendered those questions moot. He would have to disappear again. He'd go somewhere obscure this time—the Maldives, maybe—and start over. Change his name again. Change his face again. Last time, he had been too young—too vain to realize that when you were trying to disappear, giving yourself an unforgettable face was a fool's choice. This time, he wouldn't make that mistake.

He looked over his shoulder, to confirm that he was out of sight of the others. Then he dropped to one knee and lifted a half sheet of broken plywood by one edge. Holding it upright one-handed, he swept at the dirt beneath with his free hand until he unearthed a crescent-shaped edge: the soil-packed mouth of a buried pipe. Still holding the plywood vertical with his other hand, he scooped rocks away from the opening until he had exposed a six-inch gap. Leaning in shoulder deep, he reached inside until his fingers touched a rubbery hose. Grabbing it, he slid the cylindrical scuba tank and regulator out of the hole.

He checked the mouthpiece to be sure it hadn't been fouled.

Sharks or no sharks, it was time to leave.

Dragging the tank with him, Juan scooted back and let the plywood fall to the ground, revealing the silent figure that now stood behind it where, a moment before, there had been only seals.

He backpedaled, landing on his butt and dropping the tank in surprise.

Balancing on one leg like a flamingo, Jordan aimed the speargun at him. He was shocked by the hate distorting her face.

"I thought survivors were supposed to be unpredictable," she said, "but you're so fucking easy to predict, it's pathetic. That's why he left the dive gear in the blockhouse where you'd find it. He knew. As long as you thought you had a hidden escape plan, he *knew* you'd stick around."

Seeing her now, Juan felt something come unstuck inside his chest. What was he doing? He hadn't been thinking straight. He didn't want to leave Jordan. Not ever. He couldn't imagine being without her. They *belonged* together. But he'd made a terrible mess of things. He needed to make everything all right between them again.

It was his fault her face looked this way right now. He had done that to her. It was his fault her lip was trembling. He wanted to kiss her, to crush her to his chest, to wrap his arms around her and tell her he would never let her go again. He would apologize—make it all up to her. He held out his arms.

"Jordan, please—"

"Don't." She jabbed the speargun at him, and her face crumpled. "Just don't."

How could he make her understand how he felt about her? He himself hadn't realized how much he needed her. Until now.

Jordan closed her eyes, trembling. There were words he needed say to her right now. Words that *she* needed to hear him say. But he was afraid his actions had already spoken louder than any words could atone for. The words died in his throat.

When she opened her eyes again and he saw what was in them, Juan knew that his actions had damned him.

"What a sorry freak show he's gathered on this island," she said. "I know what *my* limitations are, Juan. Other people have never meant much to me. I can't help that; it's just the way I am. But you're *not* that way. Can't you see? You only *want* to be. You only *try* to be. And that makes you the worst one of us all."

"I'm so sorry," he said. "So very sorry I hurt you—"

"No." Tears burst from Jordan's beautiful green eyes. "No, you're not."

"I'll make things all right again."

"How?" She pointed at the scuba tank. "Like *that?* I guess people don't change, do they? I see that running away is still your answer to life."

Her face broke apart. "But *me,* Juan? You're trying to run away from *me?*"

She pulled the trigger.

The steel spear struck Juan's chest dead center. It hit like a hammer blow, knocking his breath away. Searing pain exploded through his sternum.

He looked down at himself.

The end of the spear protruded from his chest, wiggling as he sucked in a shocked breath that stung like flame.

He gasped, and the spear wiggled again. It stuck out of his chest at a sideways angle rather than straight.

He had been shot before. This wasn't that bad. He could survive this, too.

He looked up.

Jordan was reloading the speargun. In a rapid but graceful motion, she slid another shaft into the barrel and planted the tip in the ground. She stretched the elastic cable, letting it snap into place.

Then, raising the speargun with terrifying purpose, she aimed it at Juan's face.

The loud explosion hurt his ears, making him flinch.

Jordan's head snapped to the side.

She fell.

The speargun clattered to the rocks beside him as the echoes of the gunshot rolled across the island.

Fifteen feet behind Jordan, Natalie fumbled the Glock in an unskilled grip. Dropped it.

She looked at him with a horrified expression on her face. Sat down hard on the rocks.

Juan turned his head toward Jordan. From where he lay, he couldn't see where she was wounded. Her foot twitched once.

Maybe she was all right. Maybe the bullet had glanced off her skull, as it had when his brother Álvaro shot him in the head, years ago. Maybe one day he and Jordan would compare scars, sitting side by side on the snow white sand of Grace Beach, in front of a bungalow the two of them shared.

He pulled himself toward her. The spear through his chest snagged on the ground. He barely felt it.

Maybe they would live in Palau, sail the islands in a catamaran yacht together, his arm around her and her head on his shoulder, with calypso music playing through the speakers and their scuba tanks and gear drying in the wind.

He reached out and dragged her toward him.

Maybe she would never want to see him again. He could even live with that. He could live with anything, just as long as Jordan was all right.

Juan lifted his head and saw what was left of her face. A spreading fan of crimson soaked the dirt beneath her head.

He let go. Rolled onto his back. Stared up at the indifferent sky.

He and Jordan lay next to each other, head to toe. Without looking, he reached down and found her hand. Took it.

Juan floated in roaring silence.

Her crooked little pinky against his palm, her fingers so lifeless in his.

Shapes moved around him. People. Distant sounds, muffled, as if he were underwater. Somebody leaned over him, sweeping her curly hair away from her face and up behind her ear. A woman with tape across her nose. Why was she crying? None of them were responsible for each other here. Someone had explained that fact, but he couldn't remember who.

The woman touched his chest, saying something to him. Her warm tears splashed his face. Then she moved away, disappearing from his field of view.

Curious, he turned his head to follow her with his eyes. Now someone else—a stocky man with silver hair—came over the crest of the ridge. Juan knew these people, but their names weren't important right now. They didn't matter.

Nothing mattered anymore.

The big silver-haired man reached behind him with a shaking hand and collapsed, sitting down hard on the ground. Leaning forward, he put his face in his hands, shaking his head from side to side. The woman ran over to him. She grabbed one of his hands and tried to pull him to his feet. She pointed back at Juan, but she couldn't get the big man to stand up. She was still crying—and shouting at the man, too.

Camilla. He remembered her name.

Her actions disturbed him. They reminded him that something terrible had happened. He couldn't think about it just yet. He looked away.

A smaller woman—a girl, really—huddled on the rocks nearby, arms wrapped around her knees, face buried in her arms. She had saved his life, but she shouldn't have done it. The cost had been too high. Another woman, older, with spiky short hair, squatted next to the girl and hugged her. The older woman helped her up. As she led the girl away, she glared at Juan. Her pale eyes bored into him, furious but cold, as if this was all his fault.

He stared up at the sky again. He was starting to remember what had just happened.

It *was* his fault. All of it.

The woman he loved lay dead at his side. Dead because of him.

He couldn't run away from that.

Ever.

Juan could sense a gulf of despair opening beneath him, ready to drag him under. A bottomless void like the Blue Hole in Belize, like the Marianas Trench—an ocean of pain so vast, so black, so limitless, it promised suffering without surcease.

He now understood that he had only swum in its shallows before, even when he faced his brother on the boat and realized what he had done by running away—how he had killed his sister, his mother, his whole family. It yawned below him once again, an abyss grown so unfathomable that if he allowed himself so much as a glimpse into its depths, he would drown.

What had happened here would destroy him if he let it. So he buried it instead, pushing it down inside him.

He let go of her hand.

Juan tried to sit up but couldn't. Something snagged on the ground, holding him: the metal shaft poking out of his back near his elbow. He twisted his torso to the side and was able to sit up. It hurt, but not as much as he expected.

He stood.

Reaching behind him, he wrapped a hand around the barbed point and pulled. The shaft slid through his chest, scraping along a rib as inch after inch of blood-coated steel shaft emerged behind him. The angle was shallow. The end popped free, and a stream of blood poured from the hole in the wet suit, spattering the ground behind him. It slowed to a trickle.

Why was he alive? He shouldn't be. She had shot him in the chest, dead center. He touched his sternum, felt the rip in the neoprene. Tracing the rip sideways with his finger, he found a bleeding hole where the shaft had entered his skin at an angle, right below his pectoral muscle. Sliding his fingers back to the centerline—above his heart—he widened the gap torn in his wet suit, and felt something underneath. It felt like rock. Rock split in half.

Wincing with pain, he reached behind him to grab the lanyard and unzip his wet suit. He scooped the collar under his chin and pulled, sliding the neoprene down his chest. The *megalodon* pendant he wore was broken; the fossilized shark tooth had cracked in half when it absorbed most of the impact, shunting the spear sideways.

Camilla, Mason, and Dmitry stood a small distance away. Juan looked at Camilla's tear-streaked face, seeing her wide, horrified eyes. With the merciless clinical clarity that follows a deep emotional shock, he could read her thoughts on her face.

She thought he wasn't dealing with this right. She thought there was something wrong with him. But there wasn't. He was going to be okay.

Juan looked down at Jordan.

The black whirlpool swirled open beneath him again, threatening to suck him into its bottomless depths, but he pushed it down and chained it shut.

Jordan was dead. He needed to bury her.

Day 8

Friday: December 28, 2012

CHAPTER 166

Camilla looked down at the orange line in the sand. Ignoring the tremor in the pit of her stomach, she stepped over the line and walked briskly across the causeway toward the northern part of the island: orange territory— JT's territory.

Yesterday's tragedy tore at her heart: Jordan dead, Juan wounded, Natalie traumatized, Brent suffering a total emotional collapse. In the aftermath, the doctor had been totally useless, staggering away with the stooped shoulders of a broken man. She had found him a half hour later inside the station, kneeling in a pool of vomit, so drugged he couldn't stand.

She, Mason, and Dmitry had cleaned and dressed Juan's wound themselves, as well as they could, using supplies from the first-aid kit. Juan tolerated their medical fumbling with an air of impatience. The spear had gone through his chest at a shallow angle. But Juan needed a hospital, and soon.

His emotional and mental state worried Camilla even more than his chest injury, though. Juan's gaze was dull, his face blank. His responses, when he did respond, frightened her with their dislocated calmness.

He had buried Jordan himself. Refusing help from anyone, he had built a cairn of rocks over Jordan's body while Camilla stood sobbing nearby. Moving like a staggering automaton, his face a mask, he piled rock after rock over her, covering her.

Mason stayed some distance away from Camilla, his face sober. She was hurt by that, too—Mason didn't trust her anymore. That he could think *she* might have a part in this horror cut her to the core. Dmitry had finally taken her by the arm and led her away, still sobbing.

As sad as she was for Jordan, it was Juan who choked her up now. He reminded Camilla of the bird she saw the first day—the mortally wounded auklet stumbling through its daily routine, not understanding that it was already dead. Sooner or later, the enormity of what happened would hit Juan. It would break through his defenses and crush him in his tracks. She was afraid for him, afraid of what it would do to him when it hit.

But after spending another sleepless night alone and wide-eyed in the station, Camilla knew she had to act. She had to pull them all together again somehow. Their situation was too desperate to worry about individual risk. They were dying, one by one.

Striding past the end of the narrow causeway, her purse clamped under her arm, she crossed onto the part of the island that resembled a seahorse's head. Her heart thudded in her chest, but she didn't slow her pace. The rocky ground around her was empty, mocking her errand with its silence.

Camilla was afraid for two reasons. There was always the possibility that JT was the person they were looking for. If he was, then coming out here on her own was probably suicide. But she was even more afraid she would find that, like Heather and Jacob, JT had also disappeared. Or that she would find him dead.

In hindsight, Camilla could see how a hidden hand had set a terrible clockwork machine in motion on the island, with the contestants themselves serving as the gears. She understood only too well now how that fatal mechanism had been wound with relentless precision, turn by turn, tighter and tighter, ratcheting the tension in the springs until they snapped, triggering the cascade of violence that led to the deaths of Lauren, Travis, and Jordan.

But the machine's architect was not content simply to let it wind down and let events take their own awful course. He or she also hid behind a familiar face while prowling the shadows around them, like a predator stalking the herd, taking the unwary. Taking Heather and Jacob. Taking Natalie, whose rescue became a debt so tragically repaid.

Who was the puppet master?

Veronica was a multiple murderer—the "black widow," Mason had called her. Camilla had no doubt she had killed her second husband, also, in a carefully premeditated deception that she had gotten clean away with. She had seen Veronica kill Travis right in front of them. But she didn't think Veronica was the puppet master. She was a deeply troubled woman, but she was only another victim here.

Camilla considered Juan, and her eyes blurred. Logically, it was possible that he had set this up but the plan had backfired somehow, dragging him into the machinery right along with his victims. Her heart told her differently, though. It wasn't Juan.

She was also sure it wasn't Dmitry. The three scientists were the most unwitting victims of all, caught like flies in a web constructed for others. Two of them were dead now. She liked Dmitry's stolid, no-nonsense realism. She was sure she could trust him.

Which left Mason and Brent. The more she thought about it, the more convinced she was that one of them was the puppet master. But which one? She had genuinely liked Mason and enjoyed his cheerful irreverence in the face of even the grimmest realities. She missed the closeness they had before, lost now to distrust. And Brent had always been the voice of reason, despite the drugs. He had protected her from Travis and made her feel safe, tended their injuries time and time again. Jordan's death had been the final straw that pushed him over the edge. It had shattered Brent. Camilla had seen his face. *No one* could possibly have faked that reaction—utter, hopeless despair. Nobody. Which brought her back to Mason. But Mason couldn't have chained the scientist's boat.

She had been over and over it all in her head and was no closer to an answer.

She needed to find JT.

Turning in a circle, she scanned the rocky ground around her. Nothing moved but seals. She started forward again, and her foot met a brief resistance. A pile of rocks clattered to the ground several yards away. Leaping backward, she glanced toward the tumbling rockpile, immediately registering it as a diversion. She spun in the opposite direction.

A section of ground behind her rose up, shedding dust and small rocks. A dirty layer of cloth flipped back from the rising hump, throwing more dust into the breeze.

JT stood still and motionless, watching her with no expression on his face. He had a black tactical knife in his hand.

Camilla swallowed. She crouched and felt the ground near her feet, never taking her eyes off JT. Her fingers found the thin length of trip wire.

"If that had been a claymore," JT said, "you'd be a fifty-foot red stain decorating those rocks right now. What do you want, Camilla?"

"Jordan is dead," she said.

"I heard. Yesterday." Under his terrifying coat of dirt and camouflage paint, he looked mournful. "Didn't think that girl *could* be killed. She was something. I only met one or two like her in the service."

"Oh god, JT—I can't believe she's gone. And Juan… he's walking around acting like he's fine, but he's all shattered to pieces inside, holding himself together like a broken car windshield…"

"Safety glass."

"Yeah." Camilla swiped a hand across her face and took a deep breath. "I feel like he's going to come apart any minute. After what happened to his family, this'll kill him."

"Might not just be him it kills." JT walked over and squatted beside her. He began winding the trip wire. "In Fallujah, a guy in our unit—Robinson—caught an RPG round in the gut. But it didn't go off. Corpsman was afraid taking it out would detonate it, so he cleared the rest of us out of the room. He and Robinson's lieutenant stayed. We could hear Robinson through the wall, saying he was fine, it was nothing, he could still fight."

"What happened?"

"What do you think happened?" He shoved the coiled tripwire in his pocket and stood. "Grenade in his gut finally went off. Cut him in half—killed all three of them. But you're making a mistake, feeling sorry for Juan. That motherfucker is with Julian."

Camilla grabbed his arm. "We found Julian. Dead."

JT rubbed the back of his head. *"Dead?"*

"For days. Weeks."

He was silent for a while. "That's bad," he finally said. "Real bad. We've been watching—I don't know—canned cut scenes, like a video game."

She nodded. "I've been trying to figure out how it was done. I feel pretty stupid, actually. We should have been suspicious that Julian never mentioned anyone by name when he talked about game outcomes. It was always 'the winner' this, 'the losing team' that. It just seemed like that was how he naturally talked: kind of formal, like he was speaking to the audience, too."

JT seemed to consider this. "Juan must have killed him when they came out here earlier, to set up the cameras and stuff. There's probably some dead computer geeks, too, got turned into shark bait."

"It wasn't Juan," she said.

He shook his head. "I know it was Juan that set this thing up. What I *don't* know is why."

"What makes you so sure it was Juan?"

"Because I *saw* him, sneaking down by the dock dressed in dive gear, the first few nights. I followed him, lost him when he went into the water."

JT looked at her, and his expression hardened. "He told me he didn't have air tanks. He lied about that, Camilla. You *know* he did. Why are you protecting him?"

She turned away. "Come with me."

"Why?"

"Because I want to show you something."

• • •

The scuba tank lay, forgotten, where it had fallen yesterday. Camilla stood it upright and dusted off the hoses.

"How does this work?" she asked.

JT rotated the valve at the top. With a slight hiss, the hoses stiffened. He looked at Camilla, a question in his eyes.

She gestured at the mouthpiece. "There's going to be something wrong with it. Be careful."

JT held the regulator away from his face and pressed the purge valve. There was a loud hiss as air escaped. He sniffed at the vented gas, then moved the valve closer and did it again. Opening his mouth, he bit down on the mouthpiece.

He took a shallow breath. Then a deeper one.

Speaking through the mouthpiece, his voice was muffled. "Whatever you thought this would prove, you were wrong."

"It's working fine?" She sagged in disappointment.

"Tank air always tastes stale," he said. "I did quite a bit of diving during my training. I should know."

"I was so certain," she said. "Let me try." Taking the mouthpiece from JT, she drew a tentative breath from it, and then another, fuller one. It tasted a little funny. The air seemed normal, but she found the taste strangely familiar. Taking a deep breath, she held it in her lungs.

"I can use it to go get help." JT took the regulator back and put it in his mouth, breathing deeply. "I'll stay deep, avoid the sharks." He giggled.

Camilla sat down hard. Her head buzzed, and her vision darkened around the edges. A ringing noise filled her ears, and she tumbled sideways, catching herself with one hand. She felt like laughing, too. Then she felt alarm.

"Take the mouthpiece out right now," she said.

"Regulator." JT giggled again and sat down fast. "It's called a regulator."

Camilla grabbed the hose and yanked the regulator out of his mouth.

"Hey," he protested. He took a few deep lungfuls of air, and his face turned serious. "My head's spinning."

She recognized the dry, pasty taste in her mouth now. "That's nitrous!"

"What?"

"Nitrous oxide. Laughing gas. In college, we did whippets at parties sometimes—you know, those little metal nitrous canisters cooks use in whipped-cream dispensers? They were popular."

JT was silent, breathing heavily.

She poked him in the chest. "Juan wouldn't have gotten very far with this tank. If he had actually tried to use it, he would have passed out underwater. Drowned."

"That's messed up."

"Somebody planted this tank on the island for Juan to find. Now, because of it, he's hurt and Jordan is dead." She held his eye. "Please come back with me, JT. Juan's not the one. We need your help, or we're all going to die."

"Who do you think it is?" he asked.

"Mason or Brent. It's got to be."

"I'm not so sure what a rigged scuba tank proves. Person who did all this is one tricky motherfucker."

"None of us are going to last long on our own."

JT shook his head. "I survived five days alone in enemy territory, hunted through the Korengal like an animal, in hundred-and-thirty-degree heat, with a busted arm swollen up like a sausage. This is nothing compared to that. I'll take my chances."

CHAPTER 167

The sun was setting. Its rays painted the seals with a mellow gold light as they jostled each other on the rocks around Juan. A chilly breeze made him squint.

He stood in front of the pyramid of rocks he had piled over Jordan. The red team's flag waved above, planted at the head of her grave.

He placed a hand on the cairn and silently bowed his head.

Squeezing his eyes shut, he remembered a long-ago conversation with his father. Juan was in his late teens. They were on the veranda of the summer villa in Cartagena, which overlooked the water. Juan was eagerly awaiting his own departure for Malpelo Island in the morning. He planned to dive with Malpelo's hammerhead sharks.

Usually, he felt that the less he knew about family business the better. But this particular question had nagged at him for weeks.

"*Discúlpame, papá,*" he said. "What Gaviria says, that we killed his niece..."

"It is of no consequence." Roberto Martín Antonio y Gabriel lit a cigar and picked up a coca leaf that lay beside the crystal ashtray. A courier had brought the leaf earlier. White fungus coated its underside.

"It is like this." Roberto jabbed a finger of his cigar hand at the white fuzz on the leaf. "*Fusarium oxysporum.* The *norteamericano* DEA plans to spray our fields with this, César. Our *presidente*—Pastrana, that weak woman—is colluding with them. This fungus rots the leaf from the inside out, leaving the plant vulnerable to insects and other diseases."

"*Perdóname, papá.*" Juan slouched in his chair and looked out over the water, wishing he hadn't said anything, wishing he were already on the boat, miles away from here. "I don't understand."

"Sentimentality is like this fungus. If you let it rule your actions, it will rot you from inside. Your enemies will smell your weakness and take everything from you."

Juan's mouth tightened. "But surely, if we are seen to target women and the innocent, then how can we ensure that *mamá* and Constancia..."

Roberto grabbed Juan's wrist. "This is my fault. When I was your age I was poor, living on the street, fighting to make a name. I built this..." He waved the cigar at the walls around them. "...all of this, from nothing. But you, César, you have always been given everything. I have raised a spoiled playboy who talks to me about the 'innocent.'"

Roberto leaned toward him, and Juan looked down, wishing he had never spoken.

533

"Tell me, who among us is innocent? Is this something you have learned from those *chocha* sisters of San Bartolomé I pay to teach you?" Roberto spat on the tile floor of the veranda and looked away.

"All these fine, fancy manners and intellectual *mierda,* and you haven't learned a thing about how to be a man."

"*Papá,* if something were to happen to *mamá* or Constancia—"

"Then we would exact vengeance—a terrible vengeance. But we cannot allow fear to make us weak."

"Keyser Söse…" Juan muttered it under his breath.

"Listen to me, César, instead of mocking the father who loves you. Listen well. The nonstop holiday you live—this endless vacation—will end one day, I promise you. You will be the head of this family after I am gone. We must never, *NEVER* allow sentimentality to prevent us from doing what we must to survive. I will not have a weak son."

Standing in front of Jordan's cairn, head still bowed, Juan fought to control his emotions. Sharp pain pierced his chest. He was truly his father's son: he had destroyed everyone he loved.

He lifted the broken *megalodon* tooth—the pendant his brother Álvaro had given him—from around his neck and laid it on the mounded rocks of Jordan's grave. She had never learned to hold a part of herself back. Her ability to manipulate others had always protected her. Confident in her own dominance, she had approached her world with a childlike innocence. She had opened her heart to him, and he had killed her for it. Better that, instead, he had never been born.

The back of Juan's neck prickled in warning. He spun around and dropped into a crouch, raising his hands.

Veronica had already managed to get quite close. She hunched ten yards away. Seeing her quarry had spotted her, she straightened up and stepped closer. Juan matched her pace with a backward step toward the water.

"Where's Natalie?" she asked. Her large, pale eyes glowed luminous orange in the dying light of sunset. "I expected to find her with you."

Juan's pulse quickened, sending a stabbing throb through his side. "How long has she been gone?"

"I told her it's not safe around here." Veronica's eyes gleamed like a predator's as she moved toward him, but her voice held sad resignation. "She wouldn't listen to me. She's an adult, Juan. I can't make her do anything."

Juan stepped backward, into the water. "Julian is dead. One of *us* set this all up."

"I figured as much," she said.

"Who do you think did this?"

She stopped for a moment and tilted her head to the side, regarding him with her icy cobra's gaze.

"I don't know. Maybe Mason. He was a banker, and money clearly isn't an issue for whoever put this circus together."

"What about JT?"

She snorted. "I can't see it. He's a big, frightened kid, underneath all that tough-guy posturing. He's hiding, afraid of his own shadow right now, Juan…"

She licked her teeth. "...scared shitless."

Veronica's disturbing gaze crawled over his face. Her breathing sped up. "But we both know there's someone else here with that kind of money; I'm looking at him right now."

Her pupils flared visibly.

"Did *you* take Natalie? Maybe the first time, you brought her back just to fuck with us."

Waist-deep in the water now, Juan shook his head. "I don't have that money anymore. I didn't want it; it was filth. I took only what I needed to escape, and when I came to California I got rid of that, too. Donated it to drug rehab programs."

"Poor Natalie." Veronica stood at the waterline, watching him intently. "She was so infatuated with you, Juan. I tried to tell her, but she didn't listen. Tried to tell her what you were really like."

Juan winced. "Come any closer and I'll drown you."

Veronica stopped advancing.

"You know what's weird?" she said. "Travis's body is gone."

"Could he have still been alive?"

Her small, throaty laugh chilled him. "No chance. You didn't see him, did you? I broke his hyoid bone, Juan. I *crushed* his trachea. He was dead before he hit the floor; he just hadn't realized it yet. And then I sent the scalpel through his carotid artery."

She shook her head. "No, somebody took him, which is kind of creepy if you ask me. But it's not really all that important."

The sunset reflected in her luminous irises, its glow now fading to red. Her tongue flicked her upper teeth.

"Sooner or later, I'll find out which one of you took Natalie, Juan..."

Veronica's grin was terrifying.

"...or maybe I never will. In the end, it probably doesn't matter. I can still make sure that person doesn't leave this island alive."

With a last lingering look, she turned away.

Standing in the waist-deep water, Juan watched her retreat.

Day 9

Saturday: December 29, 2012

CHAPTER 168

Camilla squatted beside Dmitry on the beach, looking at the four logs left over from the seal barricade. Dmitry had pushed them into an eight-foot-by-three-foot rectangle. He was shirtless, his broad back running sweat.

"A raft," she said.

He swiped a forearm across his forehead and nodded.

"*Da*. But this is no good. We need more logs. Need to take them from barricade, but that crazy woman says she kill me if I try."

She inspected the raft. It looked flimsy. It needed more logs, or it wouldn't support even one person's weight without rolling.

"So how will you finish it?" she asked.

"I don't know." He raised his eyebrows and grinned crookedly at her. "Maybe tomorrow something changes; maybe not. This..." He waved a hand at the raft. "It is something to do, instead of sitting and waiting for somebody to kill me."

Camilla smiled.

"We can use the chains to tie it together," she said. "I'll go get them."

She pushed her hair behind her ear.

"Let me help."

Day 10

Sunday: December 30, 2012

CHAPTER 169

Morning. Mason was fairly sure it was December thirtieth. The days were blurring by. The island's remaining inhabitants had retreated to their separate corners and were all doing the same thing, it seemed: nothing much. Resting, operating at reduced levels of physical activity to conserve their energy. He grinned, thinking about it. It was probably instinctive behavior.

For survivor types, anyway.

Mason himself spent long hours each day just sitting or lying on the beach in the meager shade provided by the bluffs. He stared at the mainland, beckoning from across the wave-churned channel, so tantalizingly close. Watching the far shore each day, his normally overactive mind blank, the hours would pass in what seemed to be minutes. The clouds would crawl silently across the sky and the teeming colonies of seals and hopping birds would churn on the beaches around him, until the shadows lengthened and the air grew cold. Even in his low-energy meditative state, Mason's eyes were always alert for signs of human activity across the channel. But only black elephant seals moved on the distant beaches.

He found it hard to believe they had been on the island for only ten days. It seemed much longer, civilized life a fading, distant memory. Now, limping out of the station building to greet the morning, he raised his face to the sun. Despite the pain in his knee and not being able to sleep for more than an hour at a time, he felt refreshed. His original plan had been to stay awake all night again. But in the end he figured it wasn't worth it. With his knee in the shape it was in, his odds of surviving another confrontation were not great. If anyone was going to come for him in the night, at least he would be better rested when they did.

Mason had slept with the bear spray hugged to his chest, though. A calculated risk was one thing; trusting oneself fully to the whims of fate was another.

Something near his feet caught his eye, and he grinned in surprise. A plastic jug of water sat in front of his door. It was intact and appeared to be full. He was very thirsty. He lowered himself, carefully sliding his left leg along the ground to avoid bending the damaged knee, and unscrewed the cap.

Raising the jug, he drank. The water tasted clean, refreshing. He screwed the cap back on and stood with awkward movements. Carrying the jug, he limped up the scattered boardwalk, passing the broken catchment basin and the cistern where Julian's body lay.

He reached the island's high point, beside the wreckage of the fallen lighthouse tower. Leaning against the metal framework to take the weight off his leg, he scanned the island around him. To the north, in the barren rockiness of orange territory, nothing moved. Down on the beach—black territory—Dmitry dragged a log across the sand, toward a makeshift raft. Mason grinned, shaking his head.

He looked south, toward red territory, and his grin faded. Raising a hand to his forehead, he shaded his eyes.

The barricade was down. A section had fallen, or the seals had breached it, sometime during the night. Seals and sea lions humped across the open ground and lounged around the two houses. More poured through the gap in the barricade, scattering the fallen logs.

The houses themselves—the Victorian and the Greek Revival—both looked abandoned. Loose plastic sheeting flapped from the windows, dancing in the breeze. A section of plastic that had torn completely free blew across the flat ground, sending the seabirds in its path flapping into the air. The wayward plastic came to rest against the chicken coop, held there by the wind. Watching it slip free and blow away, Mason felt an uncharacteristic melancholy. Humanity's tenuous foothold in this place would never be more than temporary. They did not belong here.

Nature had once again reclaimed its own. It was erasing all traces of them.

Near the chicken coop and the steps that led down to the beach, a small figure stood on the wooden walkway. Squinting, he tried to make out who it was, and finally recognized Camilla. Curly brown hair billowing in the swift breeze, she stood very still with her arms crossed, watching the houses.

She turned her face toward him. In the distance, he couldn't see her expression. Her body language was guarded, distrustful.

He liked Camilla. He was amused to see that she had her purse slung over her shoulder and tucked under her arm, as if she were waiting for a cab on a busy Manhattan street. He waved to her. After a moment, she waved back. But slowly... tentatively.

"Santa came late this year," he shouted. He held up the jug of water, displaying it. "Did he leave you anything?"

"Yes. I found some water, too," she yelled back. "I was afraid to try it at first, but I couldn't resist."

He thought about the look he had seen pass between Lauren and Juan when they hauled the water back to shore from the boulder. The way she had counted the jugs, frowning.

"I'm pretty sure our Santa wears black," he shouted.

She pointed at the abandoned houses. "I'm worried about Natalie and Veronica."

Shouting back and forth was getting old. Mason limped down the slope toward her.

"I don't think you need to worry about Veronica," he said. "She's fine. I ran into her yesterday."

He looked down at his knee, swollen to the size of a grapefruit, and stopped to rest his leg. "Well, to be more accurate, I tried to run *away* from her yesterday. She looked like she was in great health when she broke my knee."

"Oh god." Camilla visibly cringed. "Why did she do that?"

"Someone took Natalie again."

"No!"

"Veronica's psychotic, and you've seen what she's capable of. I think she's decompensating—she's definitely a danger to all of us now. You shouldn't be out here alone."

He started toward Camilla again, but she backed away toward the beach steps. He was surprised to find that her distrust made him feel hollow inside. Empty.

"You should let Brent take a look at your knee," she shouted.

"I don't think my HMO considers him an in-network provider anymore."

"Mason!" But she kept her distance.

"Well, actually, I *did* ask him, but he ignored me. The good doc was a little busy shooting up at the time. I did snag some painkillers out of the first-aid kit, but only the ones he didn't want."

He laughed. "Like a kid with his Halloween candy—he let me take the apples and raisins but kept all the chocolate."

Grinning, he looked at her purse again, and realized what she probably had in there.

He gave her a cheery wave, and limped back up the hill.

Camilla was full of surprises.

CHAPTER 170

Dmitry peered through the doorway of the blockhouse. Juan stood with both hands flat on the table, frowning down at the map again.

"Don't you get tired of staring at map?" Dmitry stepped inside to join him.

Most of the pen marks Juan had made on the map earlier, along the shoreline and bluffs, were now crossed out with thick X marks. Dmitry pointed at one.

"This is cave where you found generators, *da*?"

Juan nodded. "Other than the generators and the fuel, it was empty. The power cables from the houses were hidden under the dirt, running down over the bluff edge and into the cave entrance."

"These other places—you think maybe you will find another cave?"

Juan indicated one of the pen marks. "This is the one you told me about, filled with concrete when they built the station." His eyes narrowed. "Over the last couple days, I've checked 'em all. I'm missing something."

"What are you trying to find in cave?"

"A communications uplink. Or at least the jammer preventing our phones from working. Does your phone still have a charge?"

"*Da.* I am keeping it off." Dmitry laid a hand on Juan's shoulder. "Thank you for water, my friend."

"The Coast Guard built the lighthouse and the two mansions in the late eighteen hundreds. You don't need pumps and boilers to run a lighthouse." Juan tapped the station buildings on the map. "So what were these?"

Dmitry had no idea.

"The big factory building—what was it for?" Pointing at the map, Juan covered his mouth with his other hand and coughed, turning away. But Dmitry didn't miss the way he wiped his palm on his thigh, leaving behind a smear of red.

A weight settled over Dmitry's shoulders. "I don't know. Is not important now. We are building a raft, to get you to hospital—"

"Come with me." Juan exited the blockhouse, and Dmitry followed him to the edge of the bluff. Juan pointed at the water of the channel. Shielding his forehead with one hand, Dmitry followed his finger to somewhere else. And then a third location.

After a season spent on the water, in the ORCA, his eyes were well trained.

"*Ras, dvah, tree, chetiree, poht, shest...*" With growing amazement, he counted the trailing wakes and gray dorsal fins.

Juan gripped his shoulder and spun him, staring into his face with a grim expression. "When I pulled you out of the water five days ago, that shark wanted a piece of you. You and I both know that's wrong, but we saw it."

There was nothing Dmitry could say.

Juan pointed at the water again. "Five days ago, there were only two or three sharks out there. Now, there are more—a lot more." He turned away and limped back toward the blockhouse. "Your raft will just be the appetizer tray."

CHAPTER 171

Veronica blinked. Her eyes strained at the gloom around her, opening wider and wider. She could feel them bulging from their sockets as she tried to see where she was. The uneven ceiling above her looked like rock.

She couldn't turn her head.

The tendons tightened in her neck as she strained to turn her face to the side. She tried to open her mouth. She couldn't move her jaw.

She was paralyzed.

She could barely breathe.

Rage coursed through her body. She would kill the person responsible. She would kill them all. Just as soon as she managed to get up.

A hollow chuckle sounded in the distance, echoing off rock walls of the small space around her. A rhythmic scraping noise drew closer and closer.

A new emotion crept into the mix of fury and frustration that twisted her face: fear. She rolled her eyes to the side as far as she could, staring, trying to pierce the semidarkness. She could see nothing.

"Ah, you're awake, I see. Good. Because it's that time again."

Something moved into Veronica's field of view, hovering an inch from her eye.

A needle.

Liquid dripped from the tip of the hypodermic syringe. Her eyes crossed, focusing on it, helpless to look away.

The person holding the syringe remained a dim, blurry outline leaning over her.

"Rocuronium only lasts an hour or so. Guessing the right amount for someone like you was tricky. Too little and you'd still be able move. Too much and you wouldn't be able to breathe. You're lucky I'm getting good at this. It took me quite a number of experiments until I started getting the amounts right."

A hand cupped her breast. Then it trailed down her stomach, touching, exploring, teasing.

I'll tear you apart, you fucking animal. I'll break you into little pieces.

Veronica strained to move an arm, a hand, a leg, a finger—anything. Her own body betrayed her. She was helpless, unable to protect herself.

"I think I nailed the correct dosage in your case. Now, as soon as we get a few uninterrupted hours, we can have lots of fun together. What do you think?"

Fingers probed at her roughly, where she was the most vulnerable.

549

Terror and fury vied for control in Veronica's mind as her eyes followed the needle's descent toward the jugular vein in her neck.

CHAPTER 172

Juan stared at the scattered rocks of Jordan's cairn. Jaw trembling, he gritted his teeth and strangled the guttural sounds trying to force themselves from deep within his chest. His shaking fingers ratcheted into fists, clenching with a brutal force that sent spikes of pain stabbing through his side.

Nearby, the flag lay in the rubble, discarded. The broken *megalodon* pendant had been trampled into the sand. Rocks were strewn in all directions, radiating outward from the gaping, empty hole where he had laid her lifeless body to rest.

Jordan was gone.

"Come, my friend." Dmitry's sorrowful voice came from behind him. "This is bad, I know, but you must come now. We need to make plan."

Shaking his head, Juan raised his fists to his temples, unable to speak. He squeezed his eyes shut against the desecration, seeing Jordan sitting on the cot in the blockhouse, the forgotten tears of an actress drying on her cheeks as she looked at him with frank curiosity. Jordan, wondering why her tears hadn't worked on him the way they always had on everyone else. Jordan asking him, *"Can you catch me a fish?"*

A shuddering breath exploded from his lungs. He lowered his arms and gripped the shaft of the speargun that had once belonged to her, but was now his forever.

I'll catch you a fish, he silently promised her. *I'll go catch you some fish, right now.*

And then he would drag whoever he caught back to the blockhouse, where the concrete walls would muffle their screams, and he would ask his questions again. But this time he would allow no evasions. He would tolerate no lies. He would fire up the portable generator and, with one hundred twenty Volts AC to help him get answers, he would learn everything.

He would find out *who.*

He would find out *why.*

Pressing a hand against his side and ignoring Dmitry's calls, Juan stalked toward the blockhouse. The hole in his chest stung and burned, and he welcomed the pain. It was all he had now. t gave him focus. It would see him through this. And he would share it a thousandfold with whoever was responsible for bringing Jordan here.

Until he found that person, they would *all* share Juan's pain—innocent and guilty alike. Because in the end, his father was right. If you hesitated, afraid to harm the innocent, it would cost you everyone you loved. It would leave you with nothing.

Leave you a ghost, cold and dead inside.
Dead but still standing.

• • •

Camilla stood in the doorway of the blockhouse, watching him approach. Her face was cold and unfriendly.

Juan shouldered past her, ignoring her. He grabbed the wet suit off the rack. He would spare no one in his search for the truth, but he would save her for last. As he peeled his shirt off, he could feel her staring at his back, not saying anything. The cold way she was looking at him now was new; she had never looked at him that way before.

"Where are you going, Juan?" So cold, too, her voice.

Shrugging into his wet suit, he didn't answer.

"We're all dying out here," she said.

He tugged the lanyard, zipping up the back.

"When are you going to understand? This is not what we need from you."

"I'll take care of it." He picked up the speargun again.

"No, you won't. You'll *die*, Juan. And so will the rest of us. We need to help each other."

"What *you* need is to stay out of my way now," he said. "Ask Jordan how well my help worked out for her. Ask Natalie."

"Natalie's *gone*. Don't you care at all what happens to the rest of us? Mason's crippled. Veronica's gone insane. Brent's killing himself with drugs. JT's hiding under a rock." She laid a hand on his arm. "We need a leader, Juan. We need *you*."

He turned away.

"Mason's ten times the man you are." She sounded furious now.

"Go lay your guilt trip on him, then."

"She told me." The fury faded from her voice, replaced by bleak resignation. "She tried to tell me about you, but I misunderstood what she was saying. You're afraid to let anybody in." She grabbed her purse to leave and looked at him with disgust.

"Jordan was right about you. You're a coward, Juan."

The strength drained out of his legs, and he sat down hard on the cot. The bands around his chest tightened with crushing force. He couldn't look at her, so he looked up at the ceiling instead. "What did she say about me?"

"She said not to trust you."

He closed his eyes.

"I can see why, *now*." Camilla gave a pitiless laugh. "But at the time, I didn't understand what she meant. I thought she was telling me you were with Julian, because of what else she said."

"What else did she say about me?"

"It wasn't about you. I only thought it was. She said that the name of the company pretty much told us who set this up."

"The Hippocrates quote?" He opened his eyes and stared at her. "*Ars longa, vita brevis*, and all that? But I don't see what it tells us at all."

"She said *what* didn't matter. *Who* did. And, Juan, I figured you would have gone to strict Catholic schools. Latin would have been part of your curriculum."

His jaw dropped. "No, don't you see? Who! Who! Hippocrates, *that's* who! That same quote probably appears in half the medical textbooks ever published."

He stood and grabbed her arm.

"Camilla, Hippocrates was a *doctor!*"

PART V

FINAL ROUND

CHAPTER 173

Mason raised a hand as they approached.

"Waiter, another mojito, please. The Cruzan Estate Silver, and easy on the ice."

He had dragged a chair and a threadbare blanket from the station to the top of the hill, where he now sat, next to the wreckage of the tower. Jordan's grisly banner stood behind him, the seal head on top a festering, flyblown horror. The corners of the blanket were wedged between the twisted struts of the tower, blocking the sun like a beachside umbrella. He lounged in the shade, bad leg extended, like a tourist on vacation.

Camilla pushed ahead of Juan and Dmitry and stopped in front of Mason.

"We know who is behind this," she said.

Mason nodded. "Brent. I figured out the answer to your question about the connection between us all. The best place to look if you wanted to find proven survivors."

"A hospital," she said.

• • •

The afternoon sun beat down on their impromptu four-person council of war. The blank-eyed seal head watched from atop the flagpole, lending its silent approval.

"Why this doctor wants to kill everyone?" Dmitry asked.

"I don't know." Camilla's throat was tight. What had *she* done to deserve Brent's hatred? "I just don't know."

"Let's ask the man himself," Juan said. "When's the last time one of us saw him?"

"Last night," Mason said. "Going into the factory building. Whatever else our Dr. Moreau is, he was drugged to the gills. You should have seen his eyes."

Juan leaned against the wreckage of the tower. Looking at his handsome features, Camilla could see no telltale signs of plastic surgery. Undoubtedly, he had used the most skilled surgeons. Any traces they left would be very subtle. But they *would* be noticeable to a trauma doctor digging bullets out of his chest—a doctor fascinated with survivor stories, who might wonder how a charter dive boat captain could afford such an expensive makeover, or why

557

he might need one. A doctor who might secretly begin an investigation to find out who his mystery patient *really* was.

She opened her mouth to say something but noticed that Juan's face was pale. She looked down at his feet instead, and her heart squeezed. "You're bleeding again."

Dime-size drops of blood sprinkled the rocks and streaked his booties. Juan glanced at them. He shrugged. And then he coughed, wiping a hand against his chin.

Camilla stared at him, dismayed to see a smear of blood at the corner of his mouth. That meant the spear had nicked his lung. He was injured even worse than she had thought.

"Confronting Brent will be dangerous," she said. "You and Mason are already in bad shape."

Juan looked away.

"You know what you need to do," she said.

He nodded. "JT."

She took a deep breath. She hated to do this to him, to hurt him again. But she had to.

She reached into her purse, pulled out a black object, and laid it on a waist-high spar of the tower. Covering it with her hand, she hesitated.

What if she did this to him now, and something terrible happened again?

She pulled her hand away to reveal the Glock.

Juan's eyes widened. He looked at her, and sorrow suffused his features.

She held his gaze. The gun that had killed Jordan lay between them—a mute harbinger promising more violence to come. For a long moment, no one said anything.

Then Juan picked up the Glock. "I know where to find JT."

$\bullet \quad \bullet \quad \bullet$

Juan walked onto the dock, the thick rubber soles of his scuba booties thudding on the wooden planks. Camilla stood on the rocky breakwater with Mason and Dmitry, watching him. Water lapped at the sides of the narrow jetty and frothed at the rocks of the shore. Nothing else moved. Camilla could see no sign of anyone else, but she didn't expect to. She had already witnessed how invisible JT could become.

Juan stopped in the middle of the dock and turned to face the island.

"Roll call, Corporal Washington." His voice echoed off the rocks. "Time to redeploy. Mission's changed. DR phase is over. It's now DA."

A splash sounded under the dock, directly below Juan's feet. Ripples spread from beneath the boards. Then a shaved head and broad, muscular shoulders emerged from the water alongside the dock. A dripping JT looked up at him.

"What does a fucking drug lord know about 'deep reconnaisance'? 'Direct action'?"

Juan gave a cold, arrogant smile. "Quite a bit, actually. We had our own private G2, our own intelligence organization, you know. When you brought your war on drugs to our country and Pastrana's 'Plan Colombia' became an excuse for the U.S. to send in your military, we studied you. We dissected your structure, equipment, doctrines, capabilities, weaknesses. We learned you inside out."

He paused to cough.

"That's all in the past, though. I'm a fellow American now. Just a dive boat charter captain, JT."

He took a step forward and held out an arm. "I'm asking for your help."

JT didn't say anything.

Camilla held her breath.

Then JT reached up to clasp Juan's forearm. He hauled himself up out of the water to stand dripping, facing him on the dock. They stood like that for a frozen moment. Then Juan held out JT's Glock, butt first.

JT glanced down at it. Then he shook his head.

"You keep it… Captain."

CHAPTER 174

The ocean lashed against the other side of the seawall. The wind had picked up. It whipped their clothes and blew Camilla's hair about her face. Juan had gathered them in the lee of the seawall, below the three connected buildings that housed the science station. The sun was setting. Shadows crawled across the rocky ground. No windows interrupted the broad shiplap sides of the largest of the three—the factory building. He knew it would be near-dark inside, between the ceiling-height rows of dusty machinery.

They would find Brent there. Juan tried to picture what the doctor might be doing, and couldn't. He faced the others.

"We clear the station room by room. JT and I lead. Dmitry, you and Camilla follow, supporting Mason. With his leg, he's going to need your help keeping up. Everybody, keep your eyes open."

He coughed, spat a dark streak onto the ground, and smeared it away with his foot.

"By now, Brent knows we're onto him. He'll have surprises planned for us. Don't get distracted. Watch out for him circling back around to come at us from behind. But no matter what, I want him alive. Is that clear?"

The taste of blood lingered in his mouth. It was constant now, like the ever-present tickling ache in his side when he breathed.

"Alive." He looked at each of them in turn, but it was himself he was most worried about. Would he be able to control his own reactions when he was face-to-face with the person who had lured Jordan here? "I want some real answers from him. He's got a lot to answer for right now, to all of you. And to *me*."

Juan chopped the air with his hand, giving the signal. JT cocked his leg and piston-kicked the door of the first building, sending it swinging inward to slam against the wall. The loud crash reverberated through the dim rooms beyond. Juan went in low and to the left, speargun in hand. The Glock stayed at his thigh. He knew that once the gun came into play, their chances of taking Brent alive would drop to zero quickly. JT followed almost immediately behind him, holding a thick length of chain doubled in one fist. He went right.

The first room of the station was unoccupied. Juan stared about him in surprise.

Shredded papers rustled along the floor, stirred up by the wind through the open door. The former science station was almost unrecognizable. The scale of destruction visited on it in such a short time defied the imagination. Mangled binders and eviscerated books and reports lay thick on the concrete floor. A chair swayed brokenly from the wall at head height, its legs driven through the plywood wallboard. Pieces of another chair were strewn all around them. The cabinets and drainboard had been ripped away from the wall and lay in a jumbled pile in the corner, splintered and flattened. The twisted frame of a cot leaned upright against another wall. Its vinyl top had been shredded from the frame and now hung in strips that fluttered like flags in the draft from the door.

The large seal skulls had been shattered, their white shards scattered everywhere underfoot. The bone fragments trailed through the darkened doorway that led deeper into the station buildings—into the room where Heather had disappeared.

Juan waved JT forward with another chopping motion of his hand. They went through, weapons ready.

The destruction in this room was even worse. The cots lay in pieces. The card table was broken in half. The remains of the LED lamp were shattered in a corner. Jagged sheets of plywood, torn loose from the wall, dangled askew from one or two corners.

Juan could hear could hear the low exclamations of surprise behind them as Camilla, Dmitry, and Mason entering the first room. But Brent had brought them here and done all this for a reason. He was sure this rampage was meant to distract them from that.

JT pointed silently. Juan followed his finger to a sweatshirt, spread and spiked to the wall like a butterfly on display. The letters "UCSC" on its front were clearly visible—University of California Santa Cruz. The upper half of the sweatshirt was no longer gray. It was stained a uniform dark red. Juan reached up and tore the sweatshirt off the wall, tossing it into a darkened corner. An unpredictable reaction from Dmitry would be a complicating factor they didn't need right now. JT nodded his approval.

Juan waved them forward. The next two rooms also bore signs of the rampage that had torn through the station, although there were no more gruesome displays like Jacob's sweatshirt. Juan and JT stood to each side of the doorway that led into the factory building. Three rows of floor-to-ceiling machinery—a tangle of pipes, ducts, and gauges—stretched like library stacks into the darkness beyond. The narrow corridors between the rows were claustrophobic in their blackness.

This was where Brent would be.

JT lowered the night-vision goggles over his eye. He looked at Juan and gave the ready sign. Behind them, Dmitry, Mason, and Camilla stood in the doorway.

Juan turned to look at Camilla. Her eyes were huge in the darkness, but he could see determination in them, too. She had her fear under tight control.

He didn't want anything to happen to her. He had to keep her safe, no matter what. He was surprised to find how important that seemed to him—more vital even than capturing Brent right now. He held up a palm and motioned her back.

Mason nodded and pulled Camilla and Dmitry a few steps back into the outer room. Juan liked the way Mason and Dmitry hovered protectively near Camilla. He forked two fingers at his eyes and waved a raised finger in a circle—*watch your back.*

Mason raised the can of bear spray and grinned.

Juan returned his attention to the rows of machinery ahead. He met JT's green insect-eyed stare. A sudden stab of pain through the hole in his side made him wince, but he forced himself to straighten.

He peered into the darkness ahead. An icy, detached calm spread through his body and down his arms and legs. His focus tightened. Senses sharpening, he raised the speargun.

Point of no return. This was it.

They slipped around the doorway into the dark, cavernous space beyond.

CHAPTER 175

Camilla watched Juan and JT disappear through the doorway. She had the dive knife strapped to her upper arm, but the thought of using it on Brent seemed inconceivable, horrific. How could someone who had dedicated his life to helping others, who had saved countless lives, be responsible for *this*? Was Brent insane? Did he have dissociative identity disorder—the condition that used to be called "multiple personalities"? She had trusted him. He had made her feel safe. Could they be wrong now? What if it *wasn't* Brent?

Mason tapped her on the shoulder. He pressed something cylindrical into her hands—the bear spray. She looked at him in surprise, shook her head, and frowned at him. What was he doing?

He grinned at her. Then he limped away, retreating through the doorway they had come through. He disappeared back into the rooms they had already cleared.

Alarms clanged through Camilla. Had Mason run away? She didn't think so—she had seen no fear on his face. But if he was betraying them, why had he given her the bear spray?

She stared wide-eyed at Dmitry, who held the concrete-capped pipe over his shoulder like a club. He shook his head, a disgusted expression on his face, and tightened his grip on the pipe.

No sound came from the darkened doorways in either direction. Camilla's pulse raced, faster and faster, thudding in her ears. Her breathing sped up. She gripped the can of bear spray tight, her palms slick with pinprick beads of sweat.

What if it was Brent *and* Mason behind this? Or only Mason?

A cramp tightened her stomach.

Had they gotten this wrong?

CHAPTER 176

The NVD goggles painted the interior of the warehouse in shades of monochromatic green. Three rows of machinery stood out from the background in high relief, stretching to the far wall in the distance. JT glanced at the six-foot wagon-wheel valve, jutting from the end of the center row like the helm of a battleship. A narrow corridor ran along each edge of the factory building, between the rows of machinery and the walls. Two more corridors extended toward the back wall, dividing the rows. The boilers, pipes, pumps, and gauges were packed densely in each row, with thick conduits rising to the ceiling.

JT looked at Juan through the goggles, thinking of their confrontation a few days ago. His bruises still ached, especially his ribs. The blows from the lead-weighted dive belt had maybe cracked one—it sent a spike of pain through his side every time he took a deep breath.

Juan's wet suit looked dark through the goggles, but his face was bright green. His pupils were huge, reflective black marbles trying to penetrate the darkness around them. JT knew he could see almost nothing. He could kill Juan easily right now. One quick blow in the darkness, to the temple or the throat, was all it would take.

But the dive captain was not his enemy.

Juan reached over and laid a hand on his shoulder. He pointed down the right-hand corridor. Then he tapped his own chest and pointed along the left hand side.

JT nodded. Flanking maneuver. But it still left the two central corridors for the enemy to maneuver in without being seen. The machinery was bolted to concrete pads on the floor, and was too heavy to knock over in any case. They couldn't deny the enemy mobility that way.

This would be tricky.

Juan raised the speargun and moved off to the left.

JT entered the corridor on the right and lost sight of him. The pipes and valves projected into the narrow passageway, forcing him to turn sideways in order to edge forward. A cluster of pipes crossed the corridor at head height. He ducked under it, grateful for the clear, green-lit view of the space around him. It would be much harder for Juan, he knew, groping through the blackness. The loss of his eye was maddening, though—a real handicap that narrowed his field of view and made his left side vulnerable. He turned to check his six, scanning around and behind him. Nothing moved.

A secondary corridor cut through the rows of machinery, perpendicular to the corridor he now sidled through, multiplying the possibilities for Brent to slip around behind them. As he passed, he looked down the side corridor, hands tensing on the chain. He was glad to see Juan at the far end, moving parallel to him.

Juan swiveled his head from side to side like a blind man, trying to penetrate the darkness with his ears. Seen through the NVDs, his wide pupils glowed like a raccoon's at night. It was clear he couldn't see JT. He probed the air around him with the tip of the speargun, but JT was gratified to see him angle it downward whenever it swung in his direction—the risk of friendly fire was high enough as it was.

JT moved beyond the side corridor, the wall of machinery on his right hiding Juan from sight once again. They had covered about a third of the building's length. He could see the rear wall now.

So far, there was no sign of Brent.

Something small lay on the floor ahead. JT paused. Wary of his own vulnerability, he knelt down for a closer look at the object: a crushed hypodermic syringe, leaking fluid. As he inspected it, a brief stuttering of light flashed bright green up ahead, accompanied by a crackling noise. JT jerked upright to scan the corridor ahead. The crackle sounded again, and green light flickered across the ground at the next intersection, where a side corridor intersected his. Then it faded to darkness again.

JT checked his six again, making sure no one lurked behind him. Then he cautiously moved forward. He peeked around the corner, muscles loose and ready, the chain held ready to swing.

Someone was coming toward him, striding fast through the narrow side corridor from Juan's side of the building.

JT tensed for action, raising the chain for a low swing to take his opponent's legs out from under him. Then he relaxed in relief. A bundle of pipes crossing at head height hid the face of the approaching figure, but the black neoprene wet suit and catlike panther gait were unmistakable.

He lowered the chain.

Oddly, Juan's speargun looked shorter than before. It now ended in two metal points instead of one. Without breaking stride, Juan raised his free hand to grip the cross-pipe and ducked underneath to stand directly in front of him.

Too late, alarm surged through JT's body. Juan's face was concealed beneath a pair of night-vision goggles similar to his own, but with a triangle of three lenses instead of just two. JT knew the additional lens was an infrared light source.

The long cylinder in Juan's hand was not a speargun. It swung up to connect with JT's neck before he could react. He felt every muscle in his body contract as his world disappeared in a crackling flash of bright white light.

CHAPTER 177

Camilla stared into the space beyond the doorway. The brief flashes of light she had glimpsed had faded. The darkness was absolute again. Her heart pounded in her chest. Raising the can of bear spray, she repositioned herself so she wouldn't catch Dmitry in the crossfire.

He nodded, hefting the length of pipe like a baseball bat.

"I hear something," he whispered, barely audible over the slamming of her heart.

The seconds ticked by, stretching into a minute... then two.

Something moved in the darkness ahead. Camilla could make out a dim shape approaching. Her finger tensed on the trigger of the bear spray. Then she realized it was Juan.

He backed toward them, his attention focused on something deeper in the building. Raising a hand in warning, he eased into the room, passing between her and Dmitry. She saw that Juan was wearing something new: a black plastic backpack with thick corrugated rubber tubes that looped over his shoulders. His shoulders appeared broader than before, his body thicker. He turned toward her, and she noticed he was wearing JT's night-vision goggles. Her finger tightened of its own volition, sending a continuous blast of orange bear spray into the insect-eyed face before she could make a conscious decision to act.

Only then did her mind scream the wet suit-clad intruder's true identity.

Brent.

The bear spray filled the room with a stinging, acrid cloud. She sneezed violently and tears flowed from her eyes. Coughing, she staggered back, still spraying the caustic stream at Brent's face.

Dmitry also coughed violently and fell back, wiping at his own face. She had sprayed him, too, by mistake.

Red-orange foam dripped from Brent's nose, mouth, and jaw. To her horror, he grinned. The spray turned his teeth orange, too.

"Doesn't really do much for me." He chuckled. "It does taste nasty, though."

The spray was supposed to stop *grizzly bears*; why did it have no effect on him? The goggles protected his eyes, but she had coated the rest of his face with it. Herself choking and gagging, with her stinging eyes half-closed, Camilla triggered another spray.

Brent let it wash over his grinning mouth again. Then he lifted his shoulders in an eerily perfect imitation of Juan's shrug.

Behind him, Dmitry swung the steel pipe.

The concrete plug caught Brent across the upper arm and shoulder, but he barely registered the blow. He spun with surprising speed to grab Dmitry's face one-handed and thrust him away. Dmitry flew back to slam against the wall, then slid to the floor, unmoving.

Brent turned back to Camilla. "All right, enough of that," he rumbled.

Streaming tears, she fearfully took her finger off the spray trigger and doubled over in a coughing fit.

Brent smiled and wagged a finger at her, like an admonishing parent. Then he stepped to the outer doorway and was gone.

CHAPTER 178

The bulky wet-suited figure emerged from the science station buildings, exiting through the same doorway the others had entered. It was clearly Brent. He scanned the area surrounding the buildings, then headed downslope toward the breakwater, coming closer. Reaching the seawall, he looked back one last time toward the station. No one had followed him. He smiled, moonlight glinting from the lenses of his night vision goggles and his teeth.

He continued toward the seawall, walking with the easy, bouncing strides of a man decades younger. Reaching over his shoulder, he turned a valve on a black plastic backpack—a high-end scuba rebreather, probably—and fitted the regulator mouthpiece to his lips. He was no doubt headed for the safety of the dark water that lay just ahead.

Hidden behind the eight-foot seawall, watching him approach, Mason grinned.

As Brent passed the corner, Mason stretched an arm to touch the stun gun to the back of his neck, and pressed the trigger. Brent was driven to his hands and knees. He dropped the long cylinder he was carrying: a high-voltage cattle prod, much larger than the stun gun Mason had just used on him.

"Oh, I'm sorry," Mason said. "Did *I* just do that? How clumsy of me." He limped closer, dragging his bad leg.

Brent looked up at him, his face dazed and uncomprehending.

"Here, let me give you a hand." Mason reached down to hold the prongs of the small stun gun against Brent's neck and tilted his head, grinning into his face.

"You've got some unhappy patients here. I hope your malpractice insurance is paid up."

He triggered the stun gun again.

Brent collapsed face-first onto the ground. Mason slid his bad leg along the dirt, dropping into a seated position next to Brent's prone form. He peeled away Brent's night-vision goggles and tossed them aside. Then he thumbed one of his eyes open. Only the white showed.

"Clear!"

Mason laughed and jolted the doctor a third time.

Camilla staggered down the slope toward them, still coughing.

"Clear!" He jolted Brent a fourth time, making his limbs flop bonelessly against the ground.

Camilla tucked her hair behind her ear and crouched beside him.

"Nurse, fifty cee-cee's of epinephrine, stat!" He jolted Brent a fifth time.

"Mason, stop it." She grabbed his arm. "That's enough."

"Oh, I don't know. Better safe than sorry."

She shook her head as a series of gagging coughs convulsed her. Then she wiped her streaming eyes and put a hand on his shoulder. "Dmitry's unconscious, and I don't know what Brent did to Juan and JT. We have to go find them."

• • •

Juan, JT, and Dmitry lay side by side on the floor of the factory building, like patients in a wartime hospital triage unit. Mason watched Camilla flit from patient to patient—laying her hand on Dmitry's forehead, checking JT's pulse, brushing Juan's hair lightly with her fingers. All three remained unconscious. The flickering orange light from dozens of candles lit their faces with soft light.

Mason sat nearby with his bad leg extended before him. When they had found Juan and JT, Camilla was so relieved that they were still breathing, she hugged Mason, squeezing him until he staggered and pointed at his knee. Together, they had dragged the three limp bodies into the open floor area where the rows of machinery began. Moving them had been difficult, but not as tough as hauling Brent's bulk.

Camilla had improvised pillows: torn blankets, a wet-suit hood, Jacob's bloodstained sweatshirt. She looked frustrated by her powerlessness and lack of medical knowledge.

"Give them some time," Mason said. "They'll be fine."

Juan coughed without waking, and a trickle of blood ran from his mouth.

Or maybe not.

The candles glowed from the machinery all around them. She had planted them in blobs of dried wax on valves, ducts, and motor housings. In the flickering light, black shadows from the surrounding pipes and machinery bobbed and danced on the walls and ceiling.

A larger shadow flickered on the wall above them: the silhouette of a human form, arms extended out to the sides, framed within a circular wagon-wheel outline.

Vitruvian man.

Mason grinned at the thought. If Brent were awake, he would probably have appreciated the irony, since Leonardo Da Vinci's iconic image of the spread-armed man within a circle frequently graced the covers of medical texts.

Brent's wrists had been chained to the sides of the six-foot wagon-wheel valve. He hung from the front of the largest block of machinery. His lower legs sagged, chained to the bottom of the wheel. Chains also wrapped his torso—they weren't taking any chances. Eyes closed, head drooping onto his chest, his face was slack but still looked severe in the candlelight.

Camilla sat cross-legged by Juan's head. Mason grinned at her.

"Look at you. Florence Nightingale."

"Where did you get the stun gun?" she asked.

He pulled it out, turned it over in his hands.

"Natalie's, I think. It was lying in the sand, outside the cave Juan found her in. Brent must have tossed this toy, seeing as how he already had the heavy-duty version." He nodded toward the two-foot cylinder lying against the wall nearby: Brent's electric cattle prod.

Camilla looked at Brent, hanging from the wheel, and her features distorted into a sad grimace. "None of this makes sense. I mean, he must have had some sort of rationale for doing this."

Mason smiled grimly. "I have to admit I'm more than a little curious, too. For a doctor who likes to quote Hippocrates, he sure forgot the 'first, do no harm' part."

CHAPTER 179

Camilla brushed Juan's hair away from his forehead. A couple of hours had gone by. He was still unconscious, and she didn't like the way he was breathing. It sounded shallow, and every few inhalations, she could hear a faint liquid gurgle. The candles had shrunk to about half their length. Mason sat nearby, thumbing through a stack of yellowed papers.

Sensing a change in the room, she looked up to find Brent's eyes open. They fixed on her with a glittery blue serenity, and her heart gave a nasty thump. He didn't say anything. She stared back at him, forcing her heart to slow.

"Why, Brent?"

He regarded her steadily for a moment. Then he cleared his throat.

"One of the downsides of my particular situation is that I can't just stop taking my meds. I'll need more fentanyl soon, or the convulsions will very likely be fatal." He tipped his chin forward, peering down at his chest. "Can you grab my small medical kit, please? It's in the chest pocket of my wet suit."

Mason chuckled.

"Nice try, Brent. I don't think so. But perhaps you can shed some light on a few things for us."

"You're not giving me much incentive to be cooperative."

"We'll see." Mason struggled to his feet. He squatted next to JT for a moment, fumbling at a pocket of his fatigue pants. Then he limped over to the wheel where Brent was chained.

Alarm raced through Camilla's limbs. "What are you doing?" she asked.

"Just asking for a little cooperation." Mason turned toward Brent and did something that she couldn't see. Then he stepped back.

She gasped.

The handle of JT's tactical knife jutted from the hollow of Brent's collarbone, standing upright between his neck and shoulder. Mason had driven it deep into his body.

Brent studied the knife handle quivering close to his chin. He raised his eyebrows.

"If you were aiming for a painful nerve cluster," he said, "I think you missed the brachial plexus. It's a little closer to the shoulder."

Mason stepped forward and pulled the knife out. He stabbed it into Brent again, closer to his shoulder this time.

Camilla tried to speak, but her throat locked.

Brent and Mason both looked at the knife handle, their heads close together, examining it with dubious expressions.

"Wiggle it, maybe?" Brent said.

Mason obliged. Blood ran down the outside of Brent's wet suit.

She gagged.

"Sorry." Brent shook his head in apology, as if embarrassed by his lack of a reaction. She pushed to her feet, finding her voice at last. "Oh god, stop! Stop it right now! What is wrong with you?"

"He can't feel pain." Mason chuckled. "That explains the bear spray, too. He didn't even feel it."

"No, Mason." She stared at him, shaking her head in disbelief. "Not *him*. What is wrong with *you*?"

"Sorry, my bad." Mason grinned sheepishly and pulled the knife out of Brent's shoulder. "But this isn't working too well. He won't tell us anything he doesn't want to."

Brent smiled at him, eyes filled with good-humored amusement. But when he spoke he directed his words at her.

"Last year, psychology researchers did a study comparing financial traders for egocentrism, cooperativeness, and risk-seeking behaviors. For a control group, they used incarcerated psychopaths. Care to guess what the research found, Camilla? On tests such as 'the prisoner's dilemma,' the traders were more egocentric, less cooperative, and more prone to senseless risk taking than the psychopaths."

Brent nodded toward Mason.

"The researchers found other disturbing similarities between financial traders and psychopaths. Both groups had above-average intelligence, were superficially charming, and had strong verbal skills. Both showed marked tendencies toward insincerity and untruthfulness, both lacked a fear of consequences, and neither group showed any remorse or shame for their actions. Sound like anyone we know?"

"Ignore him," Mason said. "He's just grouchy because he got caught. By the way, where were you going, Brent?"

Brent lapsed into a stony silence, but his jittery blue eyes stayed on them.

Day 11

Monday: December 31, 2012

CHAPTER 180

The first rays of dawn glowed bright through the small holes that dotted the roof and walls, filling the interior of the factory building with a gray light. Juan leaned against some machinery with his back toward Brent, reading through the yellowed papers they had found in the loft above. Old, handwritten documents listing dates, ship names, locations, weather conditions, and cargo manifests.

Shipwrecks. All reported within a few miles of Año Nuevo.

Something Juan had read bothered him—an oddity, a discrepancy he couldn't quite put his finger on. Yet.

He had woken some hours ago and convinced Camilla to get some rest. JT and Dmitry were still unconscious or sleeping. A makeshift bandage from a strip of torn blanket circled Dmitry's head. His brow was furrowed, and he seemed to be in pain. He had woken long enough to throw up earlier. Dmitry had a concussion at least, and possibly a skull fracture.

Juan coughed, and a streamer of thick blood drooled from the corner of his mouth and dangled toward the floor. The blood looked dark, almost black. He brushed it away, and wiped his hand on the thigh of his wet suit.

He wasn't in especially great shape, either.

In particular, he didn't like the way his injury *tickled*—a maddening crinkly itch that accompanied every inhalation. The extra oxygenating capacity of his free-dive-trained lungs would let him remain active even if the injured one collapsed completely and left him running on just one. Still, it was something he hoped to avoid.

Setting the papers aside, he stepped into a beam of light from a hole in the roof and let it illuminate his chest. He reached behind him and pulled the lanyard to unzip his wet suit, careful not to let the excruciating pain show on his face. Then he peeled the wet suit down to his waist.

He couldn't see the exit hole in his back, but the edges of the entry wound were starting to blacken. A six-inch patch of skin around the hole had turned an angry red. He probed at the wound. It didn't appear to be healing.

Juan inhaled deeply.

An ugly wheeze sounded from the hole in his chest.

He exhaled, tightening his abdominal muscles.

Tiny bubbles of dark, clotted blood foamed out of the hole between his ribs and ran down his side in a thin, lumpy stream.

That couldn't be good.

"Pneumothorax."

Juan looked up at the deep, rumbling voice. Brent stared at him with an eerie passivity from where he hung chained to the metal wheel.

"You're going to die, Juan."

Juan shrugged. "We all die sometime."

"Would you like me to take a look at that for you?"

Juan ignored the doctor. He walked over to the wall where Camilla was sleeping, next to the small pile of supplies they had salvaged. He bent slowly to retrieve a roll of duct tape, and blood dribbled from the hole in his chest, onto the floor. He straightened and scuffed the sole of his bootie across the spatters nearest Camilla, smearing them away.

She was curled on her side, her cheek pillowed on her hands. Juan stood still for a minute, looking down at her face. Her sleeping features held the sweet, guileless innocence of a child.

She looked like an angel.

He thought of the first time he had seen her, jumping out of a taxicab and running to save the little boy in the street. It had been no big deal for Juan to snatch the kid out of harm's way. He had gauged the truck's speed and distance first and seen that there was very little danger for him. But Camilla— she *would* risk her own life to save someone she didn't know. It was simply her nature.

He had no idea what she imagined she saw in him. She was a far better person than he could ever be.

Jordan's face hung before Juan's eyes. Dead because of his selfishness. His cowardice. He had been so cruel to her.

The wrenching, twisting blackness inside him tried once again to shake loose from the chains he had buried it in. He could feel it rising now, filling him, threatening to burst from his mouth in a howl of anguish. He closed his eyes, gritted his teeth, and strangled it, knowing it would annihilate him if he let himself give it voice even once. Trembling, he got himself under control again.

His injury? His physical pain? Those were nothing.

He rubbed as much of the blood as he could from the edges of the hole in his side. Then he reached behind him and, by feel, did the same for the exit wound.

He pulled a long strip of duct tape from the roll.

Camilla's eyes moved beneath their lids, darting back and forth. A frown creased her brow, and her mouth trembled. She was dreaming now.

Her dreams would not be pleasant ones, he knew. Like him, she had lost her entire family. In many ways the two of them were similar. But unlike him, she was not to blame for what had happened to her.

He would *not* let her die here.

Wrapping the duct tape around his torso, he pressed it against his skin. The patch of tape would seal the pneumothorax—a type of injury he had seen other divers sustain—and, with luck, would hopefully allow his lung to reinflate.

He welcomed the explosion of physical pain, which was a distraction from his bleak thoughts. It really didn't matter if they never found out why Brent had gathered them to the slaughter—he couldn't let any more of these people die. *Especially* her.

He shrugged back into the shoulders of his wet suit and zipped it up. Staring down at Camilla's sleeping face, he felt the full weight of his grim responsibility settle on him. What if he failed again, and she died because of it?

"*El escorpiÓn.*" Brent said.

Juan ignored him.

"That's what they used to call you, isn't it?" A rumbling chuckle. "That sweet girl you're staring at—she thinks you're some kind of misbehaved frat boy she can reform. But you and I know better, Juan. You ran your father's intelligence networks for two years. There's another word for your kind of intelligence gathering, isn't there?"

Juan walked back to where he had left the shipwreck reports. Brent's voice followed him.

"Torture."

Turning his back, Juan returned his attention to the old papers in his hands. He remembered what Julian had said, ten days ago, about the construction of the lighthouse. He flipped back through the papers, reading the earliest shipwreck dates again.

The Carrier Pigeon	1853
The Sir John Franklin	1865
The Coya	1866
The Hellespont	1868
The J. W. Seaver	1887

Juan stopped at the report on the wreck of the *Seaver*. That was the one that bothered him. He coughed, then reread the signature line on the report.

William N. Steele

Station Keeper

Año Nuevo Signal Station

A scuffling noise made him look up.

Mason limped toward him, grinning, dragging another cardboard box of old papers along the floor. He had been in and out all morning, salvaging gear and, now, documents.

They had also raided Brent's first-aid kit. Juan had dosed himself with antibiotics and painkillers. He looked at the swollen bulge of Mason's knee; Mason's mobility was undoubtedly due to the wide array of painkillers they had found.

"Ten days ago," Juan said. "The first morning we were here, Julian told us about the lighthouse. Do you remember what year he said it was built?"

Mason nodded. "Eighteen ninety."

Juan looked down at the report on the wreck of the *Seaver*. He read the signature line again.

Signal Station.

Then he rechecked the date on the report.

1887.

Somewhere in that three-year discrepancy, Juan was sure, lay the answer to their escape.

CHAPTER 181

Camilla knelt beside Juan, looking at the dozens of papers he had spread out on the floor.

"Shipwrecks?" she asked.

"Treacherous stretch of coastline." He indicated the closest document. "In 1883 it even killed two of the island's signal station keepers as they were attempting the crossing from the mainland. Their rowboat overturned while their families watched from here, helpless."

Her heart sped up. "Did you say that happened in *1883*?"

Juan smiled—it was wintry and grim, but a smile nonetheless—and something came unstuck in her chest. He tapped the 1887 report on the wreck of the *Seaver*.

"You see it, too," he said. "The dates."

She nodded. "What kind of signal station *was* this, seven years before the lighthouse was even built? There was a report on the history of this place I was reading, but it was in the other room, so it's probably confetti now. I wish we still had it."

"I borrowed it yesterday," he said. "It's in the blockhouse."

He shoved himself to his feet and swayed, almost stumbling. Her breath caught.

"I'll get it," she said.

"I'll go," Mason said. "I need the exercise, anyway, to keep this knee from stiffening up completely."

"On the table next to the map," Juan said.

Mason limped away. At the doorway, he passed JT, who carried the MRE crate in both arms. Setting it down, JT stared after his departing back.

"Where the hell is he going *this* time?"

"We need something from the blockhouse," she said.

JT frowned. "Man keeps finding excuses to leave." He tossed MREs to Juan and Camilla.

She unwrapped hers—Thai chicken with peanut sauce again—even though she didn't have much appetite.

The minutes dragged.

"I've been thinking," JT said. "Where would a doctor get this kind of money?"

She had wondered the same thing herself. She shot a glance at Juan, but he shook his head.

583

But JT walked over to the wheel where Brent hung, arms extended to the sides, and looked up at him. "Got anything to say, Doc?"

Juan's voice held quiet authority. "Don't waste your time talking to him."

"Maybe there are lots of people like Mason," Brent said. "But most don't have the money to bring their strange fantasies to life. I think this little adventure is the only reason he bought that monstrous yacht."

"I don't believe you," Camilla said, but her heart sped up.

"I got myself into deep trouble with the gambling. Ended up owing a lot of money to the wrong people. My life was in danger, so I went to my wealthiest patients for help. Mason wrote one check, and my problems disappeared. But it seems I made a deal with the devil."

Juan sounded bored. "He's lying. Nothing he says is worth listening to."

JT looked at the doorway Mason had exited through. "Man *has* been gone an awful long time."

Camilla looked at the streak of blood drying on Brent's wet suit and pictured Mason's grin as he wiggled the knife. But she also remembered how he had helped her up, hugged her, and given her water when she was sickened by Travis's senseless death. Then again, it had been his taunting Travis that almost got her killed. Which was the real Mason?

Hearing a rustle at the doorway, she turned to see him standing there.

Awkward silence hung in the air.

Mason looked at them for a moment. Then he laughed.

"Let me guess. *I'm* the man behind the curtain. A psychopathic financial trader who hired Brent to help me—or blackmailed him into it, perhaps."

He threw a languid salute toward Brent. "Nicely done. I saw you planting the seeds earlier. But there are just a few problems with your story."

Brent stared back, impassive.

"For one," Mason said, "I don't actually have much money. Oh, sure, for a while I was doing pretty well, but I made a mistake blowing the whistle on my own company. The SEC repaid my good social conscience by cleaning me out, too."

He paused and leaned against the wall.

"But I've been thinking about money, too, and you know what? I don't think we're talking millions here."

Camilla closed her eyes. "A quarter-billion-dollar yacht as a honey trap," she said. "Once we saw it, we didn't question the legitimacy. But they can be chartered, can't they?"

Mason nodded. "For about two hundred thousand dollars a day, usually to impress super-wealthy clients. The cameras, electronics, installation—let's say another couple hundred thousand." He grinned at Brent. "Especially if the technicians never left the island or got their final payments. Ten five-thousand-dollar checks with our letters, and another hundred thousand lying around the island in bundles and sprinkled on top of Julian's fake grand prize. Plus whatever they paid the Pelagic Institute—"

"Three hundred thousand dollar." Dmitry sat up, wincing, and held his head. "My cousin, he heard this."

"There you have it, then. Eight hundred fifty thousand for the whole thing. Less than the average house in the Bay Area costs. A good surgeon could put that aside in a few years, couldn't he, Brent?"

Mason tossed something, and it flapped toward Camilla in a flutter of white, like a startled bird. She caught it, surprised that she hadn't fumbled it, and looked down at what she now held in her hands. It was the report they wanted.

"But thanks for thinking of me, gang," Mason said. "Maybe we can do this again sometime. I vote for someplace tropical instead—Parrot Cay, maybe, or Bora Bora."

Camilla gasped a small laugh, mostly in relief. She felt a flood of warmth toward him. Then she noticed Brent's gaze fixed on Mason, too. His expression was heavy with malice. A tic jittered one of his eyelids, and his head twitched. Withdrawal symptoms?

CHAPTER 182

Camilla looked up from the historical report, open on her lap to a page of black and white photographs. Her eyes darted around the rows of machinery to the giant wheel valve where Brent hung in chains. She recognized it from the photograph. Her heart sped up with excitement. After all these years, could her idea actually work?

Only one way to find out.

"Who's ready to go home?" she called.

Juan was at her side in a heartbeat. She hugged him, but released him quickly when his face contorted with pain.

"Look at this." She raised her voice. "Everyone."

Mason, JT, and Dmitry joined them, looking over her shoulder in a tight semicircle.

Kneeling, she tapped the report that lay open before her. "The lighthouse itself wasn't built until 1890, but the signal station was already operating *twenty years* before that. The building we're in—all this machinery—it's been here since 1872."

She turned to Dmitry and put her finger on a black and white picture.

"Your science station was built inside of *this*."

The caption beneath the picture read "Fog Signal Building."

She pointed at the machinery all around them. "The original fog signal was a massive steam-powered whistle. This room was its engine room, generating the steam and sending it up to the whistle through that buried pipe outside."

She couldn't get the grin off her face.

"The signal was loud," she said. "Loud enough to warn ships away in the heavy coastal fog. Loud enough to be heard miles out to sea."

Juan knelt at her side, reading the captions, his face alongside hers. He tapped another picture. "The whistle itself must be buried in the pile of rubble where the steam pipe ends, at the top of the hill—"

"Next to the broken lighthouse tower." She turned her head, meeting his eyes, thrilled to see that he shared her excitement.

"We get that signal going again," she said, "and it'll be heard by every ear up and down the coast, from Davenport to Pescadero."

CHAPTER 183

Silent formations of pelicans lumbered through the sky above as Camilla and Mason shifted rocks, digging through the rubble pile.

In the distance, down near the cistern's spillway, JT's muscles flexed as he heaved the heavy high-pressure washer into place on a flat slab of broken concrete. Dmitry, his head still wrapped in a bandage, held the hose. The seals gave them a wide berth, leaving their work area clear.

Juan squatted next to them, looking into the ten-foot segment of steam pipe they had unearthed. From her angle, Camilla could see a ragged circle of light through the thirty-inch-wide pipe, but its edges were uneven—filthy inside after a century of disuse.

The roar of the power washer's diesel engine filled the air. Juan stood and nodded to Dmitry, who directed a blast of high-pressure water through the pipe. A stream of mud, bird and wasp nests, and other debris washed out the far end. After a few minutes, he turned off the nozzle. The circle of light was round and smooth now.

Juan squatted and looked down the length of the pipe again. Then he gave JT the okay sign.

JT placed his hands on the outside of the pipe section and heaved, rolling it back into its trench.

Juan stood, looking down at it to make sure it was perfectly aligned. *Like a construction foreman,* Camilla thought—*a construction foreman in a black wet suit.* Her eyes followed the path of the steam pipe, tracing the remaining sections that bulged like vertebrae from the spine of the hill, climbing to where they disappeared under the pile of rubble that she and Mason were slowly disassembling. It was so good to see everyone working together, trusting one another again. They would rescue themselves from this nightmare. Together.

They were a team again.

Mason used one hand to balance himself, holding his bad leg away from the pile. He looked awkward but energized.

"Even if we find the whistle, how do you intend to get the pumps and boilers started?" he asked her. "They're a hundred and forty years old. They must be rusted solid."

"A girl's gotta have some secrets," she said.

"Look at that grin—jeez!" Mason laughed. "And I see how you just can't keep your hands off our captain."

She slapped his chest.

589

He smiled at her. "Can't say I blame you. He's not a bad guy for a drug lord."

"*Former* drug lord."

"Don't get your hopes up," he said. "He's too torn up over Jordan."

"I liked her," she said. "I know that doesn't matter now. But I did."

"So did I," Mason said. "There was a lot going on under her little-miss-prom-queen act. She was unique."

Camilla glanced toward the bottom of the hill, where Juan stood with a palm pressed against his side, watching JT and Dmitry dig up the next section of pipe in front of him.

"Juan was probably a first for Jordan," Mason said. "The first time a guy actually tried to leave *her*."

"I don't want to talk about that. What happened is so awful and so sad—for both of them. Let's talk about Brent instead." She looked down at the factory building, where they had left Brent chained to the wheel. "Why did he bring us all here?"

"I'm still working on that one myself." Mason followed her gaze. "He won't say. He's just telling random lies now, messing with us. But there are really only three classic motives for murder: love, money, and revenge. I suppose the same motives must apply to *mass* murderers, too."

"He doesn't strike me as the particularly loving type. His family wanted a restraining order so they would never have to see him again. Money, though—could there be some truth to what Julian said about the video?"

"Well, Brent definitely was—or still is—recording all this," he said. "We've seen some playback. But profiting from illegal pay-per-view seems farfetched as a motive."

"And I can't see revenge, either." Her throat tightened. "What could he possibly imagine we did to him? We didn't even *know* him, Mason. *I* certainly didn't give him cancer or turn him into a drug addict."

"It doesn't have to be us personally. Maybe we just represent something to him. A type of person he hates and wants revenge on. Like the way some psychos target attractive women like yourself, for instance."

"Thanks... I guess."

She looked back at the factory building. It seemed dark and menacing even in the light of day. "But survivors? That's crazy. Why would a survivor hate other survivors? Does he hate himself, too?"

"Hey, look." Mason moved a rock and tugged at the corner of something rusty and metallic that poked from beneath. "Jackpot! I think we just found the whistle. Call the others."

CHAPTER 184

"What's wrong with Brent?" Camilla asked.

"You got a while?" Mason laughed. "Where do I even start?"

"No, seriously—look at him." She pointed.

The five of them had gathered once again in the machinery room of the fog signal building. Fifty feet away down one of the rows of machinery, Juan, JT, and Dmitry had taken a panel apart. They poked at the valves and gears inside, talking, unaware of Brent's plight. His head hung on his chest, jerking every few seconds. His entire body shuddered with violent trembling.

"Ah, the old Münchausen is faking it," Mason said. "Travis could have told you. It's the oldest prison trick in the book."

"No, I think he's going into convulsions," she said. "Everybody, get over here!"

JT looked at Brent with a disgusted grimace. "Who cares? Let him die."

"We don't want to be like him," she said. "Besides, he shouldn't escape punishment for what he did here."

Juan wandered over, followed by the others. He searched the pockets of Brent's wet suit.

"Phone." He held up a large touch-screen mobile phone in a Ziploc bag, then crouched and slid it across the floor to Mason. "Check it out."

To Camilla's relief, a few seconds later Juan unsnapped a small medical kit he had found in Brent's chest pocket. Taking out a needle, he uncapped it and poked it into an ampoule. "Fentanyl," he said. "How much do we give him?"

"He told us something like nine thousand milligrams," she said. "Remember? But he could have been lying."

"If he lied, then he just killed himself." Juan drew the liquid into the syringe.

With a jolt, she realized her error. "No, wait! That was the other stuff. The pills. The modafinil. I have no idea on the fentanyl."

Juan looked at JT and raised an eyebrow.

"Give him twenty milligrams," JT said.

Camilla's eyebrows rose. "How do you know?"

"Our squad medic used to carry fentanyl in the field. We cross-trained."

Juan stuck the needle into a vein on Brent's wrist, which was held steady by the chains. He depressed the plunger.

591

"Something else we missed." Mason looked up from Brent's phone. "Battery levels. After ten days, he's got a full battery. He's been recharging somewhere."

"No cellular reception, though…" Mason manipulated the phone for a few moments, then tensed with excitement. "He's got a Wi-Fi signal here. There's a hidden wireless network."

A moment later, he lowered the phone, looking disappointed. "The screen's locked," he said. "We need an eight-character code to get in. Any ideas?"

Juan shrugged. "Año Nuevo."

"Survivor," Camilla said.

JT grunted. "Shit-head."

Mason punched keys without apparent success. "I'll try a few now."

Brent's condition didn't improve over the next several minutes. The muscles and tendons in his neck and arms jumped like downed power lines.

Juan stuck the syringe into the ampoule again. "He did say he has a very high tolerance."

"Give him another twenty," JT said.

"Let's give him two hundred and see what happens."

The larger dose of fentanyl seemed to help. After a few minutes, Brent's tremors lessened considerably. He stirred, rolled an eye toward Juan, and grunted. "Modafinil."

Juan fed him some pills from the medical kit. Brent chewed them and mumbled for more. He couldn't raise his head. Fragments of pills littered the front of his wet suit and fell to the floor, the white crumbs sprinkling the patches of dried blood where Mason had stabbed his shoulder.

Eventually, he had recovered enough to raise his head. He looked steadily at Juan. "I suppose I should thank you."

Juan shrugged. "Thank Camilla. She insisted." He walked away to lean with his back against the wall. "The rest of us were okay with letting you die."

Brent turned his head toward her. His pupils were pinpoints again, surrounded by a jittering expanse of blue. "Dear, dear Camilla."

She was horrified to see genuine affection in Brent's eyes.

"You were such an adorable kid," he said. "You know, I probably saved your leg."

She felt the blood drain from her face.

"What she'd been through," Brent said, "it broke your heart. Everyone on the hospital staff wanted to adopt her."

Camilla closed her eyes. "Stop…" She could manage only a whisper.

"But then the rumors started. The EMTs, the fire crew—a kid named Garcia told me what they *really* found when they went in. Nobody wanted to believe such a thing about a little girl who looked like an angel, but it wasn't a story you could ignore."

Her mouth moved, but she couldn't make a sound. "I can't remember," she finally whispered. "I don't remember."

"But *I* do," Brent said. "I could never forget what Garcia told me. It was 1989, four days after the earthquake, when they brought you in. You were my very first survivor, Camilla. You opened my eyes."

The skin on her arms tightened into goose bumps. What she remembered couldn't *possibly* be true. She had been a child. Traumatized. She remembered it *wrong*.

Brent addressed the others. "When the earthquake collapsed the Cypress Freeway's upper deck, her family's car was under the worst section. The freeway came down right on top of it, crushing the car like a pancake. Trapping Camilla inside with her family. Breaking her legs."

The doctor's deep, merciless voice seemed to come from far away.

"She still had a little room to move about in the car. She was small, you see. But her parents weren't."

She shook her head violently, trying to shake loose from the paralysis that gripped her. A trapped-animal noise rose in her chest, fighting to break free.

"That's enough." Somebody else's voice. Juan.

Brent chuckled. "Can you imagine how terrifying that would be? For a child who had known nothing but love and security before—an only child whose affectionate mother and father had built their whole lives around her? Darkness and smoke and screaming, blood everywhere? Her dead parents crushed, immobile, alongside her? She had to get out."

"Stop right now." Juan's voice was louder.

Camilla's hands shook. She didn't want Juan to hear. She didn't want *anyone* to hear. To know what she had done. The floor blurred in front of her eyes.

Brent didn't stop.

"In extremis, some survivors are capable of nearly superhuman physical feats. There were walls of steel and concrete blocking her on all sides. When the rescue team found the car, the steel door frame was twisted like cheap cardboard. The side panels—sheet metal—were peeled and torn..."

She shook her head and shrieked, hurting her own ears.

"...but she still couldn't wriggle out. Something was in her way. Luckily, it was much softer than metal..."

"No..." Her moan was barely audible.

"...easier to tunnel a path through," Brent said. "I still find it hard to believe a child was able to do that with her bare hands, though. Can you imagine the kind of will to survive that would require?"

She heard fast footsteps crossing the floor, headed toward Brent. Soft, rubbery steps. Juan.

"They called her the 'Little Angel of Death.'" Brent's voice sped up, getting the words out before Juan could reach him. "You see, Camilla managed to escape that car on her own, several days before they found her crawling around under the rubble. The mess she made getting herself out of that car—what she did to her own dead parents—it would have followed her all her life. They were eviscerated. She quite literally tore them to pieces.

"The recovery crew pitied her, so they went back in. They disguised the damage. They covered it up, for her sake..."

Camilla stumbled toward the doorway on rubbery legs. She couldn't see properly. She heard someone say, "Not. One. More. Word."

In passing, she caught a glimpse of Juan pressing the Glock against Brent's forehead. But she couldn't look at either of them—couldn't look at anyone. She had to find somewhere to be alone, curl up, and go away for a while. She bumped into the door frame, sending sparks of pain shooting through her broken nose and radiating through her face. Realigning her body with the doorway, she made it through on the second try, leaving the others behind.

She never wanted any of them to see her again.

CHAPTER 185

Camilla stumbled out the door, and Mason watched her go. *Camilla the chameleon. I thought I had you figured out, but I was wrong.* An unfamiliar sensation ran through his body. To his surprise, it occurred to him that it was very likely fear.

Juan held the gun to Brent's forehead, leaning into his face, as if daring him to speak. Mason waited, but nothing interesting happened. Then he looked back at the door Camilla had gone through.

JT frowned and said, "Someone ought to go see if she's okay."

Mason looked at Juan. *You should go, pal. You're the one she wants—needs—to hear it from.*

Juan's fingertip was on the trigger. Brent stared back at him with amused contempt. A muscle in Juan's jaw twitched, but he kept his face impassive. His eyes never left Brent's, inches away.

Mason waited a moment longer. *I guess not, then.*

"I'll go," he said, struggling to his feet.

He found her a few minutes later in the blockhouse—Juan's blockhouse. She was slumped on Jordan's cot with her back against the wall. Her curly brown hair hung in front of her face, hiding it from him, as she stared at her hands and fingers.

Mason stood in the doorway, unsure what to do or say. His own reaction surprised him again.

She didn't look up.

"I need to be alone right now," she said, her voice empty of emotion.

"I'll be right outside if you need anything," Mason said. He limped around the corner of the door frame, and slid down it to sit in the sunshine. Seals shuffled about, curious, and he watched them.

When her quiet, wavering voice floated out of the blockhouse long minutes later, he barely heard it.

"Brent's wrong. I got out the back window."

Then came a high-pitched keen.

"I was trying to save them. I was trying to get them out. But instead, they came apart."

CHAPTER 186

"Is frozen solid with rust."

Juan watched Dmitry bang on the housings of pump after pump, walking down the row of machinery.

"This one. This one. This one. All of them. Very bad news, my friend."

Juan swayed on his feet. Fever sweat slicked his forehead, and breathing was getting harder, although he tried not to let the others see it. The itch in his side—his lung—was worse now, making it hard for him to focus.

"We could use a mechanic." JT laughed. "Too bad we don't have one anymore."

Steadying himself against a pipe, Juan tried to keep the concern off his face. The pumps were 140 years old. What was it that Camilla had in mind? She was too smart not to have considered this.

"We need new pumps," Dmitry said.

A small voice spoke from the doorway. "We have new pumps. Two of them, in fact."

Juan looked up in surprise to see Camilla. Then he realized what she meant. "The power washers."

Mason followed her into the room.

"We go get them now." Dmitry's face lit up with his crooked smile. He turned to Brent. "*Durak*. This means 'stupid.' You are very stupid to kill Heather and Jacob. Here in America you will go to jail, but in Russia they would not waste jail cell and food on you. Waste only a bullet. And *these* people here are good people, too, that you try to kill."

"Tell your bosses that, *vor v zakony,*" Brent said.

Dmitry's face blanched. *"Shto?"*

Brent spoke past him, addressing them all. "There was some truth to what I said earlier about the gambling."

"Ignore him." Juan turned away.

"I dug myself a deep hole with my debts," Brent said. "The kind of mob people I was dealing with, they were the worst sort of lowlifes. They had a sideline distributing rather unique films." He rolled his neck, looking at the ceiling. "Believe me, they loved having a doctor at their beck and call. I had access to human tissue. I had keys to the morgue…"

"Don't listen to this sick fuck," JT said.

"…and I helped them make some movies." Brent grinned. "I had to. They owned me. When the hospital administrators eventually caught on, I lost my medical license. But they had no idea of the full extent of it, and of course they didn't want publicity."

Dmitry stepped close, his face angry. "*Vor v zakony*—means 'criminal.' Thief. Mafia. Why do you say this to *me*?"

"These were bad people, and they owned me. When the video we're shooting here is delivered, all my debts will be cleared."

Brent pulled his face away from Dmitry's angry glare.

"Bad people," he said, aiming his voice toward Juan. "They made your daddy's little cocaine cartel look like a third-grade milk-money racket."

Juan ignored him.

Brent chuckled. "You see, it was the Russian mob I was in debt to. Dmitry's bosses."

"*Yob tvoyu mat.*" Red faced, Dmitry grabbed the front of Brent's wet suit. "Why do you say this lie?"

"No, Dmitry!" Camilla shouted.

Juan also realized what was about to happen, and lunged for them, sending a spike of pain through his chest. But he was too late to stop it.

Brent snapped his head forward, driving his forehead into Dmitry's bandage-wrapped temple, dropping him at his neoprene-booted feet.

He looked down at Dmitry's prone form with eerie, calm eyes. "*Durak.*"

CHAPTER 187

The fog whistle glistened in the sun, still wet from the power washing that had blasted the muck and rust from its metal sides. A four-foot-tall cylinder of steel, three feet in diameter and seamed with welds along one side, it stood upright once again on its concrete base. The surrounding area was now clear of rubble. The end of the wide steam pipe emerged from the ground to fit snugly into the base of the whistle. Camilla's eyes followed the path of the half-buried steam pipe, now a clean, straight line running down the hill to disappear into the wall of the fog signal building.

She thought of Dmitry, unconscious in the same room where Brent was chained.

"I don't like leaving those two alone for too long," she said.

"We're ready, anyway," JT said. "Pumps wired, boilers filled, and finally, this…" He slapped the whistle with a palm. "Let's go make some noise."

She turned a half-circle, looking at the stretch of California coast across the channel. Less than a mile away, just out of sight behind the dunes, a continuous flow of cars streamed up and down scenic Highway 1. What would people think when the steam whistle, silent for 140 years, split the afternoon air?

She did her best to push aside the awful turmoil that churned inside her, but it wasn't easy. Did she remember a younger Brent, his hair dark instead of silver, wearing scrubs, holding her hand, speaking gently to her? How she'd clung to that voice twenty-three years ago, pulling herself up out of the darkness that had claimed her then—the darkness that threatened to reclaim her even now.

She looked at the whistle and felt hope blossom in her chest.

Juan squatted in front of the whistle, reaching inside the narrowed section at the bottom, where a small steel door opened into the whistle's body. He frowned, and the expression on his face made Camilla's gut roll with tension.

"What is it?" she asked.

"A part is missing," he said. "A piece of the valve throat. In here, there should be a lever, with a half-gear on one side."

"Can we improvise something?" JT asked.

Juan shook his head. "Not without a machine shop." He turned to look toward the fog signal building, and his eyes narrowed.

Camilla stared at the whistle. They were missing a lever with a half-gear on one side. She felt the hope that was blossoming inside her curdle and die.

"I know where it is," she said. "I'll be right back. But don't touch that whistle again. Don't do *anything*."

She turned away and ran down the hill, headed for the seal barricade and the houses beyond.

"Be careful," JT shouted after her. "Veronica may still be around. Brent killed Jacob, but *she* might have taken the missing women."

Camilla raised a hand in acknowledgement but didn't slow or turn around. She had bigger worries right now.

• • •

Seals crowded the foyer of the Greek Revival house. Camilla nudged past them and into the living room. The big-screen monitor had been pulled off the wall. It lay in the corner, the frame twisted, the screen shattered.

Seals roamed freely through the rooms and hallways. On her way up, she passed a sea lion sliding down the stairs.

Déjà vu. Just like their first day here—the first contest. They would have to clear the houses again, she thought, and fought a hysterical giggle that wanted to turn into a sob. But only half of them were left alive now. And everybody was hurt.

She closed her eyes, fighting tears. Jordan, Lauren, Natalie, Veronica, even Travis—all dead now. The two scientists, Heather and Jacob. Dead.

Passing another seal in the upstairs hallway, she entered the room that had been hers. A moment later, she held the odd-shaped piece of metal in her hands. She remembered finding it, wrapped in newspaper, nestled in her luggage that first day on the island.

Brent had known, *even then,* that they would eventually repair the fog whistle.

They couldn't sound the distress signal now. They didn't dare.

Something terrible would happen if they tried.

Something else troubled her, too, itching at the back of her thoughts as she turned the valve lever in her hands. It was JT's shouted warning a few minutes ago.

"*...the missing women...*"

Camilla repeated his words. An ominous phrase, but familiar from somewhere. She associated it with the metal shape she held. She looked at the valve lever again. Her eye was drawn irresistibly toward something grey-white which lay crumpled in the other corner: the paper she had found the lever wrapped in.

A moment later, she was kneeling and smoothing the wrinkled newspaper pages on the floor. The headlines leaped up at her:

POLICE CONTINUE SEARCH FOR MISSING WOMEN

FAMILY OF MISSING SAN JOSE WOMAN HOLDS VIGIL

ARE WOMEN SAFE IN THE PARK?

LIVERMORE MOTHER DISAPPEARS

MAYOR CONVENES TASK FORCE

FEMALE HIKER MISSING, FEARED DEAD

IS A SERIAL KILLER STALKING THE BAY AREA?

The pages were from a variety of Bay Area newspapers: San Francisco Tribune, Oakland Tribune, San Jose Mercury Times...

Heart pounding, Camilla checked the dates. Most were within the past four years. But one article was older than the others. "**ARE WOMEN SAFE IN THE PARK?**" was from seven years ago.

Which park? Golden Gate Park?

She scanned the article, and her brows knitted.

Central Park? That couldn't be right.

Camilla looked at the bottom of the newspaper and froze.

All the other articles were from San Francisco Bay Area papers. But that particular page had come from the *New York Times.*

New York, and then California. Oh god.

The goose bumps started on her forearms, ran right up her shoulders, and met at her spine. Her hands shook, rattling the papers she held.

She could sense someone standing silently in the doorway behind her.

CHAPTER 188

"Well, this is a little awkward," Mason said. "I guess I don't really need to ask what those are about." He pointed at the articles.

Camilla stared at him. He leaned against the doorway, wearing the same familiar easy smile. Familiar, but a complete stranger.

"This whole time..." She started to rise but couldn't, and settled back to her knees. Instead of terror, she felt only the sick, bitter disappointment of betrayal. "You've been working with Brent. You're a... a..." She couldn't say the words. "Mason, how *could* you?"

He raised his hands in protest. "Camilla, you've got this wrong. I was *never* working with Brent. I'm just another innocent victim in this scheme of his. I still don't know what I'm doing here."

"Oh god, how can you say that? How can you stand there talking to me, like you're some kind of normal person?"

She could feel tears running down her face, and she wiped them away.

"I even *liked* you, Mason. I thought you were my friend."

He took off his glasses, then straightened up, rolling his shoulders back, and suddenly looked taller. Menacing. She realized with horror that the glasses and the hunched posture were simply a part of his camouflage.

"Like a cat with a mouse," she said. "Having fun. Pretending."

Mason shook his head. "No, this is the real me..." He paused. "Well, okay, fine—I'm not really gay."

"Mason!"

Strangely, she found this the worst betrayal of all. But it made the perfect disguise, didn't it? The gay friend—safe, nonthreatening, trustworthy...

"You were stalking me," she said.

"Maybe at first. But now I don't think of you that way anymore."

"You killed Heather! You killed Natalie!"

"No, not Natalie. That wasn't me." He hesitated. "Well, actually, I *did* take Natalie the first time, but Juan found her and brought her back."

"Oh god. *You* conked Dmitry and freed Travis just so we'd blame him. You smeared his paint color on Natalie's sweatshirt and waved it in front of Veronica like a red cape in front of a bull."

"But I didn't take Natalie the *second* time. I have no idea who did. It must have been Brent."

"And Veronica?"

Mason laughed—a sound of nervous relief.

"That was one scary, scary woman. She very nearly killed me, Camilla." He held two fingers an inch apart. "It was *that* close. She broke my knee like a toothpick."

He grinned. "But I got her in the end. I hope I never have to face someone like that—a *survivor*—again. I have a fairly limited capacity for fear, but Veronica was truly terrifying."

"How can you be like this?" Camilla asked. "So casual about it. Acting the same as always: laughing, joking, friendly. Oh god, this really *is* the real you, isn't it? But you're a *serial killer*..."

"Stereotyping? Camilla, I'm disappointed in you. That's just a meaningless label."

He shrugged. "I'm human just like anybody else. Ed Gein, a fellow sort of like me back in the fifties, used to say that every time he saw a pretty girl he thought two things at the same time. One part of him wanted to take her out and talk to her and be real sweet and treat her right. The other part of him wondered what her head would look like on a stick."

Spreading his hands, he leaned back against the door frame.

"To some extent, that's how everyone is. I'm just in better touch with the duality of my own nature than most people are. I guess it's one of those contradictory, biphasic survivor traits that psychologists love to talk about."

Camilla's knees hurt from kneeling. Letting herself slump to the side, she rested her weight on one hand and looked down at the floor.

"I don't want to hear any more."

"Look at me, Camilla," he said. "I'm still the same person you met on the yacht. We've been through a lot together here. We know each other pretty well by now."

"I can't have this conversation right now, Mason. I just can't." Her breath hitched. "It's been a bad day for me."

"Okay, I'll stop talking."

"Are you going to kill me?" she asked.

He shook his head. "I don't think of you that way—not anymore."

"What about the others?"

"Brent I'll kill for sure. The rest, I don't know." He grinned. "I'm making this up as I go along."

Camilla thought of Juan: wounded, vulnerable.

"You'll have to kill me first," she said.

"I won't do that," he said. "When Brent described how you got out of that car, I realized something about you. You're a girl after my own heart..."

"Don't!"

"...and I'd like my heart to stay inside my body, where it belongs. So I don't dare try anything with you. If you could do what you did to survive when you were only a kid, I'd hate to find out what you're capable of now as an adult. Veronica was bad enough."

He was afraid of her. Mason was frightened of *her*. Camilla choked back the horror that made her want to curl up and make the world go away. What kind of monster *was* she, that a serial killer was scared of *her*?

"So what happens now?" she asked.

He put his glasses back on. "Look, I may have my little hobbies, but I'm not the one you need to be worrying about right now. Brent's planning something else. He *let* us catch him, Camilla. It was just too easy."

Her heart sped up, thinking of the whistle part that Brent had hidden in her luggage. Mason was right.

"So what do we do about this?" He pointed at the newspapers.

She thought of Juan, wounded and grieving over Jordan. How could she dump this on him, too?

"We can't just pretend this didn't happen here between us," she said. "I've got to tell the others."

"If you do, I'll kill Juan."

"No!" Camilla's heart raced.

Mason grinned. "I can promise you that."

CHAPTER 189

Mason stood in the doorway, resting his leg, watching Camilla. She sat on the floor, surrounded by newspapers, thinking. She looked so vulnerable, but he knew it was misleading—camouflage, like his own. But hers was natural rather than deliberately cultivated.

The room was silent for long minutes. Looking at her made him feel strange. He liked her. He liked being around her. The thought of her rejecting him made him feel empty and hollow inside. But she would never accept the things he did.

"I could stop," he said, surprised to hear the words come out of his mouth.

Camilla looked up at him with exasperation on her face.

"How do I explain this to someone like you? This isn't a... a *lifestyle choice*, Mason. It's what you are."

The silence that followed was uncomfortable.

"Why did you come at all?" she asked him. "Why didn't you just throw the Vita Brevis letter away? I would have thought someone like you would want to keep a low profile."

Mason grinned.

He remembered standing inside his Brisbane warehouse two weeks earlier, holding the device in his hand, puzzled, his arm drenched in red to the elbow. He remembered ignoring the weakening gasps, moans, sobs, and pleas behind him as he turned the small bundle of electronics from side to side, thinking, *artificial kidney? How could someone like* her *afford this?* He remembered the trapped, panicky feeling that seized him when he realized that what he had dug out of that evening's playmate and stood puzzling over was a GPS tracker. He remembered rubbing the blood away from the round glass bubble on the front of the device to find himself staring into the lens of a camera. He remembered watching, stunned, as the iris of the lens dilated to stare back at him. Recording him.

"I don't think the letter I got was exactly the same as yours," he said to Camilla. "Mine really didn't leave me too much choice."

"We need your help," she said.

"You truly *are* a survivor, Camilla."

"Oh god, shut up." She held up the missing piece of the steam whistle. "Brent's got something nasty planned for all of us. We have to figure out what he's hiding, and when it comes to thinking like him I'm afraid you're our best bet."

She looked at him with an expression of reproach.

"We need you, Mason. *I* need you."

"This stays our little secret, then?"

"God help me, but yes," Camilla said. "For now."

CHAPTER 190

Camilla watched Juan squat in front of the steam whistle with the valve lever in his hands. He slid the lever inside the open compartment at the base and maneuvered it into place.

"It fits." He looked up at her. "You're right. Brent's taunting us with this."

Behind him, Mason craned forward as if peeking into the open compartment. But the way he leaned over Juan—the implicit threat in his posture—was unmistakable to Camilla. Mason held a fist over his mouth in a prissy gesture of concern. His eyes flicked up to catch hers almost playfully. She got the message all too well: if she let Juan suspect anything, he would die.

But now Juan was staring at her, too. His eyes narrowed.

He had caught something in her expression.

She did her best to keep her face under control. "We're all going to die if we sound this signal," she said. "Don't ask me how I know, but I'm sure of it."

Juan nodded. He put a hand on his knee and pushed himself slowly up to a standing position.

"Let's go talk to him."

• • •

"What's going to happen, Brent?" Juan asked. "What happens when we blow the fog signal?"

Brent stared back at them, looking amused. Camilla caught the tic in his eye, though. He would need more drugs soon. Maybe they could use that to make him talk.

"Shoot him in the gut." JT sounded disgusted. "Or give me the gun. I'll do it."

Juan leaned into Brent's face. "Why *Jordan*, then? You didn't discover her in any hospital. *She* wasn't a survivor story. Why did you have to bring *her* here, Brent?"

The bleak expression on Juan's face made Camilla's eyes sting.

Brent's eye twitched violently. "Are you noticing any side effects?" he asked. "The dosages you all took were moderate, and there are significant environmental stressors right now. How are you feeling? Any anxiety reactions or disorganized thoughts? Unusual sensations you can describe?"

She realized he was talking about the pills—the modafinil he had given them to stay awake. Disquiet rippled through her stomach.

"You had Julian present this all as fun and games," she said. "But I noticed he used a lot of behavioral psychology terms: 'zero-sum game,' 'double blind'... The contests were even based on Maslow's hierarchy of needs. Why?"

Brent smiled at her like a proud parent. "I'd say Maslow's pyramid made an ideal framework for our competition. Step by step, contest by contest, each of you has climbed the levels of his hierarchy. The top layer of Maslow's pyramid? It's self-actualization—realizing your true potential. Abraham Maslow said, 'What a person can be, he or she must become.' And all of you have. You have, indeed."

He raised his voice.

"Take a good look at yourselves. Other than your one defining moment, each of you has gone through your life asleep. I've woken you up again. I've stripped you of the civilized camouflage you use to disguise your true nature.

"And here on this island, we can see what you truly are—what it really means to be a *survivor*. Survival is not a gentle process, it's a brutal one. Half the seals born here will fall prey to sharks before they reach the open sea. Others will be crushed by their own parents or pecked to death by hungry seabirds. But not the survivors. *They* are the ones doing the crushing and the pecking. That's who you are. *What* you are. And anyone unlucky enough to get in your way ends up as collateral damage—chewed up, spit out. Dead."

"Why do you hate us so much?" she asked.

"I don't hate you, Camilla. In many ways, you're like a daughter to me. I've followed your progress for twenty-three years, even as I watched my own son grow up. I do hate *what* you are, though: a survivor."

She refused to see herself the way he did: as a monster.

"You're a survivor, too," she said.

Brent shook his head. He looked old.

"No, I'm not. I never was. I wanted to be, tried to be, but I'm not."

He raised his eyes to hers, his gaze steady.

"I didn't beat the cancer. I'm dying. I didn't beat the drugs. I need them to stay functional right now. At these elevated dosages, the drugs are killing me faster than the cancer. But I did beat you—all of you. None of you will leave this island alive."

Staring at him, her heart in turmoil, she couldn't think of anything to say.

"You've got the lowest body mass here," he said. "You took the same two-hundred-milligram dose of the experimental variant. Has it has enhanced your ability to function under stress? Do you feel any negative side effects, such as a heightened fear reaction?"

"I just feel sad, Brent. And sorry for you." She turned away.

He laughed. "The psychologists are ultimately misguided. The correct tool for studying the phenomenon of survival is medical science. Biology. We've learned a great deal about it since Maslow's time. We now have a decent understanding of the physiological basis of survival, and to a large extent, it's actually brain chemistry."

His voice deepened, and she could hear the dark strains of his obsession.

"Your amygdala is programmed to react to threats and stressors by triggering the release of catecholamines. Epinephrine and norepinephrine make your blood vessels constrict. Cortisol accelerates your heart rate, your breathing, and your metabolic processes so you are ready for fight or flight. Your neuromuscular system executes preprogrammed survival reflexes automatically, far faster than conscious thought. With the right pharmaceutical compounds, we can now amplify all these functions to an amazing degree.

"But chemically boosting these brain functions gives rise to a different set of problems. The chain reaction of powerful hormones and compounds blasting through your brain and body has undesirable side effects. It overwhelms the brain's neocortex—the seat of analytical thinking. Tunnel vision sets in. Irrational impulses take over. The heightened perception and analytical capability that are so critical to survival are weakened.

"The key is finding the right chemical balance. One that simultaneously accentuates both the primitive amygdala-driven limbic reactions and the higher neocortical functions. Then you would have the recipe for a true 'survivor drug.'"

At the sound of Juan's rubber-padded footsteps, Camilla looked up.

Juan crossed the floor with rapid strides to stop in front of Brent. Jamming the small medical kit into the chest pocket of Brent's wetsuit, he turned away in dismissal.

"Sorry to hear about your illness," he said. "We'll send flowers."

Standing with his back to Brent, Juan addressed them all.

"Mason said Brent's phone has an active Wi-Fi connection. That means there's a wireless base station very close to us. I think it's right underneath us, inside a second cave."

Mason started to get up. "I'll go look for it."

"No." Juan's voice was hard. "I need you to stay here. *I'm* going."

He waved a finger in a circle. "The cameras on the island are all wireless. Alongside the base station, I expect to find computer equipment for video storage, and—if we're lucky—a live communications uplink to the Internet. Otherwise, I'll find the jammers keeping our own mobile phones from working, and disable them. Either way, we're out of here."

"But we've been over every inch of this island," Camilla said. "If there was another cave, we would have found it."

Juan picked up the black backpack sitting next to the wall—Brent's scuba rebreather tank—and smiled humorlessly.

"Not if the only entrance is underwater."

CHAPTER 191

Camilla watched Juan strap the rebreather around his shoulders. He tried the air, breathing in and out carefully, then waiting, making sure there was nothing wrong with it. Then he walked toward the door, his long scuba fins bouncing against his shoulders. She felt both hopeful and frightened—he was in much worse shape than he was letting on, and she hoped he would be okay in the water.

In the doorway, he stopped and looked over his shoulder at her.

"Keep an eye on Dr. Moreau here," he said, "but don't let him drag you into conversation. That's a no-win."

He looked at JT and Mason. "For any of us."

"No sweat, Captain," JT said. A muscle in his shoulder flexed. "We'll keep him on ice for you until you get back."

"Be careful," Camilla said. "He's been five steps ahead of us all the way."

Juan touched his forehead with two fingers, throwing them all a little salute.

With a feeling of dread, she watched him disappear through the doorway. She fought back the urge to run after him, to stop him from going. But what if she never saw him again?

"He's running." Brent closed his eyes and leaned his head back against the wheel with a satisfied smile. "He's leaving you all behind. It's what he does. Looks like you finally got the captain you deserve, Corporal Washington."

Camilla's stomach churned. Brent had just put into words the doubt that she couldn't even admit to herself.

"You're wrong about Juan," she said. "About JT, too."

"Am I?" Brent didn't open his eyes, but his smile grew. "All your behavioral profiles were very clear. *Especially* JT's. Ask Julian. Oh, that's right, I'm sorry—I guess you can't."

Mason laughed. "Poor Julian was just some actor you hired."

"Was he, now? Did you check his business card?"

"Oh, shit," JT stood up. "We never searched Julian's body."

Camilla tensed. "No. It's another trick. Don't listen to him."

Brent's eyes stayed closed. "I never did find out Julian's MOS."

"What's an MOS?" she asked.

JT's brow furrowed. "Military operating specialty." He knelt and tightened his shoelace.

"He's messing with you," Mason said. "Julian wasn't military."

"Don't stereotype," JT said. "Some of the higher-ranking scientists and doctors were REMF desk jockeys—they didn't all look and dress like us grunts. Can't hurt to check."

Without looking back, he strode out of the room.

"Well played," Mason said to Brent.

Camilla was troubled.

"I'm not so sure," she said. "There's one organization I can think of with a checkered history when it comes to dangerous and illegal human experimentation. An organization that would literally *kill* to get its hands on a drug like Brent was talking about earlier. The U.S. military."

Brent opened his eyes and looked at her. His smile was paternal, affectionate. "Before his discharge, JT's MOS was oh-three-two-one— forward observer. He was very good at it. Julian promised him a full, honorable reinstatement to his previous rank if he served as official observer here."

CHAPTER 192

Juan stood at the end of the empty dock, looking down into the black water. Already, he could feel his body's rhythms adjusting, slowing in anticipation. Placing a hand over his mask and regulator mouthpiece to hold them in place, he clamped his other elbow against his wounded side. Then he stepped off the dock, and the cool water closed over his head. With a few quick bursts of air, he inflated the rebreather's integrated BC just enough to reach neutral buoyancy.

The fierce pain in his chest faded. He smiled in relief as the water's gentle support lessened the relentless pressure of his own body weight on his injury. Hovering six feet beneath the surface, neither rising nor sinking, he kicked his way into the shadows beneath the dock.

Something glinted ahead—the last section of the shiny chain that had destroyed the scientists' boat. Juan traced it to its source: a massive steel eyebolt screwed through one of the dock's support pilings.

He moved to the next piling, fifteen feet closer to shore. Another heavy chain was attached to its base as well. The second chain led away from the dock, angling down the rocky slope toward deeper water.

He remembered JT saying he had seen someone in scuba gear entering the water near the dock, at night, on multiple occasions. JT had assumed it was *him*. But it could only have been Brent, returning to a hidden base of operations. What had he been doing night after night?

Juan's eyes narrowed. He would know soon enough.

With slow, graceful sweeps of his long free-diving fins, he swam alongside the second chain. The rippling quicksilver surface receded above him as he followed the chain down the slope.

The guideline of steel links led him through a kelp forest. Cathedral rays of light beamed through the towering stalks, laddered with their scythe-shaped green and brown leaves and float bladders, swaying rhythmically in the gentle surge. A huge shoal of sardines hung in the water. The shimmering silver curtain of fish opened to let him through and closed behind him.

Passing through the underwater glade, Juan took in the beauty all around him. Yellow and purple starfish clung to the rocks, and cottony white *Metridium* anemones sprouted like flowers from the dark surface. He felt the knot that sat like a clenched fist in his chest begin to loosen.

The ocean was the only place he felt truly at peace. He wished he could have shown the underwater world he loved so much to Jordan... shared it with her... The thoughts grew too painful to pursue, so he shoved them aside.

A bright orange Garibaldi damselfish hung suspended in the water between two kelp stems. It was a rarity this far north. Standing guard over its nest and eggs, mouth opening and closing, it watched him go by.

He reached the edge of the kelp forest. The chain had taken him deeper. He scanned the blue water around him cautiously before moving out of the kelp. His pulse rose to a steady cadence. His mental radar was on full alert. Juan knew he was a mere visitor here.

He thought of Lauren, who had not known whose territory she was crossing.

A few yards beyond the edge of the kelp, the chain angled down into a narrow underwater ravine. He followed it, and the rocky walls closed in on both sides of him. Three meters over his head, the channel opened into blue water, but the passageway he swam through was only a meter and half wide—narrow enough to protect him from the massive predators patrolling above. Beneath Juan, the channel narrowed to a crack that dropped deep into the island's rocky substratum. He thought of the geological fault lines Dmitry had drawn on the map. A long-ago earthquake had created this rent in the seafloor.

Sea stars and plate-size anemones decorated the walls to each side with splashes of orange, purple, and green. Juan let the chain slide loosely through his glove as he swam. Picturing the map and trying to fix his position in relation to the island, he put himself almost directly in line with the fog signal building.

He could sense a change in the environment: a complete absence of fish around him, a pregnant stillness.

The light changed overhead, darkening his section of channel. Instinctively freezing like a sparrow crossed by the shadow of a hawk, he looked up.

The broad, pale underbelly of a great white shark slid silently through the blue water above the ravine. Its meter-high tail swept back and forth, gradually disappearing from sight.

Moments later, another great white crossed above the edges of the channel, some distance ahead. Juan could see its curving jaws, the protruding gums studded with razor-sharp triangular teeth.

A third, nearly twenty feet long, passed almost directly overhead, so close that Juan could have stroked its belly with an outstretched arm. The shark's gill slits pulsed with the rhythm of its motion. Its dark eye, big as an orange, fixed Juan with a cold stare. Then it, too, slid out of sight behind the lip of the channel.

Juan's heart sped up. He knew what drew these predators to him. He could see the wisps of red that rose from his wet suit where his blood was leaking slowly into the water. It would be an irresistible attractor, but there was no turning back now.

The ravine that he swam through grew shallower ahead. It came to a gradual end on the rocky slope, opening out into blue water.

CHAPTER 193

JT placed a palm on the rim of the cistern's dome and leaped down into the rubble-strewn interior. Four steps brought him to where Julian's moldering body lay sprawled in the circle of light from the hole above.

He knelt beside Julian, waving away the buzzing cloud of flies and holding his breath against the stench. Was it really possible that Julian had been a military scientist? He checked the corpse's slime-soaked front pant pockets. Nothing. Rolling the body to the side, he frisked the hip pockets. Nothing.

He pulled Julian to a seated position, holding him upright with one hand. Julian's head lolled forward, drooling red-orange worms and spilling a cascade of wriggling white maggots onto his forearm. JT shook them off impatiently, with Julian's cold teeth smiling against his other wrist. Then he reached inside the sodden silk coat. The pockets were empty, but he felt something lumpy against Julian's squirming chest: a locket necklace beneath his shirt.

He ripped Julian's collar open, spreading his tie. Julian's head lolled back—too far. The decomposing ligaments and tendons sloughed apart until Julian's skull dangled between his shoulder blades like the hood of a sweatshirt.

A morass of bristly, foot-long marine bloodworms churned inside Julian's sunken chest like wet centipedes. The serrated sides of their segmented bodies slithering orange and green between his exposed ribs. Reaching into the wriggling quagmire, JT fished out the shiny locket that hung from a thin silver chain around Julian's folded neck. A sharp sting pierced his wrist, and a fifteen-inch bloodworm sank its four-pronged jaws deeper into his skin and coiled around his forearm. Ripping the worm loose with his other hand, he tossed it away.

He snapped the locket chain with a jerk of his fist and flipped the elegant silver case open. Tensing, he stared at the picture of the attractive couple inside, seeing Jordan beaming up at him with her flawless smile. Her cheek was pressed against a grinning Julian's.

JT tightened his fist around the locket.

Then he relaxed, shaking his head. Brent's tricks were getting old. It was easy enough to stitch two images together with Photoshop software. Using his MacBook, JT himself could have faked this in five minutes.

But what if they had found this on Julian four days ago, while Jordan was still alive—before they knew that the real culprit was Brent? Would they have believed her?

617

He shook his head again and tossed the locket aside, not liking the answer to his own question.

Hell, they would have killed her over this.

From the corner of his eye, JT caught a flicker of furtive motion at the rim of the hole behind and above him.

He spun toward the threat as someone dropped into the darkness of the cistern's far side. The intruder landed lightly on hands and feet, like a predatory cat, then rose to a crouch, nearly invisible in the shadow of the rim.

Straightening into a ready stance, JT raised his fists. He peered into the darkness, straining to see.

Keeping out of the light, the silhouetted figure circled toward him along the wall of the cistern, staying low. Puffs of steam rose into the cold air: the intruder's breaths, a steady panting.

"Hello, JT," Veronica said.

CHAPTER 194

"It's illogical to hate survivors," Camilla said. "Nobody lives forever."

She stared up into Brent's forbidding, impassive face, needing to understand why they were here, why he had done this to them. She didn't believe any of the reasons he had given them so far. She chose her words carefully.

"Whether we're survivors or not doesn't matter in the end. We *all* die, Brent. It's inevitable."

He hung in front of her, chained to the wheel, his wet suit-clad arms stretched wide. The chains around them looked tight—agonizing, if Brent had been capable of feeling pain. His eyes rose to meet hers, and she could see no antagonism in his face—only fatherly affection.

Mason stepped up beside Camilla, grinning. Her stomach coiled in disgust.

"You're not like *him*," she said to Brent. "I know you can love."

Brent lowered his head. She tried to see his face, but couldn't.

"Survival isn't about the individual," she said to him. "It serves only one purpose. We survive so we can care about each other and help each other. So we can pass on what's best in us to future generations."

She laid a hand on his chained wrist. He raised his head, and she looked into his eyes.

"You've already done that, Brent. I know you're estranged from your family and haven't seen them for years, but that doesn't matter. Your son—he's a part of you. He always will be, no matter what. Don't you see?—you're a survivor, too. You'll live on through your son…"

"That's right." Brent's eye twitched. "When the biopsies came back positive after the second drastic course of chemotherapy—when all the alternative therapies I tried failed to arrest the disease—I told myself that. I finally understood I was not one of nature's select ten percent. I was not a survivor. But I made my peace with dying."

He leaned his head back against the wheel, looking at her steadily.

"Because of the restraining order, I could only watch his progress from afar—the way I watched yours, Camilla. But I *loved* my son. He was my legacy…"

Camilla closed her eyes.

"…and then Jonathan met Jordan," she said.

CHAPTER 195

Mason erupted in surprised laughter. Camilla stared at him in shock. His eyes were bright with amusement.

"Love *and* revenge," he said. "How classic. And how boring. We had made him out to be some kind of monster, Camilla. But he's only a bitter, grieving, lonely old man."

"Mason, stop!" she said. "That's enough."

More pieces were falling into place for her now. She looked at Brent, trying not to hate him for what her own role in this meant. What it said about Camilla herself.

Mason faced Brent, grinning. "I think you've got this whole 'survivor-guilt' thing backward," he said. "But how Jordan must have intimidated you, old man... How she must have *terrified* you. Because of the restraining order, you had to watch from the sidelines while she chewed Jonathan up and spit him out like a woodchipper."

He laughed again—a bright and manic sound that split the pregnant silence.

"She drained the life out of your boy and discarded the empty husk that was left. When he killed himself, she hardly noticed."

"There's no reason for this," Camilla said, trying to pull him away. "He's suffered enough."

Mason resisted her tug on his arm.

"You already *knew* she was a survivor type, didn't you? You'd done your homework. Even before you got sick, you'd been collecting survivors for years, and keeping track of them. They fascinated you, didn't they? They were everything you could never be."

"Stop," Camilla said. "Be better than him."

Brent's face was utterly white. He seemed incapable of speech.

"So, father of the groom... did you violate the court order to try and warn your son about her?" Mason leaned into Brent's face and screamed with laughter. "I can see that you did. But he wouldn't listen, would he? When Jordan turned her personality on full force, she got her way. *Always.*"

Dmitry stirred, awakened by the commotion. He gripped his forehead and sat up, looking puzzled. Turning her back on Brent and Mason, Camilla went to help him.

Mason paced back and forth in front of Brent like a trial lawyer in a courtroom, grandstanding for the jury.

"When Jordan got bored with Jonathan," he said, "the sun must have gone out in his world. And Jonathan was needy. Weak." He chuckled. "After all, he was a chip off the old block. Like father, like son."

Camilla had had enough. "You don't get it, do you?" she said to Mason.

She slipped an arm under Dmitry's shoulder and helped him stand. He swayed.

"Oh, I get it, all right," Mason said. "You have to admire his ambition. He decided to fight fire with fire."

He turned to grin into Brent's face. "You asked yourself what it would take to kill a survivor, and the answer was obvious: *other* survivors."

Spinning to face her with realization dawning in his eyes, he cupped his chin in one palm.

"There's your answer to what the final game was going to be: 'The Most Dangerous Game.' He was going to have the rest of *us* hunt Jordan. Eight survivors against one. To the death."

Reaching into his pocket, Mason pulled out a knife and flipped it open.

"JT's," he said.

With his other hand, he pulled out another, similar knife, and flicked it open, also. He grinned at Camilla. "Veronica's."

"Mason, put those down right now!" Camilla said.

"And finally, we know why *I'm* here." Mason winked at her. "Why he included me. I was his insurance policy. Even if the rest of you survivors failed to get Jordan, he figured I would."

He limped over to stand before Brent. "How were you going to con us all into going after Jordan? Oh, well, I don't suppose it matters now."

Mason grinned a soulless, horrifying grin.

"Surgery is open, Doctor. But I'm afraid *you're* the patient this time."

CHAPTER 196

Camilla let go of Dmitry, and he slumped to his knees. Heart pounding, she crossed the floor to grab Mason's arm again. Heedless of the knives he held, she spun him around to face her.

"You really don't get why he brought us here," she said. "How could someone like you possibly understand?"

He raised an eyebrow, puzzled.

"You were just another exhibit in the menagerie he put together for her," she said. "This wasn't about *killing* Jordan. That wouldn't have been enough. First, she had to learn to see herself the way he saw her. Brent wanted her to *hate* herself."

She pictured Jordan's face at the end: emotionless, cold, withdrawn.

"We were supposed to be a mirror, weren't we?" she said to Brent. "You brought the rest of us here, turned us on each other, and shoved us in Jordan's face to show her what she really was."

She covered her hand with her mouth. "That's why Jordan isolated herself. She figured it out. Oh god, she *knew*."

Had Jordan really thought Camilla was the same as Mason? As Veronica? *Was* she?

She recalled Jordan's words on the beach, from the last time she had seen her alive: *"I'm really sorry he brought you here, Camilla, because you don't deserve this."*

"We all liked her," she said. "We would have found a way to pull together again. We would have listened to her. She would have beat you in the end, Brent."

Her eyes filled with tears. She blinked them back.

"If it weren't for Juan. If only Jordan hadn't fallen in love with him."

CHAPTER 197

Veronica moved into the light. Fog from her breath chuffed out of her mouth in deep, steady pants. Her pale silver eyes were luminous, burning with their own inner fire. Her lips curled in a hungry openmouthed smile.

She looked bat-shit insane to JT.

He made his voice as soothing as he could. "We got him, Veronica. It was Brent all along. You're safe now."

Veronica snorted. "You're making my head hurt.I know goddamn well it wasn't Brent."

She tossed her head in an impatient predatory motion.

"You know what I think?" she said. "It's all of you together. This is some sick, secret little men's-club adventure. Male bonding. You're taking turns tormenting and killing the poor women you lured here."

A cloud of flies rose from Julian's slumping, squirming corpse and swirled in the air between them. Veronica's pupils dilated. She licked her teeth in unnatural excitement, circling toward him.

"Jesus Christ, woman." JT shook his head slowly. "You're disturbed."

"And *you* don't find any of this disturbing? Figures." She laughed, sexy and sultry. "Men."

She tilted her head sideways so her chopped gothic mop of hair hung over her cheek. Staring at him with her bulging eyes, her features twisted in horrible amusement.

"Look at you, JT—you were a good-looking kid, but not any more. Now you're a sideshow freak." Her voice dripped with malice. "Big, tough Marine... a woman half your size kicked your ass. I *ruined* you. I popped your eye like a fucking grape."

Anger surged through his body, but he fought it down.

"You've lost your shit completely," he said. "You need serious help."

"*Help?* JT, if someone did that to *my* eye, I wouldn't stand there like a fucking pussy asking them if they needed my help. You know what I'd do to them?"

Her voice rose, harsh and strident, echoing from the walls around him.

"I'd kill them. I swear to *God*, I'd destroy them. I'd cave in their face, crush their skull, twist their head around backward, rip their heart right out of their body..."

She shook her head sadly at him, moving forward with her arms raised.

Her voice dropped to a seductive purr.

"But that's me."

CHAPTER 198

The mouth of the ravine lay before Juan, opening into blue water. He scanned the water above, ahead, and all around him. Seeing nothing, he kicked cautiously forward to glide out into the blue.

Point of no return.

CHAPTER 199

"Love's a funny thing," Mason said. "I can't say I really understand it. But if this is the kind of thing that happens because of it, then I'm probably better off the way I am."

"That's not true," Camilla said. "I'm sorry for you, too, Mason."

"Don't be. I'm always happy." He walked up to Brent with a knife in each hand. "But *he* looks glum. Let's give him a great big smile that shows off those pearly whites."

A droning noise interrupted him. Camilla's eyes widened at the familiar sound, but it took her a moment to place it: the buzz of a cell phone set to vibrate. She looked down at the floor, where Mason had left Brent's touch-screen phone.

Brent's expression changed. He grinned, and she understood who was truly in control here. The blood drained from her face. He had been biding his time, waiting for this call.

He nodded toward the broad plank wall above her head.

"Take that panel off," he said. "I think you'll all want to see this."

Mason and Dmitry lifted away a six-foot section of shiplap paneling from the wall and set it aside. They stepped back to reveal another large flat-screen monitor that had been concealed behind it.

The screen flickered to life, revealing a blue and watery scene.

Camilla's hand flew to her mouth.

A wet-suited diver kicked out of a narrow canyon in the sloping seafloor, out into blue water. Behind him, a small red LED began to blink rapidly from a recess in the edge of the canyon wall. Concealed amid the rocks all around him, small packages of electronics came to life. Green LEDs flickered. Lenses focused silently.

With his senses intent on the water ahead of him, Juan did not appear to see them.

Camilla's stomach clenched in dread but she could do nothing but watch. She had no way to warn him.

CHAPTER 200

Outside the mouth of the channel, the rocky slope dropped away. Juan kicked out into blue water, feeling exposed and vulnerable. The greater depth made it hard to breathe, the increased water pressure on his chest hurting his injured lung with every inhalation. His head swam with dizziness and he shook it away.

He had to stay alert now. He was leaking blood—a magnet for hungry sharks. It was only a matter of time until one of them found him.

But would that be so bad? It would be an end to the way he felt. He would just become part of the food chain—one more animal that had lost the struggle for survival. He wouldn't have to live any longer with what he had done. Wouldn't have to see Jordan's face every time he closed his eyes.

But he thought of Dmitry, JT, Mason. And Camilla, her sleeping face so innocent and caring.

Juan's jaw clenched. He would not let *her* die here.

Now he could see the entrance to another ravine, branching away in a V from the channel he had swum out of. The second canyon angled back toward the island, providing a relatively safe route that would undoubtedly lead him to his destination: Brent's hidden cave.

But something else caught Juan's eye. He turned away from safety to stare out into the blue.

A vast, dark, spidery shape hung there at the limit of visibility, spreading across his entire field of vision. Like a giant underwater tree hundreds of feet wide, it faded into the murky distance on each side. Heavy anchor chains, bolted to the rocks nearby, trailed into the blue toward the looming branches of the tree. Glints of light reflected at regularly spaced intervals above the branches: silver float-barrels, holding the sprawling web of chains suspended in mid-water.

Juan's heart accelerated, thudding in his chest.

In the distance, massive streamlined shapes moved between the dark spans of chain. Great whites. One of the sharks seized a part of the shadowy web, and its body undulated violently, tearing something free with its jaws. The entire web shook, rippling chains all the way down to the anchor bolts in the sloping seafloor below.

Juan glanced one last time toward the safety of the second ravine. But the answer to the greatest mystery of all lay in front of him.

Drawn irresistibly forward, Juan kicked out into open water. He swam toward the vast, blurry spider web.

He had to see, had to understand.

Black shapes hung from the radiating network of chains, bobbing in the current. Human figures, their arms and legs unmoving, swayed silently in the mild ocean surge. Dozens of them. Hundreds, perhaps. Row after row—a silent army dressed in black—they floated in suspended hibernation, waiting for a general's orders.

Many of them were incomplete, he saw. Missing limbs ended in knobs of bone and trailed wisps of whitened flesh that danced in the current. Some were reduced to ragged lumps of meat surrounded by a few tatters of black.

Juan's breathing sped up, turning ragged and uneven.

The hooded army of the dead faced him in silence, floating in their neoprene wet suits.

CHAPTER 201

Camilla's jaw dropped. It was hard to believe what she was seeing on the screen. Juan looked so vulnerable—a tiny figure hanging frozen in midwater, with a giant black flower unfolding in front him. The network of chains shook violently as, a dozen yards from Juan, a great white shark three times his length tore away the lower half of a wet suit-clad body.

In a moment of horrific clarity, Camilla realized that the complex array of chains was a pulley system—almost exactly like the one Lauren had used to pull their jugs of water back to land so long ago. But in reverse. After all, nobody could possibly be insane enough to swim out and try to rebait the empty hooks.

Brent laughed. "Never having to sleep does have its advantages. You'd be amazed how productive you can be when you're operating at one-hundred-percent efficiency, around the clock."

"We wondered why so many sharks here." A grim-faced Dmitry stood next to her. "This is why," he said. "Like floating whale carcass, it draws them from up and down coast. They come for easy food—all-you-can-eat buffet."

"And this is why Lauren was attacked," Camilla said. She felt sick. "Why they tried to attack *you*..."

"Great white is very smart," he said. "Just like dolphin, they learn." He stared over his shoulder at Brent. "He is *teaching* them to associate human shape with food."

"Oh, no," Camilla breathed. "Juan."

"Quiet. Down in front," Brent said, eyes glued to the screen. His grin widened in anticipation.

"This is my favorite part—I don't want any of you to miss it."

CHAPTER 202

Juan had trouble controlling his breathing. The scene in front of him was impossible. There were too many bodies.

He swam forward and stared into the face of the hood nearest him. His heart skipped a beat. Not human—the projecting flap of knuckled gray skin had no eyes, no nose, no mouth.

Blinking, he realized what he was seeing. It was not a face at all. He was looking at a seal's flipper, curled inside the opening of the wet suit's hood.

Juan took several deep breaths, getting his breathing under control. He looked at some of the other nearby faces. None of them were human. Each wet suit was packed solid with seal meat.

At last he understood the shrinking seal populations, and why Año Nuevo's night sounds had become a chorus of fear.

A monstrous slaughter had stained the island's beaches while the rest of them slept, unaware. A butcher had been diligently at work. Like sausages, the wet suits had been stuffed with bloody seal meat and winched out into the water, night after night.

Brent had been very, very busy.

But something else hung in the center of the web of chains, surrounded by streamers and clouds of billowing white. Juan couldn't see what it was. The puffy white mass obscured it from his sight.

His heart sped up, faster and faster, hammering in his chest. He swam toward the center of the web.

A great white passed alongside, its sandpaper skin brushing against his thigh.

Ignoring it, he kicked closer.

The whiteness looked like a dancing cloud sitting at the heart of the web, where all the chains met.

Travis hung from the chains at one side of the white mass. The end of the scalpel still protruded from the hollow of his throat. His open eyes were milky and unseeing.

Jacob hung on the other side, his forehead split and gaping, the skull misshapen like a stepped-on orange, his bearded face frozen forever in a silent scream.

Juan swam between them, drawn irresistibly closer to the swirling streamers of white, as if by some terrible magnet.

And then the current shifted. The gossamer cloud of tattered white fabric parted gently, revealing what lay at the heart of the web.

Juan's eyes widened.

Bubbles exploded from his mouth as a giant, invisible hand crushed the air from his lungs.

The regulator mouthpiece dropped from his lips, forgotten.

Jordan wore a white wedding dress. Ribbons of lacy fabric from its tattered train swirled slowly about her slim, still figure. Her long blond hair drifted in a golden halo around her head. She hung suspended, one hand reaching toward Juan: a beautiful but cold sea queen, flanked by the silent ranks of her dark and terrible retinue.

The bullet's exit wound in her cheek was nearly invisible. Skilled hands had stitched it back together with delicate precision that spoke of a hate so exquisite it was almost love.

The anger was gone from Jordan's face. Her dead green eyes stared at Juan, filled with infinite sadness.

The giant fingers around his chest tightened mercilessly. He couldn't draw a breath. He clawed at his neck.

She looked lost... So very lost.

A terrible, strangled sound of despair tore out of his throat in a final burst of bubbles.

He couldn't live with this.

Juan shut his eyes tight.

CHAPTER 203

"No!" Camilla splayed her hands against the screen. She watched, helpless, as Juan sank past Jordan's bare feet. He slid from sight, hidden by the bottom of the monitor frame. A final burst of bubbles drifted up through the blue, dwindling away until there was nothing.

She shook her head. He couldn't be dead. He *couldn't* be.

She backed away from the monitor, unable to speak. A sob racked her body.

Brent spoke behind her.

"Every survivor's got a breaking point, Camilla," he said. "I think we just found Juan's."

CHAPTER 204

JT's wrist was broken, he knew. She had broken one of his cheekbones, too. He held his other fist next to his cheek, ready, watching her circle him.

A trail of blood ran from Veronica's ear. He had caught her once, slamming her against the rocks, and she was moving funny now. Her back hitched with every step.

"Don't make me kill you," he said. "Then Brent wins—he beats us both."

"Oh, don't worry about Brent," she said. "I'll get around to him, too. Right after Mason and Juan."

She wiped blood from her chin, panting in excitement.

"You know what?" she said. "I think I'll even take care of that simpering little bitch. She's like Mason's little groupie." A puzzled expression crossed her face. "I find that sort of odd. Don't you?"

"Your second husband was a police officer," JT said. "He served with honor, did his duty. What would he think if he could see you now?"

She laughed, a throaty chuckle of genuine mirth. "You're forgetting how he met me. He knew how I was. It even turned him on."

She stepped over Julian's squirming corpse, coming closer, and looked seductively up at JT.

"He used to threaten me with it, JT. He'd abuse me, do terrible things to me. Sick, *sick*, beastly things." Her nostrils flared. "Then he'd tell me how his brother officers would stand by him if I ever fought back. With my history, he could've made sure I went away for a long time. He thought I would just lie back and take it *forever*."

A finger-thick bloodworm looped over the top of Veronica's athletic shoe, the bristly serrations along its sides rippling with agitation. Looking down at it, she frowned. Then she looked up at JT again.

"Rather grotesque, don't you think?" With a sharp laugh, she flicked the worm away and focused on him with renewed intensity.

"Leo thought he was safe from me. But I found a way, didn't I? You *men*, hiding behind your pathetic little uniforms. You think they can protect you while you do whatever you want to us. Tell me, JT, how are women treated in the Marine Corps?"

"Some of the bravest Marines I know are women," he said. "You're a disgrace to everything they fight for."

"Look who's talking," she said. "I wonder what Sanchez, DiMarco, and Collins would say about you. But we can't ask them, now, can we?"

639

A weight settled over his shoulders. All of a sudden, he felt tired. Old.

"Veronica, it doesn't have to end this way."

"Oh, I think you're wrong," she said. "I think this is exactly how it ends for you."

Veronica charged him, her arms blurring in a vicious flurry of strikes.

CHAPTER 205

Juan's consciousness was fading. Crushing, invisible coils pulled tighter around his body and held him immobile as he sank. He stopped struggling and settled to the seafloor, ninety feet below the surface, letting it all go away.

A voice spoke in the blackness. In Spanish. Dimly, he recognized his brother Álvaro—laughing, happy, the way he always had been.

"When I saw that *monstruoso* shark tooth, César, I knew I had to get it for you." Álvaro's joking voice turned serious. "I know how you love the sea, but I worry about you sometimes, big brother. Keep this next to your heart. It will keep you safe from harm."

Juan remembered holding the wedge-shaped *megalodon* fossil in his hands for the first time, marveling at its timeless perfection. It was twenty million years old, and his brother had bought it just for him. His heart swelled with affection.

And then he remembered.

Álvaro spoke again. His voice sounded different now. Colder. No longer a memory.

"I understand why you left, big brother," he said. "Our life—it was not a good life. Maybe for *papá,* but not for us. We would have come with you, César—*I* would have come with you. But you never even asked us."

Juan's chest heaved. A few tiny bubbles trickled out through his nose.

"I cannot forgive you," Álvaro's voice said. "Neither can Constancia or *mamá.* Nor can *Jordan* forgive you now. We are dead, and the dead cannot forgive."

The voice in his head changed again, no longer sounding like Álvaro.

"But now other people need you," it said. "If you die, so will they. Open your eyes, *pendejo!* This, too, is a coward's choice. You are running away again."

Juan recognized the voice in his head.

It was his own.

He opened his eyes.

641

CHAPTER 206

S ensing a change in the room's lighting, Camilla raised her head.

Brent was no longer smiling. His face wasn't lit with a blue glow anymore. She swung around to stare at the monitor.

On-screen, the blue water had disappeared. In its place, she could see a rough tunnel, lit by an uneven row of fluorescent tubes bolted at head height to the rocky wall. The tunnel's walls were uneven and wet. The ceiling narrowed as it climbed out of sight, shrinking to a narrow fissure in the rock. Below, the fissure dropped into a wide crack in the tunnel floor, alongside one of the walls.

A shiny black figure came into view. Its back was to the monitor as it strode purposefully down the tunnel, holding a gun in one hand.

Camilla's heart leaped in her chest, filling with joy.

The figure was Juan.

She grabbed Dmitry's wrist, and he put his hand over hers and squeezed.

Behind her, Mason laughed.

"You can't kill a survivor that easily, Brent."

CHAPTER 207

Juan's rubber-soled scuba booties splashed through puddles on the floor of the tunnel. A rough-edged crevice a half meter wide ran along one wall, near his feet. Sea foam surged down in the crevice. Orange starfish clung to its sides. The rock beneath his feet was nearly smooth, though. The fluorescent xenon tubes lit everything with a harsh, clinical white light.

He had followed a chain through the second ravine, and it had led him here. Emerging from the water onto a rocky ledge, inside a cave roughly the size of the cistern dome that lay above, he had seen an electric chain haul, lag-bolted to the rock, beside a portable yellow Honda generator. The chain stretched up out of the water to wrap around a steel capstan the size of an oil drum, also bolted to the rock.

There had been two exits from the cave: the pool of water, and the tunnel that Juan now stalked through, gun at the ready. He didn't expect to find anyone else down here, but then again, Brent had surprised him time and time again.

His heart ached with loss. He wanted to retrieve Jordan's body so he could bury her properly, but he couldn't afford the delay. There was too much at stake right now. No more mistakes.

The ones he had already made would haunt him forever.

Reaching the end of the tunnel, Juan stopped at stainless steel double doors set into the rock with a lumpy pour of concrete. The solid-looking metal doors reminded him of a hospital morgue. A red LED blinked from the keypad of a number lock built into the handle.

Raising the Glock, he fired into the lock over and over again, sending white sparks scattering across the steel doors. In the enclosed tunnel, the pressure waves from the gunshots slammed against his eardrums, ringing loudly in his head. Tiny bits of shrapnel peppered his arm and hand, but he ignored their burning mosquito stings.

On the seventh shot, the lock gave way. The steel doors swung open a few centimeters. Raising a foot, he kicked them wide.

He smelled blood.

The gallery beyond the doors looked like a cross between an operating room and an abattoir. A sense of urgency drove him forward. Sweeping the space with his gun, he moved inside.

A row of eviscerated seal carcasses hung on hooks from the rocky ceiling. He pushed past them, bumping some and setting them swinging.

Piles of black wet suits overflowed from a stack of storage crates.

645

A half-stuffed wet suit lay on a stainless steel morgue table. The table's wheels were locked to prevent it from rolling. Dark liquid dripped into the fluid tray beneath.

Three other tables lay nearby. Unoccupied now.

His throat tightened. Brent had stitched Jordan's face on one of these cold steel morgue tables. He had changed her into her wedding dress here.

Juan turned away.

He paused briefly to pick up something that looked like a handheld power drill—a thick gray plastic pistol shape with a trigger, and a heavy battery built into the butt of the grip. Instead of a drill bit, a thick six-inch cylinder projected like the suppressor on a silenced pistol.

Captive bolt gun.

Juan recognized the device, normally used to stun cattle for slaughter. The steel bolt penetrated the skull with shattering force to destroy the brain. This was what Brent had used on his silent nightly seal hunts… and on Jacob.

Juan's fist tightened on the handle and his lips pulled back from his teeth as he imagined holding it to Brent's forehead and pulling the trigger.

Maybe his own forehead right afterward, too. *Oblivion. An end. Peace.*

He pictured Camilla's face. She would be disappointed in him right now.

Putting the bolt gun down, he wiped his fingers on his wet suit and moved on.

A steel sink with high gooseneck faucet hose stood next to a wall, alongside its pressure tank and pump.

A chain saw rested on a length of steel counter, next to a black rubber butcher's apron and curved acrylic face shield.

Juan moved past, taking it all in with rapid glances, seeing nothing useful.

He knew he didn't have much time.

Brent would have an endgame in mind, and events were moving rapidly toward some unknown conclusion. To save Camilla and the others from whatever fate Brent had planned for them all, Juan would have to move even faster.

The tunnel continued on the other side of the operating room. He could hear the faint hum of generators ahead. Raising the gun, he moved into the circular chamber that lay just beyond.

The uneven ceiling of this second cave was much higher than the first. Aquamarine light filtered from cracks ten meters overhead, projecting in diagonal rays like sunbeams through the stained-glass windows of a church. Tendrils of kelp dangled from the ceiling, drying in the air.

A row of dehumidifiers sat along the wall to his right, next to a humming yellow Honda generator. A double-wide server rack, dense with computer and network equipment and hanging loops of Cat-6 network cabling, stretched the length of the left wall. Blinking green and amber lights winked in a chaos of shifting patterns above the row of portable generators that lined the rack's base.

Just ahead, an array of six wide-screen computer monitors, two high and three wide, dominated the room. The monitors lined a long stainless steel desk that also supported a wireless aluminum keyboard and track pad.

A mesh-backed Aeron office chair sat in front of the desk.

Juan knew he had found Brent's office. This was where the doctor spent the night shift.

He crossed the floor rapidly. A plastic crate of foil-wrapped Powerbar energy bars sat near his feet. He shoved it aside with his toe as he passed.

Next to the monitors, shiny chrome nozzles and stainless steel gleamed from a high-end espresso machine.

Stopping in front of the desk, he shrugged the scuba rebreather from his shoulders and dropped it against the wall. He slid into the chair.

A framed certificate hung from the rocky wall above the monitors. Glancing at the prestigious-looking diploma—Johns Hopkins School of Medicine—Juan smirked.

A framed photograph sat next the keyboard. His smirk faded. A younger Brent smiled at him, one arm around a teenager Juan recognized from Julian's first profile: Brent's son Jonathan. Brent's wife, Mary, stood in front of them both, beaming.

A large coffee mug sat on the desk—a child's hobby project painted in bright happy colors, now faded and chipped. Large, uneven letters wrapped around the mug: a child's handwriting, saying, "World's Greatest Dad."

Another framed photograph sat nearby: Jordan's dazzling smile, laughing as she leaned over Jonathan from behind, her arms clasped around his shoulders.

The crushing bands tightened around Juan's chest again. He turned away from Jordan's picture and tapped the track pad on the desk before him.

Six monitor screens brightened, filling the room with their glow.

Two were divided into grids of smaller video windows—live shots of different places around the island, indoors and outdoors. In one, he could see himself from the side, leaning toward the monitors. In another window, his own face loomed large, staring out at him—no doubt from the camera atop the monitor.

In a third, he could see Camilla's eager face looking at him. Mason and Dmitry stood beside her. Behind them, Brent glared from his spread-armed position, crucified on the wheel. But where was JT? Juan couldn't see him.

He looked at the remaining monitors. Video editing software ran on one, displaying thumbnail clips of the work in progress: snippets from their ten days on the island, scenes from each of the games. One small preview window showed a great white shark exploding from the surface over and over, with Lauren in its jaws. In another, Jordan balanced on one leg, aiming the speargun at a cringing version of himself.

Seeing it sent Juan's thoughts back to the cattle bolt gun in the next room. An end to the pain.

The Glock strapped to his thigh would get the job done just as well.

He looked away.

The next monitor displayed a directory folder listing dozens of video files:

```
Camilla Profile.mp4
JT Profile.mp4
Natalie Profile.mp4
Lauren Profile.mp4
...
```

Juan scrolled down the list.

```
...
Shipboard Welcome.mp4
Seal Roundup Intro.mp4
Seal Roundup.mp4
Seal Roundup - penalty.mp4
Scavenger Hunt Intro.mp4
Scavenger Hunt - serious injury.mp4
Scavenger Hunt - fatality.mp4
Scavenger Hunt - multiple fatalities.mp4
Capture the Flag Intro.mp4
Capture the Flag - incomplete.mp4
Capture the Flag - serious injury.mp4
Capture the Flag - fatalities.mp4
...
```

Narrowing his eyes, he scrolled down to the bottom.

```
...
Julian's Posthumous Accusation.mp4
Most Dangerous Game - Jordan dead.mp4
Most Dangerous Game - Jordan injured.mp4
Most Dangerous Game - Jordan victory.mp4
Closing Ceremonies - the Fog Signal.mp4
```

Juan looked at the last entry. Sounding the fog signal would have certainly meant their deaths. But what would the signal have triggered? Poison gas? A cloud of some deadly virus or disease, released into the air?

Turning to the last monitor, he could see a file transfer in progress. The progress bar filled while a digital timer counted down the remaining seconds:

```
0:06... 0:05... 0:04... 0:03... 0:02... 0:01... 0:00
UPLOAD COMPLETE
```

He tapped the keyboard, and a password dialog appeared. Locked.

Motion on another monitor caught his eye.

He swiveled the chair toward it, and his stomach clenched.

In one of the live video windows, JT and Veronica circled at the bottom of the cistern, locked in deadly combat.

Out of the corner of his eye, he saw the last monitor blink. Its display changed. Swinging back to stare at it, he felt tension tighten every muscle of his body.

```
LIVE TRANSMISSION
0:00... 0:01... 0:02... 0:03... 0:04... 0:05...
```

With a countdown, at least you knew how long you had. But with the seconds ticking *upward* now, there was no way to tell. He raised his face toward the monitor where Camilla, Mason, and Dmitry stared back at him. He waved them aside impatiently, and they stepped away so he could see Brent's face.

Brent grinned malevolently at him. His expression told Juan everything he needed to know.

Endgame. This was it. They were all about to die.

Juan thrust the chair away from the desk and stood. What he was looking for—the answer to his final question—had to be here somewhere. He turned a circle, focused intently on the rock walls around him. Then he crossed the floor to stand in front of the rack of computer servers and network equipment.

He had never seen computer racks mounted like this before, flush against a wall. There was a reason you didn't do it that way: overheating. Without air circulation from behind, the servers would generate enough heat to fry themselves.

Grabbing the upper corner of the rack, Juan pulled, ignoring the pain that shot through his torso as he put all his weight into it. The racks pulled free from the rock and toppled, crashing to the ground in a burst of sparks. Four of the monitor screens above Brent's desk went dark. Juan stepped over loops of blue cable to stare into the gaping cave gallery beyond. He could hear something hissing back there.

Fluorescent tubing illuminated a large space. Multiple geological faults had come together under the island here, he knew. In some past era, water had flowed freely, widening the spaces. The gallery was vast, dozens of meters wide, fading into darkness in the distance. Irregular columns and pillars of rock held up the roof. The ceiling hung low in places, rising high in others. Juan saw fossils embedded in the rocky columns—shells, fish skeletons, even sharks' teeth—but he barely noticed them.

Cylindrical tanks ringed the columns, held against them by shiny metal straps. The two-meter cylinders were painted blue, gray, and green. The diamond-shaped labels on the nearest tanks read "Oxygen," "Nitrous Oxide," "Diethyl Ether." Medical gases. Shorter, squatter cylinders sat below, resting on the floor: propane tanks. Already he could smell something sweet hissing into the air.

There were dozens of the tanks. Hundreds of them, stretching into the distance, belted to the pillars of rock. Juan looked up at the uneven ceiling. Camilla, Dmitry, and Mason were directly overhead, unaware of the terrible trap that lay below their feet. Only a thin crust of rock and concrete separated them from certain death.

The fog whistle would have detonated the tanks, he was sure. It would have brought down half the island. But Brent would also have another way of detonating them, even tied up as he was.

Sound.

Microphones, programmed to recognize the fog signal. No doubt they would also listen for a key phrase, one Brent could say anytime, that would also function as a trigger.

He would say it very soon.

Time was running out. They were all going to die here.

Juan closed his eyes.

He knew what he had to do.

It was the only thing someone in this situation *could* do.

CHAPTER 208

Camilla brought her face close to the monitor screen, frowning. Juan had stepped back into view to look directly at her. There was something new in his face, in his body language, that caused her to tense up. Juan's characteristic reserve was gone. His composure had been shattered.

She stared into his eyes, seeing sadness. Regret.

"No." A little laugh of disbelief escaped from her lips. She shook her head. "No, you *can't,* Juan."

His chest heaving with suppressed emotion, he stepped closer to the monitor and raised a hand. He held it up, palm out.

Saying good-bye.

"No, no, *no!*" Slapping her hand onto the screen, Camilla covered his palm with hers, trying to hold him in place. She shook her head vigorously, imploring him with her eyes. "No, *please* don't do this."

From behind the illusion of their joined hands, he pressed his face nearer, and his eyes held hers in inconsolable, mute sorrow. Then his gaze flicked over her shoulder toward Mason, and his eyes hardened briefly. She understood all too well what he was telling Mason: *Take good care of her.*

Juan didn't *know.*

She pounded the monitor with her fist. "No! You *can't* leave me here!"

Shoulders heaving, he stared at her without looking away, as if he were trying to burn her face into his memory forever.

Camilla tried to laugh, but it turned into a sob.

The raw pain in his eyes held her transfixed.

She pounded the screen again, hurting her hand, not caring. She brought her other fist up to beat the screen, too. Her legs went weak and wobbly.

Juan was abandoning her.

Just like her parents had abandoned her.

One hand upraised in farewell, he watched her with bottomless unhappiness.

She hammered the screen with both fists. *Don't look at me like that.*

He raised his stare toward Brent, and his face twisted in bitter anger. She wasn't sure whom the hate in his eyes was directed at: Brent or himself.

Tears streamed down her cheeks, but she didn't care. She pounded the screen.

"I believed in you, Juan!" she screamed at him. "I *believed* in you!"

He raised his other hand, clutching something that dangled from his fist.

651

Hyperventilating, she splayed her fingers against the screen and pressed her face closer, trying to see what he held. It looked like a bundle of cables.

Juan's eyes narrowed, staring past her, at Brent again. Then he jerked his fist, yanking violently at the cables.

The monitor screen went blank.

•   •   •

Hands on Camilla's arms, strong but gentle, possessive. They pulled her away from the darkened screen. *Mason.* She turned to hug him, to let loose the sobs that were trying to tear her insides apart.

Then she remembered what he was.

She shoved him away forcefully and sank to her knees, chest heaving. He stepped back, palms upraised. Her hands hurt. There was blood on Mason's shirt, blood smeared on the monitor, too. She didn't care.

Mason didn't approach her again. He was afraid of her. *Mason* was afraid of *her.* Maybe Juan was right to leave her behind. Maybe she did belong here, with Brent. With Mason. She realized that Brent was speaking to her, and the honest sympathy in his rumbling voice shattered her last defenses.

"I'm truly sorry, Camilla," he said. "I know you had hoped for better from Juan. But now you can see what he really is. What *all* you survivors are."

She would never see Avery again, she knew. Never see any of her kids again. They would all wonder what they had done to make *her* abandon them, too. And little Avery would sit and wait for her because of the promise she was now breaking. He would wait, and wait, and blame himself when she never came.

He would wish he were dead.

Gasping, she tried to draw a deep breath, but her chest and stomach tightened like a fist, curling her body over. Pulling her elbows into her lap, she huddled on the floor, rocking, wanting to retreat into herself and leave all this hurt behind. She would just shut everything out, as she had as a child, and go away again—maybe forever, this time.

"Juan *wasn't* going to leave us," she said, her voice weak. "But he found something else that we didn't see. You put something down there that *made* him do it."

"Whatever his reasons, he won't get far," Brent said. "I left an empty scrubber in the rebreather. He'll be unconscious from carbon dioxide buildup before he makes it halfway across the channel."

CHAPTER 209

Juan moved with furious, single-minded purpose. His injury hampered him a little, but the pain was only a minor distraction—someone else's pain now, set aside. He had no time to indulge it.

His mind was ice clear and laser focused. The seconds crawled slowly by as he coursed through the caverns with brutal speed, doing what he needed to do, every movement precise and sure.

He triggered the captive bolt gun again, shattering another strap, and yanked the tank of nitrous oxide away from the column of rock. Carrying it under one arm, he scooped up a propane tank with his other hand. The weight of his load now balanced, he exited the gallery.

Hurried strides took him across the smaller room. As he passed Brent's desk he glanced at the monitors:

```
LIVE TRANSMISSION
8:32... 8:33... 8:34...
```

Juan didn't look at the scuba rebreather as he went by. It lay on the floor next to the desk, where he had dropped it.

And where it would stay.

Speeding down the tunnel, he paralleled the crack in the floor that ran along the wall. He could see the gleam of water below. He reached the point where the crack grew wide enough and, without hesitating, threw both metal tanks into the fissure. They clanged against the rocky sides, sliding into the water to come to rest two meters below the surface, atop a growing pile of gray, green, and blue cylinders.

He turned and plunged back through the tunnel, the hard rubber soles of his booties slapping against the floor.

Reentering the gallery, he picked up the bolt gun and moved to the next column. Already he had cleared all the tanks within fifteen meters of the gallery entrance. But there were so many more.

He knew he wouldn't get them all before Brent realized what he was doing, or simply decided it was time to bring things to an end. But maybe, just maybe, he could remove enough to make a difference—to give the others a fighting chance to live.

Camilla thought he had abandoned her to die. Even if he succeeded here, she would never know he hadn't.

But Juan had known that he couldn't warn them. A warning would have killed them all. Brent would have detonated the trap as soon as they tried to run.

Carrying two more tanks, he rushed down the tunnel again, passing the monitor:

9:14... 9:15... 9:16...

He had to go farther this time, because the crack was filling with tanks. He needed them deep enough to protect them from the coming explosion. Reaching the pool at the end, next to the chain capstan, he threw the tanks he carried into the water. Then he spun on his heel and plunged back up the tunnel.

He coughed, spitting blood. But he never slowed his pace, forcing himself onward relentlessly. If he was fast enough now, maybe he could save them. Maybe not.

Either way, he would never know.

Juan did know one thing with absolute, cold certainty, though.

His journey beneath the island was a one-way trip.

CHAPTER 210

Mason looked at Camilla's huddled form and felt a little concerned. Dmitry knelt beside her, speaking to her in soothing tones. He laid a hand on her shoulder, but she pulled away from him, curling tighter. Mason was reasonably certain she would be okay, but he wasn't quite sure how to help her right now, so instead, he pulled out Brent's phone.

Curious, he tapped the touch screen. The pass-code lock was gone. In its place, he saw a miniature version of the familiar scoreboard, scaled down from what they had seen on the monitors in the houses. Mason tapped his own name a few times and grinned as his score increased.

"There's an app for that?" He tilted the screen toward Brent and chuckled. "*Now* we know why you always had your hands in your vest pockets."

He swiped the screen with two fingers, and the scoreboard slid aside to reveal a grid of smaller video windows. A string of text ran below them.

LIVE TRANSMISSION... 11:26... 11:27... 11:28...

In one of the small windows, Mason could see himself, with Brent hanging over his shoulder like a big silver-headed scarecrow in a black wet suit.

In another, JT and Veronica circled in the depths of the cistern, fighting. Mason shook his head, amused. The rocuronium would have worn off half an hour ago because Juan had stopped him from leaving to redose Veronica. Now she was on the loose again. He had no doubt she would kill JT. He would have to find another way to subdue her without killing her, so they could spend some quality time together. He found Veronica very exciting.

"Mason..." Camilla's ragged voice drew his attention. She sat up partway, still hunched over, her back rising and falling in rapid breaths. "Kill him." Her head stayed bowed, hair hanging in her face. "For me."

He couldn't see her expression.

"That's what you want?" he asked.

"Just kill him," she said.

He grinned. "You don't have to ask *me* twice."

He pulled out a knife, flipped it open. Lowering the phone to put it in his pocket, he caught new movement in a third window on the screen: a wet suit-clad figure racing down a tunnel.

Mason's eyes widened. It was Juan, carrying two bulky cylinders under his arms, moving faster than Mason had ever seen him move before. Juan threw the cylinders into a pool of water and disappeared back up the tunnel.

"Kill him. *Right. Now.*" Camilla's chest heaved with contractions. "Or *I'll* do it."

"Sh-h-h." Raising a hand for silence, Mason focused intently on the phone screen. Juan was back with two more cylinders.

Watching him, Mason sucked in a breath.

Tanks of gas. Directly below them right now. A timer counting off seconds.

Sliding the phone into his pocket, he took off for the door in a limping run.

He glanced over his shoulder. Dmitry was staring at him with a shocked expression. Camilla scrambled to her feet.

Mason shouted, "Run!" and plunged through the doorway.

Behind them all, hanging from the wheel with his arms stretched wide, Brent smiled. Raising his voice, he intoned the words with slow gravitas:

"Consummatum est."

CHAPTER 211

Juan tossed two tanks—green oxygen and blue ether—into the pool. He turned away from the water, and a warm breeze blew his hair back from his forehead. A rumble shook the floor beneath his feet, growing in intensity.

His time had run out.

The far end of the tunnel glowed with orange light, brighter and brighter, racing toward him.

A roaring filled his ears.

Juan relaxed. He stood up straight, facing the oncoming glow, resolute and calm.

He had done everything he could; he only wished he could have done more. But maybe it was enough. Maybe Camilla and the others had a chance now.

He closed his eyes as the world around him exploded in flame and fury.

CHAPTER 212

A rumble shook the fog signal building, throwing Camilla to her knees.
It felt like an earthquake.

Above her, Brent leaned his head back against the spoke of the great
metal wheel. The floor at the far side of the building gave way. The rows of
old machinery collapsed into the flaming void that yawned below, dropping
like a row of dominoes as the floor unzipped beneath them. The block of
machinery that Brent was tied to tilted backward, lifting him up and away
from her to drop from sight.

She screamed. The section of floor beneath her tilted forty-five degrees,
sending her sliding toward the gaping hole that Brent had disappeared
through. To her right, the west wall of the factory building caved in,
crumbling as the island's surface collapsed beneath it. Billowing gouts of blue
and orange flame shot upward on both sides of her.

Clinging to the canted flooring, she hung on desperately, her feet kicking
in empty space. Thirty feet away from her, Dmitry stood on an unstable
section of flooring, trying to keep his footing. Flames rose around him, and
his eyes, wide with terror, met hers. Balancing on the sagging floorboards, he
looked just as he had out on the water, crouched on the fragment of the
Orca's rear deck, waiting for the great white's strike.

She clutched the splintered wood and pulled herself forward. Dragging
her legs up onto the broken, tilting section of floor, she crawled toward
Dmitry.

But this time, there was no pressure wave to warn him. The flooring
beneath him collapsed with brutal suddenness, and he fell screaming into the
flames below.

Camilla turned her face away from a jet of fire that roared up through a
gap in the boards.

All around her, the building groaned like a dying ship.

Something huge gave way in the depths underneath, shaking the whole
island. The entire factory building dropped several feet, bouncing Camilla
against the floorboards, hurting her ribs and shaking her grip loose. She slid
toward the gaping pit.

As she rolled off the edge she caught a broken floor beam and clung to it,
hanging by her arms now. She glanced down between her flailing sneakers,
seeing hungry darkness and patches of flame below. On every side, the edges
of the pit were crumbling away, dropping into the hole, widening it.

Another violent groan above her. She looked up.

The building's massive roof beams shifted and sagged against one another, collapsing in on themselves. She screamed, hurting her throat.

The section of flooring she hung from broke free. Camilla fell into the darkness below.

The roof came down, and the whole building collapsed into the void on top of her, shutting out the light.

CHAPTER 213

The floor of the cistern shook violently beneath JT's feet. Then it dropped away, collapsing into a shifting, tumbling rock slide. He covered his head with his arms, tumbling amid the debris and coming to rest in an uneven pile of broken concrete. The floor of the cistern now sloped away into darkness.

Veronica was somewhere nearby—the collapse would have caught her as well. But the gap at the bottom of the tilted floor drew his eye.

Flames danced and glimmered in the black void below, as if the earth had split to reveal a glimpse of hell.

JT stared at it. "What the fuck?"

Closer by, something moved weakly in the shadows. Tensing, he prepared to defend himself.

"JT, I'm trapped. Help me," Veronica's voice commanded.

A pile of rubble covered her legs and stomach. Her hands shoved at the rocks, trying to push them off her body like a heavy quilt. Then she stopped moving. There was a lot of blood.

"I think I'm dying here." She sounded matter-of-fact about it. "My back is broken."

She coughed. "Oh shit. I'm cold, JT."

The ground wasn't stable. The broken floor of the cistern trembled under him. He knew that it could shift or give way at any moment. He looked up at the bright circle of light from the cistern's entrance—the rim of the crumbling dome. It lay farther above now than before.

Veronica's voice changed.

"I'm so cold..." Scared now.

A billowing column of smoke and gray dust rose outside, eclipsing one side of the circle of brightness. It climbed higher and higher, expanding into a mushroom shape that blotted out the sky. Its shadow fell across him...

...like the smoke rising from a crashed helicopter. In his mind, he could hear his squadmates' voices once again: DiMarco's shouts, Collins's groans. Sanchez, whispering, *Tengo que volver a mi madre, ella está enferma... ayúdame...*

JT shook his head, chasing the distraction away. He stared up at the opening to the cistern. He knew he could make it, but he had to hurry.

He crawled upslope. Julian's ribcage cracked apart under his weight, releasing its squirming cargo of green and orange bloodworms onto the rocks beneath him.

He pictured the stunned betrayal on Sanchez's face, watching him sling the pack over his uninjured shoulder, the broken fragments of the IFF beacon still embedded in his boot sole. The kid hadn't been praying anymore.

The swirling dust cloud shifted above the cistern. A narrow ray of sunlight broke through, painting JT's face with its warmth.

He had to go *now*.

"Don't leave me down here," Veronica said behind him. "I don't want to die all alone."

Then she coughed out a small laugh of resignation. "Oh, never mind. I forgot who I was talking to."*Aw, hell...* JT closed his eye and stopped moving. For long seconds, he stayed that way, locked in a silent struggle with himself. The opening beckoned from above, pulling him. He felt as if he were being torn in two. Then he relaxed, shoulders sagging. Veronica was a psychotic nightmare, but she was no coward. She had her own strange sense of duty and honor. He couldn't spend the rest of his life knowing that he had deserved even *her* contempt.

The momentary opening in the dust cloud shrank shut again, and the ray of light dwindled and died. With one last glance at the darkening circle of sky, he turned and crawled back to where Veronica lay bleeding.

Her eyes, huge and luminous in the darkness, fixed on his face. Her body relaxed.

"I didn't mean what I said." Her breathing seemed to ease, too. "You're still a good-looking kid."

He reached out and brushed the bloody hair from her forehead. She shivered.

"I don't know what's wrong with me, why I am the way I am," she said. "But I guess it doesn't really matter anymore. For whatever it's worth, I'm sorry. For everything."

Her breath caught. "I tried, JT. I really tried. I wanted to do something good, you know? It wasn't easy, given how I am. But I found a way to help. To make the world a little better for some."

He realized she was talking about her work. Her women's shelter.

She groped for his hand. He let her take it.

Her voice turned uncertain. "I *think* I made a difference."

"That's the most we can hope for," he said.

"So cold, JT. Just hold me." Trembling, she laughed a broken version of her sultry laugh. "Sorry, that's pretty cliché, huh?"

Her eyes seemed to have trouble focusing on him. He put his other arm around her and settled into a reclining position beside her.

Lowering her head to his chest, she lay still. "I guess there's no money, then," she whispered.

He laughed even though it hurt. "No, I guess there isn't."

Veronica purred a little laugh, too. "What a waste this all was, then. What a terrible, terrible waste."

She curled tighter against his chest, shivering.

Shifting to a more comfortable position, JT stroked her hair.

His gaze wandered back to the darkened circle of sky. But it seemed impossibly far now.

CHAPTER 214

Somewhere in the orange-lit dimness that surrounded Camilla, a man screamed in agony.

Dmitry. He was hurt. She had to help him.

She sat up, bumping her head. Miraculously, other than bruises and scrapes from head to toe, she herself seemed to be uninjured. Blinking, she looked around in the light of the flickering flames.

A maze of broken rock and concrete surrounded her beneath a low, uneven ceiling. Cramped, narrow passages ran away from her in several directions, winding between crushed machinery and fallen beams.

Camilla's breath caught. She *recognized* her surroundings.

"This isn't happening." Her own adult voice sounded strange to her ears. "It isn't real."

Invisible spiders crawled over her scalp. The skin on her arms tightened, twisting into gooseflesh. Twenty-three years fell away in a heartbeat, disappearing into darkness.

Orange fire flickered nearby, lighting a curved metal surface beside her. It looked like the side panel of a car. She jammed a fist into her mouth, biting her knuckles to keep from screaming. A terrible, trapped keening noise rose from her throat instead. The hair on the back of her neck prickled and stood up.

Pulling her hand away from her mouth, she tried to crawl and started shuddering. Uncontrollably. Her teeth chattered.

She inched forward on her hands and knees, arms and legs shaking so violently they banged against the uneven walls and piled rubble.

Dmitry's screams multiplied.

They were joined by other screams, moans, and sobs from all sides, echoing through the rocky maze: the voices of men, women, children.

Not real... not real... not real not real not real notrealnotrealnotreal...

By the orange light of the fires, she could see cars now.

Crushed cars.

CHAPTER 215

Waves crashed over the low boulder, depositing something new on top. The crab scuttled forward, investigating the large inert shape sprawled across the wet rock. It crawled over the curved black surface, not liking the firm, spongy texture beneath its walking legs, but intent on reaching the pink, starfish-shaped object at the end: food.

The crab squeezed beneath the fleshy projections that curled up from the food shape, and crawled into the center of the pinkness. With its mandibular palps, it tasted the ragged flesh at the base of one of the projections. The food was too firm, the meat too fresh, but the crab was hungry. It tore away a larger piece with its claws and used its palps to guide the meat into its mouth.

The pink food shape twitched.

Alarmed, the crab tried to scramble for safety but the pink projections curled inward to tighten around its shell, crushing it.

• • •

Juan's fingers opened, trembling, and the next wave washed the crab out of his palm. He rolled onto his back.

Every part of his body hurt. He coughed up a stream of bloody water. His head pulsed and throbbed with pain. When he inhaled, only one side of his chest filled with air. The injured lung had collapsed, he knew. It felt heavy with fluid.

Sharp, piercing pain spiked the insides of his ears, like the ears of a novice diver who had failed to equalize correctly. Water foamed white on the rocks, inches from his cheek, and drained away: a wave crashing in eerie silence.

He should have heard it.

He couldn't hear anything.

Juan touched his ear and winced, pulling away fingers tipped with blood. His eardrums were ruptured. He would never scuba dive again. But he was alive. He shouldn't be—he had no idea how he had survived the explosion. But somehow he was still alive.

Grinning, he blinked up at the bright blue sky, not wanting to move. *Alive.* It was enough to lie here in blissful animal contentment...

Camilla. Dmitry. JT. Mason.

The grin fell away from his face.

A galvanizing jolt of adrenaline surged through his limbs. Hurling himself to his feet, he stood, dizzy and swaying, on the table-size boulder's surface. His vision doubled and blurred. He squinted, seeing only ocean surrounding the wet rock where he stood.

He spun 180 degrees about, to face the island, which lay a hundred yards away. A channel of churning white boiled the water in a broad line stretching toward the rock where Juan stood. Steam rose from its surface. Debris floated along its length.

Juan's eyes followed the path of churning whitewater back to the island, and horror engulfed him like a smothering blanket. His legs buckled, and he dropped to his hands and knees. Sucking in a one-sided breath, he shook his drooping head from side to side.

He had failed. They were all dead.

He gagged and vomited, spraying seawater and blood across the rocks.

Throwing his head back, he stared at the island. A towering gray mushroom cloud rose from its surface, where the fog signal buildings once stood. The billowing column of dust hung motionless in the air, dwarfing the island below. It doubled and swayed in Juan's unsteady vision. Beneath the cloud, the surface of the island had caved in. A brand-new valley stretched inland from the shore, indenting the bluffs like the rut of a giant motorcycle tire in mud.

The fog signal buildings that had housed the science station were gone, swallowed up by the collapse.

While he watched, kneeling, a crack in the earth widened. It zigzagged from the waterline up the hill in a path of collapsing ground, racing toward the cistern. The rim of the cistern's dome fell in, disappearing into the hole in awful silence and sending up another cloud of dust.

Sole survivor.

He gagged in horror. His stomach heaved.

Please not this. Anything *but this. Not again.*

The mushroom cloud rose overhead, ridiculing his failure. Mocking him for still being alive to see it.

He pushed himself to his feet and swayed, the damage to his inner ears throwing off his balance.

Juan threw himself forward in a dive.

Ears throbbing with agony, he surfaced, already swimming hard toward the island.

CHAPTER 216

JT coughed. His legs hurt. He looked at the blocks of broken concrete that had tumbled onto his shins from the collapsing cistern dome, trapping him.

Veronica shifted in his arms. She lay panting on top of him, chest to chest, as clouds of dust rose around them.

Their eyes met.

A torrent of cold water poured into the cistern through the zigzagging channel that now connected their sunken prison with the sea. The cold water churned around their ankles, rising fast over their knees, their waists... their chests. JT strained against the weight of the concrete rubble holding him down, but couldn't budge.

Game over. They were fucked.

Veronica relaxed in his arms and closed her eyes.

He kept his eye open as the water rose over their heads, chilling his cheeks. To his surprise, Veronica raised her face toward him and pressed her open lips against his in a sensual underwater kiss.

He let himself relax.

In the green-lit water, Veronica's luminous eyes suddenly opened wide. They glanced at the surface above, then focused on him with frightening predatory intensity.

JT's surprise turned to terror as she sucked in a deep breath, draining the air from his lungs.

CHAPTER 217

Juan scrambled ashore and stood at the mouth of the broken valley. Its sunken floor stretched away from him, toward the center of the island. Gray dust filled the air, a uniform haze that reduced visibility to a few meters. Fires burned in patches, dimly glimpsed through the gray. Injured and dying seals flopped and shuddered on the rocks around him. Dust coated their fur like flour, turning them into silent, bloody ghosts.

Stepping over seal carcasses and debris, Juan walked up the valley, pushing deeper into the swirling grayness. He seemed to move very slowly, almost drifting, as if underwater. The eerie silence made it dreamlike and surreal.

The ground rose ahead of him in staggered, broken steps. Walls of shattered rock sloped upward on each side to merge with the plateau five meters above. Thirty meters in, he came to a dead end: a tumbled wall of steel I-beams, shattered concrete and wood, and broken machinery—the wreckage of the fog signal building.

The sight of it confirmed his worst fears. Most of the building had fallen into the cavern below. The devastation was total.

Picking up a head-size chunk of concrete, he tossed it aside, causing a mini landslide. He ignored the falling rocks, clearing as much rubble as he could move. The collapsed lung made it hard to keep his breath, and soon, despite the extraordinary capacity his free-dive training gave him, he was panting.

Small gaps he had exposed between the larger chunks of debris gaped black. He moved his hand in front of them, testing them, until he felt the movement of air.

Placing his hands on a massive beam, he leaned forward, peering through the crack into the darkness. He could see the faint orange glow of distant fires inside. He smelled smoke.

"Can anybody hear me?" he shouted.

But how would he hear them reply? He had heard himself, though. His voice sounded muffled and indistinct, like he was underwater.

Bone conduction. Even without eardrums, he could still hear his own voice because it vibrated through the bones of his skull. It gave him an idea.

Laying his head against the metal beam, he shouted again, then closed his eyes and concentrated. Did he hear a distant scrabbling of rocks—someone moving in there? A voice, barely audible? He wasn't sure.

Something soft hit him in the face, clawing and shaking.

Juan opened his eyes to see a hand poking out of the gap between the beam and a massive chunk of concrete. A female hand. He could hear rhythmic, high-pitched sounds now, coming through the beam.

Camilla. She was alive.

He sagged against the steel as relief loosened his limbs.

Her hand crawled over his face, groping blindly, exploring. He took it in both of his own, and held her wrist against his forehead. Bone conduction. He could hear her now, although he had trouble making out the words.

Her arm shuddered in his hands. "Oh god," he heard her say. "Get me out of here. You need to get me out of here right now!"

Maybe it was his damaged ears, but Camilla's voice sounded wrong, wavering up and down the octaves. She sounded *younger.*

Juan looked at the massive beams and fallen slabs of concrete that plugged the end of the valley. They were packed so tight even a moray eel would have trouble finding a way through.

He slapped the beam between them. "We'd need a bulldozer to clear this."

"You don't understand," she said. "I can't be in here right now. I just *can't.*"

"Are you all right?"

"No."—a ragged trill that might have been a laugh or a sob. "I'm nowhere even close to all right."

Her hand pulled free from his. The fingers stretched, reaching, clawing at the open air. He could picture her, frantically pushing herself against the other side of the wreckage, as if she could squeeze through the narrow gap.

He trapped her hand again, as gently as he could, and held it against his cheekbone. "I'm sorry, Camilla. I'm trying to think of something."

"No! No! Let me out! No-o-o-o...." Her voice trailed off in a wordless little mewl.

"You're going to be okay. We'll get you out of there." He closed his eyes. "I promise."

Camilla laughed. It was the worst thing he had ever heard, brittle and horrible, chilling his spine with its hopelessness. Her hand pulled out of his and disappeared inside the hole.

Laying his cheek against the beam, he strained to hear. He could feel the faint vibration of her breathing through the steel, coming fast and shallow.

"I'm really not in a good place right now," she said.

"Camilla, listen to me. It's different this time."

High-pitched keening noises came through his cheek. Juan couldn't make out any more words. He slapped the beam again and shouted, sending a pulse of pain through his head. "Camilla!"

No response. Just her rapid breathing and those plaintive keens that made the skin on the back of his neck prickle with fear for her. It was not a sound any adult should make. Ever.

He raised his voice again. "Answer me! Please, Camilla. Just say something."

A long silence followed. When she finally spoke, Juan squeezed his eyes shut and ground his forehead against the beam.

It was the voice of a child. A confused child.

"Who's there?" she asked.

"It's me. Juan."

"Oh. Okay." She sounded as though she had absolutely no idea who he was.

"Listen to me, Camilla. There's air flowing in there. I felt it."

It was why the fires were still burning. Why she could still breathe.

"That means there's another way out. You have to go and find it." He took a deep breath. "I'm sorry, but you have to do this for yourself. Go back in there and look for it."

"Okay." She sounded dubious, like a child given hopelessly difficult instructions.

His arms and legs felt like lead. She was losing her mind in there, and he couldn't get to her. He thumped his forehead against the beam in black frustration. He couldn't even hear her properly.

"Camilla, this is very important," he said. "Don't get lost and forget what you're doing. You have to find the way out."

"Are you sure?" The baffled incomprehension in her voice was terrifying.

"Yes. You'll feel the air blowing. Follow it." He gritted his teeth, thinking hard. She cared about other people more than herself. He could use that.

"Camilla, what about Dmitry? What about Mason? Did they make it?"

A long pause. When she spoke again, relief washed over him. She sounded like herself once more.

"I heard Dmitry at first. I think he was hurt really bad. We need to find him."

"Let's get you out, first."

"Mason ran. He left me." Her voice broke. "I thought you had, too…"

She shoved her hand through the hole again, and he held her wrist to his cheek, able to hear her better that way.

Her fingers stroked the side of his face, and her arm stiffened. She tentatively touched his ear, then his other ear, softly tracing them, exploring.

"All this blood… Oh god, Juan. Your poor ears."

He laughed. "Don't worry about that. Just find the way out. I'll search for the opening up here."

"I can't go back in there."

"You can. You can do this. You're brave. You're a survivor."

"Promise me. Promise me that if I don't come out, you'll come in and get me."

"I will." Juan squeezed her hand. "I won't leave you, Camilla."

"I believe you." She squeezed back with surprising strength. Then her hand withdrew, and darkness swallowed her.

He listened to her crawl away.

He would start from the top and see if he could find a way in. He would check on JT and Veronica, too, even though he had seen the cistern dome collapse. If they were still down there, he wasn't hopeful.

He made his way painfully up the sloping side of the valley and reached the top, where a small section of seawall still stood. He leaned against the end of it, breathing heavily. The collapsed lung made it difficult to exert himself, and he felt faint and feverish. Closing his eyes for a moment, he tried to catch his breath.

A faint alarm tickled the base of his skull.

Too late.

CHAPTER 218

Mason put away the stun gun and looked down at Juan's unconscious body with curiosity. How had he survived the explosion?

He noted Juan's injuries and the blood running from his ears. The explosion had probably ruptured his eardrums. That explained why he had been so easy to catch off guard: he was deaf.

Mason took off his glasses and tossed them aside. There was no longer any reason to wear them—no need for camouflage anymore.

He took out Veronica's tactical knife, flicked it open, and squatted beside Juan.

Still unconscious, Juan coughed, and pink foam spattered his lips and chin. He didn't look good at all. Mason figured he was going to die soon anyway. He was probably doing Juan a favor by killing him in his sleep.

Euthanasia. Mason grinned.

But what was Juan *doing* here? Mason tilted his head, staring at the prone form. Why had he come back instead of saving himself? And why had he tried to disarm the bomb when he must have known it was futile?

Questions Mason didn't have answers for.

But this hesitation was unlike him. He had to kill Juan to protect himself. With no other living witnesses to what had happened here, he could tell rescuers any story he wanted to. The video Brent had recorded might well have been destroyed in the explosion. But even if it wasn't, Mason wasn't too concerned. By the time evidence techs recovered footage of his own fun and games with Heather, he would be in another state—or, better yet, another country.

He shook his head, chuckling.

"...and then there were none."

He leaned forward to begin cutting.

Then he paused again as a new thought struck him. Reaching into his pocket, he fingered Brent's phone. The caption next the camera windows had been "Live Transmission." Twelve days of video: Brent's monument to his dead son, his public vindication and revenge against Jordan, against *all* survivors—he would have made sure it didn't die with him. All that video had been transmitted someplace.

Mason was pretty sure he knew where.

Amid the lies, there had always been some truth if you knew where to look for it. Julian had described Vita Brevis's distribution methods to them

675

all: *"file-sharing sites, video hubs, peer-to-peer networks, dozens of other free high-traffic channels."*

Mason grinned, picturing a map of the world with Internet connections overlaid on it. All of them were surely lighting up right now with an expanding cascade of messages, tweets, emails, and texts. Some of the senders would be horrified; others fascinated. But all of them would be eager to share what they had stumbled upon. He could almost *see* the video spreading from server to server, phone to phone, tablet to tablet, computer to computer, around the globe.

So this was what it felt like to be famous. With all due respect to Mr. Warhol, Mason suspected they were going to get a lot more than fifteen minutes.

Knife in hand, Mason smiled and reached down to pat Juan's unconscious head, as if he were petting a dog.

The whole world knows who you are now, señor Antonio y Gabriel. I wonder what they make of you, my friend?

• • •

Twenty minutes later, Mason stood at the top of the hill, at the base of the fallen lighthouse tower. The steam whistle—Año Nuevo's rebuilt fog signal—had been knocked off its base by the explosion. It lay on its side nearby. Jordan's seal-head banner had also fallen, but Mason's chair was still upright by the wreckage of the tower. He brushed off the thick layer of gray dust on the seat and lowered himself onto it, taking the weight off his bad knee.

Night was falling.

Under the darkening sky, Mason looked across the channel toward the mainland.

The whole world knew about him now, too. This wasn't going to be easy. In a few hours, he would find out how much of a survivor he really was.

CHAPTER 219

Crawling. Coughing. Crawling. Eyes watering from the smoke. Ducking under the sagging concrete of the low ceiling, crawling across shattered rock.

Camilla's hands and knees hurt.

A propane tank lay on its side nearby, hissing out a four-foot jet of blue flame. By its light, she looked at her bloody palms.

Last time, they had been bloodier, she remembered. A slick of red had coated her arms all the way up to her shoulders.

She wiped her hands on her jeans and crawled on, searching.

The screams and moans came and went, sometimes very faint, sometimes louder. Many different voices.

Not real... not real...

She squeezed through a narrow gap between concrete and rock. What she was looking for was down here somewhere, she knew. She had to find it.

The cars were back again. She crawled past buckled steel and crushed hubcaps.

Not real... notrealnotrealnotreal...

A draft of cooler air wafted through Camilla's hair, drying the sweat on her cheeks. She crawled past the mouth of the dark circular opening where the draft came from, and squeezed under a dangling bundle of pipes. The rubble was wet with water underfoot. Raising a hand, she felt a crack in the smooth metal surface of a boiler overhead. She pushed past it.

She had been looking for hours. She couldn't find it anywhere.

Camilla swept the rough, broken ground with her hands as she crawled, searching, searching, searching.

She had dropped it somewhere down here, days ago, after getting out of the car.

Her little mermaid doll was lost.

She had to find it.

• • •

"Juan," Camilla whispered. "Where are you, Juan? I'm lost. I don't even know what's real anymore. Everyone is dead down here."

She wiped away the tears from her cheeks and touched Dmitry's face again.

677

Dmitry's cold, dead face.

• • •

Hours later, Camilla squeezed beneath a tumbled ceiling beam. She could see a small clearing in the wreckage beyond. She pushed forward and suddenly froze. Her arms and legs locked, refusing to move any further.

Her family's blue Volvo lay ahead, crushed under the massive concrete beam. The window frame of the driver's-side door was folded outward, bent double. Through the opening, she could see the two crumpled dark shapes, unmoving and silent. Dark blood slicked the door, dripping in thick, syrupy streams. Shiny, knotted wet things dangled from the window in purple ropes and sausage loops. More wet lumps lay strewn around the ground nearby, glistening in the firelight—things too awful to think about.

She stared at the bloody, smeary child-size handprints. They were everywhere. She had made them herself a few days ago, pulling at the door, yanking at her unmoving parents, trying to get them out.

Lost, she had circled back to where she started.

There was no way out.

Her arms and legs shook so hard, her teeth chattered. She couldn't make herself go forward. Couldn't back up.

"Somebody, please help me!" she shouted. "Mason... Jordan... anybody... *please!*"

The hair on the back of her neck stood up as she heard her own words. She was calling a serial killer and a dead woman for help. A dead woman she barely knew. She closed her eyes, choking in horror, knowing she had lost it completely.

She would never get out.

Something inside her gave way. It felt like wet fabric tearing inside her head.

She looked at the driver's-side window again.

"Daddy... Mama... please wake up. My legs hurt, Mama... Get out of the car... *Wake up... please...*"

Her plaintive cries turned to screams.

• • •

Camilla curled against a wall of buckled metal, tucked into a tight, dark alcove, cocooned in darkness. The fires had burned low and then gone out many hours ago. The blackness around her was absolute. Her head touched the uneven ceiling above her whenever she moved.

But she wasn't moving anymore. There was no point. She had nowhere to go. The dark, claustrophobic tumble of wreckage stretched to infinity in every direction. This place was the only reality.

Time had no meaning here. The sunlit world above—the world of her dreams and imagination—didn't really exist. It never had. She had created it in her mind to escape from this place.

But she knew now that there was no escape. There never had been.

Eyes open but unseeing, she put her cheek against the broken ground and curled up tighter.

She made it all go away.

Day 12

Tuesday: January 1, 2013

Brent's body shook with convulsions. His forehead knocked against the rocky ground. He was suspended almost upside down, inclined facedown in darkness.

Another brief period of consciousness. He knew it would be his last unless he was able to redose with fentanyl immediately.

He tried to move his arms. His left was immobilized, but his right came loose, dropping free to hang below of his face. With a trembling hand, he pushed at the rubble beneath him. A broken chain trailed from his wrist.

Fentanyl. In the small med kit. Chest pocket.

Bending his elbow, he fumbled at his chest. His fingers encountered metal pressing into his lower ribs—another mass of old boiler pipes. He was crushed between two sections of machinery, hanging head down, still chained to the wheel. That was a problem. Right now, he had more pressing concerns to worry about, though.

Fighting to stay conscious, he managed to knock the medical kit loose from the chest pocket of his wet suit and heard it spill open on the rocky floor beneath his face. He groped blindly, sending ampoules and syringes skittering and rolling, until his fingers closed on a syringe. Holding it like a dagger, Brent stabbed it into the side of his neck and thumbed the plunger down. Then his hand fell away.

Another wave of convulsions took him. He shuddered, helpless, unable to control his muscles. Bright flashes burst on the insides of his eyelids, erasing all thought.

• • •

The convulsions lessened, then stopped. Brent opened his eyes. He couldn't see anything. His brain felt fuzzy, his thoughts muddled.

Modafinil.

He slid his fingers along the ground, locating foil pill packs. In the dark, there was no telling what they were, but with his built-up tolerance, that wouldn't be an issue. *Some* of them were modafinil. Tearing each pack he found open with his teeth, he dumped the pills into his mouth and chewed them, until his fingers could locate no more.

The modafinil cleared his head quickly. Brent chuckled to himself. Now that he could think again, there was no reason to remain blind. He slid two fingers into another chest pocket and pulled out a waterproof penlight. Turning it on, he waved it around, craning his neck to see his surroundings.

His situation was worse than he had thought. Broken concrete and smashed pipes and boilers trapped him on all sides. Wedged upside down between two massive blocks of machinery, still chained to the valve wheel, he used his free hand to play the penlight beam over his own body.

Brent realized that being trapped was the least of his problems. Holding the penlight in his teeth, he tilted his chin to shine it on his injuries while probing with the fingers of his free hand.

Polytrauma.

He began a triage assessment.

His left forearm disappeared into the quarter-inch crack separating the machinery and the edge of the wheel.

Acute crush injury to upper limb. Comminuted radial-ulnar fractures. Unsalvageable.

Tucking his chin into his chest and aiming the penlight with his teeth, he could see his wet-suited thigh through the shadowy gap between the machinery and the wheel. Sharp bone glowed white from a split in the neoprene.

Compound distal fracture of femur.

He turned his neck to look on his other side. The machinery pressed tightly into his chest and abdomen there. Soft, lumpy shapes gleamed wetly in the gap alongside his torso.

Evisceration secondary to peritoneal cavity rupture. Probable omental rupture, also.

Brent took the penlight out of his mouth and flicked it off. Further assessment was unnecessary to make a diagnosis. In darkness again, he thought about his wife Mary.

He tried to picture her face, but for some reason, he couldn't remember what she looked like.

She would never approve of what he had done here, but he hoped she would at least understand why he had done it. He wished he could speak to her one last time.

It isn't right that survivors are lionized and turned into celebrities, while the ones they trample under their feet—good, innocent, normal *people like our son—are forgotten. Where's the justice in that, Mary? And* her*—why couldn't you keep him away from her? Twenty years of tracking survivors, and she was the worst I ever saw. She destroyed our boy, and she didn't even care.*

He thought about his son. Memories flooded the darkness: Jonathan as a toddler, laughing while Brent pulled him in a wagon; Jonathan at nine or ten, working on a model airplane they were building together; a teenage Jonathan, swinging at the baseballs Brent pitched him. His son's face was always turned away from him.

In his mind's eye, he could see the back of Jonathan's head, the line of his jaw, his forehead, but nothing more. He squeezed his eyes shut, trying to recall his son's face, but all he could summon was a frustrating oval blankness.

Thanks to the modafinil, Brent's thinking was all too clear now. Mercilessly clear. He longed for the earlier fuzziness. Had he really done this for his son? Or for himself? Out of bitterness, spite, and misplaced pride?

He knew that his death would be a long, drawn-out one. Even though he couldn't feel pain, he didn't like that idea at all. Too much time for recrimination. Too much time to think.

He turned on the penlight again and stuck it in his mouth.

Craning his neck, he pointed his chin at the ground. He stretched out his free arm, again reaching for the scattered syringes, but looking for different ones this time. Thicker ones.

He gathered six of the larger syringes together in a tight bundle, gripping them in his fist. He held his arm as far from his body as he could, with the needles pointed toward the center of his chest. Then he stabbed his fist inward, driving all six needles through the wet suit, penetrating his sternum. With his palm, he pressed the plungers, sending the contents of all six syringes into his heart.

Opening his mouth, Brent let the penlight fall from his teeth. He let his body sag and closed his eyes, waiting for what he had injected to take effect.

CHAPTER 221

The light danced and sparkled like a firefly, gradually intruding on her awareness. Her eyes stared sightlessly, but a tiny part of her watched it with wonder. The waves of gentle white light washed across her tear- and soot-stained cheeks, bathing them with rippling, pulsating patterns.

She couldn't remember where she was—only that it was a place of unhappiness and pain. She couldn't remember *who* she was, either, but that didn't matter anymore. She looked at the shimmering radiance, and the knots inside her loosened. The light danced just out of reach, beckoning.

It was so beautiful.

The small part of her mind that was aware watched it with delight. She knew the light was out of place down here. It didn't belong, and it couldn't stay long.

She unwrapped one arm from her body and held out her hand, stretching her fingers toward the light.

It floated back, staying just out of reach.

She had to follow the light somewhere else. It had come for her. Come to take her away.

It was time at last.

Uncurling her body, she crawled toward the light. It receded, guiding her forward, drawing her into a narrow tunnel that led up. At the end of the tunnel, radiance pulsated, sparkling white.

Camilla crawled up the tunnel, drawn toward the light. All her pain and confusion fell away, dropping from her like cut coils of rope. She left them behind. She shed her sorrow and her terror like a butterfly pulling free of its constricting cocoon.

Calm contentment washed over her. She smiled with joy.

She drew nearer, and the white light expanded to aching brightness, filling her view. A gentle, welcoming breeze caressed her face.

She was at peace.

She remembered now. The light had been there for her twenty-three years ago. It sang to her when she was a frightened child. It had always been there for her.

It was a part of her.

She closed her eyes against the blinding brightness and pushed forward.

Camilla went into the light.

CHAPTER 222

Eyes still closed, Camilla raised her face to the warm sun. The coastal wind lifted her hair and made it dance around her cheeks. On her hands and knees, she took a deep breath of cool ocean-scented air.

She smiled to herself in pure contentment, wrapped in the sheer joy of being alive. Crossing her legs under her, she sat back on her haunches. Leaning back on her hands, she opened her eyes wide and looked around her, taking it all in.

Birds swooped through the blue sky overhead. Seals swarmed on the rocky slopes in front of her and the beach down below. A cacophonous symphony of animal noises greeted her ears: the sounds of life. She felt a deep connection to the vitality all around her, filling her heart and running through her veins, bathing her in warmth. She was a part of this, and she always would be. She didn't have to be afraid anymore.

Kneeling on the island's highest point, next to the wreckage of the lighthouse tower, she looked back at the circular opening behind her. The metal fog whistle lay close by, fallen on its side. She stared in wide-eyed wonder at the tunnel's narrow mouth. She had crawled through the steam pipe that they had cleaned and refitted—all of them working together to rebuild Año Nuevo's fog signal. Her eyes followed the pipe down the hill to the flattened wreckage of the fog signal buildings. The buildings had been leveled completely, slumping into the massive crater that now deformed the island's surface.

Her joy turned bittersweet. Dmitry was still down there. And Brent.

She would track down their families, the families of all the dead. She would share their grief with them. But that wasn't the only unhappy duty she had to attend to now. Looking at the empty chair that stood nearby, she shook her head sadly.

"You should turn yourself in," she called out. "A judge might count that in your favor."

A grinning Mason limped out from behind the wreckage of the tower.

"First Juan crawls out from under a rock, and now you do, too," he said. "I guess I shouldn't be surprised, by now. It looks like there's something to all this 'survivor' nonsense after all."

Camilla stood and walked over to Mason. She didn't like the way his smile had changed when he said Juan's name. Narrowing her eyes, she prodded him in the chest.

"What did you do to him?" she asked.

689

He looked away.

"Where *is* he?"

"Well, he was in pretty bad shape already—"

"Mason!"

"So I let him get some rest." He laughed. "Don't worry, I didn't hurt your precious hero. I left him down there, in the shade next to the blockhouse."

She shoved past Mason and scrambled down the slope, rounding the corner of the blockhouse. A wet suit-clad body lay sprawled on the ground. Black dive fins splayed from beneath his shoulders, like broken wings.

She dropped to her knees by Juan's side and touched his face. Mason hadn't been joking. He looked terrible: bruised and bloody. He was breathing, though. She closed her eyes in relief.

"I think your boy toy is broken," Mason said, leaning over her shoulder. "He doesn't hear so well anymore."

Then his face turned thoughtful. He pulled Brent's phone out of his pocket and tilted it toward Camilla. "I saw him on here, you know. Juan was still down below when everything blew up. I think he managed to disarm a lot of the explosives before it did. It could have been a lot worse."

Camilla brushed her hair behind her ear and stared down at Juan's pallid, unconscious face.

"He did it for us, Mason." She blinked back tears. "He was willing to sacrifice himself to save us."

Mason stiffened at her side.

Then the hair on the back of her neck stood up.

A familiar velvety voice, edged with ragged steel, froze her in place.

"Jesus Christ, how very fucking touching," it said. "I'm getting all watery eyed, listening to you idiots."

Veronica stepped out of the blockhouse.

CHAPTER 223

Veronica walked with a hitch, holding her back with an odd stiffness. Blood ran from her hairline and encrusted her forehead. One of her eyes was a crimson, bloodshot orb.

"Young lady," she said, "you've made some poor decisions about the company you choose to keep."

Mason was no longer at Camilla's side. Out of the corner of her eye, she saw him back away, limping.

Veronica turned toward him. "How's the knee?" she asked sweetly.

Leaning forward, Camilla grabbed Juan's shoulders and shook him, hard.

His eyes opened. His hand clutched at his thigh and came up with the Glock. He shook his head as if to clear it, his eyes narrowed, and he sat up fast, aiming the gun at Veronica.

"Where's JT?" he asked her.

"Oh, he couldn't make it," Veronica said. "But he says hi."

Juan looked at Camilla, and the confusion on his face sent a pang through her chest. He had no idea what Veronica had said.

He couldn't *hear*.

She shook her head at him slowly. Sadness flickered across his face, and a weight seemed to settle over his shoulders. He held the gun on Veronica.

"Put that away, you cretin," she said. "I'm not interested in you right now." She pointed a chipped fingernail at Mason. "It's *that* animal I need to talk to. About Natalie."

Frowning, Juan rolled to his feet with feline grace, despite his injuries. His gaze followed Veronica's finger to the retreating Mason, who grinned.

Juan turned back to face Veronica and spoke with the exaggerated diction of the deaf.

"I can't hear you," he said, "but I think you're confused. This was all Brent's doing."

She growled a throaty noise of frustration. "Morons. Why do I even bother talking to you? It's a waste of time." She stalked toward them with hitching steps.

Holding the gun on Veronica, Juan took Camilla's arm with the other hand and tried to tug her away. She gently pulled free and stood her ground.

"Mason didn't take Natalie," she said to Veronica. Then she hesitated. "Well, okay, the first time it was him. And he *did* kill Heather…"

"Thanks a lot, Camilla." Mason said.

691

"...but the second time, it was *Brent* that took Natalie. Not Mason..." Her voice trailed off, because Veronica was staring at her with an incredulous expression.

Camilla swallowed.

"What the fuck is *wrong* with you people?" Veronica asked. "I swear to God, you're *all* fucking crazy."

Juan gripped Camilla's arm again, and she turned to see wide-eyed surprise on his face. His gaze swung between her and Mason, and she realized he had caught some of the conversation. Juan gave her arm a squeeze and tilted his head toward her, questioning.

"It's complicated," she said.

He looked at Mason, then back at her again, and shrugged. Then his gun hand moved, panning back and forth between Mason and Veronica.

"Get out of my way," Veronica said, shoving past them.

"Don't kill him," Camilla called after her. "I want him to turn himself in."

Mason laughed. "Not very likely. Sorry, Camilla."

"Don't worry, I won't kill him." Veronica stalked after Mason with hitching strides. "No, I'll just finish the job on your knee, Mason. I'll destroy your other knee, too. I'll break your elbows, hyperextend them backward. And then I'll break your back."

She licked her teeth in excitement. "I'll leave you flopping around on the ground in your own shit, just like a seal. What do you say to that, you sick animal?"

Mason stopped limping away.

"Shoot her, Juan," he said.

Seeing no reaction, Mason laughed. He raised a hand and gave a patronizing little wave, as if to get Juan's attention. Then he made a gun with his thumb and index finger and pointed it at Veronica, pantomiming shooting. He grinned, raised his eyebrows, and lifted a finger to his chin in a mocking *a-ha!* of realization.

Juan's expression went icy with dislike. Camilla put a hand on his wrist and pushed his gun arm down.

"Veronica, you don't have to do this," she said. "Let's help each other, instead. That's what survivors do."

"*Survivors?*" Veronica gave a sultry laugh. "What a crock of shit. *Live*, and you're a survivor. *Die*, and you aren't. Everything else is just foreplay."

A loud metallic boom, felt as much as heard, rolled across the island.

Veronica's mouth snapped shut.

Camilla stood stock-still, listening as the echoes died away. She scanned the terrain around her, trying to locate the source of the sound. Mason and Veronica were doing the same. Juan squeezed her arm again, and she raised a silencing finger to her lips.

The boom rolled across the island again, bouncing off the bluffs.

She slowly turned her head to stare at the wreckage of the fog signal building. At the near edge of the shattered heap of wood and metal, a section of shiplap wall lay inclined like a giant cellar door. It quivered and slid six inches.

Camilla stared at it, her scalp tightening. The others stood frozen in place, staring at it also.

Seconds ticked by as she held her breath.

The boom sounded a third time, and the section of wall burst open, falling aside with a crash to reveal a rectangular opening into darkness.

Icy fingers gripped her insides.

Oh god. What else was down there with me?

A six-foot metal wheel flew out of the gaping hole, trailing broken chains. It bounced once, landed on its edge, and rolled by Camilla, passing between her and Mason.

Thirty feet beyond them, it wobbled and fell over with a metallic thud, oscillated a few times like a spun coin winding down, and came to rest with a clinking of chains on rock.

Her head turned slowly back to face the opening.

Just beyond the edge of the light, something glimmered in the shadows.

Heart pounding, she strained her eyes, trying to see.

An asymmetrical black silhouette lurched up the ramp of rubble inside, moving with nightmarish speed.

In a frenzy of churning motion, it exploded into the light.

Camilla stared, and her hands rose to twist themselves into her hair. She shook her head in denial.

"Oh *god* no!" she screamed.

CHAPTER 224

Brent stood on the threshold of the rectangular opening, rippling with spastic energy. Even standing still, his entire body jerked and shuddered as the muscles contracted and contorted independently.

Drawn by Camilla's scream, his head snapped in her direction, like a raptor spotting prey. The white Frankenstein bolt of a syringe protruded from the side of his neck, vibrating in time with the machine-gun staccato of his pulse. A half-dozen larger syringes, like the one he had revived Natalie with, projected in a cluster at the center of his black neoprene-clad chest.

His pupil-less blue eyes—the merciless eyes of a crocodile—focused on her. He grinned a smeary red grin.

"The doctor is in," he said.

Camilla stared in utter disbelief at the thing that used to be Brent. Gorge rose in her throat. She clutched Juan's arm blindly, unable to tear her eyes away.

"How can anyone be alive like that?" she screamed in a voice shrill with horror, hurting her own ears.

Listing to one side like a broken tower, Brent tilted his chin down to look at himself. His left leg was oddly crumpled. Splintered bone projected from the side of his upper thigh, emerging from his wet suit.

His brow furrowed in puzzlement.

Both his legs were entangled in a ropy mass of soft, knotted coils and spongy lumps that hung from a gaping, crescent-shaped cavity below his chest. The train of blood-slick entrails stretched behind him like a tail, glistening wetly through a coating of dirt and soot.

He turned his neck to look at it.

Camilla followed his gaze to where the ropy coils of his intestines trailed out of the darkness of the opening, ten feet behind him. She sucked in a choking breath.

"Oh god!" she screamed. "Why doesn't he bleed to death?"

Brent's eyes met hers, and confusion crept across his face. He raised his left arm. Two gleaming white bones projected from a flapping sleeve of torn flesh where the arm ended, just below his elbow. He scratched the side of his head with the bones of his forearm, thinking about her question. Then his expression cleared.

"Epinepherine is a vasoconstrictor," he said.

The crescent-shaped opening below his sternum was lined with the jagged points of splintered ribs, like a shark's mouth. It sagged wider, disgorging more of his insides. They slid to the ground at his feet. Deep inside his chest, a purple lump shuddered with jackhammer speed and intensity, making the dangling coils jiggle and dance. Brent's heart.

Camilla gagged.

His head snapped away from her, jerking from person to person. He stared at Juan, Mason, and Veronica in turn.

"I'm afraid I have bad news for all of you," he said. "I see malignancy. You survivors are a cancer metastasizing through the human race, destroying the normal, healthy cells."

The twin bones of his forearm jerked through the air like pincers or prongs, their splintered ends tracing restless patterns in front of him. Brent's grin widened. His nose, cheeks, and jaw were coated with slick red from ear to ear. She recoiled in horror, realizing just how the doctor had freed his pinned arm.

"Excision is our only option," he said, "Surgical removal is necessary to save the patient."

He exploded into horrific, shambling motion, humping toward them with unbelievable speed, his arms and legs jerking spastically in a way the human body was never designed for.

Camilla knew they wouldn't be able to outrun him. He looked inhuman, like a terrible broken machine. Unstoppable.

She stood frozen.

The gun came up beside her shoulder, gripped in both Juan's hands. A litany of mumbled Latin spilled from his lips.

"*Sáncte Míchael Archángele, defénde nos in proélio...*"

She stared at him in surprise.

"*...cóntra nequítiam et insídias diáboli ésto præsídium...*"

The Glock roared in Juan's hands, making her ears ring.

Brent drew up short, rippling and jerking in place. He looked down at his chest, where Juan had shot him.

"*Tu que, prínceps milítiæ cæléstis...*" Juan pulled the trigger again. A second red bullet hole popped onto the chest of Brent's wet suit.

Brent looked up with surprised amusement spreading across his face.

"*Sátanam aliósque spíritus malígnos...*" Juan's next shot struck Brent near his collar.

Brent grinned, shaking his head apologetically.

"*...divína virtúte, in inférnum detrúde.*" The Glock roared a fourth time.

Brent raised his shoulders and spread his arms in a perfect imitation of Juan's usual shrug. His grin widened with malevolence.

Camilla shook off her paralysis. She grabbed Juan's arm, and he swung his face toward her, expression tight with fear.

Camilla pointed at her forehead as Brent exploded forward again.

Juan nodded. Turning to face Brent's charge, he raised the gun higher.

The Glock barked one last time in his hands.

The bullet caught Brent above the right eye, knocking his head back in a pink spray of tissue and bone fragments.

The gun's slide locked back. Camilla knew what that meant. Out of bullets.

Brent stood swaying, his head hanging back, chin pointed upward. He lifted both arms to embrace the sky above him, raising the bones of his forearm high.

Camilla covered her mouth with a palm. She held her breath, waiting for him to fall.

He roared a gargling laugh.

His voice changed, turning warped and discordant, doubling, as if two people were laughing at the same time. His head jerked forward again to stare at her. The upper right side of his forehead was missing, and the top of his eyeball gleamed white and wet between the grayish furrows of exposed brain.

"Why don't you just die?" Mason's voice held amused wonder.

Camilla was surprised to find him next to her, and Veronica a few feet away on Juan's other side. Instinctively, they had all pulled together in the face of an even greater threat.

"I guess I was wrong," Brent said. "It seems I'm a survivor, too."

His horrible doubled voice sent a chill down Camilla's spine; the bullet must have damaged the part of his brain that controlled speech.

She grabbed Juan's arm and took a step backward, dragging him with her.

"Change in plans." Brent's eyes were bright with happy malice. "After I kill all of you, I'll recruit more survivors. I can keep doing this again and again and again."

Veronica gave a throaty chuckle. "Don't be ridiculous. You should see yourself." She shook her head slowly in disapproval. "You look bad, Brent. Really bad. You're falling apart."

"Don't worry about me, I'll be fine." That eerie doubled voice made Camilla cringe. "I'm a doctor, remember?" He threw his head back to scream insane doubled laughter at the sky. "Physician, heal thyself!" he roared.

Camilla pulled Juan back several more steps, and Mason retreated with them. Veronica stayed where she was, crouching, ready. She raised her arms in front of her.

"You shouldn't have brought Natalie here," she said. "Maybe the rest of us deserved this, but she didn't."

The remaining half of Brent's forehead wrinkled, and he looked momentarily confused. Then his mouth stretched in a grin of pure malice.

"Natalie ruined my plans for Jordan, so I made her suffer," he said. "*How* I made her suffer..."

He laughed a spine-chilling gargle and rippled forward. "I didn't know I was capable of doing something like that to another human being. You weren't there for her, Veronica. You weren't there to protect Natalie, and I made her pay for it, in the worst ways possible. She *begged* me to kill her—"

Veronica's features twisted in torment. "You fucking monster," she gasped, standing her ground.

"Run!" Camilla yelled. "Oh god, *run*, Veronica!"

"Natalie wanted to be like you," Brent said, "and you made her into a killer. She hated you, you know."

Tears spilled down Veronica's cheeks. Her voice hardened.

"I'll rip your fucking heart out. Let's see you survive that."

"Run!" Camilla screamed again.

Ignoring her, Veronica lunged forward to meet Brent's charge.

Brent swung his good arm at her with inhuman speed. She managed to duck it, bobbing upright directly in front of him. He towered over Veronica, dwarfing her. She grabbed his jaw with one hand, driving two fingers inside his mouth and hooking her thumb into the softness under his chin. Thrusting her other arm upward, she plunged her hand into the open maw of his chest. Camilla saw Veronica's fist close around something that pulsed and vibrated between her fingers.

Veronica's face twisted in a triumphant snarl.

Then her pale eyes widened in terror.

Brent pistoned his truncated left arm into her face. The twin prongs of his jagged forearm bones drove through Veronica's eyes, obliterating them. The sharp ends of his radius and ulna punched out through the back of her skull.

Veronica went limp like a rag doll. Her arms dropped to her sides. She hung loosely from Brent's forearm, her legs dragging sideways across the ground as he surged toward Camilla.

Camilla screamed. Hands grabbed her arms—Juan on the right and Mason on the left. They dragged her up the hill, toward the fallen lighthouse tower.

Brent laughed. He flicked Veronica away, tossing her toward them with a sound like splintering sticks. Her body flew fifteen feet through the air to land in front of Camilla's feet with a boneless thump. Veronica rolled onto her back, mouth open, slack face staring up at the sky.

Camilla stared down at her in shock, too stunned to process what she was seeing: the broken bones of Brent's forearm still jutted from Veronica's ruined eyes.

Camilla shook her head in denial. It seemed impossible that Veronica, so deadly herself, was gone. Brent had snuffed her out effortlessly.

Mason and Juan pulled at her arms, and Camilla stumbled after them.

Behind her, Brent lurched toward them all with inhuman speed.

She struggled to shake her mental paralysis. *Think! Oh god, think, or we're all dead.*

She remembered Brent's impromptu brain-chemistry lecture, and a mental picture popped into her head unbidden: a propane tank spewing a yard-long jet of blue flame from its broken neck. Brent's damaged amygdala would be flooding his body with a lethal torrent of pure adrenaline right now, jetting it out just like that broken tank valve, streaming catecholamines and cortisol into his blood. How long until his chemically fueled reserves ran empty and he collapsed?

Camilla knew he would survive long enough to kill them all.

Beside her, Juan coughed and stumbled, holding his side. Mason limped awkwardly on his broken knee. She was pulling them along now. They were too slow.

She gritted her teeth.

Brent seemed invincible, indestructible. He was dying, and they still couldn't kill him. But maybe they could disable him instead. He was a lot bigger and heavier than they were. They could use that against him to slow him down.

"Come on," she said, changing direction.

Juan saw where she was headed and his eyes widened.

Mason shook his head. "No way."

"It's our only chance!" she shouted.

She clambered over the broken concrete piled at the base of the wrecked lighthouse tower, and both of them followed her down the other side.

Camilla came to a stop. This was it. End of the road.

Brent swarmed up the rubble, closing the distance between them. The awful train of ropy viscera dragged over the rocks behind him, like coils of kelp. Twenty feet away, he stopped at the top of the wreckage pile, swaying and vibrating with alien motion. He stared at her. His grin faded.

Camilla turned away from him and looked over the edge of the bluff, inches from her toes. The sand seemed so far below. The seals on the beach looked so tiny.

She reached for Juan's arm on her left.

Took Mason's elbow on her right.

Closed her eyes.

And jumped.

CHAPTER 225

Mason slammed into the sand with Camilla's weight on top of him driving the breath from his lungs. His bad knee exploded sideways in a molten eruption of pain. He tried to scream but managed only a hoarse gasp. Seals scattered on all sides, yelping in panic as they stampeded away.

He clawed at the sand as Camilla rolled off him and bounced to her feet.

"Sorry," she said. Her eyes were unhappy, but he could see no surprise in them.

She had done it *on purpose*.

The agony in his knee was no longer important. Mason stared at Camilla in fascination. She had deliberately used him as a cushion so she wouldn't hurt her own legs. She had wanted to be sure she kept her own mobility.

Every time he thought he had her figured out, she surprised him. What was even more surprising was the aching hollowness he felt at the thought of what she had just done to him. His feelings were hurt. *That* was something new.

A few yards away, Juan groaned and rolled from side to side, holding his side. Mason grinned. At least he didn't have broken ribs, on top of a perforated lung, like Juan did. *Just give up already, buddy.*

Camilla ran over to Juan and helped him to his feet.

Mason's hollow feeling got worse.

Juan staggered and coughed a thick stream of blood onto the sand. He wiped his lips with his wrist and looked up, scanning the top of the bluff above them. Mason followed his gaze. A dark, bulky shape stood at the edge, silhouetted against the sky. Brent's one arm swirled spasmodically in front of his torso, coiling loops of his intestines around his fist.

Gathering himself up to jump after them?

"A little help, maybe?" Mason called.

Camilla grabbed Juan's hand and tugged him toward Mason. Together, they yanked Mason upright.

He stood hopping, unable to put any weight on his bad leg. Below the knee, it hung loosely, his foot dragging on the sand. The knee joint was shattered.

Juan grabbed Mason's wrist and slipped his shoulder under Mason's arm. Camilla did the same with his other arm. Mason leaned on their support, and together the three of them staggered away from the bluff face.

One, two, three...

Mason counted their steps.

...fifteen... sixteen... seventeen...

The ground shuddered from the force of an impact behind them.

He looked over his shoulder in time to see the spray of sand dropping back to the beach, where a large black mound lay half buried in a shallow crater. The mound quivered, and then was still.

Mason waited, but nothing happened.

"That's it, folks, he's down," Mason said. "Move along, nothing to see here."

He tightened his arm around Juan's shoulder and grinned at him.

You know, I'm getting tired of seeing how she looks at you, my friend. I think I will kill you, after all.

Brent shot upright like a jack-in-the-box, throwing up another burst of sand, his limbs flailing in furious motion.

The grin fell from Mason's face.

Brent looked down at himself. His broken, crumpled left leg was twisted around completely, so that it faced backward.

"That doesn't look right," he said. He reached down with his good hand and grabbed the neoprene knee of his wet suit. With a savage wrench, he twisted his leg back around so it faced forward again.

The cavity of Brent's abdomen gaped empty now; the tangled, knotted coils of entrails no longer draped his legs. He had left his intestines behind, somewhere on the bluff above them.

"This isn't funny anymore," Mason said. His voice sounded strange in his ears—high and squeaky.

Camilla let go of his wrist and slid out from under his arm, surprising him yet again. His weight sagged against Juan, and they both staggered.

"Help him!" she shouted to Juan. Then she ran toward the waterline.

"Where are you going?" Mason called after her in that same squeaky voice.

She didn't answer.

Juan hauled on Mason's wrist, shoving his shoulder harder into Mason's armpit to support him better. They limped after Camilla, who had already disappeared over a dune.

"Now, *there's* something you just don't see every day," Brent roared behind them. "Mason is scared. Who's laughing *now*, Mason?" Brent's gargling laughter echoed off the bluffs. "Who's laughing *now*?"

He exploded into a jerky, lurching shuffle, far faster than even an uninjured human being should be able to move.

Mason knew there was no way they could outrun Brent.

"What a disappointment you are, Mason. You're a scavenger, not a predator. I wanted a lion, but I caught a hyena instead."

Mason reached into his pocket with his free hand and pulled out Veronica's tactical knife.

He didn't need to outrun *Brent*.

Flicking the knife open, he turned his face toward Juan's, meeting his eyes.

Mason grinned, feeling happy and in control again.

"I only need to outrun *you*," he said.

A loud elastic snap vibrated the swim fin beneath Mason's arm. Piercing pain drove through his good leg.

Juan let go of his wrist, and Mason fell to the sand, clutching at his leg. His hand closed around a long, narrow steel shaft angling up from his thigh. Its barbed point jutted from the other side of his shin.

He stared at Juan's receding back, and his mouth fell open in surprise.

Juan released the grip of the speargun that had been strapped across his back, beneath his fins. He looked over his shoulder at Mason.

"I've heard that joke before," Juan said.

The beach shook beneath Mason.

He turned, and Brent was on him.

CHAPTER 226

Camilla's breath came in gasps. Fear flooded her bloodstream with adrenaline. Her sneakers slipped and slid in the sand as she ran. Her heart pounded in her throat. She thought of Jordan, so much more graceful and athletic than she was. Camilla was nowhere near as fast. She would never be fast enough.

She sprinted up the face of the low dune and stumbled. Jamming her fingers into the sand, she pushed herself upright again.

She crested the dune, and the span of beach in front of the bluff face stretched before her. Juan stared at her, frozen with surprise.

"Get out of the way," she yelled, frantically sweeping her arm sideways as she plunged down the other side of the dune toward him, running as fast as she could. The sand shook beneath her feet.

Juan's eyes flicked to the crest of the dune behind her. His jaw dropped.

The truck-size animal that was chasing her surged over the dune in a spray of sand. Juan looked tiny in comparison. He stumbled aside, out of Camilla's path, and fell to his knees as she ran past.

The sand in front of her was clear now, all the way to where Brent crouched over Mason, thrashing him against the sand with agitated motions.

Camilla ran directly toward him.

The bull elephant seal followed her, roaring in rage.

Brent's head snapped toward her. His eerie eyes dilated, and his red-slicked mouth stretched open impossibly wide, tearing with a crack of ligament and bone. At his feet, Mason was a coiled, twisted shape, his spine bent backward, his body rolled up like a sleeping bag, looking half its usual size.

Brent popped upright and swiveled to face her.

Camilla dived to the sand and rolled aside, tumbling over and over, making herself as small as possible. The elephant seal chasing her drew up short and reared to its full eight-foot height. It shuffled in place, bobbing its head aggressively, twenty feet from Brent.

It roared a rumbling challenge.

Lying in the sand, Camilla stared in amazement. The alpha bull elephant seal *recognized* Brent.

Bellowing with rage, it faced the two-legged predator that had stalked its harem night after night, killing its females and slaughtering its young under cover of darkness. It tossed its massive body from side to side, hopping on its front flippers, and roared again.

But it didn't come any closer.

Brent turned his face toward Camilla, and she could see that anything human in him was long gone. His doubled laugh echoed off the cliffs behind him, and he pointed toward the elephant seal's scarred chest.

"You see? Even this thing is afraid to face a *true* survivor."

The seal charged him, raising itself higher as it surged forward. It threw its five-thousand-pound bulk onto Brent. His body accordioned, crushed into the sand to disappear beneath the blubbery mass of its chest.

The elephant seal roared again. It swiveled its neck from side to side, looking around itself in confusion, wondering where its opponent had vanished to.

Then it shuffled backward and turned away, rippling toward the waterline. Its tail flippers slid across a flattened, unrecognizable black shape. The shape continued to twitch, soaking the sand around it in red.

Camilla covered her mouth and closed her eyes, turning away. It was over.

A shadow fell across her.

Juan. He held out his hand.

She took it and pulled herself to her feet.

CHAPTER 227

Camilla steadied Juan as he leaned over Mason's folded body. Neither of them said anything. She turned her head and stared across the waves as he searched through Mason's pockets. She did not look down at the banker.

Juan found what he was looking for. He held up Brent's phone, still encased in its Ziploc plastic bag.

She took his arm. Passing through the clusters of seals and sea lions in silence, they walked down the beach. They reached the wooden walkway, and she supported him as they climbed the steps to the top of the bluff.

They sat on the top step, side by side next to the chicken coop.

Camilla's eyes scanned the beaches and bluffs of the mainland across the channel. Tufts of sea grass bent and waved in the breeze. A few seals lay on the sand, but the landscape was otherwise empty.

She was very aware of Juan's knee against hers. Her shoulder brushed his bicep. He pulled Brent's phone out of a chest pocket on his wet suit and held it on his lap.

Turning his head toward her, he touched his forehead to hers. She looked into his eyes, seeing a question.

"Eight characters?" she asked.

He nodded, his head moving against hers.

She took the phone from his fingers and tapped the screen eight times. The lock screen disappeared, and the normal display appeared. She handed the phone back.

He smiled another question at her.

"Jonathan," she said.

Realization dawned in Juan's eyes. He nodded. "Makes sense."

He tapped the phone's screen four times and handed it back to her.

She raised the phone to her ear, hearing a tinny voice.

"Nine one one. Can you state the nature of your emergency?"

She looked around her. At the mangled bodies down on the beach. The collapsed buildings. The caved-in center of the island.

"I don't even know where to begin," she said.

"May I put you on hold?"

She glanced at Juan.

"That's okay," she said. "I think we can manage to survive a little longer on our own."

. . .

An hour later, Camilla and Juan were still sitting on the steps. She watched the boats approaching Año Nuevo Island from every direction. Blue flashers winked atop the Coast Guard cutters that circled the island. A large fireboat was anchored offshore, its decks crawling with human activity. In the distance, she could see several helicopters in the air, heading their way. Emergency vehicles streamed down Highway 1. They were hidden by the rolling headlands, but Camilla could see the splash of their red lights and hear the faint, distant noise of sirens.

Closer to where they sat, the seals and sea lions went about their daily business of survival with the usual noisy rambunctiousness. Pelicans crossed the sky in regimented trains. The air was crisp. She looked at the island all around her, marveling at nature's resilience.

At her side, Juan stared at the water, his pale face burdened with an expression of quiet sorrow. She knew he was thinking of Jordan, still down there, unburied.

Gentle pain pierced her heart. She took Juan's hand and leaned the side of her head against his.

"She had figured it all out, you know. Jordan was frighteningly intelligent," she said. "When she saw her profile, she understood what Brent was trying to do to her, and she fought back the only way she knew how. I'm sorry I never really got the chance to know her."

Juan looked down at their entwined fingers. "I think nobody ever really got the chance to know her," he said.

"It must have been a lonely way to be."

The sorrow on his face sharpened. "She and Brent were alike in a lot of ways. More than either of them would have liked to admit."

A shudder ran down Camilla's spine. "I don't think Brent was human at the end."

"He was human," Juan said. "All too human. He could have been any of us."

The first rescue boats had reached the shore. She could see emergency personnel on the beach, carrying stretchers. She didn't feel any great hurry to go meet their rescuers. For now, she was content where she was.

She traced the back of his hand with her thumb, and a sudden emptiness spread inside her. She looked away.

"What now, Juan?" she asked. "Are you going to disappear?"

"No," he said. "I'm done running away."

She squeezed his hand, blinking, unwilling to trust herself to speak.

"Things will be different for you, too, now," he said. "You'll be recognized anywhere you go. Celebrity will take some getting used to."

She nodded, thinking of Avery. She would go see him as soon as she could. Maybe even today, if she could get away from the media long enough. She would hug little Avey and hold him tight—to reassure herself just as much as him that everything would be okay.

"We'll have our moment of fame, and then it'll pass," she said. "But I'm not going to waste mine. I'm going to make something good come of it. I'm going to use it to help my foundation kids, and Veronica's shelter." She gave a sad smile. "I bet I can raise a lot more than ten million after *this*."

Juan smiled grimly. "Interview with a double survivor: unkillable woman gets buried alive twice, defeats mass murderer, and returns to rescue orphaned children. I think you'll get more money and publicity than you want."

"Brent was wrong to single out survivors," she said. "My kids are all survivors. Every person is a survivor."

She felt Juan come alert at her side. A wide grin spread across his face and he said, "Some more than others."

She followed his gaze past the ruined houses, to where a small figure in a gray hoodie was coming out of the storage shed.

Camilla's heart leaped with surprised joy. "Brent lied."

She hugged Juan hard, and he winced.

"Behind the false wall in the shed," she said. "She was hiding this whole time."

Natalie raised a hand in a shy little wave. Camilla waved back.

"Veronica had it right all along." She watched Natalie walk away, headed toward the boats at the dock. "There's the true survivor."

The sun gleamed silver on the water. She leaned back against Juan, and together they watched the rescuers converge across Año Nuevo Island.

AFTERWORD

I'm very excited to see what you all think of New Year Island! If you enjoyed it, I hope you will consider telling people what you thought of it in your book clubs, on your social media outlets, and by writing a review on Amazon.com, Goodreads, and other favorite book review sites, blogs, and retailer sites. Here are some quick links to make it easy:

Visit **PaulDraker.com** to sign up for updates on new books.
http://www.pauldraker.com

Write a review of New Year Island at Amazon.com.
http://amazon.com/author/pauldraker

Write a review of New Year Island at Goodreads
http://www.goodreads.com/book/show/18250778-new-year-island

Write a review of New Year Island at Barnes&Noble
http://www.barnesandnoble.com/w/new-year-island-paul-draker/1116333940

Please drop by my website http://www.pauldraker.com and subscribe to be notified by email when new books are about to be released. Some select readers who sign up early will also have an opportunity to join my early readers club, which means you will occasionally be offered advance reader copies (ARCs) of my pre-release titles, or special editions of existing titles.

I'm always thrilled to hear from readers directly, too—you are the ones who make all this possible. Feel free to drop me an email, tweet, or message—contact info is on my website).

If you liked New Year Island, you're going to love what's coming next:

PYRAMID LAKE

Details at http://www.pauldraker.com

Can't wait to hear from you.

ACKNOWLEDGEMENTS

I am indebted beyond measure to my fantastic editor, Michael Carr. He saw potential in an early draft of New Year Island, and was generously willing to help a new writer over the hurdles necessary to shape the prose into something readers might actually want to read. Working with an editor of Michael's caliber is a dream come true for a writer, and it has helped me up my game substantially. Thanks, man! I owe you big-time.

I have also been very fortunate in having a couple dozen wonderful critique partners in my mystery writer's critique group and my local writing group—so many excellent writers who gave unstintingly of their time and advice to help a newbie! I would humbly like to thank the following brave souls who gave up substantial amounts of time to critique New Year Island in part or in full: Tom S., Kirsten S., Carolina A., Brian M., Donnell Ann B., Bob A., Jane F., Alice G., Chas B., Ron V., Norma H., Mike B., MaryAlice M., Dorsett B., Andrea D., Mark S., Rosemarie S., Henya D., Aggie Z., Jeanne A., Misuk P., Tony P., Julie M., James C., Tom B., Joyce K., Kent S. Without your detailed critical feedback and encouragement this book would not have happened. Their feedback keeps me grounded and helps curb my excesses—yeah, I know… But seriously, you should have seen how I originally had it.

Donnell and Aggie, in particular, were kind enough to allow a new and untested writer into the groups they ran. I am eternally grateful for that.

Any technical mistakes (I'm thinking of the climbing scene in particular) or linguistic howlers that the reader stumbles over belong to the author alone. I'm betting those are also the places where I obstinately refused to listen to Michael's guidance and adopt his well-honed editorial changes. Sometimes, you can lead a horse to water…

Finally, I would like to thank my wife, who was my first reader, and who works in the medical field. She planted the seed that grew into New Year Island. After almost two years of living New Year Island with me, I'm sure she regrets ever bringing up "survivor types," but one day she mentioned how ninety percent of people freeze up or under-react in an emergency while a small minority somehow manage to beat the odds time and time again. I was fascinated. After researching the psychology of the "survivor personality," devouring tons of real-life survival stories, and reading scholarly articles by psychologists studying the game show *Survivor*, I was left with three burning questions that sunk their hooks into my brain and wouldn't let go. Two of those questions are answered by the fictional lecturer in Chapter 7.

The third—and stickiest—question grew into this book.

ABOUT THE AUTHOR

Paul lives in Palo Alto, California, with his wife and three daughters. An avid scuba diver, he has spent much time underwater in Palau, Yap, Honduras, Thailand, Hawaii, the Florida Keys, the cenote caverns of the Yucatan, the Caribbean, the Virgin Islands, Caicos, and the "Red Triangle" off California's coast. He also enjoys skiing, swimming, and windsurfing, and has had extensive tactical training in firearms. After one too many high-speed motorcycle crashes, he is no longer allowed to own open-class sportbikes, which is probably a good thing for him and everyone else.

Paul has worked in the aerospace/defense industry on a variety of classified and unclassified programs for the Navy, Army, Marine Corps, and DARPA, ranging from strategic national missile systems to technology augmentation for small-team tactical infantry units. He has also led a Silicon Valley technology startup delivering massively-scalable custom Internet software to Fortune 500 clients including Hewlett Packard, and headed a leading videogame studio developing mobile games for top-tier publishers such as EA, Disney/Pixar, Sega, Warner Brothers, THQ, and Glu. He holds advanced degrees in electrical and aerospace engineering from MIT, Stanford, and U.C. Berkeley. This broad-ranging engineering expertise lends impeccable technical authenticity to his stories.

Made in the USA
San Bernardino, CA
23 October 2014